The Anthology of
FANTASY & THE SUPERNATURAL

Edited by
STEPHEN JONES and DAVID SUTTON

A

FANTASY
Tales

BOOK

TIGER BOOKS INTERNATIONAL
LONDON

This edition published in 1994 by
Tiger Books International PLC, Twickenham

A copy of the British Library Cataloguing in Publication
Data for this title is available from the British Library.

ISBN 1-85501-502-1

Typeset in 11/12pt Palatino by
Hewer Text Composition Services, Edinburgh
Printed and bound in Finland

10 9 8 7 6 5 4 3 2 1

CONTENTS

Contents

ILLUSTRATIONS

ACKNOWLEDGMENTS

Special thanks to Jo Fletcher and Brian Mooney for all their work on *Fantasy Tales* over the years . . .

'Introduction: A Bazaar of the Bizarre' copyright © 1994 by Stephen Jones and David Sutton.

'Child of an Ancient City' copyright © 1988 by the Terminus Publishing Company, Inc. Originally published in *Weird Tales* No.292, Fall 1988. Reprinted by permission of the author.

'The Cutty Black Sow' copyright © 1994 by Thomas F. Monteleone.

'Treason in Zagadar' copyright © 1994 by Adrian Cole.

'Fatal Age' copyright © 1994 by Nancy Holder.

'The Mouths of Light' copyright © 1979 by Ramsey Campbell. Originally published in *Swords Against Darkness IV*. Reprinted by permission of the author.

' 𝕏 ' copyright © 1988 by David J. Schow. Originally published in *Midnight Graffiti* No.1, June 1988. Reprinted by permission of the author.

'The Storyteller's Tale' copyright © 1994 by Brian Stableford.

'The Big Game' copyright © 1994 by Nicholas Royle.

'The Cat in the Wall' copyright © 1994 by Alex Stewart.

'The Shadow Queen' copyright © 1994 by Anne Goring.

'The Waldteufel Affair' copyright © 1994 by Brian Mooney.

'Up Yours, Federico' copyright © 1984 by Parke Godwin. Originally published in *The Fire When It Comes*. Reprinted by permission of the author.

'Foul Moon Over Sticklespine Lane' copyright © 1994 by Andrew Darlington.

'The Star Weave of Snorgrud Sunbreath' copyright © 1994 by Mike Chandler.

'Pele' copyright © 1994 by Melanie Tem.

INTRODUCTION

A BAZAAR OF THE BIZARRE

TAKE a journey with us into the unknown . . .

Within these pages you will discover wondrous story-tellers, vengeful deities, demons, alchemists, warriors, wizards and witches . . . superstitions, monstrous transformations, ghouls, ghosts, vampires, werewolves, murderers and madness . . . future worlds, mythic lands, outlandish lifeforms and technological nightmares . . .

Here are thirty-nine stories which span the whole gamut of fantasy themes – from sword & sorcery and science fiction to horror and the supernatural. These tales will sweep you from strange, fantastic kingdoms to the dark, half-hidden recesses within the tormented human mind.

From 1977–1992 we edited the multiple award-winning magazine *Fantasy Tales*. Our aim was to promote the popular enjoyment of fantasy in all its written and illustrated forms – entertaining the reader with as wide a variety of concepts as possible.

That, too, is the purpose of this present book. The range of fantastical fiction we have selected is the same as would have appeared in that widely regarded periodical. So, whether you dip into these pages at random, or read the volume from beginning to end, we hope your pilgrimage through these fanciful realms is imbued with a heightened sense of wonder, tinged with just an occasional shiver of fear . . .

The Editors,
London, England

CHILD OF AN ANCIENT CITY

Tad Williams

Tad Williams has been a journalist, a radio talk show host, commercial artist, lead singer/songwriter in a rock 'n' roll band and actor, before becoming the author of the bestselling cat fantasy, Tailchaser's Song *in 1985. He followed that up with an epic trilogy, the 'Memory, Sorrow and Thorn' novels:* The Dragonbone Chair, Stone of Farewell *and* To Green Angel Tower. *An illustrated, novel-length version of the story published here,* Child of An Ancient City *(in collaboration with Nina Kiriki Hoffman), was published in 1992. His latest book is a novella titled* Caliban's Hour, *while short stories have appeared in* Weird Tales *and* Midnight Zoo.

'MERCIFUL Allah! I am as a caif, fatted for slaughter!'

Masrur al-Adan roared with laughter and crashed his goblet down on the polished wood table – once, twice, thrice. A trail of crescent-shaped dents followed his hand. 'I can scarce move for gorging.'

The fire was banked, and shadows walked the walls. Masrur's table – for he was master here – stood scatter spread with the bones of small fowl.

Masrur leaned forward and squinted across the table. 'A calf,' he said. 'Fatted.' He belched absently and wiped his mouth with wine-stained sleeve.

Ibn Fahad broke off a thin, cold smile. 'We have indeed wreaked massacre on the race of pigeons, old friend.' His slim hand swept above the littered table-top. 'We have also put the elite guard of your wine cellars to flight. And, as usual, I thank you for your hospitality. But do you not sometimes wonder if there is more to life than growing fat in the service of the Caliph?'

'Hah!' Masrur goggled his eyes. 'Doing the Caliph's bidding has made me wealthy. I have made *myself* fat.' He smiled. The other guests laughed and whispered.

Abu Jamir, a fatter man in an equally stained robe, toppled a small tower erected from the bones of squab. 'The night is young, good Masrur!' he cried. 'Have someone fetch up more wine and let us hear some stories!'

'Baba!' Masrur bellowed. 'Come here, you old dog!'

Within three breaths an old servant stood in the doorway, looking to his sportive master with apprehension.

'Bring us the rest of the wine, Baba – or have you drunk it all?'

Baba pulled at grizzled chin. 'Ah . . . ah, but *you* drank it, Master. You and Master Ibn Fahad took the last four jars with you when you went to shoot arrows at the weathercock.'

'Just as I suspected,' Masrur nodded. 'Well, get on across the bazaar to Abu Jamir's place, wake up his manservant, and bring back several jugs. The good Jamir says we must have it now.'

Baba disappeared. The chagrined Abu Jamir was cheerfully back-thumped by the other guests.

'A story, a story!' someone shouted. 'A tale!'

'Oh, yes, a tale of your travels, Master Masrur!' This was young Hassan, sinfully drunk. No one minded. His eyes were bright, and he was full of innocent stupidity. 'Someone said you have traveled to the green lands of the north.'

'The north . . .?' Masrur grumbled, waving his hand as though confronted with something unclean, 'No, lad, no . . . that I cannot give to you.' His face clouded and he slumped back on his cushions; his tarbooshed head swayed.

Ibn Fahad knew Masrur like he knew his horses – indeed, Masrur was the only human that could claim so much of Ibn Fahad's attention. He had seen his old comrade drink twice this quantity and still dance like a dervish on the walls of Baghdad, but he thought he could guess the reason for this sudden incapacity.

'Oh, Masrur, please!' Hassan had not given up; he was as unshakeable as a young falcon with its first prey beneath its talons. 'Tell us of the north. Tell us of the infidels!'

'A good Moslem should not show such interest in unbelievers.' Abu Jamir sniffed piously, shaking the last drops from a wine jug. 'If Masrur does not wish to tell a tale, let him be.'

'Hah!' snorted the host, recovering somewhat, 'You only seek to stall me, Jamir, so that my throat shall not be so dry when your wine arrives. No, I have no fear of speaking of unbelievers: Allah would not have given them a place in the world for their own if they had not *some use*. Rather it is . . . certain other things that happened which make me hesitate.' He gazed kindly on young Hassan, who in the depths of his drunkenness looked about to cry.' 'Do not despair, eggling. Perhaps it would do me good to unfold this story. I have kept the details long inside.' He emptied the dregs of another jar into his cup. 'I still feel it so strongly, though – bitter, bitter times. Why don't *you* tell the story, my good friend?' he said over his shoulder to Ibn Fahad. 'You played as much a part as did I.'

'No,' Ibn Fahad replied. Drunken puppy Hassan emitted a strangled cry of despair.

'But why, old comrade?' Masrur asked, pivoting his bulk to stare in amazement. 'Did the experience so chill even *your* heart?'

Ibn Fahad glowered. 'Because I know better. As soon as I start you will interrupt, adding details here, magnifying there, then saying: 'No, no, I cannot speak of it! Continue, old friend!' Before I have taken another breath you will interrupt me again. You *know* you will wind up doing all the talking, Masrur. Why do you not start from the beginning and save me my breath?'

All laughed but Masrur, who put on a look of wounded solicitousness. 'Of course, old friend,' he murmured. 'I had no idea that you harbored such grievances. Of course I shall tell the tale.' A broad wink was offered to the table. 'No sacrifice is too great for a friendship such as ours. Poke up the fire, will you, Baba? Ah, he's gone. Hassan, will you be so kind?'

When the youth was again seated Masrur took a swallow, stroked his beard, and began.

In those days [Masrur said], I myself was but a lowly soldier in the service of Harun al-Rashid, may Allah grant him health. I was young, strong, a man who loved wine more

than he should – but what soldier does not? – and a good
deal more trim and comely than you see me today.

My troop received a commission to accompany a caravan
going north, bound for the land of the Armenites beyond the
Caucassian Mountains. A certain prince of that people had
sent a great store of gifts as tribute to the Caliph, inviting
him to open a route for trade between his principality and
our caliphate. Harun al-Rashid, wisest of wise men that he is,
did not exactly make the camels groan beneath the weight of
the gifts that he sent in return; but he sent several courtiers,
including the under-vizier Walid al-Salameh, to speak for him
and to assure this Armenite prince that rich rewards would
follow when the route over the Caucassians was opened
for good.

We left Baghdad in grand style, pennants flying, the
shields of the soldiers flashing like golden dinars, and the
Caliph's gifts bundled onto the backs of a gang of evil,
contrary donkeys.

We followed the banks of the faithful Tigris, resting several
days at Mosul, then continued through the eastern edge of
Anatolia. Already as we mounted northward the land was
beginning to change, the clean sands giving way to rocky
hills and scrub. The weather was colder, and the skies grey,
as though Allah's face was turned away from that country,
but the men were not unhappy to be out from under the
desert sun. Our pace was good; there was not a hint of
danger except the occasional wolf howling at night beyond
the circles of the campfires. Before two months had passed
we had reached the foothills of the Caucassians – what is
called the steppe country.

For those of you who have not strayed far from our
Baghdad, I should tell you that the northern lands are
like nothing you have seen. The trees there grow so close
together you could not throw a stone five paces without
striking one. The land itself seems always dark – the trees
mask the sun before the afternoon is properly finished –
and the ground is damp. But, in truth, the novelty of it
fades quickly, and before long it seems that the smell of
decay is always with you. We caravaneers had been over
eight weeks a-traveling, and the bite of homesickness was
strong, but we contented ourselves with the thought of the

accommodations that would be ours when we reached the palace of the prince, laden as we were with our Caliph's good wishes – and the tangible proof thereof.

We had just crossed the high mountain passes and begun our journey down when disaster struck.

We were encamped one night in a box canyon, a thousand steep feet below the summit of the tall Caucassian peaks. The fires were not much but glowing coals, and nearly all the camp was asleep except for two men standing sentry. I was wrapped in my bedroll, dreaming of how I would spend my earnings, when a terrible shriek awakened me. Sitting groggily upright, I was promptly knocked down by some bulky thing tumbling onto me. A moment's horrified examination showed that it was one of the sentries, throat pierced with an arrow, eyes bulging with his final surprise. Suddenly there was a chorus of howls from the hillside above. All I could think of was wolves, that the wolves were coming down on us; in my witless state I could make no sense of the arrow at all.

Even as the others sprang up around me the camp was suddenly filled with leaping, whooping shadows. Another arrow hissed past my face in the darkness, and then something crashed against my bare head, filling the nighttime with a great splash of light that illuminated nothing. I fell back, insensible.

I could not tell how long I had journeyed in that deeper darkness when I was finally roused by a sharp boot prodding at my ribcage.

I looked up at a tall, cruel figure, cast by the cloud-curtained morning sun in bold silhouette. As my sight became accustomed I saw a knife-thin face, dark-browed and fierce, with mustachios long as a Tartar herdsman's. I felt sure that whoever had struck me had returned to finish the job, and I struggled weakly to pull my dagger from my sash. This terrifying figure merely lifted one of his pointy boots and trod delicately on my wrist, saying in perfect Arabic: 'Wonders of Allah, this is the dirtiest man I have ever seen.'

It was Ibn Fahad, of course. The caravan had been of good size, and he had been riding with the Armenite and the

under-vizier – not back with the hoi polloi – so we had
never spoken. Now you see how we first truly met: me
on my back, covered with mud, blood, and spit; and Ibn
Fahad standing over me like a rich man examining carrots
in the bazaar. Infamy!

Ibn Fahad had been blessed with what I would come later
to know as his usual luck. When the bandits – who must
have been following us for some days – came down upon us
in the night, Ibn Fahad had been voiding his bladder some
way downslope. Running back at the sound of the first cries,
he had sent more than a few mountain bandits down to Hell
courtesy of his swift sword, but they were too many. He
pulled together a small group of survivors from the main
party and they fought their way free, then fled along the
mountain in the darkness listening to the screams echoing
behind them, cursing their small numbers and ignorance of
the country.

Coming back in the light of day to scavenge for supplies,
as well as ascertain the nature of our attackers, Ibn Fahad had
found me – a fact he has never allowed me to forget, and for
which I have never allowed *him* to evade responsibility.

While my wounds and bandit-spites were doctored, Ibn
Fahad introduced me to the few survivors of our once-great
caravan.

One was Susri al-Din – a cheerful lad, fresh-faced and
smooth-cheeked as young Hassan here, dressed in the robes
of a rich merchant's son. The soldiers who had survived
rather liked him, and called him 'Fawn,' to tease him for
his wide-eyed good looks. There was a skinny wretch of a
chief clerk named Abdallah, purse-mouthed and iron-eyed,
and an indecently plump young mullah, who had just left
the *madrasa* and was getting a rather rude introduction to life
outside the seminary. Ruad, the mullah, looked as though he
would prefer to be drinking and laughing with the soldiers
– beside myself and Ibn Fahad there were four or five more
of these – while Abdallah the prim-faced clerk looked as
though *he* should be the one who never lifted his head out
of the Koran. Well, in a way that was true, since for a man
like Abdallah the balance book *is* the Holy Book, may Allah
forgive such blasphemy.

There was one other, notable for the extreme richness

of his robes, the extreme whiteness of his beard, and the vast weight of his personal jewelry – Walid al-Salameh, the under-vizier to His Eminence the Caliph Harun al-Rashid. Walid was the most important man of the whole party. He was also, surprisingly, not a bad fellow at all.

So there we found ourselves, the wrack of the caliph's embassy, with no hope but to try and find our way back home through a strange, hostile land.

The upper reaches of the Caucassians are a cold and godless place. The fog is thick and wet; it crawls in of the morning, leaves briefly at the time the sun is high, then comes creeping back long before sunset. We had been sodden as well-diggers from the moment we had stepped into the foothills. A treacherous place, those mountains: home of bear and wolf, covered in forest so thick that in places the sun was lost completely. Since we had no guide – indeed, it was several days before we saw any sign of inhabitants whatsoever – we wandered unsteered, losing half as much ground as we gained for walking in circles.

At last we were forced to admit our need for a trained local eye. In the middle slopes the trees grew so thick that fixing our direction was impossible for hours at a time. We were divining the location of Mecca by general discussion, and – blasphemy again – we probably spent as much time praying toward Aleppo as to Mecca. It seemed a choice between possible discovery and certain doom.

We came down by night and took a young man out of an isolated shepherd's hovel, as quietly as ex-brigands like ourselves (or at least like many of us, Ibn Fahad. My apologies!) could. The family did not wake, the dog did not bark; we were two leagues away before sunrise, I'm sure.

I felt sorry in a way for the young peasant-lout we'd kidnapped. He was a nice fellow, although fearfully stupid – I wonder if we are now an old, dull story with which he bores his children? In any case, once this young rustic – whose name as far as I could tell was unpronounceable by civilized tongues – realized that we were not ghosts or Jinni, and were *not* going to kill him on the spot, he calmed down and was quite useful. We began to make real progress, reaching the peak of the nearest ridge in two days.

There was a slight feeling of celebration in the air that night, our first in days under the open skies. The soldiers cursed the lack of strong drink, but spirits were good nonetheless – even Ibn Fahad pried loose a smile.

As the under-vizier Walid told a humorous story, I looked about the camp. There were but two grim faces: the clerk Abdallah – which was to be expected, since he seemed a patently sour old devil – and the stolen peasant-boy. I walked over to him.

'Ho, young one,' I said, 'why do you look so downcast? Have you not realized that we are good-hearted, Godfearing men, and will not harm you?' He did not even raise his chin, which rested on his knees, shepherd-style, but he turned his eyes up to mine.

'It is not those things,' he said in his awkward Arabic. 'It is not you soldiers but . . . this place.'

'Gloomy mountains they are indeed,' I agreed, 'but you have lived here all your young life. Why should it bother you?'

'Not this place. We never come here – it is unholy. The vampyr walks these peaks.'

'*Vampyr*?' said I. 'And what peasant-devil is that?'

He would say no more; I left him to his brooding and walked back to the fire.

The men all had a good laugh over the vampyr, making jesting guesses as to what type of beast it might be, but Ruad, the young mullah, waved his hands urgently.

'I have heard of such afreets,' he said. 'They are not to be laughed at by such a godless lot as yourselves.'

He said this as a sort of scolding joke, but he wore a strange look on his round face; we listened with interest as he continued.

'The vampyr is a restless spirit. It is neither alive nor dead, and Shaitan possesses its soul utterly. It sleeps in a sepulchre by day, and when the moon rises it goes out to feed upon travelers, to drink their blood.'

Some of the men again laughed loudly, but this time it rang false as a brass-merchant's smile.

'I have heard of these from one of our foreign visitors,' said the under-vizier Walid quietly. 'He told me of a plague of these vampyr in a village near Smyrna. All the inhabitants fled, and the village is still uninhabited today.'

This reminded someone else (myself, perhaps) of a tale about an afreet with teeth growing on both sides of his head. Others followed with their own demon stories. The talk went on late into the night, and no one left the campfire until it had completely burned out.

By noon the next day we had left the heights and were passing back down into the dark, tree-blanketed ravines. When we stopped that night we were once more hidden from the stars, out of sight of Allah and the sky.

I remember waking up in the fore-dawn hours. My beard was wet with dew, and I was damnably tangled up in my cloak. A great, dark shape stood over me. I must confess to making a bit of a squawking noise.

'It's me,' the shape hissed – it was Rifakh, one of the other soldiers.

'You gave me a turn.'

Rifakh chuckled. 'Thought I was that vampyr, eh? Sorry. Just stepping out for a piss.' He stepped over me, and I heard him trampling the underbrush. I slipped back into sleep.

The sun was just barely over the horizon when I was again awakened, this time by Ibn Fahad tugging at my arm. I grumbled at him to leave me alone, but he had a grip on me like an alms-beggar.

'Rifakh's gone,' he said. 'Wake up. Have you seen him?'

'He walked on me in the middle of the night, on his way to go moisten a tree,' I said. 'He probably fell in the darkness and hit his head on something – have you looked?'

'Several times,' Ibn Fahad responded. 'All around the camp. No sign of him. Did he say anything to you?'

'Nothing interesting. Perhaps he has met the sister of our shepherd-boy, and is making the two-backed beast.'

Ibn Fahad made a sour face at my crudity. 'Perhaps not. Perhaps he has met some *other* beast.'

'Don't worry,' I said. 'If he hasn't fallen down somewhere close by, he'll be back.'

But he did not come back. When the rest of the men arose we had another long search, with no result. At noon we decided, reluctantly, to go on our way, hoping that if he had strayed somewhere he could catch up with us.

We hiked down into the valley, going farther and farther into the trees. There was no sign of Rifakh, although from time to time we stopped and shouted in case he was searching for us. We felt there was small risk of discovery, for that dark valley was as empty as a pauper's purse, but nevertheless, after a while the sound of our voices echoing back through the damp glades became unpleasant. We continued on in silence.

Twilight comes early in the bosom of the mountains; by mid-afternoon it was already becoming dark. Young Fawn – the name had stuck, against the youth's protests – who of all of us was the most disturbed by the disappearance of Rifakh, stopped the company suddenly, shouting: 'Look there!'

We straightaway turned to see where he was pointing, but the thick trees and shadows revealed nothing.

'I saw a shape!' the young one said. 'It was just a short way back, following us. Perhaps it is the missing soldier.'

Naturally the men ran back to look, but though we scoured the bushes we could find no trace of anyone. We decided that the failing light had played Fawn a trick – that he had seen a hind or somesuch.

Two other times he called out that he saw a shape. The last time one of the other soldiers glimpsed it too: a dark, man-like form, moving rapidly beneath the trees a bow-shot away. Close inspection still yielded no evidence, and as the group trod wearily back to the path again Walid the under-vizier turned to Fawn with a hard, flat look.

'Perhaps it would be better, young master, if you talked no more of shadow-shapes.'

'But I saw it!' the boy cried. 'That soldier Mohammad saw it too!'

'I have no doubt of that,' answered Walid al-Salameh, 'but think on this: we have gone several times to see what it might be, and have found no sign of any living man. Perhaps our Rifakh is dead; perhaps he fell into a stream and drowned, or hit his head upon a rock. His spirit may be following us because it does not wish to stay in this unfamiliar place. That does not mean we want to go and find it.'

'But . . .,' the other began.

'Enough!' spat the chief clerk Abdallah. 'You heard the under-vizier, young prankster. We shall have no more talk of your godless spirits. You will straightaway leave off telling such things!'

'Your concern is appreciated, Abdallah,' Walid said coldly, 'but I do not require your help in this matter.' The vizier strode away.

I was almost glad the clerk had added his voice, because such ideas would not keep the journey in good order . . . but like the under-vizier I, too, had been rubbed and grated by the clerk's high-handedness. I am sure others felt the same, for no more was said on the subject all evening.

Allah, though, always has the last word – and who are *we* to try to understand His ways? We bedded down a very quiet camp that night, the idea of poor Rifakh's lost soul hanging unspoken in the air.

From a thin, unpleasant sleep I woke to find the camp in chaos. 'It's Mohammad, the soldier!' Fawn was crying. 'He's been killed! He's dead!'

It was true. The mullah Ruad, first up in the morning, had found the man's blanket empty, then found his body a few short yards out of the clearing.

'His throat has been slashed out,' said Ibn Fahad.

It looked like a wild beast had been at him. The ground beneath was dark with blood, and his eyes were wide open.

Above the cursing of the soldiers and the murmured holy words of the mullah, who looked quite green of face, I heard another sound. The young shepherd-lad, grimly silent all the day before, was rocking back and forth on the ground by the remains of the cook-fire, moaning.

'Vampyr . . .,' he wept, '. . . vampyr, the vampyr . . .'

All the companions were, of course, completely unmanned by these events. While we buried Mohammad in a hastily dug grave those assembled darted glances over their shoulders into the forest vegetation. Even Ruad, as he spoke the words of the holy Koran, had trouble keeping his eyes down. Ibn Fahad and I agreed between ourselves to maintain that Mohammad had fallen prey to a wolf or some other beast, but our fellow travelers found it hard even to pretend agreement. Only the under-vizier and the clerk Abdallah

seemed to have their wits fully about them, and Abdallah
made no secret of his contempt for the others. We set out
again at once.

Our company was sombre that day – and no wonder. No
one wished to speak of the obvious, nor did they have much
stomach for talk of lighter things – it was a silent file of men
that moved through the mountain fastnesses.

As the shadows of evening began to roll down, the
dark shape was with us again, flitting along just in sight,
disappearing for a while only to return, bobbing along behind
us like a jackdaw. My skin was crawling – as you may well
believe – though I tried to hide it.

We set camp, building a large fire and moving near to
it, and had a sullen, close-cramped supper. Ibn Fahad,
Abdallah, the vizier, and I were still speaking of the follower
only as some beast. Abdallah may even have believed it –
not from ordinary foolishness, but because he was the type
of man who was unwilling to believe there might be anything
he himself could not compass.

As we took turns standing guard the young mullah led the
far-from-sleepy men in prayer. The voices rose up with the
smoke, neither seeming to be of much substance against the
wind of those old, cold mountains.

I sidled over to the shepherd-lad. He'd become, if anything, more close-mouthed since the discovery of the morning.

'This "vampyr" you spoke of . . .,' I said quietly. 'What do
your people do to protect themselves from it?'

He looked up at me with a sad smile.

'Lock the doors.'

I stared across at the other men – young Fawn with
clenched mouth and furrowed brow; the mullah Ruad, eyes
closed, plump cheeks awash with sweat as he prayed; Ibn
Fahad gazing coolly outward, ever outward – and then I
returned the boy's sad smile.

'No doors to lock, no windows to bar,' I said. 'What
else?'

'There is an herb we hang about our houses . . .,' he said,
and fumbled for the word in our unfamiliar language. After
a moment he gave up. 'It does not matter. We have none.
None grows here.'

I leaned forward, putting my face next to his face. 'For the love of God, boy, what else?' – *I* knew it was not a beast of the Earth. *I knew.* I had seen that fluttering shadow.

'Well . . .,' he mumbled, turning his face away, '. . . they say, some men do, that you can tell stories . . .'

'What!' I thought he had gone mad.

'This is what my grandfather says. The vampyr will stop to hear the story you tell – if it is a good one – and if you continue it until daylight he must return to the . . . place of the dead.'

There was a sudden shriek. I leaped to my feet, fumbling for my knife . . . but it was only Ruad, who had put his foot against a hot coal. I sank down again, heart hammering.

'Stories?' I asked.

'I have only heard so,' he said, struggling for the right phrases. 'We try to keep them farther away than that – they must come close to hear a man talking.'

Later, after the fire had gone down, we placed sentries and went to our blankets. I lay a long while thinking of what the Armenite boy had said before I slept.

A hideous screeching sound woke me. It was not yet dawn, and this time no one had burned himself on a glowing ember.

One of the two soldiers who had been standing picket lay on the forest floor, blood gouting from a great wound on the side of his head. In the torchlight it looked as though his skull had been smashed with a heavy cudgel. The other sentry was gone, but there was a terrible thrashing in the underbrush beyond the camp, and screams that would have sounded like an animal in a cruel trap but for the half-formed words that bubbled up from time to time.

We crouched, huddled, staring like startled rabbits. The screaming began to die away. Suddenly Ruad started up, heavy and clumsy getting to his feet. I saw tears in his eyes. 'We . . . we must not leave our fellow to s-s-suffer so!' he cried, and looked around at all of us. I don't think anyone could hold his eye except the clerk Abdallah. I could not.

'Be silent, fool!' the clerk said, heedless of blasphemy. 'It is a wild beast. It is for these cowardly soldiers to attend to, not a man of God!'

The young mullah stared at him for a moment, and a change came over his face. The tears were still wet on his cheeks, but I saw his jaw firm and his shoulders square.

'No,' he said. 'We cannot leave him to Shaitan's servant. If you will not go to him, I will.' He rolled up the scroll he had been nervously fingering and kissed it. A shaft of moonlight played across the gold letters.

I tried to grab his arm as he went past me, but he shook me off with surprising strength, then moved toward the brush, where the screeching had died down to a low, broken moaning.

'Come back, you idiot!' Abdallah shrieked at him. 'This is foolishness! Come back!'

The young holy man looked back over his shoulder, darting a look at Abdallah I could not easily describe, then turned around and continued forward, holding the parchment scroll before him as if it were a candle against the dark night.

'*There is no God but Allah!*' I heard him cry, '*and Mohammad is His prophet!*' Then he was gone.

After a long moment of silence there came the sound of the holy words of the Koran, chanted in an unsteady voice. We could hear the mullah making his ungraceful way out through the thicket. I was not the only one who held his breath.

Next there was crashing, and branches snapping, as though some huge beast was leaping through the brush; the mullah's chanting became a howl. Men cursed helplessly. Before the cry had faded, though, another scream came – numbingly loud, the rage of a powerful animal, full of shock and surprise. It had words in it, although not in any tongue I had ever heard before . . . or since.

Another great thrashing, and then nothing but silence. We lit another fire and sat sleepless until dawn.

In the morning, despite my urgings, the company went to look for trace of the sentry and the young priest. They found them both.

It made a grim picture, let me tell you, my friends. They hung upside down from the branches of a great tree. Their necks were torn, and they were white as chalk: all the blood had been drawn from them. We dragged the two stone-cold husks back to the camp-circle, and shortly thereafter buried them commonly with the other sentry, who had not survived his head wound.

One curious thing there was: on the ground beneath the hanging head of the young priest lay the remains of his holy scroll. It was scorched to black ash, and crumbled at my touch.

'So it *was* a cry of pain we heard,' said Ibn Fahad over my shoulder. 'The devil-beast can be hurt, it appears.'

'Hurt, but not made to give over,' I observed. 'And no other holy writings remain, nor any hands so holy to wield them, or mouth to speak them.' I looked pointedly over at Abdallah, who was giving unwanted instructions to the two remaining soldiers on how to spade the funeral dirt. I half-hoped one of them would take it on himself to brain the old meddler.

'True,' grunted Ibn Fahad. 'Well, I have my doubts on how cold steel will fare, also.'

'As do I. But it could be there is yet a way we may save ourselves. The shepherd-boy told me of it. I will explain when we stop at mid-day.'

'I will be waiting eagerly,' said Ibn Fahad, favoring me with his half-smile. 'I am glad to see someone else is thinking and planning beside myself. But perhaps you should tell us your plan on the march. Our daylight hours are becoming precious as blood, now. As a matter of fact, I think from now on we shall have to do without burial services.'

Well, there we were in a very nasty fix. As we walked I explained my plan to the group; they listened silently, downcast, like men condemned to death – not an unreasonable attitude, in all truth.

'Now, here's the thing,' I told them. 'If this young lout's idea of tale-telling will work, we shall have to spend our nights yarning away. We may have to begin taking stops for sleeping in the daylight. Every moment walking, then, is precious – we must keep the pace up or we will die in these damned, haunted mountains. Also, while you walk, think of stories. From what the lad says we may have another ten days or a fortnight to go until we escape this country. We

shall soon run out of things to tell about unless you dig deep
into your memories.'

There was grumbling, but it was too dispirited a group to
offer much protest.

'Be silent, unless you have a better idea,' said Ibn Fahad.
'Masrur is quite correct – although, if what I suspect is true,
it may be the first time in his life he finds himself in that
position.' He threw me a wicked grin, and one of the soldiers
snickered. It was a good sound to hear.

We had a short mid-day rest – most of us got at least an
hour's sleep on the rocky ground – and then we walked
on until the beginning of twilight. We were in the bottom
of a long, thickly forested ravine, where we promptly built
a large fire to keep away some of the darkness of the valley
floor. Ah, but fire is a good friend!

Gathered around the blaze, the men cooked strips of
venison on the ends of green sticks. We passed the water
skin and wished it was more – not for the first time.

'Now then,' I said, 'I'll go first, for at home I was the one
called upon most often to tell tales, and I have a good fund
of them. Some of you may sleep, but not all – there should
always be two or three awake in case the teller falters or
forgets. We cannot know if this will keep the creature at bay,
but we should take no chances.'

So I began, telling first the story of The Four Clever
Brothers. It was early, and no one was ready to sleep; all
listened attentively as I spun it out, adding details here,
stretching a description there.

When it ended I was applauded, and straight away began
telling the story of the carpet merchant Salim and his
unfaithful wife. That was perhaps not a good choice – it
is a story about a vengeful djinn, and about death; but I
went on nonetheless, finished it, then told two more.

As I was finishing the fourth story, about a brave orphan
who finds a cave of jewels, I glimpsed a strange thing.

The fire was beginning to die down, and as I looked
out over the flames I saw movement in the forest. The
under-vizier Walid was directly across from me, and beyond
his once-splendid robes a dark shape lurked. It came no
closer than the edge of the trees, staying just out of the

fire's flickering light. I lost my voice for a moment then and stuttered, but quickly caught up the thread and finished. No one had noticed, I was sure.

I asked for the waterskin and motioned for Walid al-Salameh to continue. He took up with a tale of the rivalry between two wealthy houses in his native Isfahan. One or two of the others wrapped themselves tightly in their cloaks and lay down, staring up as they listened, watching the sparks rise into the darkness.

I pulled my hood down low on my brow to shield my gaze, and squinted out past Walid's shoulder. The dark shape had moved a little nearer now to the lapping glow of the campfire.

It was man-shaped, that I could see fairly well, though it clung close to the trunk of a tree at clearing's edge. Its face was in darkness; two ember-red eyes unblinkingly reflected the firelight. It seemed clothed in rags, but that could have been a trick of the shadows.

Huddled in the darkness a stonethrow away, it was listening.

I turned my head slowly across the circle. Most eyes were on the vizier; Fawn had curtained his in sleep. But Ibn Fahad, too, was staring out into the darkness. I suppose he felt my gaze, for he turned to me and nodded slightly: he had seen it too.

We went on until dawn, the men taking turns sleeping as one of the others told stories – mostly tales they had heard as children, occasionally of an adventure that had befallen them. Ibn Fahad and I said nothing of the dark shape that watched. Somewhere in the hour before dawn it disappeared.

It was a sleepy group that took to the trail that day, but we had all lived through the night. This alone put the men in better spirits, and we covered much ground.

That night we again sat around the fire. I told the story of The Gazelle King, and The Enchanted Peacock, and The Little Man with No Name, each of them longer and more complicated than the one before. Everyone except the clerk Abdallah contributed something – Abdallah and the shepherd-boy, that is. The chief-clerk said repeatedly that he had never wasted his time on foolishness such as

learning stories. We were understandably reluctant to press
our self-preservation into such unwilling hands.

The Armenite boy, our guide, sat quietly all the evening
and listened to the men yarning away in a tongue that was
not his own. When the moon had risen through the treetops,
the shadow returned and stood silently outside the clearing.
I saw the peasant lad look up. He saw it, I know, but like Ibn
Fahad and I, he held his silence.

The next day brought us two catastrophes. As we were
striking camp in the morning; happily no fewer than when
we had set down the night before, the local lad took the
waterskins down to the river that threaded the bottom of
the ravine. When a long hour had passed and he had not
returned, we went fearfully down to look for him.

He was gone. All but one of the waterskins lay on the
streambank. He had filled them first.

The men were panicky. 'The vampyr has taken him!'
they cried.

'What does that foul creature need with a waterskin?'
pointed out al-Salameh.

'He's right,' I said. 'No, I'm afraid our young friend has
merely jumped ship, so to speak. I suppose he thinks his
chances of getting back are better if he is alone.'

I wondered . . . I *still* wonder . . . if he made it back. He
was not a bad fellow: witness the fact that he took only one
water-bag, and left us the rest.

Thus, we found ourselves once more without a guide.
Fortunately, I had discussed with him the general direction,
and he had told Ibn Fahad and myself of the larger landmarks
. . . but it was nevertheless with sunken hearts that we
proceeded.

Later that day, in the early afternoon, the second blow
fell.

We were coming up out of the valley, climbing diagonally
along the steep side of the ravine. The damned Caucassian
fogs had slimed the rocks and turned the ground soggy; the
footing was treacherous.

Achmed, the older of the remaining pike-men, had been
walking poorly all day. He had bad joints, anyway, he said;
and the cold nights had been making them worse.

We had stopped to rest on an outcropping of rock that jutted from the valley wall; and Achmed, the last in line, was just catching up to us when he slipped. He fell heavily onto his side and slid several feet down the muddy slope.

Ibn Fahad jumped up to look for a rope, but before he could get one from the bottom of his pack the other soldier – named Bekir, if memory serves – clambered down the grade to help his comrade.

He got a grip on Achmed's tunic, and was just turning around to catch Ibn Fahad's rope when the leg of the older man buckled beneath him and he fell backward. Bekir, caught off his balance, pitched back as well, his hand caught in the neck of Achmed's tunic, and the two of them rolled end over end down the slope. Before anyone could so much as cry out they had both disappeared over the edge, like a wine jug rolling off a table-top. Just that sudden.

To fall such a distance certainly killed them.

We could not find the bodies, of course . . . could not even climb back down the ravine to look. Ibn Fahad's remark about burials had taken on a terrible, ironic truth. We could but press on, now a party of five – myself, Ibn Fahad, the under-vizier Walid, Abdallah the clerk, and young Fawn. I doubt that there was a single one of our number who did not wonder which of us would next meet death in that lonesome place.

Ah, by Allah most high, I have never been so sick of the sound of my own voice as I was by the time nine more nights had passed. Ibn Fahad, I know, would say that I have never understood how sick *everyone* becomes of the sound of my voice – am I correct, old friend? But I *was* tired of it, tired of talking all night, tired of racking my brain for stories, tired of listening to the cracked voices of Walid and Ibn Fahad, tired to sickness of the damp, grey, oppressive mountains.

All were now aware of the haunting shade that stood outside our fire at night, waiting and listening. Young Fawn, in particular, could hardly hold up his turn at tale-telling, so much did his voice tremble.

Abdallah grew steadily colder and colder, congealing like rendered fat. The thing which followed was no respecter of his cynicism or his mathematics, and would not be banished for all the scorn he could muster. The skinny chief-clerk did not turn out to us, though, to support the story-circle, but sat silently and walked apart. Despite our terrible mutual danger he avoided our company as much as possible.

The tenth night after the loss of Achmed and Bekir we were running out of tales. We had been ground down by our circumstances, and were ourselves become nearly as shadowy as that which we feared.

Walid al-Salameh was droning on about some ancient bit of minor intrigue in the court of the Emperor Darius of Persia. Ibn Fahad leaned toward me, lowering his voice so that neither Abdallah or Fawn – whose expression was one of complete and hopeless despair – could hear.

'Did you notice,' he whispered, 'that our guest has made no appearance tonight?'

'It has not escaped me,' I said. 'I hardly think it a good sign, however. If our talk no longer interests the creature, how long can it be until its thoughts return to our other uses?'

'I fear you're right,' he responded, and gave a scratchy, painful chuckle. 'There's a good three or four more days walking, and hard walking at that, until we reach the bottom of these mountains and come once more onto the plain, at which point we might hope the devil-beast would leave us.'

'Ibn Fahad,' I said, shaking my head as I looked across at Fawn's drawn, pale face, 'I fear we shall not manage . . .'

As if to point up the truth of my fears, Walid here stopped his speech, coughing violently. I gave him to drink of the water-skin, but when he had finished he did not begin anew; he only sat looking darkly, as one lost, out to the forest.

'Good vizier,' I asked, 'can you continue?'

He said nothing, and I quickly spoke in his place, trying to pick up the threads of a tale I had not been attending to. Walid leaned back, exhausted and breathing raggedly. Abdallah clucked his tongue in disgust. If I had not been fearfully occupied, I would have struck the clerk.

Just as I was beginning to find my way, inventing a continuation of the vizier's Darian political meanderings, there came a shock that passed through all of us like a cold wind, and a new shadow appeared at the edge of the clearing. The vampyr had joined us.

Walid moaned and sat up, huddling by the fire. I faltered for a moment but went on. The candle-flame eyes regarded us unblinkingly, and the shadow shook for a moment as if folding great wings.

Suddenly Fawn leaped to his feet, swaying unsteadily. I lost the strands of the story completely and stared up at him in amazement.

'Creature!' he screamed. 'Hell-spawn! Why do you torment us in this way? Why, why, why?'

Ibn Fahad reached up to pull him down, but the young man danced away like a shying horse. His mouth hung open and his eyes were starting from their dark-rimmed sockets.

'You great beast!' he continued to shriek. 'Why do you toy with us? Why do you not just kill me – kill us *all*, set us free from this terrible, terrible . . .'

And with that he walked *forward* – away from the fire, toward the thing that crouched at forest's edge.

'End this now!' Fawn shouted, and fell to his knees only a few strides from the smoldering red eyes, sobbing like a child.

'Stupid boy, get back!' I cried. Before I could get up to pull him back – and I would have, I swear by Allah's name – there was a great rushing noise, and the black shape was gone, the lamps of its stare extinguished. Then, as we pulled the shuddering youth back to the campfire, something rustled in the trees. On the opposite side of the campfire one of the near branches suddenly bobbed beneath the weight of a strange new fruit – a black fruit with red-lit eyes. It made an awful croaking noise.

In our shock it was a few moments before we realized that the deep, rasping sound was speech – and the words were Arabic!

'. . . It . . . was . . . you . . .,' it said, '. . . who chose . . . to play the game this way . . .'

Almost strangest of all, I would swear that this thing had never spoken our language before, never even heard it until we had wandered lost into the mountains. Something of its halting inflections, its strange hesitations, made me guess it had learned our speech from listening all these nights to our campfire stories.

'Demon!' shrilled Abdallah. 'What manner of creature are you?!'

'You know . . . very well what kind of . . . thing I am, man. You may none of you know *how*, or *why* . . . but by now, you know *what* I am.'

'Why . . . why do you torment us so?!' shouted Fawn, writhing in Ibn Fahad's strong grasp.

'Why does the . . . serpent kill . . . a rabbit? The serpent does not . . . hate. It kills to live, as do I . . . as do you.'

Abdallah lurched forward a step. 'We do not slaughter our fellow men like this, devil-spawn!'

'C-c-clerk!' the black shape hissed, and dropped down from the tree. 'C-close your foolish mouth! You push me too far!' It bobbed, as if agitated. 'The curse of human ways! Even now you provoke me more than you should, you huffing . . . insect! *Enough*!'

The vampyr seemed to leap upward, and with a great rattling of leaves he scuttled away along the limb of a tall tree. I was fumbling for my sword, but before I could find it the creature spoke again from his high perch.

'The young one asked me why I "toy" with you. I do not. If I do not kill, I will suffer. More than I suffer already.

'Despite what this clerk says, though, I am not a creature without . . . without feelings as men have them. Less and less do I wish to destroy you.

'For the first time in a great age I have listened to the sound of human voices that were not screams of fear. I have approached a circle of men without the barking of dogs, and have listened to them talk.

'It has almost been like being a man again.'

'And this is how you show your pleasure?' the under-vizier Walid asked, teeth chattering. 'By k-k-killing us?'

'I am what I am,' said the beast. '. . . But for all that, you have inspired a certain desire for companionship. It puts me in mind of things that I can barely remember.

'I propose that we make a . . . bargain,' said the vampyr. 'A . . . wager?'

I had found my sword, and Ibn Fahad had drawn his as well, but we both knew we could not kill a thing like this – a red-eyed demon that could leap five cubits in the air and had learned to speak our language in a fortnight.

'No bargains with Shaitan!' spat the clerk Abdallah.

'What do you mean?' I demanded, inwardly marveling that such an unlikely dialogue should ever take place on the earth. 'Pay no attention to the . . .' I curled my lip, '. . . holy man.' Abdallah shot me a venomous glance.

'Hear me, then,' the creature said, and in the deep recesses of the tree seemed once more to unfold and stretch great wings. 'Hear me. I must kill to live, and my nature is such that I cannot choose to die. That is the way of things.

'I offer you now, however, the chance to win safe passage out of my domain, these hills. We shall have a contest, a wager if you like; if you best me you shall go freely, and I shall turn once more to the musty, slow-blooded peasants of the local valleys.'

Ibn Fahad laughed bitterly. 'What, are we to fight you then? So be it!'

'I would snap your spine like a dry branch,' croaked the black shape. 'No, you have held me these many nights telling stories; it is story-telling that will win you safe passage. We will have a contest, one that will suit my whims: we shall relate the saddest of all stories. That is my demand. You may tell three, I will tell only one. If you can best me with any or all, you shall go unhindered by me.'

'And if we lose?!' I cried. 'And who shall judge?'

'You may judge,' it said, and the deep, thick voice took on a tone of grim amusement. 'If you can look into my eyes and tell me that you have bested *my* sad tale . . . why, then I shall believe you.

'If you lose,' it said, 'then one of your number shall come to me, and pay the price of your defeat. Those are my terms, otherwise I shall hunt you down one at a time – for in truth, your present tale-telling has begun to lose my interest.'

Ibn Fahad darted a worried look in my direction. Fawn and the others stared at the demon-shape in mute terror and astonishment.

'We shall . . . we shall give you our decision at sunset tomorrow,' I said. 'We must be allowed to think and talk.'

'As you wish,' said the vampyr. 'But if you accept my challenge, the game must begin then. After all, we have

only a few more days to spend together.' And at this
the terrible creature laughed, a sound like the bark being
pulled from the trunk of a rotted tree. Then the shadow
was gone.

In the end we had to accede to the creature's wager, of course.
We knew he was not wrong in his assessment of us – we
were just wagging our beards over the nightly campfire, no
longer even listening to our own tales. Whatever magic had
held the vampyr at bay had drained out like meal from a
torn sack.

I racked my poor brains all afternoon for stories of sadness, but could think of nothing that seemed to fit, that
seemed significant enough for the vital purpose at hand.
I had been doing most of the talking for several nights
running, and had exhausted virtually every story I had
ever heard – and I was never much good at making them
up, as Ibn Fahad will attest. Yes, go ahead and smile, old
comrade.

Actually, it was Ibn Fahad who volunteered the first
tale. I asked him what it was, but he would not tell me.
'Let me save what potency it may have,' he said. The
under-vizier Walid also had something he deemed suitable,
I was racking my brain fruitlessly for a third time when
young Fawn piped up that he would tell a tale himself.
I looked him over, rosy cheeks and long-lashed eyes, and
asked him what he could possibly know of sadness. Even
as I spoke I realized my cruelty, standing as we all did in
the shadow of death or worse; but it was too late to take
it back.

Fawn did not flinch. He was folding his cloak as he sat
cross-ankled on the ground, folding and unfolding it. He
looked up and said: 'I shall tell a sad story about love. All
the saddest stories are about love.'

These young shavetails, I thought – although I was not ten
years his senior – *a sad story about love*. But I could not think
of better, and was forced to give in.

We walked as fast and far as we could that day, as if
hoping that somehow, against all reason, we should find
ourselves out of the gloomy, mist-sodden hills. But when
twilight came the vast bulk of the mountains still hung above

us. We made camp on the porch of a great standing rock, as though protection at our backs would avail us of something if the night went badly.

The fire had only just taken hold, and the sun had dipped below the rim of the hills a moment before, when a cold wind made the branches of the trees whip back and forth. We knew without speaking, without looking at one another, that the creature had come.

'Have you made your decision?' The harsh voice from the trees sounded strange, as if its owner was trying to speak lightly, carelessly – but I only heard death in those cold syllables.

'We have,' said Ibn Fahad, drawing himself up out of his involuntary half-crouch to stand erect. 'We will accept your wager. Do you wish to begin?'

'Oh, no . . .' the thing said, and made a flapping noise. 'That would take all of the . . . suspense from the contest, would it not? No, I insist that you begin.'

'I am first, then,' Ibn Fahad said, looking around our circle for confirmation. The dark shape moved abruptly toward us. Before we could scatter the vampyr stopped, a few short steps away.

'Do not fear,' it grated. Close to one's ear the voice was even odder and more strained. 'I have come nearer to hear the story and see the teller – for surely that is part of any tale – but I shall move no farther. Begin.'

Everybody but myself stared into the fire, hugging their knees, keeping their eyes averted from the bundle of darkness that sat at our shoulders. I had the fire between myself and the creature, and felt safer than if I had sat like Walid and Abdallah, with nothing between the beast and my back but cold ground.

The vampyr sat hunched, as if imitating our posture, its eyes hooded so that only a flicker of scarlet light, like a half-buried brand, showed through the slit. It was black, this manlike thing – not black as a Negro, mind you, but black as burnt steel, black as the mouth of a cave. It bore the aspect of someone dead of the plague. Rags wrapped it, mouldering, filthy bits of cloth, rotten as old bread . . . but the curve of its back spoke of terrible life – a great black cricket poised to jump.

IBN FAHAD'S STORY

Many years ago [he began], I traveled for a good time in
Egypt. I was indigent, then, and journeyed wherever the
prospect of payment for a sword arm beckoned.

I found myself at last in the house-hold guard of a rich
merchant in Alexandria. I was happy enough there; and I
enjoyed walking in the busy streets, so unlike the village in
which I was born.

One summer evening I found myself walking down an
unfamiliar street. It emptied out into a little square that sat
below the front of an old mosque. The square was full of
people, merchants and fishwives, a juggler or two, but most
of the crowd was drawn up to the façade of the mosque,
pressed in close together.

At first, as I strolled across the square, I thought prayers
were about to begin, but it was still some time until sunset. I
wondered if perhaps some notable *imam* was speaking from
the mosque steps, but as I approached I could see that all the
assembly were staring upward, craning their necks back as if
the sun itself, on its way to its western mooring, had become
snagged on one of the minarets.

But instead of the sun, what stood on the onion-shaped
dome was the silhouette of a man, who seemed to be staring
out toward the horizon.

'Who is that?' I asked a man near me.

'It is Ha'arud al-Emwiya, the Sufi,' the man told me, never
lowering his eyes from the tower above.

'Is he caught up there?' I demanded. 'Will he not fall?'

'Watch,' was all the man said. I did.

A moment later, much to my horror, the small dark figure
of Ha'arud the Sufi seemed to go rigid, then toppled from
the minaret's rim like a stone. I gasped in shock, and so did
a few others around me, but the rest of the crowd only stood
in hushed attention.

Then an incredible thing happened. The tumbling holy
man spread his arms out from his shoulders, like a bird's
wings, and his downward fall became a swooping glide.
He bottomed out high above the crowd, then sped upward,
riding the wind like a leaf, spinning, somersaulting, stopping

at last to drift to the ground as gently as a bit of eider-down. Meanwhile, all the assembly was chanting 'God is great! God is great!' When the sufi had touched the earth with his bare feet the people surrounded him, touching his rough woolen garments and crying out his name. He said nothing, only stood and smiled, and before too long the people began to wander away, talking amongst themselves.

'But this is truly marvelous!' I said to the man who stood by me.

'Before every holy day he flies,' the man said, and shrugged. 'I am surprised this is the first time you have heard of Ha'arud al-Emwiya.'

I was determined to speak to this amazing man, and as the crowd dispersed I approached and asked if I might buy him a glass of tea. Close up he had a look of seamed roguishness that seemed surprising placed against the great favor in which Allah must have held him. He smilingly agreed, and accompanied me to a tea shop close by in the Street of Weavers.

'How is it, if you will pardon my forwardness, that you of all holy men are so gifted?'

He looked up from the tea cupped in his palms and grinned. He had only two teeth. 'Balance,' he said.

I was surprised. 'A cat has balance,' I responded, 'but they nevertheless must wait for the pigeons to land.'

'I refer to a different sort of balance,' he said. 'The balance between Allah and Shaitan, which, as you know, Allah the All-Knowing has created as an equilibrium of exquisite delicacy.'

'Explain please, master.' I called for wine, but Ha'arud refused any himself.

'In all things care must be exercised,' he explained. 'Thus it is too with my flying. Many men holier than I are as earthbound as stones. Many other men have lived so poorly as to shame the Devil himself, yet they cannot take to the air, either. Only I, if I may be excused what sounds self-satisfied, have discovered perfect balance. Thus, each year before the holy days I tot up my score carefully, committing small peccadilloes or acts of faith as needed until the balance is exactly, exactly balanced. Thus, when I jump from the mosque, neither Allah nor the Arch-Enemy has claim on my soul, and they bear me up until a later date, at which time the issue shall be clearer.' He smiled again and drained his tea.

'You are . . . a sort of chessboard on which God and the Devil contend?' I asked, perplexed.

'A flying chessboard, yes.'

We talked for a long while, as the shadows grew long across the Street of the Weavers, but the Sufi Ha'arud adhered stubbornly to his explanation. I must have seemed disbelieving, for he finally proposed that we ascend to the top of the mosque so he could demonstrate.

I was more than a little drunk, and he, imbibing only tea, was filled nonetheless with a strange gleefulness. We made our way up the many winding stairs and climbed out onto the narrow ledge that circled the minaret like a crown. The cool night air, and the thousands of winking lights of Alexandria far below, sobered me rapidly. 'I suddenly find all your precepts very sound,' I said. 'Let us go down.'

But Ha'arud would have none of it, and proceeded to step lightly off the edge of the dome. He hovered, like a bumblebee, a hundred feet above the dusty street. 'Balance,' he said with great satisfaction.

'But,' I asked, 'is the good deed of giving me this demonstration enough to offset the pride with which you exhibit your skill?' I was cold and wanted to get down, and hoped to shorten the exhibition.

Instead, hearing my question, Ha'arud screwed up his face as though it was something he had not given thought to. A moment later, with a shriek of surprise, he plummeted down out of my sight to smash on the mosque's stone steps, as dead as dead.

Ibn Fahad, having lost himself in remembering the story, poked at the campfire. 'Thus, the problem with matters of delicate balance,' he said, and shook his head.

The whispering rustle of our dark visitor brought us sharply back. 'Interesting,' the creature rasped. 'Sad, yes. Sad enough? We shall see. Who is the next of your number?'

A cold chill, like fever, swept over me at those calm words.

'I . . . I am next . . .,' said Fawn, voice taut as a bowstring.
'Shall I begin?'

'The vampyr said nothing, only bobbed the black lump of
his head. The youth cleared his throat and began.

FAWN'S STORY

There was once . . . [Fawn began, and hesitated, then started
again.] There was once a young prince named Zufik, the
second son of a great sultan. Seeing no prospects for himself
in his father's kingdom, he went out into the wild world
to search for his fortune. He traveled through many lands,
and saw many strange things, and heard tell of others
stranger still.

In one place he was told of a nearby sultanate, the ruler of
which had a beautiful daughter, his only child and the very
apple of his eye.

Now this country had been plagued for several years
by a terrible beast, a great white leopard of a kind never
seen before. So fearsome it was that it had killed hunters set to trap it, yet was it also so cunning that it had
stolen babies from their very cradles as the mothers lay
sleeping. The people of the sultanate were all in fear;
and the sultan, whose best warriors had tried and failed
to kill the beast, was driven to despair. Finally, at the
end of his wits, he had it proclaimed in the market place
that the man who could destroy the white leopard would
be gifted with the sultan's daughter Rassoril, and with
her the throne of the sultanate after the old man was
gone.

Young Zufik heard how the best young men of the country,
and others from countries beyond, one after the other had
met their deaths beneath the claws of the leopard, or . . . or
. . . in its jaws . . .

[Here I saw the boy falter, as if the vision of flashing
teeth he was conjuring had suddenly reminded him of our
predicament. Walid the under-vizier reached out and patted
the lad's shoulder with great gentleness, until he was calm
enough to resume.]

So . . . [He swallowed.] So young Prince Zufik took

himself into that country, and soon was announced at the
sultan's court.

The ruler was a tired old man, the fires in his sunken eyes
long quenched. Much of the power seemed to have been
handed over to a pale, narrow-faced youth named Sifaz, who
was the princess's cousin. As Zufik announced his purpose,
as so many had done before him, Sifaz's eyes flashed.

'You will no doubt meet the end all the others have, but
you are welcome to the attempt – and the prize, should
you win.'

Then for the first time Zufik saw the princess Rassoril, and
in an instant his heart was overthrown.

She had hair as black and shiny as polished jet, and a face
upon which Allah himself must have looked in satisfaction,
thinking: 'Here is the summit of My art.' Her delicate hands
were like tiny doves as they nested in her lap, and a man
could fall into her brown eyes and drown without hope of
rescue – which is what Zufik did, and he was not wrong
when he thought he saw Rassoril return his ardent gaze.

Sifaz saw, too, and his thin mouth turned in something
like a smile, and he narrowed his yellow eyes. 'Take this
princeling to his room, that he may sleep now and wake
with the moon. The leopard's cry was heard around the
palace's walls last night.'

Indeed, when Zufik woke in the evening darkness, it was
to hear the choking cry of the leopard beneath his very
window. As he looked out, buckling on his scabbard, it was
to see a white shape slipping in and out of the shadows in
the garden below. He took also his dagger in his hand and
leaped over the threshold.

He had barely touched ground when, with a terrible snarl,
the leopard bounded out of the obscurity of the hedged
garden wall and came to a stop before him. It was huge –
bigger than any leopard Zufik had seen or heard of – and
its pelt gleamed like ivory. It leaped, claws flashing, and
he could barely throw himself down in time as the beast
passed over him like a cloud, touching him only with its
hot breath. It turned and leaped again as the palace dogs
set up a terrible barking, and this time its talons raked his
chest, knocking him tumbling. Blood started from his shirt,
spouting so fiercely that he could scarcely draw himself to

his feet. He was caught with his back against the garden wall; the leopard slowly moved toward him, yellow eyes like tallow lamps burning in the niches of Hell.

Suddenly there was a crashing at the far end of the garden: the dogs had broken down their stall and were even now speeding through the trees. The leopard hesitated – Zufik could almost see it thinking – and then, with a last snarl, it leaped onto the wall and disappeared into the night.

Zufik was taken, his wounds bound, and he was put into his bed. The princess Rassoril, who had truly lost her heart to him, wept bitterly at his side, begging him to go back to his father's land and to give up the fatal challenge. But Zufik, weak as he was, would no more think of yielding than he would of theft or treason, and refused, saying he would hunt the beast again the following night. Sifaz grinned and led the princess away. Zufik thought he heard the pale cousin whistling as he went.

In the dark before dawn Zufik, who could not sleep owing to the pain of his injury, heard his door quietly open. He was astonished to see the princess come in, gesturing him to silence. When the door was closed she threw herself down at his side and covered his hand and cheek with kisses, proclaiming her love for him and begging him again to go. He admitted his love for her, but reminded her that his honor would not permit him to stop short of his goal, even should he die in the trying.

Rassoril, seeing that there was no changing the young prince's mind, then took from her robe a black arrow tipped in silver, fletched with the tail feathers of a falcon. "Then take this,"' she said. 'This leopard is a magic beast, and you will never kill it otherwise. Only silver will pierce its heart. Take the arrow and you may fulfill your oath.' So saying, she slipped out of his room.

The next night Zufik again heard the leopard's voice in the garden below, but this time he took also his bow and arrow when he went to meet it. At first he was loath to use it, since it seemed somehow unmanly; but when the beast had again given him injury and he had struck three sword blows in turn without effect, he at last nocked the silver-pointed shaft on his bowstring and, as the beast charged him once more, let fly. The black arrow struck to the leopard's heart;

the creature gave a hideous cry and again leaped the fence, this time leaving a trail of its mortal blood behind it.

When morning came Zufik went to the sultan for men, so that they could follow the track of blood to the beast's lair and prove its death. The sultan was displeased when his vizier, the princess's pale cousin, did not answer his summons. As they were all going down into the garden, though, there came a great cry from the sleeping rooms upstairs, a cry like a soul in mortal agony. With fear in their hearts Zufik, the sultan, and all the men rushed upstairs. There they found the missing Sifaz.

The pale man lifted a shaking, red-smeared finger to point at Zufik, as all the company stared in horror. '*He* has done it – the foreigner!' Sifaz shouted.

In Sifaz's arms lay the body of the Princess Rassoril, a black arrow standing from her breast.

After Fawn finished there was a long silence. The boy, his own courage perhaps stirred by his story, seemed to sit straighter.

'Ah . . .,' the vampyr said at last, 'love and its prices – that is the message? Or is it perhaps the effect of silver on the supernatural? Fear not, I am bound by no such conventions, and fear neither silver, steel, nor any other metal.' The creature made a huffing, scraping sound that might have been a laugh. I marveled anew, even as I felt the skein of my life fraying, that it had so quickly gained such command of our unfamiliar tongue.

'Well . . .,' it said slowly. 'Sad. But . . . sad enough? Again, *that* is the important question. Who is your last . . . contestant?'

Now my heart truly went cold within me, and I sat as though I had swallowed a stone. Walid al-Salameh spoke up.

'I am,' he said, and took a deep breath. 'I am.'

THE VIZIER'S STORY

This is a true story – or so I was told. It happened in my grandfather's time, and he had it from someone who knew those involved. He told it to me as a cautionary tale.

There once was an old caliph, a man of rare gifts and good fortune. He ruled a small country, but a wealthy one – a country upon which all the gifts of Allah had been showered in grand measure. He had the finest heir a man could have, dutiful and yet courageous, beloved by the people almost as extravagantly as the caliph himself. He had many other fine sons, and two hundred beautiful wives, and an army of fighting men the envy of his neighbors. His treasury was stacked roofbeam-high with gold and gemstones and blocks of fragrant sandalwood, crisscrossed with ivories and bolts of the finest cloth. His palace was built around a spring of fragrant, clear water; and everyone said that they must be the very Waters of Life, so fortunate and well-loved this caliph was. His only sadness was that age had robbed his sight from him, leaving him blind, but hard as this was, it was a small price to pay for Allah's beneficence.

One day the caliph was walking in his garden, smelling the exquisite fragrance of the blossoming orange trees. His son the prince, unaware of his father's presence, was also in the garden, speaking with his mother, the caliph's first and chiefest wife.

'He is terribly old,' the wife said. 'I cannot stand even to touch him anymore. It is a horror to me.'

'You are right, mother,' the son replied, as the caliph hid behind the trees and listened, shocked. 'I am sickened by watching him sitting all day, drooling into his bowl, or staggering sightless through the palace. But what are we to do?'

'I have thought on it long and hard,' the caliph's wife replied. 'We owe it to ourselves and those close to us to kill him.'

'Kill him?' the son replied. 'Well, it is hard for me, but I suppose you are right. I still feel some love for him, though – may we at least do it quickly, so that he shall not feel pain at the end?'

'Very well. But do it soon – tonight, even. If I must feel his foul breath upon me one more night I will die myself.'

'Tonight, then,' the son agreed, and the two walked away, leaving the blind caliph shaking with rage and terror behind

the orange trees. He could not see what sat on the garden
path behind them, the object of their discussion: the wife's
old lap-dog, a scrofulous creature of extreme age.

Thus the caliph went to his vizier, the only one he was
sure he could trust in a world of suddenly traitorous sons
and wives, and bade him to have the pair arrested and
quickly beheaded. The vizier was shocked, and asked the
reason why, but the caliph only said he had unassailable
proof that they intended to murder him and take his throne.
He bade the vizier go and do the deed.

The vizier did as he was directed, seizing the son and his
mother quickly and quietly, then giving them over to the
headsman after tormenting them for confessions and the
names of confederates, neither of which were forthcoming.

Sadly, the vizier went to the caliph and told him it was
done, and the old man was satisfied. But soon, inevitably,
word of what had happened spread, and the brothers of the
heir began to murmur among themselves about their father's
deed. Many thought him mad, since the dead pair's devotion
to the caliph was common knowledge.

Word of this dissension reached the caliph himself, and he
began to fear for his life, terrified that his other sons meant to
emulate their treasonous brother. He called the vizier to him
and demanded the arrest of these sons, and their beheading.
The vizier argued in vain, risking his own life, but the caliph
would not be swayed; at last the vizier went away, returning
a week later a battered, shaken man.

'It is done, O Prince,' he said. 'All your sons are dead.'

The caliph had only a short while in which to feel safe
before the extreme wrath of the wives over the slaughter
of their children reached his ears. 'Destroy them, too!' the
blind caliph insisted.

Again the vizier went away, soon to return.

'It is done, O Prince,' he reported. 'Your wives have been
beheaded.'

Soon the courtiers were crying murder, and the caliph sent
his vizier to see them dealt with as well.

'It is done, O Prince,' he assured the caliph. But the ruler
now feared the angry townspeople, so he commanded his
vizier to take the army and slaughter them. The vizier argued
feebly, then went away.

'It is done, O Prince,' the caliph was told a month later. But now the caliph realized that with his heirs and wives gone, and the important men of the court dead, it was the soldiers themselves who were a threat to his power. He commanded his vizier to sow lies amongst them, causing them to fall out and slay each other, then locked himself in his room to safely outlast the conflict. After a month and a half the vizier knocked upon his door.

'It is done, O Prince.'

For a moment the caliph was satisfied. All his enemies were dead, and he himself was locked in: no one could murder him, or steal his treasure, or usurp his throne. The only person yet alive who even knew where the caliph hid was . . . his vizier.

Blind, he groped about for the key with which he had locked himself in. Better first to remove the risk that someone might trick him into coming out. He pushed the key out beneath the door and told the vizier to throw it away somewhere it might never be found. When the vizier returned he called him close to the locked portal that bounded his small world of darkness and safety.

'Vizier,' the caliph said through the keyhole, 'I command you to go and kill yourself, for you are the last one living who is a threat to me.'

'*Kill* myself, my prince?' the vizier asked, dumbfounded. 'Kill *myself*?'

'Correct,' the caliph said. 'Now go and do it. That is my command.'

There was a long silence. At last the vizier said: 'Very well.' After that there was silence.

For a long time the caliph sat in his blindness and exulted, for everyone he distrusted was gone. His faithful vizier had carried out all his orders, and now had killed himself . . .

A sudden, horrible thought came to him then: what if the vizier had *not* done what he had told him to do? What if instead he had made compact with the caliph's enemies, and was only reporting false details when he told of their deaths? *How was the caliph to know*? He almost swooned with fright and anxiousness at the realization.

At last he worked up the courage to feel his way across the locked room to the door. He put his ear to the keyhole and listened. He heard nothing but silence. He took a breath and then put his mouth to the hole.

'Vizier?' he called in a shaky voice. 'Have you done what I commanded? Have you killed yourself?'

'It is done, O Prince,' came the reply.

Finishing his story, which was fully as dreadful as it was sad, the under-vizier Walid lowered his head as if ashamed or exhausted. We waited tensely for our guest to speak; at the same time I am sure we all vainly hoped there would be no more speaking, that the creature would simply vanish, like a frightening dream that flees the sun.

'Rather than discuss the merits of your sad tales,' the black, tattered shadow said at last – confirming that there would be no waking from *this* dream, 'rather than argue the game with only one set of moves completed, perhaps it is now time for me to speak. The night is still youthful, and my tale is not long, but I wish to give you a fair time to render judgement.'

As he spoke the creature's eyes bloomed scarlet like unfolding roses. The mist curled up from the ground beyond the fire-circle, wrapping the vampire in a cloak of writhing fogs, a rotted black egg in a bag of silken mesh.

'. . . May I begin?' it asked . . . but no one could say a word. 'Very well . . .'

THE VAMPYR'S STORY

The tale *I* will tell is of a child, a child born of an ancient city on the banks of a river. So long ago this was that not only has the city itself long gone to dust; but the later cities built atop its ruins, tiny towns and great walled fortresses of stone, all these too have gone beneath the millwheels of time – rendered, like their predecessor, into the finest of particles to blow in the wind, silting the timeless river's banks.

This child lived in a mud hut thatched with straw, and played with his fellows in the shallows of the sluggish brown river while his mother washed the family's clothes and gossiped with her neighbors.

Even *this* ancient city was built upon the bones of earlier cities, and it was into the collapsed remnants of one – a great, tumbled mass of shattered sandstone – that the child and his friends sometimes went. And it was to these ruins that the child, when he was a little older . . . almost the age of your young, romantic companion . . . took a pretty, doe-eyed girl.

It was to be his first time beyond the veil – his initiation into the mysteries of women. His heart beat rapidly; the girl walked ahead of him, her slender brown body tiger-striped with light and shade as she walked among the broken pillars. Then she saw something, and screamed. The child came running.

The girl was nearly mad, weeping and pointing. He stopped in amazement, staring at the black, shrivelled thing that lay on the ground – a twisted something that might have been a man once, wizened and black as a piece of leather dropped into the cookfire. Then the thing opened its eyes.

The girl ran, choking – but he did not, seeing that the black thing could not move. The twitching of its mouth seemed that of someone trying to speak; he thought he heard a faint voice asking for help, begging for him to do something. He leaned down to the near-silent hiss, and the thing squirmed and bit him, fastening its sharp teeth like barbed fish-hooks in the muscle of his leg. The man-child screamed, helpless, and felt his blood running out into the horrible sucking mouth of the thing. Fetid saliva crept into the wounds and coursed hotly through his body, even as he struggled against his writhing attacker. The poison climbed through him, and it seemed he could feel his own heart flutter and die within his chest, delicate and hopeless as a broken bird. With final, desperate strength the child pulled free. The black thing, mouth gaping, curled on itself and shuddered, like a beetle on a hot stone. A moment later it had crumbled into ashes and oily flakes.

But it had caught me long enough to destroy me – for of course *I* was that child – to force its foul fluids into me, leeching my humanity and replacing it with the hideous, unwanted wine of immortality. My child's heart became an icy fist.

Thus was I made what I am, at the hands of a dying vampyr – which had been a creature like I am now. Worn down at last by the passing of millennia, it had chosen a host to receive its hideous malady, then died – as *I* shall do someday, no doubt, in the grip of some terrible, blind, insect-like urge . . . but not soon. Not today.

So that child, which had been in all ways like other children – loved by its family, loving in turn noise and games and sweetmeats – became a dark thing sickened by the burning light of the sun.

Driven into the damp shadows beneath stones and the dusty gloom of abandoned places, then driven out again beneath the moon by an unshakeable, unresistable hunger, I fed first on my family – my uncomprehending mother wept to see her child returned, standing by her moonlit pallet – then on the others of my city. Not last, or least painful of my feedings was on the darkhaired girl who had run when I stayed behind. I slashed other throats, too, and lapped up warm, sea-salty blood while the trapped child inside me cried without a sound. It was as though I stood behind a screen, unable to leave or interfere as terrible crimes were committed before me . . .

And thus the years have passed: sand grains, deposited along the river bank, uncountable in their succession. Every one has contained a seeming infinitude of killings, each one terrible despite their numbing similarity. Only the blood of mankind will properly feed me, and a hundred generations have known terror of me.

Strong as I am, virtually immortal, unkillable as far as I know or can tell – blades pass through me like smoke; fire, water, poison, none affect me – still the light of the sun causes a pain to me so excruciating that you with only mortal lives, whose pain at least eventually ends in death, cannot possibly comprehend it. Thus, kingdoms of men have risen and fallen to ashes since I last saw daylight. Think only on that for a moment, if you seek sad stories! I must be in darkness when the sun rises, so as I range in search of prey my accommodations are shared with toads and slugs, bats, and blindworms.

People can be nothing to me anymore but food. I know of none other like myself, save the dying creature who spawned me. The smell of my own corruption is in my nostrils always.

So there is all of *my* tale. I cannot die until my time is

come, and who can know when that is? Until then I will
be alone, alone as no mere man can ever be, alone with
my wretchedness and evil and self-disgust until the world
collapses and is born anew . . .

The vampyr rose now, towering up like a black sail billowing
in the wind, spreading its vast arms or wings on either side,
as if to sweep us before it. 'How do your stories compare to
this?' it cried; the harshness of its speech seemed somehow
muted, even as it grew louder and louder. 'Whose is the
saddest story, then?' There was pain in that hideous voice
that tore at even my fast-pounding heart. 'Whose is saddest?
Tell me! It is time to *judge* . . .'

   And in that moment, of all the moments when lying could
save my life . . . I could not lie. I turned my face away
from the quivering black shadow, that thing of rags and
red eyes. None of the others around the campfire spoke –
even Abdallah the clerk only sat hugging his knees, teeth
chattering, eyes bulging with fear.

   '. . . I thought so,' the thing said at last. 'I thought so.'
Night wind tossed the treelimbs above our heads, and it
seemed as though beyond them stood only ultimate darkness
– no sky, no stars, nothing but unending emptiness.

   'Very well,' the vampyr said at last. 'Your silence speaks
all. I have won.' There was not the slightest note of triumph
in its voice. 'Give me my prize, and then I may let the
rest of you flee my mountains.' The dark shape withdrew
a little way.

   We all of us turned to look at one another, and it was just
as well that the night veiled our faces. I started to speak, but
Ibn Fahad interrupted me, his voice a tortured rasp.

   'Let there be no talk of volunteering. We will draw lots;
that is the only way.' Quickly he cut a thin branch into five
pieces, one of them shorter than the rest, and cupped them
in a closed hand.

   'Pick,' he said. 'I will keep the last.'

   As a part of me wondered what madness it was that had
left us wagering on story-telling and drawing lots for our
lives, we each took a length from Ibn Fahad's fist. I kept
my hand closed while the others selected, not wanting to
hurry Allah toward his revelation of my fate. When all

had selected we extended our hands and opened them, palms up.

Fawn had selected the short stick.

Strangely, there was no sign of his awful fortune on his face: he showed no signs of grief – indeed, he did not even respond to our helpless words and prayers, only stood up and slowly walked toward the huddled black shape at the far edge of the clearing. The vampyr rose to meet him.

'No!' came a sudden cry, and to our complete surprise the clerk Abdallah leaped to his feet and went pelting across the open space, throwing himself between the youth and the looming shadow. 'He is too young!' Abdallah shouted, sounding truly anguished. 'Do not do this horrible thing! Take me instead!'

Ibn Fahad, the vizier, and I could only sit, struck dumb by this unexpected behavior, but the creature moved swiftly as a viper, smacking Abdallah to the ground with one flicking gesture.

'You are indeed mad, you short-lived men!' the vampyr hissed. 'This one would do nothing to save himself – not once did I hear his voice raised in tale-telling – yet now he would throw himself into the jaws of death for this other! Mad!' The monster left Abdallah choking on the ground and turned to silent Fawn. 'Come, you. I have won the contest, and you are the prize. I am . . . sorry . . . it must be this way . . .' A great swath of darkness enveloped the youth, drawing him in. 'Come,' the vampyr said, 'think of the better world you go to – that is what you believe, is it not? Well, soon you shall – '

The creature broke off.

'Why do you look so strangely, manchild?' the thing said at last, its voice troubled. 'You cry, but I see no fear. Why? Are you not afraid of dying?'

Fawn answered; his tones were oddly distracted. 'Have you really lived so long? And alone, always alone?'

'I told you. I have no reason to lie. Do you think to put me off with your strange questions?'

'Ah, how could the good God be so unmerciful!?' The words were made of sighs. The dark shape that embraced him stiffened.

'Do you cry for *me*? *For me*?!'

'How can I help?' the boy said. 'Even Allah must weep for you . . . for such a pitiful thing, lost in the lonely darkness . . .'

For a moment the night air seemed to pulse. Then, with a wrenching gasp, the creature flung the youth backward so that he stumbled and fell before us, landing atop the groaning Abdallah.

'Go!' the vampyr shrieked, and its voice cracked and boomed like thunder. 'Get you gone from my mountains! Go!'

Amazed, we pulled Fawn and the chief clerk to their feet and went stumbling down the hillside, branches lashing at our faces and hands, expecting any moment to hear the rush of wings and feel cold breath on our necks.

'Build your houses well, little men!' a voice howled like the wild wind behind us. 'My life is long . . . and someday I may regret letting you go!'

We ran and ran, until it seemed the life would flee our bodies, until our lungs burned and our feet blistered . . . and until the topmost sliver of the sun peered over the eastern summits . . .

Masrur al-Adan allowed the tale's ending to hang in silence for a span of thirty heartbeats, then pushed his chair away from the table.

'We escaped the mountains the next day,' he said. 'Within a season we were back in Baghdad, the only survivors of the caravan to the Armenites.'

'Aaaahh . . .!' breathed young Hassan, a long drawn-out sound full of wonder and apprehension. 'What a marvelous, terrifying adventure! I would *never* have survived it, myself. How frightening! And did the . . . the creature . . . did he *really* say he might come back someday?'

Masrur solemnly nodded his large head. 'Upon my soul. Am I not right, Ibn Fahad, my old comrade?'

Ibn Fahad yielded a thin smile, seemingly of affirmation.

'Yes,' Masrur continued, 'those words chill me to this very day. Many is the night I have sat in this room, looking at that door – ' He pointed. '– wondering if some-day it may open to show me that terrible, misshapen black thing, come back from Hell to make good on our wager.'

'Merciful Allah!' Hassan gasped.

Abu Jamir leaned across the table as the other guests whispered excitedly. He wore a look of annoyance. 'Good Hassan,' he snapped, 'kindly calm yourself. We are all grateful to our host Masrur for entertaining us, but it is an insult to sensible, Godly men to suggest that at any moment some blood-drinking Afreet may knock down the door and carry us – '

The door leaped open with a crash, revealing a hideous, twisted shape looming in the entrance, red-splattered and trembling. The shrieking of Masrur's guests filled the room.

'Master . . .?' the dark silhouette quavered. Baba held a wine jar balanced on one shoulder. The other had broken at his feet, splashing Abu Jamir's prize stock everywhere. 'Master,' he began again, 'I am afraid I have dropped one.'

Masrur looked down at Abu Jamir, who lay pitched full-length on the floor, insensible.

'Ah, well, that's all right, Baba.' Masrur smiled, twirling his black mustache. 'We won't have to make the wine go so far as I thought – it seems my story-telling has put some of our guests to sleep.'

THE CUTTY BLACK SOW

Thomas F. Monteleone

*Thomas F. Monteleone is the author of some eighty published
short stories, with appearances in* Fantasy Tales 7, Dark Voices
2, Pulphouse *and* The Year's Best Horror Stories *to his
credit. His eighteen novels include* Night Train, The Apocalypse Man *and, more recently, the bestselling thriller* The Blood
of the Lamb *– which won the 1992 Bram Stoker Award –
and* The Final Quartet. *He has edited five anthologies in the*
Borderlands *series and also writes for the stage and television.*

SHE was going to die, he thought.

Twelve-year-old Jamie stood with his parents and his
little sister, Gloria, around Great-Grandmother McEvan's
bed while a cold autumn wind rumbled the shutters and
whistled through the seams of their old house. Rain tapped
on the windowpanes like tiny fingers, slapped against the
shingles like sheets on a clothes-line.

Great-Grandma was a tiny bird of a woman at the age of
103. She had always looked the same to Jamie: silver-blue
hair in a bun, thin pointy face, dark sparrow eyes, and
long, spider-leg fingers. But she had always been a strong
old woman. She had never been to a doctor in her life, and
she had birthed eight children. Lost five, and raised the rest
as best she could.

Now she lay in the warmly lit bedroom, her eyes closed,
mouth half-open, breath wheezing in and out of her like a
cold wind.

'She's not going to make it, is she, Dad?' asked Jamie with
the matter-of-factness of a twelve-year-old.

'Jamie! Stop that!' said his mother.

His father sighed, touched her arm. 'No, he's right, Hon. He's just saying out loud what we've all been thinking . . .'

'Is she going to die?' asked nine-year-old Gloria with a touch of awe in her voice. 'Is she really going to *die* right here in our house?'

'We don't know that for sure, sweetheart,' said Mother. She looked at her husband. 'Should we call Dr Linton?'

'I don't think there's much use in it. You remember what he said . . .'

Jamie noted that no one was actually crying, but every-body was fighting their feelings. They were all witnessing something they had known was coming for awhile now. He was thinking about the idea of death and dying, and how it changed people into such bad imitations of themselves. His great-grandmother had always been so lively and active. She had entertained him and Gloria with stories of her native Scotland and the Highlands she loved so dearly.

Now there would be no more stories.

The sheets rustled as the old woman stirred. Jamie saw her eyelids flutter as she gathered the strength to look at him and the others around her bed. 'What day is it?' she asked.

'Thursday,' said Jamie's father, without thinking.

A pause, then: 'No . . .' Great-Gran's voice was hoarse and low. 'What date?'

'Oh . . .' said his mother. 'It's the thirtieth.'

Another pause, a wheezing of breath, then: 'Of October?'

'Yes, Great-Gran,' said Jamie, keeping his own voice low and soft.

'All Hallow's Even,' said the old woman. There was a different tone in her voice, an inflection which could have been awe or respect, or even fear.

'What? What did she say?' asked Jamie's mother.

'I'm not sure,' said his father. 'Grandma, what was that you said?'

'All Hallow's Even. I'm going to die. On All Hallow's Even.'

'Jim, what's she talking about?'

'Halloween,' said Jamie's father. 'Tomorrow's Halloween. That's what they called it in Scotland.'

'But why . . . I mean, what does she mean?' Jamie's mother held his father's arm tightly.

'I don't know . . .' His father looked at his watch. Outside a gust of wind whispered against the house. 'Eleven-thirty. It'll be the thirty-first soon . . .'

Jamie's mother leaned over the bed, tried to talk to Great-Gran, but the old woman's eyes had closed and her breathing had returned to its former shallowness. Turning back to her husband, Jamie's mother looked distressed.

'I think we'd better call Dr Linton.'

His father nodded, sighed. 'All right, I'll call him. You kids, it's time to get off to bed.'

Hours later, Jamie lay in his bed in the darkness. The storm still buffeted the house and the trees around it. He could not fall asleep, was not even feeling tired. He'd been awake when Dr Linton arrived, wet and blustery in the downstairs foyer. The tall, white-haired doctor had looked in on Great-Gran, then returned downstairs to confer with Jamie's parents. The boy listened to Dr Linton's words: '. . . and I'd say there's nothing much more you can do to make her any more comfortable. She's lapsed into a coma. Might hang on for weeks – or, she might not make it till morning.'

The words stung Jamie as he lay in his dark bed. Great-Gran dying was one of those terribly impossible things to imagine. She'd *always* been a part of his life. Rocked him as a baby, fed him his bottles, bathed him, and always the stories about Scotland. To think of her as *gone* was like knowing when you woke up in the morning your right arm would be missing. Unthinkable. And yet, true. She might not last the night.

He didn't know how long he lay in his bed without sleeping. Long enough for the storm to quiet and his parents to finally retire to their bedroom. Long enough for the heavy clouds to part and let the moonlight creep through his window. Jamie wanted to fall asleep, but he could not.

More time passed. In the silent house, he could hear every creak and groan of old wood, every tic of cooling radiator pipes.

And then a new sound: Great-Grandmother was talking.

She sounded so bright and clear that he imagined she must have arisen from her coma. A spark of hope was ignited in him, and he slipped noiselessly from the bed to creep into her room at the end of the hall. The door was open and the room was stalked by tall shadows of old furniture, cast by the feeble glow of a night-light.

Silently, Jamie approached the bed. If anything, the old woman looked worse than before and she spoke as though in a trance.

But her words were soft and clear: '. . . and down we would go to Balquhidder with the other children to gather for the fires. A-beggin' from the folk, and we would say "Give us a peat t'barn the witches, good missus!" Pile it high, we would! With straw, furze and peat . . . what a beautiful Samhnagan it would be!'

Jamie felt a chill race down his back. He thought of calling his parents, but they would only make him go back to bed. Yet he sensed an urgency in the old woman's voice.

Then he thought of his tape recorder, and moving quickly, silently, he retrieved it from his room. Turning it on, he captured the trance-like ramblings of the old woman.

'. . . and the fire would burn through the night on All Hallow's Even, and we would dance about it, we would! The fire that kept away the Cutty Black Sow! Kept it away from any soul who died on that witches' night! Till the heap had turned to bright red coals. And we would gather up the coals and ash in the form of a circle. Then into that circle we would put stones – one marked for each member of our families. The stones were our souls! And as long as they stayed inside the circle of Samhnagan, ole Cutty Black could not harm us! And in the mornin' everyone would run to the cool ashen circle – to make sure that not a stone was disturbed or missin'. For if it was, the soul that stood for that missin' stone would be took by the Cutty Black Sow!'

Jamie listened as the old woman rambled. It was some memory, a bit of remembered childhood. He tried to speak to her, to ask her what she meant, but she continued on to the end, the last words only a whisper.

He waited for her to continue, but there was nothing more. Great-Gran's breathing became ragged, catching in her hollow chest, then wheezing out as if released by a cruel fist. Suddenly her body became rigid, then a tremor passed once through her bones. Jamie watched as her drawn little body rose under the bed-covers for an instant, then fell slack, her head lolling to the far side of the pillow.

He could not see her face, yet he knew she was gone. There was a coolness in the room that had been absent before. He felt utterly alone in a vast darkness despite the pale glow of the night-light.

Slowly, Jamie thumbed off the Sony recorder as his gaze drifted to an old Westclock on Great-Gran's bureau. 4.35 in the morning. She'd been right: she *did* die on Halloween.

He padded silently back to his room, replaced his cassette recorder on a shelf by his bed, then woke up his parents. He told them he had heard Great-Gran making strange noises, and that he was afraid to go see her. His father moved quickly from the bed and down the hall. A few minutes later he returned to announce quietly that she was gone.

The time had come when they could cry. Jamie's mother held him while they both sobbed, and she whispered that everything would be all right.

But he was thinking about the recording he'd made – and he was not sure if what his mother said was altogether true.

Halloween came early that year because nobody went back to sleep. They sat in the kitchen having a very early breakfast while the sunrise burned through the autumn trees in the backyard. Then, while Jamie dressed for school, his father made lots of phone calls, and his mother cried openly a few more times. Gloria was still asleep as Jamie sat in his room and replayed the tape he'd made. To hear Great-Gran's voice, knowing she was gone, gave him a strange feeling. It struck him that he was listening to those 'last words' everybody talks about.

Listening to her words for the second time, he realised the old woman was fearful of dying *on Halloween*. She was telling him something – something important. Her people had always protected anybody who dies on that day. Protected them from the Cutty Black Sow – whatever *that* was . . .

Jamie stuffed the Sony into his backpack, along with his school books, and returned to the kitchen. His mother poured him another glass of orange juice.

'Your father's not going to work today,' she said. 'He can drive you and Gloria to school.'

She paused as though suddenly remembering something important. 'Oh God – she's still asleep. I've got to wake her up, and tell her . . .'

His mother left the kitchen, leaving Jamie alone again with his thoughts. He could hear his father's muffled voice as he spoke on the phone. Other than that, it was quiet. He thought about Great-Gran, wondering if she'd *known* he was listening to her last night, if she'd been talking about that stuff with the stones for a reason.

Jamie couldn't get the story out of his mind as he and Gloria rode into town with his father. The bonfire and the stones and the Cutty Black Sow.

At school he waited until study hall just after lunch, then transcribed the recording into his math notebook. When it was written out, he was able to study the words more carefully, and he became even more convinced that Great-Gran had been giving him a message.

Jamie asked Miss Hall, the school librarian, for books about Scotland and Scottish folklore. Usually quiet and dour, Miss Hall volunteered that she was Scottish on her mother's side, and was good to see young people interested in their heritage.

With her help, Jamie figured out a lot of what Great-Gran had been talking about. A *Samhnagan* was a ritual bonfire, burned on Halloween night to protect the people from the forces of Evil, and to save the souls of any who died on the Witches' Day. There was nothing about the 'Cutty Black Sow,' but Miss Hall told him that she would be happy to look it up when she went home that evening. Jamie thanked her and gave her his phone number, making the librarian promise to call if she discovered anything.

On his way home on the bus, Jamie planned his evening. He knew what he had to do for his great-grandmother. Gloria kept interrupting his thoughts and, finally, he knew he'd have to talk to her.

'Do you think we'll still be able to trick-or-treat tonight?' she asked solemnly.

'Gee, I don't know, Gloria. I wasn't really thinking about

it. I guess I figured we'd go, but I might have to do
something else.'

'Oh yeah? Like what?'

He considered telling her what he intended. Sometimes
Gloria could be trusted with secrets, but oftentimes not.

'You wouldn't understand,' he said after a pause. 'Something Great-Gran wanted me to do. For her.'

Gloria's eyes flashed. He had her hooked now. 'But she's
dead now . . .'

'She asked me last night – right before she died. It was like
a . . . a last request.'

'Really?' Gloria's voice flirted with true awe.

'Yeah, but this is a *secret*, you understand?'

'Sure I do! I can keep a secret.'

Jamie grinned. 'Yeah. Sometimes. Now listen, if I tell you
about this, you have to *swear* you won't tell anybody – not
even Mom or Dad, okay?'

'Gee, what're you gonna *do* anyway?'

'You swear?'

She nodded with great seriousness. 'I swear.'

'All right,' said Jamie. 'Last night . . .'

When the bus dropped them off at the house, Jamie's
mother informed them that The Undertaker had picked up
Great-Gran. Jamie went into the backyard and sat on a swing.
To his right was a barbecue pit and outdoor fireplace. If he
was going to build a fire, that was the place. The yard was
enclosed by tall oak and poplar trees, and a cool wind sifted
through the brown and orange and yellow leaves, shaking
them loose and bringing them down all around him. It was
pretty, but he found it also very sad.

The back door slammed and Gloria ran down to the
swing-seat. 'I just talked to Mommy, and she said we can
still go trick-or-treating!'

'Okay.'

'They're going to be at the funeral home, but she said I
can go out as long as *you* stay with me. Then we gotta go to
Mrs Stamrick's house when we're done. They'll pick us up
there when they get home, okay?'

'Yeah,' he said absently. 'That'll be fine. But we'll have to
make that bonfire first.'

'What?'

'C'mon, Gloria. Get real. I *just told* you about that.'

'That didn't make much sense to me.' She grimaced.

'Well, it did to me. And I gotta make that fire for Great-Gran. She wanted me to.'

After dinner that night, Jamie's parents left for the funeral home. He went out to the backyard, down toward the woods which bordered the property, and began gathering up sticks and branches from a big deadfall left from last winter's storms. He also gathered up five stones about the size of baseballs. As he began arranging the wood in his father's barbecue pit, he heard Gloria coming down the back steps. She was dressed in her trick-or-treat costume – a skeleton in a hooded robe.

'Getting it ready?' Gloria asked as she watched.

'What do you think, stupid?'

'I'm not stupid. I was just asking.'

With matches he lit the wood; it took several attempts to get the heavier branches burning, but soon the fire licked and cracked with a small, contained fury. It warmed their faces and cast a hot orange glow on the surrounding trees. Jamie piled on more wood from the deadfall, and the blaze became a small inferno, roaring as it sucked up the cool autumn air.

'It's going good now,' said Gloria, entranced by the ever-changing shapes and glowing coals.

Jamie finally pulled an El Marko from his jacket pocket and an old rag he'd taken from his father's workroom in the basement. He wiped the stones as clean as possible, then marked each one with an initial.

'What're you doing now?' asked Gloria.

'I have to fix the stones. One for each of us in the family. See that G? That's for you. And these are for Mom and Dad, me and Great-Gran. Now, we have to throw them into the middle, like this.' Jamie tossed Great-Gran's stone into the centre of the coals. Then he tossed all the others in, one by one, with a small amount of ceremony. 'There, it's done.'

'Why'd you have to do that, Jamie?'

'Because. That's the way they always did it. To protect us all . . .'

'Protect us?' Gloria giggled beneath her skull-mask. 'From what?'

'I'm not sure . . . from the Cutty Black Sow, I guess.'

'What's *that*?'

'I don't know,' said Jamie. 'I couldn't find out.'

The only sound was the wind in the tree-tops and occasional pop of a coal cooling down.

'Hey,' said his sister. 'Are we gonna to go trick-or-treating or what?'

'Oh yeah, I guess we can go now,' he said.

'Finally!' Gloria turned toward the house. 'I'll be right back out – gotta get my shopping bag!'

Then they went trick-or-treating and when they returned from a tour of the neighbourhood streets, it was almost totally dark. Jamie guided her back to their house and Gloria reminded him that they were to go to Mrs Stamrick's place.

'In a minute. I want to go check on the fire.'

'Aw, Jamie, I'm tired . . .'

'Look, it'll only take a minute. Come on, you got what you wanted, didn't you?'

'Oh, all right.' She followed him as Jamie took a flash-light from the garage and moved close to the barbecue pit. Only a few orange embers revealed the location of the small bonfire. He played the light over the ashes, searching for the five stones in the debris.

'What're you doing?'

'Just checking to see that everything's OK.' He counted the stones as the beam of light touched them: three . . . four . . . where was the last one? From the looks of the ashes and embers, the wood had collapsed, then spilled toward the edge of the firebrick. He directed the beam down to the patio and found the fifth stone, amidst a scattering of ash. It had fallen from the fire, and he remembered his Great-Gran's words: *'no stone should be missing or disturbed . . .'* He bent low and saw in the flashlight beam that it was the stone with a just-legible 'J' on its face.

His stone. His soul?

It would be best if he left it as it lay – undisturbed.

'Hey, look,' said Gloria. 'One of 'em fell out!'

Before he could say anything, his sister, costumed as a

miniature Grim Reaper, swooped down beside him and grabbed for the stone.

'No, Gloria! Don't touch it!'

But her fingers had already encircled it, had begun to pick it up. In that instant, Jamie felt a jolt of energy spike through him. His heart accelerated from a burst of adrenalin, and suddenly Gloria screamed.

Pulling her hand back, she let go of the stone in the same motion. It was flung into the darkness and Jamie could hear it thump upon the lawn somewhere to his right.

'It burned my hand!' sobbed Gloria. 'It was still hot!'

'I told you not to touch it! Oh, Jeez, Gloria, you really shouldn't have touched it! I've got to find it!'

'Let's go to Mrs Stamrick's. Come on!'

'No, wait! I've got to find that stone . . .'

'What for? It's just an old rock. You can get it in the morning.'

'No, it might be too late then.' *It might be too late already*, he thought.

Despite Gloria's protests, she helped scan the lawn for the missing stone. She must have heard the urgency and fear in Jamie's voice because she even got down on her hands and knees to grope about in the grass.

When they found the stone, it was still hot, but cool enough to pick up. Jamie carefully returned it to the spot where Gloria had first disturbed it, and hoped that nothing would be wrong. After all, she hadn't meant to touch it. Perhaps it would be all right since it was not yet morning.

He and Gloria went to Mrs Stamrick's house two blocks away, and she welcomed them with affectionate hugs and kisses and mugs of hot chocolate. She spoke in saccharine tones and made a fuss over them.

Outside the clap-board house, the wind began gusting. Jamie listened to it whistle through the gutters and downspouts as he sat in Mrs Stamrick's parlour watching a situation comedy on TV. Gloria was busy pouring her loot into a large mixing bowl on the floor; Mrs Stamrick oohed and aahed appropriately as his sister scooped up especially fine prizes from the night's haul.

Jamie sipped his cocoa and watched TV without actually

paying attention. At one point he thought he heard some-thing tapping on a windowpane, even though the others did not seem to notice. When he took his empty mug into the kitchen to place it in the sink, he heard another sound.

A thumping. Outside.

Something was padding across the wood floor of Mrs Stamrick's back porch. It was rapid and relentless, as though some heavy-footed dog, a large dog, was pacing back and forth beyond the kitchen door.

Slowly Jamie moved to the door, but could not bring himself to draw up the shade and peer out. The thumping footsteps continued and at one point he thought he heard another sound – a rough exhalation, a combination of a growl and a snort.

Moving quickly out of the kitchen, he told Mrs Stamrick that it sounded like there was a big dog on her back porch. She walked past him into the kitchen, raised the shade and looked out. Seeing nothing, she opened the door, admitting a cool blast of face-slapping wind – the only thing that was out there.

'It must have wandered off,' she said. 'Nothing's out there now.'

Jamie nodded and forced a silly grin, then let her lead him back into the parlor.

While Gloria was dozing off on the couch, Jamie tried to get absorbed in a cop-show drama. But he couldn't concentrate on anything except the sounds of the wind outside the house. And the sounds of other things he couldn't always identify.

When his father arrived to pick them up, Jamie could not recall ever being so glad to see him. He picked up his sister's treat-bag as his father carried the sleeping Gloria out to the car where their mother waited. As Jamie walked down the driveway toward the safety of the big station wagon, he listened for the sounds, searched the shadows and the shrubbery that lurked beyond the splash of Mrs Stamrick's porch light.

He sensed there was something out there, could almost feel the burning gaze of unseen eyes, the hot stinging breath of an unknown thing so very close to him.

In the car, he exchanged small-talk with his parents. It was best if he tried to act as normal as possible. But his mother turned to look at him at one point, and he wondered if she sensed – as mothers often can – that something was not right with him.

As soon as the car stopped in the driveway, he jumped out and moved quickly to the back door, waiting for his father with the keys. A single yellow bug-light cast a sickening pall over everything, but it also sparked off feelings of safety and warmth.

Finally, they were all inside the house, which afforded him a feeling of warmth and safety. While his father carried Gloria off to bed, his mother checked the Code-a-Phone; its green light signalled calls waiting. Jamie hung up his coat in the closet. In the other room he could hear his mother as she played back the tape from the phone answering machine – mostly messages of condolence from friends and relatives. He was about to go down the hall to the stairs when he heard a loud thumping noise outside the kitchen window.

He fought down the urge to run blindly to his mother and wrap his arms around her. The sound of her voice breaking the silence almost made him cry out.

'Jamie,' his mother called. 'There's a message for you here.'

As casually as possible, he moved to the table where his mother rewound the tape and replayed it.

'. . . Hello, Jamie. This is Miss Hall. I found what you were looking for in some of my books at home. I guess you're out trick-or-treating, so you can call me back till eleven, if you want. Bye now . . .'

His mother glanced at the kitchen clock as she stopped the tape. 'It's only ten o'clock. Are you going to call her?'

'Nah, it's getting late. I'll just see her on Monday, I guess.'

His mother smiled as she returned to the rest of the messages, and Jamie moved quickly up the stairs to his room. He said goodnight to his father, undressed, and slipped under his sheet and quilt.

It was at least a half-hour after his parents had also gone to bed when Jamie heard more of the strange sounds, the thumping footfalls of something in the yard beneath his window. His room faced the rear of the house, his window overlooking the roof of the back porch. Broken moonlight splintered the darkness as he slipped from the covers and forced himself to look out.

The jutting slant of the roof obscured his line of sight, and for a moment, he saw nothing unfamiliar. Then, for an instant, one of the shadows moved, seemed to step back into the deeper darkness of the yard.

Looking beyond it, Jamie was surprised to see the still-glowing embers of his bonfire at the end of the yard. From this distance, they were nothing more than points of deep orange, but he would have thought they'd be dead by now. The rising wind must have stirred up the last coals.

Again came the faint sounds of something moving with a heavy-footed gait. And the distant, snorting breath he had heard once before.

Jamie was trembling as he moved away from the window, and it became suddenly important that he speak with Miss Hall. He moved quietly downstairs to the kitchen phone, and looked up her number in the phone book.

Miss Hall answered on the fifth ring.

'Miss Hall, it's Jamie . . . I'm not sure what time it is, I hope I'm not calling too late . . .' His voice sounded unsteady.

Miss Hall chuckled. 'Well, almost, but not quite. Jamie what did you need this information for? It struck me as somewhat odd that – '

'Oh, just for a project I was doing. About Halloween and all.' There was a pause, and when the librarian did not reply he rushed on: 'You said you found it for me . . .'

'Yes, I did.' There was a sound of papers being shifted about. 'Yes, here . . . in Scotland and Wales, there was a belief that bonfires protected people from demons and witches.'

'Yeah, I already found that stuff,' he forced himself to speak in hushed tones. 'What about the . . . the . . .'

'Oh yes, the "Cutty Black Sow" . . .' Miss Hall cleared her throat. 'You see, it was a common belief back then that demons could assume the shape of animals. And it was believed that on Halloween these demons took the shape of a pig – a large black-haired creature that walked on its hind legs. Its hair was supposed to be bristly and closely cut. The "Cropped Black Sow", or the "Cutty Black Sow", was what they called him.'

Jamie felt stunned for a moment, and he tried to speak but no words would come out.

'Jamie, are you there?'

'Yes! Oh . . . oh, well, thank you, Miss Hall. Thanks a lot. That's just what I needed to . . . to finish my project.'

'Well, I'm glad I could be of help, Jamie. It must be pretty important for you to be working on it this late.'

There came the sound of footfalls again. This time, they seemed so loud in Jamie's ears that he almost felt the house move from the impact.

'Yeah, it's pretty important . . . I guess. Listen, I'd better go, Miss Hall, thanks a lot.'

He hung up the phone before she could reply, and moved quickly back to his room. He didn't want to wake up his parents, or tell them he was scared, but he didn't know *what* to do. The thumping grew louder and it was now intermixed with snuffling, snorting sounds.

The kind of sounds a pig would make.

Jamie looked out his window. The yard seemed darker than before, but the embers of the fire in the distance seemed brighter . . .

. . . until he realised that the embers were not brighter, but closer. And that the two fiercely glowing orbs were not coals at all . . .

They were eyes.

Backing away, he heard scraping sounds. Rough, abrasive, crunching sounds, as though something was scrambling for purchase on the side of the porch, something trying to climb up, towards his window.

The sounds were very loud now. The old wood of the house groaned and scraped as it was splintered. It was so loud! Why didn't his parents hear it too! Jamie jumped into his bed, grasping at the covers the way he had as a child when he had been afraid of some terrible night-thing.

Something scraped across the windowpane as ember-eyes appeared beyond the glass . . .

He must have cried out, although he didn't realize it, because he heard his father's voice calling his name. Relief flooded through him as he heard his father's hand on the door knob.

'Jamie, are you all right?'

The door swung open, and he could see his father's silhouette against the bright light of the hall beyond. Quickly he glanced back to the window, and the burning eyes were gone. He felt silly as he tried to speak.

'Dad! Yeah, it's OK . . . just a bad dream, I guess.'

His father said nothing as he walked into the room, drawing close to the bed. In the darkness, he sat on the bed and drew his son close to him. Jamie relaxed in the comforting embrace, and put his arms around his father.

He was about to tell Dad how scared he had been, when his hands touched the back of the neck of the thing which held him, when he felt the close-cut, bristly hair . . .

TREASON IN ZAGADAR

Adrian Cole

Adrian Cole is the author of several fantasy novels and series, including 'The Omaran Saga' (A Place Among the Fallen, Throne of Fools, The King of Light and Shadows and The Gods in Anger) and the 'Star Requiem' series (Mother of Storms, Thief of Dreams, Warlord of Heaven and Labyrinth of Worlds). Two novels for young adults, Moorstones and The Sleep of Giants, are amongst his other full-length works, while his short stories have appeared in four issues of Fantasy Tales, Dark Voices 2, The Year's Best Fantasy and Horror Fourth Annual Collection, Fear magazine and elsewhere. A new dark fantasy novel, Blood Red Angel, was published in 1993 and he has completed Oblivion Hand, a novelization of some of the short stories featuring his enigmatic fantasy character, the Voidal. The story which follows is a new adventure of King Kull, the character created by Robert E. Howard. As the writer explains, it was written 'as a tribute to Howard and the sword & sorcery genre he created.'

INTRIGUE IN THE PALACE

THREE men sat alone, dreaming of power and grandeur as the huge primordial sun sank down like a bloody ball of fire into the western ocean where Atlantis still held sway – three men who alone had the power of command here in the remote southern bastion of Zagadar, most outflung of the Lesser Kingdoms that still swore an unstable allegiance to Valusia, Kull's usurped throne. Far from the palaces and towers of Kull's gleaming citadels was Zagadar, its own small garrisons and crumbling edifices set close upon the borders of the vast jungle and swamp realms of the southern unmapped regions that stretched on hazily and mysteriously to the sea. Here, in this oppressive, tropical keep, shrouded in the shadows of the primeval mountains behind it, the populace watched the sun sinking and shut themselves away from the sounds of the jungle below the walls, and the nameless things that stalked there.

High in his private quarters, locked in the turret of one sun-bleached tower, sat the pensive monarch of Zagadar, the youth who had been brought here so long ago by refugees from the carnage in Valusia when bloody Kull had brought down the tyrant Borna. Borna – who had ruled with a despotic hand and who had allowed himself to become besotted with his grim power. There were still those who lamented his passing, but it was for selfish reasons, for there were always those who resented Kull – men who coveted his snatching of the bloody crown, and who would have taken it for themselves.

Gorvic was one such. He had been secretly brought here to remote Zagadar, where the new king's spies would not find him, for had they known he was kin to the dead Borna they would surely have tracked him out like demons and given his head to the suspicious Kull, whose back was ever guarded. Yet Gorvic had come here clandestinely and fought as an ordinary warrior with the poorly staffed city guards, earning many honours in the continual jungle skirmishes with the beings of the south. After the ferocious battles with the raiders from avaricious Grondar – battles in which the warriors from the north east had been finally smashed back by sheer brute strength and wild determination – Zagadar, which had been a purely military establishment, now cried out for independence and for a ruler. Hence it was the sharp-eyed and invincible Gorvic of the Ax who had stepped forward to become unchallenged monarch.

On all this grim past did Gorvic now reflect. Fate, or the Gods of the Dark Realms, had snatched him away from a chance of winning the throne of Valusia, Borna's seat, and set him here in the haunted, neglected south, and yet he had come to win a kingdom of sorts. Now he trafficked with Valusia and Kull's royal traders, but his birthright remained his close secret. To his faithful vassals he seemed content, for who else could keep back that abysmal tide of horrors that ever-threatened to press in from the southern darkness? His people respected him and his undoubted power. But as Gorvic of the Ax sat gazing out over the the spires and towers of his rock-hewn citadel, it was of a greater prize that he mused.

There was but one other in all Zagadar who knew of Gorvic's line, and this was the necromancer Xaldeev, the half-human one who preferred the caress of the night to the humid rays of the glaring tropical sun. Some whispered cautiously that the sorcerer had learned to stave off death in some pact with the demons of unguessable outer realms, while others thought it imprudent even to conjecture on this, for fear of invoking his hideous wrath. Xaldeev, alone in the slime-hung vaults below the sacred necropolis of the warriors, sat beside a glowing skull, and by its alien light he examined a dry parchment whereon were daubed strange and blasphemous sigils.

It had been wily Xaldeev who had snatched the youth Gorvic from that vile carnage in Valusia and brought him here to this place of darkness, while others close to Borna had been cut down by the Red Slayers, already won over by Kull. The cunning necromancer had long bent the ear of the now deposed Borna, and he had been the one who had already sought to bring about Kull's downfall while he had yet been in Borna's service, for Kull had control of the army. Long ago, the awful beings of night with whom Xaldeev consorted had warned him that a demi-god would come out of the west to pluck Valusia's crown, and Xaldeev, whose own power in the capital had been growing like a black, unseen canker, feared the purges of this Atlantean outlander. But his original efforts to poison Borna's mind had failed, for Kull won many honours in the field for his monarch. Thus when Borna fell, Xaldeev knew that he must flee or die, and he took with him Gorvic, seeing in the youth a ray of hope yet for Kull's downfall. There would be time enough.

Now, amongst the rotting tombs of this eerie catacomb, the hooded one briefly perused his manuscripts, but pushed them aside impatiently. He thought of Gorvic, now a young man in his prime, a magnificent fighting animal, and a man who would always reserve for the sorcerer a degree of respect for his apparent loyalty. But Gorvic would in reality be no

more than the tool by which Xaldeev would overthrow Kull
and win back his grisly power in Valusia. Xaldeev served no
one but himself, and there was no deceit so base he would
not use it to further his own foul ends.

In that ghostly chamber of the dead, shunned by all but the
lost, there was a pattering as of the feet of rats, and Xaldeev
scoured shadows for a moment, seeing a bent shape waft
corpse-like towards him. He questioned the sinister familiar
that the dark had spewed forth.

'He is without, master,' purred the obsequious creature
and Xaldeev motioned it to summon what it had heralded.
Moments later another being entered the circle of wan light
cast by the glowing skull. The sorcerer kept his distance from
the tall but strangely hunched being. Its head and shoulders
were covered in some foul-smelling garment, and it wore a
leather harness from which two swords rattled on the stone
cold floor. Green, feral eyes gleamed from that half-hood
and Xaldeev secretly gripped the cabalistic talisman he
wore about his neck, calling inwardly on his demons to
protect him.

'Is all in readiness?' said the sorcerer.

The being grunted a nod and then spoke in a reptilian hiss
that discarded the last of its human pretexts, for it was no
man, though it walked upon two legs. Its long, scaled tail
wriggled in the darkness and its bright, forked tongue slitted
out from between needle teeth.

'When you give my masters the signal, they will begin the
attack,' hissed the reptile man, and the odour of its stale
breath made Xaldeev draw further back.

'I will keep my part of the bargain. You and your masters
will have their feast. Zagadar will be yours for the taking.'

'And Kull?' hissed the sinuous lizard being.

'Yours, too. Gorvic will go back to Valusia and no one will
stay his taking of the throne.'

'We have waited long to avenge ourselves on the Atlantean
killer!' the lizard man hissed, satisfied, and turned back to
the shadows and the umbilical passages below ground that
would lead it back to its jungle environment.

While this strange meeting between the necromancer and
the reptile being took place, there was another man who
lingered late by his darkening window, reflecting on the

twists and turns of military intrigue within the growing Empire. This was a veteran of many battles, a high-ranking warrior of Kull's own Red Slayers, elite of the Valusian army. Ambellus had served the Empire for many years and had seen several changes in its kingship, but now he was absolutely loyal to Kull, a brutal but fair ruler who was bringing to the Empire new frontiers and glory the like of which it had never known. Even the untamed Picts had become less daring in their raiding of the northern shores.

Ambellus was here at remote Zagadar as an ambassador for Kull, who could not hope to visit all his outposts, as he would have liked. There was far less internecine strife within the Empire now, but border wars and conflicts with outside powers would always be a part of Valusian life. Ambellus had been here a week, studying the strength and politics of the small Zagadarian kingdom, and already he was impressed with the way in which the powerful young monarch, Gorvic, had kept at bay the grim dwellers in the jungles, where many diverse horrors were known to lurk. It was believed that the last of the terrible lizard men, who had ruled the world before the rise of Man, had their last outposts in those steaming, accursed glades, but no one ventured there.

As the ambassador looked down at the night-blackened treetops below, a sense of impending dread seemed to seep up to him as though from out of those jungle corridors a mental glow of malice beamed upwards. The seasoned warrior turned away and closed the window of his chamber. Soon he would report back to Kull in the north that things went well here. All seemed under the capable thumb of Gorvic. Ambellus would be glad to leave. He grew weary of these outlands and a return to his family in Valusia was long overdue.

While he removed his gear, shapes gathered down in the swamps, and the early moon glinted on harness and weapon alike. The lizard men waited.

SORCERER'S BAIT

Gorvic banged his silver goblet down upon the thick tabletop meaningfully and quickly an under-vassal came forward to

splash wine from a ewer into it. Gorvic waved him away
and nodded to Ambellus, resplendent in his uniform in the
morning sunlight that slanted through the high windows of
the Zagadarian palace.

'So your report to our illustrious ruler in Valusia will be
favourable, my lord Ambellus?' said the young king. Behind
the ambassador stood a company of the proud Red Slayers,
all keen-eyed men with scarred muscles that spoke of many
victorious campaigns, all veterans sworn to die for Kull.
Gorvic's face remained friendly, though beneath that smile
ran a river of conflicting thoughts.

'Indeed, sire. You have made an excellent success of
subduing the enemies that are rife in those foul jungles.
Your army is impressive – '

'Should its growing size give you cause for distress,
Ambellus, I must again point out that I pick every warrior
myself from the outlying settlements of Zagadar, and that
each man is sworn to the Tiger, Kull himself, before me. I
am the monarch here, but I serve only Kull and Valusia.'

Ambellus smiled amicably. 'Of course. And in time of
war you can rely upon the return of the compliment.
The Red Slayers will be at your side should you need
them.'

Gorvic nodded, while behind him the vulpine figure of
Xaldeev stirred as though ruffled by a breeze. Ambellus
watched the carrion-like necromancer suspiciously, though
all courts had such mystics. Had he seen that odious being
before?

'War is a constant threat as we are so close to the jungles,'
said Gorvic. 'Had I men to spare I would readily drive
a wedge into the reptile kingdom and force them back
indefinitely.'

'It seems to me, sire, that you have a strong force. Is it not
sufficient?'

'I must protect what I have, Ambellus. If I should lead too
great a force into the jungle, my city would be under siege
the day I left.'

Ambellus gave this some thought. It seemed that the
monarch was hinting at something – possibly a request.
'What would you counsel, then?'

Gorvic sipped his wine, eyes on Ambellus. 'Bring the Tiger

standard here in force. Kull's legions and mine could end the lizard men for all time!'

Ambellus nodded. 'The jungles are vast – vast enough to hide a thousand armies. I see your predicament.'

'We have some knowledge of the lizards. To the east, in the Sullen Hills, lies an old citadel without a name, older than the dawn of time, a remote and small place. There we know the lizard ones hold their evil conclaves. There it is that they call upon their vile Gods! With aid from Kull this place could be destroyed and the lizard forces scattered!'

'You say the place is small?'

'Little more than a canyon in the hills.'

Ambellus seemed puzzled. 'You have not yet set upon it?'

Gorvic shook his head slowly, drinking more of his wine. 'No – it is small, but evil. Its eon-old secrets are shrouded in the sorcerous lores of an eternity. To venture there without preparation would be madness. It is a lure. My men shun the place. I would gather them, but native Zagadarians have no wish to tempt the secret Gods of the Abyss!'

Ambellus had not become ambassador to Kull for a scarcity of tact. He thought better of suggesting that Gorvic's vassals were *afraid* of this place. Yet it seemed that this was Gorvic's meaning. With all the military might at his disposal, Gorvic had no stomach to venture forth to this nameless place. And with this knowledge, there came to Ambellus an idea. So far on his visit here he had sought in vain for a way of denting the smooth confidence of the young monarch and his immaculate retainers. Gorvic and men like him must not be allowed too much rein in the power race, and should be reminded that Kull ruled supreme. Now Ambellus had found what he had sought – the gap in Gorvic's pride.

'If I may suggest, my lord,' said the ambassador with a bow, 'instead of my returning to the king immediately, I could take my men to this place of evil and demonstrate to you both the skills and allegiance of the Red Slayers. And they need exercise.'

Gorvic winced, his tanned face seemingly evidencing confusion. 'But my dear ambassador! To go there with so small a force – '

'These are the Red Slayers, sire! There is no power living

that can withstand them! Come, give me the route to this place and let loose my hounds. See the claws of the Tiger! The lizard men will be sent down to the vaults of the dead before they are awake to it. In Kull's name I promise it!'

Gorvic appeared to consider this, then nodded. Behind him the necromancer whispered so that no one else could hear. 'Ambellus was ever a pompous boaster. See how easily he snatches at the bait, master.'

Gorvic said nothing, but inwardly he was content.

CITADEL OF TREACHERY

For steaming miles the party of fighting men had hacked its impetuous way through the dense, clinging foliage of the tropical jungles, led by the cursing figure of Ambellus. Beside the giant warrior rode a single guide, sworn to Gorvic's service, and now earning a fistful of bright gold for his part in the treachery by taking the Red Slayers up into the Sullen Hills to the feared citadel of the lizard people. All around them the entangling foliage pressed, as though its green vines and tendrils sought to envelop and choke them, living tentacles. Strange sounds came from the vaults presided over by Titanic trees, a cacophony of nerve-grating discord, redolent with fear and hatred. Through many tropical regions they had been, these stalwarts, but this place seemed imbued with an uncanny sentience of its own, dreadful and malefic.

'Forward!' cried Ambellus, wiping sticky trails of perspiration from his brow and swatting at the persistent insects that hung in a buzzing cloud around him. His skin was tough, seasoned by all weathers and climates in a score of campaigns against both men and environment. His faithful men swore crudely at the foul jungle air, but followed doggedly, hands close to sword pommels, trusting not even the stirring leaves. If there were evil eyes abroad in that impenetrable camouflage, they were hidden from the warriors – hidden, but sensed.

'How much further?' grumbled the huge leader to the diminutive guide.

'Not so far, lord. See the break in the skyline? Through

there lies a hill that leads to the citadel. Those are the Sullen Hills.'

'Well named for their miserable repose,' snorted Ambellus, for he had scarce been to such a remote region. He had begun to think himself rash in venturing so deep into an alien place, but he drew himself to his full height and thought of his Red Slayers and of their prowess. For Kull and the Empire they would triumph, even if they had to lay down their lives. Ahead of them there was a disturbance – leaves rustled and some huge body trampled off into the dense verdure. The guide looked fearful, his rat features pale in spite of the remorseless sun.

'What is it?' snapped Ambellus.

'Some things are better unseen,' muttered the puny man, his eyes darting about, searching the thick canopy.

Ambellus had drawn his blade. 'Lead on!' he urged.

The guide tried in vain to hide his evident terror and moved his restless beast on, its legs plopping down in the mud of the vague trail. Small creatures slithered aside in the weeds. Presently the party passed between huge rotting logs, thick with mosses and lichen, and then saw a break in the trees which now thinned down as a hill broke unexpectedly out of the jungle floor like some strange mound, raised by giants of the mysterious past. The guide's face twisted with fear, but he led on, Ambellus angrily insisting. Once out of the mires and bogs of the jungle and on the firmer ground of the sloping hill, the men felt a little more at ease, but this mood was quickly dispelled as they saw the foul shapes that hung from the sparse and dying trees. Skeletons and skulls – most of creatures they could only guess at – hung from the gnarled branches, the empty eye-sockets staring down as though in anger.

'The dead cannot stay us!' called Ambellus angrily, waving his blade contemptuously at the grisly relics around them.

'What manner of beings were they?' muttered some of the men, but they rode on, mindful of every shadow. As they reached the higher slopes of the hill, the trees fell away altogether, leaving behind a view like a green carpet of jungle ceiling, stretching endlessly away into an obscuring heat haze. Now they were surrounded by broken terrain, though bones littered this foothill as though strewn here deliberately by countless feasting denizens of the silent heights. The awful silence. It hung like a cloak, and nothing penetrated save the sound of the horses breathing and their footfalls on the rough stone.

A broken skyline loomed like a flattened, stumpy row of broken teeth, and from these snaggled fangs thrust up more reminders that life of some kind dwelt here, for thick stakes had been dug into the ground and upon them rested the eyeless, bleach-boned horrors that had once been skulls. Few of the grisly trophies were human remains. Scores of these grim harbingers peppered the ridge and the Red Slayers drew their breaths in sharply, gritting their teeth in a steely but shaken determination to continue.

Threading through the knife-edged rocks and erosion-smashed terrain, the party cut through the ridge and looked down at a valley, scooped like an amphitheatre out of the hilltop by the searing heat of the sun and the talons of the burning wind. Ambellus nodded. Set into the sloping walls of this natural bowl were a thousand skulls and bones, all black eye pits pointing inwards, as though watching some grisly dance of the dead within the dusty arena.

'This is the place,' said the guide beside him. 'This is where the abominations practise their foul rites to their Gods of the Abyss.'

Ambellus nodded thoughtfully, his face set in grim lines, his eyes hard as cold rock. Every stone and boulder, every jutting crag he noted, seeking out signs of an ambush, as an eagle seeks out its hiding prey. The guide saw the huge warrior's questing gaze.

'We have nothing to fear while the sun burns overhead, master. They only come by night.'

Ambellus remained silent, then called to his Red Slayers. 'Come! Destroy everything here! Rip down these filthy blasphemies!' he shouted, pointing with his drawn blade to the skulls. He goaded his steed forward, down into the natural arena, and as one his men surged forward, shouting to dispel the feeling of eerie sentience that pervaded that remote haven of devils. Then followed the crunching of bone as each warrior smashed out at the bleached relics, turning the skulls into dust and splinters. There were also a number of sinister blocks and strangely sculptured squares of basalt in the arena, reminiscent of altars, and these Ambellus decided to tear down. He gathered a knot of men to him and prepared to wipe away the sanctity of the lizard men.

'When it is done, we shall leave clear evidence that the men of Kull have been here,' he said, wiping streaming perspiration from his face. The heat had become stifling, a choking strength-sapping antagonist. Ambellus suddenly turned, for strange sounds drifted over the rim of the arena. His men had noticed, too. Bestial grunts and deep-throated calls, as of some large amphibious creature calling to marsh-bound mates, drifted across on the still air.

Then from around the rim of the dusty bowl they came. A thousand of the lizard men had secretly gathered, and now they walled off the way to the jungle and freedom. They were armed, primed for war, their vicious weapons glinting in the sun, their slit-eyes half-closed in evil anticipation of the bloody furore that must follow.

'By the Tiger!' snarled Ambellus. 'We are circled . . . there are too many for us!' He turned to look for the guide, but he was not to be seen.

'Where is the guide?' roared Kull's ambassador.

But no one knew. He had slunk away like a hyena. Ambellus uttered a crude stream of invective, but there was only time now to rally the Red Slayers, for the lizard men begun to spring their trap. As they slithered forward, their feet treading the last of the skulls into the ground, charging down upon the gathered warriors, a separate group watched the coming battle from the shadows of a nearby cave, high above the arena.

Xaldeev smiled sinuously, his hell-eyes watching eagerly. Beside him the guide from Gorvic's citadel trembled coldly, for the sorcerer set his teeth on edge.

'Good,' nodded Xaldeev. 'You have done well. Go back to your master and tell him that Ambellus's head will be sent to him ere nightfall. Go!'

Glad of the chance to quit the place of horror, the guide scuttled off down a dark corridor that debouched into the jungle. Several of the sinister reptile men stood by, hissing at him, but they let him mount his steed and race away.

Meanwhile Ambellus met the first wild rush of his enemies with a mighty swing of his sword, cutting two of the foul lizard men in twain as he did so, coating himself in a fountain of thick blood. He hacked through the defences of another, shearing off half the beast's face. Around him the ferocious Red Slayers, all men chosen from the hardiest and most efficient fighting men of Kull's Empire, leaped into the fray, wild snarls of abandonment and glory upon their lips. The laws of the jungle presided, and it was as though beast grappled with beast.

'For Kull and the Empire!' they roared as one, and such was the ferocity of their manic defence, that the lizard creatures drew back, though they were no less fanatic. Ambellus drew his men in a ring, swords thrust outwards like sharp tongues of death, and for long moments the lizards sought to breach that wall of jabbing steel. Blood showered the combatants as man and beast went down in a crimson rain of death. Wildly, exultantly, the lizards tore into the Red Slayers. Screams and curses mingled.

Ambellus crushed the heads of many a foeman, his face devoid of expression now, for he fought to remain calm, unhurried, and to preserve as much energy as he could. To win this day seemed impossible. For each beast he cut down, three more sprang for his throat like maddened dogs. Swords rose and fell, sparks flew in the heat. Slowly the Red Slayers, most heroic and determined of all Kull's fighting armies, were being cut to pieces. They fought bravely, each man fighting as well and as destructively as three normal warriors, but the fanatical lizard men were even more careless of death and self-sacrifice. Their own orders were explicit – annihilate the invader.

From over the crest of the arena came another wave of them, their scaled armour shining. Ambellus received a terrible slash on the sword arm, swapping hands to fend off further wild attacks. He saw his men falling, limbs hacked, armour pierced, their eyes glazing in death. The Red Slayers died in silence or calling out the name of their lord, Kull, and calling on him for vengeance.

'A deliberate trap!' Ambellus was thinking as he was pushed further back, his ring of defenders tightening. Now only a handful of the fighting force huddled together, backs to the cold stone basalt, where the sigils of deviltry mocked them. Across these blocks their mutilated bodies at last fell.

Ambellus sensed the wave of death closing in, and then a score of wicked blades ripped open his flesh. He was sent sprawling backwards over an altar stone and a huge sword fell and completely severed his head, his fountaining blood a libation to unspeakable Gods. Cries of bestial jubilation went up from the lizards.

Shortly after the debacle, a group of the reptile men went up into the nearby hills. Xaldeev, who had missed nothing of the bloody skirmish, watched them come. They acknowledged him, and the magician was pleased to see the fear in their slit eyes. One of them held aloft the bizarre trophy that was Ambellus's head. Xaldeev nodded.

'Wrap it before it putrefies. At midnight, cast it over the battlements of Gorvic's citadel. Leave all other arrangements to me.'

He turned his imperious gaze from them, looking out over the scene of carnage. Already the victors were at work, setting the severed heads of the slain upon stakes and lining the lip of the arena with them. Only when every one of the slaughtered had thus adorned the skyline did Xaldeev turn away, a grim smile of satisfaction playing his thin, cruel lips.

THE WRATH OF A TIGER

Kull was stretched out on a cool slab of marble beside the steaming baths of his inner sanctum, his naked and bronzed body coated in a sheen of perspiration that gleamed in the morning sunlight, streaming from an opening in the dome high above. His personal servant, the huge mute warrior, Cormus, was busily working oils into the scarred but muscled body of the monarch, hands plying his iron skin with expert precision, erasing every ache and every hint of weariness. Kull yawned contentedly. Earlier he had arisen shortly after the chorus of palace birds had heralded the dawn, and had worked hard and long at his exercises, with both ax and bare hands. There were few men that could match him at either, though he had received bruises from Brule, the Pict who seemed cast from stone.

Kull smiled in recollection of his recent tussle with the

Spear Slayer and glanced across at the pool where the dark-skinned man still relaxed in the hot water. Of all Kull's men, the Pict was his closest friend and confidant, for the crown of the usurper always sits uneasy. Kull was slowly eradicating the suspicions and doubts of his adopted people, so far from Atlantis, his home, but still he was cautious. And he could not help but feel a twinge of uncertainty while Ambellus was abroad, for the burly ambassador was one of his finest, most trusted aides. Part of the Valusian monarch felt exposed while the man was gone.

Brule suddenly swam for the side of the pool, hoisted himself from it on thick, vein-wrapped arms, and stood waiting for his own servant. The Pict's freedom of the palace was a favour granted to few, and he took full advantage of Kull's generosity – they were acknowledged equals, though both respected each other's station.

'And what has the king decided to do today?' said Brule, laying beside Kull on another slab, the servant at once massaging him.

'A few inspections. A look at the armoury,' replied Kull, yawning again.

'Forgive me, but you seemed a little slow in training today. Perhaps a little too much time spent inactively,' the Pict teased, smiling impishly. It gave his face a malign expression, which made Kull chuckle.

'Slow! If I am slow, my friend, your own reactions barely rival those of a snail! Twice I could have knocked out your brains!'

Brule growled a good-natured reply, succumbing to the waves of relaxation spreading over him as the servant roughly massaged.

Kull sighed. 'Yet there is something in what you say, Brule. This business of being a monarch tries me. Often I crave a sword in my hand and a bloody battle to whet my appetite. I am happy to have staunched the unrest within the Empire and to have kept the hounds of Grondar at bay, but sometimes I hunger for action.'

Brule grunted his agreement. It was not the first time he had heard his king utter such sentiments. They were both fighting men, and their lives had always been geared to violent action, pitting their strength and sheer survival instinct against any odds. Snatching a crown had been one thing, but fending off ennui was another.

'Perhaps I am in need of a voyage. There are places yet unvisited, and perhaps more kingdoms to win, eh?'

'Yes, and when you return? Valusia will doubtless be in the hands of another usurper. Someone of the ilk of Thulsa Doom, perhaps?'

Kull's face became sober, for he recalled his conflict with that vile mage only too vividly. It had been a grim and ageless struggle, and had brought death to many. Perhaps it was best that such a conflict was over after all. To prefer such intrigue and infamy to the present peace seemed admittedly foolish. Brule's point was well taken and the monarch rolled over, for now erasing thoughts of violence.

As he did so, a solemn procession wound its way to the portals of the royal baths. The guards were consulted and one at once sprang forward to consult the King.

'I crave indulgence, Lord. There is word from the south. Messengers from Zagadar.'

'Ambellus? Has he returned then?' said Kull, rising and drawing on a brief loin tunic. The guard bowed, motioning to the men without.

'Send them in,' said Kull. Brule sat up, also dressing himself.

The procession, four palace officials and two men clad in the harness and regalia of Gorvic's southern citadel, came slowly forward. Each man knelt and Kull bade them rise. Their faces were grave, and Kull sensed their sombre mood with apprehension. The king motioned Cormus away. One of the Zagadarian messengers addressed himself to the splendid figure that was the monarch of Valusia; before him he saw a giant of a man, hewn almost from bronze, his eyes lit with fire, his torso studded with muscge – every inch of the man was a king.

'My lord, I bring greetings from Gorvic and from the people of Zagadar. There is grave news from our troubled lands.'

Kull said nothing, his face set, and nodded grimly for the man to continue.

'The beings of the jungle, the reptile men that we thought were banished to the remote southern coast: they threaten to rise again. They harass us, and their numbers increase, for like vermin they are multiplying day by day. They no longer quarrel among themselves. They have banded. Gorvic sends you this urgent plea: can you not send forth an army to put down this pestilence? His own forces, now struggling against mounting odds to keep Zagadar's borders free, urgently need reinforcing. Gorvic throws himself at your consideration, lord. If Zagadar is to forestall this threat of invasion, it must have help from Valusia.'

Kull frowned. 'But this is not the first appeal I have heard from your master. I have answered the first with action – did I not send my ambassador, Ambellus to you? Even now I await his report. Where is he?'

The man paled, apparently quaking, and turned to his equally shaken companion, who clutched nervously at a black bag. 'There are grim tidings concerning that worthy man.'

Kull's eyes narrowed. 'Speak!'

'Ambellus bravely sought to wipe out the nest at the heart of the lizard men's growing lands,' said the messenger, nodding to his companion. The latter gently undid the strings of his bag and slowly drew forth a foul-smelling cloth. This he unwrapped and then placed the contents reluctantly on the floor before the king. Kull swore vehemently and his courtiers drew back in loathing, for they gazed upon the severed head of Ambellus, their ambassador and friend. The glazed eyes were horrified in death.

'And the Red Slayers?' cried Kull in fury, his face aflame with anger.

The messenger shook his head. 'All dead, lord. Gorvic warned the ambassador of the dangers, but the latter insisted on a foray into the jungle.'

Kull was stunned. 'All dead? A whole company of Red Slayers wiped out! How dare you bring me such news!' he roared, his thick fists clenching menacingly.

Glumly the two messengers nodded. Kull turned to Brule, who looked equally horrified. 'What do you say to this foul act?'

The courtiers made the Zagadarians cover up the grim head. Brule reached for his spear, which was never far away. He clasped it to his breast. 'Vengeance!' he snapped, his voice cutting into the air like a blade of ice.

Kull turned to the assembled men. 'So be it!' he snarled. 'Go back to your master and tell him of the anger of the Tiger!' He shook his fist in the faces of the Zagadarians. 'Tell him that Kull is not pleased with the death of his warriors, who are worth more than the entire realm of Zagadar! Tell him that he shall have his army. Valusia shall send a force made up of her finest, and Kull himself shall lead it. By all the Gods, I swear it! There will be a bloody reckoning in those jungles. The lizard people will be destroyed to a man. I shall hew a path into their nethermost haven and burn them out! Not one of them will I spare. Go! Get out of my city! Tell your master. Tell him to prepare to receive the Tiger!'

THE GATHERING STORM

Gorvic stood before his people, as many of whom as could be gathered, in the royal plaza before the palace in the citadel of Zagadar. There were men, women and children, merchants, usurers, shopkeepers, hunters, tanners, all natives of the southern city state of the kingdom, all pressing forward in a hubbub of eagerness to hear what the monarch had to say to them. Around the battlements of the large courtyard stood the silhouettes of the army, which Gorvic had built up carefully, increasing its numbers by the month, assuring the people that such a display of force was absolutely necessary; with the grim death of Kull's ambassador, the people were happy to accept such a military display. Weapons glinted, for the warriors were ever prepared for battle, particularly as the jungle outside the city walls constantly threatened to disgorge a hostile host.

As he stood, resplendent in his own war gear, high up on the balcony that overlooked the people, Gorvic waved and they responded with lusty cheers. Beyond him, hidden by the falling shadow of the palace, stood Xaldeev, himself unpopular, suspect, though he kept to himself, going about his mysterious and sinister business for the most part in and under the palace in the cold, spider-haunted vaults. Gorvic's leading soldiery stood also with him, faces set, their long spears clutched to them, swords oiled for war in their jewelled scabbards.

Gorvic raised his hand and silence dropped over the throng. 'My people,' he began, 'for too long have we lived under the threat of the reptiles. Too often they make their bold assaults on our borders, threatening the very walls of our city with their cold lust for power.' The monarch paused to let the masses agree noisily. 'Well you know that I have built up our army, training as many new warriors as possible to aid me in restraining this menace. You have been called upon to work hard to supply arms, food, clothes. You have been protected, but has it been enough?' Another roar went up, a mixture of agreement and uncertainty. The common people were wary of too strong a showing of military strength, and Gorvic was anxious to justify the even larger influx of mercenaries from nearby lands.

'The cursed lizards grow bolder. You have seen how bold – you have seen how they dealt with the ambassador of King Kull himself! The Red Slayers, the cream of our Empire's protectors, were cut down irreverently, with no respect for the King they represented. Now Kull himself, maddened and insulted by such a base and vile act, has been stung to action and to support me. Already he leads a powerful force – his elite warriors – to the lands of Zagadar. Kull, to whom we all owe our allegiance, will go forth and smash the reptile menace and trample it into the swamp!' There was a loud cheer at this. 'This will be no skirmish, no hit-and-miss swapping of forays, no mere battle. It is *war*!'

Xaldeev smiled at the way his puppet was whipping up the hopes and bloodlust of the populace. Gorvic drew his Ax and held it on high, the red sun gleaming off its magnificent workings. 'King Kull will come to fortify us!'

'Kull! Kull! Kull!' they cheered, and Gorvic masked his jealousy, thinking that one day the men of Valusia would cheer only for him. He waited for the swelling sound to die down. 'My spies have brought me news of the reptile movements in the jungle. Already they are amassing a host, made bold by their slaughter of Ambellus and his brave warriors. It seems that the spawn of the swamps are no longer content to make brief raids, slinking back into their lairs. This time their force marches on Zagadar itself – they come forth to raze this very citadel!' As expected, this news was met with a unified cry of horror. It took some

time for the hubbub to die down. Again Gorvic raised his
great Ax.

'Have no fear! The reptile tide will dash itself out upon our
battlements. Kull will be with us. Together we shall repel the
lizard filth, and then drive them back, until finally we shall
destroy them for all time. The Gods are with us, for their
oracles speak to us and tell us of our ascendancy over the
beasts. With Kull beside us, how can we fail?' This seemed
to restore the faith of the people, for again they cheered
lustily. They knew of this fabulous King Kull, of whom
many stories and legends had been told. Surely there was
no army to withstand him.

'So, my people, the war plans are already drawn up. You,
too, have your part to play. When Kull comes to Zagadar,
it will be to strengthen this citadel. It will be here that we
take the impetus of the presumptuous lizard men. Zagadar
will become a scene of bloody carnage! The streets will run
red, and the toll of the dead will be high. The vultures from
the hills will feast long into the night.' The grim picture
that he was painting made his subjects shudder. He again
silenced them.

'But you, my faithful vassals, will not be made a party to
this terrible war which will soon break. You must be sheltered
for you are the heart of the Zagadarian nation. You must be
secreted away from the crimson fury of the battle. The men
will be given arms, yes, excepting those that are too old or
infirm, and the latter, together with our women and children,
will be taken up into the mountains beyond the city, to the
sacred and secret places of the Sun Temples, there to await
the outcome of this bloody war.'

At once there was an outcry, for everyone wanted to do
what they could to help repel the invader from the jungles,
but Gorvic asserted himself as king. 'You will obey me! The
reptile legions are not human! Only the most ferocious and
bloody of warriors can stand up to them. It is my duty to
protect you all. You are my people – I will not have any of
you cast into the crimson cauldron of death that will engulf
this citadel when the war begins! Zagadar must abide. You
have heard my words – obey your king!'

For a while they seemed dismayed, but as they thought
of the coming of the reptile host, they saw the sense in

Gorvic's speech. Fear nibbled at them all. And they would only hinder the fighting defenders of Zagadar. Gradually a cheer went up, and then swelled as they cried aloud the name of Gorvic, though not so loud as they had called the name of Kull. Gorvic waved as they repeated their cries, the sound of his name ringing back from the stones of the palace. At length he drew back into the building behind him, where Xaldeev waited, a crooked smile daubing his hollow features.

'Excellent, master,' said the sorcerer. 'They hang upon your every word like obedient hounds.'

'They will accept my decree, I think.'

'Indeed. They would not stand against the lizard men. Once they are led up into the Sun Temples, they will be kept in ignorance of the coming battles. Our real plan will unfold, and they will be none the wiser.'

'You are certain, wizard, that my warriors will accept the treachery? You see how Kull's name mocked us?'

'I have access to necromantic lores and rituals that were old before the first Man walked, sire. Your men will be subjected to such a blanket of sorcery that their own wills will be a mystery to them. They will go into the fray like animated dead men, controlled by my will! And when Kull is trapped here, as a fish in an ornamental pond, and as easily speared, not only your men, but all the warriors of the Empire will bow to you, the victor. It will be seen that Kull has died at the hands of the lizards – whom you will then vanquish. Have no fears, master, the lizard men will honour their pledge to me. They will keep their part of the bargain, for they fear the things that I can dredge up to chastise them should they fail to obey.'

Gorvic shuddered at the thought of what the sorcerer meant. 'The Unborn One?'

'I will not bring it forth across the Abyss unless the lizard men force my hand. But I do not think they will. All they want is your citadel.'

'And I want Valusia. It seems an excellent bargain.'

'Have no fear. Kull's Gods have deserted him. He will be cut to shreds by the lizard men, once I have thrown open the secret passages into Zagadar in the vaults deep below us.'

WITHIN ACCURSED WALLS

Kull looked up at the soaring walls of the citadel that reared from the matted, tangled greenery of the southern jungle, cut into the base of the scorched and jagged peak behind. Beyond this were other knifed peaks over which the incessant sun poured its blistering rays. Beside the monarch of Valusia rode Brule the Spear Slayer, his hooded eyes searching the dark walls, assessing them as a warrior assesses hostile terrain, trying to gauge their strength, their accessibility. Whoever had built this southern stronghold had known how to build, for the towers of Zagadar looked secure enough. Behind Kull stretched his army, a formidable host, a long serpent of fighting men, armed to the teeth for war, helmeted and alert in spite of their long ride, a daunting array of power and spectacle. Here were the cream of the Red Slayers, superlative fighters, each man sworn to Kull, who had led them even before his ascendancy to the throne of Valusia. Not until the legions of Rome marched across the post-cataclysmic lands of Europe would such a superbly disciplined army again march across history.

High up on the parapets a score of trumpeters blew a brazen tribute to the arriving army, and at the base of the massive walls the twin gates opened. From out of them rode a party of Gorvic's retainers, though the monarch stood on his own battlements, watching the splendour of Kull and his entourage.

'See the dark-skinned one beside Kull,' hissed Xaldeev from the elbow of the lesser monarch. Gorvic nodded, noting the short, thick-set figure of Brule.

'That is the Pict, whom men call Spear Slayer. More beast than man. Be wary of him. He is no less ferocious than Kull, who is well named the Tiger. And they are inseparable, having no secrets from one another. Both men are deadly.'

Gorvic listened, lost in thought. Kull and his troops certainly made an impressive sight. He was glad that the battle would not embroil his own warriors, good though they were.

Before the gates, Kull met the retinue of Gorvic, who received him with honour and the usual gifts. Kull waved

them aside curtly and the mighty-thewed king of Valusia
was brought within the citadel, his imperious gaze studying
the walls inside and the array of warriors and fighting men
on display. Orange tunics with blue-sewn hems fluttered in
the breeze, the personal emblem of the king of Zagadar.

'This outpost king sports a strong fighting force of his
own,' said Brule, eyeing the gathered troops that lined the
way like statues. 'I wonder – is their first allegiance to Kull,
or their Zagadarian monarch?'

'For now they have no choice, Brule. The lizard men are
our common enemy. When we have avenged Ambellus, we
shall put your doubts to the test. See, how still they are. Are
they cast from marble?'

'I have smelled the reek of sorcery since first we set foot
in these remote jungles,' muttered Brule with a nod.

Gorvic meanwhile descended a broad stairway down to the
plaza, and for once the dark shape of Xaldeev was not with
him, for the sorcerer feared and despised Kull, who might yet
recognize him. The two kings bowed politely to each other,
and then, as a token of submission, Gorvic offered to Kull
his great war Ax. Kull took it, inspected it with a quizzical
expression (for it near rivalled his own weapon), then handed
it back.

'You do me great honour by coming,' said Gorvic correctly
– perhaps a shade too correctly. 'And I am greatly honoured
by your returning of my Ax.'

'A fighting man needs his weapon,' said Kull brusquely,
'just as a king needs his subjects.'

Gorvic bowed low again. 'My humble kingdom is at your
disposal,' he said, though he seethed within. Yet he checked
himself, for Xaldeev had groomed him well to be patient. Kull
nodded, apparently satisfied.

'For now, I think a bath is the thing that I desire most.
I trust you have made suitable arrangements for the Red
Slayers?'

'Of course, sire.'

With Brule beside him, Kull was led by Gorvic up into the
palace, while the warriors from Valusia were shown to their
own places in the citadel. Gorvic began talking about the dire
situation here in the south, explaining what had happened to
the lizard men and how they had suddenly become bold and

multiplied to set themselves up against him. Kull was still stung by the death of Ambellus, and his mood was dark, so that his tone was far from friendly.

'And Ambellus?' he said. 'Why was he allowed to go out into the jungle to his death?'

Gorvic remained surprisingly unruffled. 'He overreached himself, sire – he was a confident warrior. I had explained to him the dangers, and that the haven of the lizard beings in the Sullen Hills was shunned by us all. Still he insisted on taking his contingent of Slayers out to eradicate it. I told him why I had not sought to do this already, but he spurned my warnings.'

'And why had you not already destroyed this place of vermin?'

'For two reasons, sire. My kingdom is beset upon all sides, and I can ill afford to risk men in wild forays into virtually unknown territory. And secondly . . . the lands of the reptiles are shunned. They reek of superstition and elder deities. No one knows what blasphemies dwell there, or what ancient sorceries abound.'

'I see. Yet you seem to have ample forces gathered here today.'

'I hope so,' nodded Gorvic. 'Now that you have seen fit to strengthen us, we may yet smash these invaders.'

Kull sensed the man's attitude, but let the near-insult pass. Brule, though, his hand taut on his spear, looked indignant.

'Ambellus was my finest general,' said Kull bitterly.

'He ventured out with absolute confidence. I warned him, but he underestimated the enemy. Not a wise thing for a general, sire.'

'No, nor for a king,' agreed Kull meaningfully. Gorvic made no comment, but now showed his guests to their private rooms.

'Later we will discuss our plans for the destruction of these reptiles,' said Kull, and Gorvic bowed, leaving the Valusian and his personal bodyguard to their rest. Once within the sumptuous chambers, Brule grunted his displeasure.

'The whole air smells of evil,' he snapped, setting guards at the door, then moving about cautiously, as though seeking out some hidden denizen. Kull nodded soberly.

'Something is amiss. We must guard against treachery at all times. I wish that Ambellus's warriors had not died to a man. Then perhaps we would have had other news to ponder.'

'I liked not the array of strength without.'

'Nor I. Nor the silence of the dead about them. I will have the word passed. Every man must be prepared to rise up from his bed and strike at the least whisper of trouble,' said Kull.

As he went to his guards to instruct them, a tapestry at the end of the chamber rippled slightly, as though a breeze had disturbed it. To the eyes of the men, nothing seemed wrong, save for those of Brule, who like his king had been raised in the wilds, more animal than human, his instincts still honed to those of a predator, instincts upon which he constantly had to depend for his survival. He alone saw the ripple of the tapestry.

Swift as a striking snake, he had drawn his spear arm. His long shaft whistled through the silent air of the chamber and tore apart the rich tapestry. There was a strangled shriek beyond, then a flurry as of someone in flight. Lithely Kull bounded forward, his sleek body as corded as that of a tiger, his sword ringing out. He slashed at the remains of the tapestry and saw a small chamber beyond, with steps leading down uninvitingly to darkness. Brule was beside him in an instant. They heard a distant stone slab closing.

'It is useless to pursue, Brule. They have fled.'

Brule picked up his spear, which had a bloodied point. 'The smell,' he said, nose wrinkling. 'It is familiar.'

'Yes,' growled Kull. 'The smell of the reptile. We must sleep lightly this night.'

CRIMSON NIGHT

After long talks and discussions with Gorvic and his assembled generals, Kull and Brule finally decided upon their strategy for dealing with the lizard menace. The candles burned low as they argued, for Kull sought to carry the war out into the jungle, while Gorvic repeatedly warned of the dangers of doing so; the reptile men were no longer working in small units out there, they were gathering an army.

'Would it not be better to draw them to us and let them expend themselves upon our walls?' suggested Gorvic, and so the discussion went on, Kull not fond of playing a waiting game, nor of adopting a defensive stance.

At length, deep into the night, the issue was decided for them. A breathless Zagadarian warrior rushed in, eyes wide in horror, his face drawn.

'Forgive my intrusion, lord, but we are besieged! The outer walls are under attack.'

'What nonsense is this?' fumed Gorvic, hoping that his act suitably fooled his guests.

'Lizard men!' gasped the warrior. 'They came swarming out of the jungle like flies!'

There was no need for him to say more. Quickly the assembled men strapped on their armour and took their swords and weapons from the pile near the door, Kull and Gorvic wielding their war Axes.

'So we defend . . . for now,' Kull told Gorvic, who nodded grimly. Nothing else was said as they went out from the palace and up onto the castle battlements above the citadel gates. Below them they could make out the hundreds of shapes that were the reptile men, their torches bobbing in the pale light. Arrows whipped up from the gloom, while the defenders of the walls were already casting their spears and firing arrows of their own in a silent, mechanical fashion like zombies. Kull ignored the unusual movements of the defendants and took in the seething horde of lizard men, face calm. He leaned on the haft of his huge weapon and tried to take in the numbers of the enemy, who were still pouring out of the black jungles.

'They cannot hope to take the walls,' Kull said after a while. 'They must have idiots for commanders, yet I know they are not mindless.'

'They have no scaling ladders, no rams,' Brule noted. Kull realized that he was right. It seemed remarkable.

'Pah! They are ignorant and sub-human – beasts!' snapped Gorvic, his face mottled by the light of the huge moon that had broken from the clouds to hang over the noisy jungle.

'I have fought them before now,' mused Kull. 'Something of this reckless assault smacks of their cunning. They are not so foolish as to cast themselves upon impregnable walls like breakers upon rocks. Look to your defences, Gorvic. They are wily.'

Below them the din of the assault went on. Hundreds of reptile men were at the walls, some climbing sinuously upwards, some beating at the massive doors with their axes, but it was evidently going to be fruitless. Gorvic watched for a while, then excused himself.

'I will go and see that all my men are alerted, and that all our defences are plugged.'

Kull nodded, still thinking hard on the ploy of the enemy. As Gorvic left, Brule's eyes followed him until he was out of sight.

'Something is wrong,' he growled, and Kull nodded.

'It has an odour, just as the hidden staircase had an odour of reptile. Gather the Slayers, Brule. Bring them all here to the battlements. We will stand together when the killing begins.'

Gorvic had gone down into the citadel. He had no intention of looking to any defences, for he knew the night's plan better than any, save the unscrupulous Xaldeev. First the generals would be killed, leaving Gorvic master of an army doped by sorcery. Winding through the corridors that led deeper and deeper into the palace's underground grottoes and subterranean chambers, Gorvic heard sounds below – scuffling, whispering sounds. He pushed open a hidden doorway, a slab of marble that pivoted to give him access to a low-roofed chamber below.

In the gloom of this chamber he heard voices, sibilant and alien and he went forward carefully. Smoke permeated the rank and smelling air, and he saw torchlight. Limned in this were a number of grim figures, all coming up from yet another tunnel into the very earth. Swords thrust at him, and the beaded eyes of a score of reptile men observed him. Their tongues flicked out, eyes red with hate.

Gorvic cursed, hefting his Ax, for the intruders meant to kill him as they advanced. He prepared to fight, for in this cramped space he would have little time to flee, and the lizards were swift. Their swords again snaked out for him as they hissed with evil glee at his plight.

'Wait!' cried an imperious voice from the secluded shadows. Another dark being stepped into the flickering light, its face masked by the gloom. At once the lizard men paused, their eyes turning to see the one who had dared stay their bloody deed.

'Xaldeev!' cried Gorvic, the perspiration standing out on his face.

'You fool! What brings you below? I have given orders that everyone caught down here is to be destroyed.'

Gorvic stiffened. The sorcerer had never been so abrupt with him, but there was no time for recriminations now.

'Kull grows suspicious – '

'I know! I watched him and his foul companion in their chamber, and I heard their doubts. I had this for my pains!' snarled the sorcerer, holding out an arm that was bandaged up tightly, as though embalmed.

'From whom?' gasped Gorvic. 'Do they know you are here?' Panic had begun to take hold of him. The lizard men were uneasy, though they waited on Xaldeev's instructions.

'No. My identity remains masked. But Kull and the Spear Slayer shall pay for this! They were to die quickly, but now I shall see that they spend many days and nights screaming before they go to the agonies of the Abyss!'

'Have you opened the vaults?'

'Yes! The last of the entrances is open. Stand back. Go up into the palace. Before long the corridors will be writhing with the lizard men. Your warriors are under the spell I cast – they will not be touched, save for a few. And already your generals have been slaughtered. Kull's men will bear the full force of the attack. They will be smashed, just as Ambellus and his followers were!'

Gorvic smiled, standing aside as the lizard men pushed past him. He smelled their sharp, reptilian odour, his nostrils dilating. They regarded him with equal loathing as they passed, but it was all for a cause, Gorvic reasoned. To have Kull dead and to march on to Valusia's throne – for this he would endure many things. Once Valusia was his, the reptiles could have Zagadar. Quickly the unscrupulous monarch made his way up another series of stairs and corridors to the palace. He went into a small room that had a balcony overlooking the plaza and outer battlements. It was upon those walls that the last of Kull's Red Slayers were now gathering, eyes turned outwards for a sign that the attacking reptiles were making any progress. Gorvic sat and watched from his invisible retreat, his smile widening.

Kull was uneasy, his mood echoed by that of Brule, who fidgeted with his spear restlessly. Along the walls the men of Gorvic were still firing out into the night, but the Red Slayers waited patiently, not expending their own supplies of spears and arrows, quietly waiting for the command of their ruler. Abruptly an altercation broke out down in the courtyard. Guards rushed into the moonlight, yelling with terror. Kull and Brule swung round to watch, and presently they saw the cause of the outburst. A score of lizard men ran out from the shadows, swords bloodied, teeth gleaming, ready for the kill. Brule swore and made to rush for the nearest stair, anxious to get at them and begin the killing, but with a mighty jerk, Kull pulled him back.

'Wait, hothead! This reeks of treachery!' As Kull shouted this, another group of warriors – Red Slayers anxious to stem the flood – ran down from the walls and into the courtyard, swords flashing. It was too late for Kull to warn them. As soon as the Slayers rushed at the intruders, a host of the reptiles came out from the palace, surrounding the Valusians. A bloody battle ensued, with many heads rolling.

'They will be slaughtered!' snarled Brule.

'If we leave the battlements, we will all be,' countered Kull. He looked to his men. 'Hold your places!' he bellowed, his voice booming out above the ring of steel on steel. Every head turned to him, save the Zagadarians'. 'No man is to leave the walls – relay the message! You are to hold!'

Down in the plaza the battle was quickly coming to an end. Fifty of the lizard men were closing in for the kill, although the magnificent Red Slayers were cutting them down like stalks of wheat. Blood made slippery the stones, and one by one the valiant Valusians were brutally chopped to pieces. They had taken three to four times their number with them to death, though. Kull looked down grimly, his anger seething within him like a brooding volcano about to erupt. His knuckles were moon white on the haft of his weapon.

'The reptiles will pay dearly for this,' he said quietly. 'And so will the traitors who made this horror possible. We will hold these walls to the death.'

'Aye, and the Zagadarians will be of little use – are they drugged?'

Kull grimaced at the lethargic orange-tuniced warriors. He shook his head. His own men had fallen silent, ready for the real battle. The jungle was equally silent. Somewhere within the palace the main force of the lizards gathered.

SINGING STEEL

'Where are the rest of Gorvic's men?' said Brule anxiously, watching the horde of lizard men seethe down in the plaza and along most of the streets that were visible from up here. Kull shook his head.

'It seems that we fight alone. In a trap.'

Brule spat, tugging from his belt a cruel length of steel. Kull swung his Ax in an arc, teeth barred in a smile of anticipation. 'We wanted a fight, my friend – we have one.'

'They come!' cried a voice along the walls, and now Kull saw the lizard men rushing for the sets of stone stairs that led up here. Eagerly he stood at the head of one narrow stair, ready to repel the invader. They sped upward swiftly, tails flicking sideways like scaled whips. As the first wave reached him, Kull swept his huge Ax in a tremendous arc, scything into cold skin and bone, slashing three of the antagonists so badly that they fell headlong back to their doom on the stones below. Blood splashed him as its spray flew, and he spun for another terrific blow.

Brule met another rush from the other side of the stairs with a violent stab of his spear. The point tore upwards into a jaw, ripping the lizard's head near clean from its shoulders, crushing the beast back into its hissing companions. All along the wall Red Slayers were busy smashing back the fanatical reptiles, and the ring of steel sang out over the walls of the citadel. Bones snapped, heads were sent spinning and hands smote downwards, dealing death furiously. Blood ran down the stairs, daubed the walls, and the din rose madly.

The press of lizard men grew stronger as the weight from behind pushed harder, but the combined determination of the Valusians kept them back from the walls. As each of the lizards fell to join the mounting heaps of dead below, others

rushed to take their place. Kull, his tunic soaked with blood
and sweat, stood, feet braced, his Ax a blur, his arms tireless
as he cut into the clawing, snapping monsters that sought to
drag him down.

Those of the Red Slayers who could not man the stairheads
began unleashing a stream of deadly arrows and javelins,
each one aimed for the eyes and throats of the foe, the
two certain vulnerable spots. Hisses and screams of agony
mingled as the heroic defence of the walls went on into the
night. Nothing was said and there was no cry for surrender
on either side. Man fought beast doggedly, human against
sub-human, and the mixed ferocity blurred the shapes. The
moon gazed down avidly, drenching the fighting beings in
pale luminosity.

Kull kicked out and broke the neck of one huge antagonist,
and for a moment looked across at the outer wall of the
battlements. A cold fear brushed at him, for he now saw
the ends of the scaling ladders that were being swung up
from the outside. He shouted out the danger to his men,
and quickly a detachment of Slayers manned the outer wall,
thrusting back the scaling ladders of the lizards without. The
Zagadarians were standing uselessly, gazing before them as
if drugged heavily. Some died with reptile arrows in them,
falling silently.

Still the maddened reptiles sought to force their way up
the stairs. In two places along the wall they had killed the
Valusian defenders and pressed back their replacements,
gaining access to the battlements. Steel rang on steel and
blood spattered the walls thickly. Brule had lost his spear,
but was putting his sword to good use, twisting it as he
thrust it home into the abdomen of another assailant. He
kicked the carcass aside and set about the next reptile,
slashing off an arm at the elbow and driving the blade into
the beast's face.

Kull was using both Ax and sword now, for the press had
become fantastic. Faces leered inches apart. A Red Slayer
stood beside Kull, jabbing with a bloodied weapon, trying
to help stem that awful tide. Down in the plaza the seething
mass of reptiles seemed to be strengthened. The gates had
been opened, but the reptiles still tried to man the walls from
both within and without. Hundreds of them fell prey to the

arrows and spears of the defenders, but the jungle seemed to be spewing forth countless thousands. Kull's heart pounded with exertion. Although his men held the upper hand and stood in an easily defended position, they were outnumbered by at least ten to one. It would be a test of stamina, and it could not go on indefinitely. Already a good many brave Valusians had gone to their deaths.

In the turret above the battlements, Gorvic looked on with grim pleasure seeing the bestial assaults of the reptile men being checked still by Kull and his wild fighting men – but they could not survive all night. If Gorvic had chosen now to fling his own men into the wild fray, he could have turned the tide of battle and cut into the reptiles from behind. But it was not what he wanted. He dreamed of Kull's throne. This evil alliance with the denizens of the jungle would be the first and greatest step towards winning that throne. He smiled, watching another Red Slayer ripped open and flung from the walls.

'They cannot withstand such an onslaught for long,' said the soft voice of Xaldeev, who seemed to have materialized from nothing beside the dreaming monarch. He watched the killing dispassionately, holding his injured arm gently.

'No,' agreed Gorvic. 'They will be overwhelmed long before sunrise.'

'When the Valusians are all dead, have some of the bodies dressed in the orange and blue of Zagadar. A good many of your warriors have perished tonight. But not enough.'

Gorvic looked puzzled.

'When your people come back from the Sun Temples, they must see that our victory has been won at a great cost. And though Kull and his vassals are all dead, we must be seen to have suffered many losses ourselves. If your people think Kull has been betrayed, they may turn against you.'

'I fear no women, nor old men and children.'

'You should. They cannot effectively wield a sword, but they have powers of their own. They can poison in more than one way. Best to fool them, Gorvic. When you march to Valusia for the throne, you will need every one of them behind your cause.'

Gorvic, eyes still on the raging battle, nodded. 'You are wise.'

Xaldeev smiled cynically, for he could pull each string of his puppet with perfect result. He saw the wild affair on the battlements. The Tiger would be ripped down. All these great kings, whether masters of Valusia or even High Atlantis itself – they all fell. There were greater powers to be sought than mere thrones. And he, Xaldeev, would snatch the greatest prize of all. He smiled, evil as the lizards he had used, and stole away from the thoughtful, absorbed Gorvic.

Far down into the deepest recesses of the citadel went Xaldeev, down to the darkest, earthiest corner of that abysmal sub-world, stifling in the heat. Here, in a huge chamber that had been hewn from the living rock by aliens, centuries before the first sentient beings had crawled from the sea, he stopped, looking out over a fathomless pit, a gaping black wound of darkness in the heart of the earth, a veritable tunnel to other dimensions beyond the world. Raising a single, sputtering brand, Xaldeev began to speak words that contorted his lips, twisting his mouth in a primeval chant lost to elder lores for millennia.

He smiled grimly to himself, for he sensed the darkness of that bottomless abyss *rippling*.

Quickly he concluded his chant and then went away to another small chamber. Here he took certain phials and books. He sprinkled the contents of the phials out into the air of the larger chamber, and from the books he took potent spells and sigils and painted them in the air with his forefinger. Uttering further sonorous invocations, he watched the pit. Its darkness seemed to breath, to shiver with an abominable sentience. From deep below a guttural sound gurgled upwards like bubbling mire, vast and cavernous.

Xaldeev cried out a last cantillation, then turned on his heel, rushing from the cloying vapours of the awful place.

'The jaws of the trap are indeed sprung,' he cackled, finding a secret passage that led up to the palace. 'I shall be avenged on them all! Kull and his Valusians, Gorvic and his vassals, and the unwitting lizard horde. All shall perish. All shall die at the feet of Xaldeev! None shall avert the terrible death when the Unborn One rises up and crosses the Abyss to claim them all!'

HORROR FROM THE DEPTHS

Kull paused only to wipe away the coating of blood and
sweat from his face. Heaps of dead lay strewn about him.
Several more of his warriors had been dragged from the
walls while trying to push back the siege ladders of the
enemy. Lizards swarmed up on all sides. Blood ran stickily,
while swords rose and fell less vigorously, for the strength
of the fighting men slowly waned. Valusians relieved each
other while their companions tried to regain their energy,
standing back, drawing in thankful breaths of sobbing air.
Brule refused to be replaced for an instant, cutting and slicing
into the heart of the lizard attack. The plaza was a growing
mound of dead from both sides, and broken bodies twitched
where they lay.

Gorvic, quietly taking in the grim scenes of murderous fury
and sound, was the first to sense something else crawling
through the night. To him came a slight vibration, a dark
hint that something in the palace had become unstable, as
though the ground trembled in a subtle attempt to unseat
loose walls. He frowned, ignoring this weird tremor, but it
came again, and a remote gurgling sound made him jerk
away from the balcony. He went back inside and here he
could feel the movement distinctly.

Paling, he left the turret and went down into the palace.
There were dozens of corpses littering the halls, men of his
own guard, and several lizards. Gorvic noticed the seeping
smell that drifted up from below like a wind of decay from
some nether vault. A gloomy miasma that spoke of foulness
and intense evil. Running along a corridor he found a door
and was about to rush through, when he saw something
ripple from up a stairway near him, clothed in a green mist.
Gorvic gasped, for it was a mildewed and sickly growth, like
a bulbous sac, writhing along on minute rootlets that seemed
like hair. As he watched, more of the insidious maggot-things
pushed up from below and into the main hall of the palace,
coming from several stair wells, wriggling and glistening.

'Guards! Guards!' he cried as the horrific things emerged
clearly, all parts of some vile, monstrous growth, all connected to some unthinkable central segment. But no guards

came, for they had all been put to the sword. Gorvic drew back and a party of lizard men came scuttling to see who had shouted. They recognized him, and seeing the horror on his face, turned to look upon the awful thing from below. It was thrusting up from every possible outlet, its sacs of pale filth snaking forward, suggesting that it grew rapidly through the foundations of the palace, a huge plant with some wild acceleration of growth.

The lizards ran at it, swords before them, and at once a shower of bright, circular globules popped from the sickly pods and wafted forward, hungry as predators. They reached and stuck to the heads of the lizards, then burst, raining a thick, viscous substance over them, a dripping, gelatinous glue. They screamed, their flesh eaten away in a moment, their bones exposed, their bodies falling to be quickly covered over and *absorbed* by the encroaching horror.

'The Unborn! Xaldeev has unleashed it!' Gorvic cried. He ran out from the palace to the plaza, where the battle still raged madly, oblivious to the terror within. The lizard hordes were totally unaware of the monstrous horror creeping up on them from their rear. Gorvic wanted to rush to horse and flee at once, but he stopped briefly to consider. The throne of Valusia – he would be casting it away. Or would he? Could he flee, leaving them all to perish? But there was no way out now, for the gates were choked with lizards.

Gorvic rushed to the reptile men at the back of the assault on the walls. 'Behind you! See what comes!' he cried frantically. Slowly they took in his words, turning to the palace. There, slithering out of the shadows like a dozen beslimed serpents, came the first green tendrils of that subterranean blasphemy, an unspeakable mass of writhing, seeking growths, that sent forth the wafting globules of death. These came in a cloud, rising up and bursting over the lizard horde, showering them with the thick, acidic substance. Scores screamed horribly as the foul stuff ate into them, melting their skins, charring their very bones.

On the battlements Kull blanched at sight of that grim thing from the palace. He saw its filthy pods showering forth their seeds of death.

'By all the Gods – what is this abysmal monster?' cried

Brule. Seed pods were wafting dangerously higher, threatening to attack the defenders of the walls, mindless of whom they struck next.

'It will engulf us all, though the lizard men are being sucked down already. Is there another way off the walls?'

Meanwhile Gorvic was running for shelter, though there seemed nowhere in the citadel that was safe. Kull saw the running figure and watched it dash up a small sidestreet. He pointed.

'There! There is our traitor!' he cried. Before him on the stair, the lizard men were turning from the fray, fleeing the oncoming tendrils of doom and the pods of the thing from the depths. The stairways all cleared rapidly in the wild retreat, many of the reptiles plummetting off into oblivion, hurried by their terrified companions. Kull leaped after, cleaving still more of them aside with his Ax. He wanted Gorvic for his treachery.

At the foot of the stair, Kull met with only token resistance, for the entire lizard army had been thrown into pandemonium, the front ranks trying to cut to ribbons the questing greenery of the Unborn One. But new shoots sprung where swords had chopped others off, and the stench grew overpowering. Whole walls inside the palace were heaving and shaking as the unguessable bulk of its unseen body pushed upwards from below, causing earth tremors and bringing down columns and whole walls alike. All Zagadar shook, for there was no saying how vast this gargantuan creature could be.

Kull reached the sidestreet unchecked and far down it he could see the fleeing Gorvic. The Atlantean sprinted, roaring out a challenge. Gorvic turned, seeing the huge man that gave chase. He spun on his heel, waving his own mighty Ax, which had been snatched from the royal arsenal in Valusia. Kull raced towards the traitor, hair streaming behind him, forgetting the horror from below. The street shook and there came the sound of crashing masonry nearby and the awful, incessant screaming. Kull came upon Gorvic and they stared at one another like two lions.

'You have caused the deaths of many good men, traitor!' snarled Kull, unable to check his disgust. Gorvic waved his weapon menacingly.

'Your reign is at an end, Kull. The royal line of Borna will take back its rightful heritage!'

Kull bandied words no more and rushed forward. It was to be Ax against Ax, blow for blow. Kull's Ax sliced the air and was met by that of Gorvic. They were well matched and they set the air alive with ozone as their weapons clashed. Both men were coated in sweat and neither gave an inch. Kull swung and chopped, veins standing out lividly, but Gorvic was fresher, though powered by fear. It was as though he indeed fought a snarling, carnivorous tiger from the jungles. The Axes rang, the beautiful filigreed work shining in the moonlight. Another building close by crashed down. Fires had broken out. It seemed as though Zagad: had come to its hour of doom.

For a long while the two men circled, exchanging blows, trying to carve a way past each other's defence. Then at last Kull swung a low and oblique cut which took his opponent unawares. Gorvic shrieked with agony as Kull's lightning steel ripped into his thigh, almost severing the skin and bone completely. The Zagadarian toppled into the dust, pumping blood. Kull stood above him coldly, ready to finish what he had begun. It would be a quick and merciful death. But before he could strike another grim figure emerged from nearby, clad in black robes, eyes blazing with malevolence.

'So Kull – you think you have triumphed!' It was Xaldeev, features contorted in glaring hate, 'Kill him swiftly before the Unborn One sucks him to its heart! And then go to the Unborn yourself, for there is no escape this night.'

Gorvic looked up and saw the sorcerer through a mist of pain. Kull's Ax wavered. 'What is this thing you have dredged up – and who are you?' said the Atlantean.

'I am Xaldeev, last of a race that walked your world before you were raised from the slime. We tended the shoggoths of the Elder Ones. And the Unborn is from another dimension, another realm far beyond your own earthly night. The star spawn obeys only me. It feeds upon living souls. There are many here for it. In return for my gift, it will give me power.'

'Then you shall die for your pains!' roared Kull, leaping over the fallen Gorvic, Ax raised to smite the wizard down. But Xaldeev was ready. He hurled something and a ball of white light stopped the falling Ax dead. Kull's arm jolted and he was pushed back. Xaldeev laughed evilly as his opponent began to circle him.

'Your strength is nothing, Tiger,' mocked Xaldeev, raising his hand to call forth further potent spells. They circled, Kull swinging his whistling steel. It descended and smashed down into yet another ball of light and Xaldeev cackled with joy.

'See, Tiger, I call up your fate,' he said, pointing, and from down an alleyway floated a string of sickly white globules, the seeds of the Unborn. Kull paled, readying the Ax, knowing what those horrors could do. If the things burst over him, he was dead.

Xaldeev watched, enthralled by the coming death of his enemy, a cat watching its prey. As he did so he failed to see the figure that crawled laboriously towards him in the bloody dust. Gorvic, dying from his gushing wound, was making a last desperate effort. He struggled to his knees, biting back his agony and lifted his Ax. It swung back silently, then came down cleanly, embedding itself deeply in Xaldeev's unprotected back, the red blade standing out from the sorcerer's chest.

Kull turned to see the blood burst from the sorcerer's mouth, and then the wizard folded and crumpled, dead. Quickly Kull spurred himself away from the terrible scene, fearing those oncoming pods. He looked back over his shoulder as he ran, in time to see the globules descend like vampires and burst over both Xaldeev and the dying Gorvic. The king of Zagadar had atoned for his sins.

Coming to the plaza, Kull saw a scene from the realms of nightmare. Hundreds of rotting cadavers littered the place, mostly lizard men, the stench vile. The first of the grim tendrils of the Unborn were groping up at the battlements, like blind fingers. The last of the Red Slayers were fending them off. As Kull watched, the tendrils appeared to draw back a little, then pulled back more. Inside the collapsing palace there came terrible screams and gurglings, as though some gigantic being were suffering awesome tortures. It must be the fires.

Xaldeev's death, though, had blunted the will of the Unborn, and now Kull could see that it withdrew itself, slowly, back to that remote outer dimension from which it had crawled. Snatching up a fallen brand, he hurled it at the nearest of the creeping growths, and they drew back in alarm. From out of the carnage and devastation a single figure emerged.

'Brule!' laughed Kull, clapping the scarred warrior on the back.

'Aye, alive. What has turned this creature back?'

'Gorvic is no more. Nor is the alien being that gave this horror its birth. What of the reptile men?'

'All fled. The jungle has swallowed all those that survived. We were fortunate to be on the walls, otherwise we would have been engulfed by those globules. See, a thousand of the lizards lie rotting!'

'Then the victory is ours.'

'Aye, but Zagadar is finished. The walls are crumbling. The palace is a broken husk,' said Brule, shaking his head.

Kull gazed up at the moon, then into the mountains that it lit. 'The survivors will rebuild the citadel. They will find few of their menfolk left. What of the strange lethargy that cloaked Gorvic's men?'

'It is strange, for they suddenly began to awake from it.'

'Xaldeev's hand again! How many Zagadarians live?'

'Enough,' said Brule.

'We will help them, then. We must not lose Zagadar to the jungle. Doubtless the reptile men will grow bold again. They must find Zagadar prepared for them if they do. Bring the women and children back from the Sun Temples. I must chose them a monarch with care.'

Brule wiped his sword free of blood. 'Look not too hard at me,' he grinned. 'I'll go back to the Pictish Isles before I'll settle in this forsaken place.'

And Kull threw back his head and laughed at the stars, a loud, ringing sound, filled with relief that the crisis had passed.

FATAL AGE

Nancy Holder

Nancy Holder has, since 1981, published several romance novels and a mainstream thriller, Rough Cut. *Shorter work has appeared in several of the* Shadows *anthologies,* The Mammoth Book of Vampires, Greystone Bay, Women of Darkness *and* Borderlands. *She won the Bram Stoker Award in 1992 for her story 'Lady Madonna' (from* Obsessions*), and in collaboration with Melanie Tem she has written two 'sex and horror' novels,* Making Love *and* Witch-Light. *Her solo novel* Dead in the Water *was published in 1994 and she is also the author of games fiction, using the CD-ROM format, for a company for which she is Director of Mythology.*

ELISE'S husband, David, glanced from the road at her. 'Everything okay, honey?'

'Terrific,' she replied, smiling. She was as excited as Ricky, their six-year-old, who sat beside his sister in the back, bouncing and jostling and kicking Elise through the seat without meaning to. Her family, the Martin family, was in high spirits: it was her birthday, and they were off to the Jolly Clown Pizza Palace to celebrate. It was their first outing since Elise had returned from the hospital. Mom was home, and she was fine; and they only had to be a little quieter now and then, and not squabble so much, and she would stay fine.

'Pizza! Pizza! I want my own!' Ricky announced in his squeaky voice. 'I can eat a whole one!'

'Now, Ricky,' Elise began, then stopped. Why not let him be childishly demanding, greedy? She smiled in the rear-view mirror at him. At her daughter, who stared out the window, hunched and sullen. Sandy's black hair hung in curls about her face; Elise had permed it for her the day after she'd come home. Elise guessed she was pouting because they weren't going to the mall, where all her friends hung out. But then again, she hadn't done anything but pout since Elise's return.

'Don't expect too much,' Dr Passell had warned her. 'You and Sandra are bound to bump heads for a while. She's fifteen, an adolescent, and she's been through a lot. It's only natural she'll feel you're usurping her position in the household.' He hesitated, as if gauging her ability to hear what he planned to say next. 'A position, frankly, she feels you abandoned and that she, heroically, took over.'

Well, Sandy hadn't taken over the job of housekeeper, that was for sure. The house was a shambles – a year's worth of dust on the window sills, the floors never waxed; there were things in the back of the refrigerator that Elise was sure she'd placed there herself before she'd gone away. Sandy's stuff was all over the place. A sock on the kitchen counter, a bra under the sewing maching. Elise had rolled over on her daughter's hairbrush this morning. She'd cried out with pain, 'Sandy, is this an obstacle course or a house?'

'Mom, I'm Sandra now,' Sandy – *Sandra* – had groaned. '*Please.*'

Elise sighed and leaned her head against the headrest, watching the eucalyptus trees dapple the blacktop as they turned down the wide boulevards of their neighbourhood.

'I'm going to have pepperoni and sausage and hamburger and extra cheese. Double extra,' Ricky continued.

'You can't eat a whole pizza, dork,' Sandy hissed.

What did she care about a few dust bunnies? It felt so good to be out, to be listening to her children. Not so much out as in – to be back in the world, in the centre of her family, inside her own skin. Life, life was wonderful.

Life is for the living, a little voice inside her murmured. Yes. The past was over. The past was past.

They turned into the parking lot and sailed past the Radio Shack and the bakery. The cheery facade of the Jolly Clown Pizza Palace loomed into view.

The attack came without warning, without sense. Elise gripped the armrest, unable to breathe. Her eyelids flickered; her chest prepared to burst. She was in the grip of it. In the damn, dumb, thick of it.

No! There's nothing to be afraid of.
'Elise?' David queried.
It is not mine, she told herself, using the words her doctor had taught her. Her fists balled, nails pricking her palms. *This fear is outside me. It has nothing to do with me.*
'Mom?' Ricky demanded in her ear. 'Mom?'
Elise took a long, slow breath, held it, exhaled as silently as possible. Moms were supposed to be strong, and stable.
Summoning strength she hadn't possessed a year ago, she fought the fear, forced her eyes open. She wanted to scream. Instead, she fixed her gaze on the glass doors of the Pizza Palace. Over the transom, a laughing clown in a yellow-and-red polka dot jacket, a green bow tie, and a top hat, leered down at her.
'I'm fine,' she said.
Her family strained, waiting. She saw Sandy's face in the mirror, taut, lips pursed.
'Mommy's fine.' She turned around and patted Ricky's hand. Ricky blinked. As she moved to touch Sandy, her daughter's hand jerked. Sandy was the same age Elise had been when her own mother had died. And that, Dr Passell had explained, was what had triggered the breakdown. Seeing a part of her grow into that age had reminded her, terrified her –
'I'm fine,' Elise said again. They stared back at her. She wanted to beg them to be patient. The day had begun so well. It was her birthday.
'Let's go,' David said, unbuckling his seat belt. His voice was upbeat, but Elise could hear the impatience. Her husband had been wonderful through it all, but not even saints were perfect.
The kids hopped out. Elise took longer than the others to get out of the car; her pelvis still ached from the accident a year ago, when she'd lost control of the Acura, which had been totalled. The doctor said the ache in her body would go away, just as the ache in her psyche was diminishing.
The walls of the Palace were trimmed in barber-pole ribbons of red, white and blue. Little clowns chased each other up the spirals. A sign hung on the door, reading, 'Birthday Boys and Girls Today.' There was a long list. Elise

was third on it, below Bobby, 5, and Sean, 7. Her age was correctly noted: 36.

'Come on, you guys!' Ricky pleaded, while Elise leaned on David's arm and they slowly moved to the entrance. With a huff, the boy abandoned them and bolted inside. Sandy followed after with a swish of her perm. Long, slender legs ended in red high heels. Elise felt a stab of pain. Sometimes a year was a long, bitter thing.

'Don't go far,' she called. Ricky waved; Sandy ignored her.

'That girl,' David said, shaking his head. 'I think we should lock her in her room until she's twenty-one.'

'Has she been a handful?' Elise asked while he got the door.

'Actually, a couple of them.' He laughed ruefully. 'She sure can fill out a pair of jeans now.'

She raised a brow, said nothing. She pretended to fish in her purse for her lipstick. Stalling. There was nothing about the Pizza Palace that should upset her. She'd been in there a dozen times, two dozen, helping with her children's birthday parties and those of their friends. She herself had suggested it for their first family outing, thinking of the fun they'd had there before.

It wasn't the outside world that triggered the attacks, she reminded herself. It was the one inside. It wasn't what you saw now; it was something you'd seen a long time ago. Something you felt. Something you were desperately afraid of.

'Let's find a table,' David said, lacing his fingers through hers. He swung her arm. Her throat tightened. She loved him so much. He was so kind. And handsome, in his jeans and tweed jacket and chambray shirt. He was like a dream. In the hospital, sometimes she thought she *had* dreamed him.

'How about here?' David suggested, turning to the left and squeezing her into a roomful of screaming children. There were three such rooms in the Palace, designated Rings One, Two, and Three, to match the circus theme. There, in Ring Three, rows of picnic tables had been pushed together and covered with the full complement of Jolly Clown birthday regalia: tablecloth, napkins, plates. Pizza Palace balloons bobbed against the ceiling while small hands grabbed for them. A cutout sign of the Jolly Clown perched on one end of the table. Written in the conversation bubble above his head was, 'Reserved for Sean (7 Today!) and His Guests.'

'There's a booth,' David said, pointing to an empty table in the corner farthest from the birthday party. 'Is that okay with you?'

She looked at the long table covered with presents and party favours – race cars and lollipops and plastic bracelets. She'd missed both the kids' birthdays while she was away. She remembered herself in her airy little room with the bars on the windows, querying David on the phone: 'Did you buy Thundercats plates and napkins? What about party favours?' And David had said, 'What are party favours?'

And suddenly the Pizza Palace turned on its side, and whirled around like a kaleidoscope, and she remembered her own seven-year birthday party: a shipwreck party, with all the kids dressed like pirates and castaways; and the bakery hadn't understood this was a little girl's party and decorated the cake with a mermaid with enormous breasts. Elise was having a wonderful time presiding over it all at the head of the patio table, when Anne, her older sister, bent down and whispered in her ear:

'Don't drink the punch. Mom put poison in ours. I saw her do it.'

'Honey, oh, honey,' David moaned.

Elise roused herself. David was rubbing her shoulders. Sandy stood beside him, her eyes huge and angry. Her lips were blood-red, a wound of lipstick.

'I can't control it,' Elise blurted. 'It just happens.'

Sandy's eyes narrowed, grew hateful. Elise shrank. *I've embarrassed her too many times*, she thought. *She's never going to forgive me.*

'Why don't you go order the pizza, hon?' David said to Sandy.

Sandy slowly backed away. When Elise was alone with David, he sat down beside her and said, 'That was no panic attack, Elise. You were . . . imagining something.'

Mom poisoned our punch. I saw her do it.

'It was something that happened a long time ago. Something that brought on the fugue,' she told him. 'Didn't Dr Passell explain it to you?'

David frowned. 'I didn't know you had . . . delusions.'

'No. I remember things.' She swallowed. 'I'm thirty-six today, David.' When he didn't respond, she crossed her arms and hunched over the table, staring miserably at the false woodgrain on its surface. 'I've outlived her. I'm older now than she ever got.'

His arm came around her shoulders. 'Sweetheart, you promised not to think about her anymore.'

'Mom poisoned our punch,' Anne whispered.

'Mom came in our room last night and tried to smother me with a pillow. You slept through the whole thing. She heard Daddy get up to go potty and so she stopped, but if he hadn't – '

'When they're young, everyone imagines horrible things about their parents,' Dr Passell had told Elise. 'I remember once when we were driving to Texas to see my grandparents. We were going to stay in a motel – a big deal for us; we were very poor.'

Dr Passell leaned back in his chair then, in his office in the hospital. She envied him his ease; she imagined being a psychiatrist was rather like being a teacher: you sat there with all the answers to the test while everybody else strained to fill in the blanks. You were wise, and no one probed *you*. No one asked *you* to recount humiliating things you'd done –

– fainting in the Burger King, and waking up to discover you'd wet yourself in front of everyone. Sandy dying – her friends were there. She had told Elise she hated her, wished she was dead –

'So, staying in the motel was a big deal,' Dr Passell had gone on, 'but the closer we got to it, the more I began to worry. Somehow, I got the idea that there was a man waiting under the bed for me. He had a big hypodermic filled with poison. As soon as I lay down in bed, he was going to jam it through the mattress and kill me.'

Elise nodded. She'd had similar terrors. She supposed all children did.

'But the damndest part was,' he continued, 'I couldn't tell my parents. They were in on it, somehow. They knew about him and they were going to let him do it!'

He flashed his teeth at her, and for a moment, Elise was as taken aback by the feral aspect of his smile as his story. For a moment, she was as afraid of Dr Passell as she had been of her mother.

'But they weren't in on it,' Elise said.

'No, of course they weren't.' He leaned back in his chair again.

And then there was the night when she locked Elise in her bedroom, and Anne ran into the bathroom. Elise could hear the fire poker crashing down on the bathroom door. She was screaming, and her mother was screaming, and Anne was screaming. And –

'I need more quarters!' Ricky yelled as he raced to the booth.

Elise jumped. David laughed and said, 'Already?' as he fished into his pocket. 'Where's your sister?'

'I keep getting killed. Sandy's hanging out.' Ricky held out his chubby hands, frowned. 'Just two?'

'Haven't got any more.' David waved Ricky away. 'Play something easier. And tell Sandra we're ready for that pizza.'

It was Anne they sent away, Anne who was causing trouble.

'Do you remember seeing the bathroom door the next day?' Dr Passell had asked her.

She couldn't remember it; she'd blanked it out.

'Well, your father told us that when he came home that night, Anne had locked herself in the bathroom and completely destroyed it. Pulled the medicine cabinet from the wall – quite a feat for a fifteen-year old girl. And she'd broken everything there was to break. Elise, there wasn't a scratch on the bathroom door. Your mother never took a poker to it.'

Elise screamed and wept and clung to Anne as her father hoisted her sister's suitcase into the trunk of their Dodge. There was a decal of a ballerina on the hard Samsonite surface. Her father's face was white, grim. Mom watched from the doorway. She didn't come out to say goodbye.

'She won,' Anne whispered to Elise. 'Don't let her get you. Pretend you don't love Daddy, and she'll leave you alone.'

Again the Palace swirled and dipped. *Why here? Why now?* Elise asked herself, then remembered her birthday. Her mother had killed herself when she was thirty-five. Locked Elise in her bedroom (once hers and Anne's) and taken an overdose of pills.

Dr Passell said it was a cry for help, that she hadn't meant to commit suicide. But Elise's father worked overtime, then ran some errands, then got stuck behind a traffic accident and got home hours later than usual.

Elise had peed in her pants because no one would unlock the door.

'He came home the usual time,' she'd told Dr Passell. 'I heard him come in and I looked at the clock.'

The lights of the Pizza Palace flashed on and off three times, then dimmed. David groaned and said, 'I'd forgotten about this part.'

Calliope music blared into the cacophony of high, childish voices, noisemakers, and video game beeps and explosions.

'Ladies and gents, boys and girls, the circus show is about to begin!' chirruped the voice of the Jolly Clown. In ring one, the high-wire Chuckle Brothers! In ring two, the Har-De-Har trick ropin' team! And in ring three, the Clownin' Kids!'

To the left of the long row of picnic tables, a spotlight hit a pair of closed burgundy curtains flush with the wall. The curtains whooshed open, revealing two child-sized clown figures that snapped to attention as the calliope music resumed.

'We're the Clownin' Kids, ha-ha!
We love to clown around!'

The clowns jerked in imprecise rhythm to their song. Elise looked at their orange yarn hair, their plastic faces and red-cherry noses, their pirate hats and patches, and felt mildly depressed by the tackiness. Perhaps they should've gone to the mall after all; they had a food court and everyone could get what they wanted. Her son and daughter were nowhere to be seen; they weren't sitting like little Norman Rockwell creations, beaming at her and singing along, those clownin' kids of hers.

David made a face. 'This place has certainly gone downhill.'

'Here's your pizza,' said a desultory boy with pimples dressed in a polyester, short-sleeved version of the Laughing Clown's outfit. He slid the pizza off a tray and plopped some paper plates and forks beside it.

'We're the Clownin' Kids, ha-ha!'

David stood up. 'I'll see if I can round up our young'n's. You want some Coke? Some root beer?'

'Anything.' Elise smiled at him, then on an impulse blew him a kiss. But he didn't see it; his back was turned to her as he walked out of the room.

She looked down at the pizza. Pepperoni and olive, her favourite. She was very hungry. For all the hospital cost, the food had been terrible.

She eased one of the slices away from the rest and brought it to her mouth.

And froze. Because somehow, she was sure there was something very wrong with it.

She was afraid there was glass in it.

Mom put poison in our punch, and glass in our food. Anne said so. Anne didn't destroy the bathroom. Daddy didn't come home late. He let her die; he was in the house and he knew and he let her overdose.

Slowly, looking around to see if anyone was watching her, she lowered the slice of pizza, moved it in her palm as she examined it. She was being crazy. She was acting out, as Dr Passell would say. She *had* abandoned her post; she was too weak to be a mother –

There! A glint, caught from the overhead lights.

'Mom put glass in the pizza,' Anne told her.

And then Mom appeared in her shipwreck costume and stood over them; she frowned and said, 'You girls! Stop playing with your food and eat it.'

Elise didn't know what to do. Anne was shaking; she nudged Elise beneath the table with her knee. 'No,' she breathed, speaking almost through her nose. But if she didn't eat it, if Elise didn't eat it, it would mean her mother really was, that her mother was trying to –

She gasped and dropped the pizza slice face-down on the table.

'We're the Clownin' Kids,' sang the robot clowns, 'and if you don't eat that pizza, Elise, we'll get the poker.'

Elise cried out and whirled toward the figures. They froze. Everyone in the room froze: the children, the parents, the waiters dressed in polyester. Only the balloons moved, bobbing along the ceiling.

Everyone looked at her. Everyone waited.

At the other birthday party, her mother waited. The children, sensing a problem, stared at Elise and Anne in their pirate bandanas and cut-off jeans and hula skirts. The piles of presents, the party favours –

– Thundercat party favours; David told her that Sandy had bought some after all; Sandy had known what they were –

'David,' she croaked. She stood up. No one moved.

Then, as she ran, the world started up again. The kids laughed and the parents distributed pizza and the birthday boy blew out his candles. And Elise ran for all she was worth, crying David's name, searching through the other rooms for him, screaming for him.

People gaped at her; a few men rose from their chairs as if to follow her or stop her. Her body ached; her pelvis cracked again – she could feel the mending tearing apart, ripping like a seam, like a chrome bumper; collapsing inward like the fireplace poker on the hollow wood door.

'David!' she shrieked. 'David!'

What had she done, back then? What had she done?

Pretend you don't love Daddy, and she'll leave you alone.

She had loved Daddy, and Mom had never hurt her. She had loved Daddy –

– but Anne got sent away.

Her hand reached out, she paused, and heard her daughter's voice coming from the kitchen:

'Make it nice and hot, you guys, because she'll try to get out. We've got to do it quick.'

'Yeah, incinerate her,' Ricky said.

Elise pulled herself along the wall and peered into the kitchen. Her son and daughter stood on either side of an oven. David walked into view. He put his arm around Sandy, who draped a hand around his waist, slid it into his back pocket, cupping his hip. She leaned her newly permed hair against his biceps.

'This is as hot as it can get,' David said.

'Well, the pizza will slow her down,' Ricky replied.

Elise reared back. The pain shot through her body; she crumpled to the floor, hitting her elbow hard against the wall.

The three looked in her direction. 'Hi, Mom,' Sandy said brightly. 'Did you eat your pizza?'

'Oh, my God.' Elise burst into tears. 'What's happening? What's really happening?'

David walked toward her. He looked like someone she had never seen before. 'I'm going to need some help,' he said.

'Is this happening?' Elise cowered on the floor. Her elbow throbbed. She couldn't breathe. 'Why is this happening?'

'You know what your dad told me?' David said as he bent over her.

His eyes . . . she *had* dreamed him. She scrabbled backward and hit the opposite side of the hall.

He said, 'It took your mom much longer to die than it should've. Much, much longer.'

'No!' Elise shrieked. 'No, no!'

Sandy crouched beside her father. 'I love you, Daddy,' she said softly.

David touched Sandy's cheek. His fingers trailed to her collar bone.

'I never meant to hurt her!' Elise screamed. And with a final, blinding pain, all the wounds cracked open: the breakdown and the blackouts and the lies –

– Elise and her mother, *Elise*, because she loved her daddy, loved him the most, the most the most –

'It didn't happen!' she shouted. 'It isn't happening!'

Shaking his head, David grabbed Elise's ankles. 'It must be a fatal age.'

'It didn't happen!' she screamed, kicking at him.

Sandy reached down and slapped her hard. 'Oh, yes it did,' she said, and her voice was seductive and menacing and sure.

THE MOUTHS OF LIGHT

Ramsey Campbell

Ramsey Campbell, regarded as the UK's most respected writer of horror fiction, has published hundreds of short stories, edited numerous anthologies and is the author of more than a dozen novels. His most recent full-length works include Midnight Sun, The Count of Eleven, The Long Lost *plus the novella,* Needing Ghosts. *He is the editor of* Uncanny Banquet, Deathport *and, with Stephen Jones, the British and World Fantasy Award-winning annual* Best New Horror *series. His short story collections include such titles as* Scared Stiff: Tales of Sex and Death, Waking Nightmares, Alone With the Horrors *and* Strange Things and Stranger Places.

RYRE couldn't tell when he ceased to be pursued by anything but echoes. When he halted his steed, the echoes died reluctantly away. The dark held him like a fist, enormous yet so close it crushed him. It must have proved too much for his pursuers, as it was threatening to do to him. The cavern was huge as night, but far darker. He seemed not to have seen daylight for days.

Once he moved off the echoes returned, fluttering eagerly out of their lairs. Echoes stirred wakefully in the distance that was the underside of the roof, water dripped relentlessly in holes so deep in stone they were beyond echoing. He tried to hear the sounds as his steed's great veined ears must hear them, as it led him through the cavern toward the hope of light beyond.

It was no use. Everything reminded him of his folly. Had he grown so fond of the slave town of Gaxanoi that he had had to go back? For wounding a slave-driver, the priests and their bullies had given him to the vampires of the forest.

Victorious but weakened, he'd made his way back toward Gaxanoi: where else could he have found a steed? Though he had fed himself strength – he had eaten what meat he could kill on the journey – it had been winter before he'd arrived.

The echoes were mocking him. They and his memories were calling him fool. For a moment it seemed that riders were waiting ahead in the dark to ambush him. They must be echoes: how could his pursuers have outdistanced him? He would have seen their torches.

Could he not have taken the steed and left Gaxanoi before they knew he was there? But he hated slavery, for he had suffered it himself. He had cut down the guards before the slave-house of Gaxanoi, and had told the slaves they had only to break their chains to be free. He'd brought them metal bars, he'd shown them how to lever open the links of the chains – but none of them would. Where could they go? They would only be recaptured. Slavery had bound their minds more securely than their bodies. He had ridden away, enraged by their apathy, by his powerlessness. Before he'd reached the edge of the town he had heard sounds of pursuit. The guards had been found.

He wouldn't go back into the forest. He had ridden along the coast, toward the mountains which plunged into the sea. He should have been able to lose his pursuers in one of the passes, or to ambush them there, but all of the passes were blocked by snow. He'd had to go through the caverns, to trust the story he'd heard that the main cavern went all the way through the mountains.

And now he could only trust his steed. It at least was not confused by the echoes, the echoes which jabbed at his mind, already raw with memories. If he had not felt half suffocated by the dark he would have been less ready to entrust his safety. He was too enraged, and the beast was too concerned with its footing on the slippery rock, to realize that he was surrounded until the flints sparked and the torches flared.

Seven men had been waiting for him in the dark. Torchlight made them into hovering torsos with drawn swords. Though they had none of the well-fed look of the slave-drivers and their kind, their thin voracious faces were no less unwelcoming. Reflected flames ran like ghosts of blood up and down their swords.

Ryre grew tense as a bowstring. Perhaps he could drive his steed through their midst, give himself the advantage of surprise while he drew his sword. Must it come to that? He was sick of senseless bloodshed; killing in Gaxanoi had achieved nothing.

The seven were absolutely still. When the man who faced Ryre spoke, it was as though a leathery statue was speaking. 'What brings you to this place?'

'I am bound for the land beyond the mountains.' Ryre had no idea of its name.

'Why not by sea?' He brought his torch closer to Ryre's face. 'No man comes here without a purpose.'

'I had no choice. There was no boat, and if I had turned back men would have killed me.' Ryre was feeling more sure of himself. These were fishermen; he could smell that on them. They might have the advantage of numbers but not, he thought, of swordsmanship. What venture could have stranded them here, so far from the sea?

Whatever it was, it had narrowed their minds. 'What men? We heard nobody,' one said. 'It's strange you should have been driven in here just at this time. Keep your hand away!' he cried, prodding Ryre with his sword.

The torchlight must have made Ryre seem to reach for his sword. The scrawny youth kept prodding him, seeking a chink in the leaves of his armour. The dull unrelenting ache made Ryre think that bloodshed might not be entirely senseless after all.

The old man who had spoken first gazed at him. Reflected sparks glared from his eyes. He seemed to be peering through the pinpricks of light, outside which everything was dark, to be distrusted. 'It is strange, right enough,' he muttered.

A plumper man, who looked squeamish, said 'He could ride with us if we took his sword. He could help carry.'

Ryre's reaction was almost instinctive. He yielded his sword to no man without a fight. As the scrawny man's blade dug harder into him, poking uselessly but infuriatingly at his armour, he kicked his steed forward, roaring.

He knocked the old man aside with a fist as he drew his

sword with the other. Torches jerked, swords blazed, but he was already beyond the torchlight. Should he stand and fight, or lose them in the dark? If whatever they sought was worth fighting for, perhaps he should seek it himself.

There was a prize more immediately worth winning: the torches. In this darkness, light was a treasure in itself. He urged his steed faster, the better to turn before the men could see him.

He was about to turn when he glimpsed lights far off in the dark. Were there other seekers? Though reddish, these lights were not torches; they seemed to be growing. He had an uneasy impression of hungry red mouths, gaping wide. Perhaps that was an illusion, but it was enough to distract him. Before he knew it, his steed had jerked to a halt, and he was falling.

It was a long fall. His steed had baulked at the edge of a pit. When at last he hit rock it thumped the breath from him. He tried to hang on, but the rock was steep and coated with moss. Eventually he slammed against a wall, a long way further down.

He lay there, his mind and his body pounding like drums, while the men with their torches peered down at him. Their faces were so distant it seemed that he could have crushed them together in his fist. Before long they withdrew. 'We must go back and search again,' he heard the leader say. 'Bring his steed.'

A demon of fury possessed Ryre. He hurled himself upward, clawing at the slippery rock. He gouged the moss with his sword, trying vainly to lever himself up the slope. When at last he realized that he would achieve nothing, except to snap the blade, he desisted and began to grope about the bottom of the pit.

He found the exit at once. It was narrow, though high enough to allow him to crawl. It seemed to lead in the direction in which he had been riding. Cursing monotonously but silently, as though he could curse away the darkness, he crawled into the opening.

The walls were soft and moist with moss. It felt unpleasantly like crawling down an unseen throat. His sounds – his breathing that was not quite steady, the squelching of moss – pressed close to him; so did the dark, a blindfold bound tight across his eyes and round his skull. Nevertheless he was advancing steadily. His knees and elbows felt raw with crawling before the tunnel began to narrow.

What if it grew too narrow for him to draw his sword? Cursing aloud, he held the sword before him, probing the dark as he crawled. Suddenly apprehensive lest the sword be snatched away from him, he gripped the hilt more tightly. Though the darkness was impenetrable – solid as the walls which were touching his shoulders now – he could almost see the reddish lights which had yawned like mouths.

When his sword encountered an obstacle more yielding than moss he was ready to hack at it before he realized it was water. How far ahead was the tunnel flooded? He struck the water with his blade and heard the ripples chase into the distance. At least there must be air above the surface.

When he crawled into the water it closed over his head at once. For a moment he was scrabbling at the slimy walls as stagnant water flooded his nose and mouth, then he realized he had room to stand. The walls were closer than ever – he had to sidle forward between them, sword-arm outstretched – but at least he could keep his head above the water. He sloshed onward, panting, maddened by the scum which kissed his face again and again.

He was underwater without warning. The floor of the tunnel had descended, and so had the roof. There was no air at all. He couldn't drag himself backward; the tunnel was too slippery. He floundered onward, unable to breathe or to hold his breath much longer, unable to tell whether there was any air ahead.

The tunnel bent sharply. As he struggled to wrench himself out of the bend the darkness, a thick harsh fluid that had flooded his brain and his lungs, began to choke him. His chest was jammed between two ridged slabs of rock, his arm was flailing beyond them, about to drop his sword. Then he was free, and gasping above water. More – he could see lights.

They were torches, and they were in the main cavern. The cavern had descended more sharply than the tunnel through which he had crawled. The tunnel had brought him out ahead of the men who had stolen his steed. At once his rage was no longer frustrated but grimly purposeful.

By the time he had eased himself silently out of the water his breathing was under control. For a while he watched the torches. The men were ranging along both sides of the cavern, peering at the entrances to tunnels. Presumably they had marked those tunnels which they had already searched.

Though he was out of reach of the torchlight Ryre hid instinctively behind a group of mossy boulders while he planned what to do. When one of the searchers fell behind the others, Ryre would strike. His free hand was gripping the rock that hid him, gripping as though it was a throat. Or was it rock? It seemed to have grown softer. Perhaps it was only his hand that was numb.

No, it was not rock. He might not be alone in lying in ambush. The object behind which he'd hidden was writhing beneath his hand. It felt like leathery flesh, cold and overgrown, awakening in the dark. He though he heard huge lips parting stickily.

He recoiled, sword raised to chop – but must he draw attention to himself? One searcher had fallen well behind the others now. Whatever Ryre had touched, it seemed fixed to the spot. Indeed, there were several of the things; he could see their mouths now, bigger than his head – for the mouths were glowing like embers. He remembered the lights he had glimpsed earlier.

He must have a steed. He made his way quickly but stealthily toward the last of the searchers. Rocks shifted underfoot, moss made the floor treacherous. The sound of gurgling, deep in the rock, helped him avoid pits. Whenever he glanced back the mouths had not moved, except to gape wider. They illuminated nothing but themselves.

The sides of the cavern were even more distant than they appeared. As he advanced, they seemed to float away on the dark. Nevertheless he came within reach of his victim just as the other dismounted in order to peer at a blurred mark on the wall.

Ryre seized him, sword-point at his windpipe, and dragged him into the tunnel at which he had been peering. 'Speak softly when you are able,' Ryre said through clenched teeth, 'or you will never speak again.'

It was the plump man. His entire body was shaking. Ryre

should have no trouble with him, unless terror made him
foolish. Ryre let the point dig lightly into the man's throat.
'What are you searching for?'

'The treasure.' The man's whisper was hardly audible.
Perhaps the threat of the sword had closed his throat, or
perhaps he was desperate to seem cooperative. 'A ship was
wrecked where the mountains go into the sea. It was taking
treasure to a king of the Crystal Lands until a storm drove it
off course.'

'Why search for drowned treasure in here?'

'Some of the crew survived. They rescued part of the
treasure. They brought it through here because they were
afraid to go to Gaxanoi. You can understand that,' he said,
perhaps in a desperate attempt to remind Ryre he had been
vulnerable too. 'But it was heavier than they thought. They
had to leave it. All except one died in here or got lost,
nobody knows. The one who came out was mad. He'd been
wandering in here for months.'

His tone grew pleading: now he'd answered Ryre there
might be nothing to keep him alive. 'Some thought he was
raving, but we believed him. The catch was poor this year –
we could barely feed our women and children. We need the
treasure.'

Ryre was wondering who was madder – the seaman who
had survived the cavern, or these men who had forsaken
their livelihood in the hope he spoke the truth? He was loath
to kill the plump man, who had at least tried to persuade his
companions to let Ryre live. Perhaps he could send the man
ahead while Ryre took his steed.

The man still held the torch, close to his own face in case
Ryre suspected him of planning to use it as a weapon.
Suddenly it jerked free of his shaking hand and touched
his plump cheek. Crying out, he flung the torch toward his
steed, which at once bolted into the dark.

Ryre turned snarling. The beast was heading straight for
the lights which were not torches. Before he could pursue
it, the plump man hurled him aside. Ryre lost his footing on
the slippery rock. His sword flew from his hand and clattered
into the tunnel.

He scrambled after it, cursing. It had skidded quite a way;
he had to grope weaponless for minutes, and what might be

waiting in the dark? He reached it at last, and was glad of its reassurance – for out in the cavern, the screaming had begun.

The plump man's steed had baulked just short of the mouths. Had the man realized what they were? Perhaps he'd thought that to ride away would be quicker than leading the beast. But when he'd mounted, his steed had reared up, tried to throw him. As the plump man clung to it in panic the beast had overbalanced toward the mouths.

Ryre watched, appalled. Screaming, the man dragged his arm free of a mouth. The cave screamed like a chorus of demons, echoing him perfectly. The glow of the mouths was brighter now, and made the chewed stump of his wrist look molten. What was left of him tried to struggle out of reach – but his steed, already half devoured, collapsed and flung him on the upturned mouths.

Though they appeared to be toothless, the mouths sucked him apart in moments. Their raw glow was so violent now that Ryre could distinguish their bodies, stumpy glistening limbless shapes that made him think of maggots. Ripples passed slowly down their length as they swallowed their prey.

Some way off in the dark, torches were converging. The searchers had seen their companion's fate. The younger men sounded close to hysteria; one was being sick. 'We can do nothing,' the leader said, so loudly that he might have been trying to outshout his echoes. 'We must go on, and take more care than he did. Our fortune is here somewhere.'

Ryre smiled grimly. If the men were as close to panic as they sounded, they might be worse than careless. In any case, they had no idea that Ryre was still alive. They would be on their guard against things such as those which had devoured their companion, but not against him.

When they recommenced searching, he followed. Now they were searching in groups, three men to each side of the cavern; the death of the plump man had made them more cautious. Ryre thought of animals darting about in search of burrows.

At least they were slowing themselves down, now that three of them had to halt whenever they found an unexplored opening. When he caught up with the nearest group, could

he finish them quickly? Bad swordsmen could be dangerously unpredictable, especially if they panicked.

When the nearer group vanished into a side tunnel, he
quickened his pace. Rocks skittered away from his feet, but
there was no need for stealth; the searchers must be half
deafened by their own echoes in the tunnel. The other
group was too distant to be dangerous. Perhaps as the
three emerged from the tunnel, Ryre could dispose of them
one by one.

He had almost reached the tunnel, down which the
searchers were returning amid their welling echoes, when
he froze, sword raised. Had the other group crept up on
him? No, he could see their distant torches. He must
be looking at watery reflections of the torches that were
approaching down the tunnel – except that the blurred
reddish lights toward the middle of the cavern weren't
moving but widening. They were more of the devouring
mouths.

In a moment he saw why he had thought they were
reflections: they were blurred by a greenish miasma which
they were exhaling. It made him think of gases of decay. It
was drifting thickly toward the tunnel, and would reach it
almost as soon as he did.

What would happen if it reached him? These mouths
looked larger than the others, so far as he could judge amid
the dark; their lips were ragged. Perhaps age had made them
subtler, in their monstrous way.

He was still hesitating when the three searchers emerged
from the tunnel and walked into the thick of the miasma. At
once their torches began to sputter. Before the men could
retreat, the flames went out. Now the only light was the
glow of the mouths, which looked deceptively inviting, a
fire in the midst of immense darkness.

Ryre could hesitate no longer. The men were utterly
confounded, shouting in the dark; he could expect no better
chance. He ran at them, sword poised. Perhaps he could cut
down the nearest rider and take his steed before the others
knew what had happened.

Though the man was still where Ryre had last seen him,
he must have been using his torch to feel his way. Ryre's
sword chopped not into his side but through the wooden

stave. The edge grazed the man's arm. At once he began to slash at the air, crying 'Help! Someone's here!'

Ryre listened for the slashing of the blade, then parried it. The shock jerked the sword from his opponent's hand. Ryre plunged his sword into the man's guts, cutting upward. The man fell away from him, groaning.

Where were the others? The miasma filled Ryre's nostrils with a sweetish rotten stench. It made him impatient to be done with the fight, perhaps foolhardily so. As he whirled, brandishing his sword, he heard the fallen man's steed panting almost in his ear. He grabbed for its neck – if he could mount quickly, he might be able to ride away – only to find that it was empty air. He had been tricked by an echo.

He must be quick. The torches of the other party had crept nearer. No, those were the mouths – but were they very distant or very close? If they were distant, surely they must be the torches – in which case he ought to keep them in view, in case they closed in before he knew it. Or had they closed in while the dark confused him? All at once he knew it was more than the dark: the miasma had doused not only the torches but also his mind.

He was barely able to control his rage before it made him stupid. The two riders were stumbling about and shouting, but he could no longer tell how close they were. Echoes crowded him. If he moved he would be even more confused. He must stay absolutely quiet and still. The riders and their steeds must be at least as bewildered as he was.

His ruse almost saved him, until a steed blundered against him. 'What's that?' the rider cried. His blade came scything down, barely missing Ryre's shoulder. Ryre thrust his sword upward and felt it cut deep into flesh. Hands scrabbled at the blade, then faltered, fell away. As soon as Ryre wrenched the sword free, his victim toppled to the ground.

Ryre was straining to locate the third rider when he heard the man's steed lose its footing on the mossy rock. As the rider landed on his feet, he screamed. There was a loud clash of swords, then the sound of a falling body. Stupefied by the miasma, the man Ryre had first injured had killed his companion.

When the steeds fled, panicked by the stench of blood, Ryre could do nothing, even though he could see where

they were heading. They had almost reached the glow of the
mouths when they began to slither. The devourers were in a
slippery hollow. Unable to regain their footing, the beast slid
down to them. Ryre turned away, sickened by the screams,
by the sounds of tearing and slobbering.

He staggered to the wall of the cavern and groped his
way along it. He felt as though his brain had turned to
jelly, which was slopping back and forth in his skull. The
leader was calling the names of the dead men across the
cavern: 'Halanc! Erepi! Vamanth!' After a while, receiving
no answer, the three survivors moved on.

At last the blazing mouths were clear, no longer blurred
by the miasma, when Ryre looked back. Had he managed
to leave its influence behind, or would that linger? He
sagged against the wall and tried to clean his lungs with
deep breaths.

After a while he felt steadier. He was watching lights range
back and forth across the cavern; eventually they meant
something to him. The three were slowed down by having
to search both sides of the cavern. When he could stand, he
followed them doggedly.

Were they alert for him? Perhaps, since they must have
heard the steeds being devoured, they thought the mouths
had killed the riders too. In any case, they were wary of
danger. Since the leader was among them, they would be
all the more difficult to take by surprise.

Was Ryre's mind still affected? Suddenly, as the men
crossed the middle of the cavern, they appeared to be
surrounded by a multitude of jerking legs. It looked as
though enormous spiders were clutching down at them.
Before long Ryre saw they were surrounded by an inverted
forest of stalactites, some almost touching the floor. If he
could reach the searchers here they would be easier to pick
off one by one. They had moved into the open now and
were heading for the left-hand wall, but they would have
to come back.

They were quicker than he had hoped. They rode through
the stone maze as quickly as they could, apparently nervous
of being trapped while they were separated. Shadows of
their torchlight ran like water down the stalactites. Could
he reach them before they emerged? He ran, clutching at

stone spikes, which felt dangerously fragile, to keep his balance. At least he was making little noise – but he had forgotten his sword. Without warning it clanged against a stalactite.

They heard it, and froze as he did. His head was loud with his voiceless cursing. It took him a while to realize that they weren't staring back at him, but ahead. Were the acoustics of the cave helping him?

Reminding himself that he was safe beyond their torch-light, he made the sword clang against the stone. Yes, the cave was tricking the searchers: they bent low over the necks of their steeds, peering ahead for him. Their torch-flames made the stalactites grope about them.

'I am Ryre, whom you left for dead,' he said at once. 'Leave my steed and you may pass. Otherwise you will die before you see me.'

They were glaring about now, though still not looking back. Would the leader have returned Ryre's steed to him? Before the old man could respond, one of the others rode forward wildly, chopping with his sword. He must have thought he saw Ryre in the shadows ahead.

When his sword cut nothing but shadow, his momentum overbalanced him. He fell against stalactites, several of which broke off. One impaled his skull. He was dead, though still twitching, a moment after he struck the ground.

His steed came blundering back toward Ryre. Would the two survivors notice Ryre before he halted it? He cared little if they did; they were only two. But the leader was staring beyond the impaled man. 'There,' he whispered.

He seemed to have to make an effort to speak louder. 'That steed is yours,' he said to the shadows, and pointed back unseeing toward Ryre. 'You have said we may pass.'

What was making his voice tremble so, with eagerness that could not be suppressed? Ryre knew, and as he quietened the steed, he saw. Beyond the stalactites, at the very edge of the torchlight, was the dim mouth of a cave. Within it shapes glimmered like ashen embers: the shapes of a tiara, necklaces, a crown.

The two men rode furiously toward the cave. They must be frantic in case Ryre reached the treasure. Their torchlight lapped the cavern stormily, if dimly. It must be the jerky light which made the cave appear to yawn wider as they approached.

No, it was not the light. All at once Ryre saw what the riders had missed seeing, in their haste: that though the treasure and the whole interior of the cave were glowing sullenly, the torchlight had yet to reach the cave. He remembered how the devourers had reminded him of maggots – but then what form might they take when fully grown? 'Stay back!' he shouted, appalled to think that anyone should die that way. 'It's alive!'

The riders must have thought he was trying to trick them. They rode so fast into the cave that the extra steed, Ryre's own, broke free. They leapt from their mounts and knelt eagerly by the treasure. Did they think it was only moss that made the floor so soft? Could they not see how regular the ridges were that led back into the throat? Did they think it was their torches that made the cave glare, that made all the jewels into rubies, the crown and bracelets and tiara look composed of blood?

When the ridges began to shift, gulping them back into the cave, they stared about at last. It was too late; the floor was rising, hurling them backward. They began screaming as the mouth closed. Their screams were mercifully brief, but another sound went on and on: the sound of bones being crushed to pulp.

Ryre's own steed had bolted. He followed it, since it seemed to have found a clear path. Within a minute he felt a change in the air, and almost at once the cavern roof gave place to a night sky choked with clouds.

He was overwhelmed by a sense of futility. The madman who had emerged to tell of the treasure had never known how close he was to escaping the dark at once, and the searchers could never have thought to look so close to the entrance. All of them had died for nothing.

As his eyes grew used to the night, which compared to the cavern was luminous, he made out a clump of trees nearby. A grim idea occurred to him. His own steed had calmed now it was out of the cavern. He tethered both steeds, then he cut himself a heavy stave and began to sharpen its ends.

By the time he had finished, it was daylight. When he dragged the stave into the cavern, the huge raw mouth had begun to open and to glow. It had vomited up the treasure, which lay several paces inside. Could it be conscious of using the treasure as a lure?

Ryre waited hours, until the mouth was fully open; then he jammed the stave into it, propping the jaw wide. The ridges were jerking in agony, but their spasms failed to move the treasure toward him. Eventually he dodged into the mouth and snatched as much as he could carry. The stave was creaking, the roof was straining above him, the ridges seemed eager to trip him – but more than any of this, what made him rush out of the mouth was that entangled in the treasure he left behind, and staring up at him almost accusingly, was part of the old man's face.

He was labouring to carry his armfuls of treasure by the time he reached his steed. For a moment he stared at the other beast, then he loaded it with half the treasure. When he set it loose it seemed to know where it was going – back to the widows and children, he hoped. For himself, he preferred not to encounter the friends of the men he had killed. He rode away toward the foothills and whatever lay beyond.

David J. Schow

David J. Schow has written several movie screenplays, including
The Crow *for Paramount Pictures. His short stories have appeared
in various issues of* Fantasy Tales, *in three volumes of* Dark
Voices, Best New Horror 2 *and* 3, Weird Tales, *and numerous
other publications. Collections of his work are* Seeing Red,
Lost Angels, Look Out He's Got a Knife *and* Black Leather
Required. *His novels are* The Kill Riff *and* The Shaft.

THE turd had really hit the turbine, thought Eye Man,
with Jocko's small theft from the pumpkin truck. Rude had
devised a theory about Jocko. He'd told it to Strongheart and
Nobby. Nobby, scared enough to bleach piss, had repeated
it to Eye Man, not giving an airborne fuck whether he was
believed. Rude was history, too, and Nobby had watched
him die.

The theory was that the ghost of Jocko had come back to
haunt them until everybody was dead, dead, dead.

This was no trank fantasy. This was real. Growing up could
be such a scream, except sometimes you saw how simple it
would be to keep screaming until state-funded medication
erased all pain from your life. Which still didn't sound too
shabby to Eye Man.

None of them had ever thought they might actually grow
up, or grow old, or grow dead.

Jocko had always made the other Boulevard punks antsy.
The standing joke was to guess what brand of carb cleaner
he was snorting *this* week. He stood a wiry five-five, the
kind of sawed-off blood with muscle bumps in his jawbone,
and a full basket of twitches and tics. His coffee-coloured
skin had become mottled in a chemical mishap to which

he frequently alluded, yet never detailed. Eye Man thought that Jocko had been the victim of a spill in the birthmark department, and had fabricated the notion of a calamity in his misty past to make himself more mysterious, so Chaka or Lindabelle would do the bone dance with him. Otherwise, it was so solly, fuck Gash or don't fuck. But Jocko was weird enough without fictional embellishment. He'd boasted the tallest orange spikes on the street until he'd gotten clipped by the wing mirror of an RTD bus. Beat cops had hustled him off the curb, and he was muttering about Officer Piggy and the right to sit wherever he fucking well pleased, when – *whang*! The buttcrumbs staffing the emergency ward shaved Jocko's head regardless of whether it was medically necessary. Ho, ho, the name of the game is Shear the Punk. Keep Hollywood straight-edged. Big fucking deal.

After that, Eye Man swore he could see death riding in Jocko's eyes; their sclera had run to a sick ochre that reminded him of pus.

Bad trouble simmered in Jocko's glare. They'd be loitering against the brick wall facing the Orange Drive crosswalk, hustling *turistas* for coin or sneaking into the Hamburger Hamlet to foul the john, and Jocko would unleash a scream guaranteed to hamper traffic and make pedestrians cut them a wider DMZ. Jocko's wires were *beaucoup* frayed. Eye Man heard some out-of-towner farting through his face about how Los Angeles rated third in the nation for the number of homeless mental defectives roaming the streets. Right. At least Jocko never shit himself in public without warning.

The upside of Jocko's alien weirdness was power – power that could make them ten, fifteen strong on weekend nights. They sauntered down the Walk of Stars cleaving, citizens to either side. At the Seven Seas Lounge they whiffed and drank and shot up and pissed and fucked until they blacked out. Usually somebody's deathmobile could be hijacked to wherever the Scorpion Club had relocated that week, and they could skank and slam and thrash until somebody's momma called Officer Piggy about the ruckus.

Once, Jocko had bitten the ear off some dude in a fight. He always talked about wishing he'd kept it, so it could be worn on a thong like a wartime memento. The only mortal who had ever backed Jocko down, to Eye Man's knowledge, was Rude. Jocko had been pulling his raving 'n drooling bit, getting hazardous. Rude knew animal tranquilizer when he saw it, and put the flat of his hand to the center of Jocko's forehead. There was a loud, wet beefsteak *smack* and Jocko's eyes rolled yellowly toward the moon. He hit the deck and did not stir until sunrise. Nobody slept near him because he had filled his pants. He woke up with a nosebleed and no memory of having been such a sphinctroid.

That had happened back when Eye Man and his fellows maintained a nest of sleeping bags and crates and candles inside the shell of the Mecca. During the Thirties the Mecca Hotel had been pure swank, a trysting oasis for the celebrated, a stone's hurl from Grauman's Chinese. By the mid-Sixties, transients had blessed it with a permanent urinary stench, and the week Jim Morrison died in 1971 the iron security bars sprouted across the doors and windows. The next decade saw it shut down, then condemned, then gutted. When Eye Man's crew assumed residence, it was on dirt floors interrupted by the basement's ancient and crumbling support pillars.

Then the Mecca had been invaded by key lights and camera track. Eye Man and Jocko and the rest had been evicted by, of all things, a *Death Wish* sequel using the hotel's husk for local colour. In the movie, it was a hideout for dope-dealing rapist punks.

The Seven Seas vanished next. It had gotten refurbished into a yupster disco serving nonalcoholic drinkies. Eye Man didn't know what it was called now, and didn't care a rat fuck. On weekends, the lines outside the place were choked with Iranians in *Miami Vice* drag, pawing under-aged giggleboxes sporting spike heels, fat arms and faint moustaches.

Punks were losing the battle for the Boulevard; fewer and fewer manifested on Fridays, after dark. The Boulevard seemed to be evolving into something different. For different people. For eaters of frozen yogurt.

One night, they tried to raise the ghost of the Seven Seas – Jocko and Strongheart and Gash and Lindabelle and Chaka and Nobby and Eye Man and other worthies all got tanked in the Hollywood High School bleachers and wound up in the alley behind the Paramount Theatre after the parking

attendants had fled for the evening. The old Seven Seas
cul-de-sac still bore the back-door entrance sign. Punks had
always been required to enter through the rear door, and it
was a status they treasured. Eye Man felt that just a wee bit
more beer and powder would crank them enough to kick in
the now-barred access and introduce a lot of boogie feebs to
some genuine hardcore mayhem. Anyone who didn't care for
fighting could wrestle with Gash, who was dusted enough
not to care who stuck what where or how.

Fucking Gash's sliding door cunt never failed to make Eye
Man think of stirring a vat of chilli with a toothpick, or tossing
a hot dog into a swimming pool. Fat chicks were always
gushers. Staying hard was no strain; feeling any friction at
all was the challenge. Had Gash been born with that trench,
or had she dug it herself? Either option made Eye Man's dick
prefer television nights to getting slimed one more time.

Out came the spraycans and silver markers. *PUNK
DEATH SQUADS NOW! FUCKINGFUCKINGFUCKING!
ELIAS WATCHES YOU AS YOU SLEEP!* Elias had died a
long time ago.

The county had turned Jocko into a skinhead just as the
news chancres unfurled their gambit to censor punk by
linking the skinhead faction to white supremacists.

The witchunt kicked off, ignoring such plain truths as those
embodied in 'Nazi Punks Fuck Off' – a song in which the
Dead Kennedys showed the out door to punks who stirred
up shit.

They were under siege from all fronts.

Pissed, Jocko decided he wanted the rusted Seven Seas
sign to adorn their hovel at the Mecca. By standing on Rude's
shoulders, he was able to wrench it free with an opera's
worth of grunting and a few drops of sacrificial blood. Rude
re-anointed Jocko with Budweiser and got a beer shampoo.
Rude's head was mown into a tic-tac-toe crosshatch, with a
virulent streak of bright green. His eyes, generic, as colorless
as distilled water, turned to the square dead space formerly
covered by the sign.

Everyone saw the gang scrawl – part nickname, part
hieroglyphic, all incomprehensible. Anyone who lives near
a city has seen it: Cholos and low-riders bickering over turf;
Vietnamese clubs leaving memos of their passage; solos

marking their layovers and announcing their existence to an uncaring public like dogs lubricating hubcaps. This, however, was not *NIKKI-BASURA-EL MERO MERO #1* or *CATHI SUX +DIK* or *14TH ST CRIPS RULE*. This was unreadable in any tongue.

Jocko let fly one of his lunatic assault screams and obliterated the insignia with red spray paint, looping and curling and blotting out from the land of the living all trace of its faded declaration. It drowned beneath his crazed design, strangled by artful, sure strokes.

Somehow the plan to raze the disco and put the boot to wimp buttocks aplenty got buried, too. Dust and budget 'ludes can do the old cups-and-balls trick with one's attention span, that way.

Gash woke up with a quart of jism dripping out of her, and Jocko came to curled around his pilfered sign. Eye Man arose still tangled in Lindabelle. He had slept four hours, and through that time her sleeping hand had enclosed his detumescent cock as though protecting it. Lindabelle was brown-on-brown, curly-haired and freckled, with big breasts on an otherwise shapeless body. She would never be instant boner bait – like Chaka – but neither was she brain dead, like Gash. Eye Man enjoyed her smile, her smart eyes, her habit of not loudly belaboring the obvious. She provided calm to balance the stormy or extreme personalities of the rest. He did not mind waking up with her, now. When she saw his eyes open, she held a finger to her lips – shh, our secret – and smiled that smile, pumping him in the dark until he curved up painfully stiff, then rolling on top to work him like modeling clay until he shot off with enough force to bang her head against the Mecca's low basement ceiling.

Rude glided in bearing that morning's booty from the Donut Stop dumpster, off car-packed Highland Avenue, across the street from the Holiday Inn. 'Fuckin' old winos,' he muttered to whoever cared. 'They found out about the dumpster. I got there early and there was *still* one of them fuckers, ass-up. I was in no fuckin' mood. I kicked the shit outta him and told him to stay the fuck away.' He hoisted a pair of battered cartons – his cull of the Donut Stop's throwaways. 'Breaky is served.'

Getting stale donuts free meant that change could be spent

on hot coffee. Yeah, they were sure giving the free enterprise system a run for its bucks.

That afternoon they worked the Chinese, hanging near the forecourt and hustling Japanese tourists for coin. Any normal human could pose for a homey holiday snap with a real live urban punk – for a buck. It bought the beer. Jocko thought posing was pussy, but swilled his share nonetheless. No one ever tried to slap a brew from his hand.

Lindabelle and Chaka had lit off to pump the walking traffic for smokes. One round of the Boulevard generally netted plenty, especially after the layer-coiffed, hormone-crazed ax heroes strutting out of the Guitar Institute of Technology got a hind-brain-full of Chaka. She exploited a sharp Aryan physiognomy and a jailbait contour, a bleached military crop above frank arctic eyes above an elegant, chewable neck. Between those last two, almost as if in ambush, waited a pouty mouth destined for one specialty, maybe two if you were imaginative. Lindabelle caught Chaka's bounceback, and cigarettes were a smoother gimme than plain cold coin.

Again, Jocko wasn't motivated. He rolled his own from gutter butts. Eye Man guessed Jocko preferred the hand-mades for their potency – more tar! More nicotine! More rust-brown active ingredient! When he smoked, Jocko pulled *hard*, as if he was inhaling distillate of life essence, selfishly hoarding every wisp of thick grey smoke. Eye Man wondered what leftover lives Jocko was willfully packing into the dead storage of his lungs, what other psyches or failures, what ugly ends. Was he respirating the tobacco-cured breath of people now dead? Famous? Or just stuff too rank for the other Boulevard ciphers?

What load was Jocko taking on, by his own hand?

Eye Man gave it up. Too much like trying to figure out who the hell Benianino Gigli had been. A bronze LP was mounted on the guy's sidewalk star, but that said zero.

Jocko his own bad self loitered against the wall, casting about for sport and mustering a sullen sneer, until he spotted the pumpkin truck from Half Moon Bay. It slowed, gears gnashing, for the Orange Drive light just as Strongheart polished off a pair of hamhocks from Atlanta. Wifey first, then her baseball-capped breadwinner. Strongheart's kinked 'hawk made him a foot and a half taller than either of them.

He then photographed mister and missus beneath the main marquee. *Texas Chainsaw Massacre II* was afoot. The hick's eyes darted wetly about, as though he feared this monster would eat his Instamatic, but he pressed a humid dollar bill into Strongheart's hand with a shitload of full-bore rural howdy-do. Strongheart grinned back, just as fatuously. The couple's chicken-fried accents were so dense he could not comprehend a syllable.

Jocko's jaundiced eyes caught nothing but the truck, and its load of plump orange pumpkins – the colour his hair had been, before. His jaw worked and his eyes reflected back orange glints. His brain was afloat with some proposed violence, naturally involving pumpkins.

'Tricker treat,' he mumbled, a truly deranged smile carving its zigzag way across his mottled face. His teeth were as yellow as his eyeballs.

As the light changed, he highstepped out into traffic and snatched a pumpkin from the unstable pyramid weighing down the truck's rear deck. The driver should have missed seeing, but did not. He tapped his brakes, nearly causing a rented LeBaron full of townies from some Texas hog wallow to rear-end him, scissoring Jocko. But Jocko leapt deftly from the pinch line, bristling, just itching for a confrontation if this clodhopping retard was stupid enough to leave his truck and start shoving. Nobby, casing tourists near one of the poster shops, caught wind and laughed, high and shrilly. Imagine an Orthodox Jewish punk and you've got Nobby.

Jocko stood ground in the street, grinning like a sniper, pumpkin cradled, waiting for retaliation. Backed-up cars honked uselessly. The truck driver had left his spine in Half Moon Bay. He spat Hispanic invective and laid his pedal down. The wheezy Ford lurched through the crosswalk at a palsied thirty, its load of pumpkins teetering, its bald retreads feeling every crack in the slurry sealing. A workshirted arm jammed the unilateral peace symbol back in Jocko's direction. Pussy.

'I got me a punkin!' Jocko hooted.

Gash wanted to name it. Rude wanted to eat it. Jocko shunned the sidewalk trade and perched on the stone wall near the pay parking lot. He uncapped his bigmouth

silver marker and began to scrawl on the pumpkin, making
feedback noises to himself.

Eye Man sucked hard on his teeth, trying to clean them
with the rough side of his tongue. His mouth tasted foul and
his teeth were scummy. For a while he submerged himself in
the pursuit of spare change. He learned, long ago, the art of
asking for a berserk amount: 'Hey – spare sixty-three cents?'
That was good, usually, for a quarter. The Boulevard median
had bumped to nearly eighty cents. One black dude Eye
Man normally saw hanging near Frederick's of Hollywood
had the dick to ask for a buck fifty. Same army trenchcoat
(just like Eye Man's), same bedroll. Nobby said the guy had
once been a studio attorney; now he was a vagabond who
jogged every day around the track field at Hollywood High
and slept, so Nobby claimed, on the roof of the gymnasium.
Chaka said she'd seen the guy in the laundromat at La Brea
and Sunset, relating the story of how he *could* have been the
Black Valentino to a woman with too much time on three
dryers and hot mousetrap paranoia dancing in her eyes.

Your given name always changed when you hit Hollywood. That was why the names emblazoned upon the sidewalk stars meant nothing to Eye Man. You couldn't tell who
any of those people might have been. Strongheart had taken
his name from a Vine Street star; nobody knew or cared who
the fuck Strongheart might have been . . . but the name had
been resuscitated, and that was all that mattered.

Where the fuck was Sid Vicious' star? Jello's? Wendy O's?
Nothing on the Walk of Stars related to Eye Man's reality.

Fuck it. He was surly and pissed by the time he had
meandered down to Hollywood and Highland. He had one
crumpled dollar in his pocket, plus a dime. He thought of
bumming a cigarette from a PMS. They could spare the
smokes, but talking to them was like letting some yuppie
limpdick try to cornhole you. Punks with Money Suck. You
could peg them at a glance. They were too well turned out;
too much chrome and real leather. Eye Man had actually seen
one wearing a watch amid the studbands and bike chains and
custom-torn boutique hides.

Backed up sheeplike at the crosswalk, tourists gawked.
Eye Man squeezed his infected earlobe hard. The most
recent piercing had not gone cleanly. He heard an amplified

th-pow! inside his head, and pus squirted onto his fingers. He continued squeezing until he got blood, to rinse it out. The pain cleared his head while the pedestrians cut him some breathing room. He briefly felt the old power of the streets surging back into him.

'Hey, Eye Man.' It was Jocko's guttural rasp. 'Num-num-num-num-num!' His snaky tongue licked wetness from Eye Man's throat. The citizens were throughly grossed out. Both punks giggled.

'Wanna catch a flick?' Both were team experts at cinema infiltration. It was absurdly simple. You staked out the alley exit of, say, the Omicron Theatre, and when that door opened, you ittied in and laid low behind the movie screen until the next feature commenced. If a lot of movigoers streamed out, you simply walked in backwards, right through them. It worked almost without fail.

'Naah.' Jocko hefted his prize. 'Check my punkin. *Punkin*, right?'

Jocko's signature graffito adorned the pumpkin's furrowed face. On the forehead, in shiny silver, was written *POWER CHALLENGE*. Behind, *NEW ASSAULT*, plus the circled A for anarchy. Lines braided and twined. It actually lent the pumpkin a basic sort of Impressionist grimace, the scrunched visage of a fat man with burst hemorrhoids trying to squeeze out a drop shipment. There was as much logic to the artwork as there was schematic to the pigment splotches on Jocko's face.

'Know what makes punkins scary?'

Eye Man found himself cheering up. The street was still theirs, where it mattered.

'I'll show you. C'mon. Others'll follow.'

They loped east, enduring no shit from no body. A tall, satanic homeboy wearing a black duster smirked in passing, as though he knew what was going down. Jocko perched his pumpkin on one shoulder for display; the Incredible Two-Headed Punk. Street weenies goggled. Pig-eyed, scrub-shorn grunts on leave, come to shit all over Hollywood, barely noticed them. Fat-assed visitors with their squawking brats and plaid and cellulite and cameras clogged the walking pace. They think *we* look weird, thought Eye Man. None of the men looked stiff; none of the women fuckworthy. They

were the missionary-position missionaries of America. They
were doughy and dissipate. A trio of PMSs dealt some sort
of stupid power sign; Jocko snarled and gave them the finger.
He wanted to smash in their faces. He ached to battering-ram
each thunder-thighed heifer right in the bunghole, to rip out
each dinky pud and cram it into each slackjawed face; then
to take a grand diarrhetic shit over the whole massacre.

'We fucking *live* here,' was all he said.

What's a football field wide, Cal Worthington's wet dream,
ten lanes, across, and never slows to less than sixty on an
afternoon unspoiled by gridlock? The Hollywood Freeway,
that's what. Jocko loved to park between the bus stop
benches and the wire mesh, so he could stare down on
all that traffic. It made him think of coursing fresh blood,
of sharklike forward motion that never stopped, ever. To
stop was death.

Vehicles piled through the underpass, some of them
shearing away to snag at the Gower offramp at Sunset.
The divider below was thin, and battered by a million
sideswipes. Flares, oilslicks, skidmarks, car droppings – all
of it was ground fine by the stampede rush and absorbed into
the street. The tarmac was always uniform; nothing altered
its surface for long.

Eye Man took in speeding rooftops in enameled avocado,
canary, crimson, wedding-gown white, and said, 'There's no
place left to go if you die here.'

Jocko slapped on his annoyed look. 'What?' His eyes timed
the hurrying cars.

'It's all machines. Footprints in cement. Little metal records, pressed into the sidewalk. You can piss in John
Wayne's footprints. You can pry the records and TV sets
and film cameras out of the stars on the sidewalk. Nothing
lasts here. Nothing has anyplace to go.'

Jocko hocked and spat a phlegmwad through the chainlink.
The wet white comet arced into the stream of cars. Consecra-
tion. 'Don't let that shit eat at you, man.'

Eye Man turned. 'What happens, Jocko, if you fucking *die*
here, and you're not a fucking star? Who'll give a fuck?'

That made Jocko smile as though he'd figured out something big. His smile was never a fun thing to witness. '*Youuuu
walk the streeeets . . .*' It was a lyric Eye Man had forgotten.

'Get it?' They had arrived at the middle of the Boulevard overpass.

Eye Man thought Jocko was running on autopilot again.

'Look.' Jocko pointed at the graffiti-besmirched retaining wall that ran below the fence. 'We are everywhere.'

The wall resembled the side of an ancient Bronx subway car – layer upon layer of spray paint and indelible packing ink. It swooped and wove and changed colour, it seemed to move if you just glanced. A broad swatch in three colours read *STONER'S EVIL*: Fat letters, outlined and shadowed, blue shading to matte white. The labour of hours, here on the overpass, far more fascinating and intricate than the constipated 'art' Los Angeles had commissioned for its freeway web. The municipal murals were already vanishing under new coast of graffiti. *ROLLERBLADE WARRIORS*.

Eye Man kept looking at *STONER'S EVIL*. This had to have taken hours. Had nobody seen the thing being painted? Then it occurred to him that despite all the defacement he had wrought, personally, in ten years, you never really *saw* urban graffiti being implemented. It was just there. It was always just there. And it was always changing.

'Ygor, zee secret panel.' Jocko set down his pumpkin to pry back a head-high slit in the chainlink. He saw Eye Man about to ask what the fuck, and overrode with, 'Just watch. We're gonna change everybody's day.'

Eye Man played guardian of the sacred pumpkin while Jocko squirmed through the fence. The metal plaits were rusted, nearly finger-thick, much stouter stuff than basic hurricane fencing. Supposedly you could run a semi into its embrace and not sweat about breaking on through to the other side. Jocko behaved as thought the slit had always been there and he had always known about it – another fringe benefit of constantly being tuned into a station no one else could hear.

'Hey, Jocko, don't you think – '

Jocko twined his fingers in the diamonds of mesh and yawed into space, chains dangling. He shouted *hey you fuckin' aaaassholles* but the flood of cars barrelling onward below was too tight to notice him. He reeled back and extended his free hand through the gap in the fence. 'Gimme.' He meant the pumpkin.

'Jocko. Hey. Let's just book outta here, huh?' Eye Man could see what Jocko could not: A metro LAPD unit awaiting the green signal at the offramp.

Jocko flared lividly. 'Gimme the goddamn punkin, Eye Man, or I rip your fuckin' eyes out and stuff them up Gash's twat! *Now!*'

He knew Jocko well enough to know he'd have to rumble to keep the pumpkin. Then he thought, fuck it. What the hell did they owe the civil order of Hollywood Boulevard? To stop now would be pussy. To stop was death. He handed over Jocko's prize and cocked his head in the direction of future threat. 'Cops.'

'Just gimme.' The sickly yellow eyes acknowledged the warning, but Jocko swung back out, heedlessly, acting like a blood in a big hurry to finish the job. He began screaming at the traffic, dangling the pumpkin by its stalk, a deadly bomb waiting to hit a windshield and change everybody's day.

Now the drivers below paid attention. Some signaled, trying to veer from the target lane, the center northbound. Others just sped up, scooting into the dark safety of the overpass, avoiding another fleeting urban danger until another day.

Red, yellow, funeral black, mauve. They zipped past. Orange. The police car's yellow blinker was going like an impatiently tapping foot. Eye Man spotted an elderly Oriental gent halfway across the overpass on their side. The old man's eyes grew questioning beneath his hatbrim. He was leaning precariously on a knurled walking stick, and his cautious pace faltered as he contemplated the potential harassment in his path. His narrow eyes collected the sight of Jocko, hanging one-handed, brandishing the pumpkin. He stopped where he was.

Eye Man felt the compression velocity of major shit backing up the pipe. The situation was already beyond control. He gave it a try anyway, reaching forward and up to ensnare Jocko's jacket, just as the police car turned toward them.

Jocko shrieked at Eye Man, then bellowed toward the cars, olive drab, cherry lacquer, sky cyan blue, metallic flake emerald. Blood flushed his face; pink mottling red. The streets were *theirs*, Jocko screeched, and they were everywhere, and a pumpkin was scary because it could fucking *kill* you. Eye Man got a firmer fistful of Jocko's jacket. It was an old

Levi's coat minus sleeves, the rib seams split and latticed with several hundred safety pins. A downward-pointing triangle of dull green leather was stitched across the back like a shield, bordered in hex studs. Jocko's preferred bands were markered in – Minor Threat, Legion of Parasites, D.R.I. – and a wornout Asexuals sticker was pasted near his left kidney. Eye Man recalled each detail of the back of Jocko's jacket very well; when he tried to haul Jocko in, the poorly sewn leather tore loose and Jocko fell, pumpkin and all, still howling about how we fucking live here.

A loud, incoherent bray escaped Eye Man, his vision filling with the swatch of green leather as though it were ectoplasm. His lunge through the rent in the fence was determined, but ultimately lame. Jocko fell. Eye Man watched everything change, for everybody.

The pumpkin splattered the back gate of a tow truck, seeds and stringers and orange goo spraying for yards in every direction. The truck locked brakes and got bashed in the ass by a ghetto Caddy. White, blue, corroded gold. Orange and silver and more orange.

Jocko hit the blank pavement in cruciform and a Datsun longbed slewed to a sideways halt on top of him. It got broadsided by a limousine late for an LAX pickup. Skidding radials slopped crimson graffiti across two entire lanes.

A Toyota Tercel with cardboard dealer tags kissed the limo's left passenger door at forty. A muscle Mustang spun out to evade and flipped against the concrete barricade, scattering chrome and bright sparks. It slid back into the exit lane on its side, tinted windows spiderwebbing, steel grinding and twisting. After a bowling-pin pause it fell over to compact its roof and blow out the glass all around. A staved-in grille was scabbed with racing stripe by whirling fiberglas shrapnel. Surgical blue-grey meets candy apple scarlet. A summer hail of safety glass flew in diamond cubes.

Spilled gasoline mingled with Jocko's blood. It was the colour of pumpkin juice.

The overlapping symphony of collision merged into a nonstop fifteen-second wash of ugliness, sandblasting Eye Man's ears. Only the woop-woop of the police siren pierced the white noise of wreckage. Eye Man saw Chaka and Rude and Lindabelle standing behind the Oriental gent, mouths

unhinged, eyes overexposed and blank. The carnage had
stuffed them all to bursting. Rude exploded and began yelling
at the old man.

'An ambulance! Call an ambulance, you old fuck, Jocko's
fucking hurt, *what the fuck is wrong with you*, CALL A
FUCKING AMBULANCE!'

The old man recoiled, lost his footing, and stumbled,
falling on his ass like a paper sack full of fragile vegetables.
His eyes had gone so wide that his epicanthic folds seemed
about to split. Eye Man imagined the slits tearing, the eyes
brimming with blood. He saw fear in them, and panic, and
incomprehension, but no blood.

Red.

The police flashers stabbed into Eye Man's brain. He
reacted much as Rude had – bracing the first available adult
and shouting about ambulances that Jocko no longer needed.
The reply Eye Man got was a baton, introducing itself to his
temple, and when he woke up . . .

. . . he was staring at Rude, thinking, *oh, jesus, he looks like
he got the lungs kicked right outta him*.

Somebody in the bullpen had ejaculated in Eye Man's
unconsciously open mouth. He coughed up semisolid gunk
and probed with his tongue. Through some miracle his teeth
were all present, though scummier than ever.

When he could move, he leaned against Rude on a lower
bunk. When he could stand, he rinsed out his mouth in the
push-button sink above the gang toilet.

'You look like Franken-fucking-stein,' he said when he saw
Rude's gashed forehead.

'Car door. They bounced my skull off the hood a couple
times when they were patting me down. You gotta helluva
black eye, man. It goes all the way back to your fuckin' ear.'

He touched, winced. 'I can't see out of it.'

Rude almost sniggered, but it obviously hurt. 'Hm. Eye
Man.'

He was terrified at what irregularity his gingerly feeling
fingers might trip over next. His upper lip was split and
warm with new blood. He saw himself falling and striking
the curbing. His face protested the strain of speech. He said
something too mushy to decode.

Rude said, 'Huh?'

Eye Man swallowed and tried again. 'I said, he couldn't understand you.'

'Who?'

'That old Chinese fart. You were yelling at him and he was scared green because he couldn't understand what you were saying. I don't think he could speak English.' Eye Man's speech was lisping, with overlong pauses; a hard fight not to hurt.

'Cops thought I was *assaulting* him. Fuck. Stupid old fuck. This is America, goddamnit, why the fuck can't he fuckin' speak English?'

'We speak it. We live here.'

'We don't live fuckin' *anywhere* since we got kicked outta the Mecca. We got the Boulevard; that's it.'

'S'what I mean.'

Rude coughed and cushioned his head with his hands. 'Chaka was talking about moving back in with her parents. They posted fuckin' xeroxes of her *yearbook* picture, can you believe that? Our lost widdle girl. Doesn't look nothing like her.'

'It's not her,' said Eye Man. 'Did she leave?'

'Don't fuckin' ask *me*, Holmes, I got to this fuckin' bridal suite the same time you did.'

'Uh. Which reminds me. Which one of these scumbags needs broken bones in his life?' Eye Man could still taste the semen, sitting at the back of his throat like tartar sauce. Together he and Rude surveyed the bullpen's catch of the day: semiconscious drunks, overripe derelicts, Santa Monica vags and twangie boys, two or three iron-pumping chicanos and blacks, broadcasting bad. A 'groid with whitehead pustules all over his face grinned at them. Later that night, once he fell asleep under one of the bunks, Rude and Eye Man pounded the shit out of him, ramming his grin into the steel toilet rim until most of his teeth were out. Eye Man kicked him in the balls until blood soaked the crotch of his pants. Next morning, everyone swore the son of a bitch slipped and fell on his way to take a dump.

A month later, after the narrative got straightened out for everybody, Eye Man had forgotten the 'groid. The memory was always blotted out by the image of Jocko's blood, staining the 101 forever.

Hallowe'en made Eye Man feel suicidal. Jocko's distorted grin lived in every jack o'lantern. He could smell Jocko's blood in every pumpkin pie.

Past jail, fury rode in often and senselessly. Fuck the Dead Kennedys; Eye Man wanted to break a face. Dying young was a bottom line of the punk credo, but this was just too goddamn stupid. Anger and confusion went from bubble to boil, and tiny things, stupid things like rage, began to oscillate.

Eye Man aimed a pointless swing at Rude and Rude broke his nose. He would see Rude one more time in his life.

Sitting in the waiting room of Citizen's Medical Group, holding a wad of toilet tissue to his blood-caked nostrils, Eye Man told Lindabelle to write his name on the medical history form as Isadore Armitage.

Lindabelle was the only one who saw fit to help him. She sheltered him from the contemptuous stares of citizens and stole away the bite of ostracism. At the doctor's, they talked. They were not people of words, and words came painfully, aural witness to the erosion and decay that had rent their unity and stolen their strength.

Kicked out of their Mecca, they were dinosaurs, disaffiliates in Yuppieland. Adaptation was the remaining option. The antibodies were too lethal, and they were too weak. Jocko was no longer around to infuse them with psychotic pep talk and rowdy vinegar.

Four weeks after Eye Man's nose was treated, Lindabelle was humping the seven-to-three shift at Donut Stop. Isadore – Izzy – decided he had logged enough hours sleeping on bare floors and living on starch. He took on Exxon by the tiger tail. He larded his spiky flattop with Lindabelle's styling mousse and raked it straight back. Thus was he qualified for the idiot work of collecting petrodollars through bulletproof plexiglas, and hosing down the lot after midnight. He jumped to a graveyard stocking shift at the Mayfair Market. The pay was shit but the food came free. For this, he had to wear a knit tie. By pooling their incomes, he and Lindabelle could swing renting half of a stuccoed duplex, in a courtyard that had stood right on the border to West Hollywood since the early Forties. West Hollywood was now a city with its own mayor. Two useful features of the apartment were walls and a ceiling. It also had hazardously antiquated wiring, more coats of paint on a single door than Izzy thought possible, baby roaches, and the best bathroom either of them had used regularly in nine years. All over Hollywood, houses were being demolished as part of a bogus 'rezoning' project, which meant that local politicos had been heavily buttered and blown. Sprouting from the wreckage were buildings that Izzy thought resembled cellblocks, even down to the uniformed lobby guards – flashy, incredibly shoddy, prohibitively expensive. They ganged up on the stubborn homes that remained and intimidated them into rubble, until the shoulder-to-shoulder cheeseboxes formed concrete canyons, their walls ten feet from the next building. Like Beachwood Drive.

Tiny Naylor's, Schwab's, and the Brown Derby had all shut down and faded into the ghost landscape of nostalgia. Then the Seven Seas had vanished, then the Mecca. Migration would again become imminent for Izzy and Lindabelle just as soon as their Ukrainian landlord got an opportunity to sell out to the developers.

Their first common private bed was a foam pad; their next, a secondhand queen-sized that squeaked hellaciously. They treated the noise as a rueful joke, adapting. Lindabelle threw out the diaphragm she'd been using since fifteen and got fitted for a replacement. On Thanksgiving, right in the middle of the Twilight Zone Marathon on Channel 5, she announced her second accidental pregnancy and ruined the rerun of 'A World of His Own' for Izzy.

Several weeks following her abortion, some airheaded zealot firebombed the Feminist Women's Health Center and another piece of the Boulevard evaporated forever. In the same issue of the *Times* that broke the arson story, Izzy found the article on Gash's murder, page four.

Poor, fat Gash – real name, Ariel Dixon – had fled into the flesh trade on the east end of Sunset, where white meat was more in demand by the black, Hispanic, and Korean constituency. She was found with a baseball bat stuffed into her vagina, fat end first. Hemorrhage and trauma had sung the end. Her blood had been used to smear crudities and anatomical funnies on three of the motel room's four cinderblock walls.

Izzy recognized Jocko's signature graffito immediately. A few days later he saw it again – this time in silver spray paint, on the back wall of their duplex.

Crystal clear paranoia engulfed them both to the roots of their hair. Soon Strongheart was banging on their door with Rude's Ghost of Jocko theory. Eye Man and Lindabelle had ceased to exist for Rude, but Strongheart was much more frightened. Things kept on a-changin'. It was almost funny: Who ya gonna call?

Not the police. The police could not resolve this. Izzy and Lindabelle had learned via harsh play-by-play that the police were never a solution to anything. You won if you got the cops to ignore you. You won by fading into the cityscape, by becoming invisible. If they noticed you or had to spend their time on you, the booby prize was bars and hassle and little injuries that could linger for a lifetime, like the fouled vision Izzy retained in one eye until the day he died.

After Strongheart's bad news, Izzy started walking Lindabelle to and from work, head snapping around at each suspect noise. He wondered suspiciously why payphones waited until his passage to ring by themselves. Soon he was grabbing up the empty receivers. 'Jocko . . .?'

He stockpiled memories of Lindabelle's voice, her freckles, the sweep of her curly hair, the shape of her aureola, the sheathed-sword embrace of her cunt on his cock . . . just in case she was soon to be stolen.

Strongheart paid another call, even more malignantly broken out than usual in nervous fear. Stubble battled with zits for dominance of his facial real estate. Nobby, he told Izzy in a quavering voice, was in the hospital, Rude was in the morgue.

Death did not alter Rude's complexion; slab fluorescents lent him more colour than he'd ever nurtured while breathing. He'd been joyriding to Garden Grove in an Oldsmobile full of punks, following a Mentors gig at the Music Machine. For reasons never pinpointed, the Olds had somersaulted on the southbound 101. An unanchored tape deck playing a Circle Jerks bootleg had bashed a divot from Rude's crosshatch and scooped out half a cup of brains. Blond, dye green, crusted maroon, bone white. Izzy could not stare at the mangled head for long. Hydrostatic pressure had popped out Rude's clearwater eyes.

The deathmobile had belonged to some pal of Nobby's. Rude had made Nobby sit in the back. It probably saved his life. *For now*, added Strongheart, jumpy as hell.

When Izzy saw the tattoo, he vomited into the drains on the stainless steel slab. It had risen across Rude's bare chest in yellow-rimmed violet, the bas relief of a subdermal hemorrhage. It was the second time Izzy had seen it scripted in blood, and it was an idiogram he had come to hate.

Strongheart and Nobby swapped gun-shy estimates and struggled to recapture the lost warmth of camaraderie. Nobby agreed that prior to the accident, he, too, had seen Jocko's graffito all over the Boulevard – on mailboxes, defacing RTD buses (and wasn't *that* an ironic vengeance?), across the blank, dusty windows of closed-down storefronts. Nobby had been ducking payphones just as long as Izzy had. He announced his strategy to hop the next Greyhound for his stepbrother's tract home in Yellow Springs, Ohio, just as soon as he got out of the hospital.

By now Chaka was gone, too. No forwarding address.

Strongheart had discovered Jocko's mark filling a vacant star on Vine Street. Guess where. He had a hammer, and was venturing up there late at night to eradicate the original Strongheart . . . before Jocko got a chance to do it *his* way.

That was when Izzy figured it out.

'Lemme see your driver's license,' he said to Lindabelle. He fixed on it the way you triumphantly look at the final piece of a jigsaw puzzle. 'Jocko has no reason to come back and bump us off, Strongheart. We're already dead.'

Nobby hated mystery. He had bravely bulled over to the confab at Izzy's apartment on crutches. 'What the fuck are you talking about,' he said, whining nasally.

'You want to run to Yellow Springs.' He turned to Strongheart. '*You* want to smash Strongheart's star to gravel and you don't even know who Strongheart fucking *was*.' He tapped the license. 'Lindabelle has become this person here.' It listed her as *Linda Kassia MacGuire*. 'Rude and Gash flamed out. It happens. Who knows about Chaka? Maybe she did move back in with her parents. I say she *became* the girl in the yearbook photo again. And me – I stopped being the Eye Man when Rude busted my nose. The only one of us who could never change was Jocko. He *belonged* to the fucking Boulevard. And look at us now. Just fucking look at us. What a gang of weaseldicks.'

This was too much input for Nobby to track. He sat between his crutches and fidgeted, rubbing his palms compulsively against his knees. Strongheart grew more pitiful, like a dog that knows the shame of bigtime fuckery.

Izzy sighed. Once they had all been linked, unified, powerful. 'Look – have you guys seen Jocko's mark *anywhere* but around the Boulevard?'

No, all around. They still didn't get it.

They could all run, sure. The further they went, the faster they'd die, shedding their former personae like snake shuckings. The thing that had defined their existence as Boulevard punks had been Jocko, and Jocko had selfishly given the finger to the sentiment that said you couldn't take it with you. That part of each of them had accompanied Jocko right into the fundament of the Boulevard.

To stop was death. But death was not a monster movie, spooks on vendetta, slicing and dicing fornicating teens thirteen interesting ways. Death was when you turned into nothing. That brand of death had yellowed Jocko's eyes ever since the bus had dented his head. Or maybe Rude had fractured Jocko's skull; Izzy remembered the nosebleed. Either way, Jocko had smelled oncoming oblivion, and despite the punk party stance of nihilism and apocalypse, had said no thanks. He had shied from becoming nothing. Jocko never eased up; never wanted to. He always swam farther out than any of them – fucking Gash, snorting corrosives, yelling loudest, swaggering broadest, bleeding most, passing out in his own shit and puke and never ever calming from full burn. His mark was the most flamboyant. He had been enough of an egomaniac to resent becoming nothing.

If Nobby could blow off about Jocko's ghost, then Izzy felt entitled to his own theory, even if everyone was going to whizz on it.

'I think Jocko wants his, uh, presence felt,' Strongheart said after an itchy silence among them.

'Oh, great,' said Nobby. 'So he sends us greeting cards by wiping out Gash and Rude.'

'I know a lot of people who died,' said Lindabelle. 'I always thought that if they turned into ghosts, or if there was *anything* after, your friends would let you know. They'd tell you there was more. You know?'

Izzy thought again of the ringing payphones. Nahh. Jocko would never call.

Nobby squirmed. He didn't cotton to any of this. 'So why hasn't Jocko let us know. Why all this haunted house bullshit – his *mark* all over everything? Why doesn't he just fucking *say so?*' His voice veered up into a bitchy mommy caricature: *You never call; you never write, I never know where you are.*

'Maybe he has let us know,' Izzy said. 'Maybe he's screaming his head off. Maybe we just can't speak his new language.' He flashed back to the petrified Oriental gent on the overpass. Rude had *told* him, loud, blatantly – but no message had copied through.

'I want to do the Boulevard tonight,' Izzy said. 'Nobby, can you get your stuff and meet us at the Chinese?'

'No strain,' Nobby grumped. 'I hope.'

Izzy bit off setting a rendezvous time; that was just too- too fucking adult. Nobby could beard a PMS and check his Timex if he wanted to synchronize that much.

Strongheart scratched his four-day growth, cautious to avoid fresh pimples, ducking from potential pain. He was still punked out. His changes had been interior.

It hurt Izzy to see how dusty his own regalia had gotten in the closet, so quickly. A scream. As the trio walked up La Brea, he had to avoid the conscious impulse to put his arm around Lindabelle, or hold her hand, or some other happy bourgeois bullshit.

The Mecca lot was alive with transplanted green turf, and enclosed by hurricane fencing. A garish billboard proclaimed the birth of yet another mini-mall, with deco fountains and pastel and high prices and an automat cinema with six teeny screens, count 'em. Strongheart frowned and took a piss through the fence. Somebody in a passing convertible whistled. Big fucking deal.

Everywhere, graffiti.

Not only did Izzy rarely see others inscribing it, but he had painted stuff himself that he could not recall seeing a second time. At least, he never noticed it after he did it. Your eye tuned out the messages all around you. It was a filter, like the dead-ahead stare of seasoned Boulevard pedestrians. Izzy was well versed in the barrier such a stare erected. You locked eyes with no one, except to challenge, to stare down. No eye contact meant no handouts, no change to be spared. Anybody who bummed coin learned not to bother with such a stare, just as those who cultivated it ultimately did not see whoever was asking. They were *there* – but they did not exist. The multiform graffiti was *there*, omnipresent, but no one ever saw it, except for cleanup crews at election time. Those who saw it could not understand. Izzy wondered if it was even worse in New York.

He felt he heard voices all around him, jabbering some highspeed foreign gobble. It was deafening to him.

Straights stared, as usual, blubber-lipped, with the eyes of goldfish.

Nobby did not bother to show up.

Izzy held his head to still the chorus only he could hear, then said, 'Notice?'

Lindabelle's expression said *huh*? Strongheart, spooked, was still looking around for Nobby's runty little bod.

'We haven't seen Jocko's sign once during the whole walk up here.'

Strongheart got thrilled. 'Yeah. *Yeah*! Right!' He nodded enthusiastically, mohawk bobbling, his face made even more hideous by his goofy grin. 'Uh . . . so?'

'So.' Izzy grinned savagely and fast-drew a spray can of pain from the dusty depths of his trenchcoat. 'So.' He strode through the clots of footprint-oglers in the forecourt of the Chinese, and stopped at the cement fistprints of the Duke himself. Jocko was going to love this. 'So.'

Lindabelle tried to block a laugh of surprise from jumping past her mouth. No go.

Izzy pre-selected the tourist most likely to protest vandalism, and cut him off. 'Fuck with me, stud, and I'm gonna hurtcha.' He smiled, big, broad, and friendly.

Then he painted Jocko's mark right over John Wayne's remedial cursive scrawl.

The oldest doorman at Mann's Chinese (formerly Grauman's;

everything changes) is named Franklin. He migrates to pursuits at other Boulevard theatres, but always returns to the forecourt, to stand sentry at the main doors, and tear tickets (they're dot matrix slips of silver register paper, now) and direct the attention of tourists to the souvenir books and maps itemizing the Walk of the Stars. He wears a brocaded scarlet coat and a doorman's cap. He once packed a CO^2 pellet pistol to work for the purpose of plugging, quote, 'the goddamn sonsabitching pigeons' that roost in the eaves of the forecourt and occasionally soil the postcard-perfect tableau with fresh alabaster feces. Management swiftly terminated Franklin's unusual demonstration of his half-century devotion to the Chinese. They informed Franklin – nicely, since there was no clean way to cashier the old hard-on – that shooting at pigeons in the forecourt might not be such a great idea. Franklin protested, 'But I got one, I *got* one of 'em!' He resented being addressed like a child or a mental defective.

From his post, Franklin saw Izzy add to the forecourt's roster. He hid a private smile much like Lindabelle's.

'So,' Izzy said to Strongheart. 'You hangin' here?'

Strongheart spot-checked the tourist flow. The north curb was lined with buses, tip to tail, all the way to Orchid. Japanese tour groups were being herded toward one of the few remaining bastilles of a Hollywood that had existed before rock 'n roll, or AIDS, or Pruneface Ronny. Or punks.

'I'm gonna stay here a bit,' Strongheart said. His comprehension ran no deeper than an antisocial appreciation of Izzy's improvised forecourt ritual. 'You just gonna cruise, or . . .?'

'As far as the overpass,' said Lindabelle, catching on. She elbowed the spray can in Izzy's pocket. It clinked.

'Watch for us,' Izzy said.

'I'll do that.'

Strongheart saw them off with a tight grin that sat across the bottom of his face like a scar. Then he posed, with foreigners whose names he would never know, for snapshots he would never glimpse, communicating with grand, cartoon gestures, since nobody had the faintest idea of what anybody else was really saying.

Before Izzy and Lindabelle got back, he had earned an unprecedented seventeen bucks.

Izzy strolled purposefully, bracing for the first ringing payphone – the incoming call that would slam all the guesswork out of the ozone. Lindabelle spotted the phone, a block from World Book and News, still on Cahuenga after all these years. She grabbed his arm hard; pointed. It was marked for them, in red, and it was already ringing.

Eye Man jumped for it, sideswiping the Boulevard's walking dead. When his hand captured the receiver, he was ready at last for the sound of Jocko's first big scream.

THE STORYTELLER'S TALE

Brian Stableford

Brian Stableford is the author of numerous science fiction, fantasy and horror novels, including the highly acclaimed vampire epic The Empire of Fear. *More recent books include* The Werewolves of London *and* The Carnival of Destruction. *The editor of various anthologies for the Dedalus publishing imprint, his recent collection of short fiction is entitled* Sexual Chemistry: Sardonic Tales of the Genetic Revolution.

THE stars were shining brightly as the story-teller began his tale. His listeners formed a semicircle about him, and he could see the starlight reflected in their round eyes; it was as though each and every gaze was intensely studious and informed with an altogether unnatural wisdom.

'I think there was a time,' he said, 'when I could count myself a reasonably fortunate man, but that was long before this tale's beginning. Before I became involved in the escape from Kapan Kishk I had been a road-slave for six long years, but of all the men who broke their backs and hearts on the road from Dod Kadir, there was none who less deserved his fate than I, who never stole a coin or cut a throat, but only borrowed a rich man's youngest wife – and he with three more which he could by no means be said to have used up.

'You will think that I do not seem to be a strong man, and there is surely little meat on my bones, but not every road-slave is a ditchdigger or a breaker of stones; there is skill even in slavery and by day I was a mixer of concrete, which is made from broken stones, sand, lime and dross, and which binds our smooth Ancyran roads into highways fit for the hooves of horses and oxen and the wheels of carts. The

overseers were pleased to give me such light work, because
by night I still practised my old profession, and told tales to
slaves and masters alike, lightening their burdensome lives
with the labour of my tongue.

'The plan for our escape was hatched in the bold mind of
Yash Aggarwal, who had not long been a slave and could
not look forward to a long career, because he was hated by
the overseers for having only one eye, and that an evil one.
It was he, not I, who spread the tale that once the road to
Kapan Kishk was finished we would all be thrown into the
dungeons of that foul citadel – which, as you know, was
never built by human hand – and there left to rot and die
because it was not worth the empire's while to take us back
to Dod Kadir and set us to work on another road. Yash
Aggarwal it was who said that the midday sun had perforce
been our guide for nine-and-ninety days, and that we should
adopt it for our friendly star, making our own way southward
beyond the empire's bounds, into the Withering Waste.

'We knew the reputation of the Waste well enough, but we
had been living in a kind of hell for those nine-and-ninety
days, and the black caves of Kapan Kishk were one more
evil circle of that hell awaiting us. Yash Aggarwal had little
difficulty in gathering about him a dozen men of strength and
skill – mostly fighters and thieves, save for one Aor Gulamali
who knew some healing magic. I was naturally included in
his plans, for no group of a dozen men is complete without
a storyteller to lift its spirits and dissolve its drear anxieties.
And so, after the sun had set on the day when the dark gates
of Kapan Kishk came in sight, we rose against our violent
masters, and went to the work of killing them with a keen
appetite.

'Four of our own company were slain, and perhaps an
equal number of those who were not included in our plan,
but nine men survived to flee into the night, with three
donkeys and their panniers of meal – and in the morning
we had skirted the lonely mount on which Kapan Kishk was
built, and had naught but the Withering Waste before us.

'None of us knew this land, and the stories in my stock
which told of it were too dire by far to parade before my
fellows, so I spoke instead of the lands believed to lie beyond
the Waste, in the farther south – of golden cities and painted

towers and seas of sapphire blue. That is the purpose of
a storyteller, to give men heart when their minds are not
resolute. It was not a lie, but a decoration. It would have
been tactless to speak of the molochmen of the desert, or the
plants which crawl and suck the blood of men and beasts,
or those spiders which dress their webs with a poison to
blight all kinds of flesh, though I had heard accounts of all
of these things. Nor, of course, did I mention the lazarous
demons, of whom the most horrible tales of all are told – and
I even took care to keep *their* name from my own thoughts,
as storytellers have the skill to do.

'We travelled quickly that day, for we did not know
whether they would send soldiers from Kapan Kishk to
chase us. We had only killed a few overseers, who were
little more than slaves themselves, but no free man likes
to leave an escaping slave unpunished lest his example
should plant a seed in the minds of others, and spark a
greater rebellion. By the time we dared to stop we were
sorely tired, and needed more than a mere meal to soothe
our aches before we slept, so I told the excellent story of the
unlicensed moneylender of Zainul Zub and the ten temple
whores. It is a story which they all loved dearly, and which
never failed to make them laugh – though Avan Goom and
Kahin Chan, who had been on the road for three years and
more, must have heard it half a hundred times before.

'The next day we found water, which seemed fresh enough
and did the donkeys no harm, but by then we had come into
a region the like of which we had never seen before, where
no trees grew; where the grasses and grains were yellow and
brown; and where great white toadstools reared their heads
to the height of a mounted man. Poor Suleman Rham – who
was ever a luckless thief, as could be judged by his lack of
a right hand – strayed under one of these growths while
it was spilling a cloud of spores from its underside, and
having breathed in a great quantity went mad with delirium,
and turned quite black in the face before he died. We made
masks out of rags and the sleeves of our shirts to protect us,
and made our way more circumspectly after that.

'The misfortunes of that day were not ended, for one of
the donkeys was bitten by a serpent, and though it did not
seem likely to die its foot was so swollen that it could not go

on. We paused to kill and butcher it, and some of its blood
was drunk by one of our number named Anakali, who was
from the western lands where they sup the blood of beasts to
give them strength. Alas, the serpent's poison must still have
been in the blood, and rather more deadly to a man than to
the beast. Anakali was racked with dreadful pains all night,
and in the morning was vomiting up his own blood with the
donkey's. By noon he was stinking most evilly, rotting while
he lived. Yash Aggarwal cut his throat out of kindness before
we left him.

'We dared not eat that donkey's flesh, and so killed
another, but even then were reluctant to eat it, even though
our supply of meal was near run out. In the end Alaric
Lod, a northerner who had been a mercenary before he
was condemned for treason against his hirer, agreed to try
the meat, and it seemed to do him no harm. We feasted well
on the animal that night, and carried smoked meat away with
us, in good heart despite our losses.

'Only one more night was to pass, however, before another
of our company died. This was Arb ab Abassi, who slept a
little distance away from the rest of us, and far too soundly
for his own good. When we woke in the morning we found
that three of the loathsome plants which crawl had come to
him, and were sending their thirsty roots deep into the flesh
of his left leg.

'Arb ab Abassi begged Yash Aggarwal to cut out the
plant, for he knew that it would leave him naught but a
stem-entwined skeleton if left to its own devices, and knew
also that he would feel no pain when his leg was cut because
the roots kill the feeling of the flesh which they invade. Good
Yash Aggarwal did his very best, and there never was a man
more clever with a slitting-knife, but it was all to no avail,
for the tendrils of those plants grow remarkably quickly, and
Arb ab Abassi had bled to death before the last of the rootlets
could be cut away. His death was a little eased, however, by
the fact that I distracted his mind by telling him once again
his favourite of all my tales, of how the youngest daughter
of Kartar Var fared in the harem of the King of the Ghouls.

'The next day we dined well on the meat of the last-but-one
donkey, but our water supply was running perilously low.
We knew that it would take many days to cross the Withering

Waste, and that water would be the most important factor
limiting our chances of survival. When Kahin Chan climbed
to the top of an outcrop of bare rock, and told us that he
could see green foliage in the east amid the yellow dunes and
parched brown grass we unhesitatingly altered our course.
We might have guessed, of course, that where there was
water in a barren land we would likely find other drinkers,
but it could not have deterred us. If we had to fight for our
water, still we must have it, and fight we would.

'When we came close to the oasis we smelled fire on the
lazy wind, and approached most stealthily. There were a
dozen molochmen camped by the water-hole, with seven
misshapen mounts of a vile reptilian character. Because they
were twelve and we were but six we had to wait for dead of
night before attacking their tents, but before then we had
noted that four were females, and that only three of the
males were armed with iron. One of these was sent forth
as sentry, but he did not expect such enemies as us, and it
was easy for Yash Aggarwal to slit his throat. The other males
we killed with little fuss as they woke in surprise from their
slumbers. Alaric Lod slew no less than five, and it was easy
to see that he had not forgotten the way of a warrior while
he was unluckily enslaved.

'One female had to be killed, because she attacked Avan
Goom with a fury which would brook no other interruption
but a blade in the throat, but the remainder we saved. I do
not really care for molochite women, because their skins are
always leathery and their slits uncommon slimy, and they
have faces like leering apes – but a man cannot be too fussy
when he is a roadslave, and we had all learned to be less than
particular in seeking companions for our beds. The one which
I shared with Aor Gulamali was perhaps the ugliest of the lot,
with a scarred face as rough as sharkskin, but she served her
purpose.

'In the morning we killed them all – they had not the
promise of giving us sufficient pleasure to make it worth
our while to feed and water them, and had we fallen into
their hands instead of they into ours they would have
done far worse. I have heard that the favourite sport of
molochmen is to cut a man's belly, take away his intestines most carefully, and fill the empty cavity with small

rough stones and excrement, and then to stitch him up
again.

'We took the molochites' beasts of burden, their weapons
and their supplies, and had an easy time of it for two whole
days. Then, alas, Kahin Chan and Alaric Lod rode their
beasts through a thicket, not knowing that it was infested
with the poisonous webs made by the foulest of spiders,
and in a matter of hours the flesh of animals and men alike
had begun to soften and turn milk-white. They lay all night
unsleeping, terribly feverish but unable to drink because
every time we brought water they foamed at the mouth and
screamed in panic. They begged us to cut their throats, and
Yash Aggarwal had no option but to do it, though the loss
of Alaric Lod was most unwelcome, given that he was by far
the best warrior in our party.'

The story-teller paused. His mouth had run dry, and he
wondered whether he dared to ask for a drink, but when
he looked into those eyes which gleamed with starlight – so
inscrutable, so expectant – he felt that he must at all costs
continue, lest he lose the pitch of dramatic tension which he
was struggling to maintain.

'On the next day,' he continued, 'we were pursued by
another band of molochmen. Whether they had found their
slaughtered kin and followed our trail from the oasis, or
whether they had heard the screams of Alaric Lod and
Kahin Chan echoing in the desert night, we could not tell;
we simply fled from them on our stolen animals, leaving
behind the last of our donkeys. The molochites were fifteen
or sixteen strong, all of them mounted, whereas we were
only four – and though our blades were made of stronger
stuff than theirs we would have had no chance at all in a
stand-up fight.

'The beasts we rode were identical to their own, and they
must have caught us up had they continued the chase
through the day, but when Avan Goom was thrown after
his mount stumbled they stopped to seize him, and let the
rest of us go. Perhaps they only wanted a toy to play with,
and thought that they could amuse themselves sufficiently
with one hardy lad who might live for days under subtle

torture; but for myself I think they were afraid of us, and glad of the excuse to settle for one instead of risking injury to capture all four.

'Yash Aggarwal was in a foul mood that night, saying that had he taken his choice of the nine who set out he would have kept any one of the others before the two who now remained to guard him. Aor Gulamali's healing magic had not so far served to save a single man from ignominious death, and I had not told a single story which he had not heard already. But the old hedge-wizard bound a festering wound which Yash Aggarwal had on his arm, and put some ointment on it which soothed it well, and I told him the story of merchant Hamadeh who persuaded a nephew he did not like to recover a treasure from a well, and how the curse that was on the treasure caught up with him nevertheless. It is not one of my finest stories, but it was one which Yash Aggarwal had never heard before, and he was pleased enough to listen to it.

'The next day, and the next after that, we continued southwards, into a region even more frightful than the ones through which we had already passed, where even the bronzed and ochreous grasses no longer grew, and the grey ground itself seemed cankerous. There were coloured lichens on the rocks, and leopard-spotted slugs, and great lumps of amoeboid slime which shone by night with their own internal light, but there was no creature we dared to kill and eat save for the beasts we had with us, and on the second night we slaughtered one, knowing that one of us would have to walk on the next day.

'Aor Gulamali dared not quarrel with Yash Aggarwal, and I had not the courage to challenge his word, so it was left to Aggarwal to decide who would ride and when. On the next day we had little water left, which Yash Aggarwal kept entirely to himself, and one of the animals died so that we had only one to ride. We had no doubt that Yash Aggarwal would keep it for his own use, and we guessed that he would soon desert us, thinking that he could go further and faster without us, and that we were not skilled enough as fighters to make it worth his while to stay with him. There was nothing to do but kill him, and so we did – I slit his throat as he had slit so many others in his time. It was no crime to do it, but merely a matter of sour necessity.

'I took care to share what little water was left with Aor Gulamali, and to take fair turns in riding our sole remaining beast – not because I valued his prowess as a fighter, or even as a healer, but because I did not want to be left alone in that dire and awful place. I cared for him as much as I could, but he was an old man, and his healing magic had ever been too feeble to preserve his own youth and strength past their natural span. He fell sick, and I had to leave him while I searched for water, and though I returned to him when I had found it he was already half-devoured by scavengers. He was yet alive, but all sense and intelligence had fled from him, and when I cut his throat the blood that flowed from the wound was but a meagre trickle.

'Although I was now alone, and very frightened, I was determined to go on as far as I could, and I instructed myself most sternly that if there was a southern limit to the Withering Waste which a man might reach, then I would be the man who reached it. I did not fear the molochites, who were less than men; I did not fear the plants which crawled; and I did not fear the spiderwebs which blighted; for I had seen all of these at work, and knew them well enough. I did not think at all of the lazarous demons, which I had resolved to put out of my mind, and had done so – for I am a teller of tales, and I have the skill to banish from my thoughts that which it is not to my advantage to contemplate.'

As he spoke these words, uneasily – remembering that he was repeating himself – the story-teller looked around once again, trying desperately to measure the opinion of his audience. He could not do it; their eyes were like mirrors, and told him nothing of their dark and horrid thoughts.

'That is the whole of my tale,' he said, haltingly, 'as far as I can yet tell it. What end it will have is entirely up to you – but I would urge you very sincerely not to decide too quickly what you will make of me, for as I have advised you, and as you can surely see for yourself, there is very little meat on my bones.

'I judge from the patience which you have already shown me that I have some small ability to amuse you, and if this poor tale of my own sorry adventure can capture your attention I have no doubt at all that you would love the story of the unlicensed moneylender Zainul Zub and the ten temple whores, and would certainly find much to interest you in a well-crafted account of how the youngest daughter of Kartar Var fared in the harem of the King of the Ghouls.

'After all, there is surely not an intelligence in all this great wide world which does not love a well-told tale – and though I must confess that I have never before had the ambition to live among the lazarous demons, I really do believe that I could get used to it . . . if you will only give me the chance . . .'

THE BIG GAME

Nicholas Royle

Nicholas Royle's first novel, Counterparts, *was published in 1993. The author of more than seventy short stories, his work has appeared in* Dark Voices, Best New Horror, The Mammoth Book of Zombies, In Dreams, Narrow Houses, Interzone, *and elsewhere. His* Darklands *and* Darklands 2 *anthologies won The British Fantasy Award in successive years, and in 1993 he also picked up the award for Best Short Story for 'Night Shift Sister'.*

'OUT,' shouted Groom as the ball fell off the edge of the roof 140 storeys to the street below. Once again Groom had masked the bounce so that Bolton couldn't see if his return had been in or outside the painted lines of the roofcourt. Instead of protesting, which would pleasure Groom too much, he crossed to the dispenser and collected a fresh ball. He bounced it twice on the asphalt.

'What's the score?' he shouted. Bolton's facility for arithmetic was limited and Groom took advantage of it. He would usually win anyway, so there was little point.

'It's clouding over,' Groom said, ignoring the question of the score. 'We'll finish this set and we might have time for another.'

Bolton bounced the ball again and raised his arm to serve, but a cross in the sky distracted him. He blinked against the emerging sun and deciphered the silhouette of a jetliner. It moved slowly and diagonally upwards through his field of vision. He lowered his arm and watched the jet. Out of the corner of his eye he could see Groom's twisted shadow waiting impatiently, shaking its head.

Why had the planes started flying lower?

'It's only a fucking jet,' Groom complained. 'Are you serving that ball or not?'

Bolton served and failed to reach Groom's return, expertly lobbed into the rear left-hand corner of the court.

'Set point.'

Bolton hated playing with Groom but he had no choice. Groom, self-styled commercial artist – in truth, sado-pornographer, purveyor of explicit sex and violence to the discerning psychotic – put regular work Bolton's way, which the photographer desperately wanted to turn down but couldn't. His financial situation was dire. Only halfway to paying off his sister's death duties, he was also struggling to keep up with the repayments on his small apartment. If he lost that he'd be on the streets. Groom gave him regular assignments at a rate which allowed Bolton to survive. Barely.

Photography was Bolton's only skill and while he was good at it, he was unable to get work elsewhere. The photographic art had become as popular as roof tennis – from Groom's roof Bolton could see at least a dozen games in play on neighbouring courts – and so it was hard now to get work. To mention the stuff he did for Groom in support of any pitch would only prejudice most picture editors against using him.

So Groom had him. If he refused to play, the assignments would dry up. Groom liked it that way because he enjoyed watching humiliation take place.

Although he knew it was pointless, Bolton tried his hardest to postpone defeat, running, bending, stretching. But the pornographer took the set with his favourite shot: a backhander dropped just over the net with enough spin to bounce it out of the court and off the roof. Bolton swore but swallowed the oath when he saw the plane. A jetliner as big as the previous one, it seemed even lower. Maybe only a thousand feet above the roof.

Two flights down in his sumptuous apartment, where framed covers of *Paris Match* and *Stern* lined the walls, Groom wiped his face with a towel and poured Bolton a drink.

'Have a sauna. You know where to go.'

Bolton looked out of the room down the wide hallway. The

floor was chequered with black and white tiles. That way lay the bathrooms and sauna of which Groom was so proud. But to Bolton the luxury would feel like a trap.

'I'll wait,' Bolton said, clinging to the tatters of his pride, 'till I get back.'

'Did you see this yet?' Groom tossed a glossy magazine on to the raised floor section in the middle of the room. It landed next to Groom's antique ivory chess set. Bolton caught the magazine's masthead flash: *Mindfuck #7.*

'That can wait too,' he said, shivering in his film of sweat as he recalled the stench of open skulls, violated brains and semen. At least no one had been maimed or killed during that particular assignment; the girls were two-day-old auto-crash fatalities, hired out from the morgue.

'Good work, Bolton. Fucking good work,' Groom said, as he stripped off and collapsed into the tigerskin sofa like an exhausted king reclining on his throne. 'Keep that up, you'll be able to retire soon.'

Bolton tipped back his glass and swallowed its contents. Through the open window he could hear the muted roar of a jet passing close overhead. Groom had begun to masturbate languidly.

'I have to get back,' Bolton said, rising to his feet and avoiding Groom's eyes. 'Some film I have to get for tomorrow.'

He left the apartment and, slipping his ID Credit into the slot, took the elevator twenty-four floors down to the hanging corridor that joined Thomason to Jefferson. At the entrance to the corridor he needed the IDC again. The computer debited his account; toll charges were never displayed because they changed whenever the operating company was taken over, which seemed to happen once or twice a month. As he allowed the walkway to carry him along the glass corridor between the two towers, he looked down at the black ants in the sun-bleached streets and wished fervently some route would materialize by which he could escape from Groom. Instead, a jet flew over so low the glass walls of the corridor vibrated.

They *were* flying lower. He wondered if the regulations had been changed. And if so, why? It made no kind of sense, with buildings rising higher all the time.

Once in Jefferson he dropped to fifty and caught the

monorail. The trains were a health hazard but he hadn't used his car in over a year because of the prohibitive cost of the Suspended Highways.

Needles, pads and belts littered the bench seats. Before sitting down Bolton picked up a magazine that was lying on the floor. He looked at the cover and was shocked to see his own work. The magazine was 4×4 *Auto-Crash*, published by one of Groom's subsidiaries. Bolton turned the pages and wondered what sort of depraved individuals devoured the images he had slavishly photographed.

He got out at Anderson and walked home through the teeming streets cratered from tennis games. Once a week someone was hit and killed. But anyone either on the streets or beneath them was considered fair game. As Bolton unlocked the door to his apartment building a fight broke out across the street. He didn't look round. He shut the door behind him seconds too late to prevent the echo of automatic gunfire forcing its way into the narrow hallway.

He cursed, checked his trashed mailbox and headed for the concrete stairway.

The assignment was in an abandoned warehouse on the outskirts of the city. Three 16-year-old girls and an older transsexual in bishop's vestments performed a variety of sexual acts on the dirty, oil-slick floor of the warehouse. There appeared to be no script or attempt at role-playing, not at least until the masked gunmen stormed into the cold, resonant chamber, at which the girls feigned surprise. The gunmen wore black balaclavas and hefted ARX-53s, safety catches off.

Bolton used an automatic winder and self-loading cartridges to get through 30 pictures a minute. Because of the poor lighting and conditions – Groom's shoots were illegal and last-minute location changes very common, requiring a minimalistic approach to sets and equipment – thirty per cent of these pictures would be rejected for use in the home market and sold on to third-world syndicates.

In the interests of maximizing profit, a second freelance operative was present on this occasion to film the action for the video market. He and Bolton weaved in and out of each other's paths without a word being exchanged. Both were professionals.

The gunmen, understood to be random terrorists, opened fire on the three girls and the transsexual. The intention was only to maim, never to kill, Groom maintained. They aimed at arms and legs but some shots inevitably went wide, for they were not terrorists by profession, but actors. The participants were paid extra for the risk of sustaining fatal injuries.

Bolton watched a volley of bullets tear into skin and shred the muscle of young limbs. Off target, one bullet opened up a crimson wound in one girl's stomach. He gagged and dropped the camera from his eye. The video cameraman, however, did not cease filming and Bolton knew that if he didn't carry on shooting Groom would not pay him. With great effort he ignored the girl's cries and flexed his shutter finger.

The terrorists continued their assault upon the girls and the transsexual. Serious wounds were sustained, fingers crunched, kneecaps shattered. The girl who had been shot in the belly, he noticed, was lying curled up and still. Avoiding the lines of fire he circled the group until he could see the girl from the front. Blood flowed from her abdomen and formed a greasy pool on the floor.

He faced an excruciating choice: avoid intervention and hang on to his job, or try to save the girl's life, thereby risking his own.

Instinct drove him as he dropped the camera and screamed at the gunmen: 'Stop it! Stop shooting, for fuck's sake!'

He threw himself in front of the girl. Pulling a lens duster from his pocket he pressed it hard against the wound. She had already lost a lot of blood. He felt her pulse; it was low, and her face was so white it looked overexposed. A shadow fell over them. Bolton glanced up and saw the cameraman filming them. He increased the pressure on the girl's stomach. The gunfire grew sporadic, sputtered and died out. Rubber-soled footsteps faded away towards the exits. The video camera stopped humming and the girl moaned. Bolton bent right over to keep her warm, shrugging off his jacket to wrap around her. She moaned again.

'It's all right,' he murmured. 'It's all right.'

The other two girls and the transsexual had left. A trail of dark spots on the concrete showed the way they had gone. Groom's money would reach their accounts in the morning, and it would be less than Bolton's fee.

When she had come around sufficiently to apply the compress herself he lifted her up and carried her from the warehouse.

'Bolton.' Groom sat on the edge of his desk in the office beneath his apartment. 'You know the score, Bolton. Don't touch. It's the golden rule. Look but don't touch.' Behind him was a bank of monitors and a Steenbeck. The screens multiplied an image of Bolton shielding the girl from the gunmen. 'Don't get involved. You're an observer.' He jumped down off the desk and paced the room. 'You're just there to take pictures. That's what you exist for. And that's how you exist.'

'What can I say? They shot her in the stomach. I couldn't watch her bleed to death in front of me.'

'They aim,' Groom continued, 'to avoid killing anyone. Naturally. I mean, what do you think we're doing here? But there's always a risk and the girl was being paid to take it. People sell their own and others' lives to survive. It's all a big game.' He glanced at the ivory chess pieces then took a lilac-coloured pill from a small tin and swallowed it without offering one to Bolton.

'Obviously,' he was saying, 'your fee will have to be adjusted. You lost us five or ten minutes of shooting. It's out of my hands,' he lied easily, as he perched once more on the edge of the desk, chin jutting towards the mirrored ceiling.

At least you don't know I've still got the girl. In silent defiance Bolton thought of the girl in his bed. Of his night spent alternately watching over her and bent double on the couch trying to snatch a moment's rest. For so long he'd moved forward one step at a time, earning a little money to pay off a little more debt. Now, with the girl, he'd taken a diagonal move right under Groom's nose and Groom didn't know. Wouldn't even suspect. He had been exposed for so long to his own callousness that he could no longer be sensitive to the possibility of compassion.

Groom's windows rattled in their frames as a jet passed overhead. The soundproofing failed to keep out its bass roar and Bolton felt its cruciform shadow cross his heart.

Groom was still pacing, deciding, perhaps, what to do. Bolton knew he was cruel enough to want to punish him. Would he merely drop Bolton back into the street where he had found him a year ago photographing addicts and scavengers? Or did execution seem the more appropriate option? *Why should the fucker have such control over me?*

'I must think about this,' Groom declared as he lit a cigarette. 'We can play tennis.' He inhaled deeply. 'It helps me think.' Smoke poured out of his nose like dry ice from a machine. 'Be available.'

Bolton was in the glass-walled elevator going down.

Total bastard, he thought and his ears popped. A dark shadow fell across the engulfed streets seventy storeys below. He looked up. A huge jetliner flew so low it appeared to pass between the two towers. Bolton searched at the round windows lining the jet's sleek body and thought he saw faces smeared by speed and panic.

Walking home he plugged into a credit box and found that his fee had already been paid in, sixty per cent of the normal amount. That was still good, though, because it would cover the withdrawal he had authorised the girl to make in the event of her feeling well enough to book an airline ticket. He'd encouraged her to leave the city and found the only reason she hadn't already flown out was money. He had enough to buy her a flight to the coast where she could wait on tables for tourists and live like a human; the price of a flight being roughly equivalent to that of a clean conscience.

She was up and looking better.

'I booked a flight,' she said. 'I want to thank you.' Her hands fell by her side. She appeared at a loss. One hand began to play with the tail of her shirt which had fallen between her legs.

'No thanks needed,' he said, realizing with a stab of regret she was offering all she'd ever had to use as currency. 'I'm glad.' He began to smile and felt tears welling up inside him out of the struggle between self-disgust and happiness.

They spent the evening eating pizza and sitting at the

open window that looked out over the slum quarters of the
city where no building rose higher than twenty floors and
all of them infested with rats, criminals and viruses. The
streets and walkways were patrolled by self-styled vigilante
knights.

He had to stop himself putting his arm around her at one
point in case she misinterpreted his affection.

'Stay here until you go,' he said, feeling glad of her company in the unfriendly neighbourhood for a few more days.

Bolton threw the ball, twisted backwards and swung his
racket. Straight down the centre line, a long bounce, but
Groom got to it and scooped it high and deceptively, deep
back to Bolton's base line. He ran and reached for the
spinning ball, just managing to pull it back. It fell mid-court
and high enough to give Groom the optimum position from
which to spin it backhand over the net by the sideline.

Ignoring a dark shape in the sky, Bolton lunged for the
ball, knowing that if he failed to make contact the momentum
would almost certainly carry him over the edge of the roof
– the exhilarating risk for which the sport had become so
popular. He felt the racket pull his arm out towards the ball
as the shape suddenly mushroomed overhead and roared fit
to pierce his eardrums. The ball seemed to hang in the air as
if controlled by the jet. On the other side of the net Groom
had almost ceased to exist.

The jetliner passed over and Bolton smashed the ball across
the court to the far corner. Groom had anticipated a long ball
knocked down the near side and was badly placed to make
a run. It was his first concession in the game.

Bolton served for advantage but Groom's lob tricked
him again.

'You're too good to let go, Bolton,' Groom shouted, returning his final serve with ease. 'Otherwise I would do so.'

Bolton ran to the net and struck wildly. There was a lucky
bounce but Groom was there.

'There's more work,' he grunted as he drove the ball
horizontally with topspin across the net. 'There's a new
game season starting this weekend. Come along.'

Bolton's racket was in the way and the ball ricocheted back
over the net. Groom swung for a lob, Bolton hung back, but it

was a trick: he pulled the racket back a fraction upon impact
and the ball lost its energy, falling tiredly on Bolton's side
to bounce once and roll off the roof before Bolton could
reach it.

'Season of what?' he asked, exasperated.

'Come to the game,' Groom ordered, spitting onto his
palms. 'Bring your camera.'

'Turn towards the window. Just a fraction. That's it.' He
pressed the trigger. 'OK, move.'

The girl leaned forward slowly so that her hair fell about
her face and caught the transverse light. Using the automatic
mechanism he shot a dozen pictures. The high-speed film
would keep her features sharp and the movement would
melt the light into her hair like hot gold.

'That'll do,' he said. 'Do you want a drink? You must be
tired. I'll get you a drink.'

'I'm not tired,' she said, leaning back again to look out of
the window at the slow-burning sunset. Jetliners droned in
the distance low over the city's towering structures. Bolton
returned with two thick tumblers of Slivovic. She smiled at
him, confusing his emotions all over again.

'Maybe I shouldn't go,' she said, referring to her flight
booked for the following morning.

He looked down into his drink. 'You must. It's your only
hope. You've got to get out and live your life.'

She swung round on the bench seat and stuck her head
out of the window. 'The planes are so low,' she remarked.

'Yes. I read a report which said it had something to do
with pollution levels. Though how aircraft can alleviate the
pollution problems by flying lower I don't know. Maybe they
want to preserve the upper atmosphere and concentrate all
the shit down here.'

He watched the short shirt ride up her back as she leaned
further out. He wanted to touch the delicate hairs lining her
spine, but swallowed the remainder of his drink.

'It wouldn't work if you stayed,' he said, more to convince
himself than persuade her.

'Why not?' She twisted round and found that he was close
behind her. Her eyes were very wide. She seemed to think
it would be easy. Without repeating the words she asked

him again. He raised his hand to his face but outstretched it towards hers. She closed her fingers around his wrist. Over her shoulder he saw the long, low light thicken like honey and with the monotonous buzz of a fat queen bee drunk on the pollen of a lazy afternoon a jet pursued its trajectory across the sky.

Bolton met Groom at his apartment in Thomason and together they set off in Groom's Mazda on SH62. It was the third time that morning Bolton had used the Suspended Highways.

He had risen at 5 am and resuscitated his own car, an old Ford model, to go and get his film developed and then take Anna to the airport. He drove onto SH6 without paying; he'd take the chance on the fine. The lab where he regularly took his films was open 24 hours. A lot of people in Groom's line of business used it because of that convenience.

When he came back an hour later he was completely wiped out. Anna found him sitting in the kitchenette with his head in his hands, sobbing. She tried to comfort him but he was inconsolable and wouldn't talk.

She climbed reluctantly into the passenger seat clutching a small bag he'd bought her the day before. It contained a wallet and some money, a small mirror and a novel. They drove across the city; it was the first time she had seen it from that perspective and maybe now she saw the sense in leaving. The Highways were busy. Jets flew above the car. Bolton tried not to look at her as he selected the right exit to take them out of the city, through the desolate suburbs, in the direction of the airport.

A line of low hills separated the airport from the suburbs. As Bolton negotiated the contours and they watched the scenery, they both noticed incongruous constructions perched like castles on top of some of the hills. More closely they resembled grandstands and stadiums and they seemed hastily erected and temporary. Bolton and Anna exchanged some brief comments but their words sounded brittle in the small car and they fell silent until they reached the airport.

He kissed her goodbye and felt her tremble. Her skin was like a river to his lips. Last night had not been a dream. *She's too young*, he told himself. Once in the car he didn't look

back. Just drove. After the hills he pulled off into a burnt-out
suburban lot and cried until he felt empty.

He drove back home and some time later took the monorail
to Thomason. Inside he was just numb.

'What's the game, Groom?' he asked as they sped out of
the city.

'Wait and see, huh?'

He raised his pitch: 'What's the fucking game?'

'Hey, hey!' Groom pointed a gloved finger at him. 'Don't
you fucking talk to your employer like that.'

Bolton was in turmoil beneath the surface and he barely
contained it. He had to hold his left arm down to stop it
reaching over and grabbing the wheel to send them careening
into the crash barrier and over the edge.

Keeping his voice level: 'Where are we going?'

'Why don't you fucking sit tight and see, boy?'

*Groom, you're filth. You're slime. You're Hitler. You're the
Devil. You aren't even fit to be buried in the earth.*

He recognized the route from the earlier trip. They were
heading out towards the airport. Once in the hills, though,
Groom drifted down an exit road and then eased the Mazda
up a narrow unmarked side road. The slope levelled off and
Bolton was surprised to see hundreds of parked cars.

'Let's go,' Groom barked as he marched away from the
car.

Bolton followed, undecided what to do. A jet buzzed
overhead, frightening a mixed flock of rooks and crows.

Around the next bluff was another surprise. They had
climbed up to one of the strange erections he and Anna had
noticed from his car. Constructed out of wood, with speed
in mind rather than durability, it looked like a sketch for or
the skeleton of a football stadium. Two long grandstands
on either side, nothing at either end and just rough ground
in the middle where the pitch would be. The stands were
packed with thousands of spectators.

Bolton felt the camera by his side and saw again in
his mind's eye the horrible pictures he'd seen four hours
earlier at the lab. He looked at Groom's back as the sado-
pornographer began climbing the wooden steps to find their
reserved seats.

When they sat down Bolton put the camera bag on

his left-hand side away from Groom. In addition to his
camera, film and lenses, it contained a small automatic
pistol – the only weapon he had been able to find in the
apartment. He was just waiting for an opportunity. Or was
he trying to fathom the depths of Groom's evil soul before
he extinguished it?

Groom spoke: 'Can you hear?'

The crowd had fallen silent as if stricken by pre-match
nerves and Bolton could hear nothing except the ever-present
distant roar of a heavy jetliner.

Down at the front, men started shouting and signalling.
Wads of bills changed hands and pencils scribbled as if in
some atavistic rite. A book had been opened. But on what?
The jet engines drew closer. Still there was no sign in the
clear sky of the jet they propelled. The air between the
two grandstands seemed to crackle with electricity. The roar
intensified. Bolton pressed his hands over his ears. Suddenly
over the top of the hill a massive jetliner appeared, less than
a thousand feet above the ground, travelling at speed.

Groom nudged him and pointed to the corners of the stands.
Men wearing protective clothing wheeled out medium-sized
laser cannons at all four corners. Bolton felt sick in the pit of
his stomach. All eyes around him were on the approaching
jet, still climbing. Petrified, he knew he could do nothing.
If he took out his pistol and shot one of the marksmen
the crowd would lynch him. And someone would take the
marksman's place. Shooting Groom would achieve nothing
either. He had probably set up this whole thing as an entertainment, and he'd invited Bolton along to take pictures for
the magazine specials that would follow. Somewhere in the
stadium would be the video operator Bolton had encountered
in the warehouse. But martyrizing the impresario would be
ill-conceived.

'The point of the game is to try and get it down inside the
stadium,' Groom explained. 'That's what they were betting
on. That and the number of survivors.'

Bolton recalled a spate of air crashes eighteen months
previously. Had they been caused by Groom and his sick
colleagues and rivals? He remembered the other ad hoc
stadiums they'd seen on the way to the airport. This jet
was not the only target of the day.

The shadow of the plane fell over the crowd and the laser cannon operators unleashed their fire as one. Struck in four places the jet was instantly crippled. An explosion ripped apart the undercarriage. A gaping hole was torn in the fuselage beneath the nose. The plane toppled from the sky.

Bolton had begun to pray to a God whose name he had mocked since his sister's death. He prayed that this was not Anna's flight. Prayed that hers would not pass over any of the neighbouring hilltop stadiums. *Please God, she's already gone, she's half-way to the coast!* He did frenzied calculations in his head to work out how long a delay there might have been after he left her at the airport before her flight was due to leave. All planes for the coast would have to cross the hills. There was no other way.

The jet was falling. Snapped in the middle like a stale cigar it twisted and dropped. Passengers still strapped into their seats fell out of the wrecked fuselage. Baggage showered the grandstand. The crowd cheered, screaming with excitement. Couldn't they see that one of the wings was directly over their heads?

The jet fell between the two stands with an explosion of fire like an exquisite waterfall. One wing crashed onto the ground and ignited upon impact. The other smacked into one of the stands and ignited with a brilliant flash.

Bolton and several others had begun to run before the jet landed. As the wing hit he was five yards from the wooden stand. The explosion rocked him off his feet and he fell, grabbing at his bag. The ground shook again and a tremendous gust of heat like a solar wind shoved into his back, curling him up. A further explosion wrenched free the strap of his bag. Fire showered around him like a rain of lava and quickly faded.

He looked up. The wrecked plane was ablaze, passengers become human torches, some torn from their seats, some still bound down and flung forward from the waist. Arms and legs lay scattered like charred matchsticks.

In one stand the spectators gazed enraptured. Some took snaps with melting cameras, others mouthed expressions of wonderment. Down at the front they queued up for winnings.

The other stand was on fire. The wing had shed its fuel, spreading its blessing of fire beyond the fall of debris.

Bolton's bag had been shredded. He picked up his camera and adjusted the settings. Narrow aperture. Speed compensation.

Many spectators in the stand were already dead, others in flames screamed in agony. One of these was Groom. The sado-pornographer had staged his final atrocity and he wouldn't live long enough to cash in on it. Bolton thought of the thousands Groom would have made from this 'game', far more than from *Rape Inferno*, in which the pyrotechnics had gone disastrously wrong, incinerating the featured young 'actress'. Even covered with third-degree burns, Bolton's sister's body had been clearly recognizable in the photos he'd seen lying about at the lab. ('What are these?' 'An old job for Groom. We're clearing out the old stuff.') The photographs were a shock but the realization not surprising. His sister's death had eventually been reported to him as a auto-crash statistic and he'd supposed, since she didn't drive, that her luck had simply run out – most traffic stayed on the SH network, from which pedestrians were excluded. But you didn't ask questions of the police in the city: 'protect and serve' was history.

His sister's murderer – for whom he'd worked to pay off her death duties – burned on the stand. Bolton aimed and squeezed. *These* pictures were for himself. *Groom in Pain*, *Groom Dying*, *Death of Groom*, *Groom in Hell*. He itemized the exhibits in his own private gallery.

His tears flowed as he continued shooting and were dried by the fire. Cinders landed in his hair. The terrible stench of cremation crept up his nose and he thought of Anna.

She was safe, airborne beyond reach of the city and its insanities. She looked out of the small window and saw the coastline approaching. In her lap she tightened her grip on the little bag. She was safe.

There was just a *chance* that she was safe.

People sell their own and others' lives to survive. He remembered Groom's glib justification of his work. *It's all a big game*. Bolton now realized that the jets had only begun flying lower when the game season was approaching. How much did Groom and others like him have to pay the airlines to get them to play? How could one put a price on so many lives. He wondered as he surveyed the charred devastation if the airlines even sent people to the games to place bets.

Helping the girl get to the coast was not enough. He had to chance it himself as well. If he made it he would find her and they would work out a way to survive together.

And if he didn't, he would still have the satisfaction of knowing that Groom's game had ended in checkmate and he would not profit from Bolton's move back to pawn.

THE CAT IN THE WALL

Alex Stewart

Alex Stewart is the editor of Arrows of Eros *and the critically acclaimed shared-world series,* Temps, *which he created with Neil Gaiman. Aside from anthologies, his fiction, articles and comic strips have been widely published.*

THE drizzle had thickened to solid rain again by the time Martin swung off the A12, and began to thread his way through the narrow, high-sided lanes of North Essex. He slowed instinctively, changing down to third, as the Volvo churned stoically through the layer of topsoil running from the fields to silt up the gully of the roadway. The weather had been bad for weeks, but it hadn't seemed to matter much in London. Now, as the thin slurry hissed against the bottom of the car, he was beginning to think he'd made a mistake in coming out here.

The places he thought he knew had changed with the coming of autumn. The cereal fields had been harvested, scarring the familiar yellow landscape with dark gashes of clotted mud. The trees were brown and partially bare, shedding their leaves into the rotting mess that slithered alarmingly under the wheels every time he braked or tried to turn. Even the landmarks were different, changed with the alchemy of the seasons, obscured by the rain and the gathering dusk, to leave him perpetually convinced he was about to get lost.

'What the hell . . .?'

Something small and animate streaked across the road in front of him, its shadow dancing in the headlights. He stamped on the brake and spun the wheel, felt the rear of the car slide eagerly towards the waiting ditch,

overcorrected, and slithered to a halt in a bow wave of filth
a few yards further on. The blur paused briefly at the top of
the embankment, meeting his eyes with a cold yellow stare
of malevolent contempt, and disappeared through a hole in
the hedge.

'A cat. Christ.' Martin shuddered, feeling sick. He hated
cats, with the absolute loathing of the phobic. That was
something else Carol had never understood. 'Pull yourself
together,' she'd hiss, while his throat contracted and his
heartbeat drowned the voices around him, and someone's
cherished pet ghosted round the corners of the room.

As the drumming in his ears began to fade, he realized
the wretched animal had done him a favour after all. He'd
almost overshot the narrow cart track leading to the cottage.
The remains of the rotting gate were visible a few yards
further on, set back from the road, entwined with the
dripping brambles that held them up. He engaged the gears
cautiously and set off through the woods, wallowing along
the ruts carved by Dyson's tractor.

The house was on the right, about thirty yards from the
sagging gate, set back against the trees. In daylight, and the
summer sun, it looked picturebook perfect; the original structure subsumed into nearly four centuries worth of extensions
and additions, which somehow managed to blend together
to form a harmonious whole. Tonight, though, little could
be discerned beyond its silhouette.

Almost opposite, across a narrow clearing, Dyson's barn
loomed black against the sky. Between the two buildings
the track broadened, opening on to the fields that fell away
gently into the vale, and the distant, huddled hills of Suffolk
beyond. Martin coasted to a stop, stretched, and killed the
engine.

The sudden silence unnerved him. In London there were
always human sounds, the murmur of voices and traffic, as
constant and comforting as the rhythm of his pulse. Here he
could hear his own breathing, and the rattling of the rain on
the car roof.

Well he'd wanted to be on his own, hadn't he? He reached
across to the passenger seat and hefted the suitcase, trying to
lose himself in the routine of unpacking.

Thirty cold, wet seconds of fumbling for the door key

with his hands full convinced him the luggage would have been better left in the car. But the lock gave at last, and he stumbled into the narrow hallway, dropping his burden and groping for the light switch. It clicked derisively, leaving the house dark.

'Damn!' He burrowed under the stairs for the main switch, banging his head painfully on the doorframe. He found it eventually, behind the usual detritus spontaneously generated by rarely-opened cupboards, and rewarded himself with the civilized amenities of light and heat.

He couldn't get much wetter, he decided, so went back to the car for the rest of his luggage. Three trips were enough; a sagging cardboard box for each year of the marriage. The thought was profoundly depressing. It was while he was balancing the last one on a raised knee, trying to close the tailgate with his elbow, that he saw the cat again.

It was sitting on the edge of the copse, by the side of the house, watching him with the air of amused disdain cats reserve for most human activities. Seeing him look up, it turned and melted away into the shadows.

Martin felt his breath stop for a moment, then shook himself angrily. It was only an animal, damn it. He went inside, and slammed the door with hardly more violence than necessary.

The next day was perfect for late September, warm and bright, the clouds moving on to disperse over the North Sea. Martin dug out an old T-shirt, relishing the change from his city routine, and started unpacking. By mid-morning most of his books and computer disks were neatly shelved in the study, next to the work station, and he was back in the kitchen, distributing the small stock of groceries he'd brought with him around the cupboards. The coffee machine was just finishing its death rattle when he heard the faint susurration of tyres along the muddy lane.

It was Dyson of course, he realized that even before he saw the familiar Toyota pickup coasting to a halt beside the Volvo. By the time the farmer climbed out, smiling a greeting, Martin was waiting for him beside the front door.

'Morning.' His eyes took in Martin's casual clothing, and the parked car. 'Thought you were up here.'

'How could you tell?' One of the things Martin had never got used to about the countryside was the way everyone seemed to know what was happening around them by some form of social osmosis.

'Saw the lights.' Dyson nodded across the open field behind them; he lived the other side of it, a few hundred yards as the crow flew, but over a mile round the narrow, twisting lanes. Straining his eyes, Martin could just make out the low outline of the roofs of Valley Farm. Up here, on the hillside, the lights of the cottage would be hard to miss.

'Nice of you to check, though.' Dyson nodded.

'Never hurts to make sure. Staying long?'

'A while.' What the hell. He'd know soon enough. 'Maybe for good.'

Dyson digested that slowly, extracting the implications.

'Both of you?'

'Just me.'

'Ah.' He nodded slowly. 'Well, you know where we are if you need anything.'

'Thanks.' Unspoken embarrassment curdled the air between them, and Martin cast around desperately for a safe subject. 'Whose cat's that?'

Despite his automatic shiver, he was almost pleased to see it again. It had strolled around the corner of the barn while the men were talking; now it stretched, flexing its claws, and paused in a patch of autumn sunshine to wash its face.

'Barn Puss? Mine, I suppose.' Dyson shrugged. 'But she don't like the farm much. Don't get on with the other cats, and she don't like people much either. So she come up here about a month ago.'

'You mean she lives in the barn?' Martin felt his shoulder-blades contract. Dyson nodded.

'Lucky for you, really. Keeps the vermin down.'

Martin nodded too, not trusting himself to speak. It looked as though Dyson was right; in daylight the little tabby seemed sleek and well-fed.

'Well, best get on.' Dyson collected a tool bag from the pickup, and strolled away towards the barn. As he approached it the cat turned, and skittered away into the undergrowth. Martin muttered something non-committal, and went back indoors.

Despite his misgivings, he saw very little of the cat in the following weeks. She seemed as unsociable as Dyson had said; though they caught sight of one other now and again, she seemed to be avoiding him as enthusiastically as he avoided her. He hardly gave her a thought after a while, except when some barely perceived motion in the corner of his eye set off a reflexive shudder.

To his pleased surprise he found himself settling easily into the rural life. Freed from the distractions of the city, and the endless quarrelling with Carol, the work seemed easier, and more fun than it had been for years. The firm didn't interfere, happy to let him work at his own pace, provided he came into London now and again to discuss the current project; he'd make a day out of it, going to a movie or the theatre, or for a meal with a friend, before catching the last train back from Liverpool Street. He began to relish the feeling of freedom it gave him, setting his own hours, logging on over the net whenever he felt like it.

And then there was the cottage. After a month or so it was permeated with his presence, unmistakably his, in a way the flat in London could never have been. Even the furniture Carol had chosen became overlaid with his own sense of possession, the chair cushions moulding to the shape of his body, driving the last lingering traces of her from his surroundings.

'In fact,' he said, 'It's perfect. I should have come out here years ago.'

'Shame you didn't.' Terry, Dyson's eldest son, swallowed the dregs of his pint, and set the empty glass down carefully on the table between them. 'Maybe we'd only be second from bottom.'

Martin grinned. They were about the same age, and between them they made up the core of the Shepherd and Dog's enthusiastically inept darts team.

'Strategy,' he said. 'We're lulling them into a real sense of security.'

'Right.' Terry nodded, and glanced at his watch. 'Got time for another?'

'Silly question.' Martin waited for him to return, savouring the warmth of the saloon bar, the smell of stale beer and old tobacco, the feeling of simple companionship. Outside the wind was malicious, sudden gusts rattling the leaded panes behind his head.

'There you go.' Terry was back from the bar, pints and a packet of crisps in his hands. Martin took one of the glasses, and waited for his friend to settle again.

'Got much work at the moment?' he asked. Terry nodded. He owned a small building firm in the next village, and seemed to be in steady demand around the district.

'Enough,' he said. 'Do you need something done?'

'I'm not sure.' Martin sipped at his drink. 'Can you drop by tomorrow and see?'

'It looks like your damp course all right.' Terry straightened up, stuffing his hands back in the pockets of his donkey jacket. His words were visible, appearing as little puffs of vapour in the chill December air. 'Trouble is. I can't see how far it goes.'

Martin nodded. They were standing outside the cottage, on the small flagstoned area next to the kitchen door.

'So what do you reckon?' he asked.

'I'll have to get in there. See how far it's spread, what other damage it's done.' Terry shrugged his shoulders. 'It's not really urgent. But the longer you leave it, the worse it'll get.'

Martin nodded thoughtfully.

'Best to get it done now, then. Before the weather sets in.'

'Would be sensible.' Terry produced a battered and incongruous-looking palmtop from the depths of his donkey jacket. 'Reckon I can start Thursday, if that suits you.'

Martin sighed, and stared at the screen. It stared unhelpfully back.

Syntax error: line 8510 it blinked. The trouble was, line 8510 was definitely error free; Martin had checked it twice to make sure. That meant the bug was somewhere else in the program, or even in one of the subroutines accessing that particular block of coding. Or possibly the data record it was supposed to be handling. But then why would it show up here? Perhaps . . .

His thoughts scattered in the face of another fusillade of hammering from the kitchen. This was hopeless. He sighed again, typed *tron*, and the code for a hard copy. The printer buzzed obediently into life.

It was going to take at least twenty minutes to get the printout he wanted, so he wandered into the kitchen for more coffee.

'How's it going?' he asked. Terry was out in the yard, attacking the wall of the cottage with a hammer and cold chisel. As he leaned out of the back door to speak to him, Martin could see he'd made a pretty large hole there already, piling the dislodged bricks carefully to one side. The builder glanced up.

'Not too bad,' he said.

'Good.' Martin shivered a little in the northerly wind. 'I'm taking a break; feel like a coffee?'

'Thought you'd never ask.' Terry grinned. 'Be with you in a couple of minutes.'

The hammering continued as Martin made the coffee, counterpointing the gurgle of the filter and the faint insect hum of the printer in the study. Then suddenly it fell silent.

'Martin.' Terry's voice sounded odd, as though he wasn't quite sure what to say. 'Come and look at this.'

Martin went outside, shivering again as the icy wind ripped through his pullover, and a few stray drops of drizzle spattered his face.

'What is it?'

Terry moved aside from the hole, to let him look. Something was wedged in the gap between the inner and outer walls, a grey, amorphous shape, encrusted with the grime of centuries. He gazed at it, repelled and fascinated, tracing the outline with his eye. It looked a little like . . . it could almost be . . .

'It's a cat.' Terry reached into the hole, touching it carefully, then grasping it with a featherlight touch. He moved it, gently, then lifted it out. 'A mummified cat.'

'Get rid of it!' Martin leapt away, practically screaming the words, his stomach knotting. He sagged against the wall, an arm flung up over his eyes to blot it out. Terry stared at him curiously for a moment, then realizing his friend wasn't joking, carried it away round the corner of the house.

Martin watched him go, wondering if he was going to be sick, and trying to control the panic rush of adrenalin. He was still trembling from the reaction when Terry returned, and, for the first time he could remember, he didn't react at all when he caught sight of Barn Puss watching him idly from the branches of a nearby tree.

'I've just got a thing about cats, that's all.' Sitting in the warmth of the kitchen, a mug of coffee in his hand, Martin felt vaguely embarrassed. He'd almost got over the reaction now, except for the tingling in his fingertips. Terry nodded.

'I know. My youngest's the same, except it's spiders with her.' He sipped at his own drink. Martin hesitated.

'What did you do with it?'

'Put it in the barn for now. Dad won't mind.'

Martin thought about that. He'd have to dispose of it somehow, even if he wasn't quite sure what to do with it yet. The thought of picking the thing up, even at arm's length, even with gloves on, made his skin crawl. But at least he knew where the loathesome thing was, and at least it was out of his way.

'How did it get there?'

'The people who built the place, most like.' Terry gestured vaguely, taking in the room and the cottage itself. 'Most of the brickwork's original, sixteenth century.' He grinned. 'Sound, too. It's only your modern plumbing causing the trouble.'

'But why a cat? I mean . . .' Martin petered out, not quite sure what he did mean. 'You didn't seem all that surprised.'

'It's not the first one I've found. Most of the old houses around here have one.' Terry sipped at his drink. 'They're supposed to be guardian spirits; you know, protecting the place from demons and such.'

Martin laughed.

'Sounds daft to me. What do you do with them?'

'I put 'em back.' Terry smiled shyly, almost sheepish. 'I mean . . . Well, it can't do any harm, can it?'

That night, for the first time in weeks, Martin found it hard to sleep. The image of the mummified cat kept invading his mind, all the more haunting for not having been seen clearly. And in his wakeful state the noises of the house sounded different, louder, the familiar creaks and rustlings, long ignored, scraping away at the edge of his awareness.

The next day he was tired and irritable, unable to concentrate, the bug in the program as elusive as ever. Every time the problem started to make sense his attention was snatched away by some stray particle of sound. At first he thought it was Terry, still working energetically on the delinquent damp course, but most of them were too soft for that; gentle creaks, like stealthy footsteps on the floor behind him, faint rustlings as though the curtains were being disturbed.

He shivered. The weather was getting colder, the wind coming straight from Scandinavia, and the house was bound to react to the sudden drop in temperature. He hadn't realized it would be quite so draughty in winter, though, and made a mental note to ask Terry about double glazing.

Eventually he gave up trying to work, and wandered back into the kitchen. The builder was there, repacking his toolbag, and Martin suddenly realized it was already growing dark. He'd wasted half the day struggling with the recalcitrant coding.

'Ah.' Terry looked up as he came in. 'I was just about to call you.' He led Martin outside. In the gathering dusk, the hole in the side of the house gaped like an open wound. 'I've just about finished now.' He indicated the polythene sheet, fastened across the gap like an oversized band aid. 'I'll be by on Monday to replace the bricks and tidy up.'

'Fine.' Martin shivered again, the cold cutting through his clothing like a razorblade. 'I'll expect you at the usual time.'

Monday came and went with no sign of Terry, but Martin wasn't really surprised. The snow had begun early on Sunday morning, and by the following day the drifts were five feet deep in places. Gazing out of the window of the tiny lounge, he could see the wind-driven powder rising from the fields like whirling smoke, to mingle with the thick, heavy flakes still falling from the slate-coloured sky. He put another log on the fire, and turned up the stereo.

He felt terrible. He was still sleeping badly, kept awake by the noises, which seemed to grow louder every night; when he did fall asleep he had nightmares, where strange, formless shadows coiled through his dreams, questing, malevolent. He began to suspect he had flu, was feverish, but couldn't be sure.

The music was broken by a sharp burst of static, which receded rapidly, but remained audible below the melody, like the whisper of waves on a faraway shore. Martin shut his eyes, trying to block it out, concentrate on the sound of the orchestra, but it kept scratching at the fringes of his mind. It seemed rhythmical, somehow, like the murmur of voices in another room. Drifting in the warmth of the fire, the hypnotic flicker of the flames on his eyelids, soothed by the music, he found himself listening to the fluctuating hiss, almost as though there was a pattern there he could decipher with a little more effort . . .

A raw, inhuman shriek tore through the room, snapping him back to wakefulness. Heart racing, he glanced around.

It had grown darker while he dozed. The fire was burning low, the shadows in the corner of the room advancing as the illumination dimmed, and the speakers were humming emptily, the record long over. Martin kicked the burning logs together, the flames flared, and the shadows retreated.

Something dark and shapeless was huddled against the window. Hands tingling, Martin walked over to look at it.

It was the cat, Barn Puss, pressed against the glass. Seeing him, she howled again. She was shivering, her fur damp and matted.

'Piss off.' Martin drew the curtains, and switched on the light. The last traces of his fright, and the waking dream that had preceded it, faded away. He made up the fire, and selected another record. Outside, in the bleak winter night, the cat kept on howling.

Damn it. He couldn't just leave it out there to freeze. On the other hand, the mere thought of allowing it inside the cottage flooded his palms with sweat. He hesitated for a moment, breathing deeply, trying to fight down the surge of irrational fear.

'Puss puss puss. Here puss.' He stood at the kitchen door, battered by the wind, and hoped it couldn't hear him. For one brief, relieved moment he thought it must have gone back to the barn; then he saw it, floundering towards him, chest deep in the snow.

He flinched away as it entered the house, sniffing the air, and ignoring his presence. It shook its paws fastidiously, each one in turn, then sat, and started to lick its coat. Martin closed the door behind it, keeping as far away as he could.

'I suppose you want feeding, too.' He was surprised at how well he was coping; he still felt uncomfortably queasy this close to the animal, but the usual panic reaction was muted. After the horror he'd seen on Thursday, he supposed, the live cat was a bit of an anticlimax.

He opened a tin of tuna, upended it into a saucer, and put it on the floor as close as he dared to the little tabby. It padded over, sniffed at it for a moment, then gulped it down. Martin set a saucer of water down too, and fled to the lounge.

With the connecting doors closed, and the hi-fi turned up, he could almost forget it was in the house. Even so, he found himself straining his ears for some sign of its presence.

The record ended, and the silence closed in on him again. This time he was certain he could hear something, a rustling in the fabric of the building, audible even over the hum of the speakers. He turned his head, questing the source.

A faint scuffling, marginally louder, came from beyond the door. The cat! It must have got out of the kitchen!

His breath froze at the thought. The room seemed darker, somehow, the shadows gathering in the corners flickering before his eyes. He found himself striding forward, propelled by hysterical courage, grasping the handle of the door, and flinging it open.

'All right, you little . . .'

The narrow hallway was empty, but gloomier than it should have been, as though the light bulb couldn't be bothered any more. The shadows seemed to move as he glanced around, flowing away from him, staying in his peripheral vision. Martin stared at the kitchen door. It was firmly closed, just as he'd left it.

He returned to the lounge, and made up the fire. Luckily he'd brought a fresh stack of logs in when the snow began, so he had plenty of fuel. Even so, the room felt unnaturally cold. He shivered, certain now that he'd caught the flu, and was running a fever.

He ought to go to bed, he thought. Soon . . . The idea of moving, climbing the stairs, weighed him down with the thought of the effort required. Better to stay here for now, close to the fire . . .

The hissing was back, flowing through his mind like the static on the speakers, slowing and clogging his thoughts. His vision seemed blurred too, the lounge darker, slim tendrils of shadow flexing from the corners of the room, coiling around the ceiling and the walls. As Martin watched, distantly fascinated, they reached the lights.

Gradually the room dimmed, the illumination absorbed by the hovering cloud, which thickened as it fed. Abruptly the lights went out, plunging the room into darkness, relieved only by the flickering flames.

Martin stared at the fire, seeing the first faint tendrils of shadow reach out towards it. One of them touched a rising thread of smoke, shyly, like a lover, and entwined with it. The hissing in his ears grew louder, triumphant, leaching away the will to move. As it rose to a crescendo, he first felt the touch of the darkness.

It didn't hurt. It was the antithesis of feeling, a crushing wave of negation that rolled through his body and mind, obliterating both as though they'd never been. For a moment he held on, resisting fiercely, trying to concentrate on his name, the sensation of *being*, then felt even this begin to slip.

Then something howled, far away, and the grip of the darkness loosened. Martin strained to see, to hear, to seize some part of the real world, some simple affirmation he could use as a weapon, however feeble. Slowly he became aware of a frantic scrabbling, and the repeated thudding of something soft against wood. Then the darkness dropped him, flowing away suddenly, as if something more urgent had attracted its attention.

He returned to awareness lying prone on the rug before the fire, the last few glowing embers warm against his face. After an eternal second of frantic paralysis, he turned his head towards the sound.

The door, closed firmly behind him when he entered the room, was now ajar. Even as he watched it swung wider, shouldered aside by the cat from the barn.

It paused on the threshold for a moment, its glowing, golden eyes transfixing the pulsing heart of incarnate darkness hovering in the centre of the room. Then it stalked towards it. Tail swishing, lips curled back from its teeth, it hissed a challenge. As Martin watched, incredulous, the shadows retreated.

Moved by instinct, he seized a handful of the sticks he used for kindling, and thrust them into the remains of the fire. It blazed up, suddenly, illuminating the room, hurling the darkness back into the corners. It writhed there, indecisively, while Martin heaved a couple of logs onto the leaping flames.

'Gotcha, you bastard!' He jumped, suddenly, as the cat brushed against his ankle, and glanced down. It settled itself in the centre of the rug, eyes fixed on the deepest knot of shadow, and hissed again.

Martin sat down next to it, and reached out a hesitant hand. The cat sniffed at his fingertips for a moment, then looked down and started washing its chest. Martin laughed.

'You and me, eh? Saw him off all right, didn't we?'

They sat together for the rest of the night, basking in the safety of the fireglow, while the shadows writhed around them. From time to time the darkness would thicken, slinking closer to the refuge of firelight, until the cat stepped forward to challenge it. Inevitably the darkness retreated, driven back by the animal's advance.

Eventually the shadows grew fainter, slowly at first, so Martin couldn't be sure they were really fading, then faster, more noticeably, until they finally withered and died as the grey glow of dawn seeped around the edges of the curtains.

As the lights came back on, startling Martin with their sudden brilliance, the cat crawled into his lap and began to purr.

Dyson and Terry arrived a couple of days later, battering their way through the partially-cleared drifts in the young builder's Land Rover. Martin waved as they appeared at the edge of the clearing, and stuck his shovel in the pile of cleared snow by the back door.

'I see you survived all right.' Terry strolled over to meet him, his hands in his pockets, and bent down to inspect the hole in the wall. The polythene sheeting was torn, and flapped loudly, exposing the gap intermittently as the wind tugged at it.

'We managed.' Martin turned to greet Dyson. Burdened with a box full of groceries, the older man was picking his way cautiously towards the house, placing his feet down carefully in his son's bootprints.

'We?' The farmer looked puzzled.

'My little friend and me.' Barn Puss wrapped herself round Martin's legs as he spoke. He bent down to scratch her between the ears, and she purred loudly.

'Well I'm buggered.' Dyson's expression was almost a parody of astonishment. 'I've never seen her take to anyone like that.'

'Reckon she's found out where the food is, that's all.' Martin turned his attention back to Terry. 'Is everything all right?'

'I reckon so.' The builder was still looking carefully at the gap between the walls, checking for signs of damage with a pocket torch. His voice changed slightly. 'I see you've put it back, then.' When he turned to look at Martin, there was an air of faint relief on his face.

'It seemed the best place for it.' Martin shrugged, controlling his own expression carefully. Terry nodded.

'Isn't the saucer of milk overdoing it a bit?'

'Maybe.' Martin grinned, suddenly. 'But like you said; it can't do any harm, can it?'

He scooped the little tabby up, holding her gently in the crook of his arm, and led the way into the kitchen. Dyson put the box down carefully, and Martin started burrowing in it for the coffee.

'When you've finished up out there, do you think you could put a cat flap in the door for me?'

'I could do.' Terry pretended to think about it, the grin growing wider on his face. 'But I don't think you'll fit . . .'

THE SHADOW QUEEN

Anne Goring

Anne Goring has written many short stories and articles, plus five novels and several radio plays. Her horror and fantasy fiction has appeared in Weird Tales, Blood Review, 2AM *and the acclaimed* Women's Press anthology, Skin of the Soul. *Her most recent novel, a Gothic saga called* A Turning Shadow, *was published in 1993 by* Headline.

'MAM's got a new baby.' The candle Clara held flickered its trembling, golden light across her round face. She looked solemn, older, as though the weight of the news had bestowed burdens, responsibilities. 'It's a little lad.'

Lizzie felt her mouth drop open.

'What she got that for?' she demanded, struggling to free herself from the demanding softness of the feather mattress and sit upright. 'Is Mam here? Has she come to take us home?'

'A message just come from Dad for Auntie Bea,' said Clara, importantly. 'She said I could tell you straight off if you hadn't gone to sleep.'

'I was nearly. You woked me, our Clara,' The plaintive note in her sister's voice caused Clara to toss her head so that her heavy red plaits bounced against the frills of her pinafore.

'I'll get back downstairs, then, seeing as you're not interested.' Clara flounced round so sharply that the candle flame streamed in a long horizonal streak and black shadows did a wild dance over the walls, giving momentary life to the stiff cabbage roses imprinted on the wallpaper.

'But I am int'rested. Honest,' Lizzie cried, penitent. Even though the news was puzzling and unwelcome. How could Mam . . . after what happened to Peter . . .?

She shivered. She didn't want to remember about Peter.

Instead, she said pleadingly to her sister, 'Aren't you coming to bed?' She felt lost in the big bed without Clara. And there were noises. Not the friendly noises she was used to, clogs on cobbles and yowling cats and trains shunting and puffing in the junction yard. The country night, was different. Full of strange cries and hootings and screechings. At home, when the wind got up and blustered round the houses, it gave her a warm cosy feeling to be safe indoors. Here, the wind moaned and scratched at the windows like something, some THING, about to break in and get her. And now there was this worse horror. Tom had told her today. Whispering in that sly, grinning way of his, the words slithering between his small brown teeth, telling her of the evil witch who lived right over her head in the cockloft and came out at midnight, looking for little girls to gobble up . . .

'It's not half-past-eight yet,' Clara said, but she relented. She wandered to the washstand and stood for a minute primping at her reflection in the glass. Auntie Bea had decreed that Clara, who was nearly ten, should have an extra hour downstairs if she sat quietly and helped with the mending. 'I always learned my girls to be useful with the needle,' Auntie Bea had said, tut-tutting over Clara and Lizzie's lack of accomplishment. 'I don't know what our Mary-Ann can be thinking of. Not even showing you simple hemming. And in her circumstances an' all . . . 'Words like "daft" and "feckless" hovered unspoken. 'Here, take this mutton cloth, Lizzie and I'll show you . . .'

Lizzie, silently and rebelliously attacking the square of muslin that mangled itself under her clumsy fingers to something so grey and blood-spotted that she feared it would even be rejected for its intended use as a dishcloth, knew exactly what her mother, Mary-Ann, thought of when she sat chin in hand, smiling dreamily, over the warm, tumbled, dusty clutter of her kitchen. And it wasn't about dull things like polishing furniture and putting sheets side-to-middle and scouring the scullery flags, things around which Auntie Bea's day revolved. Mam had secrets, lovely golden secrets that she shared only with Lizzie. But she wasn't going to tell about that to Auntie Bea. Auntie Bea would sniff and look down her nose. And, worse, she might let on to Tom.

The thought of Tom knowing something like that about Mam, of twisting things in his vicious way made her go cold inside. She'd hated and feared him from that very first day, nearly two weeks ago, when he'd snatched her beautiful Ruby, and dangled her over the water butt outside the scullery door. Ruby had real hair that Lizzie put in rag curlers every night and proper clothes that you could take on and off, even drawers with frills on and black shiny boots with tiny buttons.

'Shall us see if 'er can swim, then?' Tom had grinned.

'Don't!' Lizzie had cried, anguished. 'She'll drown!'

''Er's only a daft ol' doll.' He jerked his grubby fist down. Ruby's shiny black boots disappeared with a splash, the hem of her green skirt darkened as it soaked up the water.

Lizzie flew at him.

'Give her back!' She hammered with her fists on his stomach, 'Give her back or I'll tell on you!'

Tom's grin broadened. 'You do an' you know what? Owd Johnson's bull'd be right after you. Tell-tale-tits allus gets chased by Johnson's bull.'

His words brought her up short. Johnson's bull was a fearsome creature. Lizzie and Clara had already walked down the lane to the farm for eggs and milk. Mrs Johnson had let them help to gather the warm eggs that the hens had laid only that morning and shown them the baby calves with the big beautiful long-lashed eyes. And on the way they'd passed the dark odorous barn where the monster was penned. It was hard to believe that this great brown beast had once been a gentle, timid calf. It swung its heavy head sullenly as it spied them over the half door. It had little angry eyes and cruel curving horns sweeping up from the tight packed curls on its head. It shifted restlessly, the brass ring shuddering in its nose as it snorted. Lizzie could feel how angry it was, how powerful and puffed up with wickedness. She had no need of Mrs Johnson's warning that they mustn't ever go near it.

So when Auntie Bea came crossly out of the scullery to see what Lizzie was making a fuss about and Tom casually tossed Ruby back at her and said, 'Oh, she nearly dropped her dolly in the butt. If I hadn't been here it'd have sunk right down,' she didn't say a word. She just hugged Ruby, damp and dripping, to her chest and hung her head while Auntie Bea scolded her for being such a nuisance.

'Does Tom know about our Mam and the baby?' she burst out now, to Clara's back, knowing before Clara spoke what the answer was. He was sitting downstairs, wasn't he? Having a game of cribbage or draughts with Uncle Sammy. He'd known before she, Lizzie, had. She felt betrayed.

And Clara was making it worse. ''Course, *I* knew about Mam getting the baby, ages ago,' she announced, full of self-importance.

'You didn't!'

'Did. That's why we're staying here.'

'You're fibbing me, our Clara. Mam would've told me an' all.'

'I'm big and you're only little.'

'I'm not little. I'm six.' Her voice quavered, then strengthened. 'You're telling big fibs, our Clara. Auntie Bea only fetched us 'cos Mam was poorly and needed a rest.'

Mam had lain in bed, white-faced and weary looking, her long hair, so like Clara's in colour but lank and dull now, spread untidily on the pillow.

'You'll be a brave girl, won't you, lovey?' she'd said softly. 'It won't be for long and the country air will do you good . . .'

Lizzie had thrown her arms tightly round her mother's neck.

'But Mam, I don't want to go. I like it best here. Besides,' she'd added miserably, wanting to say so much and finding the words difficult because of the tight ache in her chest and because Lizzie and Auntie Bea were hovering impatiently to make their own goodbyes, 'besides . . . you know . . .,' her voice was a thread of breathy sound in Mam's ear, 'when . . . when we open the secrets box . . .'

Her mother smiled and whispered so that only Lizzie could hear.

'It's easy, Lizzie love. Just shut your eyes and think very hard and the secrets box will be there, waiting for you to lift the lid. Your very own private, personal box, filled with all the lovely things you could ever want . . .

But it hadn't been the same. She'd tried it. The pictures wouldn't come. She needed Mam to make her see the beautiful princesses, the castles, the magic landscapes, the adventures . . . without Mam there wasn't anything.

She turned her thoughts reluctantly to the prospect of a new baby in the house. She supposed there was nothing she could do about it, but she was troubled all the same. And there was something she had to ask. Something important.

'Did she get the new baby from the same garden as our Peter?' Her voice came out loud and challenging.

Clara giggled. 'Garden? You're a right daft lump, you are. Babies don't come from gardens.'

'They do! Mam told me.'

Clara hesitated, a look that was both calculating and wary. Presently she said, 'What did Mam say – about this garden?

'That there are lovely flowers there, like rainbows, and babies grow in 'em and live there until there's a nice Mam and Dad as want 'em. But Mam said our Peter was only loaned so he he had to go back to be a rainbow flower.' Her bottom lip stuck out mulishly. Mam had said he was happier in the lovely, sunny garden. Lizzie had allowed herself to be comforted by the thought of him gurgling in the sunshine, rosy and plump-limbed, instead of thin and listless as he'd been when he'd lived with them. But it still hurt inside that he hadn't wanted to stay with her. She'd loved him so much. His special sister, Mam had said, because he always stopped crying when she rocked his cradle by the fire and smiled his sweet toothless smile, his eyes following her round whenever she was in the room.

'You'll have to ask Mam about that when we get home,' Clara said carefully after a moment.

'But when are we goin', Clara?'

'Dunno.' Clara shrugged and walked to the door. 'Week or two yet, I s'pose. Any road, I'm not bothered. It's nice here an' Auntie Bea's going to learn me to crochet.' She held up the candle, grinning, 'Course it might snow or somethin' – it gets right cold on t'moors, y'know – and we'd be trapped here all winter. No one'd be able to find us 'till they dug us out in spring.'

She closed the door, giggling, on Lizzie's wail of protest.

Lizzie pulled the sheets over her head and tried not to cry. It couldn't snow yet. The leaves were still on the trees and the hedges full of fat purple blackberries and red rosehips.

She wouldn't think about winter and snow! She wouldn't listen to the creaks and rustlings in the walls! She wouldn't think about the witch in the cockloft, waiting until the clock struck twelve when she would pounce out with long fangs and reaching claws!

Mam . . . Mam . . . why aren't you here? Where's the secrets box with all the lovely princesses and magic castles? I don't want to think about nasty, frightening things. An' why did you get another baby? We didn't want another after our Peter! I loved our Peter. I didn't want him to go away . . .

Everybody had been a baby once. It was hard to think about that. To imagine that Mam and Dad and Mrs Perkins-next-door, who was so old that her face had shrivelled up all scribbly, and Auntie Bea and Uncle Sam . . . people so big and clever . . . had once been small, helpless babies like their Peter. They must once have waited their turn for a Mam and Dad. Waited in the rainbow garden where the sun never stopped shining and the butterflies with soft powdery wings guarded them and birds sang for them and the air was full of lovely smells like when Mam baked bread or when you sniffed the yellow rosebush in the backyard after it had rained.

Even Tom must once have been a baby.

But he couldn't have come from the same place as our Peter! Tom was an orphan, any road. He didn't properly belong to Auntie Bea and he'd never had a Mam and Dad. It was only because he worked with Uncle Sammy at the mill down by the river and Auntie Bea had room now her girls were married that they'd took him in as a lodger. Orphans like Tom couldn't never have come from anywhere nice because a Mam and Dad hadn't taken him in. The place where he'd come from could only be nasty. Black as night when the moon didn't shine and full of nettles and squirmy slimy slugs and bugs and soot and smelling like the gas works or the privy when it needed emptying . . .

A board creaked. She burrowed further under the sheets, hugging them so tightly about her head that the little pocket of air under the bedclothes grew stale and beads of sweat broke out on her face. Oh, why didn't Clara come to bed? The old witch in the cockloft was moving about already. Perhaps they'd forgotten the time downstairs. It must be long after half past eight. Nearly midnight.

The creak came again. She squeezed her eyes shut, gasping now, but not daring to raise the sheet an inch to let in fresh air in case . . . in case the someTHING she feared spied her through the gap and put its evil face close and hooked her out with a bony talon.

Mam, Mam, where are you?

She didn't want to think about the cockloft, but her thoughts crept like disobedient mice up and up. Through the ceiling, into the dusty, musty, beetly, spidery space under the slates . . .

Mam! The secrets box! I can't open the lid. I can't see the nice magic things. And the old witch'll get me any minute! I know it. Tom said . . .

And suddenly, blissfully, the picture was there behind her screwed up eyelids. Mam, laughing, reaching out with a gentle hand to touch her hair, to draw her onto her lap, as she always did.

'There, there, love. Nobody's going to hurt you. I'm here. And look, here's the box, just as it always was. Made of silver and gold and precious stones. Shall we open it and see if there's a story inside, waiting to be told? I'll just lift the lid . . . and look, Lizzie, look! There's the cockloft – no, don't be afraid – see, it's not like you thought it would be. There are fireflies and stars glowing everywhere like tiny lanterns. And can you see who's there in the corner, seated on a downy couch of angel's feathers? It's not a witch, is it? It's a princess – no, a queen! She's wearing a diamond crown, and a dress woven from cobwebs and moonbeams and there are sapphires and emeralds braided into her long black hair. And you know what, Lizzie, love? She's come there specially all the way from a magic land far, far away beyond the icy mountains of the North Pole just so as to watch over you and keep you safe as long as you're at your Auntie Bea's.'

'Oh, Mam,' she breathed. 'I can see her and she's smiling – an' she's beautiful and kind.'

"Course she is. Would I let anything ugly and horrible like a wicked old witch near my good little Lizzie? Now, remember, love, while I'm not with you you must be brave . . .' Mam's hold slackened. Lizzie could see that she was going sort've shimmery, fading. She felt the touch of her mother's lips against her hair. 'We'll be together again soon. Put your trust in The Shadow Queen. She'll not let harm come to you.'

'But the baby, Mam,' Lizzie cried. 'I wanted to ask you about it . . .'

'Joseph, that's what he's to be called.' Her mother's voice was faint as a whisper. 'You're the very first . . . the first to know . . .'

The very first to know

The words sang in Lizzie's head. She smiled as she slept.

She woke the next morning with the usual sinking feeling that Saturday brought.

At home she loved Saturday and Sunday. No horrible school when she might be picked out by Miss to spell a word or do a sum with the whole class watching. She could play hopscotch or bowl her wooden hoop in the street. Or perhaps Mam would take her into town ever so late to look for bargains in the market when all the lights were fizzing on the stalls and the prices were knocked down to get rid of stuff before the market packed up. And Mam said there was no need for anyone to go to chapel more than once on Sunday. They'd sometimes spend the whole afternoon in the park listening to the band. Or friends would come for tea and there'd be special things to eat like ham and seed cake.

It was different at Auntie Bea's. There was a lot of work to be done on Saturday. On Saturday everywhere had to be extra clean in readiness for Sunday. Lizzie was always given the ornately carved legs of the heavy table and chairs to polish before she was sent out with Clara to do the errands. 'And no skimping, mind, or you'll do them over again,' Auntie Bea said, in her sharp voice. Sunday meant stiff clothes, chapel three times and listening to Uncle Sammy read stories from the Bible with long words she didn't understand. Her picture books were put away and she wasn't even allowed to take Ruby to chapel like she did at home. 'It's not seemly,' was Auntie Bea's final judgement as she rammed a hat pin into her black straw hat. 'And it's no use trying tears on wi' me, Lizzie. I'm not soft as duck muck like your Mam, so put your

face straight and get on out.' She would feel the hard prod
of Auntie Bea's finger between her shoulder blades, but that
didn't hurt nearly as much as leaving poor Ruby all alone
and pining in her best frock when Lizzie knew Ruby *wanted*
to go out.

But worse than all these things was the fact that Tom was
at home. At dinner time on Saturday he and Uncle Sammy
came up the valley road from the mill. He'd be grinning or
whistling and as soon as he saw Lizzie he'd shout, 'Watch
out little 'un. Tom's back. I've got me eye on you, so don't
you get up to no mischief.' And though Uncle Sam would
laugh and ruffle her hair as though what Tom said was no
more than a joke, Lizzie felt fear shiver up her spine. Tom's
grin never reached his eyes. She knew his jolly words really
meant *Watch out, I'm going to get you. And when I do it'll be the
worse for you, little brat.*

Though she did her best to keep out of his way at
weekends, he was right crafty. He knew just when to
sneak up on her and wrench off the big white bow that
fastened her plait and throw it into the brambles, so that
she got herself all scratched finding it and a telling-off from
Auntie Bea into the bargain for losing it in the first place. He
knew exactly how and where to pinch her arms and legs with
his big rough fingers so that it hurt most and showed least.
And he knew how much it terrified and pained her when he
tortured her lovely Ruby. Rudely lifting her skirts to show
her drawers, pulling her hair so hard that some of the fine
yellow strands came out of the china scalp, snatching her
from Lizzie's arms and whirling her round by her leather
foot until her boot came off and she pitched into the muddy
ground.

Lizzie knew better than to run to Auntie Bea. 'Can't do wi'
mardy babies,' was all the sympathy she got. 'Got to learn to
take a bit o' teasin' else you'll grow up wi'out any backbone.
Now get from under me feet . . .'

This morning Lizzie lay in bed and tried to recall the warm
comforting feeling she'd had last night when Mam had talked
to her, *'Put your trust in the Shadow Queen.'* Last night she'd
been so certain, so relieved, that it wasn't a witch in the
cockloft but a beautiful and kind lady who would watch
over her. Last night she hadn't been afraid at all. Now she

stared up at the whitewashed ceiling and felt the tendrils
of fear creeping back like a clinging unpleasant mist. Tom
was as real and big and solid as Johnson's bull. She could
reach out and touch the both of them if she dared. They
could certainly touch her. Harm her. The Shadow Queen
might be as brave and beautiful as Mam said, but she was
elusive, like the secret box. It was difficult to imagine the
storyworlds of the secret box when Mam wasn't there.
Perhaps it was the same with The Shadow Queen, Perhaps
her magic only worked after dark, when Mam was talking,
whispering, holding her safe.

All her certainties fled as the morning wore on. Clara was
full of herself which made everything worse. Auntie Bea
was letting her help with the baking. She whisked butter
and sugar in a bowl with a wooden spoon, her face almost
as red as her hair. 'Have you done the dusting properly?'
she asked in the same sharp tone as Auntie Bea when Lizzie
wandered into the kitchen.

'It's not fair,' Lizzie said sulkily, 'me havin' to do your
dustin' as well as me own.'

'Nowt in this life's fair,' snapped Auntie Bea, straightening
up from the oven with a great, brown crusted pie. She laid it
on the table and stared at it in satisfaction. A smell of savoury
steam filled the kitchen. 'Sooner you learn that Lizzie, the
better. Now while Clara finishes that you can go to Johnson's
for a dozen eggs.'

'By meself?'

'It's nowt but a cock stride.' She lifted a basket down from
its hook on a black beam. "Sides you can look out for your
Uncle and Tom and tell 'em to get a move on or their dinner'll
be spoilt . . . And you'll need two hands, so don't go taking
that doll.'

Lizzie took the basket. If it hadn't been a Saturday she'd
have felt important going to the farm by herself. Not that
she had any intention of going alone. Away from Auntie
Bea's eagle eye she snatched up Ruby from where she'd
been sitting on the step taking the air because of the Bad
Head she'd woke with and hid her in the basket. Perhaps if
she was very quick she'd be there and back before she saw
Tom . . .

She ran into the lane. She could see almost all its empty

length from here. It wriggled like a dusty grey worm down the hill, between the drystone walls that marked Farmer Johnson's fields, past the farmhouse, then down to the village, across the river by a humpy bridge and on to the big square block of the mill.

She ran as fast as she could down towards the farm, it was only as she turned the last corner that she saw Tom trudging towards her.

Alone. Oh, no! Uncle Sammy must've stopped as he sometimes did for a glass of stout at the Red Lion and there was Tom an evil grin splitting his face when he saw her. He began to run.

She stopped dead, then in a mad panic flew for the wall and climbed over it into the field. The grass was tussocky. She stumbled so that Ruby nearly fell out of the basket. It wasn't far. She only had to get down the field, through the open gate and she was in the farm-yard. She'd be safe in the farmyard. Mrs Johnson would be sure to be about or Farmer Johnson or one of his men.

'Eh you! Come 'ere!' Tom was thudding after her. He had long strong legs that could eat up the ground. She could almost feel his breath on the back of her neck, his hands reaching out for her . . .

'Mam, Mam,' she screamed in her head. 'He's going to get me.'

'Remember what I told you, The Shadow Queen will keep you safe.'

The words floated into Lizzie's mind, calm and sure . . . And, suddenly, there she was! The Shadow Queen. Drifting across the grass, like a stray pearly moonbeam in the mellow autumn sunlight. Fragile, indistinct as a wisp of mist, her jewelled garments billowing and fading, her long hair streaming behind her like black watery silk.

'Don't be afraid, Lizzie. He won't hurt you.' Her voice was comfortable, gentle, a bit like Mam's. Lizzie felt a cool incandescence drift around her. It was like being masked in dappled shade when the day was too hot. The thought sprung into her head. 'I mustn't run. You can't run away from people like Tom.' She stopped so suddenly that Tom almost cannoned into her.

'You daft beggar!' he yelled, his boots slithering as they fought for purchase on the damp grass.

'Stop followin' me,' she said, her voice sounding thin and pitifully squeaky, even though she was trying to be brave.

The field stretched round them. Empty. Useless. She thought she could hear voices, shouting. Down in the yard, perhaps. Farmer Johnson's men. Too far away to save her . . .

Tom thrust his face down to hers. His eyes were piggy little slits. He bared his teeth. 'Ah'll follow you if I feel like it. An I'll do this if I feel like it.' He caught the soft flesh of her cheek between his rough nails and squeezed tightly. 'And this.' He released her and made a grab at Ruby hanging perilously over the basket's edge. She swung the basket away, her cheek stinging so that tears came to her eyes.

'Aye, I'll mek you cry,' he sneered. 'Nobody to run to 'ere, is there? Nobody to *see* . . .'

'There is!' she cried. 'There is, right 'ere. An' . . . an' she'll punish you . . . 'cos she's magic . . .!'

He chuckled evilly. 'Magic, eh? Come on then. Show me.'

She stood very still, staring past him. She felt suddenly very peaceful, very secure. It was happening. The Shadow Queen was going to rescue her. It was like Mam said. She'd had no need to be afraid.

'What yer starin' at? What's that racket?' Tom's head swivelled round. She'd thought of the worst thing that could happen to Tom. Now it was about to happen and she would watch and be glad because of all the nasty things he'd done to her and to Ruby.

'Oh, help . . .'

Tom looked about wildly.

'It's a punishment,' she said, calmly taking Ruby out of the basket and settling her in the crook of her arm so she could watch too. 'You're to be punished. That's the magic.'

'T' bull's out!' Tom screamed. 'And t'gate's open . . . it's coming this way.'

'It's coming for you,' Lizzie said. 'Me an' Ruby's all right.'

The bull paused in the gate, head down, pawing the ground with its hoof. Behind it men, puny little figures against its angry bulk, ran with ropes and sticks. They waved their arms, shouting to Tom and Lizzie, 'Get out o' t'way! Get over t'wall.'

Lizzie stood. No need for her to go. Tom began to run, mindless of her, thinking only of his own skin. The bull roared, spying the running figure with its evil, bloodshot eye and began to lumber forward.

Tom tripped and fell. His scream seemed to echo up and up towards the clouds, back and forth from the green flanks of the moors. He floundered helpless on the tussocky grass.

'This is what you want, is it Lizzie?' Mam's voice, The Shadow Queen's voice, she wasn't sure which. 'There'll be no rainbow garden for him, remember.'

'I know,' she said. 'Just a nasty black stinky place. Which he deserves.'

'Well?'

The bull was gathering speed, thundering up the field towards the shrieking flapping object on the ground. The thing that it instantly hated with all its angry, frustrated heart.

The question hovered. Lizzie felt the power of it surging in her veins. She had an odd feeling of detachment. Of standing apart watching herself, the bull, the frightened boy on the grass as though all three were frozen, unmoving, waiting for her to give the answer. The right answer.

And flowing between them, the shimmering form that curled and wreathed and flowed like moonlit water.

Lizzie sighed. 'I don't want him really to be hurt,' she said. 'I don't like anyone being hurt. But he didn't care about hurting me. Or Ruby.'

'He knows no better, Perhaps no one has ever shown him how to be kind, how to love. Will you give him the chance to learn?'

Lizzie considered the boy spreadeagled helplessly on the grass. Not such a big lad, after all. Skinny really, his feet swamped by over-large boots, his legs like thin sticks below his rough cord breeches. Or perhaps in some funny way she herself had grown in the last few moments so that they were more evenly matched in size.

She sighed again. And answered.

Afterwards it was reckoned a miracle. The way the lad picked

himself up and hurled himself over the wall in the nick of
time. The way the bull had slowed to a halt, staring around
in a bewildered sort of way until they'd managed to get ropes
on him and lead him back to the barn, gentle as a lamb now
he'd worked off his bad temper. The way that little lass had
stayed so brave and still.

Only Lizzie knew.

She'd watched fascinated as the ethereal, shadowy drift of
jewelled mist swept across to Tom. She saw how the slim pale
arms had raised him as though he weighed feathers rather
than flesh and bone. And, so swiftly and easily, he'd been
lifted over the wall away from danger.

Once the bull was caught, she went across and climbed
onto the wall. She lifted Ruby to see Tom cowering below,
his face the colour of ash, tears of fright and relief squeezing
from between his pale stubby lashes.

'See, Ruby,' she said, smiling. 'Nothin' to be afraid of, is
there? He's crying just like the new baby that's come to live at
our house. You didn't know he was going to be called Joseph,
did you Tom?'

He's only a poor orphan she thought, calmly. Nobody
really loves him. Not even Auntie Bea and Uncle Sammy.
They only give him house room because they feel sorry for
him and there's no one else to care.

Tom blinked up at her. He looked as bewildered as
the bull.

'What you on about?' he said sullenly, knuckling his eyes
with a grubby fist and scrambling unsteadily to his feet, but
the fire, the threat had gone from him.

She continued to smile at him. She wasn't going to explain
now. There'd be time in the next week or two. Plenty
of time.

Tom turned away, as though her smile somehow defeated
him. He began to walk up the lane, limping, shoulders
bowed against the weight of her victory

It wasn't right, Lizzie thought sadly, that someone should
be as lonely as all that. And she didn't really need what he
needed . . . She was strong enough now, loved and with
love to spare . . .

She stood there lost in thought, her lips moving silently
as though she spoke to herself. And presently drifting away

from her up the lane she saw the jewelled mist that flowed round the indistinct, shimmering figure of a woman. It hung for a moment in Tom's wake, then in a tender, gentle, graceful movement, it wrapped itself protectively around his thin frame.

Tom hesitated, lifting his head, staring round in surprise as though he heard someone call his name. Then he shrugged, squared his shoulders and walked on with a lighter step, while Lizzie skipped away down the field hugging Ruby to her heart.

THE WALDTEUFEL AFFAIR

Brian Mooney

Brian Mooney is a Customs Officer in Wales. Although not prolific, his short stories have appeared in Fantasy Tales, Dark Voices 5, Final Shadows, London Mystery Selection *and* The 21st Pan Book of Horror Stories, *amongst others.*

'*ACH, scheiss!*'

Slightly winded, Willi Becke pulled himself to an awkward sitting position and aimed a feeble kick at the root which had sent him sprawling to the ground. His hand reached for his jacket pocket, guided by instinct, and he cursed again when he found it empty. '*Wo ist es?*' he muttered, scrabbling his hands through the dirt of the forest floor. After several frantic seconds he felt the familiar shape of the schnapps bottle and with a sigh of relief he unscrewed the cap to take two or three long swallows.

Grunting with effort, he pulled himself to his feet and stuffed the bottle into his pocket. He swayed and staggered, bleary eyes peering about into the twilight to orientate himself. Day was fading quickly and a thin, patchy mist crept from the soil. The forest could be bad at night, filled with hidden hazards even for one who had spent his whole life in the region.

Got to get home, such as it was. In for another nagging tonight, he shouldn't wonder. In for naggings every *verdammt* night, the way it had been for years. First his wife and then, after *her* death, his daughter – daughter, ha! She'd been born old, that one. She acted more like his blasted mother. And people wondered why he drank. Willi stopped for another pull of Steinhäger before lurching onwards.

'Better hurry,' he grumbled, 'Else *der Waldteufel* will catch

me. He sniggered at himself. Fancy believing old myths like
that. Still, one could never tell. He stumbled, falling against
a small tree, and his shirt was soaked by the chilly moisture
dripping from the quivering branches. Snarling at the tree,
Willi lumbered towards a nearby sound, a sound which he
knew to be the rushing water of the small stream which
passed through the forest near to the main Dürckheimerdorf
road. He tottered to a standstill on one slippery bank.

Tugging the bottle from his pocket again, he shook it.
Experience told him that it was about three-quarters empty.
Might as well get it finished now, then *she* won't be able
to take it away. Anyway, the stupid, narrow-minded bitch
didn't know about the bottle hidden in the lavatory cistern,
nor about the other one secreted in the woodpile.

The cap came off the bottle for the last time and was tossed
aside. Willi tilted his head back and drained the fiery spirit.
It was as he lowered the now-empty bottle that he thought
he glimpsed something out of the corner of his eye. He
turned slowly and faced the *thing* which stood, glowering
and malignant, on the far bank of the stream.

'*Du lieber Gott, der Waldteufel!*' gasped Willi.

He stared for a moment, unkempt head shaking numbly.
The Steinhäger bottle fell from nerveless fingers, thudding
to the ground and rolling into the river with a tiny splash.
The old man raised a shaking hand, crossed himself.

The *thing* took a single step forward, halting by the rushing
waters. '*Nein, nein . . .*' Willi whispered as he backed away.
Almost without volition, he started to run, frantic to reach
the road. As he ran, he whimpered like a child.

The old castle known as Schloss Dürckheim was beautiful in
the clear Tyrolean light. A two-storied building of century-
mellowed stone, it was fronted by a great stone-flagged
patio, enclosed in part by a low balustrade, and flanked by
two onion-domed towers. Wide, worn steps descended to a
gravelled carriageway which swept in a slow curve towards
the distant public road. Neat flowerbeds were set at intervals
on the lawns and much farther away could be seen a small,
stone building, formerly a gate-keeper's lodge.

Behind the Schloss were meadows, several hectares in area
and rich with wild summer flowers, which rose gently on

three sides towards the forest covering the lower slopes of
the surrounding mountains. Beyond the tree-line could be
seen the high pastures which in turn gave way to crags, some
still lightly tipped with white.

The day was perfect for the al fresco luncheon which was
taking place on the patio. A number of people sat around a
table which was covered with fine old linen, and sunlight
glinted from polished silverware and priceless Austrian
crystal.

A simple, delicious meal had been served and now the
quiet, efficient housekeeper had departed, leaving the members of the party to relax over coffee. The conversation had
turned somehow to the nocturnal prowlings of an as-yet
unidentified animal which had made several attacks on local
livestock. It seemed to Reuben Calloway that the time was
right for him to interrupt with a provocative question.

'Have any of you stopped to consider that the thing may be
a werewolf?' he asked. Someone dropped a piece of cutlery
which rang upon the stone flags. As faces turned towards
Calloway he raised his glass in silent salute and drained it.

His companions, two men and three women, stared at him.
'A werewolf, Herr Professor?' said Emil Harmer at last.

'A werewolf.' Calloway made an elaborate gesture with
his Turkish cigarette, sketching a fleeting, smoky image of
a muzzle and pointed ears. 'You know, a shape-shifter, a
loup-garou, an unfortunate soul who is transformed into a
ravening beast at the time of the full moon.'

'The moon is barely new,' Harmer pointed out, 'It won't
be full for several weeks yet.'

'Ah yes, that's right,' said Calloway, unabashed, 'May I
help myself to some more of your excellent champagne?' He
reached a huge hand across to the ice bucket.

'I do believe that the Herr Professor is amusing himself at
our expense,' said Frau Hamer, her voice tart, 'An example,
no doubt, of the celebrated British sense of humour. Do you
not agree, Madame Levoisin?'

The dark and elegant Frenchwoman to Calloway's right
shrugged. 'British humour leaves me cold,' she said, 'A
certain type of puerile mind might appreciate it.'

'Putting aside the fantastic and the ridiculous,' continued
Frau Harmer, 'What can the thing be?'

'A very large dog turned feral, perhaps?' suggested her husband, 'Even a wild boar.' He glanced at the pale, blonde girl beside him, as if seeking approval for this idea. 'I believe that occasionally wild boar are seen around the Dürckheimerwald.'

'And how would your wild boar theory account for the savage wounds on the cattle, my dear?' asked Frau Harmer.

He shrugged. 'Wild boar are known scavengers. It could be that the cattle were dead from some other cause, disease, say. A boar – a number of boars even – took advantage of an easy meal.'

The third man at table, who had been listening quietly while he smoked a cigar and sipped a Kirsch, turned a cropped head towards his host. 'An appealing proposal, Herr Harmer,' said Inspector Lohmann, 'But quite wrong, I regret. It's fairly certain that the various animals were alive when attacked and all of the wounds were consistent with those likely to be made by a large carnivore of some kind. The tracks found tend to bear this out. A boar's tusks would inflict a quite different wound and its spoor could not be mistaken for anything else. The exact species of animal has not been established so far, but give us time.'

'Can't you call in a zoological expert from Vienna?' said Harmer, 'Or even Munich, which is so much closer.'

'We are following certain lines of enquiry,' said the policeman with professional vagueness.

Calloway filled his glass yet again. The vintage champagne seemed to have little effect on his massive frame. 'I heard it rumoured that a local man saw the beast,' he commented, 'Can't you get a good description from him?'

Lohmann nodded. 'Willi Becke. The village drunk. He thinks that he saw a forest imp or somesuch.'

'Then he's sure to be unreliable,' said Madame Levoisin. 'He probably sees forest imps every day.'

'He often sees things, *ja*,' admitted Lohmann.

Madame Levoisin shivered theatrically. 'Whatever it turns out to be, let's hope it's not rabid.'

'Have you no romance in your soul, Madame?' said Harmer, 'Don't worry about rabies, enjoy the enigma of an unknown creature, think of the little frisson it gives to the lives of those who may be affected. You have mystery beasts in Britain, don't you, Herr Professor?'

Calloway pulled a battered leather case from his pocket, extracted another flat cigarette. Lighting it, he nodded at Harmer. 'There's the so-called Beast of Exmoor,' he said, 'and there have been some others, in the Scottish Highlands, for instance.'

'But no werewolves, eh, Herr Professor?' asked Inspector Lohmann.

There were some chuckles at Calloway's expense.

'You've said nothing yet, Fräulein von Wohl.' Emil Harmer turned to the pale girl. 'What is your opinion of our uniden-tified forest creature?'

Anna von Wohl turned large eyes towards her questioner. 'I haven't thought much about it,' she whispered. Her full-lipped, scarlet mouth twisted with what could have been distaste.

'Oh, come now, Fräulein, it must be the most interesting thing to have happened in Dürckheimerdorf for many years,' said Harmer. 'You're surely as curious as the rest of us?'

Lovely hands, with long, red-tipped fingers, clenched nervously at a napkin as Anna shook her head. 'I do not like to think of unpleasant things . . . they disturb me . . .'

'But surely – '

'Herr Harmer,' cut in the icy voice of the Frenchwoman, 'Can you not see that Anna does not wish to talk about this matter? She has not been at all well recently and is easily disturbed. It was only with difficulty that I persuaded her to accept your kind luncheon invitation today.'

Harmer reddened and mumbled an apology.

Madame Levoisin lowered her head in fractional acknowl-edgement and then turned to Frau Harmer. 'You will excuse us if we leave now – Anna is tired and I think that she should rest.'

The male guests rose at once, thanking the Harmers for their hospitality. Calloway took a dark cape brought by the houskeeper and held it open for Madame Levoisin. As he helped her he spoke, switching from German to French with ease. 'You will forgive my rudeness, Madame, but through-out our meal I have become more and more convinced that I know you from somewhere. Have we met previously?'

She stared at him, eyes hard and suspicious. 'I think not. It's unlikely that I would forget someone of your . . . remarkable appearance. Good afternoon, Professor Calloway.'

'Truly, an Ice Queen that one,' said a voice at Reuben Calloway's elbow. It was the police inspector. 'You have transport, Herr Professor?'

'No, Harmer is arranging for his chauffeur to drive me to my hotel.'

'Don't bother, please. I have my car here and will gladly take you. Let's just bid farewell and go.'

Lohmann did not speak again until they were on the main Dürckheimerdorf road. Then he said, 'If you are free for the moment, perhaps you would care to join me for a drink and a chat. I know a rather pleasant little beer-garden nearby. I think you'll approve of the brew they serve.'

'A pleasure,' said Calloway. For a few moments he watched the road ahead then added, 'You have an ulterior motive.' It was a statement, not a question.

Without embarrassment, the policeman said, 'Yes.' He took a thin cigar from a box on the dashboard and accepted the light offered by Calloway. 'There is something I wish to discuss, to ask your opinion and perhaps your help. You know, since I've been here, most people have seen me only as a plodding country cop, a man of limited ambition and even more limited intelligence. I don't mind that, it suits my purposes most of the time.'

A thin stream of smoke hissed from between his teeth. 'I'm more aware of what goes on in the world than they give me credit for. For instance, I've always taken a great interest in the bizarre and the unusual, not only in my own country but in others too. I have heard of you, Herr Professor. In certain – shall I say social circles? – you have an enviable reputation for your knowledge of the . . . odd, the outré.'

Lohmann laughed briefly. 'I am not the sort of person the Harmers would normally invite to their table. They are wealthy but *parvenu*. Most summers she likes to rent somewhere with a little class, a little history, so that she can enjoy playing lady of the manor. She's done it in England, France, West Germany. This year she has honoured us.

'Most of their guests have achieved great success or fame or perhaps high social standing. You are an acclaimed scholar

of international repute. I believe that the von Wohl girl is old
blood, she has aristocratic antecedents. The Madame is her
house-guest, so by implication worth cultivating. Me, I'm
nobody, Herr Professor. Ah, here we are.'

He turned into a driveway and stopped the car before a
small *Gasthaus* but made no move to get out. 'When I heard
that you were visiting the village and that you were to be the
Harmers' guest for lunch, I persuaded them that it might
be to their advantage if I was present too. As a quid pro
quo, the small matter of some unpaid parking fines might
be resolved without unpleasantness. So I attended, and at
an appropriate moment, and without too much difficulty,
turned the conversation to the mystery beast. The result . . .
well, you did not disappoint me, my friend.'

'Lohmann, what is your point?' asked Calloway.

'My point, Herr Professor, is that I might just believe your
theory that the unidentified beast is a werewolf.'

'Might you now?'

'Yes.' The inspector lit another cigar. 'Yes, for some days
now I've had the feeling that there is something very
unnatural about this affair.'

Calloway stared appraisingly at his companion and then
nodded. 'In that case, Herr Inspektor Lohmann, let's go and
have a beer.'

Lohmann led Calloway to a secluded table in the garden
and ordered two tankards of draught Kaiser from a plump
waitress. When they were alone, he reached into an inner
pocket and produced a sheaf of large, coloured photographs
which he spread across the table. Each one depicted a farm
animal, savagely torn apart.

'These show the first attacks,' he explained, 'As you may
know, in the summer our farmers take their cattle to the
high pastures and leave them until the fall. We began to
get reports of attacks on the cattle about three weeks ago,
and you will see that the injuries inflicted were appalling.
Most of the poor creatures were partly devoured and some
were still alive while being eaten.

'At the outset it was assumed to be wolf predation,
although personally I doubted this. Wolves have been absent
from these parts for many years and anyway, in summer one
would expect there to be sufficient natural prey to satisfy

them. Furthermore, wolves are pack animals – they rarely hunt alone.

'However, hunting parties were sent out, traps were set at the various pastures . . . nothing. The creature, whatever it is, is cunning. It made its attacks in places where there were no guards, or where the hunting parties had checked and moved on. Then one morning after there had been rain, we found tracks in mud at the tree-line.'

Lohmann brought out a further set of photographs, large and clear monochrome prints, and passed them to Calloway.

The pictures were numbered progressively and Calloway laid them out in order. The first few showed what appeared to be paw marks, with clearly delineated pads and claws but in the sixth frame there was a change. A little way past the final pugmark were several odd, half-moon indentations.

Lohmann pointed to the odd marks. 'At this point the ground was turning rocky. The tracks were becoming incomplete and eventually faded out.'

Calloway took a small magnifying glass from one bulging pocket of his shabby jacket and peered at the prints. 'Any sizes?' he grunted.

A stubby forefinger indicated two prints. 'That one is seventeen-and-a-half centimetres in length, and that one is twenty-five.'

'Rather long paws for a wolf, I'd guess,' said Reuben Calloway.

'And what do you make of those, my friend?' said Lohmann, pointing to the photograph with the peculiar half-moon marks.

Again Calloway scrutinized the picture carefully through his magnifier. 'It could almost be part of a naked human heel,' he said at last, 'A pity that the ground grew too hard at that point. Any particular territorial pattern to the attacks, Lohmann?'

The policeman dug into another pocket and unfolded the map he took from it. It was of the local region and was heavily annotated with black marker-pen.

'These crosses mark the places of attack. The thick lines join the points of the furthermost attacks and give an area of about five kilometres square. Now here –' Lohmann pointed, '– here at the river is where Willi Becke had his fright.'

'What did he claim to have seen?'

Lohmann offered a cigar to Calloway who shook his head brusquely. 'We must make certain allowances. It was almost dark at the time of the sighting, and Becke had at least a bottle-full of schnapps inside him. And when I questioned him he was almost incoherent with terror. He claims to have seen what appears to have been a quadruped, perhaps a metre or so high at the shoulder and covered with a coarse, darkish hair. He said that its eyes were fiery red and he mentioned immense fangs.'

Calloway smiled. 'That could almost be a description of Harmer's hypothetical wild boar.'

'Agreed.'

'Any tracks found there?'

'Nothing useful. This is a small mountain river. On Becke's side the ground was soft and grassy, and there are plenty of signs of his blundering around and making a panicky flight. There was an empty Steinhager bottle in the river at that spot. The other bank is more rocky with only a few clumps of plants. There were indications that something had been there, but nothing substantial.'

Calloway took out his worn cigarette case. 'So the river was between them – is it swift?'

'Normally, yes. It runs downhill and after rain it can be torrential.'

'I see.' Calloway fired his lighter, held it to his cigarette. 'Madame Levoisin was convinced that Becke was seeing things. What's your opinion about that?'

'I think he's telling the truth. Becke is an habitual drunkard and he's often had the DTs while a guest in our cells. They usually last a long time, at least until he passes out. If his forest creature had been an hallucination it would probably have pursued him all the way into town. As it is, Becke is sure that it did not follow him.'

'And could it have been a wild boar, do you think?'

Lohmann considered briefly. 'It's just possible,' he admitted, 'But I doubt it. Like wolves, wild boar are in short supply around here. This is tourist country, not a hunter's paradise. We have walkers and climbers in the summer, winter sports when the snow falls. Wild animals are adverse to such conditions – they tend to move away to less populated places.'

He gestured towards the map. 'Take another look at the marked area. Notice anything in particular?'

Calloway did as bid and nodded. 'The Schloss is almost exactly central in the square.' He indicated a minute, black square. 'And this will be the gatehouse. I believe that's where Madame Levoisin and the Fräulein are staying.'

Abruptly, Lohmann changed the subject. 'Tell me, Professor Calloway, why are you here in Dürckheimerdorf?'

Calloway's smile did not show in his flint-grey eyes. 'I suspect you know exactly why I'm here. I'm researching a book on the occult in European history. Certain primary sources have been made available to me in Salzburg and this area has some relevance to my work.'

'The Graf Helmut von Dürckheim,' said Lohmann and at Calloway's nod added, 'Tell me what you know of him.'

The Englishman shrugged. 'Very briefly, von Dürckheim was a fifteenth-century nobleman, an alchemist and an alleged witch. He built the original Schloss and became the feudal lord of this part of the Tyrol. Legend has it that Satan gave to him the one true secret of total power over the world, a knowledge said to be so terrifying that von Dürckheim could not bring himself to use it. This secret was thought to have been cached somewhere in the environs of the Schloss but it was never found. There have been many assiduous searchers, including the Nazis, but to no avail.'

'Are you interested in von Dürckheim's arcane knowledge, Herr Professor?'

'Good lord, no! I'm a scholar, not a politician. Oh, it would be academically interesting, but any gift from Satan would be sure to have a nasty sting in the tail.'

Calloway stubbed out his cigarette and immediately lit another. Generous quantities of ash were scattered about his clothing. With an abrupt movement, he stood and, watched by Lohmann, stalked about the garden, beer-krug in hand. After several minutes, he returned to examine again the collection of photographs.

Then he said, 'You think that the mystery beast may be a werewolf, you seem to think that the Schloss and my research may have some bearing on the matter, and you believe that together we may be able to reach a solution.'

Lohmann's nod was almost imperceptible.

'You are a very unusual policeman, Inspector,' said Calloway.

'So I have been told before, Herr Professor. It's the main reason for my not having reached a higher rank. It's also one of the reasons that I was sent here a year ago. Still, I have no regrets about that. Can I count on your help?'

Reuben Calloway extended a big hand for the Austrian to shake. 'It will be a pleasure, my friend, if only for the unique experience of working with an open-minded police officer. Now, I am committed to an appointment in Salzburg tomorrow but I will come to see you on my return – I should be here by about six pm.'

Lohmann nodded his thanks. He stood up, drained his tankard and then remarked, 'It's a pity I'm not psychic, I could possibly have solved this problem weeks ago.'

Calloway grunted, 'That's it!' He saw Lohmann's puzzlement and explained. 'I've just recalled where I met, or rather saw, the Levoisin woman before. It's unimportant. I attended a public séance in London, about a year ago, where a so-called psychic was showing off his powers. A charlatan, of course. Madame was in the audience. She had the look of one who wanted to believe.'

As the two men were leaving the beer-garden, the professor turned suddenly. 'One last question – were any of the attacks made during the period of the full moon?'

'Some were, others not. The puzzle doesn't exactly fit the legends, does it, Herr Professor?'

'No,' said Calloway, 'I'm afraid not.'

With a murmured '*Bitte schön*', Frau Ebel placed the after-dinner coffee on Calloway's table. As she gathered up empty dishes she said, 'An enjoyable lunch today, was it?'

'Excellent,' said Calloway. He lifted his cup and sipped. 'And so is your coffee, Frau Ebel.'

The woman smirked. 'The temporary housekeeper at the Schloss is my sister-in-law, a good cook. Forgive me, Herr Professor, but we're both proud at the moment. Two celebrities in the village and we have one each.'

'Two celebrities?'

'Of course, yourself and the Herr Harmer.'

'Herr Harmer, perhaps. I'd hardly consider myself a celebrity. Anyway, during the ski-ing season you must have a surfeit of real celebrities here.'

Frau Ebel shook her head. 'Most film stars and their like prefer the grander places. Our trade here is mostly package tourists. Perhaps no bad thing, they are not as rich but neither are they as demanding.'

Calloway lit a Turkish cigarette. 'You've forgotten Fräulein von Wohl and Madame Levoisin.'

She sniffed. 'Levoisin? Who knows who she is? As for the Fräulein, I can't think of her as a celebrity. After all, she is one of us – from the village, you understand. As a matter of fact, she owns the Schloss rented by the Harmers.'

'I didn't know that,' admitted Calloway.

'Oh yes, Herr Professor, the von Wohls were related to the von Dürckheims. When they died out, the von Wohls inherited. Fräulein Anna is the last one.'

Calloway poured another coffee. 'I take it she's always lived at the gatehouse?'

'No, only since the Levoisin woman arrived early this summer. Before that the Fräulein had a small apartment here in the village. The von Wohls were never very wealthy, and in recent years their income has derived mainly from renting the Schloss to summer visitors.' Frau Ebel sneered a little. 'Mostly *nouveau riche* acquiring a patina of class. The Fräulein, now, such a nice girl, and yet what a change since the arrival of the Frenchwoman.'

'Change? What manner of change?'

'Anna was always quiet, yet very pleasant. Now she seems to be both nervous and stand-offish, won't talk to her old friends. Madame arrived from nowhere to stay with her, insisted that the apartment was too small for two persons, which is a nonsense, and they moved to the gatehouse. That was – let me see – about two weeks after the Harmers took residence.'

Calloway sat in a museum reading-room, enjoying the warmth of sunlight on his back. Had he turned to gaze out through the tall windows behind him he would have seen a panorama of the city, split by the Salzach with its many bridges, spread out before him. Beyond the Salzach was the Kapuzinerberg with its famous ski-jump and the streets were busy with both commercial and tourist traffic.

The table in front of Calloway was littered with a medley of books and documents. An assistant librarian, laden with several heavy files, approached the big professor quietly.

'The other papers you requested, Herr Professor.'

'Thank you.'

The man gave a gentle cough. 'If you will forgive my impertinence, Herr Professor, the subject of your research must suddenly have become of very great interest. These papers have remained undisturbed for many years and yet you are the second person within a month to work on them.' ·

'Indeed?' Calloway put down his fountain pen and leaned back in his chair, stretching to ease himself. 'Would you by any chance know the identity of the other person?'

'I'm sorry, no. I did not attend her personally.'

'Her, you say?'

'Why, yes, Herr Professor, it was a woman. Very tall, dark brown hair, elegantly dressed. Very chic. I only heard her say a few words as I was passing, but I think she was a foreigner. Her spoken German, like your own, was excellent but there was a slight accent – not British though, possibly French. I do hope that her purpose is not the same as your own. To have important work pre-empted is most annoying.'

Calloway smiled briefly as he prepared to resume work. 'I will have to take that risk,' he told the man.

'Oh, one trouble I can save you, Herr Professor. We do not have the clandestine diary amongst the von Dürckheim papers.' He started to move away.

'Wait!' snapped Calloway, 'What do you mean, the clandestine diary?'

'You may not have come across the reference yet, Herr Professor, but the Graf mentions his clandestine diary a number of times. Our understanding was that all of the Graf's papers had been passed to the museum, but that is one item not catalogued. The French lady was very keen to see it and was apparently most piqued that we do not have it.'

'You know,' said Calloway, 'I think it might be a very good idea if I had a word with your colleague who attended the lady.'

It was about 5.30 pm, when Calloway alighted at the
Dürckheimerdorf station and he was immediately hailed
from the far end of the platform. A uniformed police officer
came running towards him.

'Herr Professor, the Inspector has sent me to fetch you to
the Schloss. The beast has attacked Frau Harmer.'

'In broad daylight?'

'Yes, sir. The Frau was not injured but she is in shock and
has been taken to the hospital at St Andreas.'

By the time they arrived at the Schloss, the blue sky was
marred by storm clouds like viscous whorls of oil-paint and
Calloway guessed that there would soon be one of the cloud-
bursts typical of this mountainous country. Lohmann was
waiting for them together with a pale-visaged Harmer. The
inspector beckoned Calloway towards the Schloss entrance
and pointed.

There were a dozen or so long, deep gouges in the thick
door, as if gigantic claws had ripped at it in frustration.
Shreds and splinters of wood were scattered about the steps,
while much further down, the gravel path showed signs of
considerable disturbance for some distance.

'Frau Harmer?' said Calloway.

'Unscathed but sedated and in hospital,' whispered Harmer.
He looked as if he, too, could use sedation. 'I will be leaving
here this evening. I'll stay in an hotel at St Andreas and take
my wife away in the morning.'

'Do you know what happened?'

Lohmann stepped forward. 'As far as we can make out,
the Frau was some two or three hundred metres from the
house, gathering flowers. The thing came out of those far
woods and went for her. She made the Schloss just in time
and was able to slam the door in its face. You see the result.
She was lucky.'

'Yes, wasn't she?' Something in Calloway's voice, an
element of doubt, perhaps, made Lohmann smile.

Leaving the patio, Calloway walked down past the flowerbeds, part way to the forest edge and back again, all the time
studying the ground. Harmer slumped, still stunned, against
the balustrade, while Lohmann watched the professor with
smiling patience.

'Did you see the creature, Harmer?' asked Calloway as he
remounted the steps.

'A glimpse, that's all, through the dining-room window.'

'Describe it, please.'

'What?' cried Harmer, 'Good God, man, I was far too
worried about my wife to take a description.'

'Don't be foolish,' said Calloway, 'If you glimpsed it, you
must got some kind of impression.'

'Very well, just an impression. Large, dark hair, that's
about all. I tell you this, it was fast. It regained the forest
in a blink.'

Early, spattering drops of rain gave notice of what was
to come and thunder grumbled gently behind the distant
mountain range. 'I for one am not going to stay here and
get wet,' announced Calloway, 'Harmer, you have made the
right decision. Pack and leave here now! I suggest that you
dismiss the housekeeper and pay her well. Lohmann, I want
a word with you – I'll wait in your car. You can send your
men back to their normal duties, they'll accomplish nothing
by standing around. All understood? Good!'

When Lohmann reached his car, Calloway was already
seated, enveloped in a fug of Turkish tobacco smoke. He
said nothing until he finished his cigarette, then, 'A test for
you, Lohmann – what was peculiar about that attack?'

The policeman grinned. 'I knew you'd spot it, even if
Harmer didn't. There's an excuse for him, but none of my
men spotted the flaw, either. If the attack had been genuine,
Frau Harmer should be dead. Over that distance, it would
take an amazing human to beat a racing animal of that size.
And Harmer did say it was fast.'

'Precisely. And this suggests . . .'

'That the intention was to terrify, not to injure.'

'Good. I noticed that some people were missing out
there.'

'You mean Madame and the von Wohl girl. Yes, it's odd
that they should be so incurious about all the excitement.
Madame's car is there, so they're not away.'

'That's what I thought,' said the big man, 'Now, I want to
show you something.'

He rummaged in an inside pocket and handed Lohmann
a small slip. 'What do you make of that?'

It was a piece of tracing-paper, cut in the shape of a face and with pencilled-in features. It was darkening rapidly outside and Lohmann switched on the roof light. 'It's almost . . . lupine . . .' he suggested.

Calloway's face was impassive. 'That's just part of it,' he said, lighting another cigarette, 'See anything else?'

Lohmann continued to study the paper. A long moment, then he said, 'It looks a little like Madame Levoisin – in fact the more I look, the more obvious it becomes.'

'Now turn the paper and look at it from the other side.'

Lohmann did as he was bid, toying with one of his thin cigars. 'Yes, of course. It's like a mirror-image. Strange I never noticed when they were together. Style, colouring maybe. What is this thing, anyway?'

'I took a tracing from a one of the documents I was working with today. It's from a contemporary woodcut of the first Graf Helmut von Dürckheim. There was also a little comment, an aside almost, in a letter from a contemporary local scribe to a friend, just a piece of gossip.

'Now, where's my notebook. Ah, here . . . now listen to this, Lohmann. ". . . [about our local lord], *es geht das Gërucht, er Werwolf ist* (rumour has it that he's a werewolf) . . .'

'To change the subject, Lohmann, how do you feel about burglary, or should I say an unofficial search without warrant?'

Lohmann laughed. 'Why not, I've put my head far enough on the block already. Where do we go?'

'Not now, tomorrow morning. Do you have any contacts in Salzburg, some person you can trust without question?'

'My brother-in-law – we were boyhood friends.'

'Good, phone him this evening, ask him to send a telegram as late as he can but without despatch being postponed until tomorrow. It's to Madame Levoisin and it's to purport to come from the Alt Museum. It must read: "Missing diary found. Will hold until noon before notifying Calloway." Sign it as from Linz, the Chief Librarian.'

'Suppose she calls the museum to check authenticity?'

'That's a chance we take. I think she'll be too eager to get there for opening time. Now you can drive me to my hotel. I am going to take a bath and fill myself with *Wienerschnitzel* and *Kirschetorte*.'

The search of the gatehouse was disappointing. Other than for necessary furniture, the place was oddly bare.

Calloway and his companion had arrived at about six in the morning and their vehicle was parked so that they would have a good view of the building while themselves remaining unseen. Lohmann had brought a huge flask of coffee well-laced with Sliwowitz and the two breakfasted on tobacco, each according to his personal taste.

At a few minutes before eight, the front door of the gatehouse had opened and Madame Levoisin had emerged, almost dragging behind her an ill-looking and seemingly reluctant Anna von Wohl. She pushed the girl into the passenger seat of her car and within a few minutes they were gone, the sound of their engine fading quickly.

'That poor girl looked wretched,' Lohmann had observed as he locked his door. 'I know that it suits our purpose, but I wonder why Madame took her to Salzburg.'

'I don't think she'll want Anna out of her sight,' said Calloway.

The solid front door was firmly locked but the back door was altogether different, being flimsy and with an old-fashioned tenon lock. 'Typical,' sighed the policeman, taking a large ring filled with an assortment of keys from his raincoat pocket.

'I'm glad you thought of those,' grinned Calloway, holding up a slim wallet. 'It saves me having to use my set of burglary picks.'

The fifth key worked and they entered the lodge through the kitchen, which was simple and functional. As well as the kitchen, the ground floor comprised a wood-panelled sitting-room and a small hallway. The sitting-room contained only a dining-table with several matching chairs and two easy chairs positioned one on either side of the fireplace. The wooden floor was bare.

The upper floor was reached via a steep and narrow stair-way. Three doors opened from a square landing, one into a bathroom, the others into two bedchambers, one slightly larger than the other. Calloway gave the bathroom a cursory glance and then entered the smaller of the bedrooms.

Like the rest of the lodge, it was no more than functional.

It contained a narrow bed with a duvet, a wardrobe and a chest of drawers. Calloway glanced first into the wardrobe and then rummaged quickly through the drawers. He found only a few items of clothing. The top of the chest was empty, containing nothing decorative or personal, nor was there any mirror.

He and Lohmann moved quickly into the second chamber and found the furnishings to be identical to those of the first, with the exception of a low bedside table. Calloway opened the wardrobe. 'This is Madame's room,' he told Lohmann. 'I recognize the cape.'

With care, the inspector slid open the drawer in the bedside table. 'There's something here, Calloway,' he called. 'Seems to be some kind of fashion belt or girdle. There's a book, too.'

The belt was a wide one, and was covered with a coarse, grey hair. There was a curious, locking clip on the buckle and a handle-like retaining groove at one end. Calloway examined the belt closely then gave a curt nod.

'What an ugly thing,' said Lohmann, 'Fashion can be so damned crazy.' He shrugged. Having passed the belt to Calloway, he had opened the book and looked puzzled. 'I can't make anything of this, Herr Professor,' he added, 'It's printed in what looks like Greek. Any ideas?'

Calloway took the volume and quickly scanned through the pages. 'Ah yes, that's very interesting.' He said nothing more, ignoring the policeman's expectant look. Instead, he indicated that Lohmann should replace the items in the drawer as found, then he headed for the staircase.

By the time that Lohmann had checked the lodge for tidiness, Calloway was outside, smoking a cigarette as he waited. 'A soulless place,' the inspector commented as he refastened the door, 'Most people, even temporary visitors, leave some kind of imprint on a house, but that was . . . well, it was almost like an operating theatre, it was so clinically neat. A waste of time, wasn't it, although I've no idea what you expected to find anyway.'

'On the contrary, it's told me quite a lot.' Calloway looked smug, self-satisfied.

Lohmann sighed, exasperated. 'Do I have to beg you to tell me what you've found out?'

The Englishman grinned. 'Better not, I could be wrong even yet. But I do think that we can end this matter by tonight.'

'And in the meantime?'

'For me, nothing except perhaps a leisurely afternoon in a beer-garden. For you, I expect you have other duties to keep you busy. There is one thing you can do for me, though. Get someone to phone the Alt Museum – Madame Levoisin should be arriving there very soon – and leave a message that she has been the victim of a hoax, perpetrated by myself. The anonymous caller is to suggest that I have discovered what she wants, and I am going to the Schloss after dark tonight to claim it for myself . . .'

Calloway and Lohmann made their way towards the shadowy bulk of the Schloss, walking on grass rather than gravel so that they made no noise. The night was fine and warm, and a gentle breeze caressed their faces, bringing with it sweet night scents. The sky above them was dark velvet, with a lighter afterglow limning the black silhouettes of mountains to the west. The Great Bear and its related constellations were splendent overhead and the new moon, a tilted silver crescent, rose in the east.

Calloway stopped, turned his back on the Schloss and pointed to the sky with the thick walking-stick he carried. 'Look at that, Lohmann. Faced with beauty like that, who could doubt the existence of a creator.' His huge chest expanded as he breathed deeply. 'I love this country, it's so clean.'

Lohmann's attitude was more prosaic. 'At least the moon's not full,' he muttered. 'Why the stick, Calloway, you've not used that before?'

'Oh, a touch of rheumatism, nothing to worry about.'

They mounted broad steps to the massive oak doors, where Lohmann turned to the professor. 'You seem to be a practical man, Calloway, and I presume that you've planned on how we get in. None of my keys could cope with these doors.'

Calloway lifted his hand, showing a big iron key. 'Harmer's,' he explained. 'I sent a messenger to St Andreas last night to retrieve it.' From one of his capacious pockets he took a slim flashlight, directing the beam at the keyhole.

The lock was kept well lubricated and the doors swung open with ease.

'I'm so glad that I didn't have to be involved in such business in bygone centuries,' said Calloway as he flicked a light switch, 'Electricity is a great boon in places like the Schloss. I think we'll wait in here.'

The dining-room, into which he led Lohmann, was long and dark-panelled, with a huge fireplace at the end wall to their left. Light came from two ornate chandeliers and the room was dominated by an immense refectory table surrounded by carved, high-backed chairs. The wall to their right was obscured in part by a blackened, antique sideboard, above which were several gloomy oil-paintings.

Calloway investigated the sideboard and produced from its depths a bottle of Martell Cordon Bleu. 'Might as well be comfortable,' he told Lohmann as he poured two generous measures.

They sat at one end of the table and sipped cognac. 'And now?' said Lohmann.

'And now we wait,' replied Calloway.

It had been close to ten o'clock when they had arrived at Schloss Dürckheim. It was almost midnight when they heard the main doors crash back, the intruder caring little for stealth. Calloway motioned Lohmann to stand in the far corner by the sideboard, where he would not be readily visible at the opening of the door. The policeman moved across as bid, making little noise, and as he went he drew an automatic pistol from his pocket.

There were sounds from the corridor, a scrabbling such as would be made by the claws of an eager dog as it sought purchase upon the wooden floor, and there was a guttural snarling. Although no words were clear, the men heard Madame Levoisin's voice rapping orders and then there was a cracking sound followed by whimpering.

With a finger to his lips and a curt shake of the head, Calloway commanded the policeman to silence. Then he took one stride forward and threw open the door. 'Good evening, Madame Levoisin, please do come in.'

She did so, and brought *something* with her.

It took a strong effort on the part of the concealed Lohmann not to cry out with surprised fear. In contrast, Calloway's face showed nothing but an academic interest. He looked almost benevolent as he stood leaning casually on his cane.

'A fine specimen,' he told the Frenchwoman, 'Your first attempt at the ritual or have there been others?'

The woman's creature, restrained from attacking Calloway only by her firm, twisting grip upon the broad leash fastened around its middle, was frightful.

The body was high at the shoulder, sloping down to a tailless rump, and rumbling barks emanated from the deep, broad chest. It was covered with a blackish hair which sprouted in tufts from dark and blotchy skin, covered, that is, except for the legs which were naked and showed the knotted muscles. There were several vicious claws upon each foot and a hideous mouth gaped to show long, drooling fangs. The snout was short and wrinkled, the maddened eyes red, the neck almost non-existent. The thing's ears were small, almost unnoticable, and were round rather than pointed.

It lunged again and again at Calloway, the leash pulling it short each time. Cursing, Madame Levoisin lashed at the creature with a short whip held in her left hand. It yelped with pain and turned to snarl at the woman, whose blows became even more wild and brutal.

'Where's that diary, Calloway?' the woman screamed.

'Oh that,' said Calloway, making a dismissive gesture, 'That doesn't exist. Or if it does, I don't have it. I simply concocted an elaborate charade to test your stupidity level.' His grey eyes hardened. 'You rate very low, Madame.'

She spat at him. 'Hear me, you *cochon*, if you hand the diary to me now, I will let this thing kill you outright. If not, I'll just let it maul you. You know what your fate will be then.'

'Empty threats,' Calloway said, 'Inspector Lohmann's over there pointing a gun at you.'

As her head turned from Calloway he twisted the handle of his cane to draw a long, razor-edged blade which he slashed across the woman hands. She shrieked with pain and shock and lost her grip on the leash. At the feel of slackened pressure, the beast turned and reared up, tearing away the woman's throat with a scything movement of its head. She fell backwards and the thing followed her, snapping and worrying at her body.

Lohmann was moving in, aiming his pistol, but any
attempt at a good shot was foiled by the intervention of
the professor's bulk. Calloway seized the leash and sliced
through it with his sword-blade. The creature's head went
back and it howled, a mournful sound filled with anguish and
terror. It lurched away from the torn corpse and stumbled out
into the hallway. They heard a heavy fall.

Wary, the men stepped into the hall, Calloway placing a
restraining hand over the policeman's weapon. The creature
writhed upon the floor, and as they watched a transmutation
took place. Before them lay the unclad, bruised body of Anna
von Wohl.

The girl raised her head to stare at the men. She crawled to
the wall and dragged herself upright, trying vainly to cover
her body. Her mouth was bloody from the death of Levoisin,
but it was the torment in her eyes that held their gaze.

'You poor child,' said Calloway. He held up the hirsute
leash. 'It was this, wasn't it, this and the book?'

Anna nodded. 'She . . . she tricked me into wearing it . . .
I was . . . helpless against her . . .'

'But you were both losing control? Sometimes it happened
without the belt?'

Again she nodded. 'Help me . . .' she whispered, 'Help
me . . .' She threw back her head and screamed twice.
The first scream was a sound of unrelenting human terror,
the second the dreadful baying of a hunting beast. Then,
fingers crooked like talons, she snarled and threw herself at
Calloway, to be impaled upon the blade of his sword.

The two men sat in Lohmann's car watching the flames
destroying Schloss Dürckheim. Lohmann said, 'You took a
deadly risk back there.'

'Perhaps,' said Calloway, 'I was quite sure that that poor,
tortured creature would turn on Levoisin.'

The policeman sighed. 'Illegal entry, illegal search, two
unlawful killings and now arson. I should feel some guilt,
I suppose.'

'Don't!' said Calloway, blunt as ever. 'You've helped rid
the world of something that shouldn't exist, something that
your laws would not recognize and could not deal with. Anna
had no chance of recovery from this appalling thing.'

He lit a cigarette. 'The irony is that Frau Harmer was right, at that luncheon party I mean. I was indulging in a little drollery at your expense when I suggested a werewolf. It was your appeal for help and those photographs which made me rethink.'

Lohmann reached for his cigar-box, found it to be empty and accepted one of Calloway's pungent cigarettes. 'Tell me how you reasoned it out, Calloway. What did I miss?'

'Nothing really, I just picked up a little gossip that is unlikely ever to have been mentioned to you. That, and some specialized knowledge.' He lit the cigarette for Lohmann, returned his lighter to a side pocket.

'The proprietor of Haus Ebel mentioned to me that Anna von Wohl owned the Schloss. She was a long-time village resident and a von Dürckheim descendant. As a comparative newcomer here you couldn't be expected to know all of that, neither was there reason for anyone to tell you.

'Then a librarian at the Alt Museum told me that Madame Levoisin had been researching the von Dürckheim papers. This and the fact that I had once seen her at a séance suggested that she might have an interest in the occult.'

Calloway fumbled for his wallet and produced the tracing he had made, handing it to Lohmann. 'The resemblance to Madame was strong and then that to Anna became obvious. Despite the difference in ages and colouring, the two women were like mirror-images, which you observed when I first showed you this.'

He reached for another cigarette, lighting it from the stub of the first. 'I think that if we were to enquire deeply enough into the life of Levoisin, we'd find that she was a distant relative of the von Dürckheims. I'd guess that she was probably a bit mad, and very likely considered the legendary secret to be her birthright. She must have researched her family, found that Anna was her only living relative and proceeded from there.'

Calloway wriggled, trying to get comfortable. 'When we searched the gatehouse, two things suggested the truth to me, what we found and what we didn't find.'

Lohmann carefully extinguished his cigarette. 'What we didn't find – the strange behaviour of the dog in the night?'

His companion grinned. 'A good analogy. What we didn't

find was cosmetics. When we lunched with the Harmers, I noticed that Anna von Wohl had exceptionally red lips and fingernails, and yet there was trace of neither lipstick nor nail-varnish among her belongings.'

'Couldn't she have used Madame's make-up?' said Lohmann.

'Their colouring was so different, I think it unlikely. Now, extreme redness of lips and nails can be an indication of werewolf activity, not conclusive but a sign.

'Then we found the belt and the book. Contrary to popular belief, a full moon is not essential for were-change. There are a number of ways in which it can be accomplished, among them using a girdle of animal skin together with an appropriate spell. I think the belt we found was wolfskin. The book was a fourteenth-century printing of the *Lukanthropia of Anaxathes*, a very ancient treatise which includes the spells essential for transformation.'

Calloway rubbed his eyes, shook his head. 'Poor Anna. I daresay that there was a werewolf strain in the family and its by-blows, doubtless starting with Helmut von Dürckheim and probably dormant until triggered. Levoisin recognized the signs in Anna and decided to use the girl. I think the intention was to create such a bad reputation for the Schloss that people would shun the place and then she could seek her ancestor's secret at leisure.'

'And what about the secret?' asked Lohmann.

'If it existed at all, it's probably burning with the Schloss. Good riddance!'

Lohmann reached to switch on the engine. As he set the car in motion he said, 'Tell me, was it really necessary for you to kill Anna von Wohl?'

'I didn't kill her,' said Calloway. 'She committed suicide.'

UP YOURS, FEDERICO*

Parke Godwin

Parke Godwin's recent books include the historical fantasies Sherwood *and* Robin and the King, *plus a science fiction novel,* Limbo Search. *His current projects include a novelization of the narrative poem* Beowulf.

AT four o'clock in the afternoon, exactly four in the afternoon in Chihuahua in the sun-baked clay of Juarez, the Plaza del Toros.

Hurry: it is time for the brave festival, the festival of bulls. *Ai, los toros perdidos*, the lost bulls. So many, their courage scarlet on the sand. The *afición* rents its cushions and eyes the *toril*, the Gate of the Fright, that will expel a ton of death to the clean-raked sand of the ring.

Ai! Listen! Now the clock strikes four. In a strutting thrill of brass, the tinny, booming band strikes up 'La Virgen de la Macarena.' With the rigid march of the matadors in gold and silk, in the suit of lights, with the *cuadrillas* and mounted picadores behind them, now the *corrida* begins.

It has been said by men who know the Hour of Truth, that *corridas* are a marketplace where men buy courage they can never own. At four o'clock it has been said (by bitter men, thinking men) that the Hour of Truth is known only to the killers on the sand, and that for the briefest moment.

When the cape has made its flight, the *banderillas* placed, the *muleta* stilled and when the killing horns are lowered, tired. When the matador's *montera* has been lifted to the judge, permission for the kill received, the dedication mouthed – then it seems there passes, eye to eye, from the

---

* With no apologies whatsover to Federico Garcia Lorca.

killer to the killed, whatever truth or poetry the world can find at four o'clock.

There are those matadors who die from time to time, but not a single bull that lives beyond the Hour of Truth – and this, to the embittered thinking men, falls short of the intent of the tragic play. This smacks of some disparity, and 'Macarena' would turn flat but that such men know the world and how it goes.

Consider the breeder of bulls, Don Esteban de Caliente y Escobar, a man of acrid vision far too clear. His son has studied in Madrid, a surgeon of the delicate brain, a balancer of cells upon a knife. A *brujo-médico*, bearer of a torch, thrusting light into the dark places of the brain where intelligence has not gone before.

The bulls have made their family rich and given them the time to think. But then reflection is a bitter path, seeing the world and how it goes. They know the feel of *corrida* and what it means or what it meant. But Esteban was in Madrid in '37 when dreams and blood did not bray out in a skirl of brass at four of a Sunday afternoon, but were bought and sold the usual way the unpoetic world gets on.

Father and son: they have the Castilian look, the thing called *casta*, though their eyes are chilled with knowledge far more northerly: that death is not nor ever was a thing resembling poetry, but an irrelevance except as end to the pulsing single prize of life. Narrow-eyed in seats of honour, both of them are here today to watch their new idea of a bull. (Look at this bull. It moves too quickly for a bull's weight and with a precise deliberation that wastes no energy.)

This bull's sire, at his *tiente*, the testing of his will to fight, charged the lance but once and stopped. Don Esteban frowned. The watching vaqueros sighed in disappointment. One charge is a pallid showing for a bull calf born to fight. But even as the lancer turned with a shrug to Don Esteban and his son, the bull trotted casually to place himself between the rider and the entrance to the corral. Then it pawed the ground absently, as if reflecting on the most efficient means of killing horse and rider both at once and, satisfied with its equation, charged again, a tutored death that dodged the lance and killed the horse and, with a certain detached flair, the rider as well.

'Father,' said Esteban's surgeon of a son, 'this is a bull to breed with.'

And that they did. The bull was only fair at love – all clumsy passion, perfunctory as a human at times – but much more meticulous at death, though for most of his fighting sons with enzymes planted in their brains, intelligence was far too brief before the fever closed their eyes. But now one son of this reflective bull is making his brave festival today, where courage in the face of death is bought (to watch) for the ticket price. And the crowd comes roaring to its feet –

'¡Toro!'

'¡Torero!'

'¡Magnífico!'

– all but the Escobars, that is, who sip cerveza as they wait. Their bull has taken the iron like milk. His hide is spined with ribboned cruelty and blood rivers the lathered hump. But the picadores are scared; the ones he's left alive, that is. This devil-bull gets past the lance as easy as a *gringo* cheats upon the tax of income. Three horses are dead with their digestive tracts rearranged artistically in view. Their riders hadn't even time to pray.

The bull has charged and whirled and hooked – 'To the left. See, Father? Always to the left' – following the cape and not the matador. It isn't time for the matador. The game's not done.

'The greatest of bulls!' cries the *afición*. 'Both ears should the *torero* have, and the tail and a hoof as well!'

'¡Toro . . . torero . . . magnífico . . .'

But the Escobars with sharp, sad eyes know magnificence is yet to come: new poetry for a bartered world at just past four in the afternoon from a fighting bull too quick for a bull to be, with odd-lit eyes that never glare but only watch and measure.

The *torero* lifts his little hat and asks permission for the kill – which, to the waiting Escobars, is optimism of a tragic cast. The killer dedicates the kill to the noble son of Escobar, to the *médico* and his science, and never knows how right he is.

A hush – the Hour of Truth has come. *Ai*! Pity the bulls who went before, who always died before they learned that brains can keep a bull alive; that killing bulls requires of men a deal of courage and a sum of skills, but killing a clown in a shiny suit is easy as rutting and twice the fun.

The bull pauses. He considers the matador, that slim objective in the shiny pants. Enzymes planted in his blithely murdering brain retain far more than how to charge. He is not a disparity, no more than the matador was to his lumbering ancestors who charged once from the chute and died and never had the time or brains to remember. This bull remembers everything, and if in his inexorable efficiency he strips the drama from the play, so has the world. The bull only states what is. He is a bull for today.

And now the matrix behind his watchful eyes remembers the object of the nimble game. The bull knows it's time; the rag is short. He reflects, fiddles at the sand. computes the distance and the waiting sword – and charges, hooking to the right. Surprise.

The shiny pants go all red and leak their insides on the sand. The terrified pics lure the bull away, and the bull is pleased to comply. This is part of the play, and insofar as a bull can love, he loves the game on the scarlet sand. He lets them lead him far enough for hurrying peons to lift the matador – then turns too fast for a bull to turn and punches the matador's ticket for good and one of the peons just for the fun.

No doubt the matador dies with a prayer and a sense of drama, however aborted. The peon just knows he's been screwed. *Corrida*, after all, is a tragic poem but not so tragic as the truth known to the Escobars: in the hollow-hearted world, the festival of courage, the spectacle at four in the afternoon, is a sweet fed to children against the aftertaste of a world never won in glory but sold since Judas and Madrid, since Munich, Saigon and Watergate and above all since tomorrow by bloodless men who somehow never lose and have no time for bullfights.

The crowd is hoarse but the Escobars are still. Their bull will have to die of course, but not a virgin like most fighting bulls. This one sired calves of a brilliant breed. Amazing what the younger Escobar can do with a scalpel, an enzyme and a truth. God knows what promoters will promote if future bulls are half this smart. Matadors like being alive much the same as buyers and sellers, and there's just no percentage in going against a bull that remembers or knows the whole game coming out of the chute. Like other men they will be, in the Hour of Truth, less inclined to drama than to flight.

The pics are coming to finish the bull for whom this was never a poem. It will be harder to kill his children and theirs will kill the sport, though not before good money's made by betting on the bull at three and four to one (seeing the world and how it goes).

The picadores close on the bull, and he wonders which of them to cancel first. He knows he can and knows besides, in bull-fashion, the clear, cold truth of the world as seen by the men who bred him. He waits, computes and paws the ground and loves the sudden red of it all.

And insofar as a brave bull can, he grins.
Olé.

FOUL MOON OVER STICKLESPINE LANE

Andrew Darlington

Andrew Darlington works freelance for the music press and is a stand-up poet on the alternative cabaret circuit. Additionally he has written for and recorded with the electronic group U.V. Pop. He has interviewed Robert Plant, Deep Purple, Shamen, Kraftwerk and many other individuals and popular groups. In the fiction field there have been interviews with William Burroughs, M. John Harrison, Kurt Vonnegut and others. On the short story side, his science fiction, fantasy and horror has been published widely, in such magazines as Fantasy Tales, Science Fiction Monthly, Space & Time *and* Dark Horizons. *He is also the author of several collections of poetry.*

FLEXING and writhing. Warted black tentacles uncoil around the buttress. Thrashing into the dark tide beneath the arches. Long ribbons of weed caught in the rush of tide hurtling out from the warrens into the canal. His footfall squelches back in echoes, he's hunched into his anorak against the slow drizzle, slouching through the gathering gloom. Dark Arches. Sticklespine Lane leads off the strip, down through the arches, to the neck between canals where the locks leak and hiss, where the caravan sits. Terry doesn't like the arches, even in daylight. They back off into a black nothingness of subterranean ducts, sluices, and channels that stink of decay. The imagined haunt of winos, muggers, junkies and . . . worse. But the caravan lies beyond. And he needs the stuff.

The cobbles underfoot tilt unevenly. Pools of water extend out from dead Victorian masonry. He's walking a slow curve that slews him away from his last over-the-shoulder glimpse of the lights of the strip, the flesh-pale sodium street-glare, the crawl of headlights, the blare of pubs and store-fronts massed in damp huddles. The cheap movie-set city with its puppet-shapes of people suddenly eclipsed by faces of brickwork. And as yet he can't see the light of the caravan beyond either. Only the piss-smelling underground passages splashing away through a glittering forever of disturbing sound. It's a place that whispers secrets. Horrid secrets. Then the walkway cants left. He could see the uneven wedge between the canals. Could see the caravan that squats on it. The luminous frames of its windows.

Coming out of the arch it was drizzling hard. Everything glistened or was veined with wetness, in a low liquid dirtscape. Beneath the parapet deep water surges in eddies. A black bin-liner caught up at a gradated depth marker was inflating and pulsing as though something inside was trying to escape. A trapped animal. A butchered corpse. It deflated, slinking glossily free, whipped away into chilling depths. Terry can't swim. Consequently intimations of such deep water frightens him.

Too late to turn back, he's carried by some other current, he squishes across to the caravan. A long cold silence follows his sharp rap. Jazz's caravan was old. Oval. A customized creature with wires, plugs, and pipes disappearing into a variety of orifices from flasks and cylinders. It was rooted deep into tall grass and sodden nettles that presumably hid punctured and perished tyres. Wheels chocked with bricks to stop it rolling down the sharp incline into the canal. The caravan had been there forever. How'd they ever get it here in the first place? There was no access except the Dark Arches walkway. And that was too narrow. The lock gates had parapets you could cross. They creaked in a bad state of repair. A man could edge across, sideways, if he was careful. But not a vehicle. His thoughts revolved stupidly as he waited. Barge. It must've come on a barge and . . .

The door imploded. Carolyn. He squinted up into the sudden brilliance. 'Jazz said I should come. Shitty night out here.'

She was framed by the fluctuations of calor gas glow, as if she gave off light.

'Oh yeah. Suppose you'd best come in. Full moon too.'

He shouldered in past her. Stamping wet away in shimmers. 'Foul moon? Whaddya mean?'

She's just smaller than he is. Black hair, long but unkempt. Dark sweater and faded jeans. 'Full moon. Not "foul" moon. I mean that somewhere up past the drizzle and rainclouds there's a full moon.'

He slumps down onto a seat that folds out into a bed. She sits on the bed across from him, swinging her legs irritably. The carpet pile is as thick as the coating on his tongue. There's a smell of something that might be cat-food. No, cat-vomit. Or something else. 'It was Jazz' he begins. 'He said I should come. It's alright?'

'If that's what he said it must be alright.' There's a portable TV. It's a dazzle of static. 'He's not here, but you can wait. He . . .'

Silences pile up in the air between them. He'd seen Carolyn at the 'Duchess' or the 'Royal Oak'. She hung back on the periphery of whatever was happening. Jazz was always the epicentre. He was scoring or making deals, setting up all manner of strange arrangements, schemes and scams. While she waited, palely loitering, until he'd done. Then she'd melt away with him to other assignations.

'Are you still with Eileen? Does she know you're here?'

He shrugs expansively. Things with Eileen were entering an odd phase. Their room was suddenly too small. Her Dali prints from Figueras annoyed him where once he'd found them quaint. 'No. She knows I'm out. That's a tautological statement, isn't it? I'm not there, so obviously I'm out somewhere. That's self-evident. But no, she doesn't know where I've gone. Probably she no longer cares. I don't know.' His eyes ransack the room. There's a frail door partitioning off the other half of the caravan. He wonders – does Jazz keep the stuff here, or there? On top of a bookshelf there's a row of Dixie-cups drooped and melt-distorted into bizarre shapes. They are part over-filled with off-white furry fungus. Perhaps he's growing something of his own? Perhaps that's whatever Jazz had slipped him last Sunday in the yard behind the 'Duchess' by the empty crates and the cistern-trickle of the Gents?

The TV is tuned to Saturn.

He coughed self-consciously, absorbing her tension, her

on-the-edgeness. Absorbing it by osmosis. To think, he'd once fancied her. She was . . . comely, in a neo-hippie loose-limbed toothy sort of way. Jazzie doesn't treat her right, doesn't appreciate her. He ignores her more often than not. What if some other guy showed a friendly and concerned interest in her. She'd respond. Sure she would. She'd be all over him. Except, of course, she hadn't. When he'd finally made his move she met it with an expression of derision. And later he'd seen her sniggering with Jazz. Telling him how Terry had tried it on. Laughing at the absurdity of the very idea. 'Is he gonna be long, Jazzie?' he managed.

She uncoils like some animal coming out of hibernation, tousled and blinking, as though she'd been reading him. She leaves interesting burrows in the quilt. 'Did he give you something?' Her smile smears across her face as slow as the spread of a pool of low-grade oil.

There's a strange charged silence, like the silence that comes after a scream. Through it he can detect the pulsing of a huge alien heart beneath the floor.

'And he told you to come here to pick up some more?'

He slumped back seat-ways and sat soaking up the low couch. 'Yes, I guess so.' This wasn't how it was done. You don't just come out and state things like that. Hell – there's an etiquette to scoring that must be observed. You just don't trash traditions like that. And why is it cold as a grave-digger's toes in here?

'What do you think it was he gave you?'

'Don't know. But shee-it, it was pretty.'

For a moment her eyes seem to shine with sparks of fear. But no. He must be mistaken. The carpet pile is as thick as the fuzz inside his skull.

'You want to know where it's from?'

'Sure. Sure – if you want to tell me.' There's a small fold-down cupboard beneath the bookshelf, but above the bed-head. Bet it's in there.

She looks down at her watch. 'We've got time. You want some wine? I've got some cheap red.' She fills two Bart Simpson mugs from a bottle without a label. 'He told me this story, Jazz did.' She passed him a mug. You know the Arches? You know how far back they extend.' The wine was sharp and raw. 'This part of Yorkshire's been mined for some

500 years. The earth beneath us is riddled with more shafts than a Gruyère cheese. Some of them go back centuries and aren't even marked on any charts. The canal network and the Arches are part of the infrastructure that grew up around the Mines when they were at their most operational. Ventilation shafts come up from underground. Some of them come up within the Arches complex.'

I don't want to know this, thinks Terry. He gags back a mouthful of wine, washing its acid residue around his teeth. He turns and pulls back a curtain to look out. Black air slithering away into numbness. Distant buildings beyond the canal seem to smudge before his eyes. Huge ungainly forms move in the shadows of Dark Arches. The drizzle has receded slightly. Slivers of moonlight lance down uncertainly. It's full moon, she already told him. Foul moon over Sticklespine Lane. If he got out now he could make it through the arches while there was some light, between the worst of the drizzle. Perhaps if he gets out now and goes back to the flat it'd be worth the effort. Eileen would be there. The bitch. But he wanted the stuff. He wasn't a real user; he did a dab of this, a touch of that – nothing serious. But he *did* want the stuff. No – he wanted it badly. He'd used it twice. Pellets of rubbery gunk, like dried Amanita flakes. Fungus. It was good. Only, ever since he'd used it he'd had this uncontrollable itchiness to do it again.

He turned back. Concentrating his attention on the book-shelf above the bed where Carolyn sat. The wine was loosening his tongue. The paperback spines said Lovecraft, Derleth, Ramsey Campbell, Simon Clark's *'Blood and Grit'*. The TV screen surged with squalls of static.

'Do you read all that stuff? Horror. The Undead. Black Magic.'

'Black Magic? There's no 'black' or 'white' magic, there are just forces, forces without morality. All that black and white stuff came along later. It's the Christian mythology that invented that kind of moral duality and put it onto the older craft. 'Black' and 'White' are *their* concepts – borrowed from their myths, nothing to do with what's real, but subsumed to such an extent that some people, some adepts who should know better, even believe all that rubbish themselves.' She smiles with eyes like portals into

Hades. But no. He's mistaken. She's . . . odd. Carolyn. She's 23-ish. Sat on the quilt. That's the bed they use. She and Jazz use that bed for all manner of gymnastic things. The slag!

The erotic image made him smirk uncomfortably. She was looking at him as if reading his mind. His crotch crawls weirdly. Where the hell is Jazz? The pulsing from beneath the floor grows louder. No – it's just inside his head. He revolves the Bart Simpson mug with exaggerated care. And she's still talking. All those other times he'd hardly ever heard her speak. Now he can't shut her up.

'There's no 'black' or 'white', just forces. Like hallucinogenics, narcotics. They're forces made up of chemicals and substances that act and interact in different ways with different effects. They don't plan it that way. It's not deliberate. It's just an accidental combination of elements thrown up by millions of years of accidental evolution. That's just how it is. Jazzie told me all about it. About the mine workers, the pitmen excavating the shaft. Two hundred years ago give or take a decade. Right below where we are now. They were using explosives to open up the tunnel, but the charges set up a series of seismic shocks along a geological fault which caved the ceiling in, but simultaneously breached this series of huge pockets, a kind of cave system. And that's where they found it growing.'

This is stupid. Where's Jazz? Where's the stuff? It must be in that fold-down unit beneath the books. But concentrate. 'They found what?'

'That's where it grows. In those labyrinths, those luminous grottos. Can you imagine how weird it must have been for them. Trapped down there, but finding this network of gleaming caverns, with dense carpets of mossy fungus. Its spores, seeds and flesh hallucinogenic. By the time they'd discovered the air-ducts, scrabbled and expanded them through to the surface, weeks had gone by. They'd been given up for dead, and many of them had died. The shafts tombing them had been sealed off. And anyway – by then, they'd changed. They'd taken to cannibalism to survive. And by then the stuff was growing inside them. Eat the fungus flesh and you just get the buzz. Eat the spores and it germinates in the gut. They bring it to the surface through the ventilation ducts that open into Dark Arches.'

'Who do what?' The wine was gone. His attention drifting.

'The Mine Workers. The Pitmen. They bring it up. Me and Jazz are careful just to use the fungus flesh. But for them – and now for you, it was too late. By then it was growing inside them. As it's growing inside you. The spores rooting in their intestines, growing and branching through their bodies. Didn't William Burroughs say that narcotics keeps you young? Something to do with cellular rejuvenation . . .'

He looked across at her. Stupid slag. Full of junkie tales and spook romances. He opened his mouth to speak. But there was nothing sensible he could find to say. Instead he lurched up to his feet. 'It's alright Carolyn. Think I'll give tonight a miss.' He unconsciously scratched at the irritation in his crotch.

She looked at her watch. 'It doesn't matter anyway.'

'Why doesn't it matter? What do you mean?'

'They're almost here.' She paused. Set the anonymous wine bottle on the carpet pile. 'Wait', an admonishing finger held out like some kind of hex. She clicked through the partition door and was gone. The sound of rummaging. A curtain swishing back. A baited silence. He glances at the out door, then at the fold-down cupboard beneath the bookshelf above the bed. Bet it's in there. The silence extends.

In a series of rapid decisive movements he's across the room, the catch comes free, the panel paging down. Inside is phantasmagoria. The scent of it is instant, headily arousing. Small blocks in silver foil wrapped in polythene rammed in stratas as far back as they'll go. He reaches into the coldness. The blocks are light and faintly gelatine-soft. He stuffs two deep in his pockets. Reaches for the next.

'What the . . .!'

Carolyn is behind him. Clawing for him. He turns too quickly. The heartbeat beneath the floor huge and deafening. He shoves her away harder than he'd anticipated. She careens across the room. Hits the sink unit with a sharp thud. Her head snaps back viciously. No sound as she bounces back, then slithers forward. The hair at the back of her head instantly blood-matted.

He's breathing hard, caught in indecision.

She's still. Small gurgling noises come from deep in her throat.

He goes to close the cupboard. Takes another fistful of blocks. Thrusts them deep into his damp anorak pockets. Then shuts the unit up.

There's no reason for stealth, but he tiptoes. Opens the door. It's ice-chill beyond. Silvered by a foul moon. The black wall of Dark Arches smudges before his eyes. The ground is sinking moist. His shoes wetting into his socks already. A ghost drizzle that's hardly visible but silts everything with a sheen. Huge ungainly forms flow through the shadows, more bestial and primordial than anything he'd imagined possible. A bad trip of a night. But try as he might he couldn't grab a clear view of any specifically abnormal phenomenon. Nevertheless he was scared to approach the Arches. Irrational. He turned towards the nearest lock. He could cross there. He could cross in the sense that it was *possible* to cross. But dangerous, treacherous underfoot. And it brought him out a long inconvenient way from the strip.

A noise from Dark Arches, only coming closer. A sound like someone ripping the lid off Hell. He thought of the liquid noises Carolyn was making, a secretion of blood, mucus and saliva drooling unhealthily through tissue not designed for its passage. It was like that, but louder, and more of it. The shapes were real. He turned for the lock. Shapes there too, inflating and pulsing, glimmering moisture and stench. The moonlight angled and indistinct. The drizzle liquefying forms into a lurching slither of blacknesses.

They were coming for him.

He spun back for the caravan. The movements closer now.

He skidded and squelched through pools of filth towards the caravan's wavering light. Something huge lurching at his heels.

Then he was inside the caravan, the floor trembling under his feet. He was slamming the door closed behind him, it went so far but wouldn't go further. He rammed himself at the door with the increasing urgency of desperation. A liquid roaring coming from outside. Looking down he saw that the obstruction was a hand, clutching and grasping for him, but trapped by him at the wrist. Just as suddenly the obstruction shattered, severed, the hand spun free and the door shut hard. He rammed at the catch with the heel of his hand so hard it grazed. His back gratefully solid against the locked door as the obscene exhalations outside intensified.

Carolyn's eyes were wide and accusing. 'Bastard' she said, strands of bloody spittle drooling.

A window detonated inwards. There were massive shudders of impact. The whole caravan lurched. 'What's *happening*, Carol? Wha-in-*Hell's* happening?'

The severed hand oozed glutinous fluid. The flesh was pale, white, semi-transparent. But more, it was thickly veined with tiny filaments, capillaries . . . roots? The whole hand . . . and presumably the grotesque body it had belonged to, was a dense mass of micro-fine fibres forking and branching.

'The Pitmen' she breathed. 'Why do you think you're here? They don't trade the stuff for free.'

Again the floor canted, the entire caravan upending, slithering and crashing a yard down the incline. The lights slammed off as the life-support system of wires, plugs and pipes were amputated. In total darkness now. The hand lost and invisible. Spasms of fear coming at him that said 'they can't get in, but they've unchocked the wheels'. The sound of moist fists beating on the outer panelling with strangely dull hollow rhythms.

'Get out' hissed Carolyn. A hostile presence in blackness. 'Or we're both in the canal.'

Another sickening tremor. The thought of a blackness of swirling water stinking with decay. The Dark Arches receding away into a terrifying nothingness of deep rushing currents.

Or . . . the door was bucking insistently behind him. He thought of the severed hand.

That's when he turned and began screaming.

THE STAR WEAVE
OF SNORGRUD SUNBREATH

Mike Chandler

Mike Chandler began writing fiction when he first read Fantasy
Tales *in the late 1970s. He has published several stories, but admits
he writes mainly for his own enjoyment and for the escapism it
provides. The story which follows forms the basis of a novel he is
currently working on, amongst other projects.*

I thought about it a while, then I said: 'Three.'

'Is that all?' He sighed fragrantly, insulted.

'They're the best they could buy.'

He loomed and blinked and squinted at me with rheumy
eyes the colour of peacock's tails.

'And who are these three so worthy of gold coin and
me?'

I kicked a scapula, a yellowed tibia and an ominously
charred skull from under me, folded my rain-damp cloak
and sat. Not a good move. He looked even larger.

'Thorin Icethorn, Javez Hod, Laskar Tremayne.'

'*Hmmmm.* Known Names. Names of Valour. I'm impressed
and flattered.' The saurian neck snaked towards me with the
speed of a cobra, a distant but rarely discussed relative. 'What
more do you know, more than mortal, less than god?'

'Call me Cal, it's shorter.'

He scratched an ear with a talon and curled smoke at the
roof. A scale half hung from his flank and he turned to gnaw
irritably at it. It drooped a few more degrees.

'Icethorn, Hod, Tremayne. Archers all. It's to be an
ambush, then?'

I shrugged. 'I don't know. They don't trust me.'

'Understandable.' He ignored my pout and faceful of wry.

'So why should I? What did you come here for, Cal? My treasure?' He waved a heavily spined tail at the shadowy mound behind him. His own voice was his mockery and I turned away, stung by the acid of his bitterness.

He shifted through a subtlety of greens and rainbows flecked, the long tail curled until the tip twitched like a second tongue resting on the dank cave floor beneath his chin.

'Is it raining outside?'

'It was when I came in.'

The massive, horny head lowered until the tail tip cradled it. Back flared nostrils pointed at me like the muzzles of flamethrowers, which, of course, they were. The lizard's cold kaleidoscopic orbs regarded me lidlessly, impassively, no hint of the thoughts unreeling in the calculating mind surfaced.

Hidden from me. Shielded where once his feelings, his dreams and wants and sunken desires had rolled upwards like bubbles in tar. Now his soul was guarded and barriered and he would not let me in.

'What did you come for, Cal?' The harsh, rasp-sweet voice wriggled amongst stalagmites, tickling nape hairs upright. A flush was lightly colouring his throat and the neck spines had lifted, just a mite. I sat my ground, thinking runes and hoping they'd work if I told him the truth and he did not believe me. Not that I'd blame him.

'To warn you. You're a friend.'

For an instant the flush deepened, spines rising and a slight whoosing indicated the preliminary intake of oxygen.

My gut knotted.

Then he laughed.

At least, I call it 'laughter'. It's a sort of rumbling, coughing wheeze. The snake head lifted, weaving hypnotically, then curved over me like a question and I turned my face from his fetid breath, ripe with hellfire and corruption.

'Friend? Friend? If I remember a-right, you used me once when you had a need and I was younger and more gullible and made the mistake of trusting you with my back.'

'We all make mistakes.'

'And you took the best, you bastard! How much did you get for it?'

'A baronetcy and the hand of the king's third eldest.'

'You were conned. It was worth a kingdom and a harem of princesses.'

'That's what I thought.'

A silence then. Was he remembering?

I was.

The glittering hoard and the deep, rich smells of clean earth and bone dust. Cobwebs and the musk-bitter-fetid stench of dragon. The emerald the size of an ostrich egg I christened Mammon's Eye.

Just the third eldest. But she was worth it.

But he followed me. Hunted me across the Plane until I shifted, just a little, taking Melanie and WeirKeep with me.

'So you've come back to ease a wounded conscience?'

'If you like.'

'And if I don't?'

'Then I'll tell you anything that suits you. That I need you again. That it's all a trick and I'm part of the ambush hired to lure you out.'

He shook his great head and puffed a little smoke.

'Just once. The truth.'

I rubbed finger and thumb down the sides of my mouth. Water dripped somewhere and I wondered if the lower parts of the passage were flooded.

'I came to help a friend.'

He was old.

People like us, we forget time. It means nothing. A day comes and goes like a blink. Start talking centuries and we might grasp the concept, but a second? And it makes you forget, it makes you careless until you see old friends, and even old enemies, gone grey, gone to dust. Then, for a while, you might contemplate, reminisce if that's the way you're built, drink a flagon or two to bless or curse them through the Eblis Gates and store them away for campfire tales.

But Snorgrud . . .

The kiss of sunlight on the water-shimmer of iridescent scales. The head held with all the haughty power of long youth. A roar to shiver courage and quail walls, a breath to melt rock or lightly roast a knight in his own red-hot armour. The sighing silences of Dragon Moot; the sage-whispers of croaking, dull-scaled ancients passing on knowledge and secrets to feisty, impatient youths. Red blinding passions, and the snapping, snarling, ichor drawing rutting lust of the Swollen Moon; the rough tenderness of mating.

Not now.

Now was amber rheum clotted at the corners of lacklustre eyes. Trails of mucus dangling in slimy strings from gaping nostrils, ribbons of pearl and yellow saliva from drooling jaws. Softening teeth and weakening joints that ached in the cold and the rain. The wide spread, cyclone beating wings of veined membrane that were once umbrellas of wind fire and were now dark and dirty and faded scarce able to lift the once glitter-sleek body.

Age. The Ravener, the Gnawer, the Slow Corrupter, had struck insidious as ever.

Snorgrud the Roarer was much changed.

He snuffled and shifted a little closer, smoking torchlight rolling oil over his bulbous, warted body, leathery wings rasping as they dragged over the cavern floor.

'Not long ago they scampered from me like ants from a flame. Not long ago they'd have hired an army to fight me.'

'Not long ago,' I murmured, 'They wouldn't have hunted for you in a cave.'

It struck home.

The long neck stiffened and those spines started rising again and I cursed my tongue and tactlessness.

Snorgrud tilted back his head and stared at the fanged roof, dull rumbling a mocking roar. The tail lashed once, twice, smashing a thousand years of dripping water and solidified rock, sweeping away stalagmites with splintering crashes. The dragon chased his tail for a moment, rage flaring him near to madness. Breathless, panting, he flopped down, spraying puddles of icy water, baring his pale green belly, scratching it fitfully with a twisted foreclaw, an old wound from some ancient, terrible fight.

'Damn you, Caliban!'

I bowed acceptance of his bane.

'They're all gone, my friends. I'm the last of Gnorri Southbrood.'

'Elbion? Regestor? Dashwind?'

'You sound surprised. You didn't know?'

'I've been away a while.'

'Too long, it seems. Elbion just died. Gave up and died.

He flew back to Dragon Moot, curled his wings on a ridge high up on Galesong and went to sleep. Regestor was fed poisoned carcases by those worms up there. Eight days, it took. Eight days with him clawing and ripping at his belly until he wore his own guts for a garland, then one of their heroes went down the tunnel and shot a quiverful of poisoned arrows into him.' His head lowered and the great eyes glistened with anger and sorrow. 'Dashwind went out in style. You know they said she was a little crazy since the dragonslayers killed her young? Well, something finally snapped because she upped and went after John Stormspear in his own Keep. Fought most of the day, so I heard, and in the end Stormspear went to the roof of his tallest tower and faced her alone, bow against breath. They both lost. She took a clothyard through the eye and smashed into the tower taking him with her.'

'I didn't know,' pathetic and helpless but true all the same. 'I didn't.'

'For once I believe you. What the hell do they want with me, though? I'm too old to fly much, I don't bother them except in winter when the cold makes my wings ache so I take a sheep or cow or two. I sleep most the time. So why now?'

Scratching my nose, I wished I'd brought my pipe, shifted a little uncomfortably on the moist cloak and dampness soaked through my breeches.

'I think,' I said, dryly. 'That they're running out of virgins.'

'A rare and desirable commodity, I'm told.'

'A gourmet feast,' I agreed. 'But a little too expensive these days for a poor village.'

'That bastard priest! Is he the one stirring them up?'

I nodded.

'Hypocrite! He was the one started the whole thing!'

I frowned. I was doing that a lot.

'Don't tell me. He never told you?'

'Right.'

'Understandable, I suppose. Wouldn't want to broadcast the fact. What did he say?'

'That the village could no longer pay the blood dues you demanded.'

Snorgrud moved with alarming speed, claws and scales rattling on rock. The saurian head lashed out, vanishing into the mouth of the tunnel. The throat purpled and the back spines lifted. A furnace wind laced with tendrils of yellow-blue flame washed into the cavern, rippling the surface of a nearby rockpool as the dragon sent jet after jet of flame towards the surface.

Snorting, eyes filled with anger-ghosts, the dragon sauntered back to his favourite spot, settled down. The stench of baked earth and singed stone. Grey curls of smoke like half-formed wraiths, billowed from the opening.

'Were you followed, Cal?'

Why lie? 'Yes.'

'Oh dear.' The rest he left unsaid.

He lapped some water contentedly. 'It was his idea to send me girls. I prefer sheep, myself. Virgin meat is too milky and tasteless. But to be fair, they're usually quite pretty. He does dress his meals nicely.' He belched sulphurously, waved a talon before his grinning jaws. 'Yes, it all started about five winters back. Do you remember that one? No? Real ball-breaker. Trees exploding in the cold; men lighting fires on the river ice; snow deep enough to bury a horse and cart. Well, this place isn't like my old lair and when I'm cold I get hungry. So I went out for a snack.'

I could imagine. A herd of cows here, a flock of sheep there . . .

'But the farmers weren't pleased. They went to the priest for some guidance from the gods. After the usual mumbo-jumbo he pronounced they should placate me with an offering every six moons. Naturally, they weren't too pleased. It meant more of their stock. Then that pile of demon dung played his ace card. Said, no, not animals, the sacrifice must be human. A virgin.' He stretched out a wing, studied it for a moment. 'The scales get so dry here. I can't make as much oil as I used to. When the skin cracks it hurts like hell. 'Shaking a mournful head he returned to his story. 'That perked them all up. The farmers were happy because their livestock was safe, the village boys were happy because the girls were rutting like rabbits. The only ones not happy were the lemon-faced girls even the village idiot wouldn't service.'

'You didn't have to eat them.'

He dug a claw up a nostril, belched again. 'Sorry. All that fire breathing gives me heartburn. No, quite right, I didn't. But the first poor creature they sent down came on the coldest night of the coldest month of the coldest winter ever. She was all swaddled in sheepskin and my eyes aren't what they used to be. I thought some poor little bleater had wandered down, all innocent, like. By the time I'd cooked it and peeled off the skin it was too late.' He half closed one eye. A droplet of mucus splashed his cheek unheeded. 'You ever had virgin?'

'Not in the culinary sense.'

'You haven't missed one of life's great treats, I promise you! Especially if they're all like that one! Next to no meat and stringy as hell. I've eaten better donkey. And on top of that she gave me indigestion! So I sent the next one back!'

'You did what?'

'Another thing he forgot to mention, I suppose. Yes, poor child. My eyes might be going but the old hearing's still as sharp. Heard her creeping and sniffling down the passage. When she got here she smelt something awful. I think she soiled herself on the way down. Anyway, I told her to go back, that I wasn't hungry, which was a lie, and that I didn't want her or any more of her kind, which was true. You know what she did?' I said I had no idea. 'She fell on her knees and blessed me in the name of her father, four sisters, three brothers and the children she had not yet borne. Made me feel rather good, to be honest.'

'So what happened?'

Calloused lips turned back from jaundiced ivory teeth. A canine was visibly rotting.' They killed her. Said she lied. Said she never went near me, just hid in the passage for a while. Cut her throat and rolled her back down.'

'And you did what?'

'I ate her! It was getting on for summer and I didn't want that stinking up the place, did I?'

Thespar, all benign smiles and soft words, coaxing and cooing, agreeable without fawning, a flatterer but no sycophant. His hand on my arm, fingers gnarled, the backs speckled with kidney-coloured marks. But the nails held me. So clean and cared for, unlike the villagers with hands forever darkened with ingrained grime, nails chipped and chewed and broken. His white aureole of hair the hawkish nose and the cruel-kind curve of a mild-lipped mouth. He could do it. He was demagogue enough to sway those damn fools any way he wished. Had he swung the knife that night? Grabbed a handful of dark hair and told the shocked moon-white face it was for her own good as he drew sharp steel over taut flesh? I could almost hear his soft but penetrating voice cajoling the farmers, ordering the corpse tossed casually into the pit. Thespar, when this is all over . . .

'And since then?'

'I eat 'em. Why not? If I send them back they're killed.'

I saw his point.

'A pity they couldn't wait a couple more years. Then I'd follow Elbion's example.'

'Not you, Snorgrud Rainbow-Weaver. Never you.'

He rose then, long neck waving slowly from side to side.

'Good times then, Caliban. Good times. The soaring, cloud hopping, diving through the snow mists of the sky, laughing at lightning, roaring thunders while we kissed the sun! I walked rainbows and quivered mountains! Then I *was* Rainbow-Weaver! Then I *was* Walker of Thunders, the Shining Scourge, Snorgrud Sunbreath whose names were legend and the legend lived!' He sank down, head drooping, the shimmer from the incandescent eyes fading to age-dampened embers. 'Now I'm just an old lizard, a walking fossil too stupid to die. Look at me! Eyes and teeth almost gone, out of breath if I snort, my scales falling, joints all swollen up with cold. Even my Hoard's all gone. No more shining mountain of tribute and loot. The youngsters came and took it, bit by bit, as I did myself when I was their age. They come and posture and challenge and I'm too weak, too cowardly, too keen to eke out the last seconds of life to try and stop them. But a dragon must have a Hoard . . .' he shuffled towards me giving me my first clear view of the dark heap.

Torchlight shone on . . .

. . . old breastplates and rusted ploughshares, pieces of broken harness, a small cart with a broken axle, heaps of mouldering rags, broken pots. Nothing. Rubbish. Junk.

'That's it, Caliban. That crap's all I've got. They don't have to kill me for it. I'd give it to them. Make me more room.' He snuffled. I patted his scaly hide, small comfort.

The wedge-shaped head turned, forked tongue flickering. 'Pathetic, isn't it.'

'We all get old. Someday it'll be my turn.'

'Do you? Will it?'

He was tottering away, tail dragging when I said: 'I can make you young again.'

He halted, tail poised in mid-sway. With creaking slowness he turned and studied me over his humped back.

'You can *what*?'

'Not for long. Maybe an hour. Perhaps a little longer, perhaps a little less.'

His stare held the life of a corpse, the slit pupils expanding, the scaled lips drawing back in a rictus.

'Why?'

And to that I had no answer.

'They sent you down here, didn't they?'

'You knew that all along.'

'To coax me out. Lead me onto the bows.'

I said nothing, studied my nails.

'Old I'm easy, but if you did as you said . . .' He turned clumsily, favouring the scarred left side, twisted claw held protectively high. 'Why?'

'You want to touch the moon again. You want to hear starsong on the ether. You want to tumble windsprites and make those humans tremble in their beds just one more time.'

'Yes! Oh, yes!'

'Then I can give it to you. For a while.'

He squinted. 'Just long enough, you mean.'

'Take it or leave it, Snorgrud. They'll get you either way.'

He washed me in stenchbreath and bile rose to the back of my constricted throat.

'Icethorn, Hod and Tremayne. Names of Strength. Good names to go down in legend with.' The eyes slitted. 'Is that bastard priest with them?'

'He stayed in the village. Said it was not priest's work.'

'That's his style.' A pause, then: 'Do it, Caliban.'

What followed . . .

A chant; a pledge to something better unseen and undescribed; a promise of blood hissing amongst flames;

a faint but definite alteration in shadow patterns and the fleeting impression of a gigantic maw.

The weight of The Presence left the cavern when I spoke the last Words soft and rocked as the tremor smote harder than usual.

And opened my eyes on Splendour.

He was Awe.

He was Terrible Glory.

He was the last experiment fantastical God made before buckling down to staid Creation.

Even in the weak torchglow there were rubies and rainbows and diamonds dancing laughter amongst ripe greens and pale limes of his scales. Head held high, throat wattle virile and swollen, teeth polished sabres. He lifted back spines in a salute to youth and his voice was an earth shout of defiance. He turned to me, coins of brilliance in the peacock orbs and the cavern was loud with the sounds of his breathing and my beating heart.

He held me, a butterfly pinned, and I read the knowledge in his gaze and looked away. Moving with a flowing, reptilian wriggles, Snorgrud was halfway up the tunnel.

Hastily tossing my paraphernalia into the satchel I dashed after him.

Burnt earth and baked rock surrounded me, starting sweat from my brow and sticking my shirt to my back. Too hot air flapped in lungs, making them struggle. As I drew near the slight fold in the wall where Tipper, Helvan and Race had waited I looked neither left nor right, which might have saved my supper if I hadn't trodden in something that crunched and squished together and curiosity was faster than sense.

I looked down.

Pale and gagging, I stumbled after the rapidly vanishing reptile, wiping sour bile from a loose-lipped mouth with the back of my hand.

Cooler. A breeze? Or had my sweat chilled? No, light! I saw Light!

I bumped into him on the brink of the tunnel entrance.

'Where are they?'

I shook my head. 'I really don't know, Snorgrud. I'd tell you if I did.'

He was very still, etched in moonsilvers and youth. The

stars were brighter than when I'd entered, colder, somehow more distant, aloof, a haughty audience awaiting the
last show.

'I ought to thank you. Ought to make a speech, a few
last immortal words, something noble and touching that
will echo in Time's dusty corridors.' He turned the lamps
of his soul upon me and I saw it burning ambers and
yellows and balefires. 'So harken to the final words of
Snorgrud Sunbreath, Eldest and perhaps unwisest of Gnorri
Southbrood.' We were locked together by grappling gazes
that neither would break. He showed me things no mortal
has seen nor will have the chance to see again. He unravelled
himself like a tangled skein and laid bare his being bright
before me.

Then something hard and flexible smashed into my chest,
hurled me, winded and hurting, down the passage in a small
avalanche of dirt and loose stones and the last words of
Snorgrud Sunbreath mocked me.

'See you in Hell, sucker!'

I shielded my face, head bowed, and he struck his wing
wind and was gone, up and banking hard port before any
of the lurkers could knock an arrow. He was young and the
ichor pulsed faster within him. He was not to be denied the
Rite of Star Weave, the Death Threading.

Panting, a rib gone, maybe two, hands bleeding, breeches
tattered about the knees, I crawled to the lip and hauled
myself painfully clear.

He was the silver comet that mirrored stars, mocking the
moon with his brilliance. Snorgrud wove the patterns of his
honeycombed mind, creating shapes no human brain understood, making sense from the chaos of reptile geometry. A
soar; a loop; a triple turn; a wing straining starboard twist
that disintegrated into a corkscrew dive and the whistle of
tormented air as he banked out.

Figure beside me a few paces off. A bow.

I threw a rock and he took it on the side of the head. When
I throw, I throw hard. He went down, bow spinning.

I knew what Snorgrud meant to do.

Up, up, a victory roll followed by an Immellman, then a
long, lazy circle that carried him over the village . . .

We all heard the faint, strident wails, like an aeolian harp

in a tempest, and someone close whispered: 'Parsus save us!'
And someone else just said: 'Shit!'

He was still eighty, one hundred feet up when the back
spines rose against the moon and a sort of hush snuffed
the wind.

Hard hands helped me up. I leant on a strong shoulder,
against a stocky body smelling of pigs and rain.

'Snorgrud . . .' It was almost a plea.

Hell came.

The first half dozen cabins just vanished in a nova of heat
and the dragon was silhouetted by the glare, zooming over
at zero feet, spines upright like a death salute of swords,
flaming anything he saw but heading always for the massive
building at the very centre of the square.

'The temple . . .' a shape gasped.

Goodbye, Thespar, your oily character should fry well.

Snorgrud made very sure.

He landed.

Amid spiralling sparks and exploding timbers, screams
and yells, the dragon touched down with all the grace of
a dove. Snout feet from the door, he savoured the begging,
sobbing voices, head tilted to pick out one in particular. Then
the long neck curled back and slashed forward like a whip.

The front of the temple turned into an inferno. Glow
worms staggered from it, burning men and women tottering,
swaying, blackening as they moved, flopping in weary defeat
to the ravening flames.

The dragon went skyward.

Coming toward us.

'Take cover! Cover!'

I was down the burrow like a greased rabbit, biting lips
bloody against the talons of pain.

He passed low and slow and did not flame at all.

Bass of bows.

Soprano of arrow flight.

Snorgrud barely faltered.

He had drawn our fire and knew our sting and our
positions.

I started to mutter runes.

A running figure, Tremayne, I think, moving cover for a
better shot and Snorgrud snared him like an owl with a

rat, lifting him high and effortlessly into the sky, a thin, despairing wail trailing into the night.

My pig-stinking friend sobbing and praying.

Me? I just hoped.

He described a long, slow, sine-curve and at the peak let Tremayne go, folding his wings and following the hurtling body almost to the ground.

In the few seconds it took between ending the dive and curving away, Hod and Icethorn shot four shafts.

One high in the neck. It made him scream.

One off the flank. It splintered, sending the heavy iron head spinning, whining off into the flame streak darkness.

Two in the soft belly, sinking in to the flights.

Snorgrud staggered. Hurt but not dying.

They fired again, more deliberately this time, masters of their trade.

I think it was Icethorn who did the damage. Cold, blond Icethorn with a temper as brittle as glass and a heart like a glacier. He had the northwind for blood, did Icethorn.

His shaft severed the main wing muscle.

Snorgrud fell brokenly.

They poured in arrow after arrow.

But the spell was fading and his majesty was growing dull.

A clothyard pinned his tongue to the soft, pink palate. He fell on his side, waving the shrivelled claw.

Icethorn shifted two paces left. Hod, beside him, drew string to ear.

With clinical precision they planted both arrows in the dragon's left eye.

His death scream ripped me.

His heart cry sprang tears.

I heard his great head fall but did not see it, hanging my head and blaming my ribs.

The tail shivered for several seconds. A back leg kicked. The dangling scale finally fell off. An acrid stench above the smell of burning straw and roast meat as his bowels voided in death, then the only fires in the one good eye were cold reflections.

Scorched, coughing survivors attacked the corpse with scythes and knives, boots and bare fists, screaming their hate, spitting in the dead and gaping maw with hyena courage.

Holding my ribs I tried to breathe softly so it did not hurt so much.

Icethorn unstrung his bow, placed the string carefully in the oilskin pouch sewn inside his helmet, then, bowshaft in left hand, he faced me.

'You did well. When all that flame and smoke came out we thought . . .' he shrugged. He didn't really give a damn. 'I don't suppose any of the others . . .' He was mock mournful when I shook my head. 'Had to be expected. They're bastards to kill, especially when they're as old and tricky as that one. You all right?' He pointed the bow butt at me.

'Got too close to the tail. Broke a rib.'

'Soon get you strapped up. Pity about the village. Still, long time till winter.' He half turned, then remembered, hand going inside his jerkin. 'This is yours.' He tossed it deliberately high, a smile on bearded lips while I gnawed a groan to the bone.

'Thanks.'

'You earned it, Minstrel. Wouldn't get me going down a burrow for all the silver in the Shires. You want a souvenir?'

'A what?'

'Tooth? Claw? The women go crazy when you show them. Little bending of the truth and suddenly you're . . .' He tapered off, his cheeks ghostly as he saw something in my face, my eyes, I had tried, God, how I'd tried! to keep hidden. His hand snapped down to the leather wrapped hilt of a short sword and he took a couple of paces back.

I went down in a crouch, nursing ribs, but not taking my eyes off him.

'Go away, Icethorn. Just go away.' He backpedalled until certain he was out of range then walked briskly towards the yelling, hacking mob, bellowing unheeded orders. I gripped a tussock of grass, white knuckled. 'Go to hell, Icethorn,' the words shredded through clenched teeth. 'Go directly to hell. Do not pass peace. Do not collect happiness.' But I was in no state to make the curse stick.

Not right now, anyway.

A woman with a bright pink burn on her cheek and the

perfume of singed hair about her bound my ribs with rough tenderness.

Slepnir snuffled, pranced away, smelling dragon and soul sickness and self-hate on me, crude wine flowering my breath. I hauled myself into the saddle with the luxury of a long yell of pain, then heeled him southward, turning my back on death and burning, and I heard Hod call after me. I pointed at him, then at the horse's rump and left it at that.

Long after the wineskin was empty and tossed aside I rode, following the winding trail of the Unicorn.

In a dell, by a rivulet, I let Slepnir drink and tugged the purse from my jerkin.

I held it, the weight of a friend's life in my palm. What the hell? He was old and a man had to eat.

I counted the coins one by one, moonlight turning them silver.

They were all there.

All thirty.

PELE

Melanie Tem

Melanie Tem's short stories have appeared in such anthologies as Dark Voices 3 *and* 5, Best New Horror 2, The Mammoth Book of Vampires, Snow White Blood Red, Women of Darkness, Skin of the Soul, Final Shadows, The Ultimate Dracula *and* The Ultimate Frankenstein. *Her first novel,* Prodigal, *won the Bram Stoker Award in 1992, since when she has published* Blood Moon, Revenant, Demodis *and, in collaboration with Nancy Holder,* Making Love *and* Witch-Light.

THE drive up Haleakala took less than ninety minutes, and they climbed ten thousand feet. The very air changed. As the sky lightened with the dawn, Hilary could see rocks and ground cover and pine stands reminiscent of the Rockies, but with groves of eerily twisted eucalyptus reminding her that she was not at home. Here the hairpin turns seemed – impossibly, of course – to overlook ocean on all sides. Eight, then nine, then ten thousand feet below them, and perpetually dissolving in the blue-grey mist, water glimmered everywhere and the land receded so nearby that it could hardly be said to have a horizon.

She cut open papayas for breakfast, drizzled grey-green lime juice over the nest of slimy bitter black seeds, and fed bites of the orange pulp to Joel while he drove. They laughed together, and she patted the juice off his beard with a white napkin, giddy with the pleasure of touching him so easily again, fearfully taking note that this was the closest they'd been in a long time.

'What happens to marriages?' she'd cried during one of their interminable discussions, lengthened by Joel's interminable silences.

After a long pause he'd said sadly, 'Everybody learns what everything means, I guess, and then nothing means anything anymore.'

This was their last chance. If things weren't better after this vacation, they wouldn't live together anymore when they went home. Already they'd been in the islands nearly their full two weeks, and the sheer sensory presence of the place could make Hilary forget why they were here.

Fourteen days and thirteen nights in utterly unfamiliar surroundings. First the pink highrise hotel on Waikiki where the beach was a narrow spotlighted strip and the buildings and litter and avenues and hucksters of Honolulu clung fiercely to the thin moving crust of the earth. Then Maui, which was altogether another world, where colours had familiar names but were deeper and richer, plants had parts she recognized but were so tangled that she couldn't see where one stopped growing and the next began, rocks looked as if only recently they'd been alive. The two of them alone together in a place so spurting with impetuous life, so alien, that maybe, for the first time in years, their relationship would send out new growth and claim their notice.

'I think it's working,' Joel had told her on their first night. She knew what he meant, though she didn't know if it was true. He'd smiled at her and cupped her face in his hands, which were damp from the ocean spray and from his constant sweat mingled with hers. Hilary had thrilled at being able to hold his gaze like that. At home, he was in the habit of glancing at her a hundred times a day, then as quickly glancing away, and there were always little avalanches between them. Here, with no apparent effort, things took hold.

The air here was viscous, hard to take in. Her throat had clogged with her first breath off the plane, and the cilia in her nose had seemed to swell and stick together. But once the air got inside her body, she couldn't imagine ever getting it out, and she could feel the random energy of things growing.

Hilary aligned herself here with the structure of the earth, the continental plates sensuously drifting, the islands continually erupting and sinking back into the sea. The knowledge that rock could exist in a molten state and still be rock now amazed her, though she'd known it for a long time. She shivered with the teeming of the ocean and the building up of the coral reefs, the rotting away and hollowing out of millions of tiny bodies, the vivifying of their skeletons. In the soles of her feet and the palms of her hands, nerves tingled with the rampant powers of growth and decay. On the islands, anything would grow, whether there was room for it or not, and anything would decay.

'This place makes me nervous,' she kept saying to Joel. 'It's all so *lush* that it's just one step this side of decay.'

Two nights, then three nights in a row she had dreamed: Joel melting at her touch, sensually, and she couldn't stop touching him. In the dreams she left her body and entered the ocean, entered the thick wind, entered the hot flowing lava, but she still couldn't stop touching Joel, even though her hands and her love passed right through him. His face was a skull without flesh, but soft and lovely, the forehead dimpled wherever she touched it, the eyes liquid. She had walked with him along an endless beach at night, endlessly forming and re-forming, and his fingers had carried the imprint of hers in their flesh. A dim phosphorescence had glistened out to sea and moved toward them like footprints across the waves.

Around them now, on this volcanic mountain, it was snowing. Ninety minutes below, the air would be steaming and hissing like the ocean on the beach. Here you could see your breath. Hilary shivered and pulled on her sweatshirt. Briefly, Joel took her hand.

'Civilization,' he said, as if they'd been talking about it, 'is nothing but a holding action anyway, and so are relationships.' He moved his hand to her knee for a moment before putting it back on the wheel. Through her jeans, her knee stayed warm from his touch, a patch of flesh heating like lava and then stiffening uncomfortably until she put her foot up on the seat and massaged her leg and thigh with both hands.

Awake, she was afraid of the ocean. In the dreams, she went in, and the ocean floor dissolved under her feet like Joel waiting alone behind her and like the warm water closing over her head. In the dreams she wasn't afraid; someone was waiting for her out there, an enemy, but also a guide. Awake, she was the one who waited

on the shifting beach every night while Joel went swimming.

Each time she woke up, Joel would be beside her. Solid.
Impenetrable. She would feel his breath on her arm. The
cries of strange birds would plait over the constant hiss of
the ocean under their hotel window, and she'd be sure there
was someone else in the room, in front of the mirror, under
the covers, in the sweet warm living air she couldn't help
but breathe.

They arrived at Haleakala Crater just in time for the
ranger's sunrise lecture. Hilary leaned back against Joel in
the crowd, and he put both arms around her waist. The
ranger was Polynesian, with a charming accent and the crisp,
folksy, passionate patter of park rangers everywhere.

'Looks pretty foggy today.' He gestured toward the windows, through which mist was just visible in heavy peaks
and eddies. 'Sometimes it burns off, sometimes not. Be
careful in the crater on a day like this.'

He lectured them about the crater, its flora and fauna,
its geologic history, and read to them from Captain Cook's
account of its discovery by Europeans. The ranger's tone was
both playful and reverent, but the words of the old explorer
sounded downright testy, as though he'd been offended by
the mystery of the place, its liquidity and unpredictability.
Hilary listened, pressing Joel's fingers against her sides and
staring out the window. From here she could see nothing but
the fog, growing steadily whiter as the earth turned toward
the sun.

She wondered suddenly what Joel was thinking, and
couldn't even imagine. She glanced up at him. He was
watching the fog, too, but she knew his thoughts wouldn't
be like hers, the words and images he used to shape his
thoughts would barely be recognizable to her. Here on the
islands, where everything grew, they sometimes seemed to
be understanding each other, but Hilary knew that wasn't
true. Watching the mist, she shivered. Joel's arms tightened
around her, and she had to settle for that.

Hands on hips, the ranger strode to the centre of the group.
'The sun, ladies and gentlemen, is preparing to rise.' There
was an excited murmur, as if these people had never seen
the sun before, and the ranger held up his hands. 'But before

you go out to meet it, I must tell you the most important thing about Haleakala.

'These islands are inhabited by the Goddess Pele. Madam Pele is the Goddess of the volcano, and the Goddess of the ocean, and all the Pacific Islands are her domain. But because Haleakala is not extinct, only dormant, it comes under her special protection.

'It is dangerous to cross Madam Pele, and almost as dangerous to be loved by her. She has been known to change both her rivals and her lovers into lava, bit by bit, starting by hardening the palms of the hands. She can set fire, she can drown, she can melt.

'It is said that the curse of Madam Pele shall be forever upon anyone who takes anything from this place. A rock, a flower, anything. Pele claims her own. This place belongs to her. Remember that.'

The ranger was not smiling, nor was he looking at the crowd. He stood with his legs firmly apart and his hands on his hips, gazing into the crater full of mist where the sun was preparing to rise.

Then suddenly, dramatically, he turned. 'We have proof!' he cried, waving a newspaper clipping framed under clear plastic. 'A family from Montana took home one rock, just one little scrap of lava, and in the next year they had $20,000 in medical expenses. We get packages in the mail all the time, full of rocks and dried plants that people have taken away from this place, people like you who scoffed at Pele, and she has followed them. Accidents, illnesses, financial reverses, romantic difficulties.

'This place belongs to Madam Pele!' He waved both curved fists over his head as if in a hula. 'If you try to take anything from here, she will take it back, and she will take you, too!'

'Can we take you home with us?' giggled one of the matrons in the crowd. 'Or are you under Madam Pele's special protection, too?'

The ranger dimpled. 'Well, now, that all depends, ma'am. Some of us have tried to leave the islands and have discovered that Pele wouldn't permit it. But for the right offer . . .'

'Is it all right to take pictures?' someone else asked.

'You may take all the pictures you wish. Pele has no

objection, and neither do we. Of course,' he added solemnly, 'anything Madam Pele regards as her own won't show up on your film anyway.'

They stood at the rim of the crater – or where they imagined the rim to be, since the fog was so thick they couldn't see more than a few feet below – and watched the sun come up – or thought they did, since the fog hid the sun, too. The earth turned. The sun came up very gradually, until they were flooded by clouds of brilliant burning white. The sun and the earth were not distinct from each other; there was no horizon, and they couldn't see the rim of the crater at their feet.

Hilary could hardly catch her breath. 'Let's go down.'

As they descended the narrow path – if, indeed, there was a path; the stones seemed random – the fog closed around them so that they could see nothing above or below, and the fog or the presence of Pele hushed footsteps and voices. Joel reached for her hand, but Hilary shook her head; it was hard enough to keep her balance alone.

Every night on the islands they had walked along the beach, at the very edge of the land where the ocean came in. The hugeness and opacity of the water stirred her, the smallness of the land, the sense of being alien and powerless. The sky was moist tropical black, with a haze over the moon. The sand was dark and wet, sticky between her toes, and warm from the day's hot sun; it accepted her footprints and absorbed them before she could even look back over her shoulder. Her feet stiffened from the hardening sand; she thought of Pele's lava and hastily went to wade in the sea, which, of course, was Pele's, too. She went in farther than she meant to; the blood-warm water was up to her knees before she knew it, and she had cupped some of it in her hands, splashed it onto her face, rubbed it into her dripping hair.

She ran out of the ocean. Her footprints on the sand glistened for a moment, one after the other, and then filled in. She'd thought she could bury herself safely in Joel's arms, but he had run off down the beach and was only a black silhouette against the pearly black sky and the black sea. She heard his voice, playing, calling her name, but in syllables just slightly altered so that she wasn't sure it was really her

name at all. Other silhouettes milled just at the periphery of
her vision, rippling away when she looked.

Standing again at the edge, Hilary couldn't understand
how the ocean could *have* an edge, a beginning or an end, any
more than fire did, or the constant quiet drumming which she
hardly noticed anymore until it stopped. There was a story
about Pele, wakened in a dream by a distant drum like that
which announced a hula, assuming her spiritual form and
leaving her physical body, an old woman asleep in a cave,
to go and investigate. She was gone for a long time.

Backing up from the ocean, feeling the drums at her back
like breath, watching the mysterious points of phosphoresence
in the air and across the water, Hilary understood how that
could happen. Land was only an interruption of water.
Silence was only an interruption of drums. It wouldn't be
hard for her to move in and out of her body, or for Joel to
move in and out of his. She knew they would not be allowed
to leave this place together.

Joel went in.

His hands would leave her and she would faintly see him
run into the surf, his body blurred and then swallowed. She
would hear a dim splash, glimpse spray from his first stroke
or two, and then he'd be gone. Hilary would retreat a few
more steps from the lapping sea and try to wait for him on
the shore, unable to see him among all the light and shadows
or to hear him through the island's cacophony, unable to
distinguish him from all the other presences, unable to fix
on anything she could believe was the horizon.

Joel went in every night. 'You can swim,' he'd say to her,
every night. 'We used to swim laps together at the pool,
remember? Come on in with me.' But she couldn't bring
herself to go into this water. She couldn't even stay very
long near the ocean. The land wasn't much better, for she
knew that at its core the land was on fire.

Finally he would emerge, wet, laughing and shaking,
breathless, and she'd rub him down with a white towel. Then
they'd walk back to the hotel hand-in-hand, arm-in-arm;
sometimes he'd carry her like a bride across a threshold,
or she'd wrap her arms and legs around him from behind.
In the hotel they'd take a long steamy shower together, and
then make love.

On the islands they made love more than they ever had.
In the giant vibrating bed, on the sea-green carpet, in the
shower, on the open-air patio that overlooked Waikiki. The
drums never stopped. They drank MaiTais and smoked the
good Hawaiian weed that Joel had casually scored in a
scrimshaw shop on the main street of Lahaina from a spacey
pony-tailed kid from New Jersey and his pretty Polynesian
lady. Hilary was on a constant, horizonless high.

She knew she couldn't live like this forever; this was
not her home. She couldn't love Joel like this forever, not
knowing where she was, and anyway the loving seemed to
have little to do with either her or Joel, seemed to seep out of
the very air like the mist or the fragrance of orchids, seemed
to tremble and erupt out of the sea like Pele's island chain.
Hilary held onto Joel's hand, but she had to look down now
and then to make sure it was there.

A few hundred feet down into Haleakala Crater, they
stopped and sat down together on a cold outcropping of
lava rock. Mist swirled between them. On the path beside
them someone went by with horses, huge silent beasts with
muffled hoofbeats and icy tails. Hilary ran her hand over her
hair and brought it away with snowflakes on the palm. Joel's
beard was tipped with silver.

'It's beautiful here,' she said.

Joel put an arm around her. 'It's beautiful with you.'

'Let's get some pictures.'

'All you'd get is fog. You wouldn't get a sense of the
vastness of it, the perspective.' He grinned. 'You wouldn't
get anything important. Pele would see to that.'

Hilary stood up, slipped, made her way a few steps down
the slope. With every step she seemed to be on the edge of
something, but when she peered over all she could see was
fog and the dim outline of more volcanic rock. She held her
hands protectively away from her body and thought maybe
someone would take them, but the offering was refused, or
ignored.

The hike back up to the crater rim seemed endless. On the
way, making sure Joel didn't see, Hilary picked up a small
nondescript brown crater stone and put it in her pocket.

Again and again she touched parts of Joel's body with her
fingertips and tongue. In the hollow behind his ear, she

listened to his pulse like the beating of the sea in a shell. He lay across the bed under her and she rubbed coconut oil into his back, his neck, his thighs. His muscles slid and separated under her hands. There were still grains of sand rough on his skin, between his ribs and in the hollows of his knees; he flinched when she scraped them away with the heel of her hand. In the daytime, the light was watery, rippling; at night, there was always a dim fire. 'Mouths were made for kissing,' Hilary murmured, quoting Pele, and like Pele felt the fire come into her eyes.

A breeze came in the open patio doors, stirring the bamboo shades. The trade winds had picked up again. From the outdoor cafe just above the beach proper – where only communal illusion kept the tables and dancers, the palms and eucalyptus and flickering gas lamps from sliding off into the sea – flowed rhythms of ukeleles and steel drums. There was a show every night, haunting tenor ululation from a man with sleeves like white wings, alto from a woman whose hair the colour of cinders fell straight to her waist.

It seemed to Hilary that on the islands she'd hardly slept at all, or that there was no real boundary between sleeping and waking. Pele was known to disturb the sleep both of her rivals and of those she loved, because she could make dreams seem real and reality seem like dreams. It seemed to Hilary that everything was in constant motion: the sea, the sand, the music, the winds, the molten core of the earth, the many aspects of Pele who was goddess of fire and goddess of water and goddess of the islands themselves. Her own love for Joel and his for her moved, too, struggled to hold on, grew frenetically even though its roots, she knew, were precarious. Hilary could hardly keep still.

She leaned over Joel, laid herself against him. She absorbed the sweet smells of his body, tasted the salt in his hair, whispered, 'I love you.' As she said it, it grew in her, until she was nothing but her love for Joel.

'I love you, too,' he answered, like a chant, and rolled over, tumbling her onto the bed and taking her in his arms. Her back burned where he'd touched her; her eyes burned with hot tears.

That night, their last in Hawaii, Hilary for the first time dared to walk alone on the beach. It was very late, but the lights and the music hadn't stopped, any more than the ocean had stopped, or the intimations of Pele everywhere.

Hilary walked barefoot through the pools at the very edge of the ocean and stared out in the direction she thought was home. Immersed as she was in the dangerous magic of the islands, she couldn't really imagine going home, but somewhere beyond those mythical black waters was a high, still, dry place where growing things had to be cared for and feet could be kept solidly on the ground. She waded farther out into the sea and spread her hands on its undulating surface, trying to understand this element that seemed so alien and yet that filled so much of her own body, trying to feel what force it was that held the water together, thinking desperately of Joel.

Then, suddenly enraged, she flung the small brown stolen crater stone as far as she could out to sea, away from Pele's islands, toward home. The stone disappeared; she couldn't have thrown it that far. She had a sudden image of its springing to life, *growing*, arching back toward her. Mourning Joel, knowing this would be their last time together, she stumbled back to shore so as not to see where the stone sank into the sea.

Joel caught her. At first he frightened her, coming out of the dark like that; she pushed him away, then clung to him. 'I don't want to go home!' she said against his chest. She could hear his heartbeat, the air in and out of his lungs, the blood in his veins.

'We have to.' She could hardly hear him over the surf and the cacophonous undertow of voices, magnified as if there were crowds nearby, although no one else was in sight. 'Our tickets are non-refundable without a death certificate or a doctor's excuse. And we both have to be back to work on Monday.'

'Things won't last at home.'

He held her at arm's length and smiled down at her. She could see his eyes, reflecting the phosphorescence of the sea, or of her own eyes. She could feel the rich air all around her, hear the voices, female voices, whispering and rumbling. 'Everything that's happened between us here,' Joel said, 'we can take home with us.' He was firm; he believed what he was saying. But she knew it wasn't true.

'I love you,' she said, helplessly.

'I love you, too.' He kissed her. She opened her mouth under his, braced her feet wide apart so that her legs were spread, but she couldn't get him close enough, couldn't keep him from moving away from her and saying, 'I'm going in one last time.'

'Don't, Joel.'

'There won't be time in the morning, and who knows when I'll have a chance to swim in the Pacific Ocean again? Come in with me.' He held out his hand to her.

'No.'

'Wait for me, then.'

She watched him for as long as she could see him, which wasn't long. The ocean waves caught all the lights and made moving shadows among themselves. She listened to his rhythmic splashing until it melted into the other island sounds.

Then she heard him cry out.

She took a few steps. Her heart filled her ears. Water surged around her ankles, so close to her own body temperature that she could barely feel it. 'Joel?'

'Hilary! Help!'

She saw him go down, at about the place where the crater rock she'd stolen and then returned had disappeared. She saw his head go under the waves. There were a host of other forms out there, crowding around. She screamed, 'Joel!'

His head came back up. He was choking. He made a sound that was not her name, but she knew he was calling her.

She could swim. She was afraid of the ocean, especially at night, but Joel knew that she could swim. Frantically she glanced around; there was no one else on the beach, although the sounds and scents of life were everywhere. She waded in up to her waist, two steps, then half-fell forward with her face in the water and took a few strokes out to sea, in the direction of the spot where she'd last seen Joel.

When she shook the salt water out of her eyes, she didn't know where she was. There were lights everywhere, shadows everywhere, horizons near and far. For a terrified instant she thought she couldn't touch bottom. Then she stood up, her feet on the molten floor of the ocean in the tepid water but the rest of her exposed. There, she saw

Joel, flailing, making his own cloud of spray. She heard him cry out again and again, her name like the drums in Pele's dream.

But he had been claimed. She didn't go to him. Skin stinging with tears and sweat and spray, stinging as if with hot ash, she turned and went back up the beach alone.

They found his body without much searching, discarded onto the shore. It had already been possessed by the sea, of course, invaded by the hot salt sun. It was already decomposing, so that the boundaries between Joel's flesh and the sand on the beach were blurred.

Hilary was there when they found him. She ran to him, crouched beside him. She could hear herself keening, taste it in her throat. She took one of his hands in her own, though the bare-legged men of the search party told her not to; the fingers were bulbous like fat roots, and her fingers sank into them. She tried to be careful that they didn't pass all the way through. The palm of Joel's hand was hard, like lava; it did not accept even a deliberate scratch from her nails.

Hilary let go. One of the dark-skinned men in the bright shirts pulled her away from Joel's body, muttering kind admonitions. Hilary looked around. In the crowd she saw women, shrouded, with eyes reddened from tears or from fire; in the brilliant reflections off the sand and the waves, their backs seemed to be gorgeously on fire.

Joel had had no family but her. She had had no family but him – none she counted, anyway; none who would care. She and Joel were still each other's family. They had grown together, and now would always be. Planning his cremation, watching his smoke drift up into the watery blue sky, Hilary was as joyful as she was griefstricken, as filled as she was bereft. She had been about to lose him, and now that would never happen.

On the plane home, she took her seat by the window behind the wing. The urn of Joel's ashes was in her carry-on bag behind her feet. There was no need for her to stay in the islands anymore, and she was eager to escape. Already, in the thin dry cabin air, her head was clearing. The thought of spending the rest of her life in the mountains was like a strange fruit: inside the pulpy layers of widowhood, of aloneness, would always be Joel.

. Hilary fell asleep over the ocean. When she started awake, there were presences in the aisles. A haggard old woman sat beside her where an empty seat had been, asleep, her uninhabited body breathing lightly and regularly on its own. A beautiful young woman, in countless forms, filled the walking spaces and breathing spaces of the plane, eyes blazing, back afire.

'When you come to the islands,' Pele said gently, as she had always been saying, 'I possess you and you possess me.'

Through the golden cloud pile, toward the perpetual sea, the plane began to fall.

ALCHEMIST'S GOLD

William Thomas Webb

William Thomas Webb is the author of eight published novels, including After the Inferno, The Eyes of Hollerl-Ra *and* The Time Druids. *His numerous short stories have appeared in* Fantasy Tales, Science Fantasy, Nebula, Science Fiction Adventures, New Writings in Horror & the Supernatural 1 *and* 2, *and* New Writings in SF. *A novel in progress is titled* Moloch.

'HE'S a heretic, isn't he?' the soldier shouted, nudging the Dominican aside and seizing their naked victim by the neck. At the same time, his comrade grabbed a hammer to nail the man to the door of his own spacious laboratory.

'That may be so,' the friar said, staring with obvious concern at the great, iron-bound door through which they had just forced an entry. 'But this is hardly the way to bring a heretic back to the fold.'

'Your brethren in the Inquisition don't share your dainty scruples,' Gabrion de Saxe said, gripping the hilt of his sword. 'Nail him up, I tell you!' he shouted to the brawny, helmeted soldiers. 'We'll soon make him repent of his heresies. And furthermore,' he added with a smile, 'we'll make him reveal where he hides his gold.'

The nobleman, who, in contrast to his hirelings, was tall and slender, had a short, green, fur-trimmed cape over a silk gown with silver buttons and trailing sleeves. His legs were dressed in silken hose. And from his low belt hung the jewel-hilted sword he was constantly fingering.

As well as being an alchemist, and a philosopher of renown, Dr Johann Darston was an outspoken freethinker. And, more to the point, he was a constant critic of Gabrion de Saxe; and lost no opportunity to rail against him. De Saxe made a handsome income by luring pilgrims to the Shrine of St Bernard, which stood on his family estate, on the outskirts of Avignon. The shrine claimed to possess, among many saintly relics, the largest fragment of the True Cross outside of Palestine. But Darston had ridiculed this claim so fiercely that pilgrims were decreasing in numbers.

Until recently the alchemist had enjoyed the protection of Jacques de Molay, the Grand Master of the Templars. But Jacques was now in disgrace, and in peril of his life. So Gabrion de Saxe had decided the time was opportune to silence his enemy and relieve him of some of the gold he was said to manufacture.

Taking the friar along to give the venture a semblance of legality, de Saxe and two of his mercenaries had burst into the laboratory early that June sabbath morning, when the alchemist, who slept among his tools and treasures, still lay in bed.

'Recant your heresies,' Friar Hubert pleaded with their wrathful victim as Pierre pressed the man's hand to the sturdy door. 'Repent of your sins. And I'll instruct the noble Gabrion de Saxe to order his men to desist.'

'That's right,' said Gabrion, who had been searching the bed, throwing off the sheepskin rugs and linen sheets, and peering beneath the goose-feather mattress. 'Recant your heresies, and produce your gold; and we'll leave you in peace to manufacture more of it.'

'I have no gold,' Dr Darston declared in his loud, ranting voice. 'And my so-called heresy is nothing but the truth as I see it after a lifetime of study and contemplation. I honour the Nazarene as staunchly as anyone. He stands for ever among the world's great teachers. But he is no more, and no less, the son of God than you or I.'

'Blasphemy!' said the friar. And he closed his eyes as Renaldo, with a grin on his bearded face, hammered a flat-sided iron nail into the alchemist's left wrist. From some distance away a bell began to toll for matins.

'Hold him, you fools!' Gabrion shouted as the man slumped forward. 'You haven't killed him, have you? I'll finish off the pair of you if you have. We don't want him to give up the ghost until we know where he keeps his treasure.'

'He's all right, my lord!' said Pierre. 'Come, Renaldo! Let's fix the other arm.'

'Wait!' the black-robed friar moistened a piece of linen from the jug near the bed. Then he wiped the alchemist's brow, and spoke to him softly: 'Johann, I implore you to recant your heresy. Repent of your sins before it's too late. For at any moment you may leave this life for the torments of Hell.'

'Life has no joy for me now,' Darston said in a voice which, although no longer loud, had lost none of its defiance. 'And Hell, if there be such a place, can hardly be worse than this evil kingdom ruled by Philip and his band of assassins.'

'That's both blasphemy and sedition,' the friar said with a resigned glance at the leering soldiers. 'And each of those crimes is punishable by death.'

'Try his other hand!' ordered Gabrion, who was still rooting round for the alchemist's gold. 'Let him hang like a fox on a barn door. It may help him remember where he's put the stuff.'

As the friar turned his head away, Renaldo stretched the alchemist's right arm across the door, leaned his weight against the naked body to keep it still, and gripped the forearm and the tightly-clenched hand. Then Pierre, grunting and cursing, hammered a big, rusty nail into the sinewy wrist. Johann Darston cried out and fainted.

'You haven't killed him, have you?' Gabrion repeated, reaching for his sword.

'God knows!' Pierre retorted insolently. 'But it's thirsty work in here, with that furnace smouldering like the hobs of Hell; and all these stinking pots filling the place like a pest-house. Come, Renaldo! Let's see what the magus has to drink!'

He threw down the hammer. Then, followed by the furious gaze of their master, the soldiers swaggered across the untidy room, with its alembics and cucurbits, and vessels of acids, herbs, spices, and many other substances in solid and liquid form.

But they could see nothing that enticed them. And eventually they forced a door at the rear of the premises for access to a cellar where the savant kept his skins of wine. They helped themselves to this without delay, laughing lustily as they guzzled it, and splashed it on their beards and jerkins.

They were three parts drunk when they staggered back to the laboratory, each carrying a skin of choice Burgundy. And there they saw that the alchemist, who stood with his hands pinned in line with his ears, had regained consciousness and seemed to be lecturing the nobleman and the friar.

'Gold in itself is worthless; and I would waste no time making it even if I knew how. It is as nothing compared with some of the treasures I have here. But you are both too blind to see them.'

'What treasures? Where?' Gabrion jerked his head from side to side as he glanced round the room, taking-in the tables, the furnace, the shelves and niches, and the ornate metal lamps. A large, sloping overhead window filled the place with morning sunlight, which picked out bright surfaces of glass and metal. 'Do you mean diamonds, rubies, sapphires, pearls . . .?'

'Nothing of the kind,' the alchemist said weakly. 'For many years I have given up the vain pursuit of gold and the Elixir of Life. And I have laboured instead on the manufacture of drugs, potions and unctions to cure or alleviate disease. And the day will come when all right-thinking men of my calling will devote their efforts to a similiar pursuit.'

'Hypocrite!' Gabrion shouted, waving a hand. 'All the world knows that you make gold in this laboratory. You have presented many a talent of it to his holiness Clement V, and to Charles, the king's brother.'

'That, my lord, is simply untrue.'

'You lie!' screamed Gabrion, slapping the doomed man's sweating face. 'But we'll have the truth out of you before we're done. Soldiers! Nail his feet up clear of the floor.'

'Yes, sire!' Pierre said, knuckling his narrow forehead. And after swigging more wine, he and Renaldo bumped into each other in their eagerness to grab the hammer and another long nail.

Johann Darston had been taking most of the weight of his body on his feet. But when, with the utmost brutality, they bent his knees and hammered a blunt nail through his crossed ankles, he hung there crucified, with his body sagging painfully, and his weight dragging on his nailed wrists, from which trails of blood trickled down the door. His naked torso squirmed with every shallow breath he snatched into aching lungs.

'There is yet time,' said Friar Hubert, who had been kneeling on the wet floor and now stood in front of the tortured man, with his own arms raised in sympathy and entreaty. 'Repent of your sins, Johann my child. And I'll command these men, were they servants of the king himself, to pull out the nails and free you, on pain of offending against the law of the Holy Church . . .'

The man gasped so noisily that death seemed to rattle in his throat. To the soldiers, violent death was a feature of their trade; and they paid little heed to the condition of the alchemist. They glanced instead at their master, who had his back to them and was striding across the room in his search for gold. But to the friar it seemed that the sinner had died unrepentant. He felt himself partly to blame for this; and, with a groan of despair, he sank to his knees again, his head thrown back, and his hands clasped before him. Then, like one stirring painfully from death, the alchemist snatched several shallow breaths in quick succession and pulled himself up on gory wrists. When he spoke it seemed to the friar that his prayers were being answered, and he had saved another soul.

'Lord forgive me!' Johann Darston murmured. And outside the building all the bells of Avignon seemed to start ringing at once.

'Come on, you two!' Friar Hubert cried, springing to his feet. 'Help me pull out the nails!'

He beckoned also to Gabrion de Saxe. But he was at the far side of the room now, searching among some parchments on a table. The friar, impatient to release the penitent, and distrustful of the fumbling soldiers, found a large pair of pincers and tugged at the nail that pinned the man's ankles to the door. It came away quickly from the wood. But it took longer to wrench it free from the struggling, blood-drenched limbs. And Darston screamed when the nail was eventually removed.

Hubert wiped some of the slippery gore from his hands and brandished the pincers at the soldiers as if he were St Dunstan attacking the devil.

'Hold him still while I get the nails out of his wrists!'

Pierre and Renaldo were almost blind drunk by now. But they were accustomed to obeying orders. And they held on to the naked, squirming body while the friar tugged out the other nails. Then, staggering and stumbling like a pair of clowns, they helped to drag the tortured man over to his bed, leaving behind a trail of blood. Suddenly Gabrion de Saxe, looking round towards the door, realized what was going on. And with a shout of anger he came clattering across the laboratory knocking over carboys, retorts, and pelicans in his furious dash.

'You drunken sots! Who told you to take him down?'

'They acted under my orders,' the Dominican said, raising a hand. 'The sinner has repented, my lord. Another soul has been saved.'

Gabrion trod angrily towards him.

'You keep out of this! These men are under my orders. The repentence of one heretic means little to us. But his gold, when we find it, will be used to maintain my family shrine, which may cause hundreds of pilgrims to repent their sins.' He drew his sword with a well-practised flourish and pressed the point of it against Johann Darston's naked body. 'Where is your gold, Master Alchemist? Speak now, or I'll have my men nail you back against that door.'

The man on the bed laughed wheezily. His broad brow gleamed with sweat, yet he lay there shivering as if with cold. Saliva dribbled from his bearded lips. His eyes had a dreadful glaze to them, as if he were dead already and only waited for someone to close them. And his voice, when he spoke again, was the husky whisper of an animated corpse.

'There is much treasure here, Gabrion de Saxe. Yet you and your ilk will never see it.'

'Hach!' Gabrion jabbed forwards and downwards. As the sword pierced the flesh of the helpless man, the friar turned his head in disgust and even the drunken soldiers looked shocked. But Gabrion, undaunted, pointed his gore-tipped blade towards the heart of Friar Hubert. 'Where is this treasure he babbled about? Did he confess to you?'

'I had no time to shrive the penitent,' the friar said, crossing his forearms over his breast. 'But he recanted his heresy in my hearing; and his soul is now at the gates of Paradise, waiting to be welcomed in.'

'There's gold here,' de Saxe shouted. 'The alchemist admitted as much with his dying breath. Search for it, men! Leave no crock unturned until we find it.'

Barely pausing to sheathe his sword, he began to dash about like a madman, hurling costly vessels of glass and earthenware to the floor, over-turning tables, and emptying shelves and niches, with his flailing arms. Some of the liquids splashed the black robe of the friar. More of it dashed against the walls and on the dead man on the bed, and spurted over the wine-guzzling soldiers, who sloshed about in it like demons in a brimstone pit.

'Stop it!' the friar shouted when this had gone on for some minutes and showed no sign of abating. 'Have you no respect for the Order of St Dominic and for the corpse of a penitent?'

But the wreckers were deaf to his words. Like rampaging vandals, they were more intent to destroy the premises than to continue their search for any treasure it might contain. The friar turned away from them, raising his cowl in an attempt to banish them from his thoughts. Then, muttering prayers, and listening to the bells outside, he reverently closed the dead man's eyes, and covered him with a sheet, hoping to prevent further insults to his earthly remains.

Eventually, when hardly a vessel remained intact, Gabrion de Saxe came to accept it as a fact that he was not going to find Johann Darston's treasure. But at least he had silenced his vituperative tongue. So he called to his hirelings to desist. But by now they were quite berserk, and beyond taking orders from anyone. They continued to shatter glass and pottery, and even pieces of wood; splashing and churning liquids and unctions everywhere, until the stuff mingled into a stinking, foaming froth that covered the floor, spilled over priceless books and parchments, and spattered against the walls, to ooze down them in hideous *ruches*, like curtains in some alcove in vilest Hell.

Gabrion shouted to his men once more. And then, with no more compunction than a serf would have when killing rats, he ran them through with his sword and watched them slump to the floor and expire in a froth of blood and chemicals. And the room, save for the chimes of bells outside, and the monotonous murmurings of the friar, was strangely silent.

Feeling sick and extremely weary, Gabrion returned his sword to its sheath. Then, desperate for a breath of pure air, he staggered towards the door. But as he was about to step outside, he heard the Dominican call out.

'My lord! There is something here you must see.'

Gabrion, who a moment ago, had been weary to the point of collapse, felt new energy spurt through him. He swung round immediately, his hand trembling on the hilt of his sword.

'What is it, Friar Hubert? Have you found the gold.'

'Something much more splendid.'

'What? Where?'

'Clearly we have here a sign that Johann Darston has been accepted into Paradise.' With a wondrous smile on his face, the friar stood pointing down at the body of Dr Johann Darston. It seemed to glow miraculously in the shaft of sunlight piercing the overhead window. 'Look! The sheet which lies upon him like a shroud, bears an impression that might almost be the likeness of our crucified Lord.'

'By Jesus, you're right!' Gabrion pulled the sheet off the corpse and held it up. 'A miracle! This might well be the very shroud that covered Him when He was lifted down from the cross by Joseph of Arimathea.'

'A miracle indeed!' said the friar. 'Dr Darston has been truly honoured.

'You're right!' said the jubilant Gabrion de Saxe. 'And for every pilgrim who journeyed to my family shrine to pay respects to the fragment of the True Cross, which Darston so scurrilously derided, a hundred, nay a thousand, will flock to see the *True Shroud*. How wondrous are the ways of Providence!'

The Dominican shook his head, and crossed himself very slowly.

THE HORROR WRITER

Allen Ashley

Allen Ashley has had stories published in Fantasy Tales, The Best
Horror from Fantasy Tales, Interzone, Back Brain Recluse,
The Golden Void, Chills, Dark Horizons *and* Mystique,
*amongst other titles. As well as short stories, he has written a
novel,* Inside the Viper, *and an acclaimed study of the rock band*
Hawkwind, *with whom he has occasionally performed.*

IN his time, Nigel Norwood was rightly acclaimed as a modern master of the macabre, a weaver of webs of witchcraft and
wizardry to rank with the finest produced by Lovecraft, Poe,
Machen, Bierce, Bradbury, M. R. James, *et al*. Even now,
some years after his untimely death, his many novels and
anthologies continue to figure consistently in the bestsellers
lists. As one might have expected, the critics have gathered
like literary coroners to dissect his work. Most have tried to
rob it of meaning, to dismiss the jewels of his career with
one or two glib phrases, and thus enhance their own critical
reputations. Needless to say, the people who really count –
the book buyers and readers – have not been swayed.

My abiding interest in Nigel Norwood began many years
ago, when I was in my teens. A friend lent me a copy of
Norwood's first, and at that time only, novel: *Necromancy
Night*. I started reading it after dinner one evening, intending
to peruse a few chapters before getting on with my history
homework.

However, once I opened the book I did not put it down
until I had read the whole story. I even carried the book
with me into the kitchen when I went for a mug of water,
and into the bathroom when I simply *had* to go. Just after
midnight my quivering hands finally let the paperback slip

to the floor. I looked over my shoulder for about the eighth time in the last ten minutes, expecting to see some ghastly zombie standing statue-like against the wall. I was, of course, relieved to find no such thing. Even so, I was scared out of my mind and my fired imagination was running riot so that I had to continually blink away delusions. I was so tensed up that I could not sleep at all that night. Instead I drank several cups of black coffee and helplessly relived the horrors I had encountered within that terribly beautiful book. As for my history homework – well, Franz Ferdinand and the Kaiser just ceased to exist!

When my friend asked me to return the book I did so, but rushed immediately to one of the specialist science fiction and fantasy bookshops in London where I bought my own copy of *Necromancy Night* and also every professional and fan magazine that had even so much as a mention of Norwood. I was hooked, good and proper. When his second novel, *Death in Dark Water*, hit the shops I was one of the first dozen or so people to purchase it. In hardback!

I had shown artistic inclinations in my schoolwork and had even been fortunate enough to have some poems published in the school's annual anthology. One of these was later reprinted in the local newspaper, which was a great thrill for yours truly. In short, I secretly wanted to be an author. My boyhood tastes had been towards detective stories and I dearly longed to create a character to rank with Father Brown, Nick Charles, Sherlock Holmes, or Philip Marlowe. But after my introduction to Norwood's fiction my ambition was permanently changed and I wished only to be a master of the horror genre. To this end I set out to study the works and lives of all the major figures within the field, past and present, and Nigel Norwood in particular.

I immediately began by writing to him, via the publisher. My letter was full of youthful enthusiasm for his work and rather impassioned pleas for any advice he could offer an aspiring author, namely myself. No doubt he was too busy to waste time on callow youths wanting the secret of success; he was gracious enough, however, to send me in reply a signed paperback copy of his first collection, *The Twelve Nightmares Of Doctor Spiritus*. No bill was enclosed, it was a gift.

Throughout his career Norwood avoided every interviewer's attempts to get him to talk about his art. Often he was rather rude in doing so. It didn't matter; his books spoke for themselves. I well remember when I managed to speak to him at a fantasy convention he ignored my every word and seemed intent instead on discussing the merits of various wines and beers, although he was not at all addicted to alcohol.

When he died there was great sorrow in many a heart at such a tragic loss, but there was also a feeling that at last one might be able to penetrate the veil, to find out the truth about the man. Deciding to temporarily forget my floundering career in fiction – although one published story in ten years can hardly be called a career – I began to delve ever deeper into the late Norwood's affairs.

Even at the beginning of my search I found it curious that he had died of a heart attack on the same day that three police helicopters had collided in mid-air over southern Spain; that all the President's bodyguards had failed to save his grandson's dog from being run over by a Cadillac; and the great romantic author Samuel Sutcliff had also died of a heart attack.

And so, I set about my mission, collecting and collating all the available data. Now, it can all be revealed.

I have seen it written of Ambrose Bierce that he was a misanthropist; of Howard Phillips Lovecraft that he had fascist sympathies; and of Edgar Allan Poe's work that it carries racist overtones or undertones. All this may be true. Thus, there is a tradition of dark hearts producing dark fiction.

At the tender age of twenty, Nigel Norwood temporarily possessed as dark a heart as any man one might care to name. His rent was two weeks in arrears and he was under threat of eviction. The loose change in his pocket would feed him for another two days at most. His dole cheque was not due for another four. His parents refused to help him out, stating categorically that it was up to him alone whether to sink or swim. He had left his last job under such a cloud that he dared not even ask them for a reference.

In short, he was on life's scrapheap at the age when the world was supposed to be his for the taking.

Sitting in his local library, poring methodically over the employment vacancies only served to further depress him. Nearly everybody asked for skills he simply did not possess – typing, book-keeping, machine operation, and the like. Norwood was literate and numerate, but that was about it. As for the jobs he was capable of doing, the salaries offered were such pittances that he was financially better off unemployed.

Tiring of this useless quest, his eyes strayed over the page, across the used car and vacuum cleaner columns, onto the PERSONAL section. A strange mix this: whores offering euphemistic 'relief massage'; spotty boys seeking Miss World; a mature gentleman seeking similar for 'sports and entertainments'; and lastly, the one ad which caught his attention. It read simply, 'Help given – financial and otherwise. *D.M.T. Enterprises* invite you to ring Melantha.' There then followed a telephone number and an address for personal callers.

'It's probably another con,' he thought aloud, causing a few people to glare momentarily in his direction. However, Norwood was desperate enough to try anything. When no one was looking he almost soundlessly tore the ad out of the newspaper and hurriedly departed.

Melantha's voice over the phone would have been enough to convince him of the appropriateness of a visit even if she had not invited him to come round and see her. He fell in love with her delicious vocal cords, and if she proved to be even a quarter as attractive in the flesh, well . . . who knew what might happen? . . .

His destination was some four or five miles away and being unable to afford the extravagance of public transport he had to walk. It took him a good hour during which his anticipated pleasure simply grew and grew.

He found the right street easily enough. It was in a somewhat shabby area and he was expecting the plush offices of *DMT* to stand out like a rednosed reindeer. But they did not. He wandered up and down for a while, alternately confused and then thinking himself the victim of a rather stupid hoax. At last he stopped in front of an old wooden door off which the yellow paint was almost visibly flaking. And there it was, between the names 'Louise French' and 'Danish Dana', a tiny notice bearing the legend *Dreams Made True*. At once intrigued but also a little mistrustful, Norwood rang the relevant doorbell.

The rest of the visit took on the quality of a dream and many of the details were somehow lost into the haze of memory. Suffice it to say that Melantha proved to be a hypnotic beauty and was only too willing to help the young man. They may have made love – Norwood could never afterwards remember. Certainly he felt a lifting of his spirit when first she touched him, as if a great weight had been removed from his shoulders. But after that, everything became incredibly jumbled and he could not tell what was real and what was fabrication.

At length he seemed to be back in the real world. Some hours had passed for it was now late afternoon. Melantha, he realized, had just suggested that he mortgage his soul, leaving it in her safe keeping, and she would keep her part of the bargain and help him gain success and riches.

'But,' he objected, the remnants of his religious education stirring into temporary life, 'I would be condemned to eternal damnation.'

'Not necessarily,' she assured him. 'If you can be successful – and I'll make sure you are – and can gain a full understanding of the whole of human nature, then you can have your soul back when the appropriate time comes.'

It sounded nonsense but he was too bemused to argue with the delectable witch. He merely asked, 'How do I go about becoming successful?'

She smiled, dazzling his tired eyes. 'You decide,' she stated. 'Here,' she added, handing him a wad of notes, 'this will help you get started.'

The next thing he knew, he was back out on the streets, money in pocket, waiting for a bus to take him home. Riding back to his tatty flat, he vainly tried to recall the strange events of the day. He did not go in for all that talk about selling one's soul and yet there was something intangibly plausible about the deal he had made with the lovely Melantha. And the money she had given him – that possessed an undeniable reality.

Just before his stop, he was gazing out of the window when his attention was caught by the signs in the stationery shopfront. They were having a typewriter sale and all of a sudden Norwood knew how he was going to achieve fame, fortune, and also an understanding of human nature. He was going to be an author.

He bought the best typewriter he could afford with the cash in hand, and a ream of paper also. He was left with just enough cash to get a takeaway from the local Chinese restaurant.

Back home, he wolfed down the fried rice and sweet and sour pork, rinsed his hands and face, then put a forbiddingly blank sheet of paper into the typewriter. Then he did nothing for half an hour. And another half hour. At last, tentatively, he began to type with two fingers.

He worked until the early hours of the morning, not caring whether he disturbed the elderly couple downstairs or the family next door. When the story was finished he made himself a well deserved cup of coffee and set about reading the piece he had written. He was expecting to find that it was a rather ordinary story with maybe just one or two inspired phrases or snatches of dialogue. He expected someone might accept it but doubted they would offer him much for its publication. This writing business wasn't as easy as most outsiders seemed to think.

He began to read the story and could hardly believe his eyes. It was his story all right, but it was yet somehow different. And better, much much better than he ever thought he could write. It was a masterpiece, without question. Reaching the end with an involuntary shudder he thought again of his meeting with Melantha that afternoon. He shook his head, then looked back to the pages in his hands. He pursed his lips.

He worked all night, typing out a neat version of the story. In the morning he boldly sent it off to the top magazine in the fantasy field. Within a week they had accepted it and contracted him to write another half a dozen for them. That story was *Begone Vampire!*, now a standard horror work reprinted in countless anthologies and translated into several languages. Nigel Norwood's writing career was on the move.

In hardly any time at all, with just half a dozen stories to his name, Norwood was a minor celebrity. His fictional works, particularly his first story and the award winning *Eight by Eight*, had helped take his name off the unemployment register and out into the literary world. Publishers and magazines were starting to write to him asking to publish his next piece and offering surprisingly high sums for his services. A transatlantic company made him an offer for a novel which literally caused his mouth to fall open for fully five minutes. He decided it was time he flexed his literary muscles and aimed for eighty rather than eight thousand words.

It was about this time he met up again with the girl who had been his sweetheart at school but who, after a torturous year of coy passion, had run off with Motorcycle Mike. Her name was Monica Mason and, meeting her with the dubious benefit of hindsight, Norwood realized she had mistreated his younger self; but he still found himself inevitably attracted towards her. Her affair with Mike had broken down when she found out that bikes would always be tops with him. Since then it had been a downhill slide, leaving her disillusioned with life and lust, and gaining her a rather regrettable reputation in one or two local drinking establishments. In short, she needed picking up and was quite willing to give Norwood his second bite at her well-chewed cherry.

Impressed by his new-found success, Monica accompanied him back to his flat. With the hefty advance received from a major mainstream magazine, Norwood had paid off his debts and was indeed intending to move to a classier neighbourhood at the earliest possible moment.

Proudly he showed her his latest piece, a terrifying novelette which would immortalize his byline. The story was, of course, *The Cabinet Of Professor Eden*, later beautifully filmed by the precocious British director Bill Ellisberg, which also assured his name of its place in the history of artistic achievement.

Finishing the story with a frightened shudder her first reaction was to hug Norwood frantically for the comfort he could offer her. Then she asked, 'Are they all like this?'

'I think that's the best so far,' he answered.

'No, I mean are they all horror?' she explained.

'Yes,' he replied, inevitably reminded of Melantha's instruction that he gain an understanding of human nature. Well he was getting that understanding but, so far, only of the dark side. There would be time for the lighter side.

Monica was wrinkling her dainty little nose. Justifying his output, he said, 'It's what I've been able to sell.'

Cash signs veritably sprang to life inside her head, burning behind her green eyes.

'I think,' she began, 'that you should concentrate on your writing and find someone to look after the business side of things. You know, to get the best deals and make sure everyone pays up, and all that.'

'Someone like you?' he asked, smiling.

'Well, why not? I'm your friend, you can trust me,' she answered with unconscious irony.

They kissed for the first time in three years, sealing the deal.

Within two months Nigel and Monica were married. It is fair to say that he loved her dearly until the end of his days. She was his first love and because of that he forgave her numerous indiscretions, the first of which happened less than three months after the wedding. It seems she had become accustomed to a certain way of life and could not break away from the behaviour pattern built up over the last few years.

Before too long Norwood found himself also starting to stray from the straight and narrow. Of course his new lifestyle as a rising star, an ever more popular celebrity, presented him with more opportunity than when he was just an unemployed clerical worker. Many close to him say that he was simply trying to fight fire with fire. That may well be partly true. But I believe he was also conducting a search: for Melantha. Though his hitherto secret diaries do not say this in so many words, my opinion is implicitly substantiated. Also adding weight to my hypothesis is the fact that, at the various conferences and conventions he attended, Norwood showed a strong tendency to chase after redheads. One of the few things he clearly noted about the mysterious Melantha, his benefactress and soul-keeper, was the distinct fiery colour of her hair. It was Melantha's help which enabled him to become famous and successful and Norwood, it appears, expected that she would at some time or other check up on him. But she did not, at least not till the very end. But I am getting ahead of my story.

Of course, Norwood occasionally paired up with blondes or brunettes and even, once, an East African princess. Maybe he thought Melantha would come in disguise . . .

At the age of thirty he reached a crisis point. Success had taken him a long way. He now lived comfortably in a country cottage, keeping a flat in London for whenever he had to attend conferences or give interviews for the media. He was still married to Monica and finding that their armed truce was the best of compromises. He was, to his knowledge, childless – but this did not worry him, his stories would carry on his name after he died. He had as much of material wealth as he had ever desired. Whatever one may say of Monica Norwood, she proved to be an excellent financier, seeing that not too much of her husband's money was squandered on the luxuries of drink, drugs, holidays, lovers, and charitable contributions.

Norwood was virtually at the top of the tree. As he wryly remarked in his diary, 'It's all downhill from here!' Every one of his books was currently in print and earning him handsome royalties. The film rights for his early novelette *Truth Or Dream* had just been sold for something more than three thousand dollars a page. And, of course, he had recently completed *Fly Like A Vulture*, the novel many consider to be his finest work. Certainly it was his most successful, sales figures being listed in the millions in Britain alone. I need hardly state that financial success does not always equate with artistic achievement and though I greatly enjoyed *Vulture*, I do not regard it as Norwood's magnum opus. My choice, for what it's worth, is his last, semi-factual novel, *Of Hawks, Doves, and Vampire Bats*.

Suffice it to say, then, that Norwood should have been delighted with life, but in fact he was sorely troubled. In the inevitable slack period following the creation of a major novel, his mind began to dwell on Melantha's carefully chosen words of advice just ten years previously. She had certainly kept her part of the bargain and he had tried to keep his. But he had been only partially successful. He now believed he fully understood the darker side of human nature and the phenomenal success of his macabre works seemed to confirm this. But what of the lighter side?

In truth, he remained a literary novice as far as being able to portray the nicer aspects of Humankind. Oh, he had tried! *How* he had tried! Every time he started a new novel he meant it to mark out a new direction in his distinguished career. His works began life as love stories or fables or romances, but before very long they turned sour and dark and ever more terrifying. Indeed, it is this false sense of security in his tales which has most delighted critics and readers alike and it springs very obviously from the repressed, humane core of Norwood's otherwise very dark heart.

His abiding problem was, simply, how would he ever win back his mortgaged soul with only half an understanding of the human consciousness?

At such soul-searching times he wished most fervently that Monica herself had been a writer. If she had written, she would most certainly have turned out romantic fiction and could have helped him; for although she was marvellous at selling his horror stories she could never bring herself to read them. Still, Norwood realized, she had three bookcases stacked full of her kind of book. He was under no contractual obligations to produce his novels within a given length of time – Monica had seen to that – and so he decided to spend the next year engaged in research. He could write well, there was no doubt about that. It would merely be a matter of learning to write in a slightly different manner and to have somewhat different concerns.

Monica was all in favour of Norwood changing genre. Indeed, her very influential mother kept asking why young Nigel didn't write 'a nice story for once'. Monica picked out a representative section of her collection and left Norwood to get on with things.

He spent fully six months reading everything from *Romeo And Juliet* to the formula-written doctors and nurses sagas. He found that his favourite author was a young man named Samuel Sutcliff, whose career had been curiously similar to Norwood's own, and was the living lord of the light and fanciful in much the same way as Norwood was the modern master of the macabre. Nigel resolved to write to the man but before he finished the letter he was invited to appear on a TV chat show on which Sutcliff would also be a guest. Considering their respective positions this was not such a remarkable coincidence; rather it was a smart piece of planning by the programme's producer.

In the event, however, Norwood contracted influenza the day before filming and a well known astrophysicist was hurriedly drafted in to fill his place. Watching the show from his sickbed Norwood perceived Sutcliff to be an affable, blond, bearded fellow but not very forthcoming on the subject of his own creativity. Still, Norwood thought to himself, one author to another ought to make a difference.

Thus, when he was well enough, Norwood completed his epistle and duly posted it. To his dismay, the letter was returned a week later with a covering note from Sutcliff's agent/brother informing him that the romantic author had embarked upon a pilgrimage to India which could well last several years and, for the moment at least, he could not be contacted.

Unperturbed, Norwood set about writing to as many of the lesser love story writers as he thought would be able to help him to any degree. Eight of his enquiries were returned by executors of estates, informing him that the ilustrious authors had been deceased for periods varying from one to ten years. Norwood saw this as poetic justice. Two people did not reply to him, another said she'd love to help but was expecting her third child and would be out of literary action for some months yet. The last half a dozen people he contacted turned out to be mere pen-names for one person. Although in her mid-sixties she claimed to be a sprightly woman and signed her letter 'Suzi Stendahl', suggestive of the young girl remaining alive inside the aging body. Indeed, Norwood rated her books as amongst the raunchiest he'd read.

Much of her advice was either incomprehensible or unusable. The gist of her message, however, seemed to be specifically: 'get a dog and take him out for walks in the country' and, more generally; 'enjoy life'. Norwood took her at her written word but six months later he was no nearer the desired object of writing a romantic novel.

Despairing of the seemingly paltry advice others could offer him he set about searching on his own for the secret of creating a good, readable, believable love story. He read and read but to no avail. He watched every 'tearjerker' film which appeared at the local cinema or on the television, but this did not help him either.

Then, almost three years into his quest, he had the idea which he truly thought would solve his problems. He decided to interview everyone he knew and obtain from them a picture of the brighter aspects of existence. In short he would end up writing a compounded, fictionalized account of their love lives. Even this, however, did not lead to success. To both his surprise and his sorrow, Norwood discovered that even the seemingly happy marriages were but a mere sham and that husband and wife concealed hatreds for their spouse and children and, often, passions for someone else, someone unobtainable. In fact, his new found role as psychiatrist almost drove him mad and he had to give it up.

Dejected, he once more tried to write romances. Again, without success. He did actually complete one short story and send it off to a magazine, wisely using a pseudonym. Three months later he received the story back through the post accompanied by a printed rejection slip. To add insult to injury the concluding line 'Try Again' had been crossed out and a junior editor had scribbled 'Don't Bother' in blue ink.

It was now several years since anything new had appeared bearing the byline of Nigel Norwood. He did not need the money, not at all. He could live comfortably for more than a century on the royalties piled up in his bank account. But Norwood had an understandable professional pride and also felt he owed something of a debt to his hordes of fans to again come up with the goods. He began to write once more; horror stories, this time. They were not as good as the best of his earlier work but his years in the wilderness had not totally deadened his touch and he was widely welcomed back.

At the age of thirty-eight he produced another novel, the aforementioned *Of Hawks, Doves, and Vampire Bats*. I feel this is his greatest work because it carries the touch of a man who has entirely realized both the strengths and limitations of his own talent and vision. Norwood's forte was horrific fiction and this book was his greatest gift to the genre.

In all events, it was to be his last novel.

In this critique I have, perhaps, been a little too damning of Nigel Norwood's wife, Monica. Let me state now that she has been personally very kind to me, allowing me access to Norwood's hitherto secret diaries and other autobiographical writings. She herself possesses no literary talent whatsoever and was rather thrilled when I offered to go through the whole collection with a view to editing them for future publication. Much of this material consists of undated scraps of paper liberally sprinkled with Norwood's rather untidy, barely legible handwriting. Monica had tried to make sense of them shortly after he died but understandably soon gave up the task.

It is mainly from these pieces that I have been able to throw some light onto the matter of Norwood's character. My depiction of his demise is largely conjectural but, I think, fits the facts perfectly.

But what else of Monica? Certainly she relieved Norwood of all the business pressures attendant upon a successful author, leaving him free to concentrate upon the actual writing. Also, to her credit, she has not allowed any rubbish or juvenile work to appear with Norwood's byline since his death – she has not cashed in, so to speak. Just one work has appeared posthumously, and that completed a month before his death, the short story *Unlucky Leviathan*. A creditable obituary, indeed.

In trying to understand Norwood's writing I have sought to understand Norwood the man. Many of his early works have young female antagonists – vamps, as they used to be called. Gradually his stories show a shift so that in the later fantasies the female antagonist is often fat and middle aged, a repressive mother or a spinster witch. That all these characters are firmly based on the lady Monica seems beyond doubt, but the fact reflects only one side of his ambivalent feelings towards her. For he never fell out of love with her and she, in her way, remained constant to him.

Today finds her a rich, rather portly, middle-aged woman whose blonde hair has turned white and frizzy and for whom life has little more to offer. Matronly and somewhat subdued is how I would describe her. The men no longer flock around her at parties and these days she shows a taste for precocious thirteen-year-old schoolboys, giving them some sort of playground credibility, no doubt.

The ringing of the phone woke him. Usually Monica dealt with all calls, particularly those in the morning, for Norwood sat up late to write his atmospheric tales of horror and consequently rarely rose before noon. But Monica was away, visiting her mother. He staggered out of bed and went to answer the ringing. As he lifted the receiver his gaze caught the date on the calendar and he realized with a mild shock that it was exactly twenty years since the fateful meeting.

'Hello,' he said, somewhat hesitantly.

'Judgement Day,' said a voice long forgotten but now instantly recognizable.

In a daze he took down the details of the appointment, time and place. So this is it, he thought, as Melantha rang off. The end of the line. It was tragic, but he'd certainly had his money's worth. He could not honestly complain – Melantha had more than fulfilled her part of the bargain. But he had been unable to keep his, though God knew he had tried.

Norwood made himself several cups of coffee and cooked himself a thick, juicy rump steak. Knowing it would be his last meal, he must have relished every mouthful. Then, after a brief notation in his diary and a last scribbled message to Monica, he set off for the offices of *DMT Enterprises*. There was no question of him *not* going, it was *that* sort of summons.

There Norwood's diary ends. Although he was found dead in bed, of euphemistic heart failure, the coroner noted that the body seemed to have been moved, but this line of enquiry was never followed up and foul play was ruled out by the end of the hearing. I maintain that Norwood did actually go to the offices of *DMT Enterprises*, finding it in the exact same place, surrounded on all sides by call girls' parlours in that shabby neighbourhood.

And Melantha? She still looked like a twenty-five year old beauty queen which, knowing her powers, did not surprise Norwood. She had fulfilled her promise to make him rich and famous but he had only half kept his side of the bargain. Thus he forfeited his soul, or consciousness, or whatever. Invoking poetic, or more correctly prosaic, justice, Melantha confined Norwood to one of his own hells – perhaps the arid wasteland of *Fly Like a Vulture* or the nerve-tingling limbo of his novelette *Life Has Just Begun*. Even now, as his body becomes *hors d'oeuvres* for worms, his soul suffers a fate unthinkable for even one's worst enemy . . .

No! I cannot bring myself to believe Norwood was punished in such a manner. Maybe I'm being naive or romantic but I can't accept that, after working so hard on Norwood's behalf, Melantha would take great pleasure in gloating over his ultimate demise. Perhaps I'm blinded by her beauty but I have a theory that she gave Norwood a safety clause in his contract. For, at the same time as the pact with Norwood, it seems Melantha had also made a deal with Samuel Sutcliff, the erstwhile romantic author. He understood the better side of human nature so well, just as Norwood knew the dark part to excess. Their knowledge was complementary – a case of between them both they licked the platter clean. Maybe she went easy on the pair of them because of this. Or, and this is not such a fantastic conjecture on my part, perhaps the two authors were in fact the divided halves of just one personality?

Certainly it can be no coincidence that they died on the same day and that their careers ran in parallel lines. Sutcliff was found dead outside Danish Dana's door just one floor below Melantha's. The prostitute did not know him from Adam and to find him in such a place was entirely uncharacteristic, for he was a handsome man who regularly did the rounds at women's institute meetings and the like. He did not need to pay for sex.

Did Norwood pay the ultimate price for his success or did he get the best of both worlds? I visited the offices of *Dreams Made True* but the spiders and cockroaches had taken over. My research has been useful to an extent, and some of Norwood's techniques and thoughts on literature have influenced my own efforts. But success still eludes me. I need a helping hand from somewhere.

So, sweet Melantha, if by chance you're reading this . . .

THE HEALING GAME

Laurence Staig

Laurence Staig was an arts administrator for several years, and a jazz and blues guitarist, before expanding his horizons into writing fantasy and thrillers for young adults. His books include The Network, Digital Vampires, The Glimpses, Shapeshifter *and a collection of short stories,* Dark Toys and Consumer Goods. *A new book for younger children,* The Invasion of the Wire Ones, *has a planned sequel entitled* The Empire of the Lost Sock. *The author has also recently completed an autobiography about growing up in London,* Smokestack Lightning, *and he's at work on an adult psychological thriller,* The Milk of the Moon.

FOR ROBERT JORDAN

MID-MORNING has crept up on Drood unnoticed. The day arrives with a tell-tale shaft of light, a cruel brightness that pierces the gap in the curtains with the precision of a razor. The makeshift drapes, rummaged from the housing-estate skips, allow peppered points of daylight to cast a ray of stars across the place where he lies. He is huddled, ungainly, like a broken mannequin.

Drood cautiously opens a single eye. Sticky eyelashes blur his view of the room as he peers over the frayed edge of the tattered eiderdown. He pauses for a moment, uncertain if he has awoken, wondering if perhaps he still dreams. His hand emerges from beneath the cover, which stinks of something sweet and sickly, like bad yeast. Outstretched searching fingers, fumble for his spectacles.

He coughs and almost gags from the stench of the air. For a moment his hand crawls across the surface of the chair, like a pale-coloured spider, and then the tips of his fingers discover something wiry, which surround two thick smooth circular wedges.

He pulls his spectacles towards him and winds the hooks of the wire arms around his ears, greasy knots of hair become fastened to the sides of his face. The cold metal almost holds his features, as though steel fingers were trying to hold his head steady, so that he might recall where he is.

But now, he knows exactly where he is. Exactly.

Another day in the pit.

He groans, his voice almost touches bottom.

A new day is always unkind, it brings the usual vermin: the brats downstairs in the estate courtyard; milkmen clattering bottles and crates whilst eyeing lonely mothers, half-hidden in doorways leering back at them, sheathed in cheap market-stall nylon nighties. Sometimes the milkmen's tuneless whistling stops whilst an overdue bill is paid, one way or another.

Babies squawk. Dogs howl. Eventually it will become a cacophony: a symphony of blaring radios that will crowd the air with rubber-band music. The washing machine on the floor above, will rattle and shake his ceiling.

For a moment he clenches his teeth, remembering the past week: as if living itself wasn't enough, there had been the doorstep callers to contend with. Young children often knocked, daring one another as to who would stand their ground the longest, before he opened up. Usually they would run away with shrieks of terrible laughter, knowing that he wouldn't dare leave his doorway to give chase.

Recently another kind of caller had troubled him: The God Squad, drawn to the estate's hive of decaying souls like flies to meat.

There were many who needed saving here.

Perhaps it was something to do with the challenge? Was that why they came?

The Sally Army Band came first, risking a half hour in the yard last Saturday with clapped-out brass and broken tambourines. Roaming groups of Jehovah's Witnesses followed. They had knocked repeatedly at his door, asking whether he had found the way, the truth and the light. They always called when he had finally managed to doze off, or late in the evening when he was beginning to get into a game or write a new virus.

There were others too, all wishing to take you away to paradise.

Drood's knuckles still sting, grazed and sore from a recent doorstep encounter. The pain reminds him yet again that he is alive, feeling returns in increments, slowly searing his body with a poker heat. His mouth is full of puffy gum, swollen and sore. He groans, the abscess that throbs hot beneath his tooth hasn't healed; it is as raw and infected as everything else around him.

How he hates the place.

Drood considers for a moment whether to put his head back beneath the cover and to drown out the day. It would be easy. Drood is a night creature, and for that the pit suits. Spurned by the day, he has long grown used to the dark, rejecting the cruelty of sunlight. But there is something he must do. He remembers with a small monkey-grin, that he is to listen to the news again this morning.

Throwing the cover to one side, he swings his spindly legs round to sit on the edge of the couch. A fluttering feeling inside his head, like the flurry of a captured moth, makes him feel dizzy and there is a pain across his eyes. He had fallen asleep around the middle of the night. After he had reached for the remainder of the bottle. He glances at the radio and discovers that he has time to gather his thoughts.

This morning the room looks worse than usual. The day has brought with it a brightness that somehow shows too much, which reveals his secrets: piles of dirt and dust, magazines are strewn across the floor, cardboard boxes of second-hand paperbacks are stacked against nicotine-stained peeling wallpaper.

The day corrupts. It casts a reflected glare across his computer screen, tainting and obscuring, casting a dust-grey sheen. Spoiling.

In the cloak of night, alone and undisturbed, he can melt into the world of programmed dream and imagine impossible worlds, to live unimaginable lives. To fight and quest with dragons and demons, to hide away from the drum of reality in his adult fairy-land and, of course, to plot new ways of revenge. He has his mission, of course.

Drood currently has another burden to bear: there has been little time for game playing these last nights. He has spent acres of time swapping cables, discs and disc-drives in the hope that perhaps the problem was a simple software fault, unlikely as that might be. Then he re-copies and edits discs in a frenzy until, feeling sick and confused, he can take no more.

It has been the same every night, all week. He lifts his body and slouches into the chair that faces his screen. A mass of wire feels soft around his feet like loops of slow worms. A jumble of discs that he had swept off his plywood desk, in a sudden surge of explosive frustration, lay scattered across the wires.

He moans, realising that the fault is still with him, and pushes his lank, unwashed hair, back from his face. He stares towards the screen, a knot tightens inside and he grinds his teeth like a slow coffee mill. The screen is as he left it, locked in a reverse video with that awful shining face grinning out from the centre of a jumble of text. It mocks him, taunting with the same usual expression: a hideous clown face, frozen into a laugh. There is that message too:

'Have a nice day.'

He wipes his forearm across his face. There is a frightening justice here that confounds him. It sits uncomfortably inside his conscience like a stone. After all, is it not Drood that writes programmes to cause chaos? Is it not his talent that destroys and eradicates?

Now, at last, his own system has fallen foul of someone else's trick: a victim of the Mirror Clown Virus.

It was a work of brilliance. He had to admit that, part of him was fascinated, mesmerized by its ingenuity whilst being puzzled how it had entered his computer system. He'd heard the rumours: that it was mean and could corrupt everything.

The first and most startling thing it did was to turn the screen into a silver sheet, like the scales on a dead fish. His first encounter scared him to death. It was late. One minute he was devising a way to get out of the Castle of Dromeda, from the third level, and the next he was staring at his shadowed jowls: pin-prick eyes intense and set like an animal's.

He next encountered it when the text of another adventure
game was transformed into its opposites in seconds, just
simple words to their antonyms: good to bad. Full to empty.
Open to shut. It even worked on images and numbers: a
negative number to a positive, and of course that made
garbage of number crunching.

He cries out suddenly as the clock radio breaks the silence.
This is what he has woken for.

Local news dribbles its way through mundane items.
He listens carefully, there has to be something. A young
girl's emotionless voice announces that, 'the "mysterious
computer virus" that had hit the city has now contaminated
the Hospital Mainframe computer. The havoc was sweet.
One patient undergoing computer-monitored surgery is in 'a
serious condition.' Drood smiles as he listens to the whining
of the Hospital Administrator as he is interviewed. It is the
same little shit that lost him his porter's job when he worked
there, and now *he* is in trouble. Drood's virus is spreading
quicker and better than he had ever dreamed. A programme
that scrambles everything.

He turns to his monitor.

The stare of the clown face dampens his good feeling.

He reaches out his hand and searches for the off switch.
The room plunges into the more natural gloom of curtained
daylight as the after-glow of the screen dies.

Feeling restless, Drood stares at his mail for several minutes.
The black coffee, which he was sipping has gone cold. He
knows what is in the envelopes. There are the usual crop of
red reminders, unpaid bills; there is a renewal subscription
to a computer games magazine, *Orange Dwarf*; and a long
grey envelope with the words CompuRead Ltd in the top
left-hand corner. This envelope, he places against a china
lamp. They are good payers and the money is running out
from the last contract he'd taken, he might value another
'one-off' from that company. It pays for his 'mission'.

His other items consist of junk mail and a stiff card
envelope, postmarked Charleston, USA. This will be more
goodies – pirate stuff from Jim, his American contact.

This morning, the envelopes feel sticky between his fingers
and he half wonders if they shouldn't go straight into the

trash. Could he really be experiencing guilt? Could something from the spate of God Squad knockers be rubbing off on him?

Drood replaces his mug on a side table for a moment and, yet again, thinks deeply about the mirror virus. Had it come from any of the programmes Jim had sent him? Not intentionally, surely? After all they'd exchanged things for years now.

'No,' he mutters, 'not Jim Rigney. Not knowingly. He warns me of problems, he doesn't send them.'

'Bad-fuck virus,' he mumbles as he falls back in his seat allowing the remaining envelopes to drop to the floor.

He feels tired, washed out and lower than he's felt in weeks. The virus has deprived him of his toy and made restless days worse. It fills his thoughts, angering and frustrating him. A sick feeling inside contains the fear that he might have to junk every programme he'd lovingly stolen over the years.

As he stretches his head back and yawns he reaches out and switches off the radio. Suddenly, a sharp rap on the front door disturbs the drum of stillness.

'Kids? No,' he thinks, 'not kids, not so early. I'll break their fucking legs if . . .'

He perches himself on the edge of his chair and gazes into space, what should his next move be? His chin rests in his hands.

The knock returns. Unusual.

'Perhaps not kids after all?' He considers. 'Not to knock twice so soon.'

He stretches himself out of his chair and shuffles towards the curtains. He peers through the gap. At first he thinks it is the police. Several dark figures stand there, all dressed in a similar uniform style, navy blue or black. Then he realizes that there are two children as well, a boy and a girl.

He pulls his face away from the chink. Drood cannot understand what he has seen. After a moment the knock returns, a third time. He leans forward to take another, longer look.

His adult visitors are tall, there is something about them too, a distinguished air maybe? Both are elderly men, with large black books tucked beneath their arms. Their skin looks smoother than marble, despite their age. Each rests a hand on the shoulder of the boy and the girl who stand, almost ceremoniously, before them. The detail of their dress is clearer now: they wear a thick cloth, heavy with loops and folds – almost capes, with large-brimmed circular hats, pulled firmly down on to their heads.

More God Squad, but very out of place here.

'Shit no, Mormons!' he cries.

Drood allows a grin to stretch his face, he can hardly believe it.

'Mormons, on Stockwell Park Estate! Witnesses, the Sally Army, Baptists and now Mormons. God help them if any of the McHugh kids catch them on the stairways.'

As he pulls the curtains shut, another, harder knock rattles the door.

'Let them rot,' he says, hauling himself over to the couch.

Another, shorter knock follows, and after that there is silence.

Drood dreams of laughing clown masks that smother his face, and of mirrors that ripple like shining pools. Suddenly, the dream dissolves into an aerial view of his computer screen. A knocking, far-off at first, moves closer. It is a persistent rapping, it now comes from the disc drive – urgent as if somebody or something wants to get out.

He sits upright, awakening with a start, a trickle of sweat runs down his face, his gums hurt more than ever.

The knocking continues. It takes only seconds for his roving eyes to settle, and to realise that the noise is coming from out in the passage-way.

'Fuck it, I'll have their balls so help me,' he says.

Drood does not know why, but he adjusts his spectacles and gets up off the couch. He scratches his back-side and proceeds to the front door not bothering to check who might be there. He knows who it is, and he is angry.

Without engaging the security chain, an automatic move usually, he opens the door and looks out into the day. The brightness of sunshine stings his eyes at first, he might be staring into a furnace. The quartet whom he had spied through his curtains earlier stand again before him. Black wedge shapes peek out from beneath the folds of neat and sombre dress.

'Good day, neighbour,' smiles the man to his right, with a polite bow. His partner, an older man with a white pencil-thin moustache, touches the brim of his hat. The children remain silent, their wide eyes stare upwards with serious angel-like expressions.

Drood stares back.

'I don't understand this,' he whispers, 'what . . . just what am I doing here on the doorstep?'

'We have come to tell you of the Coming of the Kingdom, neighbour, of the news that those who open their hearts may receive healing through the power . . .'

'Wait, wait, just wait a minute . . .' Drood tries to collect himself waving his hand meaninglessly.

'Neighbour?' enquires the older man, frowning.

Drood stops waving, talking isn't helping his abscess.

'You ain't my neighbour. My neighbour's a sixteen-stone black dude with a wife who's fucked off out of here, leaving him with a bunch of children.' Then he adds, with uncharacteristic pleasantness, 'I . . . I work nights, you've got me at a bad time . . . and I can't . . .' he takes a deep breath, wondering why he is bothering with an explanation.

'We understand. We'll call back, we know you are in need.'

'*Shit, you will,*' he thinks. 'Need? No. No I'm not religious and I don't follow the Mormon preaching and . . .'

'Mormon?' Asks the small boy with an uncomprehending gaze.

The group laugh. Even the little girl manages a smile as she turns towards the boy, making a gesture suggesting they might share a secret.

'We are not Mormon, neighbour, oh no. We are messengers, healers.'

'What is your work?' asks the older man.

'Computers, and . . .' he could have bitten his tongue, he realizes that he is walking into their gambit, actually talking, exchanging with them. 'Look, I have to get back to bed and catch up on a heavy night. I'm not interested anyway.'

The older man removes the black book from beneath his arm and holds it out like a gift.

'The Word, neighbour. The Book. The Method. In Christ, you see? Just take and read, perhaps we might call back on a more opportune occasion when . . .'

Something tightens like piano wire inside Drood. His irritability shifts within him like coarse sand.

'I'm going. I don't read. Just . . .'

'We have all kinds of media, sir,' says the little boy.

'Video. Perhaps you have a machine? Or maybe a talking cassette will be easier if you cannot read? CD ROM too?'

'Of course I can read you little . . .'

'We are aware of the twentieth century, neighbour,' says the older man in a gentle but firmer voice.

'We even provide a way for you,' smiles the little girl holding out a black envelope. She turns to the boy. 'Our neighbour has said he works with computers.'

For a reason Drood cannot fully understand, something makes him recoil, he shrinks with fear or loathing, he is uncertain which. He steps back, allowing the door to swing fully open as he does so.

All four of his visitors are smiling now, their heads tilted to one side, eyes hard as orbs in statues. Their faces are powder white, reminding him of the Mirror Clown. The sunlight etches their outline, which is now filled with solid shadow. They are becoming a mysterious blackness. For a few seconds he feels the skin on the nape of his neck prickle and crawl. He can stand it no longer.

'Jeeesus . . .'

'Indeed,' says the girl. 'Healing? Do you require healing?'

He slams the door hard with a sudden urgency, surprised at his breathlessness.

Quickly returning to his room, he curls into a ball beneath the quilt cover and sucks at his thumb like a child.

Drood starts back at the computer later than usual. The night has brought dreams of solutions to his problems, of vaccine discs that will protect and eradicate the menace that has dropped into his life. He decides to try to save what he can from the hard disc and maybe reformat it. He wonders if the virus has been lurking within the machine for years.

Drood runs his fingers across an unopened software

package and decides to try something new first. The game
that he opens is, of course, a copy, recently acquired.

The screen starts up as usual. Everything is as it should
be. Perhaps it is too normal.

He loads 'The Valley of Mists'.

The drive purrs softly.

At the C> prompt he types MISTS.

A purr accompanies twisting fog, which stretches across
the screen.

'Good graphics,' he thinks, as the grey weaves a series of
shades, promising special adventures.

The sudden rap on the front door makes him catch his
breath. He is very nervous today.

'Hell!' he spits.

The knocking returns, harder, longer and much more
persistent this time.

Drood pushes his chair back.

The door will burst.

'I'm coming!' he yells.

He pauses on his way to the front door, and decides to
check through the window. Crossing to the curtains he peers
out. Evening is settling in, but a single paint-spattered bulb
on the balcony casts light across a dark outline. A huddled
figure stands beside his front door, like a dark elf. At first he
is uncertain who or what the visitor can be.

He pulls his head back.

'They're back. They're back, the bastards!'

His face feels flush and full as, with wide strides, he
continues to the hallway and unhooks the security chain.
He holds the door wide.

'Sling it!' he screams, and then finds himself gawping
downwards.

He had expected the entire quartet, but here instead is the
little girl, alone. The girl is smiling again, she searches out
his eyes.

The next few moments are blurred. A soft beating, like the
blow from the wings of a huge bird, fills the space behind his
eyes, each blow tilts his view of the world. The girl stretches
out her hand, he isn't sure why.

He registers the movement as an act of aggression. Surely
all that she is doing is offering him something, a book maybe?

Already the door is swinging shut from the full weight of his push, and still the girl's arm is outstretched towards him.

The black sleeve jams in the opening. Drood panics as the door swings back. As the sleeve withdraws, the latch clicks and the door shuts on the tips of tiny fingers.

A terrible scream rents the air, as wetness trickles down the door jamb.

Drood falls back against the door, his breath coming fast, the cries continue outside. Something black, the shape of a card, flutters down by his feet.

The girl's cries are frightening. He lifts his hands to his ears and tries to drown out her voice.

'Invasion!' he cries, 'Invasion of privacy! It was an accident and it's your own fucking fault!'

He runs from the hallway and back to the living room.

The computer screen has already turned to a perfect mirror, bouncing back and reversing everything that it sees. He lowers his face to the monitor and stares long and hard as muddled voices outside, come and go. He half expects to hear a knock, for footsteps to return, but instead, the sounds of crying and comforting whispers, disappear with slow footsteps, down towards the stairway. They have gone without complaint.

He continues to stare at his reflection. He cannot see his eyes, there are only dark spaces set in a paste face.

Suddenly the mirror screen shatters like a crazed windscreen and the laughing clown face pushes through, grinning back at him.

'Have a nice day.'

He whimpers like a whipped dog.

An amusement arcade laugh fills the room.

Drood listens by the window, resisting the temptation to peek outside, but he listens for any tell-tale footsteps, any snatches of muffled conversation, which might announce the police or the return of the God Squad. But there are none.

The night is uncommonly quiet.

Feeling braver, he goes to the front door, unable to recall whether he had replaced the security chain. He hadn't.

He stops for a moment and listens carefully. He is vaguely aware of stepping on something soft like a sheet of paper. He

crouches down and notices a black envelope. Something pale
that oozes a dark coloured softness spoils the edge of it.

Isn't there a piece of tiny finger-nail there too? Like a
child's?

Not wanting to consider this further he brushes it off
against the door mat and rises with the envelope in his hand.
The unsealed flap is tucked within the body of the envelope.
Creasing the opening reveals a computer disc. There is
nothing else inside and a quick inspection reveals that there
is no writing or printing of any kind anywhere on the disc.

He returns with a drunken walk to the sitting room. The
computer is switched off.

'New disc,' he mumbles. 'It's a bible tutor, or a publicity
disc of some kind. Who did they say they were?'

He thinks for a moment, recalling the words.

'We are not Mormon, neighbour . . . we are messengers . . .'

A nagging feeling inside begins to irritate him. A curiosity
he finds hard to resist surges through his thoughts. It will
not go away.

'Why not?' he sighs.

Switching the computer on, he waits whilst the operating
system purrs.

'Keep off my back, Coco,' he hisses between clenched teeth.

Drood hesitates but then eases the disc into his drive,
snapping the gate lever shut with a flick of his finger.

At the screen prompt he types A:Dir to show him a list of
files on the disc.

Three file names flash up:

The Word.Exe.

Jesus Christ.Syst

Healing.Exe.

Drood considers these for a moment and types: Word.

The screen goes black, there is a soft tinkling sound, like
winter crystal.

It brings peace, calming him. A message spreads across
the centre of the screen, his command has worked:

'Enter into his gates'?

Drood frowns. He presses ENTER.

The same message returns.

'You're not thinking, Drood,' he murmurs, 'it's asking you
a question.'

He types Y to accept.

The fairy notes float out on to his desk as the programme runs.

'He sent forth his word, and healed them, and delivered them from destruction.'

Drood's eyes widen.

'We are messengers. Healers.'

Now he remembers. There was something about the file name too. He presses the Enter key.

'Is any sick among you?' appears on the screen.

Drood types Y.

For a moment a brown wash of light flickers about him as though the bulb in the corner lamp were about to die. The twinkle of the disc returns, but this time it is different. It is sweeter, more musical, like chimes.

His fingers freeze, poised above the keys. The screen goes black again, and the corner lamp goes off. The room becomes a sticky darkness.

The black that fills his vision is too black, as though shutters have dropped down from beneath his heavy eyelids. The effect lasts moments only.

Drood gradually becomes aware of a shuddering, a low rumble as if a spring was bubbling beneath the floor, it seems to echo in the flat below. The notion of a burst pipe, flashes across his mind, but these sounds are natural-organic. Quickly the rumbling changes to an urgent rush – like a far off wind.

The screen flashes white.

Poker white.

Molten white, like the heart of a furnace.

Drood tries to push himself away from the desk, but as he drops his hands across the keyboard he realises that his fingertips have become fastened to the keys. Suddenly, he finds that he is typing in code, leaving blood prints on the keys as he taps.

Shafts of brightness, sharp as lasers cut around the edges of the keys. They shine up from the keyboard and into his face. His mouth falls limply open, he is unable to help himself. A great wind rushes around him. He tries to turn his gaze away from the screen, but it is impossible.

Something is coming. From out of the light.

Angel voices fill the room as a slender fingered hand reaches out towards him. He catches sight of the edge of a robe and the hand gently turns as with a gesture, he sees something within the palm – a mark.

'Jeeesus . . .' he whispers. 'What graphics!'

'Thou dost show me the path,' flashes at him from deep within the screen.

Drood's hands feel hot and the cavern of his mouth, now filled with light, tastes sweet. So so sweet.

The name 'Christ' ripples into view.

'What fucking graphics!' he whispers again, as the light fills his mind.

Several hours later, Drood sits before the computer again, the disc is set within the drive, ready to go.

His hands are cooler now, but still he holds them before his face in amazement. The grazes from last week's doorstep encounter have completely healed. He feels better in himself, better than he has felt for months, maybe even years. His mouth is fresh and clean, not stale and sour. There is no longer the taste of abscess.

He slides the disc into the drive.

Quickly, he executes the loading tasks, eager to see what will happen. So far the 'Mirror' virus has failed to click in. If the programme can heal his mouth perhaps it will heal his computer – cleanse the goddamn virus. As before, the files flash across the screen and he loads The Word.

The message, 'Enter into his gates?' drops into view.

Drood presses the Y key.

The tinkling resumes.

He watches and waits, his tongue lolling from the side of his mouth, like a panting dog.

The sound from the drive stops.

An aching silence follows.

'Come on, come on,' he murmurs.

The screen pixels appear to flex threateningly, to crumple like foil.

'No,' he thinks, 'not the fucking virus, just let me load the programme.'

A message ripples across.

'He sent forth his word, and healed them, and delivered them from destruction.'

He presses the Enter key and holds his breath.

After a moment he is asked the question.

'Is any sick among you?'

He types Y and raps out a wild card path, to examine all the files on the hard disc, and to run a system check.

The music box chime returns.

Drood's fingers grip the sides of the desk, he leans forward, hungry to know more, getting so close to the screen that he can smell the heat of it.

The screen turns black and the room falls into darkness, he waits as if beneath an eclipse. This time he can feel the blackness. Taste it on his lips, sense its pressure.

As before there is a rumbling, a far off crackle of thunder. The patter of scurrying rats flutter around the edges of his room, behind the skirting. He feels the floor move, just a fraction, as if the concrete that divides the flats might be cracking.

Does he hear a sound over his shoulder? Ancient hinges creak wide somewhere behind him.

The computer screen melts into space, the surface is barely visible. Red shimmering letters cross before him, floating there, turning his face the colour of glowing coals.

'Him that stole, steal no more.'

'Do no more harm to any man.'

Drood pulls back.

The message appears to drip and pool like wet paint daub, but perhaps it is not paint?

The message changes to another.

'Welcome to the kingdom of the holy.'

The crunch of broken glass seems to surround the place where he sits. A low growl follows.

'Thou dost show me the path,' flashes up on the screen.

Drood swallows, he feels icy sweat trickle down his back. A silvery glow, like the beam of a flashlight creeps in from the corners of the monitor.

He freezes with fear. The Mirror virus. It is coming.

More crunching glass sounds cut into the murmur of the room. This time there is a grating from inside the computer. It is as if metal were being twisted.

The empty gate of disc-drive B spits a fine blade edge of orange out from its slot.

Drood's jaw slackens, the air smells bad and hot, not bright and clear as before.

The light on the screen grows, the message dissolves, reforming into other words. The word 'show' dissolves into 'hide'.

'Thou dost hide the path from me.'

The mirror virus is almost there.

The noise of laughter explodes inside his head, as he reaches out a trembling hand. He struggles to find the switch.

The new message, the entry to the programme, shines, just as before.

'Christ'

A dull thud sounds within the darkness, as though something has fallen to the floor behind him from a great height. The moment freezes time. There is something at the disc drive gate. At first Drood thinks that the disc has ejected.

He quickly recognizes that the thing that shoots out at him, is not a disc. It comes from Hell's letter box. He stares down in horror as a tangle of cables rush towards him and rip through his shirt, into his chest.

But they aren't cables.

They are an unholy mixture of sinew and bone and nail.

A searching claw cuts under his ribs and squeezes his heart, cajoling as if it were fondling a breast. He screams with the music of artificial laughter.

The pre-fix 'Anti-' has dropped into place before the word 'Christ'. He watches in disbelief as the word *holy* dissolves into *unholy*, at the top of the screen.

A great wash of colour, like shimmering silk, gushes generously on to the keyboard. The screen reflects the agony of his last breath just before the familiar smiling face of Coco the Clown fills the monitor frame, having corrupted another programme.

The computer crashes.

The clock radio fizzes into life, the glow from the digital letters pick out his twitching body, which is huddled across the desk.

'Have a nice day.'

THE LOVE-GIFT

Josepha Sherman

Josepha Sherman is the prolific author of a number of novels and short stories. Her book-length fantasy includes The Shining Falcon, The Horse of Flame, A Strange and Ancient Name, Windleaf *and, more recently,* The Chaos Gate *and* King's Son Magic's Son, *amongst others. With nearly one hundred short stories published, her appearances include* Sword & Sorceress *(four volumes),* Vampires!, Sisters in Fantasy, Alternate Warriors *and* Dragon Fantastic. *She has also scripted an episode of TV's* Adventures of the Galaxy Rangers *and is the author of a number of non-fiction titles such as* Indian Tribes of North America, A Sampler of Jewish-American Folktales *and* Once Upon a Galaxy: Folktales, Fantasy and Science Fiction.

WENA looked about the cabin yet again, desperately holding herself under control, amazed and, despite the control, a little frightened at how little she wanted to take with her. The spellbook, of course, Grandfather's prize. The fine new tunic for town wear, the warm woollen cloak Grandfather had had woven for her in exchange for a protective charm for the weaver's kin . . . Wena bit down on her lip, hard, to stop a sob. There must be something else! This was – this had been her home for all the twelve years of her life!

Or nearly all. If the girl stretched her memory back as far as it would go, she thought she could remember being brought to this mountainous place by her father. Her father, the wizard's son who had inherited not one glimmering of the Power, who had wandered bitterly far afield and at last wed an outlander woman. Wena couldn't remember her at all, or her death. But Wena had somehow inherited the Power her father had missed, and so he had come briefly home again to leave her here like some unwanted pup.

But Grandfather had wanted her. Grandfather had raised her and taught her and loved her. Wena bit her lip again, fighting a quick blurring of tears. Even when the old wizard had been at his harshest, instructing his grandchild in the dangerous ways of magic, the girl had still revelled in that love.

And it was for love that he would have sent Wena away.

'You'll go to Mererid, girl, your grown cousin in Caerlloches. She has a school there, in magic mostly, but also in all the things that go to make one truly human. In her, the Power is a gentle, healing thing; you'll like her. Ach no, Wena, don't argue with me. You were an unexpected love-gift to me, even though I had never expected to find myself with the raising of a girl-child. But now you're too old for babying, too young for womanhood, and while this hermit life on a mountain top is fine for an old man who's seen the world, it's no place for you.'

It's true, I can't live here, not any more!

Wena froze, jerked abruptly from her misery, alert in every psychic sense. Someone was climbing the rocky, treacherous path up to the cabin. For one wild, foolish moment she thought, *Grandfather!* But of course that couldn't be. This was some stranger. If she focused her mind as she had been taught, she could *feel* the foreignness.

She could *feel* something else . . . faint swirlings of cold, terrible Power, the hint of a grim mind behind it –

The door! She had left the door wide open with never a Guarding on it! Wena raced in sudden panic to shut it, but even as her hands pushed at the wood, stronger hands pushed back, sending the girl staggering. A handsome, bearded face looked in, smiling.

'Now, that was small courtesy, lass!'

Wena watched in tense silence as the man entered, neatly brushing dust off himself and his fine clothes, glancing casually about as he did so. The sense of cold strength, of Power gone wrong, was stronger now, sharp as the smell of iron, and the girl fought down a shudder. Grandfather had told her a horrid thing once: When a wizard died, his Power flew free upon the winds – unless he died at another's hand.

Then that Power flew directly from slain to slayer. Wena *felt* the stolen magics in this man, swirling like storm clouds. Grandfather would have known what to do, Grandfather would never have let a sorcerer come anywhere near the cabin . . .

The man seemed oblivious to Wena's fear. 'A difficult path up here,' he commented blandly, 'all edges and dangers. You can't see many strangers.'

Wena glared, fiercely wishing this stranger away. The man smiled, eyes cool and blank as grey ice. 'Are you all alone, lass? Surely you don't live here all by yourself.'

'Yes!'

'Tsk, has Cystennin never taught you not to lie? Oh yes,' he added at Wena's involuntary start, 'I know the old wizard. We met, long ago.' His gaze roved the room once more. 'He's done well for himself. The place fairly reeks of his Power. But to waste it, keep it pent up in a little mountain hovel with only a girl . . . Who are you? No kin, not with that pale outlander hair.' The cold eyes raked her still child-slim body with contempt.

'Certainly not his lover. His servant?'

With a shock of relief, Wena realized that the stranger, sorcerer or no, couldn't read minds. And, unlike Grandfather, he held the old, foolish prejudice that stated, in defiance of fact: Women can't wield Power. He didn't suspect. 'I . . . live here,' the girl said evasively.

'So I gathered.' The man stirred impatiently. 'I've business with Cystennin. Where is he?'

What manner of sorcerer couldn't sense the answer for himself? Wena hesitated. 'I don't know.'

'Why girl, I've already caught you lying once. Where is he?'

'I told you. I don't know. I – '

The force of the slap sent her sprawling. Stunned, Wena stared up in sheer disbelief, fighting back tears of pain. The man bent over her, still smiling. 'Liars are punished. Did Cystennin never tell you that? Now, where is he?'

He had her trapped in a corner. Sickened, Wena *felt* the fog of cold, twisted Power all about him and knew, *If I tell him the truth, he'll kill me.* 'He's out there. In – in the woods below. I'll g-go and look for him.'

A harsh hand pulled her down again. 'Oh no, girl. He'll be back before nightfall, surely. We shall both wait here for him.'

And when Grandfather didn't come . . . 'Who are you?' Wena cried. 'What do you want?'

'Call me Fychan,' the man said with mock courtesy; the name had been given so freely it must be false. 'And I'm here, girl, for new Power.'

'Wh-what?'

'Don't be dense! I'm here to kill your wizard.'

Wena nearly choked subduing a shout of anguished laughter. 'Why?' she gasped. 'Why?'

'Hasn't he told you anything?' Contempt dripped from Fychan's voice. 'Look you, if you slay a wizard, the Power flows from his life into yours and – Ha, I see you do know this!'

'I . . .'

'I really did meet Cystennin once, long ago.' Though his voice remained level, the flat grey gaze wavered. 'Picture a child,' he murmured. 'Not like you, no. A boy unwanted, alone, struggling to live, the prey of those who prey on youth.'

Wena winced, the familiar not-quite-fear of *What if Grandfather hadn't wanted me*? racing through her mind. Dimly she knew Fychan was playing to her sympathy, trying to get her to lower her guard, but she couldn't not listen as he continued softly:

'Can you feel his terror, his pain, his want? Now, picture that boy finding a way to escape, to be safe: Magic.' He said that with a child's awe, and for a bare instant his eyes were a child's eyes, wide and wondering. But then they hardened to grey ice once more. 'I went to your Cystennin. I begged him to teach me. But he . . .' Fychan shook his head. 'He refused me. Cystennin warned me away from the one thing that could help me, with some such nonsense as: I hadn't the inner strength, the Power would warp my spirit.'

Caught up in his story, Wena protested, 'But it's true! There *are* folk like that, Grandfather told me – '

Wena clamped her jaws shut in horror, but it was already too late.

'Grandfather!' The man's hand shot out, catching the girl's

chin in a fierce grip. Grim eyes studied her face. 'There isn't
all that much of the old man in you, but still . . . Well now,
I never expected to find Cystennin not at home. I certainly
never expected the chance of taking his grandchild hostage!'

Fychan's face was sharp with savage hunger that sent an
atavistic terror racing through Wena's mind. What men she'd
met till now had been honest farmers or crafters, not the sort
to harm a girl-child even had she not been wizard-kin, but
she wasn't so young or naive she couldn't guess at the
vengeance Fychan might take on her. And there was so
much worse than physical abuse . . . Wena cried out her
horror, fighting wildly to free herself, unable to do more in
that cramped space than claw at Fychan's arms. He released
her chin and snared both her wrists with painful strength,
pinning her back into the corner.

'Stop struggling, girl! Now!' Eyes blazing, he shook her
till her head swam. As Wena sagged in helpless surrender,
Fychan asked her sharply, 'You *will* obey me, won't you?
Won't you? Yes . . . that's better.' His face so close to hers she
could taste his breath, the man continued in a soft, hurried
voice, 'Look you, girl, I've taken lives before this, small,
sorcerous lives, and felt the new Power flowing through me,
sweeter than sweet. But there was never enough, not from
those petty souls. Now, with all Cystennin's store of Power
waiting, now, with the chance for true strength at last, I'm
not about to let a fool of a girl stop me! Do we understand
each other?'

Breathless, Wena nodded, and Fychan gave her a quick
grimace of a grin. He released her and got to his feet, but
he stood between her and the door. Wena huddled where
she lay.

Grandfather, help me, I don't know what to do!

Oh, foolish, childish! Grandfather couldn't help her now.
Couldn't he . . .? What if . . .?

A breeze stirred just outside the cabin. The door creaked,
then swung open. Fychan drew in his breath in a startled
hiss, for there in the doorway stood Cystennin himself, tall,
lean and Powerful.

'How?' gasped Fychan. 'I would have heard, sensed –
No, no, there's so much stray Power here I couldn't sense
anything – '

He cut himself off abruptly. Wena felt the sudden tense heat of hastily gathered magic, and told herself, *Now!* She pushed off from the wall and threw herself at the unguarded doorway and freedom –

'No! Damn you, no!'

The girl cried out as Fychan's hand clamped shut on her shoulder and hurled her back into the cabin. How could he have known – Ach, he'd known because Grandfather's image had faded! In her panic, Wena had taken her attention too quickly from the illusion she'd cast.

'You clever little bitch! You tricked me. I never even felt the surge of Power!' Fychan dragged her to her feet. 'He's not coming back, is he? Oh no, he's dead, isn't he? *Isn't he?*'

'Yes!' It was an anguished shout.

The cruel grip on her shoulder relaxed so suddenly she stumbled. 'Dead,' breathed Fychan, and the echo of a slum-boy's grief quivered in his voice. 'All the years of learning, planning, savoring what I'd see on his face as I killed him and took his Power . . . Dead. All that Power wasted.' His eyes pierced Wena, savage with despair. 'But I'll have your life. The wizard's grandchild – at least I'll have your little flickering of Power.'

Aching to scream, Wena bit down on her lip till she tasted blood. If she started screaming now, she wouldn't stop till Fychan had torn the mind and life from her.

Grandfather, please, please help me!

She couldn't fight back, she didn't know how. Cystennin had never taught her spells of offence because he'd said such things were too advanced for a child –

But she wasn't really a child, not any more. In that moment of utter despair, memories she had been trying to forget came spilling back into Wena's mind: the thought of those treacherous mountain paths, the horror of that fall two weeks past that in one cruel moment had turned Grandfather from wizard to broken, dying man . . .

'Listen to me.' Cystennin's quiet voice echoed again in Wena's mind. 'I had thought to take you safely to Mererid, but now you must go alone. Ach, Wena, girl, don't pull at me. There's no feeling at all in my arms and legs, you know enough to know what that means. There's damage within me beyond magic's healing. Ah, but my poor, dear child, I can't let you go out into the world all unshielded! I . . . will give you a love-gift, Wena, a gift to protect you forever, the greatest gift that is mine to give. But in return, my dear, I must ask a terrible thing of you. In return, you must grant me a love-gift even greater.'

And she had. Somehow. With one quick stroke of her knife, she had freed Grandfather from the helpless prison of slowly dying flesh, and felt the wild, warm tide of love and Power surging into her . . .

Wena shrieked, dragged back to the present as Fychan's will engulfed her, searing her mind.

I can't let him have Grandfather's gift, I won't!

Cystennin's last words had been a warning:

'It is all too easy to use Power as a weapon, all too tempting to turn tyrant. The flood of so much sudden magic is going to be intoxicating, Wena. Resist it. You must have time to assimilate the Power.'

There wasn't time. If she must die, Wena thought, let it be from Grandfather's love, not Fychan's sorcery. She sensed the new Power awakening within her as she called on it. She felt it blazing through her, stronger, more wonderful than anything she'd ever known. Dizzy, dazzled, Wena nearly laughed aloud in savage joy. She would make Fychan pay for hurting her! She would burn him up, play games with his soul and send it screaming –

She would degrade Cystennin's love-gift.

Oh Grandfather, no!

Aching, Wena shut out the inner voice whispering she could be queen of the world, the universe. Aching, she pulled the unruly waves of Power to her, forcing all her magic, all Cystennin's magic into a shield of force to block the fiercest attack and . . . And send it blazing back upon the sender!

'Fychan!'

Oh, she couldn't hate him any more, not after nearly being trapped by the lure of Power herself! How much stronger that lure would have been for a poor, tormented little slum-child –

'Turn back!' Wena screamed out, mind to mind, *'You'll die! Oh please, turn back!'*

'Girl-fool!' The scraps of thought blazed at her, barely coherent. *'Helpless! Prey!'*

Before she could think to move, Fychan's hatred flashed about her, flame against stone. And, like flame, it recoiled, searing back into the sorcerer's mind. For one brief, terrible moment, Wena shared the man's agony, his horror, his broken stammering:

'*Cystennin's Power – but . . . he's dead. Power . . . could only have been taken by force – but this is a girl, only a – she couldn't – she –* '

Then those other thoughts were gone. Fychan's empty body slumped bonelessly to the cabin floor. Wena held herself rigidly guarded as she *felt* the sudden release of his Power. She didn't want any of that twisted strength!

Then it was gone. Almost sobbing from weariness and shock, Wena let her shield fall, feeling Grandfather's Power settling back throughout her being as though it had always been there, warm and soothing as a caress.

'You couldn't know how it was,' she told Fychan's body. 'I didn't matter so much. I mean, whether or not you killed me. But I couldn't let you have his love-gift.'

Quickly Wena took up her pack and left, pausing outside to look back at the cabin, shifting her weight from foot to foot in indecision, refusing to weep. Oh, she'd had enough of weeping these last two weeks!

She would go to Cousin Mererid. Even without Grandfather's warning, Wena knew she would need help in mastering the new Power if she wasn't going to end up like poor, deadly Fychan. But first . . .

Fire surged up in answer to Wena's will, fierce white flame blazing into the sky, a beacon to the world that a wizard had died. And another had been born.

And then, dry-eyed and determined, Wena started down the mountain for Caerlloches.

A NEW LEASE

David Riley

David Riley's short stories have appeared widely in such anthologies and magazines as Fantasy Tales, The Year's Best Horror Stories, The Mammoth Book of Terror, The Mammoth Book of Zombies, New Writings in Horror & the Supernatural, The Satyr's Head & Other Tales of Terror, The Pan Book of Horror Stories, Fear *and* Whispers. *A resident of Lancashire, his regional horror story, 'Writer's Cramp', is published in* Northern Horror, *an anthology celebrating the works of writers and artists from the north of England. He has also written three novels,* The Satyr's Head, *its sequel,* Cursed Be the Ground, *and* Goblin Mire.

GILLIAN Willoughby pulled her face into an ugly grin, then spat. Red light from the sun, setting low over the factory roofs further down the dark length of the Leeds–Liverpool canal as it wound its way through the outskirts of Accrington, made her deep set eyes glow like ingots of molten brass as she stared at the boy standing by the wall below her.

'Mark Dillon is a snivellin' little coward,' she sneered as she raised her four-and-a-half foot, twelve-year-old frame to its full height, so that she seemed to tower above him. The other children, one more boy and two other girls, joined in until she stamped her foot and the jeering stopped. A cold wind whispered along the otherwise deserted canal bank as if to emphasize the sheer loneliness of the place. The nearest houses were separated by rows of ill-kept allotments, to loom like fallen battlements in the dark along the purple skyline. Here and there a lit window accentuated the dismal gloom elsewhere.

'If you don't come with us, Mark,' Gillian said, 'we'll never let you play with us again.'

'Never, *ever* again,' repeated Jenny Duxbury, a dark-eyed, willowy eleven-year-old with greasy plaits.

Mark looked from one to the other, but in none of their cold, wind-chapped faces did he see anything other than an ugly, relentless determination. If he did not fall in with their plans they would shun him, he knew, from now on. Reluctant tears forced themselves from the corners of his eyes, hidden in the gloom.

'Well?' Gillian's round face stared at him intently. 'Are you comin' or not? If you're not, you can bugger off like the squirmin' little coward you are. If you are comin' with us, then come with us now.'

Mark lowered his head.

'I'm comin',' he muttered. His throat felt dry, drained of spit.

Gillian grinned once again. She'd known she would win. She always did. With a *'Whoop!'* she jumped from the wall and cuffed him playfully on the shoulder, though the playfulness had a hardness about it. She was a tough little girl, with cuts and grazes all over her, and calluses on the palms of her hands.

The third girl, podgy little Wendy Bullen, and her brother Paul, joined together in congratulating Mark.

'We're glad you're with us,' Wendy said, her broad face beaming a strained smile against the cold. 'I knew you weren't a coward. I knew that all along.' She held his arm for a moment and squeezed it. Mark grunted what sounded like: 'Thanks.'

Paul grinned, gap-toothed. 'I knew you weren't a coward too.'

Gillian frowned.

'Come on, you lot. We've no time for bein' soppy. He's with us. That's all that matters. Come on!'

A shadowy group, they raced down the tow path with highpitched screams, leaping stones and clumps of weeds, as the evening darkened and street lights twinkled between distant houses beyond the pens. An off-colour rind of moon kept total darkness away from the canal, but it was a poor, shadowy, misleading gloom, in which commonplace objects took on strange and frightening shapes. Derelict warehouses loomed like grotesque cliffs. Old newspapers, carried by the

wind, swooped towards them like living creatures, battered
and almost dead. Tall rushes, growing from the stagnant soil
alongside the canal, reached up like impossibly thin fingers,
tipped with claws.

'This way!' Gillian urged, as the others suddenly paused
behind her. She pulled a small, Woolworth's torch from
inside her anorak and shone it on the unpainted wooden
door that was set deep in the rough stone walls of a disused
factory,

> *Hogg & Co*
> *Canal Street*
> *Church*
> *Accrington*

faintly etched in faded paint on an old sign board fixed
above it.

'This is it,' she whispered. Her voice was much lower
than before as the others, advancing slowly from behind
her, fingered the padlock fixed to the door. It looked oily
and new. Each in turn lowered their heads to look down
at the lock, then backed away again. Freshly pasted notices,
warning against trespassers and of the building's dangerous
condition, were fixed along its walls.

'Shine your torch through 'ere,' Mark urged, pointing to a
boarded-up window several feet to the left of the door. He
reached up on his toes for the edge of one of the narrower
boards and tried to pull it free. A piece splintered from it,
leaving a narrow gap.

Gillian pursed her lips.

'*Fuck* the window. We're gonna go in, not peep into it.'

'But the door's locked,' Mark protested, pointing at the
heavy padlock.

Gillian smiled. Mark noticed something glint in her other
hand as she moved the torch. It was a knife, a sheath knife,
its blade at least five, perhaps six inches long, shiny with
newness.

'My brother bought this two weeks ago. I "borrowed"
it.'

Gillian handed Mark the knife.

'You prise it off,' she told him. For a moment Mark

hesitated, feeling the warmth from her hand on the hilt. Her eyes stared at him impatiently. 'Go on,' she urged.

Reluctantly he turned to the door. Gillian stepped up close behind him, perhaps to make sure that he didn't back out. She shone the torch on the padlock and the rusted iron pin it was fastened to.

'Put the knife under the pin,' she told him.

Its narrow base was already loose, with deep grooves and scratches in the wood surrounding it, as if someone had previously had a go at freeing it, and Mark, his hands trembling so much that he was sure that Gillian would see his nervousness, even in the gloom, easily slid the blade beneath it.

'Don't put too much of it under,' Gillian said. 'You'll never be able to prise it off if you do. Don't you know anythin'?'

Mark pulled the knife out a little, then levered it upwards, gritting his teeth.

'Harder!' Gillian whispered in his ear, uncomfortably close. *'Harder!'*

There was a snap. Mark fell back against her. His shoulder jarred into her chest with a solid thump that made the girl stagger, her face suddenly ashen with pain. The torch beam danced about the bottom of the wall as she gasped for breath.

'I'm sorry,' Mark said. He held out the sheath knife, showing her where the blade had snapped, an inch from the end.

Paul swore, his plump face dark with anger, but Gillian merely shook her head dismissively.

'So my brother'll 'ave to do without 'is knife. I wasn't even sure whether I was goin' to give it back to 'im anyway.'

'But the lock?' Mark nodded at the door.

'There's enough of the blade left, isn't there?' Her eyes bored into his intently, as if daring him to raise any more objections. 'Push what's left of the blade under the pin. The rest of it's thicker, so it shouldn't snap again.'

It didn't. Fraction by fraction, sweat smearing his face as he grunted and pushed, the pin was gradually prised from the door. The bolts holding it showed an inch, then two inches of brown rust as they were forced from the damp wood. With a final grunt Mark pulled against the knife and the pin fell with a leaden thud on the ground, less than an inch from his trainers.

Gillian gripped his shoulders in a brief hug as the others closed in, gathering round.

'Let's see what in there. Come on.' She turned to the others. 'Are you ready?'

Sickly sweet, like rotting fruit, the air from inside the dismal factory hung about the open door as they looked inside, making them pause momentarily, unsure if they could breathe it in and not be sick. Even Gillian, intent on what she'd planned, was made to turn her head away and gulp in fresher gasps of air before facing that fetid, festering darkness again.

'There's somethin' awful in there,' Mark muttered, almost to himself, too much in awe of Gillian even now to raise his objections openly to her.

'Awful my foot!' Gillian snapped. 'That dead cat we found last week was worse than this.'

His stomach rolled with revulsion as he recalled the maggots disgorged from the cat's open mouth when Paul experimentally trod on its wet carcass. Mark had to admit that she was right. That was worse. That and the smell that swept up at them as its dead flesh, almost molten it was so far decayed beneath its matted fur, split apart like an over-ripe melon.

'Come on, you soft-arsed babies,' Gillian scoffed, sucking in breath as she led them into the darkness inside. The torch beam darted about the ground in front of her, highlighting lumps of debris littered across the concrete floor. A length of chain hung from somewhere high overhead. Thick with rust, it swayed stiffly as Gillian pushed it aside, shining the torch beam up at the iron girders that spanned the ceiling twenty feet or more above their heads, dark with dust and grey cobwebs that hung between them like massive, misshapen hammocks and nets and tattered flags.

'We'll not find anythin' 'ere,' Mark said, his voice barely more than a whisper, the immensity of the space surrounding them bearing down upon him.

'What did you think we'd find?' Gillian asked. The others were silent, listening behind them.

Mark shrugged.

'I don't know.'

'Then wait an' see. If you didn't know what we'd find 'ere, you couldn't be disappointed, could you?' she sneered, heading onwards. The darkness drew in suddenly about the rest of them as she walked away with the torch. Mark hurried on after her, the others at his heels, until the torch beam was only a few feet away, an oasis of light in the intimidating dark.

In the afterglow reflected back from the concrete floor, Mark saw the self-satisfied look on Gillian's face. A tight little smile curled upwards at the corners of her mouth as she walked with unswerving certainty between the wreckage of old machinery, where lathes and grinders and large electric drills had once been used on the shop floor. Ahead of them, faint in the gloom, were offices where the foremen and manager would have once looked down, empty now except for what insect life had made its home inside them.

'You said you saw someone usin' this place for storin' stuff in,' Mark whispered. 'Crates of it, you said.' That had been the lure she'd used initially. Like her own family, with her overweight, drunken stepfather and her older brothers, half of whom were in Risley Remand Centre now for doing over an Asian off-licence on Audley Range in nearby Blackburn only three months ago, they came from families that skated close to the edge of the law. Petty theft, burglary, things like these were a fact of life. None of them could be shocked, even at their age, by a break-in. All that mattered was that when they did it there was something worth breaking-in for. And that they could get away afterwards with what they wanted without being caught. 'No one's used this place for years,' Mark added.

Gillian stopped, turned on her heel and shone the torch in Mark's face, trembling with tension.

'You callin' me a liar?'

Caught off balance by her anger, Mark stuttered: 'N-n-no.'

'You are, you little turd!'

Mark looked at the others for support. Just like before, when they intimidated him into agreeing to come here to start with, they again stared at him with a relentless determination, less like friends than . . . than . . .

Than what? he wondered, unable to find a word to fit. Even Wendy Bullen stared at him vindictively, as if he had no right to voice his doubts.

'Hey,' he said. 'What is this? I only said as 'ow it didn't look to me like anyone 'ad been usin' this place.'

'And I said they 'ave.'

Mark blinked his eyes, dazzled by the torch.

'Okay then. They 'ave. If you say so, they 'ave. All right?'

'All right.' Gillian lowered the torch. The darkness seemed even denser than before once its glare had gone from his eyes. Gillian's face was all but invisible to him in the afterglow now. A dim shape, like a misty, egg-shaped blur, hovering in the dark. 'Then we go on,' the girl said, swinging round.

Disorientated in the darkness, Mark stayed close to her, following what light the torch threw out. Behind him Mark felt Wendy Bullen press close to him, urging him on. Her brother pushed his fist into his back.

'Stop pissin' 'er about,' he whispered to Mark aggressively.

Mark glanced round at him, and shrugged. 'I'm not.'

Paul grunted his doubts. 'You said you were with us. Remember?'

'I am.'

'Then shut up an' stop acting like a prat.'

Gillian led them across the shop floor towards the offices. Going past these, they came to a door set in the bare stone walls of the factory. Unlocked, it opened with a dismal creak when Gillian pulled it, jamming halfway. Inside, stone steps spiralled down into an even murkier darkness – a thick, cloying, damp-filled darkness that smelt of earth, overladen by an obscure sourness, like ancient milk.

Mark would have protested again, despite the growing hostility of his friends, but Gillian started down the steps without a pause, taking the sole source of light with her. The advancing darkness urged him onwards. To stay at the top of the steps would have been to let the dark sweep over him. Unthinkable as a prospect, he retreated down the steps after her, grasping at the walls for support.

As the steps wound deeper and deeper into the earth, he felt in the torn pocket of his anorak for the knife Gillian had given him, disturbed and frightened by the way things were going. He knew that Gillian had lied to him. No one had used this place for years. No one, for sure, had come down here. So why was she leading them here?

Why?

They must have descended at least twenty feet as his mind replayed this question again and again before the steps opened out into the black expanse of a cellar. Gillian's torch beam shone across tall racks of cardboard boxes stuffed with papers – invoices, receipts, record cards and orders – stored here as a dumping ground for the factory above. The ground was covered in cobblestones like some of the streets in town that had not yet been tarmaced over.

'What 'ave we come 'ere for?' Mark asked, as he and Gillian waited for the other three to catch up.

Gillian smiled.

'I told you,' she said. 'Even though you don't believe me. But you'll see. I'll show you.'

A moment later the others emerged down the steps. They paused, glancing at Mark and Gillian suspiciously.

'Is 'e stallin' again?' Jenny asked, her plaits thick with dust from where they'd swung against the walls as they came down the steps.

Paul stepped forwards, his podgy face set hard with determination. 'If 'e's at it again . . .'

His sister put a hand on his arm. 'You're not, Mark, are you?' she asked, though Mark felt repelled by the tone of her voice and the hint of a threat that was in it.

''Course I'm not stallin',' he said. He turned to Gillian for support. 'I'm not, am I?'

'No,' Gillian said with a thin smile as they set off again, though Paul kept mumbling beneath his breath as they passed between the racks of paperwork. The arched, red-brick ceiling pressed close overhead, matted with webs. Some of the overburdened racks almost reached up to it.

'There you are.' Gillian pointed through a broad archway to where a number of racks had been pushed to one side. In the space left by them, five heavy wooden boxes lay on the ground. Getting them down the staircase must have only just been physically possible, Mark thought, unsure, in fact, if it really was possible at all, even though it *must* have been for them to be here.

The boxes were roughly six feet long by three feet wide, strongly made from plain timber, grey with dirt. Old-looking, they were caked with mould.

'You never saw them brought 'ere,' Mark said accusingly. 'They've been 'ere for years.'

Gillian's tight little smile grew fractionally broader, dimpling her cheeks.

She stepped nearer the boxes and shone the torch on them. One was open, its lid smashed in at one end, then forced away to lean at an angle to the ground.

Mark felt hot spit rise in his throat as if he was going to be sick. *This wasn't what they were supposed to have come here for!* He looked at Gillian, scared at the strangeness in her face, her eyes inscrutable.

'Paul? Wendy? Jenny?' He stared at his friends, vague in the gloom away from the torch. Vague, but not so vague that he couldn't tell that something was wrong with them. His fingers tightened on the knife in his pocket, securing them firmly round its hilt. 'What is it?'

A faint echo chanted: 'What is it?' – mockingly.

Gillian took hold of his arm, pulling him nearer the opened box.

An arm – skeletal and grey, with worm-eaten tufts of ragged flesh sticking to it – reached out suddenly. It clamped a hand, like a leper's claw, round his wrist and dragged him forwards. Mark screamed, as Gillian released him, letting the hideous, rotting arm tug him to it. Instinctively Mark pulled out the knife and hacked at the arm with its broken blade. A fibrous finger, chopped off at its second joint, flopped to the floor, and a sticky grey ichor jetted out of the stump. Again and again he hacked at the thing, frantic with terror, his screams re-echoing back and forth in a growing frenzy of hysteria.

Almost severed in two already by the knife, a tendon snapped in the creature's arm. In that instant of limpness, as its fingers relaxed their vice-like grip, Mark backed away from it, unwilling to look at the rest of the creature that had risen from the box, grey and thin, with a pock-marked, raddled, rotting face that gaped a snag-toothed, drooling mouth towards him.

In a surge of anger, Mark whirled on his companions, hating them all suddenly. Gillian stumbled back from him as he swung round at her with the knife, wanting more than anything else in the whole wide world to feel its blade cut through her face. Her smile had gone. Confusion and fear had replaced it.

'You fuckin' bastards! All of you!' Mark gasped, watching them as they stepped away from him, drawing back into the darkness. 'You bastards!'

A thump of something falling on the ground behind him warned him to move.

He looked back, saw the creature stagger from the box towards him, its naked body a grey obscenity, like a Death Camp victim brought to life.

'No!' Mark hacked through the barrier of his 'friends', cutting about him to drive them away as he ran back, onwards, on into the dark, heading for the stairs.

What light the torch had given went out suddenly. Total darkness, a darkness so dense he could almost feel it, blinded him.

He bumped past the racks of cardboard boxes, his back prickling with apprehension, as if he could sense the creature reaching out for him, its claw-like fingers only inches from his neck.

Driven by fear, he ran heedlessly on, until a vivid flash of light shot through his eyes as his head hit the wall with a sickening *thwack*, rebounding backwards. Nausea swirled about him for a moment. Unable to reorientate himself, he reached for the wall and used it to climb back onto his feet.

Out in the darkness, as he leaned weakly against the wall for support, he could hear furtive sounds of movement. There was a scraping somewhere to his right. A bump elsewhere. A harsh rasp of breath came from some distance in front of him. His ears tingled with the effort of listening. Desperately he reached along the wall, feeling his way, hoping for the edge of the staircase, hoping . . . hoping . . .

'It's no good, Mark.'

A girl's hand, calloused on its palms, grasped his own.

'No!'

Mark swung at Gillian's unseen face in the dark. The knife hit the wall, stinging his fingers.

Other hands, stronger than Gillian's – Paul's? – took hold of his arms and forced them up his back till his shoulder screamed with agony and he bleated: 'No!'

Someone grasped hold of the knife and prised it free of his fingers. Then the torch came on, and he saw that his friends surrounded him, Paul behind him, the three girls crowded on either side. Gillian held the torch at his face. The knife jutted out in front of it, pointing at his eyes.

'Don't be stupid again,' Paul warned.

Mark twisted his head round as far as it would go, looking in terror for the creature, beyond what light was cast back into the cellar by the torch.

'That th-thing,' he stammered.

Gillian smiled. At a nod of her head Paul forced him round and pushed him, step by step, towards the racks, then on between them, back to the boxes beyond the arch. Mark tried to struggle, but Paul had an unbelievably strong grip on his arm, forcing it up so far behind his shoulder blades when he resisted him that it seemed as if it would be torn from its socket. The pain almost made him faint, it was so intense. Helpless against it, he ceased his struggles as they pressed relentlessly onwards, on towards the opened box.

'Gillian . . . *please!*'

Their lack of fear almost unnerved him even more, in some strange, inexplicable way, than the prospect of seeing the creature again.

'Why are you doin' this? Why?'

A hint of amusement passed briefly across Gillian's face. With a flick of her hand she indicated for Paul to lead him towards the other boxes.

'No, Gillian, *please!* Don't do it!' Mark pleaded. He kicked against Paul's legs behind him. Suddenly his heel connected with his captor's knee, and Paul fell sideways. In that instant Mark felt himself slip free. He darted forwards, but as he did so Paul thrust one of his legs out, tripping him with it. With a cry, Mark tumbled against the box in front of him. Its lid had not been fastened down, but merely lay across the top of the box, covering it. As he grabbed hold of it, it fell off, clattering on the floor. As it fell, Mark screamed.

Inside the box lay a shrivelled, dried-up, mummified parody of Gillian Willoughby, its bloodless, blackening lips drawn back in a frozen scream of terror. Its dead eyes, staring sightlessly upwards like melted marbles, were already starting to sink in decay.

'Don't worry,' Mark heard the Gillian behind him say as the children took hold of his arms once more. 'It won't hurt for long. But our brother must have a new lease of life, just like the rest of us, you see.'

From close behind him Mark heard the unmistakable sound of unshod feet being dragged across the floor.

'Some bit of you will still live on, though,' Gillian added, as if to comfort him in some small way as they held his head in an unyielding grip, 'like some of the Gillian you once knew lives on in me.'

Mark screamed as he felt the soft, rotting lips of the thing from the box transfix themselves to his neck, and its jagged teeth bite into him.

'In some way, Mark,' his terror-filled, fading consciousness heard as he felt his life – and something *more* than his life – being sucked from his flesh, 'some bit of you will live forever. Forever and ever and . . .'

A FLY ON THE WALL

H. J. Cording

H. J. Cording is a freelance journalist in Kaitaia, New Zealand. As well as working for local newspapers, he has sold articles to Omni *and* Classic & Sportscar. *Short fiction has appeared in* Starry Nights, *an anthology of erotic fantasy, and in* Forum Fabulatorum *(Denmark),* Maplecade *(Canada) and* Beyond *(USA). A small collection of the author's poetry,* Homeless Souvenirs, *was published in 1990.*

ELAINE arrived home from the auction considerably later than she had intended. She got out of her car, glanced at her watch, and realized she would only have time for the most cursory rummage through her promising boxes of oddments. The crystal and silver had been out of the question; even the porcelain miniatures, tempting though they were, had gone far too high for a collector at her level of involvement. But they were only a minor disappointment. All things considered, she was quite pleased with her bidding. It was among the oddments that the most serendipitous gems often came to light.

She lifted one of the boxes out of the back of her station wagon and set it on the workbench that divided the double garage. It was surprisingly heavy, and made her belatedly appreciate the insistence of the older man in the tweed coat who had loaded the five boxes for her. She had tried to dissuade him at the time, having taken him for the sort of antique dealer who would not be above removing a small but valuable item from an unguarded job lot.

The incident was soon forgotten as she began to unpack the box. There were two lacquered wooden jewellery cases, lined with red plush, their inlay only slightly chipped, a grotesquely large tortoise-shell comb, three large glass plates and four small, carefully wrapped in yellowed newspaper – Elaine dared to hope that the remainder of the set might turn up in the other boxes. These were followed by a pair of wooden shoe-trees just like her grandfather's, and an alligator-skin purse with a dozen compartments, empty except for a faded cash register receipt. An ancient box camera surfaced next, then three brass candlesticks and something else of brass, ornately scrolled, that might have been the chamber of a hookah. And, poking out of a clutter of kitchen implements at the bottom, an enormous silver teapot.

At least it looked like a teapot, with its elegantly curved handle and spout, only the lid was impossible to remove. She turned on the light and examined it more closely. The lid and the body were in fact a single piece of metal demarcated by an ingeniously fashioned seam.

There was no inscription on the base to indicate its composition, but its weight and sheen left Elaine in little doubt that the object she held in her hands was solid silver. The late Vivian Prescott could certainly have afforded such an item. There had been rumours at the auction about Mrs Prescott's only son; gambling debts had been mentioned, and a messy drunken-driving episode. Whatever the reasons, Elaine could not help being glad he had disposed of his mother's household effects so hastily.

She found a clean rag on the workbench and began to rub the smooth, polished sides. Engrossed in admiring the metal, she did not notice the smoky vapour issuing from the spout until it had formed a large cloud in front of her. As she stared in astonishment, it coalesced into a tall, imposing figure in flowing robes who bowed and introduced himself.

'Ibn Muhal al-jini, at your service, my lady.'

Elaine started and gasped, and a split second later realized she had lost her grip on the teapot. She braced herself for the crash of silver on concrete that never came. Instead she watched with deepening amazement as the teapot righted itself in midair, rose up, and floated gently to rest on the workbench.

'Please do not be alarmed, my lady. I am the jinn of this

urn. You have summoned me by rubbing it, and now I am yours to command.'

Elaine could only continue to stare, open-mouthed. After a brief pause the resonant voice resumed. 'Forgive me, my lady, if my sudden appearance has caused you distress. I presume you have never met a jinn before, and therefore you may not be aware of the powers at my command. The jinn's credibility has declined greatly over the last few centuries with the growth of science and loss of faith in magic. This is most unfortunate, for a jinn is a willing, obedient, and very useful spirit whose only desire is to serve. I am capable of dealing with the most modern technology, as well as being a qualified practitioner of levitation, necromancy, and transmutation. Under the terms of my spell, I disappear as soon as I have fulfilled a wish or command. If you have further need of me, you only have to rub my urn again.'

Elaine had a hundred questions she wanted to ask and no idea where to begin. 'Would you mind telling me . . . that is . . . how did you wind up in an auction?'

'Through no fault of my own, my lady, I assure you. It is beyond my powers, alas, to guarantee my master eternal life, and so I must inevitably be handed on from time to time. But . . . how may I best say it . . . the knowledge of my presence is not always passed on with the urn. My masters have generally found it in their best interests to keep my existence a secret. Thus, if a misfortune occurs, such as befell the venerable Rashied Hamdul, who died after receiving a kick in the head from a donkey, at the age of 108 . . . He had outlived all his sons, so my urn went to the widow of his second oldest son, who gave it to an aged servant woman for polishing. This crone's one wish was to join her long-lost love in Paradise. I arranged this for her, and then . . . Forgive me, my lady, for going on at such length, but you must understand, thirty-five years have passed since I was last summoned. When I came into Mrs Prescott's possession, I was once again entrusted to the care of a servant. This girl took fright when I materialized and wished never to have to polish my urn again. And so I have remained until now, gleaming and idle, as the years . . .'

He was interrupted by the phone ringing.

'Excuse me,' said Elaine as she went inside to answer it, still holding the urn. Ibn Muhal dutifully followed.

'Hello . . . fine, darling, and you? . . . oh . . . oh, not again! Well, what time should I expect you? . . . all right . . . see you then.'

David was working late. Again. A marketing conference . . . His job had been occupying more and more of his evenings lately, what with conferences, meetings, Institute of Management seminars, extra paperwork. There had been other periods when David had had to put in extra time at the office, but it had never gone on like this. And, if she remembered correctly, it was shortly before all this started that a new receptionist had taken one of her calls. Most receptionists had bland, impersonal voices, hardly distinguishable from one another, but not this one. Her slightly husky tones brought to mind someone young, confident of her attractiveness, with an easy, familiar manner bordering on the provocative. Elaine tried to tell herself that her imagination was working overtime, but she was not convinced. Although she was still fairly good-looking, thirty-six was, undeniably, no longer young. And on those nights when he had stayed late at the office, David was invariably too tired to do anything but sleep when they went to bed.

Furthermore, she was annoyed at having cut her afternoon short for nothing. Stephen had gone to the Wilkinsons' after school and was spending the evening there, so she could have accepted Deirdre Simpson's invitation for coffee and had a good, envious look at her glass figurines. At least she hadn't started dinner yet; it couldn't be ruined like the soufflé she had gone to so much trouble over last Thursday. She had still not entirely gotten over that.

She caught sight of Ibn Muhal hovering solicitously nearby, and had an idea. Ten minutes ago it would have been nothing more than an idle fantasy, a figure of speech, but reality had been transformed in that short length of time, so that it now became a feasible plan of action. She said, 'I wish I was a fly on the wall at this marketing conference.'

Delighted to have a wish to grant, the jinn proudly announced, 'It is done!'

In the next instant Elaine found herself clinging to a smooth vertical surface, head down, facing a vast expanse of woolly beige. Her initial moment of terror at the sheer drop soon passed as she realized she would not fall. She crawled to her left on six unfamiliar legs, turned a corner, and met an undulating vista of grey polyester blend. Ibn Muhal must have been slightly out of practice, for he had landed her, not on the wall, but on the leg of a chair.

A sudden knee-bend startled her into flight. She gained altitude and circled the high-ceilinged room. Gravity no longer existed; her wings vibrated with a will of their own. Her new body's reflexes took complete control, leaving her mind free to savour a joy the equal of any she had ever known.

She was jolted out of her rapture in the middle of a figure eight when a man complained about the goddamn flies in the air conditioning again. The animosity in his voice made her realize the need for a safe hiding place.

The twenty-first floor conference room of the Harper-Cowles Building featured a wide window nearly the full height of the room. Heavy drapes were drawn to one side, revealing a hazy urban panorama feebly lit by the late afternoon sun. Elaine secured a vantage point amid the voluminous folds from which she could take in every detail of the scene below.

It was something between a relief and a letdown to find no cute receptionists, no couches, no passionate infidelities, only David and six other men seated around a long, polished mahogany table, papers and drinks before them, discussing in exhaustive detail the promotion and marketing of the new Primal range of men's toiletries. Cigarette smoke eddied upward into a blue haze, irritating her spiracles. She was ashamed of her mistrust, and wished she were home.

Nothing happened.

She could not help being disappointed, even though she had not really expected it to work. There was undoubtedly more to this business of wishing than she had imagined. Recalling her words to the jinn, she realized she was almost certainly stuck here for the duration of the conference, which had barely started when she arrived.

Time dragged on. Market research surveys were quoted, sales figures of competing brands compared, projections analyzed, promotional campaigns debated. The upper level of air grew thicker. Elaine decided she would rather wait out the rest of the meeting at David's side. She had a sudden longing to be close to him, as well as a need to escape the pall of smoke.

David was on the far side of the table, opposite the man who had complained about flies. It seemed important not to let this man notice her again. She told herself he was not likely to do anything but complain some more, but she still felt unpopular, conspicuous, and vulnerable. She had always reacted to the buzz of a fly's wings, and was afraid hers would be unpleasantly obvious.

After carefully considering various flight plans, she decided on a wide sweep around the head of the table, keeping close to the ceiling. Reaching the other side, she descended in a gentle curve that landed her on the back of her husband's chair. He was leaning forward, busy with a calculator. She hopped onto his jacket and crawled under the flap of the right-hand pocket. It seemed a perfect shelter: warm, completely hidden, with a comfortable foothold, unlikely to be disturbed – David never carried anything in the outside pockets. She stroked her wings with her back legs, as she had seen flies do, and found it surprisingly relaxing.

A mosaic of odours permeated the cozy darkness: a faint tinge of mothballs, Primal body cologne for men, the slick impersonal vinyl of the chair upholstery, a harsh blend of tobacco residues in the suit fabric, and the reassuring familiarity of David's personal smell, from which her heightened olfactory sensitivity was able to glean nuances previously unimaginable. His delicious, well-groomed, manly scent generated a warmth she had not felt toward him for far too long. Poor David, he had suffered her unvoiced suspicion, her coolness, her lack of sympathy, when all along he had been guilty of nothing more than putting in extra hours at tedious sessions like this for the sake of his job. She hadn't worked since before Stephen was born, and could still afford to indulge her penchant for collecting would-be antiques, thanks to the man she was spying on. How could she ever tell him? She wouldn't have to, of course, if the jinn returned her to normal when the meeting was over. It only now occurred to her to wonder if he would . . .

Papers rustled; a series of clicks bespoke the closing of

briefcases. David stood up, and after a moment began walking. When he stopped, after perhaps twenty paces, she ventured to the edge of the pocket flap and peered out.

An elevator soon appeared and the men filed in. Elaine withdrew into the lee of her shelter to avoid possible scrutiny. Conversation died so simultaneously with her retreat that she could not help wondering if she was somehow responsible. The faint hum of the elevator seemed to impose a rule of silence. As the doors slid open on the ground floor, a flurry of farewells burst forth.

The tang of the street was vivid after the bland conditioned air of the office. An appetizing aroma loomed on the olfactory horizon, waxing steadily stronger. As she neared its source it revealed a rainbow of individual essences: salami, cheese, garlic, tomato, pepper, anchovy, ham, mushroom, and . . . yes, it was really pineapple.

David turned a corner and stopped walking. The air was saturated with floating molecules of hot pizza. Elaine heard him order a slice of Hawaiian to go and remembered that she hadn't eaten for hours – at least, her human body hadn't. She had no way of knowing how long her fly body had been without nourishment, but it certainly felt in need of some.

It was evident from the way he chatted to the counterman that David was a regular customer. She had always thought he was not particularly fond of pizza. Could there be further surprises in store? Perhaps she had been allowed to remain a fly for reasons yet to be divulged . . .

Speculation was drowned in a flood of tantalizing odours as the counterman opened one of his ovens. Her wings trembled with excitement. It was dangerous, it was madness, it was finally impossible to resist the urge to find a tasty crumb or two. She darted behind David and up to the high counter, landing beside a fat blob of crust smeared with cheese and tomato and still slightly warm. She kept a compound eye on the counterman as he wrapped David's slice, cheerfully made change from a ten-dollar bill, and turned back to his stainless steel bowls without noticing her. She, in turn, was so engrossed in feasting that it was not until she turned to get at the rest of the cheese that she realized David had gone.

Suddenly panicked, she flew out into the street, circling frantically. She glimpsed a figure walking away, dark-suited in the shadows. There was no one else in sight; it had to be David. Before she could be sure, he disappeared.

She hurled herself desperately in the direction he had been going. A third of the way down the block, an air current nudged her into the entrance to an underground parking station. Footsteps echoed from somewhere out of sight along the curving ramp. After a second's hesitation she plunged down it. David was by the far wall, unlocking his car.

By now she was in such a state she could not even feel relief at finding him. She drew on every resource she had and reached the car just as David was starting to close the door. This presented a taxing aerodynamic problem: she had to turn at maximum speed into an ever narrower opening at an ever more acute angle. She veered sharply to the right, almost doubling back, the door crunched shut, she slammed into something invisible and fell like a stone.

The darkness vibrated gently. A hum that had been there all along grew noticeable. She lay on her back between two rubber ridges that cradled her like the sides of a bath. She flexed her legs gingerly, one by one, and felt no sign of damage. Turning over with an effort, she found that her wings had also survived intact. The stultifying ache between her eyes could not entirely overwhelm a confused, grateful wonder that she was still in one piece. The door had been within an inch of its frame as she flew through it. Her life had begun to pass before her mind's eye. Then came the stunning blow and the slow, disoriented return from oblivion. She had hit the windshield, bounced off the dashboard, and rolled under the front passenger seat. She wondered where they were as the engine droned on and on.

A sharp pull on the handbrake startled her into alertness. She was suddenly aware that the engine had stopped. It was a struggle to shake off the drowse she had fallen into, but she managed to hop onto David's trouser leg as he got out of the car.

'What the hell . . .' he wondered aloud, disturbed to find the station wagon in the garage and the house in darkness. He glanced at his watch. He had called her a little over two hours ago, and she had not mentioned going out then. It was possible, with Stephen not due home until later, that she had gone somewhere on the spur of the moment in one of her

friends' cars . . . He shrugged and went inside. He turned on
several lights, threw his coat over a chair, and made himself
a drink at the bar. Glass in hand, he sank into an easy chair
with a sigh of relief and opened the newspaper.

Meanwhile, Elaine flew over to the urn, which she had left
on the counter by the phone. She landed on the side where
she had rubbed and began to walk across it, at first in random
zigzags, then back and forth in a methodical line, gradually
widening her turns until she described a fat ellipse.

After several thousand steps she reluctantly conceded that
she could not imitate the rubbing of a human hand. She
climbed up the spout and peered down it into blackness,
wondering if the jinn was aware of her presence. She
concentrated her entire being on the wish to return to
human form.

It was no use. She dredged her memory of the encounter
with the jinn. She had not actually specified a return to
normal – it had not occurred to her. The jinn should have
known – but on the other hand, it was his business to carry
out wishes, not to question or interpret them. Then again,
jinns were reputed to be treacherous, which was the reason
they were imprisoned in lamps, bottles, fake teapots . . .
There was no point in putting it off. Unappealing though
the idea was, she could think of nothing better to do. She
would have to go down there after him.

As she rounded the curve of the spout, total darkness
engulfed her, and her wings were pressed against her back.
Suddenly she froze in terror, certain that she was about to
be squeezed into a horrid oozing pulp. She huddled there
for eternal minutes, unable to move forward or back, until
at last the fact that she was still alive penetrated the fog
of fear and gradually made it recede. Eventually she was
able to rationalize with a name the sensation she had never
before known: claustrophobia. She told herself she had
broadened her horizons, in a sense, and doggedly forced
herself to go on.

The spout widened, descended vertically, then returned
to the horizontal to join the body of the urn. A shorter
descent led her down to the base. She felt her way around
the perimeter for a while, then cut across toward the center.
Reaching the side, she climbed until she was hanging upside

down in the peaked dome that crowned the urn. She stayed there several minutes, lost in perplexity, before dropping down to the bottom.

She was almost ready to admit defeat, having found nothing but a faint musty smell that might have been the jinn's molecules in suspension. As a last resort she fanned her wings in the hope that the noise and disturbance of the air would cause him to materialize. But when she stopped, the darkness was as still and empty as ever. Unless . . . but of course, the jinn would not appear inside the urn. Heartened by this remaining possibility, she climbed a short distance up the side, guessed correctly that the entrance to the spout lay to her left, and groped her way back out.

But when her eyes had readjusted to the light, she saw only David, still reading the paper. Her only hope was to get him to rub the urn. But how to communicate with him? She would have to convince him quickly that she was no ordinary fly. She had seen him greatly irritated with flies, not to mention vindictive. Her own record was no better – she recalled with shame how, just the other day, she had aerosoled a hapless fly at point-blank range and watched with satisfaction as it expired on a bookshelf.

She landed as quietly as she could on David's shoulder to consider her next, crucial move. The likely consequences of a wrong strategy weighed on her oppressively. Feeling the need for a moment's distraction, she began to read the paper. A single-column headline, 'Help Promised for Flood Victims', germinated an idea.

She hopped down to Help and began walking around it in an effort to imitate a moving finger, watching David as she went. His attention was elsewhere. Struck by a new inspiration, she started buzzing: dot dot dot, dash dash dash, dot dot dot . . . He shook the paper halfway through her second sequence. She resisted the instinctive urge to flight and buzzed more insistently.

David suddenly turned the page, forcing her to take off in a hurry. She zigzagged around the room despondently, knowing she would have to provoke him to get his attention, unable to work up the nerve. Finally she ventured a lap around his head, and a second, slightly closer. He shook the paper irritably but did not look up. She grew bolder, hovering in front of his eyes one moment, darting away to the urn the next. David folded the paper with a muttered curse and stood up, glass in hand, contemplating a second scotch.

Elaine redoubled her efforts. He tried to wave her away with his free hand – and turned the right way! She swooped within inches of his nose in excitement. He watched her land on the urn. She flew back toward him, not so closely this time, and showed the way again.

David shook his head as if perplexed – and started toward the urn. She looped a loop with joy, touched down, and began to walk circles around the place she had rubbed, buzzing frantically all the while. In her enthusiasm she failed to notice him reaching for the can of fly spray on the windowsill.

AT DIAMOND LAKE

William F. Nolan

William F. Nolan's stories have appeared in more than 200 anthologies, including Fantasy Tales, Best New Horror 3 *and* Weird Tales. *He is the author of some 1500 published items – novels, short stories and non-fiction. His sixtieth book, a novel called* The Black Mask Murders, *was published in 1994. Another of his works,* Yankee Champion, *is currently being adapted by film director David Cronenberg for Warner Bros., under the working title* Red Cars, *while* The Black Summer *is his own adaptation of Peter Straub's novel* Floating Dragon, *which is being produced as a two-part mini-series by NBC-TV. An extensive interview about his TV/film scripting career recently appeared in the magazine* Filmfax, *and* Night Shapes *is his latest collection of short horror stories.*

'I don't understand why you won't go,' his wife said. 'I just don't understand it.'

'We'll go to Disneyworld,' Steve told her. 'They say it's a real kick.'

'To hell with Disneyworld!' she said sharply. 'I want to go up to the lake.'

'No, Ellen.'

'Why no?'

'It's too damn cold up there in the fall.'

'And this summer, when I wanted us to go up for the Fourth of July, you said it would be too damn hot.'

He shrugged. 'I'm going to sell it. I've got it listed with a realtor.'

'Your father dies and leaves you a beautiful redwood house on Diamond Lake and you won't even let me *see* it!'

'What's to see? A lake. Some woods. An ugly little cabin.'

'It looks charming in the scrapbook photos. As a boy you seemed so *happy* there.'

'I wasn't. Not really.' His eyes darkened. 'And I'm not going back.'

'Okay, Steve,' she said. 'You can spend *your* vacation at Disneyworld. I'm going to spend *mine* at Diamond Lake.'

Ellen worked as an artist in a design studio; Steve was vice president of a local grocery chain. For the past five years, since their marriage, they had arranged to share their two-week vacations together.

'You're being damned unreasonable,' he said.

'Not at all,' she told him. 'What I want to do seems perfectly reasonable to me. We have a cabin on Diamond Lake and I intend to spend my vacation there. With or without you.'

'All right, you win,' he said. 'As long as you're so set on it, I'll go with you.'

'Good,' she said. 'I'll start packing. We can drive up in the morning.'

It took them most of the day to get there. Once they left the Interstate the climb into the mountains was rapid and smooth; the highway had been widened considerably since Steve was a boy. When his father had bought property on the lake and built a cabin there the two-lane road had been winding and treacherous; in those early days the long grade to Crestline, five thousand feet up, had seemed endless. Now, their new Chrysler Imperial swept them effortlessly to the summit.

'We need something special to celebrate with,' Ellen said as they headed into the heavily-wooded area. 'I want to get some champagne. Isn't there a shopping centre near the lake?'

'The village,' Steve said, his hands nervously gripping the wheel. He'd been fine on the trip up, but now that they were here . . . 'There's a general store at the village.'

'Are you okay?' she asked him. 'You look sick. Maybe I'd better drive.'

'I'm all right,' he said.

But he wasn't.

Coming back was wrong. All wrong.

A darkness waited at Diamond Lake.

The village hadn't changed much. A boxy multiplex cinema
had been added, along with a sports clothing store and a
new gift shop. All in the same quaint European motif, built
to resemble a rustic village in the Swiss Alps.

Ellen bought a bottle of Mumm's at Wade's General Store.
Old man Wade was long dead, but his son – who'd been a
tow-headed youngster the last time Steve had seen him – was
running the place. Looked a lot like his father; even had the
same type of little wire glasses perched on his nose, just the
way old Ben Wade used to wear them.

'Been a long time,' he said to Steve.

'Yeah . . . long time.'

Afterward, as Steve drove them to the cabin, Ellen told
him he'd been rude to young Wade.

'What was I supposed to do, kiss his hand?'

'You could have smiled at him. He was trying to be nice.'

'I didn't feel like smiling.'

'Can't you just relax and enjoy being up here?' she asked
him. 'God, it's *beautiful!*'

Thick pine woods surrounded them, broken by grassy
meadows bearing outcroppings of raw granite, like dark
scars in a sea of dazzling fall colours.

'Do you know what kind of flowers they have up here?'

'Dad knew all that stuff,' he said. 'There's lupine, iris,
bugle flowers, columbine . . . He liked to hike through the
woods with his camera. Took colour pictures of the wild life.
Especially birds. He loved scarlet-topped woodpeckers.'

'Did you walk with him?'

'Sometimes. Mostly, Mom went, just the two of them,
while I'd swim at the lake. Dad was really at his best in the
woods, but we only came up here twice after Mom died.
When I turned fourteen we stopped coming altogether. I
tried to get him to sell the place, but he wouldn't.'

'I'm glad. Otherwise, I'd never have seen it.'

'I'll be relieved when it's sold,' he said darkly.

'Why?' she turned to him in the seat. 'What makes you
hate it so much?'

He didn't answer. They were passing Larson's old mill-
wheel and Steve had his first view of Diamond Lake in fifteen
years – a glitter of sun-bronzed steel flickering through the

trees. A chill iced his skin. He blinked rapidly, feeling his heart accelerate.

He should never have returned.

The cabin was exactly as he remembered it – long and low-roofed, its redwood siding in dark contrast to the white, crushed-gravel driveway his father had so carefully laid out from the dirt road.

'It looks practically *new!*' enthused Ellen. 'I thought it would be all weathered and worn.'

'Dad made sure it was kept up. He had people come out and do whatever was needed.'

He unlocked the front door and they stepped inside.

'It's lovely,' said Ellen.

Steve grunted. 'Damp in here. There's an oil stove in the bedroom. Helps at night. Once the sun's down, it gets real cold this time of year.'

The cabin's interior was lined in dark oak, with sturdy matching oak furniture and a fieldstone hearth. A large plate-glass window faced the lake. On the far shore, rows of tall pines marched up the mountainside. A spectacular panorama.

'I feel like I'm inside a picture book,' said Ellen. She turned to him, taking both of his hands in hers. 'Can't we try and be happy here, Steve – for just these two weeks? *Can't* we?'

'Sure,' he said, 'we can try.'

By nightfall, he'd conjured a steady blaze from the fireplace while Ellen prepared dinner: mixed leaf salad, angel hair pasta with stir-fried fresh vegetables and garlic, and apple tart with vanilla ice cream for dessert.

She ended the meal with a champagne toast, her fire-reflecting glass raised in salute. 'Here's to life at Diamond Lake.'

Steve joined her; they clinked glasses. He drank in silence, his back to the dark water.

'I'll bet you had a lot of friends here as a boy,' she said.

He shook his head. 'No . . . I was mostly a loner.'

'Didn't you have a girlfriend?'

His face tightened. 'I was only thirteen.'

'So? Thirteen-year-old boys get crushes on girls. Happens all the time. Wasn't there anyone special?'

'I *told* you I wasn't happy here. Do we have to go on and on about this?'

She stood up and began clearing the dishes. 'All right. We won't talk about it.'

'Look,' he said tightly. 'I didn't want to, but I *did* come up here with you. Isn't that enough?'

'No, it isn't enough.' She hesitated, turning to face him. 'You've been acting like a miserable grouch.'

He walked over, kissed her cheek, and ran his right hand lightly along her neck and shoulder. 'Sorry, El,' he said. 'I'm letting this place get to me and I promised myself I wouldn't. It's just all this talk about the past.'

She looked at him intently. 'Something bad happened to you up here, didn't it?'

'I don't know,' he said slowly. 'I don't really know *what* happened . . .'

He turned to stare out of the window at the flat, oily-dark expanse of lake. A night bird cried out across the black water.

A cry of pain.

The next morning was windy and overcast but Ellen insisted on a lake excursion ('I have to see what the place is like.') and Steve agreed. There was an outboard on his father's rowboat and the sound of the boat's engine kicked echoes back from the empty cabins along the shore.

They were alone on the wide lake.

'Where *is* everybody?' Ellen wanted to know.

'With the summer people gone, it's pretty quiet. Too cold for boating or swimming up here in October.'

As if to confirm his words, the wind increased, carrying a sharp chill down from the mountains.

'We'd better head back,' said Ellen. 'This sweater's too thin. I should have taken a jacket. At least *you* were smart enough to wear one.'

Steve had turned away from her in the boat, his eyes fixed on the rocky shoreline. He pointed. 'There's someone out there,' he said, his tone intense, strained. 'On that dark pile of boulders.'

'I don't see anyone.'

'Just *sitting* there,' Steve said, 'watching us. Not moving.'

His words suddenly seemed ominous, disturbing her. 'I don't see anyone,' she repeated.

'Christ!' He leaned toward her. 'Are you blind? *There* . . . on the rocks.' He was staring at the distant shore.

'I see the rocks, but . . . Maybe the wind blew something over them that looked like – '

'Gone,' he said, not listening to her. 'Nothing there now.'

He pushed the throttle forward on the outboard and the boat sliced through the lake surface, heading for shore.

A hawk flew low over the wind-scalloped water, seeking prey.

The sun was buried in a coffin of dark grey sky.

It would be a cold night.

At one am, under a full moon, with Ellen sleeping soundly back at the cabin, Steve had crossed the lake to the boulders. He felt the cold knifing his skin through the fleece-lined hunting jacket; the wind had a seeking life of its own.

He was able to ignore the surface cold; it was the *inner* cold that gripped him, viselike. A coldness of the soul.

Because he knew. The motionless figure he'd seen sitting here on these humped granite rocks was directly linked with his dread of Diamond Lake.

And, just as he had expected, the figure reappeared – standing at the dark fringe of pine woods. A woman. Somewhere in her twenties, tall, long-haired, with pale, predatory features and eyes as darkly luminous as the lake water itself. She wore a long gown that shimmered silver as she moved toward him.

They met at the water's edge.

'I knew you'd be back someday,' she said, smiling at him. Her tone was measured, the smile calculating, without warmth.

He stared at her. 'Who are you?'

'Part of your past.' She opened the slim moon-fleshed fingers of her right hand to reveal a miniature pearl at the end of a looped bronze chain. 'I was wearing this around my neck the last time you saw me. You gave it to me for my twelfth birthday. We were both very young.'

'Vanette.' He whispered her name, lost in the darkness of her eyes, confused and suddenly very afraid. He didn't know why, but she terrified him.

'You kissed me, Stevie,' she said. 'I was a shy little girl and you were the first boy I'd ever kissed.'

'I remember,' he said.

'What else do you remember,' she asked, 'about the night you kissed me, here at the rocks? It was deep summer, a warm, clear evening with the sky full of stars. The lake was calm and beautiful. Remember, Stevie?'

'I . . . I can't . . .' His tone faltered.

'You've blocked the memory,' she said. 'Your mind dropped a curtain over that night. To protect you. To keep you from the pain.'

'After I gave you the necklace,' he said slowly, feeling for the words, trying to force himself to remember, 'I . . . I *touched* you . . . you didn't want me to, but I – '

'You raped me,' she said, and her voice was like chilled silk. 'I was crying, begging you to stop, but you wouldn't. You ripped my dress, you hurt me. You hurt me a lot.'

The night scene was coming back to him across the years, assuming a sharp focus in his mind. He remembered the struggle, how Vanette had screamed and kept on screaming after he'd entered her virginal young body . . . but then the scene ended for him. He could not remember anything beyond her screams.

'I wouldn't be quiet and it made you angry,' she told him. 'Very angry. I kept screaming and you punched me with your fists to make me stop.'

'I'm sorry,' he said. 'So sorry. I . . . I guess I was crazy that night.'

'Do you remember what happened next?'

He shook his head. 'It's . . . all a blank.'

'Shall I tell you what happened?'

'Yes,' he said, his tone muted, dreading what she would say. But he *had* to know.

'You picked up a rock, a large one,' Vanette told him, 'and you crushed my head with it. I was unconscious when you put me in your father's boat . . . *that* one.' She pointed to the rowboat that Steve had used to cross the water. 'You rowed out to the deep end of the lake. There was a rusted anchor and some rope in the boat. You tied me, so I wouldn't be able to swim, and then you – '

'No!' He was breathing fast, eyes wide with shock. 'I didn't! Goddamn it, I *didn't*!'

Her voice was relentless: 'You pushed me over the side of the boat into the water, with the anchor tied to me. I sank to the bottom and didn't come up. I died that night in the lake.'

'It's a lie! You're alive. You're standing here now, in front of me, alive!'

'I'm here, but I'm not alive. I'm here as I would have been if I'd been able to grow up and become a woman.'

'This is all – ' His voice trembled. 'You can't really expect me to believe that I'd ever – '

'– murder a twelve-year-old girl? But that's exactly what you did. Do you want to see what I was like when they took me from the lake . . . after the rope loosened and I'd floated to the surface?'

She advanced. Closer, very close.

'Get away from me!' Steve shouted, taking a quick step back. 'Get the hell away!'

A little girl stood in front of him now, smiling. The left side of her head was crushed bone, stark white under the moon, and her small body was horribly swollen, blackened. One eye was gone, eaten away, and the dress she wore was rotted and badly ripped.

'Hi, Stevie,' she said.

Steve whirled away from the death figure and began to run. Wildly. In panic. Using the full strength of his legs. Running swiftly through the dark woods, rushing away from the lake shore and the thing he'd left there. Running until his breath was fire in his throat, until his leg muscles failed. He stumbled to a panting halt, one hand braced against the trunk of a pine. Drained and exhausted, he slid to his knees, his laboured breathing the only sound in the suddenly wind-hushed, moonlit woods. Then, gradually, as his beating heart slowed, he raised his head and . . . oh, God, oh Christ . . .

She was there!

Vanette's ravaged, lake-bloated face was *inches* from his – and her rotted hand, half mottled flesh, half raw gristle and bone, reached out, delicately, to touch his cheek . . .

*

Two years later, after Ellen had sold the lakefront property and moved to Florida, she fell in love with a man who asked her what had become of her first husband.

Her reply was crisply delivered, without emotion. 'He drowned,' she said, 'at Diamond Lake.'

SATAN CLAWS

Randall D. Larson

Randall D. Larson is the author of numerous articles on films and film music for Cinefantastique, Starlog, Soundtrack!, CinemaScore *and many other publications. His survey of music in horror films,* Musique Fantastique *was published in 1985 and forthcoming are* Films Into Books: Movie Tie-Ins & Novelizations *and* Music from the House of Hammer. *On the fiction side, he has published short horror stories in* Fantasy Tales, Eldritch Tales, Space & Time *and others, as well as editing and publishing his own small press magazine,* Threshold of Fantasy. *Bibliographical works include three books about Robert Bloch (a reader's guide, bibliography and collected interviews), plus* Works of Joseph Payne Brennan *and* Natural Horrors, *the latter an analysis of animal horror novels.*

NICK Lazenby kicked aside the half-crushed Pepsi can and stepped over a wadded litter of MacDonald's wrappers as he crossed the street, ignoring, or trying to ignore, the fuming exhaust, the obnoxious drivers, and the panicked crowds of holiday shoppers that swarmed in all directions. Nick felt their jostles, breathed the foul odour of their cigarettes and cigars, heard their muttered grumblings about how much to spend on so-and-so, or what should we get Aunt Flo and why does it really matter because she'll only return it anyhow, and he tried to ignore all of it. He passed angrily by the endless throngs, that seemed to move with universal purpose, through the various shops and department stores and other merchant habitats that besieged the sidewalks and crowded the skyline.

As darkness dimmed the twilight, Nick drew the collar of his coat tighter about his neck, a momentary shiver running through him as he realized how cold it was getting. He should have taken a heavier coat, but he really hadn't intended to be out this long. He had just wanted to get away from those drunken morons at the office party, but he had no desire to head home just yet. There would only be an empty apartment waiting for him anyway, and he had felt a walk might do him some good.

It had hardly done him any good. It merely reinforced the irritation he felt during the holiday season. People scattering about everywhere, buying gifts out of love, duty, guilt, for assorted friends and loved ones. Nick had no family and no need of gifts. The song of scattered groups of carollers invaded his ears briefly as he walked past them, their melodious sound quickly swallowed up by the discord of the crowd. Nick hardly felt like singing, and the religious words never meant anything to him anyway. The tolling bell of a Salvation Army Santa Claus, who resembled more a sagging geriatric than the rotund gift-giver of Western myth, chimed its way through the crowds, its incessant ringing a convicting plea for donations. Nick looked at the red-garbed, cotton-bearded Santa with disdain; he felt no need to buy indulgences from a practitioner of lies.

That's what they were, after all. Just lies.

When he was a child, his parents had told him the cozy story of Santa Claus, the cheery-faced bringer of gifts who 'knows if you've been good' and will reward you annually for your good works. Nick had trusted Santa Claus throughout the days of his youth, working hard at being good, by whatever standards seemed to apply at the time, and he felt confident of his righteousness when he found all those presents on Christmas morn. But his hopes had been rent when his mother sprung it upon him one blustery fall day that, nope, it was all a grand myth, just fun and games, Nicky, ho! ho!, no need to worry, we were just *fooling*. It had just been a game, they'd told him, but he had put his youthful confidence in the image of that portly, red-suited jolly friend of reindeer, and Nick learned his faith had been betrayed. It taught him a hard lesson. And later, when his parents tried to tell him of another bearded gentleman, one who wore a purple robe and a pained but loving face who brought spiritual gifts and offered them to anyone, even to those who weren't 'good', well, Nick had similarly rejected putting his faith in this man lest it be crushed once again.

Nick's eyes met those of the dressed-up Santa Claus, and he noticed an odd twinkle in the Santa's eyes, as if he had read his thoughts. Nick grunted to himself and walked on. Up ahead a mottled green station wagon pulled up to the curb and unloaded its cargo of children, who excitedly darted into King Norman's toy store, enthusiastically clambering for much-wanted items. Nick grumbled, aware that his annoyance was simply souring his disposition all the more, but feeling no desire to be cheerful. He just felt like being away from all this foolishness.

He turned into a small shopping mall – really only a large one-time department store turned into a series of compartmentalized shops – in the hopes of avoiding the streaming crowds on the street. He breathed in the pleasant aromas of pastries mingled with broiled turkey as he walked past tiny restaurant counters, bakery tables and other small businesses offering their holiday wares. In the centre of the mall was an open space in which had been constructed a gaudy red, white and green Santa's Village – really only a tiny octagonal hut with an opened side, beyond which sat another clone-like Ho-Ho-Hoing man in a red and white suit, bouncing a giggling tot on his knee and promising the world's riches in exchange for the child's goodness.

Goodness. As if anyone could really be good, Nick mused sourly. He'd long ago put aside the notion that there was any inherent goodness in mankind, maintaining instead that there were only varying degrees of badness. History and the six o'clock news certainly bore this out. The cheap department store Santas only perpetuated the lie, selling an unrealistic fairy-tale optimism that collapsed when held against the light of reality. Jolly Santa filled the minds of young people with the creed that they were all good, brand-spanking wonderful tikes who could do no wrong, and Santa would cheerfully reward them, even if they did secretly sprinkle salt on snails and threw cans at puppies and stole comic books from Walgreens and plotted to hide Jimmy Bowman's clothes during gym and told naughty, untrue stories about Miss Greer the English teacher.

Something was fuming now inside of Nick, some vile,

seething anger that had been pent up since the holidays began. An anger that made him stand glaring at the cardboard Santa's Village, gazing past the mechanical wobbling elves and staring inside at the jiggling fat man in the red suit. Nick chewed contemplatively on his lower lip as he watched the boy climb down from Santa's knee and trot away, confidently smiling, as a second youth climbed up and began to describe his list of everlasting wants to the cheerful god of the season. The cynical anger and frustration boiled inside Nick, and he found himself hating passionately the myth that filled the heads of young people with these lies; hated it so much that, even though he had nothing better to offer, he couldn't allow this impatient line of youngsters to be victimized any longer.

Nick strode up to the hut, shoving aside the children, and grabbed the young boy on Santa's knee. Nick pushed him away, yelling viciously at the Santa to leave the kids alone, to stop telling them lies, to stop perpetuating a vile myth.

The gruff paw of a mall security guard pulled him out of the hut while its owner ordered him to depart hastily. Nick, embarrassed, glanced about at the affronted children and parents who stared back and he walked rapidly away. He turned once to look back into the hut, and was startled by the burning gaze of the man in the Santa suit, who stared at him ominously. Nick made his way out of the Mall and back onto the crowded streets.

A little further along, he passed another costumed Santa, who stood in front of a Woolworth's store and advertised vocally the sales of the day. But the man stopped shouting as Nick walked past, and the eyes of the red-suited barker seemed to follow him, accusingly, as if he sensed Nick's opposition. Nick stared back and made an exaggerated grimace at the Santa before turning the corner onto a side street.

It was with relief that Nick realized he was leaving the major commercial district, and the crowds were thinning, even though it meant he was also entering the seedier side of town. But at least he would be free of the pestering throngs and stupid howling Santas.

Maybe not. Up ahead, on the other side of the street, stood one of the red-garbed, bushy-bearded denizens of sleighs.

This one was unusual because he wasn't surrounded by hordes of begging children, wasn't ringing a monotonous bell soliciting donations, wasn't even near a shop or other commercial establishment. He simply stood there, staring at Nick.

Nick kept on walking, glancing curiously at the costumed man every so often. Santa continued to stare at him with blank eyes and firm-set bearded jaw. Nick passed by, and as he glanced back to see that, yep, the Santa was still staring at him, he noticed another red figure heading up the sidewalk behind him. It was the Santa from the Woolworth store, turning the corner and walking up the way Nick had just come, eyes blazing at him from behind blooded-cheeks and whited beard. Nick looked back across the street. The first Santa was keeping pace with him along the opposite sidewalk, watching him, and it seemed as though a sinister gleam twinkled in his eyes, and the firm-set lips seemed a mite gruesome beneath the billowing beard.

Nick cursed and walked faster, wondering what these dime-store clowns were up to. Maybe they had all decided he had been bad by scolding their fellow in the Mall, and were after him, he chuckled. He stopped it when he saw two more Santas turn the corner ahead and walk, both abreast, toward him. His face wrinkled with concern. He turned and stared behind him. The Woolworth's Santa was striding quickly toward him, eyes slanted wickedly. Nick looked across the street. The Santa there had left the sidewalk and was crossing the pavement in his direction, manipulating around the parked cars. Nick turned back to the pair of Santas approaching, eyes set upon him, marching footsteps echoing in the dark, deserted streets like the ominous footfalls of a part of executioners gloomily approaching in a dimly-lit castle dungeon.

Panic filled him, and he glanced about, spying a dark alley on the other side of the street. Nick bolted, running across the pavement past the surprised Santa, and darted into the alley, legs pumping desperately as his feet pummelled the ground. He raced to a shadowed, inset doorway and clung to the wall, heart-pounding, breath-wheezing. He sucked his body into the space, trying the door-knob and finding it locked, gazing through the window in the door and seeing only blackness.

Nick looked back to the entrance of the alleyway, his breath halting with a gasp. All four Santas stood there, staring in, and Nick could hear their whispered mumblings and deep grumbles. They were joined by a fifth Santa, and Nick could see shadows of more of the blood-coloured, shroud-bearded, tomb-bellied elf-keepers approaching from the shadows beyond. They all stood there, ranks swelling, all of them glaring into the alley with evil intent as Nick huddled in the doorway, barely breathing, shaking with panic. A movement, a silhouette, appeared in the corner of his eye, and Nick turned to look into the window in the door.

An evil, leering figure with yellow eyes, white beard and red suit cackled at him as the door swung inward. Crimson-cloaked arms thrust out toward him, but Nick beat them aside, slipping on the rough pavement as a pounding myriad of footsteps grew louder from the alley's entrance. Santa was coming.

Nick shrieked and regained his feet. He pushed away the Santa who emerged from the doorway and ran fiercely down the alley, his eyes watering with desperation, his gut twisted with panic, his forehead awash with sweat, his legs tearing through the alley, feet slipping in the slime of litter, ankles scraped by sharp-edged, overturned trash cans; and all the while the pounding pursuit of the heavy Santas and their husky breathing and deep growling spurred him on.

The alley took a sharp turn to the left ahead, and Nick cut the corner close, scraping his shoulder on the bricks of the corner building. He smacked heavily against a solid concrete wall ahead of him, the alley ending suddenly against the backside of some massive structure. Nick whirled around, shoulders hugging the wall, hands scraping the cement, eyes peering through the blackness, waiting.

Waiting for Santa Claus.

But he heard nothing, saw nothing, only dim glimmers of garbage cans, strewn crates, and wet pavement shining through the shadows. Nick wondered what had happened to them, his head pounding with pain. He sighed; perhaps he had only imagined it, after all. Imagined the hulking sea of jolly, chortling Santas chasing after him, hungry for his blood. Another imagined myth. The silence calmed him, and he stepped away from the cold, concrete wall and shook his head in amusement. He started to walk back out of the alley.

The hand grabbed him from out of the darkness, roughly shoving him back into the wall, his head cracking against the hard cement. A sharp, taloned fist emerged from a white-fringed red sleeve, and pointed claws raked the side of his face, leaving in their wake a cold and trickling sensation.

They all stepped out of the blackness, growling to themselves, staring at him with ghoulish faces. A dozen or more leering Santas stood before him, yellow eyes peering from beneath white-fringed, scarlet hoods. Black mouths lined with sharp white teeth huddled behind bushy white beards. Flared noses snorted above.

'Get away!' Nick cried with a broken voice, struggling against the restraining arms. 'I can't *believe* this!'

'You don't believe in anything anymore, do you?' a cacophonous voice croaked, and its owner stepped forward into the dim alley light. Nick recognized him as the Santa from the Mall. 'Few people believe the Truth anymore. It's better we keep it that way!'

The Santas began to press in on him, and the sharp fingers that clamped his shoulders began to cut deeply. 'None of this talk of lies!' the Mall Santa said. 'Someone may listen to you!'

'Hey!' Nick cried, aghast. 'What is this! Who are you guys?'

'You haven't been good, Nick!' the Mall Santa grinned, his reddish cheeks gleaming. 'You should have believed.'

'In Santa Claus?' Nick gaped. The cheery faces, fluffy white beards and bright red suits closed in.

'No,' the voice rung in his ears. 'In the Truth we try to hide! But it's too late now . . .' The yellow eyes, flaring nostrils, sharp teeth bore down on him, and soon everything melted into darkness, except for the voice.

'Even the demons believe,' it cackled. 'And shudder!'

THE MAIDEN & THE MINSTREL

Dallas Clive Goffin

Dallas Clive Goffin works mainly as an illustrator, with 400 pieces of artwork already published in the small press. His work includes illustrations for Simon Clark's Blood & Grit *(BBR Books) and his own collection of stories,* Legends of Fogrophol *(British Fantasy Society). In 1992 the Scaremonger Certificate was awarded to him for artwork published in* Peeping Tom *magazine. His short stories have appeared in* Dark Dreams, Peeping Tom, Dementia 13, Flickers 'n' Frames *and* Auguries.

ONE humid night, Pashonnio the Minstrel happened to be crossing the Meadows of the Moon, on his way to woo the nymphs who dwelt upon the verdant slopes of Mount Olyddria. His lyre – the scarlet shell of a torripelnesian turtle, strung with the sinews of gryphons – was slung across his shoulders, and a flute of drilled bone – the shin of a unicorn – hung at his waist. He had walked for five days without companionship and Olyddria was still many leagues distant.

Discerning the glimmer of a brook and made aware thereby of his thirst, Pashonnio dragged his aching feet towards the water. He pushed through the shrubberies growing upon the bank and was about to take his refreshment when a marvellous vision smote his eyes and halted him like a man petrified by a gorgonian gaze.

Among the rushes at the edge of the brook knelt a naked young female of breathtaking beauty. She shimmered as pale as ivory in the darkness and her back and shoulders were mantled by poppy-crowned tresses of elfin gold. She too had come to the brook to drink and water sparkled like beads of spilt quicksilver upon the luminous spheres of her milk-pure breasts.

Hardly had Pashonnio recovered his wits than the object of his attention caught sight of him and sprang upright.

'I crave your pardon,' apologized Pashonnio, 'but I beseech you to recline yourself once more among yon rushes and allow me to mount you; for I am weary with journeying and lonesomeness and would have such a one as you carry me to the peak of pleasure.'

Dark eyes burned with affront.

'I have money with which to pay you,' Pashonnio persisted, drawing a purse full of silver faerie coins from within the breast of his doublet.

'You insult me!' accused rose-petal lips. 'I have no use for your money. But I see by your lyre you are a minstrel! Sing me a song, you bold bard, and if it pleases me I shall loan you my body, as you have asked.'

And so, unstrapping his lyre, Pashonnio seated himself upon the bank and proceeded to sing his mournful 'Epitaph to Empires'.

'It is beautiful,' complimented the ruby lips, when he had finished, 'and yet so very melancholy. Have you nothing lighter, with which to brighten my spirit?'

'Aye, that I have,' obliged Pashonnio, plucking his lyre once more and reciting the limericks of his hilarious 'Ballad of the Clowns'.

Before he was halfway through, his lovely companion was giggling hysterically and, when the song was over, it was several minutes before she could control herself.

'Have I pleased you sufficiently to win my request?' inquired Pashonnio, himself laughing.

'You have made me too frivolous!' she complained, good-humouredly. 'Sing me one more and I shall give you my answer.'

Smiling patiently, the minstrel bent a third time to his lyre and sang, in his noblest tones, the 'Ode to Love' – three verses of which praised the physical union of man with woman.

Now the listener was fully captivated by this shameless songster and, when he had laid down his instrument for the final time, she gave him her smile of approval. With his heart beating wildly against his ribs, Pashonnio watched her recline herself and stretch in yielding abandon.

'Come,' she invited, beckoning with one pale hand.

Rising to his feet, he approached her with trembling eagerness and then lowered himself gently upon her; straddling her, hugging her lithe torso in his arms and resting his head against her blonde locks. She arched up beneath his weight and he clasped her tighter at the first rhythmic movements of her flanks and loins, feeling the rapid throbbing of her heart and hearing her sharp intakes of breath. Her taut muscles quivered against his thighs as he rode her and he grew damp with her fragrant perspiration.

Then, of a sudden, her smooth movements ceased and, drawing a deep breath, she pointed to the green slopes that rose up steeply in front of them.

'You have done me a very great service, my lady,' said Pashonnio gratefully, sliding from the back of the milk-white centauress.

Bowing his thanks, he turned to ascend the foothills of Mount Olyddria, the legendary peak of pleasure.

SIGHT UNSEEN

Jean-Daniel Brèque

Jean-Daniel Brèque has been a full-time translator since 1987, producing French versions of novels by major horror writers such as Clive Barker, Fritz Leiber, Stephen King, Dan Simmons, Dean R. Koontz and many others. He began translating in 1984 with Arachne, *a small press anthology which included stories by Michael Bishop, Ramsey Campbell and Charles L. Grant. His own short fiction has appeared in* Fantasy Tales 5, Dark Voices 5, Best New Horror 2, Darklands 2, Antares *and* Territoires de l'Inquietude, *amongst a number of other European publications.*

I didn't see at once who had called me from the other side of the crossroads.

Standing still on the pavement, I was looking up towards an optician's board: a huge pair of electric blue eyes peering behind an equally huge pair of circular spectacles announced to the crowd of indifferent passers-by the nature of the shop situated on the corner of Rue Saint-Georges and Rue Saint-Dizier. Sightseers and locals, all scantily clad, were slowly loitering around me, struck down by the unusual heat that plagued the city of Nancy on that day in July.

I heard my name a second time.

I walked towards the crossroads, looking for the person who would call me in this manner. I only knew a few people in this city and the slightly highstrung voice didn't suggest anyone to me. Something caught my eye to my left. When I looked up, I discovered another board, similar to the one which had frozen my steps a few moments ago, except that its eyes were brown rather than blue. I felt pinned down by the convergent gazes of two all-knowing gods, two glass and metal *Big Brothers* whose eyes would

surely never leave me afterward, would follow me wherever
I went.

I eventually managed to shake myself free and looked
down, instantly locating a man sitting outside a café who
was waving his hand at me.

Who could that be? I thought, crossing the road. When I
reached him, I still didn't recognize him.

'Forget your old friend, did you?'

The man who was sitting at the empty table had no
noticeable features. He was lightly clad, like all the other
patrons, but the outfit he was wearing was paradoxically so
colourful that nobody paid any attention to him. He had a
soft, round face, his eyes were hidden behind mirrorshades,
and his hands were occasionally seized by nervous spasms,
as if he had waved them for a long time and had decided to
give them a rest, only to see them tentatively try to continue
waving.

I said nothing for a few moments, feeling a bit self-
conscious, and I was getting ready to utter a confused
apology when he said, 'Why, it's me! Bressault!'

I would like to say that, at that moment, a flood of
recollections came running into my mind, but it wouldn't
be quite true. As a matter of fact, only two incidents were
associated with that name in my memory. Both of them went
back to a time when I was a high school pupil in Bordeaux.

The Commandant-Arnouldt High School for boys, located
in a street of the same name, stood in the middle of a prostitutes' hunting ground, a fact that caused despair in teachers
and parents alike. My mother had once come to wait for me
after classes and several men had approached her, looking
for venal pleasures. The ladies were rather bold and would
frequently offer tantalizing looks to teenagers whose cheeks
were devoid of the slightest trace of down. Said teenagers
generally fled in a hurry, for the beauty of the ageing courtesans left much to be desired. I used to wonder how many
alumni of that school had been viscerally afraid of the opposite sex after having been confronted by these sad, soiled
doves during their so-called formative years. The year of my
graduation, the school board, moved by some aberrant logic,
had transferred all the pupils in the nearby Michel-Montaigne
High School and had converted Commandant-Arnouldt into

a secondary school, aiding and abetting the emergence of a new generation of twisted boys.

Among all my friends, among all the pupils in my class and in the others, Eric Bressault was the only one not to be sought out by the prostitutes. He wasn't the ugliest duckling in that farmyard and was less acne-ridden than some, but none of these creatures – so the outraged parents called them – had attempted to seduce him. The fact had come to the attention of one Audignont, an Upper Sixth pupil who boasted of his frequent encounters with the hookers, and he had started to pester Bressault about this matter, in the tried-and-true tradition of the high school bully. He eventually became obsessed with the idea of engineering Bressault's coming of age and stopped buying the charms of the prostitutes for himself, trying instead to convince them to rescue the unfortunate boy. These efforts had abruptly come to an end when the police, alerted by a virtuous woman living in the neighbourhood, had arrested Audignont on a charge of procuring. They released him quite quickly, of course, but the school board had expelled him equally quickly and nobody had heard from him since.

Bressault himself reminded me of the second incident I associated his name with. 'Do you remember the graduation file crisis?' he asked.

Shortly before the French oral exam – a prelude to the exam we would have to pass one year later before officially graduating – each pupil had received a sealed envelope containing his school file, which was to be opened only on the fateful day. After all the envelopes had been given out in my class, a shaky voice had asked, 'What about mine?' It was Bressault. The Chief Monitor, an old drunkard whose favourite pastime was waiting for retirement while gazing at the blooming trees in the schoolyard, had lifted an eyebrow, looked at the empty table before him, and asked our classmate to follow him to his office. Bressault had come back fifteen minutes later, ashen-faced. His school file had apparently vanished.

A few days later, as I was trying to cram into my head the fundamental differences between Voltaire and Rousseau, the telephone had rung at my parents' and I had been summoned to the office of the Headmaster, who wanted to have a look at my school file. Filled with dread, as only a high school pupil can be filled with dread when an exam is near, I had walked down the Rue du Commandant-Arnouldt, hardly noticing the ubiquitous courtesans – even more scantily dressed in the spring heat – to discover, once I was in the sanctum sanctorum, Bressault and his parents. The Headmaster solemnly unsealed the envelope I had given him, pulled a file out of it – and pulled my file out of Bressault's. It seemed that all the files had been laid on his desk, opened at the appropriate page for him to sign them, and when he had closed mine, he had put it inside my classmate's – Bressault, unexpected victim of the alphabetical order – which he had obviously not signed. When Bressault had left the office, squeezing to his bosom the duly sealed envelope sheltering the duly signed file, he had given me a dark, contrite look, and I had not been able to stop from laughing.

'What do you want to drink?' he asked me.

'Oh – a beer.'

After a few moments, he asked me, 'Could you call the waiter when you see him?'

I gave him a puzzled look, then mentally shrugged and began to look for the waiter. He came bearing a tray full of glasses and I ordered a beer for me and a ginger ale for my old classmate.

When our drinks came, Bressault pounced on his and drank it in one gulp. 'You can't imagine how thirsty I was,' he said. 'Could you order another one for me?'

I complied, hailing the waiter, who was going to and fro between the bar and the terrasse, trying valiantly to slacken the thirst of the crowd of patrons sitting in the sun.

'I've been waiting like this for an hour,' Bressault said when he had gulped down his second ginger ale as fast as he had the first.

'What's the matter?' I asked. 'The waiter couldn't see you?'

Then he lifted his mirrorshades and stared at me as fixedly as the optician signs which were gazing at the crowd on the other side of the crossroads. There was a rather long silence, after which he said, 'That's right. You got it exactly right.'

Then he started to gaze at his empty glass, turning it in

his hand and drawing hazy reflections on the metal table's white surface. I felt he was impatient to confide in me, but when he finally spoke, it was to ask me an utterly mundane question.

'So, what're you doing these days?' he said.

I had no intention of telling the story of my life to someone I had not seen for several years, and who had not been especially friendly to me when we were younger. I mumbled some evasive answer, which he didn't even listen to, then asked him, 'What about you?'

He shrugged. 'I work in an office. A real cushy number. Nobody pays any attention to me.'

Then he burst into laughter.

I looked around me, ready to scowl an apology to any patron startled by his outburst. But all the people sitting on the terrasse seemed besotted with the heat and only their cold drinks apparently interested them.

'Don't bother with them,' Bressault said. *'Nobody pays any attention to me.* Look!'

Before I had time to act, he got up, unbuckled his belt, let his trousers and jockey shorts slip down.

I was totally taken aback and had only one thought in mind: *There is no problem so complicated that it can't be solved by flight.* I was getting ready to jump out of my seat and let Bressault handle the police who would certainly show up very soon – *and to let him pay for the drinks*, a malicious voice whispered within my skull – when I suddenly realized something was definitely wrong.

All the people who were around us, whether sitting outside the café or walking on the pavement, kept on minding their own business as if nothing was happening. I almost thought I was watching a *Candid Camera* number in which all the innocent bystanders had located the camera and had decided to leave the actor to his own, grotesque devices, refusing to play the parts which had been assigned to them.

Bressault looked in my direction, noticed my reaction, pulled up his trousers, and came back towards me. 'A little demonstration is worth a thousand words,' he said. 'And what do you think now?'

I truly didn't know what to answer.

'It can be a bother sometimes, but it is quite handy, too,' he went on. 'For instance, you can go away now and leave me here. I'll wait for a few minutes and then I'll go without paying. The waiter won't notice anything. Not right now, anyway.'

I was still struck dumb.

'I don't really think I am invisible,' he said. 'You did see me, eventually. And I still can be photographed. But, like I told you earlier about my work, nobody pays any attention to me. I wonder how they managed to hire me. When I went to the job interview, the person I met seemed to be wondering what the hell he was doing there. But my power must not have been fully developed at the time, and maybe I could somehow control it.'

'Your power?' I babbled.

'Yes, my power. Can you realize the possibilities? The first time I became aware of it, I spent two hours sitting at my desk, thinking about all I could achieve with it. But I soon came to know its limits.' He stopped and looked at his empty glass, then went on, 'I always wanted to know what women were doing when no man was around. Once, I slipped into a women's changing room – the things I saw and heard! Did you know that women could be even more foul-mouthed than a bunch of sailors on shore leave? But when I wanted to snatch a pair of knickers they were throwing around in a fit of hysteria, they realized I was there and I was nearly skinned alive. And I can't go into a bank and empty the safes. I can look, but I can't touch.'

I remembered the prostitutes in the Rue du Commandant-Arnouldt and how they had been indifferent to Bressault. Was his so-called 'power' already active then, or did this indifference frustrate him to the point of developing so bizarre a neurosis? He had told me he had waited for an hour before I could order a ginger ale for him, but he might have sat down outside the café only five minutes before he saw me walking on the other side of the road. *No*, a voice in my mind whispered. *Try and explain his unseen flasher performance by neurosis.*

Bressault was still smugly elaborating on the various advantages of his gift, but under his self-satisfied facade,

I glimpsed an undercurrent of dread which made his blue eyes shift nervously.

I listened to him, thinking of the old James Whale movie in which Claude Rains takes off his bandages that hide only nothingness. My mind was filled with a horrible picture: Bressault tearing the skin off his cheeks to reveal no facial muscles streaked with pulsing veins, but an empty space in which float his eyes, their gaze at once evasive and overbearing. I shivered and recoiled from him.

He stopped his pitch, which I was no longer hearing. 'What's the matter? You find me disgusting? You would have me using my gift to help mankind, like some comic book hero? The world has always ignored me and I owe nothing to it, do you hear me? Well; I'm off. You'll wish I hadn't left, you could have had a free drink!'

And he was gone.

Five minutes later, I paid for the drinks – *maybe you shouldn't have pissed him off*, a voice laughed in my mind – and went back to meet my wife, whom I had left in a store deciding which dress to buy.

The remainder of our stay in Nancy went without incident. The following days we went blueberry-hunting in the Vosges mountains, and when we came back to Paris on the Tuesday evening, I had completely forgotten my reunion with Eric Bressault.

How did he manage to locate me? I had told him next to nothing about myself during our brief encounter; he couldn't know that I had settled down in Paris and that I was working from home. Later, when everything was over and I had ponder about what had happened, I thought that he might have contacted my parents, who were still living near Bordeaux, in order to get my new address. Even though I have a lot of cousins in the southwestern part of France, my name is not very common and he probably had no trouble in finding them.

Anyway, near the middle of August, a few weeks after our return from Nancy, I was interrupted from my keyboard – and from the rather difficult report I was sweating over – by a ring at the flat door.

I thought my next-door neighbour had once again decided

to let me in on a bit of the gossip that enlivened her otherwise humdrum life, and thankful for this welcome break in a frankly dreary job, I went to the door and opened it without checking through the spyhole.

It was Bressault.

I was taken aback for a few moments, then asked, 'How did you manage to get into the building?' It is impossible to enter the premises if you don't have a key, unless you call one of the occupants by the intercom and he opens the door for you.

He had a weary smile. 'I waited for somebody to be let in and I slipped in behind them.

That near invisibility power again. He did not seem to have profited by it. He was dirty, unshaven – *can he see himself in a mirror?* a sardonic voice asked in my mind – and his clothes were soiled and rumpled.

I suddenly realized he was not standing on the landing any more. I turned around and saw him slumped in an armchair beside my desk. He had taken advantage of my lapse of attention to enter my flat.

'Could you take me in for a few days?' he asked.

I refused instantly. We would sometimes put up with a friend in our tiny flat, but it would only be for a day or two, and I feared Bressault was of the root-growing kind, as the way he had gotten in seemed to prove. Moreover, I need solitude and total silence in order to get my work done and I couldn't write a single paragraph with someone constantly looking over my shoulder. And he was no friend of mine. Merely a vague acquaintance, somebody you only see from time to time.

He threw me a defiant glance. 'You know, I've been very polite in asking. I can live here without you noticing anything out of the ordinary – '

A few seconds went by until I grasped the meaning of this threat. I remembered his unseen flasher number on the pavements of Nancy and a shiver went up my spine as I imagined him spying at me while I was at my desk, at the dining-table, in the lavatory or in my bed. That was too much. I went to him, grabbed him by his collar and dragged him towards the door.

'Get out of here,' I said, throwing him onto the landing,

next to a battered suitcase which I hadn't seen when he arrived – *maybe it catches*, I thought. 'I've had enough of your rantings. This building is off-limits to salesmen, Jehovah Witnesses and other pains in the ass. If you're not gone in five minutes, I'll call the landlord, who'll certainly call the police.' I was bluffing. The landlord lives in the fourteenth *arrondissement* of Paris, but Bressault was not supposed to know that.

'Look,' he said with feigned regret. 'I'm in trouble. I've left Nancy in a hurry. You're the only one who can help – '

'What happened?'

He remained silent for a few moments, obviously looking for the best way to formulate his answer, then scowled and said, 'Well, I've given birth to an unknown variation of the oedipan drama – '

This non sequitur would only reveal its full meaning a couple of days later; for the time being, I thought it was both ridiculous and crazy.

'I'll go to the balcony and watch the door of the gardens,' I said. 'If you don't pass through it within five minutes' time, I'll use the phone. I won't go with you, you know the way out of here.'

Then I closed the door. Double-locked it.

According to my watch, three minutes and forty-five seconds passed between the time I left him on the landing and the time I saw him leaving the gardens. When he had headed towards the Rue de Ménilmontant, I returned to my work in progress and was surprised to realize it was no longer dreary, but rather reassuring instead.

The following morning, after I had opened the flat door for my wife, who was leaving for work, and after I had carefully closed it behind her, I spent an hour searching through the premises; I even went so far as closing my eyes and feeling my way through the rooms to assure myself *de invisu* – so to speak – of Bressault's absence.

Then I went back to my typing and completely forgot my old classmate.

So completely, in fact, that I did not remember him when, the following day, my wife gave me a press cutting her mother had enclosed in the letter which had just come from Nancy.

That jolly woman knew about my taste for the macabre and she had noticed how attentively I had perused the crime pages of *L'Est Républicain*, the local paper, especially interested in the story of a female corpse which had been found with the hands cut off. The report she had sent me that day told an even more horrible story.

A ten-year-old girl had killed herself in the commercial district of Nancy, using an original and awful method. She was with her mother, shopping in the Saint-Sébastien market, and had taken advantage of the woman's lapse in attention to snatch the house keys from her purse and run towards the nearest crossroads. Once there, according to witnesses, she had started to scream, 'I don't want to see you! I don't want to see you!' and she had gouged out her eyes with the keys. When her mother had rushed to the scene, alerted by the police sirens, her first words had been: 'The keys! Where are the keys?' Thinking she was distraught, the policemen hadn't paid attention to her screaming. Mother and child had been rushed to the nearest hospital.

The little girl had succumbed to her ghastly wounds, as the reporter put it, and her mother seemed to have gone mad. 'The keys! The keys!' she cried unceasingly. When a compassionate nurse had started to look for them in order to quiet her down, it appeared that the keys had vanished. Since the police needed them as exhibits, they had gone to the woman's house, which had been totally ransacked. Its door had been left open, which proved that someone had found the keys, but there was no trace of them. The police met no success when they started to look for the woman's car, either.

I read the matter-of-fact account very attentively, looking for the best way to use these events in my fiction, but any thought of creation flew from my mind when I learned the victims' names. The woman was divorced and was legally called by her maiden name, Nathalie Rouvier. But the little girl had kept her father's name.

Her name was Christelle Bressault.

I instantly understood what must have happened, using my own terrors to sketch out the two victims' fate: Bressault had been infuriated by the divorce. Using his power – which I did not doubt any more – he had imposed his unseen presence on his wife and daughter.

I could imagine him, hidden behind a half-closed door, still unseen, observing Nathalie Rouvier fixing Christelle's lunch, or watching the television with the two of them, or gazing at the mother bathing the daughter.

What had happened? Had he overstepped his bounds? Had he succumbed to the desire to kiss his wife or to caress his daughter's hair? Harassed by this perverse persecution, expecting no help from the authorities – who would have laughed in their face when hearing about an 'invisible man' – Nathalie Rouvier and her daughter must have led a hellish existence, constantly on guard, wary of all the shadowy corners and cupboards in their house; both looking for the merest sign of Bressault's presence and fearing to discover him behind a door or window carelessly left open.

Maybe it was because she had seen her father's hand go into her mother's purse, looking for the keys of the home he had been chased from – for the umpteenth time – that Christelle had grabbed them, then fled from the market, followed by Bressault, who must have been furious to be denied his pleasure.

When I read the report for the second time, I realized that the drama had occured where Rue Saint-Georges and Rue Saint-Dizier cross, right where I had been frozen on the spot, caught by the twin gazes of the monstrous signs . . .

You are supposed to eschew the *deus ex machina* when you plot a piece of fiction. According to critics and historians alike, readers don't accept hat tricks from writers any more. Things happen quite differently in real life, and our direst problems are sometimes solved by chance alone, when it is not by fate.

During the two days which followed the arrival of that letter, my life was hell. I was even afraid to go out to buy groceries. I would telephone my friends rather than mailing the letters I had written to them. I had a very strained conversation with an editor who I called in order to convince that I simply couldn't go and see him at his office about the pieces I was going to write for him. And my work in progress was stalled.

My wife, who had always known me for a recluse, nonetheless began to worry about the way my habits were becoming obsessive, and I had to tell her the whole story. As I expected, she didn't believe one word of it – I could understand that: had I not disbelieved Bressault's talk of power myself?

Things were becoming tense when I got a phone call from the Hôpital de la Salpêtrière. Did I know a man named Eric Bressault? Could I come and see him at the hospital, and take care of the paperwork for him? After I asked a few questions, I managed to understand what had happened.

Bressault had forgotten to look both ways before crossing the street.

It is rather difficult to ignore a man who lands in your car after shattering its windscreen and who starts to bleed all over your steering wheel. Despite his power, Bressault was lying on a hospital bed, with several bones broken in interesting ways.

I slept quite peacefully that night, knowing that my old classmate wasn't hidden under the bed and wasn't counting my snores to pass the time.

In the morning, I went to the Hôpital de la Salpêtrière and my troubles began.

My friend was unknown among the registry for traffic victims. His name was on no doctor's listing. Was I sure I was in the right hospital?

I vaguely realized what must have happened; I managed to locate the hospital wing where traffic victims were housed. I saw several casualties lying among immaculate sheets, surrounded by nurses who cleaned their wounds and changed their dressings, but there was no Bressault to be found. As I reached the end of a corridor, I heard a feeble voice call my name.

A stretcher lying on the ground materialized right before my eyes.

The sight of Bressault was not a pretty one. Nobody had taken care of him since his arrival, obviously. The dressings he had been given in the ambulance were beginning to show some sickly colours, dark red and pale yellow. Bruises grew unattended on his face. Under his prone body, a puddle of liquid attested to the fact that no nurse had ever presented him with a bedpan. In the middle of his shattered face, his blue eyes threw me a pitiful and totally demented glance.

I knelt down to hear what he was saying.

'. . . can't control . . .' he said, '. . . nobody hears . . . nobody sees . . .'

'What happened in Nancy?' I asked. 'What happened to Nathalie and Christelle?'

There was a worried light in his eyes when he understood that I knew much more than he had deigned to tell me. Then his hideously bruised features distorted even more as he tried to smile – at least, I thought it was a smile.

'Christelle . . .' he said. 'She didn't want . . . to see me any more . . . *but she still did!*'

Then I did something I am still not proud of. I could have called a nurse, forced her to *see* the mass of pitiful flesh which lay in the corridor, forced her to give it some first aid. I could have managed to find a bed for Bressault, to have him taken care of and saved.

But I did nothing of the kind.

Instead, I stood up, threw a last glance towards his broken body – one half of his shin was set at a weird angle from the other; a piece of bone was jutting from his torn trouser leg – and I said, 'It seems flies are immune to your power, Eric. Look, they're buzzing all around you. I'll leave you to their care.'

And I was gone.

The end of the story?

Not quite.

Unlike what had happened after my two previous encounters with Bressault, I didn't forget him this time. Not an hour went by without my thinking of the bruised body I had abandoned in the corridors of the Hôpital de la Salpêtrière. Remorse gnawed at my mind for a few days, of course, but it eventually left, to be replaced by something else.

I remembered the words that had come out of Bressault's mouth. He had told me about his daughter: 'She didn't want to see me anymore, *but she still did!*' And I remembered Audignont, the school bully who had eventually become obsessed with Bressault, who had seen no one but him, so to speak.

Bressault was invisible to all mortals, all right, except when he decided otherwise – and this gift of deciding when to be seen and when not to be seen had been denied to him during his last hours. But could it be that some people couldn't do anything except see him?

Some people who were so involved in his life, or who loved him so much, that he started to worm himself in their mind, to claim each and every one of their thoughts?

People like Audignont who, for the sake of power or for the hell of it, had wanted to engineer the coming of age of the boy the hookers ignored. People like Christelle, a little girl whose father was the centre of her world.

People like me.

I had something to comfort me at first: Bressault couldn't survive for long in the condition I had left him, not to mention the eventual consequences of the lack of food and water. But several weeks have gone by since the day I left him rotting in the hospital corridor, and I get more and more worried each night.

Suppose he has managed to find somebody who is aware of his presence and who can nurse him back to health? Maybe he is licking his wounds even now, maybe he is even cured.

Or – and this is the reason for those sleepless nights which plague me with increasing frequency – maybe he has decided to crawl back to me, unable to stand on two legs and dragging himself along the streets, leaving a trail of blood, lymph and urine, like a gigantic slug resolved to reach its goal, no matter what the cost.

Or – and this thought is even more horrible – maybe he is dead and his corpse is rotting, forgotten by all except the feasting flies, in a hospital corridor from which nurses and patients alike shy away without knowing why.

If so, the image which haunts my days and nights will always be with me, unless I follow Christelle's example and decide to take a cutting instrument – scissors, a knife, even a key – and raise it towards my face and strike.

That image which haunts me the most when I am in front of a mirror, washing or shaving myself, and what I see, behind the glasses of my spectacles – which seem for a moment to stop being transparent and become opaque mirrorshades – eyes. Eyes that are sometimes brown, like mine, and sometimes blue, like his, and which remind me of that gigantic board under which I froze one July day, when the sun was shining, when terror hadn't yet come into my life.

Eyes at once evasive and overbearing.

Eyes . . .

THE MALSPAR SIGIL

David Andreas

David Andreas has published short stories in various small press magazines over the past few years; these include 'King Amphitrites and the Hierophant' and 'Gobolesti' in the British Fantasy Society's Dark Horizons, *and 'The Awful Incident at Drover's Firs' in* Mystique 4.

ALREADY they were getting careless. After several days on horseback they had reached the moorland to the north of Aedhremoria, and perhaps the mild air of the hills had lulled them into incautiousness. It was not so far as they might have imagined between them and the old man in his shop in Lacsu.

Ahead of them, on the other side of a short defile, the road forked, the one branch being the route to the east, the other the old road north to Malspar. The wind surrounded them with silence and they spoke little, not needing to speak, as they rode on; around them the impoverished moorland grass was broken by curiously outcropping rocks with the semblance of crouching figures. At the end of the defile, one of them of a sudden rose, immense and menacing, before them.

'Get off the horse, you,' the man commanded. He nodded to the other. 'And her.'

Evidently he was a man who did not mean to be argued with; was it better to be safe now than sorry later, or could they turn and escape the way they had come?

'And don't try to make a run for it or I'll break the legs of your horses,' the man threatened, 'before I break yours.'

Pharazeon dismounted.

'Who are you? What do you want?' he asked, hoping this

was only a common robber. 'Perhaps you'd better do as he says, Elhisia,' he said to his companion.

'I am Ctoron. You heard of me in Lacsu?'

Oh yes, they had heard of him in Lacsu. This, then – this coarse and monstrous creature – was the man with whom the old dealer had sought to intimidate them. It is said that a drowning man sees the events of his life flash by before him; in Pharazeon's case the events of the last week vividly re-lived themselves in his mind.

Pharazeon was not even *the* younger son but merely *a* younger son of a prominent merchant of Trest and, as such, was more or less obliged to make his own way in the world as best he could. Trade being the field in which he was least ignorant, this was the living that presented itself to him. In his brief career he had made some outstandingly impertinent deals and had his share of irremediable failures; it was the others, unremembered, that brought him his bread and butter. The previous week's somewhat underhanded little ruse had perhaps been one of his less worthy efforts but on the other hand, as time went by, his expedition half a dozen years ago to Aedhremoria seemed increasingly to reveal true acumen on his part.

Having underestimated the poverty of Trest's north-eastern neighbour he had had no great hopes of bringing off his deal with the elder of the village of Gaorhàn until the latter offered his daughter in payment. As is the way of her people she was dark of eye and hair, well-made and far from unattractive, and Pharazeon noted something in the way she held herself that suggested it was not such a bad deal, all things considered. There was also the not insignificant argument that it was evidently either her or nothing.

Elhisia, it turned out, was able and intelligent and had a canny eye for a deal herself, and was so quick at learning the language of Trest that he had voluntarily taught himself hers. He fed and clothed her and did her the honour of marrying no woman of Trest, although in the eyes of the law he could never be wedded to Elhisia; she was happy in return to do all that he desired, and he was well pleased with the arrangement. Every now and then her father would visit her, leaving a basket of pigeons which she would release at intervals to carry messages home. There the priest, the only man in Gaorhàn who was literate, would read them aloud to the marvelling villagers while Elhisia's father sat bathed in the radiance of his reputation for driving a satisfactory bargain.

It was in search of trinkets to please his wife, common in law but in nothing else, that Pharazeon had come to the shop of the venerable Borenius. Elhisia's liking for bracelets hung with charms and periapts that tinkled plentifully about her person was not regarded as the acme of taste in her adopted land but what was more important, it seemed to Pharazeon, was that it was regarded as the height of taste in her native Aedhremoria.

Accordingly, Borenius brought out a tray of assorted charms, some of which might even have been as genuinely efficacious as he said they were, and left Pharazeon to examine them. Without a doubt they were what she wanted, but he surveyed the shop in Borenius' momentary absence, hoping to spot something that would make it worth his while. In a little bowl nearby he noticed a collection of semi-precious stones, seals perhaps. Curious, he studied them more closely, then peered intently at a reddish stone, a garnet or a tormeryl.

Skilfully cut in the surface was an intricate design that Pharazeon seemed to have encountered before: there was an echo in his mind of something primordial, something of primal and limitless power. While he was trying in vain to place it Borenius, returning, distracted him; of a sudden Pharazeon remembered.

'Thirty for the lot,' Borenius suggested.

Pharazeon accidentally, as it were, let the stone drop from his fingers into the tray.

'Fifteen,' he said. 'It's all rubbish, of course.'

'Then why do you want it? Twenty-five.'

'Eighteen,' Pharazeon countered.

'Done,' said Borenius.

'Yes, you have been,' said Pharazeon to himself.

As Borenius emptied the tray into a bag, Pharazeon's seal caught his eye. Snatching it out, he seemed to recognize it, though endeavouring to give no sign of it.

'This is different,' he said, glancing guardedly at Pharazeon. 'It doesn't belong – '

'The deal's done,' Pharazeon interrupted, invoking the unwritten laws of commerce. 'I have paid for the tray, no more and no less.'

Restraining his haste, he took the bag and made off as unhurriedly as he was able.

'Do you see the design?' said Pharazeon later. 'There can be no doubt – it is one of the sigils of Malspar. Just lying there in a shop in Lacsu . . .'

'But what is a sigil?' Elhisia enquired.

'A sigil is a seal or signet,' said Pharazeon, 'an occult sign or device supposed to have mysterious powers.'

'You talk like a dictionary. What does it do?'

'Everything,' Pharazeon breathed. 'Anything and everything. Who knows? It is said that in the right hands its power is infinite.'

Elhisia suggested drily that if this were the case, they would almost certainly be the wrong hands.

'But how can it have such power? And why do you mention Malspar?' she asked. 'That is the Wasted Land.'

Quieter now, suppressing the wild, wild ideas beginning to kindle within him, Pharazeon spoke of the mystical history of Malspar – of how, in the distant past, its prosperity had declined when the king received a grievous wound – of how decay set in like a gangrene and the land began to die.

'Yet it seems that the mages and hierophants of Malspar had made a last attempt to save their land. By means of arts whose nature we can scarcely guess, but whose secret is not entirely lost, they encapsulated the vitality of Malspar, its life force, in a number of stones – the sigils. Then, with the strength and identity of Malspar preserved, the Ailing King could be allowed to die of his wound in peace.'

The death that came to Malspar in the meantime would be transitory. If, in the fulness of time, all the sigils were returned together, and the appropriate cantrips practised, the land would be recalled from death and Malspar resurrected. Nevertheless the life in a single stone, if taken on its own to Malspar, would drain away into the earth as water into the sands of the desert, and with it the life in its bearer;

and for a while something green might flourish there in the wilderness.

'But there was treachery, and the sigils were lost. This is the hieratic symbol of Malspar.' Pharazeon seemed to stare into the depths of the sigil. 'Think of the power in this stone . . .'

Elhisia tried, but not with much success. To her the sigil was no more than an ordinary stone, heavier than one might have expected, perhaps, and with an admittedly enigmatic image incised thereon. It was always her role, as she saw it, to help him tell the difference between his brilliant inspirations and his impulsive plunges into self-delusion, and she suspected that the Malspar sigil fell into the latter category. Nonetheless, like him and because of him, she wanted it to be so.

Her doubts were soon to be dispelled: on the following day Borenius turned up.

'You have something that is rightfully mine,' said he elliptically. 'It was not part of the deal. You deceived me.'

'This was resolved to my satisfaction yesterday,' Pharazeon commented. 'There is nothing more to be said. Except that you have a way with you when it comes to keeping customers.'

'I might be prepared to name a price.'

'That's my prerogative, isn't it? What did you have in mind?'

Borenius named an undeniably generous sum. That he should want the sigil so much threw a new light on the mysterious stone.

How dare you try to put us off, you horrid old man, Elhisia thought. It was, indeed, a bad step on the old man's part, not only illogical but ill-advised.

'No deal,' said Pharazeon. Elhisia breathed again.

Knowing better than to appeal to their good natures and to plead for the return of the sigil, Borenius tried another approach.

'You need time to think about it. If it is not returned by this hour to-morrow I will send Ctoron for it. Do you know Ctoron? I thought so. His powers of persuasion are a little greater than mine.'

Of this there could be no doubt. Possibly there was

something good to be said of Ctoron, but life was too short for it to be worth anybody's while to discover it. His status, in Lacsu at least, was almost legendary; it was tempting to forget that he was as real as any other thug.

'What a hateful creature,' said Elhisia when Borenius was gone. 'And I used to think that he was a nice old gentleman . . .'

Pharazeon was silent.

'What can we do?' Elhisia enquired hesitantly.

'What we originally intended. Only we must be quick. The best place to be when Ctoron is about is somewhere else.

'The problem is that we don't know how to use the sigil – how to release its power. But I do know of a man, an eremite in the mountains to the north of Aedhremoria who is said to understand these things. They spoke of him in Rostirior. Maybe the man would want his cut, but I am sure we could accommodate him. As a specialist in these matters he is probably interested in the art for its own sake, and not for profit. I would trust him more readily than Borenius. Whatever is his name? I think it begins with a D,' Pharazeon concluded helpfully.

'Then there's no problem,' said Elhisia in the ambiguous tone that Pharazeon recognized but could never quite fathom.

'You'll have to come with me,' he said. She was ready to set off there and then; there was no time to waste if D the Sigillist was to be found. Within her a wild excitement arose, for this was a quest of which her ancestors would have been envious. That Pharazeon felt the need of her presence at such a time completed the circle of her happiness.

'I dare not leave you behind,' said Pharazeon.

'No,' said Elhisia. 'Of course.'

'I know you understand,' said Pharazeon.

Her understanding was deeper than he could imagine. She sighed to herself, but not for long.

Her understanding was deepened when Ctoron stood before them. Defying the panic that assailed her, she kept her presence of mind enough to realize that Ctoron seemed to consider her beneath his notice, and to be thankful that it was she who was carrying the sigil. Yet in this there seemed no advantage, for Pharazeon, no fighting man, found himself seized by the neck in a paralysing grip and hammered repeatedly against the wall of the defile.

'Give me the sigil,' Ctoron growled, 'or I'll turn you into pulp and get it out of you with a sieve.'

In vain Elhisia wrestled with him, tried to bend his fingers backward, bite his hands – in spite of the strength that was the child of despair, he kicked her brutally aside.

'Run for it!' Pharazeon appealed to her through bleeding lips. 'Don't worry about me.'

He too had the presence of mind not to reveal that it was she who bore the sigil. Elhisia, distraught, could not think of running but stared desperately about for inspiration. At the end of the defile was a roadman's hut and, leaning against the wall, a shovel. She ran for it, took aim at Ctoron's head, then almost fell as he deflected it and the iron chipped sparks out of the rock. Not giving in yet, she pushed the shovel between his legs and brought the blade back sharply; but he was ready for it and, catching the handle, jerked it out of her fingers. Despairing now, she saw Pharazeon almost senseless and knew that this was the end of it.

'Here, take it!' she cried. 'Take it and leave us alone!'

Reaching inside her shirt she retrieved the sigil from where no gentleman would have taken it. Insignificant and unconvincing it lay, still warm from her body, in the palm of Ctoron's hand.

'You have a warm heart,' he leered. 'That's nice. Perhaps I should take advantage of it.'

Elhisia stared at him in terror, but clearly the sigil was a greater temptation. Moving over to where the horses stood, superciliously ignoring them all, Ctoron took out a knife and cut the bridles and the saddle girths. Lashed savagely, the frightened animals stampeded out of sight. With a mocking laugh Ctoron walked away.

'You should have run,' Pharazeon protested, coming to himself a little.

Elhisia gently dabbed his bleeding face and held him to her. 'It wasn't worth it. Nothing can be worth the pain.'

'I can take the pain . . .'

Elhisia said nothing. His was not the pain she was thinking of.

Some time afterwards, having rested for want of anything better to do, they set off for home. In the distance, hurrying northwards, they could still discern the huge and brutish figure that was Ctoron. Suddenly it dawned on Pharazeon that he was heading in the direction of Malspar.

'Doesn't he realize? Maybe we can catch him up and tell him.'

'It's *his* problem, isn't it?' said Elhisia crisply, to the point as always.

'But we could do a deal. If we warned him we might come to some arrangement and share the profits.'

'Why ever would he believe us? Would you if you were in his shoes?' It irritated her to think that he was serious. 'Let him go. Write it off as a bad debt.'

Somewhere in the nether regions of the shop they could hear his eager steps, hastening to meet them. It was evident whom he was expecting, for he stopped abruptly in the doorway when he saw them and his jaw dropped.

'Surprised?' Pharazeon remarked. His tone was not friendly.

Obviously Borenius was trying to make some sense of the situation. In the dim light of the cluttered shop they could see the muscles of his face at work beneath the ashen skin.

'Why are you here?' he managed to say at last.

'Just to keep you informed,' said Pharazeon sardonically. 'Just to point out that because of your greed and Ctoron's, nobody has benefited from the power of the sigil. But we, at least, are still alive to tell you.'

'What do you mean? Where is Ctoron?'

'When last seen he was heading for Malspar. With the sigil,' Pharazeon added. 'It was all his own idea. He was very persuasive.'

Borenius clutched blindly at the door, stumbled and sank to the floor, crumpling slowly and silently.

'Ctoron, Ctoron,' he moaned. 'He didn't understand . . .'

Elhisia ran to help him.

'Fortunately,' Pharazeon continued without sympathy, '*we* are safe.'

'Ctoron,' the old man was weeping now. 'I should have

warned him. I didn't think . . . I thought there was no need.
He always wanted to do things his own way. He must have
thought the secret of the sigils lay in Malspar. I am sure
he was doing it for me. Although he did things that were
wrong he was his own man and I admired that. I always
admired him. You must know,' he confided to Elhisia, 'he
was my son.'

Pharazeon was tempted to observe that this was hardly
something of which to boast, but wisely thought better of
it.

'At least,' he said, as if it ought to have been some
consolation, 'your son has helped to bring life back to
Malspar. Perhaps, even now, a few blades of grass are
springing up where there was none before.'

'Wait for me outside,' Elhisia ordered, 'if you can't help.'

Afterwards, sensing an atmosphere, Pharazeon said, 'They
brought it on themselves, you know. It was greed, that
was all.'

'That's something you should know about,' said Elhisia.
'What about the way you took the sigil in the first place?
That was a deceitful trick.'

'I was only buying you a present of some charms and
suchlike things.'

'Thank you,' said Elhisia stiffly, 'but I don't think I could
wear them now.'

CRACKING

Steve Green

Steve Green is a former newspaper journalist. Since 1991 he has been a freelance writer, contributing to a number of genre periodicals, such as The Dark Side, Interzone, Fantazia *and the counterculture magazine,* Headpress. *His short fiction and poetry has been published in* Dementia 13 *and* Works, *amongst others. Along with Martin Tudor, he publishes the European science fiction and fantasy review,* Critical Wave.

IT wasn't so much that Eddie Stewart loathed his brother, or even harboured an excessive dislike for that matter; it was merely that he considered holding Jeff in sharp contempt to be a perfectly natural duty for an elder sibling to discharge.

He'd always stopped short of actual cruelty, of course, and he tried to erect a veneer of intellectual justification for his sneering standpoint, but those afternoons he had to collect the younger Stewart from school never failed to inject an element of irritation more genuine than usual.

And so that October sunset found the pair engaged in yet another instalment of the long-running drama: Eddie, combat jacket swung over his right shoulder despite the chill autumnal breeze; Jeff, bolstered against the elements in duffle coat and school cap, his shorter stride adopting an air of Mack Sennett absurdity as he frantically accelerated to keep pace whilst they headed homeward.

Eddie's own speed was partially inspired by his desire to have enough time to change clothes before leaving for his date with the well-proportioned Jayne Middleton (whom he strongly doubted to be a natural blonde and had determined to unmask as soon and as regularly as possible), and partially because the breathless march was one certain way to staunch his brother's incessant babbling.

It was the dull impact of Jeff's frame upon the pavement which forced a halt to their speedwalking marathon. Eddie spun around to see the youngster sprawled across the concrete, a satchelful of exercise books disgorged over the rotting leaves lining the gutter.

'What the hell are you doing *now*?' he snapped, reluctantly proferring an outstretched palm. Then, realizing returning Jeff to the family bosom in too frightened a state might threaten his rendezvous with Jayne's pelvis, Eddie tried a little nervous humour to lighten the atmosphere: 'I thought it was only the Pope that kissed the ground when he arrived somewhere.'

It appeared to work, Jeff's momentary slide towards tearful hysteria deflecting into an injured sulk. 'I tripped. I was trying to avoid the cracks, but you were going so fast.'

Although Eddie's jaw didn't exactly drop, he allowed it to fall a little, mainly for effect. 'The *cracks*? You mean, the spaces between the paving slabs?' As the crouching youngster gave a cursory nod, his brother allowed the rare emotion of affection to well inside him, albeit still tainted with a fair degree of pity; at nine years old, Jeff was a little under half the other's age, but there were times it felt more like a century divided them.

'You know what people say,' Jeff was saying as he finally clambered to the vertical. '"Step on a crack, break your mother's back." You must have heard them, you *must*.'

Eddie tried to resist the temptation to grasp the schoolboy by the lapels and shake some sense into him, then sighed and began salvaging homework from the gutter. Their mother was going to burst a blood vessel if she saw the green and brown stains now decorating the expensive textbooks.

He'd long since diagnosed Jeff's bizarre trust in petty superstitions, nursery rhymes and old wives' tales, but this was beginning to border on the obsessive. Avoiding walking under ladders was one thing, he could almost accept it as sensible, but steering clear of black cats and throwing salt over his shoulder to blind imaginary devils was plain stupidity. Hell, the last time he tried the salt routine, someone had caught the barrage face-on and only

Eddie's intervention had prevented a bloody nose. Any day now the idiot would be investing in a ouija board and trying to raise the dead.

'Jeff, grow up for chrissake. You're starting to get on my nerves with all these ridiculous stories – it's all a pile of crap and you're acting like a real baby to swallow it.'

The words were harsh, but Eddie wasn't finished. Thrusting the sodden books into the satchel, he turned to face his brother. 'Here, I'll show you just how stupid you're being.'

Scanning the pavement beneath his feet, Eddie selected one of the wider seams between the slabs and slammed his right boot directly at it with a thespian flourish.

It never connected. Jeff watched in mute horror as the slabs swung open like a theatrical trapdoor, exposing a vast abyss, a limitless passageway into Hell. For a split-second he appeared to hang in mid-air, his uncomprehending gaze meeting Jeff's across the brink of the unknown, then Eddie pitched out of sight, as though wrenched into the darkness by massive, invisible tendrils.

The slabs swung shut, the seams hidden once again. Below, there was a muffled explosion, like a giant grape bursting between the fingers of a colossal hand, then a sound like wet glass scraping stone. Finally, silence fell upon the street like a shroud, disturbed only by the breeze scattering a few leaves and the stray pages Eddie had yet to rescue from the ground.

The spell shattered, Jeff dropped his satchel and ran the quarter-mile back to his home without stopping to catch his breath, too terrified to pay attention to the bursting pain in his chest.

The house came gradually into view, its frontage almost completely painted in shadow, shielded from the last afternoon sun by the trees lining their driveway. A scream stillborn in his throat, the youngster ran onward, his fear growing with each footfall.

Step on a crack, break your mother's –

In a mind now old far beyond its years, Jeff knew the nightmare had scarcely begun.

ANGEL COMBS

Steve Rasnic Tem

Steve Rasnic Tem won the British Fantasy Award in 1988 for his story 'Leaks'. His short work has been widely published, in such anthologies as Best New Horror, The Mammoth Book of Vampires, MetaHorror *and magazines like* Fantasy Tales, Fear *and* Weirdbook. *Collections of his work can be found in the chapbooks* Fairytales, Celestial Inventory *and* Absences: Charlie Goode's Ghosts. *His first novel is titled* Excavation.

THE morning had sharp edges. Annie could see them.

Her mother had gotten her up an hour before dawn – the earliest she could remember ever getting up, except for that Christmas Uncle Willy had stayed with them, and she knew she was getting something nice that Christmas because she had seen a half-moon sliver of the doll's face with the long blonde hair in the big brown sack Uncle Willy had carried in. That night she hadn't slept at all. She had dreamed of the doll's hair, how it might be arranged, how long it might grow. Maybe the doll was a little magical and the hair might grow forever. She dreamed of it stretching around her little room, catching her other toys up in its waves, carrying them along like colourful boats in a river. She dreamed of drowning pleasantly in the flood it made. Most Christmases it didn't much matter. Most Christmases Momma couldn't afford much of anything.

Her bedroom window looked out on the back yard. In the brownish streetlight: the rough darkness of her dead father's old car, wheel-less, drowning in weeds. The occasional razor-sharp gleam of a discarded tin can.

Annie kept thinking maybe they should clean up the backyard a little. Maybe turn it into a garden or something.

They could have fresh vegetables, their own peas and lettuce
and corn. But Annie was too scared to be in the back yard
very long: the weeds were too tall, and sharp, and things
were always moving there. And her mother kept saying she
just didn't have the heart.

There was usually a little bit of a fog in the backyard. A
mist. This morning was no different. This morning the fog
looked torn, like some ferocious beast had ripped into the
middle of it, pulled it to shreds. Great long pieces of it
hung from tree branches, eaves, and junked machinery like
fingers, or teeth. It fascinated Annie, but it also made her
nervous to look at. Eventually she turned away and started
getting dressed.

She could hear Momma getting dressed in the next room.
Humming, happy. Only now and then snapping at one of the
twins to get a move on. 'Tommy! You don't want me to dress
you! Nossir. You *don't* want *me* to squeeze your scrawny little
butt into them tight jeans!' Then she'd go back to humming,
singing, as if nothing had happened. It had been a long time
since they'd made, as Momma put it, 'a major purchase.' She
always said that with a soft, serious voice, like she was talking
about somebody that'd died. Her mother was almost funny
when she talked like that.

Momma had found this ad in the paper. 'Bedroom Sets.
REDUCED! $40!' And they had just a little over forty dollars
saved. The little over would go for the tax, Momma said. And
if the tax didn't take all of that, they could use the left over
for an ice cream treat. The twins were excited by that, all
right. They didn't care much for the idea of bedroom sets,
but the prospect of a special ice cream, a separate one for
each of them without having to share, that had kept them
talking most of the past evening.

Her mother said it was like a miracle, the way they'd just
gotten that very amount saved, and for sure a hard saving it
had been, too, and here this furniture store comes out with
this nice sale. And them needing the bedroom furniture so
bad. Like a dream, Momma said. A fantasy come true. She'd
shown Annie the picture in the paper. It was a drawing so
you really couldn't tell that much. That's what Annie had
told Momma, but her momma had said, 'No. They couldn't
do it up in the paper like that if it wasn't true.' And of course

that wasn't what Annie had meant at all, but she just nodded and let her mother point out each piece and tell her how fine it must all be.

There was a bed with four posts (the sketch in the paper showed wood grain so Momma said it must be oak and 'oak is about the best there is'), a bedside table with two drawers (not just one like most bedside tables had), a set of drawers, and a little dresser with an oval mirror ('they call that *fine detail*').

'Now maybe I can buy my children something that will *last*,' Momma said.

Maybe it was because Annie hadn't shown enough enthusiasm about the 'major purchase' to satisfy Momma, or maybe it was the way Annie had looked at that dresser. But last night, after she'd gotten the twins into bed, her Momma had said, 'You know I've been thinking. I think maybe you should have the dresser. I've got that dresser Grandma Smythe willed me, and it's special enough. Why, it's an antique. And you need a private place to comb your hair. Every woman, or about-to-be-a-woman, needs a private place to comb her hair.'

Unconsciously, Annie began stroking her long, brownish-blonde hair with her palm, then opening the fingers slightly – as if they were the teeth of a huge, heavenly comb – and catching her hair now and then with those finger-teeth, using them to melt away the day's filth, making the tangles and snarls vanish one by one into the cool night air.

Annie had looked up at her mother, seen her mother's satisfaction, then realized what it was she'd been doing. And stopped it immediately. She'd seen herself in that dreamed-of oval mirror, seen herself combing the hair that was so much like her mother's, hair that was the only thing even remotely special about her. Hair even the rich girls in her class envied. She'd seen herself combing herself in that fine and private place that once was her bedroom, that special place because the dreamed-of dresser was there.

And at that moment Annie was almost angry with her mother because of the dream.

They arrived at the furniture store only a few minutes after it opened. There were a few other customers already inside: two well-dressed women, an older man in a ragged overcoat with dark spots on its sleeves, and a tall young man casually dressed, but Annie thought his clothes might be expensive since she'd seen some just like that on one of her favorite detective shows.

Her mother looked a little panicky when she saw those other customers. She'd wanted to be at the store *before* it opened, but the twins had gotten in a fight at the last minute – Momma tried to slap at least one of them but they got away from her – and then their old car had stalled three times on the way over. Annie had been wondering the whole time how they were supposed to get the new bedroom set back to the house. Surely they just couldn't tie it to the top of the car. She'd heard about having things delivered but she didn't know if the furniture store would do that, especially for something on sale like that, or even how that sort of thing was done. She doubted Momma knew how that sort of thing was done either. It would be just awful if they couldn't get the bedroom set after all because they didn't have a truck and somebody who had a truck got there first, or because they didn't have enough money to pay for the delivery.

Again, Annie found herself absently stroking her hair, seeing her reflection in each display case they passed, something glinting between hand and hair, and almost hating her mother. Suddenly she just wanted to get out of there. She just wanted to go home where no one could see her.

Her mother made her way quickly to the back of the store, clutching the newspaper ad, looking around to see if any of the other customers were looking at the bedroom set.

As they stood there waiting for someone to notice them, Annie looked around the store. Nobody seemed to be paying them any attention. A man in a blue suit and tie was talking to the casually-dressed young man, who was looking at sofas. Two other men in suits were talking to the well-dressed older women, showing them something in a huge book on one of the counters. The man in the dirty overcoat was going from chair to chair, sitting in each one, occasionally saying something aloud to no one. Nobody seemed to be paying any attention to him, either.

All the bedroom furniture had been shoved into a far corner of the store. From that distance Annie didn't see anything that resembled the picture, but she reminded herself that you really couldn't tell anything from those sketches. One of the well-dressed women was making her way toward the bedroom furniture, and Annie's mother was watching the woman, licking her lips nervously, her back rigid, hands fisted tight. But still she didn't try to get the attention of one of the sales clerks. It was all crazy. Annie's face was growing warm with anxiety and unfocused embarrassment. The man in the filthy overcoat looked at her and grinned with broken, brown teeth. Annie closed her eyes and imagined herself combing her hair with a beautiful curved, silver comb. Gazing into a mirror that made her look far better than she thought possible. Combing away all her nervousness, all her fear. Combing peacefulness and beauty back into her.

'May I help you?' a practised male voice asked.

Annie opened her eyes. A tall man in a suit leaned over them. Annie's mother bobbed her head spastically, as if she had just awakened from a trance. 'This ad,' she said, shoving it into the salesman's hands. 'We'd like to buy . . . to *purchase* that bedroom set.' Then, anxiously, 'You still got it, don't you?'

'Oh, yes. Several, in fact. Right over here.' The salesman started toward the bedroom furniture. Annie's mother breathed deeply, relieved, and hurried after him. For all her hurrying, Momma was trying to look queenly.

'Here we are. A *fine* set. And a very good price.'

'Oh yes, a very good price,' her mother said. 'We're not against paying the money for quality, mind you,' she said hurriedly. 'But why pass up a bargain, I always say.' Momma laughed off-key.

'Hmmm. Yes. Of course. Anything I can tell you about this particular set?'

Annie could see that her Momma could hardly look at the set, she was so nervous. She just kind of moved her eyes around the furniture, going 'Hmmm, hmmmm, yes, oh yes,' all the time. Not really seeing anything. Annie, on the other hand, looked at every piece. It wasn't much like the newspaper sketch. A slightly different style, and of lighter colour than she had imagined. Certainly not oak. The colour, in fact, was unlike any wood she had ever seen. She

went around to the back of the headboard and the set of
drawers and discovered some other kind of board with little
chips pressed into it, and plastic. But still it was nice enough
looking. Certainly better than anything else they had.

And the oval mirror was real nice. Not expensive and
elegant like they'd imagined, but clear and shiny. Her hair
looked good in it. It caught the highlights. At a certain angle
her hair seemed to grow dozens of brilliant sparkling places,
as if she had filled it with all these tiny silver combs.

Someone touched her hair, softly. But she didn't see
anyone in the mirror, and when she turned there was no
one there.

Her mother was crying. Louder and louder, until she
was almost wailing. People were turning around. The two
elegantly-dressed women were whispering to each other.
Annie saw all this, looking all over the store before she
could bring herself to look at her mother.

'But the ad says *forty dollars!*' her mother cried.

The salesman looked embarrassed and a little angry. He
was looking around too, as if he were trying to find someone
to come help him, to help him shut up this bawling,
embarrassing lady. For a panicky moment Annie imagined
him calling the police. 'That's forty dollars reduced, ma'am.
The price has been *cut* by forty dollars. Four sixty down
from five hundred. It's . . .' He looked ready to plead with
her. 'It's still really a very good price.' He looked around,
maybe to see if his boss had shown up yet. 'Maybe you
could finance?'

Annie's mother looked thunderstruck. The casually dressed
young man was looking their way, smiling. The raggedy
old man was smiling, too. Annie wanted to kick them
both in their smiling mouths. Annie wanted to kick them
all. Something cool and metallic was in her hair, stroking
it. She turned to the salesman. Her mother was like a doll,
a dowdy mannequin. 'We can't . . . *finance,*' Annie told the
salesman. 'We don't have the money.'

The salesman nodded, and for a moment it looked like he
was going to reach out and touch her hair. But her mother
had moved behind her, and now was breathing cold and
sour into her hair. 'How *dare* you,' her mother whispered
harshly. 'We're going,' her mother told the twins.

'What about our *ice cream*?' one of the twins cried. Annie didn't know which one.

Her mother turned around and grabbed both the twins by the arm and started dragging them toward the door. They both screamed, and her mother had to threaten them with slaps and worse before they faded into sniffles and whimpers.

Annie took one last look at the mirror. In her reflection, sharp-edged glints of silver seemed to be attacking her hair. She broke away and followed her family out to the car.

That night Annie had been sitting in the kitchen, just staring out the window, absently stroking her hair. Her mother came into the room, looking drawn and pale, but at least she had calmed down. She pulled an old purple brush out of her robe and began brushing Annie's hair. 'I just wanted to get you something *nice*,' her mother said.

Annie squirmed away from her mother and walked quickly to her bedroom. Her hair felt warm, uncomfortable.

The next morning Annie found the first comb under her pillow. She had had bad dreams all night, of sick smiles and dirty poor people and of teeth, mostly teeth. Biting and ripping, or sometimes just pressing up against her soft skin and resting there, as if in anticipation.

When she woke up she'd still felt the teeth, working their way into her skull like the worst kind of headache. Then she'd lifted her thin pillow and discovered the comb. Long, curved metal. Not silver, she didn't think, but something like it. The teeth long and tapered, spaced just the right amount apart, it seemed, so that they wouldn't snag the hair, but pass through softly, like a breeze through the woods.

Tentatively she pressed the beautiful comb into her hair. It was as if all her nerves untangled and flowed as softly as her hair. She could hear a soft buzzing in her ears. Her skull went soft as moss. She hated to take the comb out of her hair. Her hair clung to the comb, making it hard to take away. She could feel her skull pull toward the comb.

Annie took the comb, holding it like a baby to her chest, into the kitchen where her mother was drinking coffee. 'Oh, Momma. *Thank you*,' Annie said.

Her mother looked up at her out of ugly, red-rimmed eyes. 'What's that supposed to mean?'

Annie was suddenly confused. 'The comb. You put it there, didn't you?'

Her mother pursed her lips, put her coffee down. 'Let me see that thing.'

Anxiously, Annie handed her mother the comb, already thinking about what she would do if her mother refused to hand it back.

Her mother dropped the comb onto the kitchen table. It made a musical sound, like a triangle or a very small cymbal. 'You steal this at that store yesterday?'

'Momma! That was a *furniture* store! Besides, I don't *steal*. I found it under my pillow this morning; I thought you had given it to me for a *present*.' Annie felt on the verge of tears.

Her mother grunted and stood up, took her coffee and started back to her own bedroom. Much to Annie's relief, the beautiful metal comb was still on the kitchen table. 'Well, I don't care if you stole it or not,' her mother said as she was going out the door.

When Annie got back to her bedroom, moving her beautiful new comb through her hair rhythmically, in time with her steps, she thought she saw two silver wings resting on the edge of her bed. When she got a closer look, however, she could see that they were two small, metal combs, only a couple of inches long.

Something unseen whispered through her hair. Insects buzzed at her ears. The comb moved rapidly through her hair, dragging her hand.

Annie thought she could see bits and pieces of her reflection in the air around her. Slivers of face, crescents of shoulder. Long flowing strands of hair, floating through the air like rays of silver dust.

Row upon row of long silver teeth dropping through the morning air.

'You dream too much. You eating junk before bed?' her mother said, when Annie told her about the eight metal combs she had found around her bedroom.

'Just a glass of milk.' Her mother looked at her sceptically.

'But see,' Annie said, reaching into a worn paper bag and dropping the musical assortment of combs onto the table. 'This isn't a dream.'

It gave Annie satisfaction to see the dumbstruck look on her mother's face. Her mother stared at the assortment of combs for a very long time before actually touching one of them. 'This one's cool,' she said, running her finger along the spine of the longest comb. 'Like ice.' She picked up the smallest comb, one so curved and delicate it resembled the skeleton of a tiny sunfish. 'And I swear this one's warm as a kitten.' She stared at them a while longer, then looked up at Annie. 'But what good are they goin' to do us?'

Over the next few days Annie discovered combs everywhere. In the silverware drawer, nestled cosily among the forks and knives. Arranged in a circle under the front door mat. Hanging from the ivy that grew up the back wall of the house. Flowering from otherwise dusty mason jars in the cellar. Planted in rows in her mother's flower boxes. Jammed into the house foundation's cracks along with leaves and twigs. Raked into the weeds that had swallowed the back yard. The combs' positions changed a bit each day, so that Annie imagined a steady drift of combs, grooming the weeds into ornate stylings.

Annie felt blessed, richer than she could ever have imagined. Who needed a fancy mirror when the combs seemed able to make each window, each shiny surface the clearest of mirrors? She tried out each comb she found, at least once, spending hours sitting, humming to herself, the combs harvesting all the tension from her head.

And still it was the original comb, the one she had first found under her pillow, nibbling at her head, that was her favourite. She let it mouth her long hair every chance she could.

But her mother was not as enamoured with the things. 'They scare me,' she'd say, 'all these shiny, sharp, toothy combs. Where'd they all come from? Can you tell me that?'

Annie just smiled a lazy smile, the only kind of smile she could manage these days. Broad smiles, grins, they all seemed just a little angry to her now. 'I don't know. Does it matter? Maybe the angels left them,' Annie said.

'That's crap,' her mother said, trying to remove a particular sharp-toothed comb that had gotten snagged on her sweater. She got it out finally, but in the process lost a small swatch of material.

Annie just smiled.

Like their mother, the twins grew to dislike and distrust the combs. They'd sit down in front of the TV to watch cartoons and a wayward comb would work its way out from under the living room rug, snag their socks and scrape their ankles. They'd reach into their toy boxes for a truck or gun and one or several combs would bite them. And early one morning Tommy found his pet kitten stiff and matted in the front yard, a long shiny rattailed comb protruding from one ear.

More and more the family found combs soiled with the occasional fleck of red.

At dinner a spoon might arise from the soup with a small comb nestled in its hollow. The hamburger grew crunchy with their discarded teeth. They collected in boxes, in bags, in suitcases and every unused pocket. They gathered in the cold dark beneath the steps. They held meetings in the mailbox.

'I'm gonna sell some,' Annie's mother announced one day. 'You can keep that first one you found; you seem to like it best anyway. But we need the money. I'm sellin' the rest.' She waited for Annie to say something. The twins were cranky, complaining about going with their mother, afraid to help her pick up the combs. They didn't want to touch them. Annie said nothing, just continued stroking her hair with her favorite comb. Her mother looked almost disappointed that she didn't get an argument.

Not bothering to repackage them, her mother carried them away in the vessels in which they'd naturally gathered. She filled their old car with suitcases, jars, bags, and boxes, cans and glasses and pots and pans full of combs. The car jangled musically as she and the twins sped off for town.

While they were gone Annie dreamed of unseen presences, riches by the bagful, and a quiet place where the combs could make love to her hair. For hours she waited for her family's return.

'They wouldn't take 'em, *none* of 'em!' her mother shouted, slamming through the door. 'The recycle man said they weren't any metal he'd ever seen, and all the other stores said they weren't good as combs anyway. Too sharp. Might hurt somebody, they all said.'

'Where are the combs now?' Annie asked quietly, stroking her hair.

'At the *dump*, that's where! That's where they *belong* – bunch of junk! Lord knows I wasn't going to haul 'em all the way back here!'

If her mother expected an argument, she wasn't going to get one from Annie this time, either. Annie held her last remaining comb to her ear, then looked up at the ceiling. Her mother looked up, too. 'What the hell?' she began.

'You wanted things. That was your dream,' Annie said, as the metallic rain began. 'You gave me the dream, Momma. And now we're rich. Just *listen* to all we have.'

The sound on the roof was unmistakable. Metal against metal. Metal against gutter, against shingle. Comb against comb, a steady downpour.

Her mother ran to the front window. Annie could see past her, through the window and into the front yard. Where thousands of combs fell in a shimmering, silver-toothed deluge.

Her mother turned from the window. 'Annie!' she screamed. Her mother dashed across the room. The twins were bawling.

'Annie!' Her mother reached for her, angry and scared. 'Annie, give me that comb!'

The comb flew from Annie's hand like an escaping bird. It landed in her mother's hand, pulled her mother's fingers around it like the individual bits of a fancy-dress ensemble. Then it pulled her hand to her head and began to comb.

Annie smiled her lazy smile. The floor grew soft with the thick pile of her mother's harvested, blood-clotted hair, her mother's discarded pain.

THE WATERS OF KNOWING

S. M. Stirling

S. M. Stirling is the author of several fantasy novels, including three sharing the same universe as the story which follows – Snowbrother, The Sharpest Edge *and most recently,* The Cage *(in collaboration with Shirley Meier). Science fiction/alternative history novels include* Cops and Robbers, Marching Through Georgia *and its sequels,* Under the Yoke *and* The Stone Dogs. *More recent work includes developing a novella, 'The Children's Hour', into a full-length book, a World War Three novel, and a science fiction anthology titled* Cold Fusion.

IN the Tecktahate of Fehinna, in the city of Illizbuah, hard by the Old Harbour, stands the Weary Wayfarer's Hope of Comfort and Delight. Behind a screen of marble fretwork on the rooftop terrace a wizard, a thief and a mercenary sat together over wine.

Naturally, they made conspiracy.

The mercenary opened another oyster with her dagger. 'Ahi-a, bliss,' she sighed.

Long fingers closed around a cup of carved wood. The shell clacked on the smooth brown tile of the floor.

The wizard ignored the attempt to bait him. Few Fehinnans would have dared; that made the foreigner more valuable, for his purposes. The mage's seamed face reflected a faint, sardonic amusement.

'Shkai'ra Mek Kermak's-Kin,' he said formally. 'Will you accept the contract?'

Shkai'ra stretched with fluid grace. She wore the embroidered tunic, cloth belt and open sandals of the Fehinnan middle class, but nobody would have mistaken her for a low-country native; that breed did not run to grey eyes and copperblonde hair. The face was more alien still: hawk-handsome, scarred, older than her years with the eye-creases of a steppe-dweller.

She leaned back and picked out familiar constellations among the huge soft stars of the southern night: Eh'donna's Lance, the Shield . . . Around her were the muted sounds of the Illizbuah night, and somewhere the plangence of a harp. Moist, mild spring air; rose-scent, brackish water, tar, spices, city-smoke . . .

'Your pardon,' she said, her Fehinnan fluent under a thick, clipped accent. 'Never met a shaman who came to the point so fast.'

She flexed her hands. There were pads of hard callus on them from rope and rein, lance and bow and saber. Warfaring, she thought: hunger, heat, exhaustion like lead on your helmet, runny guts in an unclean camp. The smell of gas gangrene; going up a scaling-ladder and listening to the screams above as red-hot sand flayed warriors alive. The southrons had other ways of killing, yellowdeath, stickflame, power-driven casters.

Still, she thought, we Kommanza are bred to war. If I were home I'd be fighting to keep the nomads off the crop, this season. Yet . . .

'Why me?' she asked bluntly.

'Kaina over the mountains,' the wizard Bashuln answered. 'The Free Canton War.'

She blinked. Not many east of the Blairuh range knew of that. She remembered the chill shock of the pikepoint slamming up into her thigh and the sound of the wounded.

'A good reason,' she nodded. 'What are yours? The high-thief here I understand: a ruler's troubles are a bandit's luck. You have the name of one who cares mainly for his . . . art. What gain, to balance the risk to you?'

His fingers traced lines that glowed briefly on the tabletop. 'It is the nature of our kind to become what we may. True, I have enough trade-metal to last me what years the Sun leaves me: wine, food, the caresses of youths and maidens – these delight me less that you, who are closer to the fires of Prebirth. Ah, but knowledge, and the Art, and power . . . these do not fade. Each of us will receive what we seek to fulfill our needs: for you, treasure; for

Jahlini, the chaos her kind need to flourish; for myself the Waters of Knowing, a treasure beyond the grave-goods of the Maleficent herself. And for our backers, *their* choice as next Tecktah and Sun-on-Earth.'

'eKlar,' Shkai'ra said, in her own language: all clear. She remembered an old tale of her people, of a woman who had mated with a snow-tiger. She had been asked how she did it, and replied in one word – "cautiously". This shaman was the scariest old *zteafakaz* she had seen in a long while.

Aloud, she continued: 'I'll start recruiting: most of you Fehinnans fear the sunwrath too much to strike at the Heir . . . We'll meet again in three days.'

Jahlini stared after her retreating back. 'Why do we need the outlander?' she said. Illizbuah-bred, she had that city's odd mixture of cosmopolitanism and provincial snobbery. And professional jealousy: crime was as tightly organized in Fehinna as any other trade. The jowly bulldog face scowled, and fingers curled unconciously toward the knife slung hilt-down along one flank beneath her tunic.

'Adderchief,' the magus said, 'I would not instruct you in lockpicking, or the selling of "protection". You would not lesson me in potions or starlore. Does not the Second Collection of the Orthodox Philosophers enlighten us: "In the well-ordered state, each caste shall cleave to its own for the good of all?" Is this not the expression of the Sun's Divine Harmony?' He smiled thinly.

'This is not assassination. We shall require professional soldiers to face the Guard. And are you really so anxious for your Adders to face the blade and the bow? Besides this,' his smile widened, 'do the fallen require trade-metal?'

The crimelord nodded satisfaction. 'If you can't steal, cheat,' she said.

'Indeed,' said the wizard. 'The old Tecktah has entered the Shrine of the Holy Wisdom: the Waters of Knowing are being prepared. Our backers expect their candidate to drink them, rather than the Heir. After we sieze them. We are to be paid generously – for giving them Fehinna and everything in it.'

Jahlini looked up sharply. 'You mean . . .?' At his nod she whistled sharply. That meant raising the stakes. No matter how much religious reverence attached to the Waters it was still one thing for the elite to accept a coup among themselves and another to swallow a commoner. A thought occurred to her.

'That would leave our accomplice sitting out waiting for a word that never came, wouldn't it?'

'Ah,' the magus sighed, 'So tragic.'

Alone, the wizard Bashuln brooded. Fourty years of research it had taken to garner the knowledge he required; soon he would strike, he who alone in millennia of power had penetrated the secrets of the Waters and the Sun-on-Earth. He held up hands liver-spotted with age.

'Soon,' he mused, smiling slightly. 'Very soon.' Yes, he would strike. But temporal power would be the least of the prizes.

Shkai'ra whistled gaily as they left the Weary Wayfarer's gate. Already the morning air bore a hint of the day's wet heat; in this climate, the odd Fehinnan habit of washing all over was easy to follow.

'Produce plaza,' she said to her companion. That was the best place in town for a private conversation, as long as you were cautious. Jaibo grunted, surly as usual until the sun warmed his blood.

The market seethed. Straw, dung, spilled grain, rinds, less nameable things hid the brick pavement. Booths covered the great square, shading the sellers and their goods: cornmeal, fruit fresh and dried, pickles, tomatoes, cheeses of every shape, fried locusts in honey . . . Heat baked down, and smells of sweat and decay, spices and dung rose up to meet it. Buyers swirled through the narrow lanes, bargaining, arguing, cursing; fights broke out to be quelled by the Watch; children screamed for their kinparents; peasants gawked; an occasional haughty upper-servant stalked through, grand in robe and staff.

Most were native Fehinnans of the lowlands, swarthy snub-featured folk in tunic and sandals, many stripped to loincloth or less in the heat. But a port city showed many other breeds; Middle Sea traders in folded cloaks, black Haytin sporting goatskins and feathers, New-Fai sweating in furs. In so mixed a throng Shkai'ra attracted little notice in native dress, and her Fehinnan companion less. He was of average height for his people, barely reaching Shkai'ra's eyes, but broad-faced and broad-shouldered, thick arms and legs heavy with muscle and seamed with white scars vivid on the dark brown skin. His movements were quick, economical, precise: he was one of the fast heavy men, rare and very dangerous.

'Why?' he demanded plaintively, running a hand over his cropped black hair. 'Why get involved in politics? Why not stick to sellswording and honest crime?'

Shkai'ra shrugged, smiling faintly. 'Jaibo, I didn't leave home to be poor,' she said patiently. In fact, the prospect of a slit throat had sent her wandering from the gaunt stone Keeps and huddled villages of the Komman of Granfor; two would-be High Seniors was one too many.

She felt a touch on her belt. Without turning she grabbed, twisted, locked and wrenched. There was a grisly popping sound; the cutpurse lurched away, keening.

Jaibo resheathed the shortsword he had been just too slow to use and continued. 'There are other ways to make money.'

'Yes, but *safe* ways?'

'Wellll . . .' He sighed. 'If I'd wanted to be safe, I'd have stayed on the farm and spent my life shovelling pigshit and pushing a plough. We'll need about sixteen blades, then?'

'*Ia*, and it'll be tricky. Fehinnans wild enough to strike at the Sun-on-Earth's get are likely to be a treacherous lot . . . nothing personal.'

He grinned. 'No offence.' Actually, the blasphemy did bother him a little; on the other hand, there wouldn't be much of his soul left after the Lake of Fire anyway. Easy enough for an outland pagan like Shkai'ra, he thought.

They wandered on, mulling over names and records. Drift brought them to the edge of the market-square. In theory the Plaza of Healthful Delights Naturally Satisfied by the Fructifying and Beneficent Sun was reserved for fresh produce; there were a dozen other markets, ranging from the Liquid and Translucent Depths Yield their Denizens to the Light, for seafood, to the Strange and Effulgent Products of Heavenly-Inspired Hands, for the jewellers and goldsmiths. Practice was otherwise.

Here near the whitewashed boundary-wall were less commonplace goods, draught-dogs, homing pigeons, and a few small coffles of slaves. Not the skilled cooks, fancy bedmates or muscular litter-bearers that could be found at the Houses of Sun-Sent Deliverance from Annoying Toil, as the municipal pens were called. These were the type of purchase a visiting peasant-farmer might decide to pick up.

They would have passed by with a glance in the normal course of events. But events were not normal that day.

Two of the slaves had been freed from the forked wooden poles. Both were young, alike in their brown-haired leanness, naked bodies showing the elaborate tattoos of the western mountain tribes. The prospective purchaser prodded and peered, alert to the tricks of the trade. Crouched listlessly, the female of the pair picked at the ironwood manacles on her wrists as the slaver eyed money in the wagoneer's fist and sang the praises of her merchandise. All was normal to the point of boredom. A guard's attention wandered from the tribeswoman.

The next instant she half-rose, turned, and drove her fist up under the guard's tunic into his groin. His eyes bulged, and a whinny of astonished agony burst out shrill as a wounded horse.

The slave lunged and wrenched away his staff with a savage yell of glee. The manacles hampered her, but a minute of skilled wood-on-wood left one guard moaning over a broken wrist and another clutching her ribs as she slid down the wall. The slave whirled the staff in a blurring circle, chanting hoarsely, her face twisted with exultant rage.

The others of the coffle shrank away. Her companion wasted no time: the first guard's scream brought him up, slamming a kick into the base of the slaver's spine, hard. A quick swipe left her fighting-knife in his hand, and only a frantic scramble took her out of reach before it gutted her. He swung back-to-back with his fellow rebel and they lifted their tribal screech, alien and chilling in the warm seacoast air. The menace of staff and long, glittering blade brought a moment's hesitation. Events balanced in silence.

Shkai'ra studied the scene and made a swift decision.

'Follow me,' she said to Jaibo. 'No killing or crippling: here's where we get two loyal fighters.'

'Sweet Sun Herself, Shkai'ra – ' he began.

'Shut up, and do it,' she snapped. The slaver was furious enough to order saleable property shot down, as soon as someone thought to bring out a crossbow. Jaibo shrugged, drew blade and trotted forward at her heels.

Without taking her eyes from the pair she called: 'How much for these two, if we get them under control?'

'Kill them – I'll pay *you*' the slaver snarled. This was a family business, and the guards were members of her own kinfast. Then the words penetrated.

'You want to *buy* these!' she exclaimed, rubbing her bruised tailbone. 'What for, show fighters?'

'No, to eat,' Shkai'ra said with heavy sarcasm. 'Before the Watch get here. Two silvers.'

'Three silvers for both,' the slaver replied.

Shkai'ra shrugged and began to turn away. 'I paid two to the military on the border!' the slaver said. 'They ate like horses all the way east – ' She trailed off. The slaves should not have been here, it was just that the bribe was less than the regular fee at the pens. Ghastly visions of confiscation, losses, lost licences, fines, delay flitted through her mind. Once the officials got their teeth into it, they would strip her down to her earrings. She fingered the brass loop in one ear and reflected on the ingratitude of the western animals she was forced to buy. Still . . .

'Done,' she said. 'May they give you as much trouble as they did me.'

The two mercenaries circled to enclose the slaves. Shkai'ra stared into a hating blue gaze, nodded, smiled slightly. Her hand moved across her body and the long curved sabre flicked out as she flowed forward. Wood jarred on steel in a flurry too blurring-swift to follow. The tribeswoman blinked and settled her stance for the next passage.

Shkai'ra breathed in; time slowed, until every moment was jewel-edged; smell of dust and sweat, the balance of muscle and nerve uniting with the weight of the bone hilt in her palm and the smooth flicker of her mind weighing a thousand subliminal clues from her opponent's stance and expression. A tingling ran over the skin on shoulders and breasts and belly, and she felt the hard joy of a difficult art performed supremely well. Nothing else made you feel so much alive . . .

'Drop the weapon,' she said in the Blairuh mountain dialect. 'Listen.'

'You know the hill-tongue?' the woman said, hard suspicion in her voice.

'I'm from the lands beyond the Great River: I travelled through the hills on my way east. And learned enough to know those skinpaintings mean you're of a chiefly kinfast.'

'You should know we'll never be Fehinnans' servants!' she snarled, feinted a sweep and thrust with the end of the staff. That earned her a stinging cut along the forearm.

'I'm no Fehinnan,' Shkai'ra continued calmly. 'A bargain, service for freedom. Refuse and the Watch will have you blinded and chained to a pump. There's always time to die.'

Her companion burst in. 'No! It's a tra – ' There was a quick scuffle of feet, a single clash of metal, a thump and the loose sound of a falling body. Before she could move the mountaineer felt a slight sting in the small of her back; the point of a Fehinnan infantry shortsword pressed, very lightly, over her kidney.

Shkai'ra reached foreward, flicked her fingers off the staff and rested the slanted-chisel point of her sabre at the base of the other woman's throat.

'No time left,' she said quietly.

'I swear,' the tribeswoman said thickly.

'Your kinsib there, too?'

'I'm senior; he'll follow.'

Shkai'ra stepped back a few paces before sheathing her blade: there was no sense in offering temptation too soon. And now there would be paperwork; she thought with a wry grimace that it might have been better to live among unlettered folk. At least, if they decided to rob, kill or imprison you it would be for a better reason than not having your papers in order.

Fed, bathed and clothed, the slaves glowered nervously at Shkai'ra and her lieutenant from the floor of their room at the Weary Wayfarer. Eyes flickered nervously at patterned carpets, carved furniture, inlaid mosaics in abstract patterns, all common enough in Illizbuah but beyond the dreams of the wealthiest mountain chief. Shkai'ra judged there was still spirit there; these two would be dangerous slaves even if broken, but fine retainers.

She poured chilled pomegranate juice and sipped, tapping thoughtfully at the chair.

'You speak Fehinnan, you two?' she asked.

'Better than you,' the hillwoman replied. It was fluent, although closer to the peasant patois of the border than the cityspeech. 'I hight Deevhla; this be Haain; both Soosn-Kin, of the Black Ravens.'

'So. How were you taken?'

'By treachers,' Deevhla said. 'The Fehinnan garrison commander at Rannak fort couldn't keep us from lifting heads and cattle, so she sent trade-metal and weapons to the Wild-wolf tribe, and to Keena Two-Knife Soosn-Kin our – ' she paused to spit on the carpet, '– relative. He bespoke a peace-feast; they fell on us when most were drunk or blown on dreamweed. Those that lived were sold: now the Wild-Wolves have most of the Black Raven lands, and Two-Knife rules what's left.' She barred her teeth. 'May the Fehinnans have joy of them: the Wild-Wolves eat the Meat, and Keena would skin a roach for the hide or sell his kinchildren to a Kaina fuckhouse.'

Shkai'ra nodded. The Fehinnans often found Intelligence work more useful than armies sent into the wilderness, and the border traders did good business in furs and captives when the wild folk fought. 'So you couldn't go back?' she probed.

Haain laughed sourly. 'Two-Knife would take our heads for his godhut. The Wild-Wolves would do the same, and put the rest in the stewpot.'

Deevhla rose. 'You bespoke a service,' she said.

Shkai'ra nodded. 'Can you fight?' she said.

The mountaineer shrugged. 'We're Black Ravens, and chiefs,' she said simply.

'Prove it,' Shkai'ra said, and flipped her own dagger through the air. 'First blood, and you both go free.'

The tribeswoman snatched the weapon out of the air and looked doubtfully at Jaibo. He leaned against the door, a repeating-crossbow cradled in his arms, wishing he could use it and showing the fact.

'No meddling, Jaibo,' his leader said. He nodded curtly.

Deevhla crouched, left foot foreward and right hand holding the blade, hilt low and point up, well back with a three-finger-and-thumb grip; her left-hand stiffened into a chopping weapon, held across her body. Shkai'ra nodded in approval and stood relaxed, hands held loosely before her.

The mountaineer shuffled forward cautiously: she had sampled the other's speed. But that had been at a disadvantage, bound and fighting steel against wood. The knife gave her extra reach, and she only had to score once, so . . .

A feint lunged toward the face. Shkai'ra backed, blocking forearm to forearm. Deevhla shifted her feet as if for another lunge, laughed distractingly and threw herself forward in a flying thrust, the whole momentum of her body behind the point as her feet left the floor. An attack almost impossible to counter without a serious cut.

But Shkai'ra made no attempt at a handblock. She went back before the attack, back and down, almost seeming to float dreamily before the blinding speed of the thrust. The long legs slashed up, crossed at the ankles, cords and long flat sheathes of muscle rippling as her feet turned inward to lock the hand. In the same instant, just as her back touched the floor, she arched and twisted up on the crown of her head, twisting with all the leverage of her long body. With a wild yell Deevhla threw herself forward in a midair summersault and came down with a crash, releasing the knife.

Shkai'ra came erect with a flickering shoulder-roll and kicked, stopping the calloused edge of her foot just as it touched the other's throat.

There was no need for words. Warriors all, they knew that the foothold would have torn Deevhla's arm off at the shoulder if it had been held.

She looked at Haain and raised her eyebrows. He shrugged.

'Never could handle Deevhla at close-quarters,' he said. 'Better with a bow, but not knife or hand-to-hand.'

Jaibo grinned.

Shkai'ra looked down at the fallen mountaineer. 'Not bad,' she said. 'Not bad at all. Come.'

Bewildered, the two slaves followed.

Shkai'ra hired a gang-pedicab for the journey; faster, and she remembered how her first sight of a city's streets had left her mazed and shaken for days. And that had been a village compared to Illizbuah; better to let the tribesfolk take it in slowly.

Brick tenements over tiny shops and workplaces gave way to the courtyard-centered homes of the professional and merchant kinfasts. The gang leaned into their work, pumping the pedals in time to a soft chant. The smells of cooking-oil and garlic and sweat gave way to incense and greenery once past the internal wall into the Old City; the glittering tower-and-dome architecture Fehinnans favoured surrounded them, amid tiny manicured parks and fountains and sculpture and wall-mosaics of irridescent glass.

These drew back around Temple Square: the hierarchs wanted no competition for their masterpiece. Two hundred meters, the dome of the Sundwelling lifted before them, the light of afternoon glinting off its gold-leaf covering. About the square stood low stone-faced public buildings with pillared arcades. In one such was the office Shkai'ra sought.

She addressed a bored, pregnant woman in white. 'These slaves here; freedom papers.'

The clerk nodded without expression and began to assemble forms and papers. Behind the counter another made a quick sketch for the archives: a copy would serve as original for a woodblock wanted-poster at need.

Haain flushed, then went white. Deevhla made a low grunting sound as if a fist had hit her in the belly and went on her knees, gripping Shkai'ra's hand.

The clerk ignored them until she was ready. 'There's a transfer tax,' she said. 'This is treated as a sale to the slave.' The new freedperson's identity cards were handed over.

'Fingerprints here,' she continued. 'I don't suppose you can write? Mark here – good. Now, you're – ' She stopped to puzzle over the foreign name '– Deevhla and Haain doMek Kermak. Your patron is still responsible for your behaviour: you cannot marry, change residence or fast to any kin without her permission. She has a right to two-tenths of whatever you earn. You may apply to her for help when in need. Next!'

Aygah Clahruh's-Kin, prince, Heir of Fehinna, and soon to be a god, was bored. The fact that this state was, as usual, self-inflicted, did very little to relieve it.

On the wall opposite his couch, stone warriors raised pike and bow in triumph, while arch-necked horses trampled the banners of foreign rulers and the Sun shed Her light on Her people. The relief was boring too. There must, he reflected, be thousands like it in every realm from the sea to the Great River: Fehinna had not been the only state to recover its independence when the Maleficent's jury-rigged empire fell apart. Of course, it might have been different if she hadn't died of marsh-fever in Sainlu . . . That was a new thought, and such had been rare enough in his fifteen years to make it fascinating.

'Excellence!' his tutor said sharply, looking up from her scroll. 'Will you attend!'

He looked at her coolly; the drone had been merely part of the backround, with no more meaning than a fly's buzzing. Grey under her lined brown skin, the old scholar rose, silently made the prostration, and left. Aygah yawned and swung to his feet, smoothing down the thin silk of his robe.

Behind him four troopers of the Guard fell in, moving soundlessly. They were armoured from head to foot, leather and fiberglass eked out with fabulously expensive steel for helmets and joints. Shortsword, halberd and repeating crossbow were poised, great oval shields ready to snap around their charge at a moment's notice.

Aygah ignored them. They were part of the background of life; no more to be noticed than the lamps of fretted silver, the rose-marble of the floor or the arched roof of stained glass that made the corridor a fantasy of shifting colour as he walked toward the distant door.

That gave on a sunken garden, walled in blue lapis-glaze tile traced with golden fish; potted jasmine and dwarf fruit trees artfully trained stood among stone benches. Aygah signalled the guards to wait outside; they obeyed after a quick, thorough inspection. The prince took that chance to give a quick glance at his reflection. What he saw reassured him, a slim taut body and a regular face just firming toward adulthood, framed by silky black hair.

'Siddo!' he cried. A man in the green tunic of the Guard's undress uniform rose and made the deep bow his rank allowed. A tall man, sharp-faced for a Fehinnan, white teeth showing against his close-trimmed beard as he smiled.

'My lord Aygah,' he said. The familiar address and quite illegal.

'Ah, no "my lord" between us,' Aygah said as they embraced. 'When I have my inheritance, you'll be fasted to the Clahruh's-Kin. It will be "my lord general" to *you*, then, from those.' He jerked his head toward the palace.

'Not everyone will be pleased at that,' Siddo said. That was the Sun's own truth: starting with the General Staff, and including most of the nobility. Favourites had died before, and his own Cahwic's-kin was more ancient than wealthy or powerful. But . . . the chance of seven lifetimes, gone!

Aygah pulled his head down for the kiss and smiled. 'But let's not talk politics now. We've so little time, with all the ceremonies. Until you lead the escort to the Shrine, next week.'

Siddo stiffened. 'You did it, my lor – Aygah?'

'Yes, of course! Those greybeards were slow, but they daren't oppose me now. He clung closer. 'But now there's no time to waste, before the priests come.'

'Indeed,' Siddo laughed as they sank down on the bench. 'But time enough.'

Siddo was nervous. Worse, he was convinced that the others here knew it. He looked around the table: ancient wizard, silent black-clad thief with her closed, jowly face, the red-haired foreigner sprawled like a sleepy leopard in her chair. He knew he was a brave man, and not only on the battlefield: nobody reached Vice-Commander in the Steel-Walled Guard Surrounding the Personage of Infinite Worth to the Beneficent Light without a full share of deviously ruthless cunning. But he was in a trap, and knew it.

Best to make a bold front. 'You still offer too little,' he said. 'As it is, I stand to be fasted to the Tecktah-kin.'

'Incorrect,' the mage's dry voice rustled. 'As it is, you stand to spend several days of accute discomfort being flayed and pickled, when it is found exactly how you augmented your inadequate funds. There are limits even to the protection of the Infinite One . . . and you have many enemies.'

Siddo sweated. Why had he done it? It had been like madness, and he was a cautious man.

'Very well,' he said. 'But there will be no harm to the Heir? And you have the backing of the Cai'tuh-Kin as well as the Maacluns?'

'Could we attempt such a substitution otherwise?' the wizard answered. It amused him to lie with a minimum of outright falsehood; it was only with such limitations that the game had any savour, these last few decades.

The door slammed to his exit. 'That man is fey,' Shkai'ra said slowly, making her people's warding-sign against bad luck with her swordhand.

More briskly: 'To points: I and my band clip the bird on the way to the Shrine; you put in your substitute; I hold the Heir until it's all over, then we scatter until the fury dies down?'

The mage nodded. Around them the shadows lay thick, hiding the corners of the huge chamber. Flickering lantern light caught on the glass of beakers, coils, strange shapes and vessels; a throat-catching chemical stink lingered in the air, the smell of fourty years of magic. On one wall curled the divided-circle emblem of the Guild of the Wise, one half black, the other golden, divided by an S-line: superimposed was a double-helix spiral.

'Here,' he said. The first bag he handed the mercenary chinked heavily. 'One thousand silvers' value, in minted Pensa and Bailfon gold.' He opened a wooden box to reveal two glass spheres. Within the thick, translucent barriers coiled and eddied a stuff half liquid and half gas, acid green and viscous.

'Be careful,' he said, tapping the straps that held the globes in their padding. 'The substance is introduced into the balls chilled. At normal warmth it presses strongly on the glass, and will burst and spread if they break.'

'Ahi-a,' Shkai'ra grunted. 'Like steam in a closed pot.'

'Indeed.' the wizard said with surprised respect. 'And for the space of twelve heartbeats, it will kill. After that, the air renders it harmless.'

'Why isn't it used in war, like yellowdeath, or flame-throwers?' She had a healthy respect for the powerful weapons of the southrons.

The wizard shrugged. 'For the same reason firearms rarely are,' he said. 'Expense. Much effort went into these, many lives and much magic. A year of my life.'

Shkai'ra tucked away money and weapon. 'The plan still seems too rigid to me,' she said. The Kommanz warmasters always said victory went to the one who could improvise.

Jahlini snickered. 'My kinchild Davhit will be with you for liaison,' she said. 'With pigeons for messages. Almost as fast as the public heliograph. Are you afraid your part will fail?'

'No, yours,' Shkai'ra said, ignoring the silent flare of rage in the Adderchief's eyes. 'No more communication except in an emergency.' Her heels clacked toward the door.

'That one could see through a millstone sooner than most,' Bashuln mused.

'Why not use the "waters of believing" on her, then,' Jahlini said, smiling nastily. 'It worked well enough on Siddo.'

'No gain without loss: they impair the wits, and we need hers. But that was why I chose a foreigner; no matter how shrewd, it will not occur to her to ask the questions a Fehinnan might. Until too late. And now, shall we study the details of our part?'

Shkai'ra stood beside a rough map-board at one end of the disused factory. Dim space hid the fibre-braced concrete walls, silent except for the creak of a rotted powershaft that had once run to a rooftop windmill. The scents of dyewood and coffee, rum and molasses and pepper lingered on the air; a place for trade of the more discreet variety.

She shifted the round bullhide shield on her back and let her hand drop to the shotpistol at her waist, symbol of past prosperity and present authority, a weapon whose ammunition cost the price of a trained warhorse per round. Before her were the fighters, squatting with cool alert predator patience. Discharged soldiers, bravos, deserters from foreign armies, part-time bandits when opportunity offered: the elite of their trade. Most wore full cavalry armour and carried crossbows and the straight single-edged swords easterners favoured;

one was a Pensa, a two meter giant leaning on a blade near as tall as he.

Haain and Deevhla crouched to one side. She had fitted them out with their native camouflage smocks, shortswords, throwing-axes; Haain bore a long elm bow. Deevhla a grip of short darts across her back and a staffsling. That had caused trouble: all the eastern realms had blood feuds with the mountaineers. Fist and boot and the menace of Jaibo's crossbow had brought them to order: the prestige of her name and the gold she had spread would hold them, at least for a moment.

'Listen up!' she barked, pushing back her flared helmet by the nasal. 'Sheepjackers, the oath's sworn. The Sun can have your scabby souls, but for the next two weeks your arse belongs to *me*. I'll not mealymouth it: we've been hired to kidnap the Sun-on-Earth's Heir, and hold him while someone else takes the Waters of Knowing and the Tecktahate.'

There was a moment of stunned silence, then a confused roar of anger from twenty throats. Shkai'ra waited until hands began to reach for hilts before she raised the shotpistol and fired over their heads: it was the extravagance as much as the noise that quieted them. Jaibo lowered his crossbow with an unvoiced sigh of relief. Sometimes he wished the boss wouldn't leave things quite so long.

There was a rattle as the pellets fell back to the floor. Shkai'ra put a foot on a chair and swept them with her eyes.

'*Soooo* pious the thought offends you?' she drawled.

'Shit on piety, I'm not a sellsword to end up on the flaying table!' one of them snarled. 'You've gone *ahrap*, Red.'

'You petty larceny apple thieves,' she replied with a nicely calculated show of passion. 'Do you think I'd go into this without backing? Do you really want to spend the rest of your lives fighting bandits for fat merchants and lifting an occasional horse, when this could set you up for life?'

The idea penetrated; she could see the cold thought behind the hard scarred faces. No one here was going to die for a cause, but each and every one was ready enough to take risks if the prospects for profit were good enough.

'You all know Dieter,' rumbled the huge Pensa, leaning

on his two-handed sword. 'You know Dieter doesn't like *her*, no, not at all. But Dieter likes money, yes, much. So let's listen.'

Dieter, you *zteafakaz*, she thought, for that I'd almost forgive you for trying to steal that drummer-boy from me back in Kaysbuah. Almost.

'What backing?' another asked.

She beckoned, and a figure in the black overalls and padded harness of the assassin brotherhoods ghosted out of the corner, eyes black slits in his mask.

'The Adderfangs, and others,' she said. 'And Tiera, what you don't know you can't spill.' The woman subsided; that was plain sense, and the figure in black a powerful argument.

Shkai'ra grinned without humour. 'Now, here's how we'll do it –'

She spread her blankets near the door: it was the only exit, and there was no sense tempting anyone with the thought of an informer's reward. Jaibo would take the first watch, so –

'Care to join me for a while?' she said to her newly freed retainers. Haain grinned with delight: Deevhla hesitated.

'You asking, or telling?' she said.

'Asking. You're free now. But I always did like to get nice and relaxed before a fight.'

Deevhla began unlacing her vest. 'Good idea,' she said cheerfully. 'That Fehinnan commander at Rannak, when we were captured, she tried telling. Got some teethmarks in a very sensitive spot. Right here –'

Seventy kilometers from Illizbuah Shkai'ra woke to false dawn, and lay for long moments studying the sky. Around her the night was full of rustles and buzzing and the chirring of nightbirds. This was a lush land, and the scents were strong and alien, spicy, rank, wildflowers and weeds and vegetable decay.

This might be the last time she would see the stars. Not that she awaited defeat, but Zaik held the scales of victory, and the world was very beautiful. It was strange, she thought, how she saw that more as she grew older. A youth did not *think* about it: she recalled lying on the spring steppe watching a prairie hawk circling in immense blueness, or standing in a captured Minztan village enraptured before a swirling, arabesque design in enamelled copper. But those sensations had been merely *there*, like heat or cold, hunger or thirst or lust, acted on without reflection. Perhaps her years of wandering had driven her to seeking inward more than others of her folk . . .

Enough, she thought. I'm not a greyhead yet: too much thinking weakens you. Work to do.

She rolled erect and began the stretching exercises that would leave her limber and ready. Her mind ran through the patterned responses of the Warrior's way, disciplines that dampened fear and pain and tapped the last reserves the body hoarded against extremity.

Haain ghosted over as she went to check on the horses. She froze, and they leopard-crawled to where the supplies lay stacked. A figure came erect, half the height of a human, a packet of dried fruit clutched in its hands. The tribesman touched the handle of his throwing-ax.

Shkai'ra shook her head and pitched a pebble to startle the animal away, grinning at the scurrying panic that followed. The giant racoons were rare in Fehinna and unknown in the far West; she had heard that they had been filtering down from the unpeopled deathlands north and east of Pensa these last few generations.

'Good, chieftain,' Haain said. 'Lucky to spare the little thief, they're too smart to be animals. Must be a devil.' That was a compliment from a Blairuh tribesman, they being devil-worshippers themselves.

'A fellow-plunderer,' she said. 'Dog doesn't eat dog. Time to wake the others.'

The Fehinnans among the mercenaries knelt to face the morning sun, chanting softly; then all joined in donning their warharness, a complicated process that needed time and help. Being professionals, they ate and drank sparingly, a few sips of water and a bite of hardtack; it was never wise to load the belly before a fight.

Shkai'ra and her lieutenant crawled to the edge of the ridge through the trampled wheat.

'Pity we don't have enough to cover the other side of the road,' Jaibo said, taking her binoculars and scanning the forest-roof that reached nearly to their level right and left.

'Necessary risk,' she shrugged. 'That's thick woods down there; our hillfolk will be useful, if we need to pursue.' At his grimace she sighed. 'Jaibo,' she chided, 'stop thinking like a Regular: it's been years now since I dragged you out from under that heap of bodies up in the border country. We need those skills.'

He rolled over and checked that the rest were far enough back to be invisible from below. 'Sometimes I think you don't get excited about anything,' he grumbled.

'Training,' she said. And remembered her time with the Warmasters: herself in a line of other children, each balanced on two rocks and holding a practice-sabre out at shoulder height in each hand. The Tactics Master stood before them, snapping out problems and demanding instant analysis and solution; behind them prowled a ten-year-old Senior with a riding crop. Tears, errors, trembling brought a flick of the whip and sometimes it would slash down with no reason at all, except to remind them of the unfairness of life. She had left a child behind in Granfor; physical parentage was not very important to her people, but for a moment she wondered idly how it was doing with the child-herd.

Carefully, Shkai'ra uncased the two spheres the wizard had given her and handed them to Deevhla; a sling would be the best method of delivery.

'Be careful with these,' she said. The mountaineer nodded fervently. She had seen the results when the Fehinnans pitched yellowdeath among hill warriors trying to storm a fort; hideous blisters, clansfolk blinded or coughing out their lungs.

'You sure the spirits won't break loose?' she asked.

'Not until the glass breaks,' Shkai'ra assured her. 'Remember: one at the head of the line, the other right behind the litter as long as the wind holds steady toward their face.' She was confident enough the other woman would hit what she aimed at; a quick test had proven her claim of being able to drop a moving squirrel at a hundred paces.

'Dieter!' she called. The big man nodded, his little eyes shadowed through the narrow slit of his barbut-helm. 'Remember, don't just *hold* the head of the column; push it back.' He signed agreement. 'All right, no more talking. Keep your positions.'

The sun rose, and Shkai'ra waited with endless hunter's patience as sweat trickled down her flanks and insects dug their way under her armour. Below them the crushed-rock surface of the road gleamed white, standing out vividly against the dark green woods below and the grassy slope.

An hour later the first sign came, less a noise than the absence of the normal country sounds. Then the multiple soft thudding of rubber-shod horseshoes with ceramic insets sounded, muffled through the trees to their left and north. No sound came from the waiting mercenaries, but suddenly the air was thick with tension.

Shkai'ra raised the glasses and strained to catch the first sight through the trees. Jaibo's breath hissed as he caught the image of their prey.

'There – just like you said,' he marveled. 'Two *laituns*, forty lances. No dragoons, no holbars, no infantry. Sweet Sun's tits, who would have believed it?'

'Siddo has influence,' she said. 'Also, this is a secret rite, and feared.' She chuckled softly, exultant. 'You Fehinnans rely too much on specialist troops. If those were Kommanz horse-archers we'd be in trouble.'

She carefully pulled a dozen shafts from her quiver and stuck them point-down in the ground. The spring morning air was sweet; she felt almost giddy, yet strong, vital, alive. Zaik, Godlord, she prayed. You of Might, give me victory or rebirth among the folk of the Ztrateke ahKomman.

The escort swung into sight from her left, lanceheads throwing back the light and pennants snapping. A standard-bearer, then the first laitun, then the horse-litter for the Heir and the rest to follow; it was as she had planned. Siddo beside the litter; he was wearing an actual steel breastplate, and the sight made her teeth ache with envy. On second thoughts, it would be an invitation to bandits on an ordinary person.

These troopers would be the best, lifetime soldiers and fanatics when fighting for one of the Sun-on-Earth's kinfast; by Shkai'ra's standards their weapon-skill was no more than middling, but they would die hard. She waited until the whole column was clear of the woods and stretched out around the foot of the bluff. She filled her lungs.

'Now!' she shouted.

The escort halted, heads snapping up, quivering-ready for Siddo's order that never came. Before they could bunch around their charge, Deevhla's sling was buzzing. The first sphere whipped down, to shatter on the standardbearer's shield. The second followed while it was still in flight, to crack on the ground four ranks back from the litter. There was a muffled double thump as the pressurized liquid exploded into gas, green for an instant and then clear.

The Guard troopers were used to the war gases used in the eastern realms, burning vesticants. This was different. Where it touched, men, women, horses were down, every muscle in their bodies locked in a single spasm, a spastic wrenching that snapped bone, tore veins apart, sent thin jetlets of blood spurting from the body orifices. Terror was loose; more than half survived, but their morale was shattered for brief, crucial seconds.

The mercenaries threw themselves forward to the rail fence that lined the bluff and shot, the twanging throb of their repeating crossbows filling the air. Six shafts per magazine, and power for six shots in the coiled spring; these at a range where even the best armour would not stop a square hit. And there would be many hits, with experts firing from prone position.

Shkai'ra rose to one knee, drawing and loosing, fast and machine-accurate, thinking the bodkin-headed arrows into their targets. Haain stood to use his long bow, chanting his glee. Deevhla's sling hummed.

'The horses! Get the horses! Baiwun Thunderer hammer your greedy souls, kill their mounts!' It went against Shkai'ra's own grain to slay something as beautiful and valuable as a trained warhorse, but she could allow no messages to ride out of this ambush.

Quivers and magazines were empty. 'Down!' Shkai'ra yelled. 'Down and *in!*'

Finely trained, her mount leaped forward as she vaulted into the saddle and plunged down the slope. That was a mad scrambling half-fall, and no others of her band dared try it in the saddle. But she had ridden before she could walk, and came of folk who claimed kinship with the Horse Spirit.

Feet braced, she leaned forward in the saddle and extended

her sabre point-first, arm and shoulder locked. The point slammed into a Fehinnan trooper's gorget, breaking through the tough leather with the momentum of horse and rider behind it. She ripped it loose, and he fell with blood bubbling past clenched teeth. Shkai'ra shrieked, a high exultant wailing falsetto, and then she was boot-to-boot with the next. For a moment they traded cuts while their mounts savaged at each other with hooves and teeth. The Guard trooper's mount stumbled, and while she struggled with the reins Shkai'ra got her point home in the vulnerable spot under the arm. The Fehinnan's shield dropped. The Kommanza's blade blurred, overhand, backhand, then thudding down on the exposed swordhand. Even through a horn-backed gauntlet the pain was too much; the weapon fell from nerveless fingers and Shkai'ra landed a drawn cut under one ear. The Fehinnan toppled.

Elsewhere the fight intensified. Dieter stood like a tower in the roadway, flanked by his squad. A Fehinnan tried to rush him, relying on the weight of her horse and lancehead to clear the way. Dieter crouched, pivoted with a speed astonishing in so large a man, cut downward with his two-handed sword, through lance and arm and into the horse's neck. The Fehinnan went to the ground, and lived just long enough to see the great blade falling toward her shock-wide eyes.

Haain and Deevhla bounced about, yelling, relying on sheer agility as they hamstrung horses and tore riders out of the saddle, tactics honed in the endless guerrilla warfare of the frontier. The air was loud with the sharp sound of metal on metal, dull thudding of blade on sheild and armour, the sudden astonished noises of human beings in agony greater than they had ever thought to bear. A single pair of feet went thudding off into the woods.

'Deevhla! Haain! Get him,' Shkai'ra barked. The mountaineers vanished into the shadows, on a trail marked with blood.

Shkai'ra sat her saddle, breathing slow and deep as her followers finished off the enemy wounded; her own casualties were astonishingly light, no dead, only three too hurt to fight. She smelled the sharp stink of blood and stool and urine that goes with violent death; with a sigh, she cleaned and sheathed her sabre. There were no nicks, thank Zailo Protector: good Minztan steel was almost impossible to get this far east.

Siddo had scarcely moved through the fight, except to snap the neck of a trooper who attacked him; the stone-headed warhammer rested on his saddlebow as Shkai'ra rode up.

'It took long enough,' he snarled as she rode up on his left.

'Perhaps,' she said, with a wide smile. Something alerted him, but seconds too late. She reached out, gripping the edge of his shield and pushing it across his body and pinning his other arm. The dagger appeared in her other hand and whipped forward to slash behind the buckle of his neckguard. She grinned into his eyes and twisted the blade. 'Baiwun Avenger of Honour sought you out,' she said: in her own language, but he would know her thought. The fight had been satisfying, but this was a real pleasure. 'Betrayal for a traitor.'

On the hill a figure in black released two pigeons. The panting mountaineers ran back from the forest; Haain swung a severed head from one hand.

'No trouble,' his kinsib grinned. 'Couldn't run worth donkeyshit in all that gear.'

The Heir had climbed from the litter and watched Siddo die without expression. 'Are you going to kill me too?' he asked coolly.

Shkai'ra shook her head and jerked a thumb toward a riderless horse. 'You come with us, hand-tied,' she said.

'I'm ready,' the lordling said. The mercenaries' commander began to admire his nerve. 'Just one thing first.' With slow deliberation he leaned over and spat into Siddo's glazing eyes.

Fear and boredom were the companions of the guard detail at Raisak Staiun, the Shrine of Holy Wisdom. A low brick wall surrounded a complex of buildings in the massive style of four centuries ago, with beam-ends carved into demon faces to frighten the nightwalkers. Peasant legend and the secret records of the Guild of the Wise both whispered of earlier structures on the site, and the lands about were left in forest by decree of the Sun-on-Earth. Even poachers avoided them by night.

The section leader watched her ten troopers closely as she marched them out to relieve the gatewatch. Discipline was her cure for uneasiness, and it held even on this midnight watch. Under that eye the *hayn* marched with a stiff precision, ox-obedient in the manner Fehinna demmanded of its infantry; five pikepoints slanted at the regulation angle, five repeating crossbows slung neatly over right shoulders, ten hobnailed sandals crunching down as one.

'Hayn – *halt!*' she rasped, in a voice roughened by a decade of drillfields. She wheeled, grounded her halberd smartly and waited for the *aykukah* to report and request relief.

The wooden lattice gate was ajar, against regulations. Baijo would catch punishment-drill if the officer of the day saw it. She was still grinning at the thought of him trotting around the parade ground in weighted armour when the blowgun dart sank into her neck and pumped its poison into an artery.

Swift and silent as their namesakes, the black-clad Adders flowed over the wall. Caught off guard and without leadership, the troopers could do little; an Adder went down with a pikepoint in his belly, another took a quarrel in her forehead. Then the soldiers were all down under a rain of darts and spiked steel disks.

Bashuln and Jahlini walked out of the nightblack woods and stood by the gate as messengers came and went.

'All secured,' Jahlini said at last. 'The perimeter guards are dead, and we have the rest bottled up in the barracks; no alarm got through.'

Bashuln smiled quietly. The Tecktahs had relied on secrecy and superstition to guard the Shrine, which meant there was little physical force to fall back on if fear failed. Once again, he thought, I see the advantages of daring to think the unthinkable.

And in no other place would so many of Fehinna's mighty have gathered without private guard forces of their own. No such display of power was permitted here in the royal sanctum.

The wizard led the last of the strike force through the gates of the centrum. Idly, he noted the unusual depiction of the Godwar on a corridor mural; it showed the Mighty One rising above the Cities of Darkness, not in the inverted-pyramid symbol used in modern art, but with a more organic image. Much like a tree, or a mushroom, he thought: interesting archaism.

The gates of the Chamber of Initiation burst open. Jahlini reflexively pulled up the black cover of her hood, leaving only a slit for her eyes. Scorning concealment, the magus strode into the centre of the circular room, feeling with satisfaction the collective astonishment of the Fehinnan nobility ranked around him in rising tiers. There was a rustling as he was recognized, an added shock for the pious as they realized a magician had entered the holy of holies. Someone called harshly for the guard, a voice accustomed to authority and obedience.

'Call for your guards in Darkness,' he laughed. 'But my professional opinion is that ghosts will do you little good.'

The head of the Maaclun-Kin had come to his feet. 'What is the meaning of this!' he shouted, beside himself with fear and rage. 'We agreed – ' He bit off the words, too late.

'Ah yes, our agreement,' Bashuln's voice higher than his usual high whisper. Red spots burned high on his cheeks. 'That I should put your kinchild on the throne, for a pittance and a dagger in the back as soon as the task was done . . . All without revealing your treason to your fellow Tecktahs, brainless fox-hunting oafs that they are, licking the spittle of the priests.'

Hookswords, knives and blowguns kept the unarmed aristocrats in their seats, but the Maaclun blanched visibly at the mutter of outrage. Bashuln pointed; Jahlini nodded to her followers, and darts struck the man and the adolescent girl beside him as they twisted in their seats.

'So much for the candidate of the thrice-born,' the mage said drily. Before him were the chiselled-bronze gates of the Sanctum, priceless and ancient. Before it stood a row of impassive priest-acolytes of the Shrine, their hands folded in the sleeves of their yellow robes.

'Fools,' he said quietly. 'Stand aside.'

'Though you slay us, we will not,' came the calm answer. The shaven heads followed his movements with the silent intensity of snakes. Even the Adders would hesitate to touch these, from well-grounded fear rather than piety. Bashuln knew that fear's foundations, and acted swiftly.

His arm swept across their front, a faint hissing sounding in the tense silence of the chamber.

The chief acolyte frowned and raised her hands before her. Slowly, an expression of horror replaced the cold fanaticism in her eyes.

'Melting,' she whispered, gaze flickering across the room. A shrill scream erupted, saw-edged and startling in the hush. She sank to the floor and curled herself into a ball. 'Don't eat me, mother, no *nooo*' she whimpered, sobbing. The priests collapsed into madness; Bashuln saw that the audience was utterly cowed as no threat of mere violence could have done.

'The Tecktah is dead,' he intoned. 'The Waters of Knowing are prepared. I go within; when I return, prepare to worship.'

And they would . . . as long as the Adders remained. That would be long enough for him to set the escape plans in motion; perhaps even for Jahlini to do likewise. But *he* would have the knowledge of the Waters, and he was no unformed youth to be overwhelmed. No, he was strong with the discipline of decades of study, a lifetime of psychomotor control and self-conditioning. With the knowledge and a sample of the mother-culture in its blank state he could find a suitable subject for his own transfer. No more nights of sleeplessness, no more sour old-man's smell in his nostrils . . .

The doors swung open under his hand, soundless on their oiled crystal bearings. 'My purpose is achieved!' he cried.

A shouting from the corridor; the thudding rattle of hooves. He spun around.

'I think not,' came a familiar voice.

The manor where the mercenaries took their captive was small and old-fashioned; it had belonged to a kinfast of minor gentry whose line perished in the Four Nations War, a generation ago. Since then the Maacluns had held it, visiting infrequently to collect rents and hold the sort of entertainment that needed discretion. The local peasantry came only to pay dues and render boonwork; the staff were slaves, and had learned to be close-mouthed. The warband kept to the long-disused family wing of the rambling two-story brick structure.

With blunt Kommanz practicality, Shkai'ra had confined Aygah to the top floor of the manor's single tower. The only window overlooked a courtyard, and there was a four-storey drop on to hard stone. Guards kept the roof and the shaggy garden below as well as the door, and none but her own followers were allowed to attend the Heir. That was one face the staff might recognize, from a poster seen in town on a feast-day if nothing else, and the reward would be large enough to overcome a good deal of fear.

'Noonmeal, lordling,' she said as she came through the door with a tray. Jaibo yawned, hitched his swordbelt and made for the exit.

'Over to you,' he said. 'Our prize here is still as haughty as if he were Sun-on-Earth.'

'Here, eat,' Shkai'ra said. She was mildly worried: the lad seemed to be pining.

'I'm not hungry,' Aygah said, using the superior-to-inferior tense. 'Just leave it there.'

Shkai'ra shrugged. 'If you're not, I am,' she said, squatting on her heels and eating with wolfish speed. There was fish in batter, glazed yams with honey, herb-and-greens salad and white wine. It was a relief to feed naturally; her folk did not use forks or chairs.

The prince stared at her, indignant. 'You – you need a lesson in manners!' he cried, aghast.

She swallowed noisily. 'So do you,' she said. 'In the Zekz Kommanz, a youngling who talked that way to a blooded warrior would get the whip, chiefkin or not. I was hired to hold you: the contract didn't say you had to be able to sit down in comfort.'

Aygah gaped, began to speak, thought rapidly and held his peace. Shkai'ra nodded at him and relaxed. She had brought up one of the shoulder-guards of her armour; undoing the bindings, she carefully began checking the curved strips that linked lobster-tail fashion and laced on to the breastplate. The leather surface was in good condition, but she went over the fibreglass backing as well; armour needed careful maintenance, and she never delegated that task.

She turned to her wheelbow. Aygah had been watching with curiosity, and at the sight of the unfamiliar weapon he asked:

'What . . . is that thing?'

'A wheelbow,' she said. Unbolting the arms from the rigid centrepiece with its handgrip, rangefinder and cutout, she continued. 'They're the main weapon on the steppe west of the Great River. See these little bronze wheels at the ends of the staves . . .' Unhurriedly, she explained how the pulley-action halved the draw on the bowstave and increased the speed of the arrow's flight. It was something to talk of, and seemed to draw the boy out of his sulks; she guessed that the practicalities of warfare were strange territory to him.

She oiled, polished, fitted, then gripped the stave at each end and held it at arm's length, flexing against the strain to strengthen arms and shoulders. She was stripped to the waist in the mild heat, and muscles stood out in flat sheaths and long smooth curves beneath the sweatslick skin, moving like living metal. Veins stood blue against skin that was milk-pale where the sun had not touched.

At last he asked: 'What do you think will happen to me?'

She laid down the bow and rolled her head to loosen the neck. 'Can't say,' she replied. 'Probably comfortable exile: most plotters would rather not kill royalty if they can help it, it sets a bad example. Or they may decide you're better out of the way. Why bother about it, since you can't do anything?'

He sighed and fell back on the bed. 'What else is there to think about,' he said bitterly. Except Siddo, he thought, and grimaced.

Shkai'ra watched him with detached sympathy. If it was called for she would slit his throat without hesitation or qualm, but he did seem to be bearing up quite well, for an untrained *gakaz*, a non-Kommanza. He treated them all like servants, which bespoke a certain courage, or at least the heedless confidence of the young who cannot imagine that they can die. She smiled wryly at memories of her own.

Rising, she went to the bed and put a rough hand under his chin, raising the handsome sullen face.

'Always something worthwhile to do with a bed on a fine afternoon,' she said cheerfully.

With a surprising shyness, he answered: 'Well . . . I haven't before, I mean with a woman . . .'

She laughed throatily. 'High time you learned to "walk

on both legs",' she said. Mentally she counted on her fingers. Good, the precautions might have spooked him, she thought.

Several hours later, they lay curled together, sipping at the last of the wine, drowsily content.

'Again?' she asked.

'I don't think I could,' he said dreamily. 'That was nice. Strange, but nice.'

'That's one of the advantages to being female,' she said, yawning and stretching hugely. 'Even at your age, with you males it's sting a few times and die, like a bee.'

He moved closer. 'Maybe I'll grant you a pardon, when the conspiracy is broken: I could come and visit you in your cell, when you're *my* prisoner.'

'I wouldn't advise it,' she said with grim humour. 'It's been tried . . . Besides, you're never going to be Tecktah and Sun-on-Earth.'

'But nobody else *can* be,' he insisted.

'Why not? The spook-pusher who hired me has been working on it for years, learned all the rites. He's been grooming the little Maaclun-kin for six months now.'

Aygah stared. 'Then he can't know as much as you think: the priests told me that a year is the minimum, for the preparatory potions to take hold.'

He felt Shkai'ra stiffen. 'What's . . . what's wrong?' he stammered.

Her mind raced. It could be simple ignorance on Bashuln's part, but he had impressed her as a man supremely competent in his Art. Aygah shrank back from the expression of pure hatred on her face.

'Tiera!' she shouted.

The door jerked open, and the guard looked in with her crossbow ready. Her smirk lasted only seconds.

'Get – me – Jaibo!' Shkai'ra bit out.

'What's the matter?' Aygah said.

'Tem-ok moi zhivuh-na eshk'hroga graai – ' she snarled in her own language, then dropped back into Fehinnan: 'We just stopped being enemies. Help me dress.'

She found Davhit the Adderfang talking to Dieter in the

stables; by then she had schooled her face to a semblance of calmness. But Davhit's trade demanded skill in reading a thousand clues of stance, muscle tension, eye movement that spoke as loud as speech to the trained mind. He knew a killing rage when he saw one, and there were two mercenaries behind Shkai'ra as well as her mountaineers and Jaibo.

'Kill her, Dieter!' he yelled. Even as he spoke, a spiked steel disk slipped into each palm from the magazines in his sleeves. Fractionally faster than his targets' reaction, they sank into the throats of two of Shkai'ra's followers; one of them, dying, slumped into Jaibo and saved the Adder's life, spoiling the single shot he was able to fire. Then he bounded backward as Davhit attacked, drawing his blade.

The giant Pensa's blade slid over his shoulder into his hands. Shkai'ra had seen Dieter in action with his great two-hander before; she did not make the mistake of underestimating it. The advantage of speed and numbers was with her, but Dieter had armour and she did not. And the long blade gave its wielder extra reach.

She circled, shield up, moving crabwise toward the vulnerable spot on the right rear, trying to pin his attention for Haain and Deevhla to attack the weak points of the armour with their light weapons. Dieter backed, holding his sword blade down with the hilt level with his eyes. A stroke would leave him open, but no parry could stop that blade.

Suddenly he realized that others would come soon, with crossbows. Astonishingly quick for a man of his bulk, he surged forward, sweeping a great figure-eight cut before him.

Deevhla rolled in and tried to cut at his legs, getting an armoured knee in the face for her pains: Shkai'ra could hear the solid meaty smack of it, and knew that she was out of the fight. But the mountaineer's move gave her a fractional part-second. Time slowed. Shield up, she surged forward under the cut, trying to put herself as near the hilt of his weapon as she could, and stabbing low. The blow thundered on her buckler, smashing her to her knees and leaving her shieldarm numb – but she felt the point of her blade slice into meat.

A bellow of rage split the air as Dieter saw the steel slide through the slit in the divided skirt of his hauberk and ram through thin leather into his inner thigh. Incredibly, he managed to reverse the huge sword and bring it down in an overarm cut. Shkai'ra bounced back as it glanced off her helmet, and even as she sank into whirling darkness she wondered at the awesome display of sheer strength.

She woke with the taste of metal in her mouth. Her eyes opened, and she winced at the stab of sunlight, saw straw-covered brick before her face, smelt horsedung and her own sweat.

Jaibo lifted her shoulders from the ground. 'Hai, all right?' he asked anxiously.

'*Ia*,' she replied, brushing him aside. From the shadows, only a few minutes had passed. 'Ignore the brains running out my nose. They got away?'

'*Tia*, I had to break off with the Adder to help Haain keep Dieter from finishing you off. Dahvit came up leading a second horse; Dieter almost didn't make it aboard, you nicked him good. Haain – ' he nodded direction.

The mountaineer lay a few paces away, silent: a great rent across his body from hip to breastbone showed why. His kinsib kneeled beside him, and as Shkai'ra watched she smeared his blood over her cheeks. From what she knew of uplander customs, that boded ill for Dieter.

'I hope the Pensa sheep-raper bleeds dry as he rides,' she said vindictively, fighting back the nausea and dizziness of mild concussion.

Jaibo spread his hands. 'Be in Illizbuah by now.'

She shook her head. 'Not Illizbuah: the Shrine of Holy Wisdom.'

'Why?'

'That crazy spook-pusher,' she said disgustedly. 'That's what this is about; he stabbed his backers as well as us. He plans to take the Waters *himself*.'

Jaibo sucked breath between his teeth, a Fehinnan's expression of awe. 'Never get away with it,' he said hopefully.

'Either way, we're in a sea of shit without a sail. Two choices: we run for the border, or we hit the Shrine and try to turn it all around. Davhit didn't have time for his pigeons, we'll arrive right on the heels of any warning.'

'Risky,' Jaibo winced. 'Will the Heir go along?'

'No choice, and he and I got . . . friendly. A sensible lad, and he's madder at the ones close to him than at us, betrayal hurts worse than open enmity.' She looked up to see the others of the band gathering, unease in their eyes.

'Gather, children,' she said, using the classic Illizbuah street storyteller's cry. Levering herself erect she rubbed at her neck, thanking Zailo Protector the blow had not landed square: that would have snapped the bone. Suddenly she laughed, with mocking good humour. 'Gather and hear how each and every one of you is going to save his ass.'

Deevhla ghosted up to where the warband waited in the woods outside Raisak Staiun.

'Like you called it, warchief,' she said mushily through bruised lips. 'Bodies and blackcoats at all the gates. More around the tower, an' I'd say there's holdouts there. Nice neat job, Black Ravens couldn't 've done better.'

Shkai'ra considered a moment, looking up to where moonlight filtered through the cathedral stillness of the great trees. The scent of leafmould came from the forest floor, and jasmine from beyond the walls that bulked black ahead. This was no time for stealth; only she and Deevhla had the skill to play hide-and-seek with the Adders in the dark.

'Anybody sight you?' she asked.

'Devils, maybe. Even blackcoat Fehinnans breathe too loud. Lowlanders,' she said with contempt.

Shkai'ra began to shape the air with her hands. 'There aren't too many Adders here – more than us but they rely on speed and darkness, mostly. Not equipped or trained for a stand-up fight . . . and the garrison aren't all dead yet. I'll punch through to the central shrine; Jaibo, you hit the ones holding the barracks and follow behind to stop the ones on the walls from falling on my rear.' She turned her palms up in a curious curled-finger gesture. 'Keep it simple. Zaik Godlord send the victory.'

'Or the Sun herself,' Jaibo said with a tight grin. 'No point in waiting.'

The Adders at the barrack's gate were formed up when the attack hit. It did no good; blowguns and knives were not much use against warriors unsurprised and in full armour, and the crossbows reaped among the cloth-clad assassins. Then Jaibo led his detachment forward shield-to-shield. This was the sort of fighting he liked, fighting the way the drillmasters had taught it in The Bounding Marshcats Advancing Reckless against the Foe, Protected by the Glorious Light, known to other regiments as the Bouncing Kitties.

Left foot forward *smash* with the shieldboss stab-stab-stab *stamp* smash with the shieldboss –. He hunched his shoulders and drove his shortsword up into the belly of an Adder who was trying something fancy with a spiked ball on the end of a chain, the low-angled regulation gutting thrust, and found himself looking over her body at a startled Guard trooper: the garrison holdouts had sallied.

'Attention!' he screamed, the parade-ground bark of the professional *aykukah* he had been. 'Right, there's work to do. Fall in with these irregulars, and head for the Shrine!' There was no time for explanations. And a leaderless group would follow the voice of authority by conditioned reflex. The Adder thrashed at his feet, trying to stuff the intestines back into her stomach. He swung his short, heavy blade in an arc that connected with the back of her head, as much to stop the shrieking as to kill. Then his redoubled force pounded off into the night at a trot.

The assassins at the entrance to the Shrine died hard and quickly. Dieter had been the only heavy-armed fighter with them, and one glance at the situation had sent him into a prudent professional's retreat. There was a brief murderous scrimmage before the tall brassbound doors; hooves scrabbling on marble, long cavalry swords flickering in moonlight, clashing on the Adders' knives; shouts and the tearing scream of a wounded horse echoing off walls and pillars; the sudden gruesome popping crunch of a skull when a hoof came down on it. The fight ended and there was an eyeblink of silence before a horse went over slowly with a clatter of gear. Mounts were bigger targets than riders, and wore less armour, but it took poison longer to work through that bulk.

Shkai'ra bared her teeth with carnivore glee and urged her mount forward to the doors. 'Gaaaaiiiiii, *up*!' she called, urging the animal with hands and knees. Rearing, it crashed forefeet against portals built for show rather than strength. On the third thunderblow they parted, booming back against the interior walls. Sickly-sweet incense gusted out from the high-ceilinged corridor.

The others hesitated at riding into an enclosed space, but Shkai'ra had a Kommanza's reflex, never to walk where she could ride at all. Spurring, she bore down at the knot of Adders who stood shock-still at the other end of the long hall. Incredulous, they were still trying to accept the sight when her mount finished a series of great slithering bounds over the slick stone. Its hooves filled the space between walls with a roaring clatter of echoes: then it was among them, savaging with teeth and killing feet, weight alone a terrible weapon in cramped quarters with no room to dodge.

'*Eeeeeeeeee* – ' Shkai'ra keened and chopped, left, right, felt the heavy sabre chop home and drew the cut. In moments half a dozen were down, bleeding out their lives on the granite flags. Her followers arrived to complete the work.

The next door was thick, massive squared timbers, but it was barred on her side, meant to keep escapees in. She shot back the bolt from the saddle, sheathed her blade and pushed back the leaves. They swung inward with only a whisper of displaced air. Across the circular chamber the wizard stood triumphant at the entrance to the inner shrine, while the Fehinnan aristocrats waited motionless and impotent.

'My purpose is achieved!' Bashuln cried.

'I think not,' Shkai'ra called out: the wheelbow leaped into her hands. 'Fh'aaikaz ah-izzo to-a puz'ha,' she said slowly, in the tongue of the Zekz Kommanz: 'I lift against you the Bow of Truth.'

The shaft slammed into his side just below the ribs, a wet thump audible under the great bass throb of the bow. Shock threw the magus back against the bronze doors, doubled over as the broadhead shaft drove through liver and spleen to grind home in the pelvis.

Shkai'ra locked eyes with the leader of the Adders: that was one kill that would attract too many avengers. Jahlini thought, considered the dying wizard and the long bright arrowhead pointing at her stomach, and decided. 'Out!' she called. The bow followed the last of them out the door.

The audience murmured. 'Gaaimuns!' Shkai'ra called. Her

head indicated the rest of the mounted party, and Aygah in
their midst.

Ignoring the startled intake of breath, with a single glance
of vindictive satisfaction at the spot where Bashuln lay
making the animal noises of slow dying, Aygah stepped
over the line of fallen priests and into the sanctum. He
lifted the chased silver cup and drank in full view of the
assembly.

For long moments there was nothing. Then the goblet fell
from his fingers; the pupils of his eyes grew to enormous pits
of darkness, staring sightlessly at some infinity beyond the
walls. His face writhed, and he gave a single shrill scream.
Staggering, he called out, in a language two millennia dead,
on a god that even the legends had forgotten.

'Jesus Christ, what the fuck is happening – !'

Shkai'ra felt an unfamiliar sensation. It took her a moment
to realize that the hair was trying to stand up along her spine
under her gambeson. Unthinking, her sword hand made the
sign against witchcraft.

The new Sun-on-Earth, who had been Aygah, looked
around and ran a questioning hand down his own arm.
'A male this time,' he muttered. Bending to touch the priest
curled into a fetal ball at his feet, he continued: 'Talk about
a bad trip!'

He looked up at Shkai'ra and smiled.

'Ah, I remember you,' he said. She nodded, keeping a tight
grip on her bow. Steel was the best counter to magic, the
godsayings held: scant comfort here. What had been Aygah
chuckled, and walked forward to grip her bridle with fluid,
inhuman grace.

'You wouldn't know what I was talking about if I mentioned "RNA" or "filterable virus" or "memory transfer",
would you?'

'I'm a fighter, not a shaman, Mighty One,' she said. 'But
you wouldn't be here, but for me.'

'Perhaps. Or perhaps that old fool might have found more
in his drink than he expected. So, what with one thing and
another, we'll say neither of us has a debt. Perhaps you'd
better leave.'

Sweating under her armour, Shkai'ra carefully backed her
horse toward the corridor, ignoring Fehinna's new god-king

as he began tonguelashing the assembled nobility. The smell of blood and incense and wizardry sickened her: she longed for the open and the cleanness of the night air. Wheeling swiftly, she heeled her mount into a trot and rode into darkness.

Mellow afternoon sunlight glanced from the awning above their heads as Jaibo mopped up the last of a serving of the Weary Wayfarer's famous seafood stew. Pushing the heel of cornbread into his mouth he asked:

'Four hundred silvers left. Not a great fortune, but more than a pig's fart . . . What'r' we going to do with it?'

Shkai'ra leaned back and sipped at her wine, a far-away expression in her eyes as they gazed absently at two birds squabbling in a potted dwarf apple tree. The sea breeze cuffed at her hair, whipping strands around the narrow face.

'Well, we won't buy a farm, or put it out with a shipping firm.' Jaibo felt a sudden thrill of alarm. 'No, I've figured out a way to turn it into real money, and since we'd better leave the country for a while anyway . . .'

He groaned and buried his face in his hands.

JUST A VISITOR AT TWILIGHT

Charles Wagner

Charles Wagner has written for a wide range of fiction and comic markets, in addition to creating and writing adaptations for Clive Barker's Tapping the Vein *(an illustrated series derived from the* Books of Blood) *and scripting an entire issue of* The Twilight Zone *comic book. One of his short stories, 'Deadlights' (from the comic book* Twisted Tales), *was selected to appear in Karl Edward Wagner's* The Year's Best Horror Stories XIII, *and his fiction has also been published in* Night Cry *and* Dark Voices 3.

NEVER overlook the good properties of anger. As an emotion, it has uses above beyond fuelling racists, soldiers and football players. Anger, properly directed, can keep you alive when all else fails.

My mother probably understood this. Elderly and in failing health, anger could rouse her from her bed when nothing else (including my frequent visits) could.

Often I would visit her in her private room at Sunnyside Rest Home, and she would be sitting there – in the hallway, in the lobby, or on her bed – glaring. It didn't seem to matter much what was before her – television shows, the outside world, or the other ladies – whatever was in her view was to be glared at.

Surprisingly, she had a few friends. They took humour from her lack thereof. They would even agree with her in her complaints.

They knew it was all an act.

Mother had not always been this way. She once had been a quiet, pleasant, even pious person. But failing health changed that. When the illnesses ravaged her, made her suffer for years (she was actually the youngest patient in the

home), she finally lost the temper that I had always believed
to be infinite. She raged at her doctors, blaming their opera-
tions for her state. She complained about the caregivers,
accusing them of being thieves behind their backs.

But she was kind to me, and what little of our family that
visited her. We loved her, and couldn't stand to see her mood
twisted like it was.

But I understood. Her anger gave her an occupation. A
way to pass the time. It also gave her the strength to go on
– especially since she was not to the point where she would
die immediately.

So things trundled on. I continued my regular visits. The
home continued to offer care. Mother's friends continued to
smile at her off-remarks. And Mother just continued.

Then one day, while making my usual visit, I noticed
something.

The usual cast of ladies (who outnumbered the few male
residents more than three-to-one) was scattered in the hallways and lobby. The aroma of stale skin, faeces and vomit
hovered just below the disinfectant reek and aroma of per-
fumes and colognes from other eras. I made my usual walk
to Mother's wing. It was as I was passing Mr Rydell's room
that I noticed it. Inside, Mr Rydell lay on his bed, which faced
away from the door. There was a silver-haired elderly woman
in a dated, floral dress sitting beside him with her back to
me. They both faced out the window, and appeared to be
intently watching something outside. I didn't think much of
the scene until I realized that the woman wasn't Mrs Rydell.
At least from the back, this woman didn't resemble her, and
Mrs Rydell was nowhere to be seen.

It seemed odd, so I returned to the desk.

'Say, Wade,' I asked the young orderly, 'who's the lady
with Old Man Rydell?'

'Don't know. Probably a volunteer. We get people who
come in to read to the residents.'

'I see.'

I hadn't seen a book in the woman's hand, nor had I heard
any spoken words. Shrugging, I forgot about it and went to
my mother's room.

Mother gave no indication of being glad to see me, nor
did she sit up or ask to be taken out in her wheelchair. She

just sat in bed and spoke for a short while. Then she rested, gathering her energy for another round. I listened to her for half-an-hour total. Then Mother ran out of steam. I told her goodbye, remembering to look in Mr Rydell's room on the way out.

Nothing in his room seemed out of place. Mr Rydell still lay there, staring out the window.

His visitor was gone.

On the way out, I noticed Mrs Rydell sitting in the lobby talking with other ladies. She was wearing plain slacks and a blouse, confirming that the woman in the Rydell's room was not Mrs Rydell.

But what difference did any of this make? I forgot the matter for awhile.

A few days later; I returned.

Mom was in a more sullen mood than usual, but she pushed herself up as I entered. Her short frame was tiny in the bed, her face grey and beaten as it turned toward me. Her arm shook as it propped her up.

I went over and calmed her, easing her back to the mattress.

'I signed the papers,' she said. 'I did it. You won't have to worry . . .' Her voice trembled too much for her to continue.

'What, Mom?' I said, pulling up a chair. 'Why would I worry?'

I flicked off the TV with the remote which always sat on the tray-table by the bed.

'You don't have to worry about me rotting away on some infernal machine. I called the doctor. The manager of the home just left. I signed the Code Blue papers. If something happens, they'll just let me go.'

'I'm glad, Mom,' I said, a little clumsily, wondering what I meant. Glad she was going to hasten her death, or glad she was doing something she wanted to do?

Tears welled up in her eyes. They magnified the pupils, making them look wild with fear and loathing.

'You want me to die, don't you?!'

'No, Mom, I didn't mean it like that – '

'I'm afraid to die!'

'I know, Mom. I can't imagine what it must be like.'

I reached over, clumsily taking her shoulders, and gave her a hug. It seemed a long time since I had given her one. I almost cried, but fought it down for her sake.

I wondered about my own death. What would it be like to face this? The tears almost came again.

After awhile I calmed her, and got her talking about other things. Soon she was smiling and telling tales about one of the other, more cranky residents of the home. A nurse came in to join us. He knew what had been said between us, had seen our conversation forecast in the new orders on Mom's chart. He offered more kind words, then returned to his rounds.

I left after another minute. Mom did not seem unhappy to see me go. I had hastened the time, though, making up false pretences. But I didn't leave the home immediately. Instead, I meandered around the hall. Mom would not be coming out, so I knew I wouldn't be caught in my lie. As I walked, I thought about my life with Mother, and all the slow steps that had brought things to this pass.

Some of the staff offered words to me, which I acknowledged. But conversation wasn't expected, so I kept walking. As I passed Mother's hallway again, I noticed the lady I'd seen in Mr Rydell's room the other day. At least she seemed to be the same woman. From the back, I could only recognize the floral pattern dress she wore. Mrs Rydell was leaving the room as she entered. In fact, Mrs Rydell looked at the old woman, almost in sorrow, as they passed each other.

Again I was curious.

I approached Mrs Rydell.

She started as I came up to her.

'I didn't mean to surprise you, Mrs Rydell,' I said softly.

'I'm sorry, David,' she said. 'My nerves just aren't what they used to be.'

She gave a quick glance back to her room.

'How's your mother, David?' she asked, turning back to me.

Her nervousness was palpable.

'About the same,' I said. 'Say, Mrs Rydell, I was just wondering . . .'

She looked at me, her wide eyes intensified by the thick glasses she wore. 'Yes, David.'

'That lady – '

'Lady?' she said, too quickly.

'Yes, the one you were just speaking to.'

'*Oh*, that lady,' she said, sounding neither relieved nor calm. 'She's just a volunteer who comes around.'

'I see.' It was obvious I was bothering the poor woman. 'Well, nice talking to you, Mrs Rydell.'

'Bye now,' and she hastened off as rapidly as her crippled gait would allow.

I watched her stooped frame recede. I wondered if my mother had heard my voice. There was no one to see me at the desk down the hall, so I loitered outside of the Rydell's room. Inside, the visiting woman sat by Mr Rydell's bed, just as she had the previous time I saw her. Her back was to the door, and she appeared to be doing nothing, unless she and Mr Rydell were watching the wind blow outside the window.

Again it made no sense. The woman had nothing with her, and was reading no book. I was about to move off when there was a change.

The woman turned toward Mr Rydell. She reached out and touched a hand to his forehead. It stayed there, as if she was feeling for a fever. I watched, waiting for her to remove her hand, but she didn't.

After several long seconds – or could it have been a minute or more – I got nervous about being discovered and walked back to my mother's room. I peered inside.

Mother was asleep with the TV blaring. She probably hadn't heard my conversation with Mrs Rydell at all. I turned the volume down a little and left her again.

On the way out, I noticed that Mrs Rydell had rejoined her husband. He hardly seemed to have moved. She sat in the chair by his bed, staring at him.

The elderly visitor was nowhere to be seen.

Two days later, Mr Rydell was dead. The room where he had lived with his wife was empty and devoid of signs of recent habitation. The beds were made up with those saffron bedspreads popular with hospitals and state homes.

The walls lacked the obligatory pictures of loved ones. The few pieces of personal furniture were gone.

'Where is Mrs Rydell?' I asked the orderly.

'She's with her son's family for awhile,' she said. 'When she gets back, she'll probably move in with Mrs Greene.'

'She won't keep her room?'

'They usually don't if the spouse dies in it.'

'I see.'

The orderly looked into my eyes. 'Hey,' she said. 'Don't feel too bad. Your mom's doing okay. She took Mr Rydell's death quite well.'

'That's good,' I said, 'thanks.'

I left the orderly to her business and turned for my mother's room. At the door, I stopped. First I leaned in to check the situation. I smiled. Mom was sitting in a chair – the first time I'd seen her like that in some time.

She was dozing.

Deciding to give her a few more minutes of rest, I turned back to the hallway. For something to do, I walked back to the main nursing station. No one was there, so I leaned against the counter, listening to the talk show blaring on high volume in the lobby. Down the hall of the full-nursing wing, I saw a familiar figure emerge from a room.

It was the old lady, the one who had visited Mr Rydell.

As I watched, she turned on down the hall away from me and went into a second room. I walked on down that way and looked into the first room she had come out of.

Inside were a pair of living, wrinkled corpses. Tubes sprouted from their noses and from beneath the sheets on their beds. I couldn't tell if they were man or woman, or even if they were alive, save only for the click, ping and whoosh of machines.

Saddened, I looked away and started for the room which the volunteer lady was now visiting.

'Looking for someone?' asked a polite voice at my shoulder.

I turned around and saw a nurse.

'No, uh, my mother's a patient on the other wing.'

'I see,' she said, and went on about her business, not really caring if I was there or not.

After all, what harm could I do.

A few minutes later, I found Mother awake and ready for a visit. She seemed well, but her spirits were misplaced: she told me that Mr Rydell had indeed been lucky, and since she lived near him, her turn must surely be coming.

'I'm not afraid,' she said to me.

Not knowing what else to do, I took her hand.

'But, Mom – ' I began.

'I'm not afraid anymore. I'm tired of being in this – this – *death camp.*'

'Mom, have you told your doctors you feel this way?'

She looked shocked. 'Of course not. And don't you tell them either. The last thing I want is interference. Or a bunch of do-gooders sapping my resolve. I signed all the papers. No interference.'

'Whatever you say,' I mumbled.

Two days later I received an urgent phone call from the rest home. My mother was much worse, they said, and she asked to see me. Of course I left at once.

Upon arriving at the home I immediately went to the station to announce myself and learn the worst.

'How is she? What's happening? Will she die?' I asked in staccato succession.

'She's in pain. Been this way since dinner. I think she'll be okay come morning, though.'

'Her doctor?'

'She wouldn't let us call,' the man told me, and before I could protest he added, 'she did sign all the papers.'

'Of course,' I agreed, and headed down the hall.

Though I was in a hurry, each step down the hall seemed to take longer. Finally I was lingering outside her room.

The orderly appeared at my side.

'Shall I come in with you?' he whispered.

I shook my head.

'You can go on in,' he said, then went away.

I waited until he was gone. Bracing myself, I eased the door open and peered in.

To my shock, my mother was not alone. The lady – the one that had been called a volunteer – was in the room with her. She sat on a chair near the bed, dressed in the ghastly floral dress she wore each time I saw her.

Mother lay on the bed, scarcely acknowledging this company. From what I could see, she seemed to be asleep, her face looking up from the bed.

As I watched, the visitor reached out and laid the palm of one hand on my mother's forehead.

My mother made no sound or movement, but I could feel a mewling sound slip from my throat.

The woman stopped and drew back the hand.

'What are you doing there?' I managed to hiss.

The woman slowly turned toward me. For the first time, I saw her face.

It was lightly wrinkled, the skin almost white. But her eyes . . . that was what I noticed. The pupils were black and round and wide. She had no iris, no colour at all in either eye.

She made no answer, but only turned back to her charge – my mother.

I understood. Tears started from my eyes as I remembered the words my mother had said that day:

'No interference.'

As the visitor laid her hand back upon my mother's brow, I turned and closed the door and headed down the hall.

In the lobby, the day was surrendering to twilight.

AND MAKE ME WHOLE

Joel Lane

Joel Lane lives and works in Birmingham as a desk editor and freelance writer. He is the author of numerous horror tales, which have been published in Fantasy Tales, Best New Horror 3, *four volumes of* The Year's Best Horror Stories, Ambit, Skeleton Crew, Darklands *and* Darklands 2, *amongst many others. A number of his poems appeared in* Private Cities, *a three-poet anthology, whilst a selection of his verse won him the 1993 national poetry competition, the Eric Gregory Awards. Aside from fiction and poetry, he has also published critical articles on Ramsey Campbell, H.P. Lovecraft, Robert Aickman and Dr Seuss.*

IT was late on a Saturday night, in early spring. The two men got off the bus on the main road. This wasn't a district that James knew well, and the presence of his companion defamiliarized it. He tried to see it through the eyes of a resident. His perceptions were also affected by his recent experiences of looking for a flat. There seemed to be two kinds of run-down area in Birmingham: new and old. Close to the city centre, the industrial region had been redeveloped in a half-hearted way, little housing estates appearing like film sets against a background of motorways and factories. These estates were already deteriorating: the council were slow to repair the damage done by vandals, and tenancy of the flats was often a step away from vagrancy.

Further out in the suburbs, some of the formerly prosperous residential areas had undergone a rather alarming kind of recession. While property values in the approved suburbs had shot up, those in these areas, isolated from their neighbours, had actually declined. Generations of neglect had reduced the Victorian houses to awkward hulks, rented

out floor by floor, room by room. Landlords could collect property in bulk, while cutting costs on maintenance
and refurbishment. Poverty bred poverty: the more owner-
occupiers moved out, the more land passed into the hands
of property agents who found it easier to let than sell.

The area where Adrian lived was closer to the latter type
than the former. The main road was an outgrowth of the city;
but just off it, the suburban character of the district reasserted
itself. The houses were old, and impressive in their outlines.
But few of them showed any signs of recent attention. Many
had FOR SALE notices in their neglected front gardens; some
were derelict, wholly or in part, with windows smashed and
boards nailed across doorways. Adrian's house was in a
relatively well-populated road, with a church on the corner
and a primary school a little way uphill on the far side. Still,
the house could well have been one of those closed up on
itself. It had a steeply angled roof and porch; the front had
been painted black a long time before. The narrow windows
were smeared with dust, over whitish net curtains that were
obviously left shut. The window-frames were split and
warped. An overgrown privet hedge, interwoven with the
brambles and weeds it enclosed, walled off the front garden
from the street. But Adrian seemed unembarrassed by this
disorder, as he led James through the gate and opened the
front door. James wondered if he ever had visitors in the
daytime.

The house's interior was surprisingly domestic, by com-
parison. Adrian prepared some filtered coffee. They sat at the
living-room table, avoiding eye contact. James occupied himself with making a covert inventory of the room's contents.
Its appearance of disorder was due less to neglect than to the
sheer accumulation of things, gathered on shelves and little
tables, and on the floor: records, pictures, books, antiques,
stereo equipment. Another piece of the jigsaw fitted into
place. Adrian was a born collector. The kind of person
for whom useless possessions always took priority over
living space or decoration. You could see where attempts
to organise the collection into some kind of display had
been submerged in the mass and variety of new objects.
Competing for space on the same shelf were an assembly
of cigarette lighters, from the ornate to the most basic, and

another of brooches, including an unpainted iron butterfly whose wings were a delicate but hard lattice.

At the same time, James tried to weigh up the owner of these archives. It helped to have got Adrian on home ground, where he could not avoid being himself. First impressions were usually deceptive; people weren't the same in public and in private. This was their second meeting. The first had been in a club a few days before, and this evening they had gone to see a band perform in a pub on the far side of town. Music was one thing the had in common. James was an inexperienced vocalist who'd worked briefly with a group from the technical college. Adrian was all but a professional keyboard player and composer. His band, Silent Majority, had just produced a debut album. It hadn't sold well, but it was the kind of thing that would go on selling slowly for a long time.

James' impression of the album had been that its sound lacked consistency. The elements of the music – drums, keyboards, guitars, voice – didn't belong together in any intrinsic way. The singer, who should have been a focal point, was just another oblique element within the pattern. Adrian defended the group's approach: they weren't concerned with unity, he said, but with conflicts. Harmony could be provoked in the listener, but it couldn't be taken for granted. The two had spent most of their time together discussing music. So far, they hadn't talked about much else.

Aware that Adrian was doing the same to him, James tried to read the face across the table. It was sharply featured and intense, the eyes underlined by dark creases that gave him a look of perpetual anger. He was twenty-three, a year older than James; but the seriousness in his expression made him seem older than that. And yet, James thought for the first time, there was a child's face hiding somewhere behind the hard outlines. You could see it in the eyes themselves, how wide open and receptive to the world they were; and in the way the mouth flickered between a smile and a protest. As though he were saying to the world, *do your worst*; but to each individual in it, *don't hurt me*. What face did Adrian have in the dark? James had the feeling of being drawn into the other's thoughts. For an uneasy moment, it seemed that he was falling while everything around him remained still.

'Are you wondering about this place?' Adrian said. 'It used to belong to my mother. I lived here till I was sixteen, then moved out. Moved back in when my mother died, a couple of years ago. Still don't understand why. It's trapped me in the past, hasn't it? But still, it's cheap, and I'd probably never sell it. So I'm stuck here, basically. How's your search for a home going; any luck?'

James thought back over the past week. 'Don't know. It doesn't look too good. I might still be renting a room this time next year. The only properties I could afford really aren't worth having. Unless I want to end up like you, with a place I can't sell. All the things I've seen are either tiny apartments near the city or old houses in areas like this. Or else they're places in such a desperate state of repair they've cut down the asking price. Like the last place I saw, a maisonette in Hockley. Only a short walk from the city. It was on this rather unhealthy housing estate. Every flat in the block seemed to be for sale. The estate agent said it was because they'd originally been let to tenants who'd fallen behind with the payments and got evicted. Now the owners had repossessed all these flats and maisonettes and were trying to sell them off cheap. The one I saw was derelict. The former occupants had taken out their frustration slightly on the building. There were smashed windows, doors unhinged, messages carved in the walls . . . You'd have to replaster and redecorate the whole place to make it habitable. And nobody who could afford that would move there anyway.'

Adrian nodded. 'Sounds like the kind of place that would only go for rent. And be taken up *by* rent, if you get my meaning. It's that kind of area. Right next to the city, so you've got money on your doorstep. But nothing around you except alleys and subways and multi-storey car parks. Imagine being young and unemployed and living there. What would *you* do? Should have stayed there. At least you'd never be lonely.' He smiled. 'No, I should go for a little flat somewhere. If it's too small, you can always sell it again. Don't buy an old house, it's not worth all the hassle. Maintenance, repair, redecoration. I wouldn't live here if I hadn't inherited it. I hate the place.'

'Why not move?'

Adrian shrugged. 'I will, soon enough. But I feel like . . .

at the moment, I'm using the house for something. I grew up
here. Moved out as early as I could. And then I came back. I
suppose I'm taking revenge on the house. Or fighting a war
against my childhood. Doing everything I couldn't do when
my mother was here.' He paused, lost in thought; then went
on, choosing his words carefully. 'There's more to it than
that. This house is full of hiding places. I'm filling it up with
things that remind me of the past. Or that express things in
myself that were never realized. When I finally move out I
want to be clean and whole. I want this house to keep all
the ugly and crippled parts of myself. But to do that, I need
first to bring them out of hiding.' He was staring into the
table, his expression a mixture of sadness and excitement. 'It
doesn't make sense yet. Does it? It will eventually, though.
If you want to know what I'm really like, look at the house.
Or if you'd rather leave, go ahead.' He smiled again. James
realised that he was being challenged, and kept his eyes level
with the other's, saying nothing.

There was a pause, during which some obscure link
was forged. James wondered what lay ahead. A swarm
of ill-defined questions and warnings filled his mind; he
decided to let Adrian do the talking, for now. His inner
fidgeting combed out three dangers from the swarm. The
first was a familiar threat, against which he had learned
to be on guard. The best defence against a hungry ego
was to be inarticulate. It was a matter of keeping one's
discursive legs crossed. The second was half in darkness,
and provoked his curiosity. What had turned Adrian inward
on himself in this way? Whatever it was, it made him seem
both alien and real. Adrian's loneliness was a fierce vacancy
that shadowed his expressions, facial or verbal. For James,
loneliness was a relative thing: a pressure that accumulated
gradually, and took as long to dissipate. A love affair reduced
it by degrees, clearing a space and restoring a perspective.
For Adrian, it seemed, loneliness was absolute. And James
suspected that, for him, it was unalterable. Was that why
he had returned to the house: to break down a door long
ago sealed in his mind?

The third danger was entirely hidden from view. James
felt, without being able to find words for it, that something
was badly wrong with Adrian. If he became too involved

without knowing what the something was, then it would
touch him without his knowledge or consent. But in the
meantime, he had no idea what kind of clues he was looking
for. This fear was too difficult to examine, and he allowed it to
filter downward through his thoughts and be ignored. Much
later, when it was all over, he would realize how the same
fear had controlled his actions.

Adrian crossed the room to the stereo. 'Silence makes me
nervous. Let's have some music.' Hazel O'Connor's discord-
ant voice limped from the speakers, against a background of
flat piano chords. Adrian turned the volume higher. 'Don't
worry about the neighbours. They're used to it by now.'
The additional power brought out all of the conflict and
suppressed hysteria in the singer's voice. She seemed to
be crying from a still and isolated place, beyond human
contact. James noticed a similarity to the effect of the Silent
Majority album; looking at the stereo, he realized what it
was. A simple trick. Adrian had turned up the bass and
treble to maximum while cutting out the centre frequencies.
The effect was to preserve the frail edge of the voice and
the hard pulsing of the drums, while silencing everything in
between. No wonder that Hazel O'Connor seemed to flicker
between elation and despair: *It's getting kind of late now, I
wonder if you'll stay now – stay now – stay now – Or will you
just politely say goodnight?* Adrian was staring at him. James
took the hint, and smiled in mock shyness. Inwardly, he was
laughing: hard, with a bitterness that he couldn't explain.

'I've always been obsessed with music,' Adrian said. 'Ever
since I was a child. Not playing it, really; just listening to it.
I like distorting sound. Getting notes so low they make the
walls shudder, or so high they can break glass. This is the
fifth pair of speakers I've had for this stereo. I put too much
bass through it, it just blows the speakers – turning sound
into energy . . . I've got an idea about analysing sound. Like
a Fourier pattern, you know? All the components separated
out. You can do that in your head with most music, because
the elements belong to different sources. But a voice is harder
to disintegrate. Because it's something human, you know?
It's more unified. Belongs to one person . . . Would you sing
for me?' The question caught James off balance; he shrugged.
Adrian's mind seemed to work by means of what a friend of

his, a psychiatric nurse, had called knight's-move thinking. Two steps forward and one step sideways.

Hazel O'Connor was still stumbling through the torment of hope. *Take up your eyes, bare your soul, Gather me to you and make me whole . . .* In that moment, James decided he would rather accept than understand, at least for the time being; he needed relief and rest. The night that dissolved instead of resolving. Adrian stepped out into the hall. 'Have a look in here.' The front room was filled with musical instruments: an electronic keyboard on one side; an old piano on the other; brass and woodwind instruments displayed in variously-sized cases around the room. Adrian lifted a folk guitar from the corner by the doorway and tuned it carefully.

The walls and mantelpiece, as well as the low windowsills, were decorated with some of the oddest items that James had yet seen in the house. A grey child's head, inexpertly carved in clay, with pale blue marbles for eyes. Vivid and obviously childish paintings of monstrous figures, against backgrounds which separated the four elements. Photographs of a woman, changing in age from about seventeen to about fifty; the oldest prints were of superior quality, an intense black on white, matt where the recent prints were glossy. Smaller photographs of a boy who, as the sequence progressed, became Adrian. It was like seeing the same image in different stages of resolution.

The room drew James out of himself; he was hardly aware of the other man's presence, until Adrian placed the guitar in his hands. 'Would you sing for me? Please. I like your voice.' James mentally flicked through a file of songsheets. None of his own songs felt appropriate to a solo performance in a strange house. He strummed the guitar, his awkwardness lending an aggressive precision to the notes. His mind made a vicious-seeming connection between the low opening chords, the unreal atmosphere of this room, and his blurred doubts about Adrian. The image of the iron butterfly stamped itself across his view. He began singing one of the Jam's lyrics, something he was sure Adrian knew.

So you've finally got what you wanted . . . He stepped back, as near to the middle of the room as the clutter of objects would let him; he stared hard at Adrian, framing him in the doorway, against the unlit hall. Adrian glanced down and then sideways, avoiding the other's gaze, stepping backward; but there was only darkness around him. James moved into the doorway and let his shadow pin Adrian to the wall. *And I don't feel any sorrow, Towards the kings and queens of the butterfly collectors*. He sang these words very close to the other's face, letting proximity make his voice quieter but no less hard. At the last moment, James turned aside, facing down the hall towards the front door. He moved forward. Adrian stepped into his path, first blocking and then holding him. James felt his questions short-circuited by contact; he wondered which of them was the collector.

Not being alone was always worth something. James lay alert for much of the night, listening to the house. He imagined its presence around them, heavy and silent. It seemed possible to him that tonight had effected some crucial change in Adrian, or in the house itself. They had both been uneasy: unsure of their roles, keen to withdraw into the privacy of sleep. The childish aspect of Adrian had seemed clearer than ever, in the unfinished look of his face and body in the half-light, and in the way that he was both demanding and passive. Before falling asleep, Adrian gripped James by the throat; not tightly enough to be threatening. 'I want your voice,' he whispered. James woke up in a room swarming with silver-grey dust, and thought that it had indeed been transformed. But it was only the effect of dawn, filtered through the net curtains. In a while, the air had clarified, and the room looked much the same as it had by night.

A few months later, James was in Nottingham, working for a printer. It was similar to his former job; the only difference was in location, which had also been his incentive for taking it. He had been there for several weeks, living in a rented flat, when he heard the news of Adrian's breakdown. It came from Derek, the drummer with Silent Majority; Adrian had evidently given him James' new telephone number. Derek sounded as though he held James to blame for what had happened. All he knew was the name and address of the hospital, and that Adrian might not be out for some time yet. 'Why did you leave him to himself like that?' he asked resentfully. James held back the truthful answer; under the circumstances it would have been tactless. He decided to go back at the weekend and visit Adrian in hospital. In the event, it was another fortnight before he could make himself pack an overnight bag and catch the train to Birmingham.

In the intervening phase, James picked over the fragments of his recent experiences, searching for clues. He had moved into Adrian's house and stayed for two or three months, until Adrian's instability and his own growing unease had fractured their affair. The questions which had stirred at the back of James' mind on that first evening had never been answered. Perhaps James was not clever enough to resolve them; more likely, he didn't care enough. Because concern was often the key to the most obscure of people: it enabled you to step into their skin and speak with their voice. At the back of all James' anger, all of his inward protests that Adrian was a head case and a bloody waste of time, there was a whisper of guilt. James knew that he had begun by tolerating instead of understanding; and that tolerance had become the foundation-stone for the wall of rejection which he had built during their time together. In the end, walking away had felt like the fulfilment of a contract drawn up on the first night.

Adrian's story had only come together in bits and pieces, like a mosaic. There was the time when he had sat in the front room for a whole evening, hardly speaking. Then at midnight he had started hunting through drawers full of unsorted papers. James had gone to bed; a couple of hours later, he had come back down to see what was the matter. Adrian pushed a folder into his hands. 'Have a look at that. You know what it is?' Squatting on the floor in a blotched and tattered dressing-gown, surrounded by heaps of paper, Adrian looked like a desperate teenager on the night before an exam. The folder contained various photocopied documents and bank statements. James stared at them for some time before realising that they dealt with the divorce of Adrian's parents and his father's maintenance payments to his mother. They were more than a decade old.

'That's my life,' Adrian said, 'a few badly-photocopied sheets of paper. That's why my mother kept me. Why I lived here. Because I was worth the cheque every month. I'd have gone into care otherwise. And that's what I was to my father: a crumb flaked off his bank account once a month.' Adrian stared up at James without appearing to recognize him; hatred was lodged in the darkness of his eyes and mouth. 'There's one other reason why my mother kept me. So she could punish me for being my father's son. I hated every day of my life until I left home. That was on my sixteenth birthday. Five years later, my mother died of a heart attack. Only reason I went to the funeral was so I could know where she was buried. So that I'd know where to bring the radio and start dancing. One thing I couldn't understand. Why she'd left me the house. She'd never given me anything before.' He lapsed into silence. James stood until cramp forced him to move; and he was about to go back up to bed when Adrian continued: 'I know why, now. She knew I'd be stupid enough to come back. To lock myself up with the past. That way, she could go on hurting me.'

James dropped the folder to the floor. 'Old papers, love. That's not your life any more. Neither is this house. Why don't you pull yourself together, just a bit?' He gripped Adrian's shoulders and lifted him, surprised by how heavy he seemed. Like something inert. As Adrian stumbled up the stairs behind him, James had a sudden fantasy of going up a second flight, past the upper floor and out onto the roof, where they might be able to sleep in peace. The stars were too far away to give back even partial echoes. *You're only tormenting yourself, you know.* Irritation and fear made him incapable of saying it out loud.

There was the time when James tasted something metallic in Adrian's mouth, a taste that reminded him of garages and rush hour traffic. Adrian looked at him sarcastically, but said nothing. His lips were dry and flaky. A day went by before James would kiss him again. Eventually they talked about it. Adrian was defensive. 'Lighter fuel's cheaper than alcohol, isn't it? Let alone dope. I've almost given it up now anyway. It made me feel like I was drowning. Literally, I mean it was damaging my lungs. I couldn't run without choking. But also in my mind. It dissolves your sense of identity. So does sex, if you think about it. You can use other people to help you forget yourself. Just dissolve in someone else. But then you get up in the morning, and what does the mirror show you? A face with no skin.

'Don't worry, it's the way I've always been. Getting high on solvent doesn't change me. It just makes me happier with myself. I started at twelve. That was when I knew my mother hated me. At the time I didn't blame her, I thought everyone was bound to hate me. Do you know what it's like to feel split up like that, eh? To not even have yourself to talk to? I was dehumanized like that at home. It's all a matter of dissolving, isn't it? Like an embryo in a jar. The way I keep going back into the past, when I hate the past so much.'

It wasn't really that Adrian lived in the past. Rather, the past seemed to live in him. James couldn't understand how it worked; but he thought of the Hydra, which grew two new heads for each one that was cut off. The more damage, the more heads, more voices, more hunger. Adrian seemed to be driven by a limitless need for everything that was human. And whatever he took in, he rejected just as quickly. The photographs bore out Adrian's story that, as a child, he'd been grossly overweight. At twelve, he had begun starving himself; he'd lost five stone in a few months. Through his teens, he'd alternated between fasting and gorging, sometimes drinking soapy water to make himself vomit. His eating patterns were still irregular. But it was really in deeper and less physical ways that the ritual persisted. Need and denial.

There were all the times when Adrian took James around the local area. He had a passion for window shopping; what he collected in his mind exceeded his actual possessions many times over. Sound equipment, furniture, clothes, pictures, antiques of all kinds . . . the range of Adrian's knowledge was incredible, even if it had the erratic quality of what was self-taught. 'I used to buy a lot of really new things. When I was young. I had nice clothes, a decent stereo, all that. It's only recently I've started buying all this old crap. Somehow it's taken over.' His eye for the unusual detail made him a disconcerting companion. He led James through all of the abandoned places nearby: the alleys, railway bridges, canals, bits of wasteground. All the time, pointing out and commenting. On the history of something left for weather and vandalism to destroy. On the minor wildlife that improvised a living there. On the characters of silent and enclosed people who passed by with carrier bags or speculative glances.

'When I was fourteen or fifteen I spent half my time walking round here. It got me out the house. I used to like sitting on the walls outside public toilets, watching everyone go in and out. After a while, you learned to spot all the types. Rent, punters, police. I never used to do anything, just watch. And talk to people. They can't arrest you if that's all you do. I still go, but it's just window shopping.' Passages of Adrian's uneven chatter passed through James' mind as the train neared New Street Station. The open view led him to scan his memory at random, before fixing on a key episode. It might explain so much that was merely typical.

A few days before James left, the two of them were walking through the park. Adrian was in one of his agitated moods: he was talking fiercely and laughing, not really concerned whether James was listening or not. 'Real dump, my school was. None of the teachers knew how to control a class. You'd get fights going on in the lessons and the teacher wouldn't do anything. Best thing was, one day we were sitting in a history lesson and someone out in the playground threw a brick through the window. You should have seen the teacher's face. Not many of them drove into school, either. They'd park down the road, hoping nobody would notice. But they still got tyres slashed, windscreens shattered, paint taken off with solvents.' It was a chilly night in April. The footpath leading diagonally across the park was lit by sodium lamps; in their yellow light, the falling sleet was like the tails of rockets in a firework display. James felt his senses dominated by the grainy intensity of the scene. His hands were shaking; he pushed them into his coat pockets. The mention of solvents reminded him of what Adrian had said before, about mirrors and dissolving.

That was how James felt at that moment. As though his face were flaking away into the sleet. An unexpected rush of sympathy for Adrian made him reach out and grasp the other's hand. At the top of the park, a bench faced downhill across the flowerbeds, to the hospital on the far side of the road. The beds were planted with bulbs: daffodils, crocuses, hyacinths. The flowers had the hard delicacy of things sculpted in wax. The bench was crusted with melting sleet, but the couple sat down anyway. 'This is my favourite view,' Adrian said quietly. 'I've been coming here since I was a child. It's all just the same. Nothing ever changes.' The muscles in his face were rigid, and his eyes blinked repeatedly. James gripped his shoulder; it was like touching a dead body.

By this time, of course, they both knew that James was leaving. He had the new job and accommodation already sorted out. But he and Adrian had not talked much about the reasons why. Two months later that was still true: neither had felt the need to spell out what they both understood. Which was that Adrian was beyond reach; or, alternatively, that James lacked the will to try. It was a matter of self-preservation: James could already feel how dealing with the cracks in Adrian's character had made him divided within himself. That evening in the park, he could only protect his sanity by becoming indifferent. He had once thought that Adrian's misery made him more real; but in crisis, it seemed to cancel him out. James had anticipated the chance to be with Adrian at a time like this. Now that he had it, his being there made no difference at all. 'I'm losing it,' Adrian whispered. 'Everything's going away from me.' There was no resolution. Adrian got up unsteadily, and they walked back home together. He seemed to be in shock, though whatever had hit him was hidden. James had the feeling that, if he were not guided home, Adrian would stumble like a blind man into the traffic.

The train passed through the outer edge of Birmingham, and the view closed in. Struggling through New Street Station in the Saturday rush-hour crowd was worse than James remembered. Halfway down the ramp to New Street, he stopped and shut his eyes. *Leave me alone, all of you. Let go of me.* But he only really had one person in mind. By the time the bus reached Adrian's neighbourhood, it was getting dark. James decided to try the house, and then to walk on to the hospital, which wasn't far away. With a shock of unease, he asked himself if it was the same hospital that they had seen across the road from the park. He checked the address that Derek had given him in the A–Z street atlas; it was.

The black house seemed to have deteriorated further, like a bad memory that became more abstract with time. But a light was on in the front room, behind the clotted net curtains. James rang twice, then knocked on the door with his fist. He was about to go away when a figure stopped at the gate, behind him. Adrian walked up to the doorstep, nodded without speaking, and unlocked the door. Inside, they stood in the hall as though neither of them had been inside the house before. Adrian looked pale and tired. 'They shut me up,' he said. 'Then they let me out.' His eyes seemed to be looking inward. The two men embraced in the dim hallway. Adrian drew back and gestured toward the living-room. 'Someone found me in the street. You'll understand, when you see what I did. But nobody else will. They think I was just trying to kill myself.'

Somebody had tried to clean the walls and floor, but the bloodstains were still visible. 'It's in all the rooms,' Adrian said. 'I thought it was going to change everything. But nothing's any different. Just redecoration, eh?' James gripped Adrian's hands and turned them palm upward. The wrists were crossed by raw-looking streaks of scar tissue. He dropped the hands as though they were dead. The patches of blood remained on the stairs and in the front room, though attempts had been made to scrub them off there as well. A faint odour of bleach thinned the air. Adrian remained standing in the hall, looking at nothing in particular. James went into the living-room and sat at the table. After a few minutes, Adrian sat down opposite him. There was a feeling of truth in their silence, as though it were the basis of all the words the two had used. Two monologues, one spoken and one in thought; neither belonging to any dialogue.

Eventually, when it was completely dark outside, Adrian asked: 'Where are you staying?'

James shrugged. 'Don't know.'

'Do you want to stay here tonight? Just to sleep, I mean. I'd like to talk to you, but I'm too tired now.' His forearms on the table were tense under the weight of his shoulders. Seen against the curtains, his face was a sketch; it carried its own shadow within it.

'Okay.' James felt tired as well. The tension that had been gathering in him for days ebbed into the wood of the table and floor. As the blood must have done. He was unable to picture the manic ritual that the other must have attempted. If he stayed the night, there was a danger that he might start to understand how it had been. He remembered how, that first morning in the bedroom upstairs, the air had appeared to swarm with grains of light. Now this room was becoming grainy in the same way, except that the bits were dark. Like fragments of carbon in the heat-haze above a bonfire. Or particles moving through plasma on a microscope slide. Their background was a reddish fluid that darkened slowly, dissolving Adrian's still head and shoulders from view.

'My God.' James shook his head; the stiffness in his neck suggested that he had been asleep for some time. Adrian was slumped over the table, his face hidden in his arms. James stood up, and a blind rush of vertigo pushed him back into the chair. This was something like Adrian must have experienced in hospital. *You bastard. Do you think you'll get my sympathy that way?* Fighting off numbness, he got to his feet. His eyelids beat against the light. 'Adrian? Wake up.' The other lifted his head and stared in fear. 'Come on, let's go upstairs.' What had he been thinking about? It made no sense to believe that Adrian could touch his mind. James led the way up the stairs, Adrian following each of his movements at close range. When James sidestepped what could have been a bloodstain in the hallway, Adrian did the same.

In the bedroom, James was afraid to switch on the light. Adrian felt thin and fragile in his arms: a metallic angel. The bed was a more perfect sink for vitality than the table had been. It seemed to make him insubstantial. Beside him, Adrian was asleep almost at once.

James woke twice during the night. The first time, the complete darkness unnerved him. He was unsure where his own body ended and the room began. Cautiously, he reached out and touched Adrian's face, which was turned toward him on the pillow. The cheek and upper lip were wet. Intolerable images flared up in James' mind. He switched on the bedside lamp. Adrian remained fast asleep; he was breathing slowly and deeply. And he was crying. The tears drained from his eyes like plasma, across his face and into the pillow. James didn't know what to do, and the sight troubled him. He switched out the light and went back to sleep. Much later, he would come to believe that those few moments had been his opportunity. For what, he would never know.

The second time, it was still dark. James realized that his left arm had crossed Adrian's side of the bed without touching anything. He held his breath and listened; no sound. He reached across to the lamp. Its light showed up a faded rusty patch low on the wall opposite. Where had Adrian gone? At once, an image came into his mind: the white building the two had seen from the park, its windows screens of light against the darkness, its porch light holding up a thumbprint of sleet. *They shut me up.* James pushed himself onto his knees; the air was cold against his skin. Shivering, he stepped onto the floor.

Sounds from downstairs jerked him back to common sense. Adrian was playing something on the stereo. It sounded as though he was going from one radio station to another, getting more static than anything else. Hints of voices and instruments stumbled towards clarity and were lost again. James went down the stairs cautiously; his nakedness made him feel incomplete. 'Adrian?' No light was on downstairs, but he could see a pale flickering in the doorway to the living-room: the TV set on the blink. Among the confusion of partial voices, he thought he could catch Hazel O'Connor singing 'Will You'. But that could be association: Adrian had played it over and over again during their time together. *Take up your eyes, bare your soul, Gather me to you and make me whole* . . . It was so like Adrian to sit on his own in the dark and listen to something like that. Well, the drama had no principal actor now. James felt a mixture of anger and guilt pressing from within his chest, leaving him no air to breathe.

The light in the living-room was faintly discoloured, making the wallpaper look something like flesh. It was concentrated in a far corner, opposite the window, where somebody was crouching to hide from it. The figure was naked, but it wasn't Adrian. He or she was a child, or perhaps a midget. Its hands, which were pressed against the wall, seemed enormous. James stepped forward, then stopped. He had realized two things at once. One was that the creature was not hiding from the light; it was giving off the light. The other was that it was trying to turn round and face him, but was unable to detach its giant hands from the wall's surface. Its limbs were not very strong, James could see. Its body looked as though it had once been fat, but had been starved, so that the skin was in flaps. James stared in curiosity and disgust, then retreated. In the front room, Adrian's music room, there was a similar flickering of grey light.

Inside, he could see two more children. One was sitting on the mantelpiece, staring back at James with eyes that were intensely blue, very beautiful, and nearly as big as light-bulbs. Its arms and legs were crumpled like empty sleeves in a shirt before ironing. The other child was trying to climb out of the piano, whose wires appeared to penetrate its body. Its face, turned upward, was nearly all mouth; a stream of something like ectoplasm drifted out of it and trailed downward to the floor. James smiled. The cold was making his limbs shake, and his eyes stung until he wished he could cry. In the hallway, another spoilt figure was stuck to the inner door. He turned away from it and began climbing the stairs, his arms wrapped across his chest for warmth. Against the murmur of all the wordless voices, he could hear his own teeth chattering.

There were more figures in the bathroom; the other bedroom, nearly filled as it was with Adrian's possessions; the closet; the loft. The more he saw, the more there was to see. A family of deformed and injured children. James was shaking uncontrollably, both with the intense cold and with a violent feeling of rage. As he staggered from room to room, from one abortive ghost to another, he wanted to confront each in turn with the same bitter question. *What are you like?*

THE LAST CHILD OF MASFERIGON

Darrell Schweitzer and
John Gregory Betancourt

Darrell Schweitzer is the author of a number of fantasy novels, including The Shattered Goddess *and* Conan the Deliverer. *He has been the editor of the revived* Weird Tales *for several years, and his own stories have been published in* Fantasy Tales, Amazing, Fantastic, Whispers, Twilight Zone, Cemetary Dance, Heirs of Cthulhu *and others. His collections include* We Are All Legends *and* Tom O'Bedlam's Night Out. *He was a finalist in the short story category of the 1992 World Fantasy Awards, and won jointly with George Scithers for* Weird Tales *the same year.* John Gregory Betancourt *is one of the former editors of the revived* Weird Tales *magazine, senior editor at Byron Preiss Visual Productions, and owner of his own small press imprint, the World Fantasy Award-nominated Wildside Press. Recent collections of his short stories are* Slab's Tavern *and* Performance Art, *he co-edited the anthologies* The Ultimate Zombie *and* The Ultimate Witch, *and he is the publisher of* Horror, *a regular newszine.*

THROUGHOUT the long summer day, the guards on the walls of the city watched the storyteller's approach. At noon he was a dark speck on the horizon. Dust rose as he walked on the barren plain. In the evening he was a black, ragged shape against the sunset. Still a column of dust followed him. Flocks of sheep scattered at his passage. At night they lost sight of him. He walked among the squat mud buildings beyond the city's walls.

He came to a small gate left open for late travellers. Somehow, by the look on his face, the sentry there knew he was not as other storytellers. Unchallenged, the stranger passed by. He walked through the dark maze of buildings.

Many eyes were on him. These were dangerous streets, but no hands were raised, no alarms given.

Shortly before midnight he came to a great square. He sat by a fountain in its middle. He looked at the drab, stone buildings, at the hundreds of gaudily-dressed people wandering about on this night of festival, and he knew there was almost always a celebration in this idle city. Lit by torches was a great arch commemorating the past glories of the place. It was built of black stone. The figures carved on its sides were squat and ugly, like toads.

Children pointed at the ragged stranger. Parents hushed them. Then a crowd gathered and the square was thick with people, with torches, with shadows.

When there was silence, he began his tale:

Masferigon did not create the Earth. He was a bemused elder relative of Shon Atasha, who did. But when the creation was done, the elder god walked over the lands. He swam in the oceans and made love to Aeldach, the Mother of Waters. It was not improper that he should love a river. That was the way of things, near to the beginning of time. She followed him wherever he went, her tributaries and streams watering the soil. Where he walked, forests grew, and great grasslands, and all the magical beasts Shon Atasha had created came down to the water's edge to drink.

One night Masferigon slept between two hills. The Mother of Waters circled around him, and the brown hillsides were green, the air thick with the smell of flowers. Night birds sang.

Content as he was, the god dreamed of the valley in which he rested. In his dream he saw it as the most beautiful of all the places on Earth, where winter was unknown and fruit always ripe on the vine.

The god slept with his hands closed, his fingers curled. As he dreamed, he opened his left hand, and the animals were there, large and small, stately, delicate, coloured like nothing else that lived on the Earth. They scattered among the trees and underbrush of the valley.

Then Masferigon dreamed of men, more perfect of mind and body than any others, and he opened his right hand, releasing a man and a woman, the first two of his children.

In the morning he rose and went out of the valley, following his beloved river.

Centuries passed. The offspring of the first couple grew numerous. They dwelt in perfect harmony with themselves, with the animals of the valley. The greater beasts did not pray upon the lesser, nor did men kill them in return.

The valley drifted through the years like a delicate ship, all the parts perfectly in place, yet with no hand to guide it.

Still the children of Masferigon multiplied, and in every generation there were those who asked, 'What is beyond the valley?'

The answer was always the same: 'Places less beautiful than this, and people less happy than ourselves, for they were not created by Masferigon.'

Then there was born among them one whose spirit could not rest. He was not like the others. He had a name, but it is unworthy of mention.

This one was filled with pride, not simple curiosity. He wanted to know what was beyond the valley so he would be greater than his fellows. He did not ask what was out there, nor did he announce his intentions. He simply went.

Many years later, when he came back, he did not have to tell anyone where he had been. They knew by the look on his face and the strange clothing he wore.

He was filled with indignation and shame.

'We are not like other people,' he said. 'We are barbarians. We are little better than the animals that graze.'

'How are we different?' the elders of the valley asked.

'They are mighty. They are hardened by winter. They wear the skins of beasts they have slain, even as I do now. They do not live as we do.'

'How do they live?' the elders asked.

'They build great cities. They tear up the fields and sow their crops. They herd animals into pens and slaughter them. They do not regard their neighbours as we do.'

'How do they regard them?'

'As potential slaves. As prey. As foes. Therefore they make war on them.'

Later, the one who had been outside the valley killed the elders and made himself king.

More years passed, and the valley was transformed. Trees

were cut down. Sharp ploughs tore up the meadows. The magical beasts of Masferigon's dreams were slaughtered, their skins made into garments, whose wearers were very proud.

A city was built, first of wood, then of stone. From out of the gates an army marched, to conquer and subdue other nations. And they were victorious more often than not.

By this time Masferigon had gotten over his romance with the river. Perhaps they had quarrelled. Perhaps they had merely grown apart. In any case, the god had long since returned to Theshemna, the palace of gods in the sky, whose windows are lighted with lanterns that blend among the stars.

In an idle hour Masferigon gazed out one of those windows. He looked down on the Earth and wondered what had become of his valley. He swept down from the heavens like a falling shadow, then strode across the land.

He walked a long time to get there. The city in the valley had become the capital of a vast empire. Its roads girdled the world. Nights echoed with the tread of its tireless army.

He drifted through that great city in a wisp of fog. He saw how the people fought among themselves, how they murdered, how they amused themselves with cruel games. He looked in vain for the two hills between which he had slept. They were covered over now, bristling with battlements.

In the darkness he floated through a window, into a great hall. There he met the Emperor, who had blood on his hands from sacrificing a child. He was planning future wars by what her entrails revealed.

Masferigon appeared to him as an old man. His face glowed like a paper lantern.

'Do you not know me?' he asked.

The Emperor scowled. 'You are a god. What of it? I have conquered the worshippers of many gods. I worship the greatest god of all, which is the spirit of this city, the god of might and glory.'

Masferigon listened. He heard the voices of revellers in the city, and the shouts of the evening watch, repeating that all was well and the army victorious. The only other thing that moved among the rooftops was the wind. There was no spirit in the city. It was a dead place.

'Do you not remember this valley as it once was? Was it not beautiful then?'

The Emperor laughed. He threw a sacrificial dagger at the god, who vanished. Later, when he asked the soothsayers what this apparition portended, they told him the downfall of a city.

High above, drifting in a cloud, Masferigon wept. Then he was angry. Then, firm in his resolve, he lowered himself from the cloud and walked through the night again. Where his footsteps touched, where his tears fell, the ground trembled.

He sought out the Mother of Waters for consolation, but she was covered with warships, and ran thick with blood and the ashes of burning cities.

In his despair, the terrible despair and anger of a god, he came to a dark place, and opened the secret doors of the Earth, releasing all those evil things which Shon Atasha the creator had shut away. They gathered around him and even he grew pale with fear at their nearness.

'Go,' he said, 'and drink of the souls of that doomed city. You will find them to your liking.'

They flew and hopped and slithered. They drifted like a foul mist. They entered the dreams of the people of the city, and the night was filled with shrieks of terror, with cries of madness, as fathers smothered their children, as husbands strangled their wives. The dark spirits crouched in corners, on windowsills, on bedposts. They drank deep. They feasted on souls.

In the morning they returned to Masferigon, like dogs to their master.

'Do any remain alive?' he asked.

'Yes, but we are sated.' They looked up at him, their eyes dull.

'Return when you are hungry again.'

The following night they fell upon the dazed survivors in the dark streets, upon the refugees in the roads. Screams filled the night.

'Do any remain?' he asked them, when they gathered in a cavern to hide from the sunrise.

'There is only the Emperor, whose magic is powerful. He sleeps alone in a locked room. He does not dream.'

Masferigon went with them on the third night. He raised up the sacrificed child from her grave. He caused her to walk, naked, mud-smeared, her entrails hanging out, to the Emperor's golden door. She pounded on it with her fists.

'Great Lord,' she cried with her dead voice. 'Open the door. I have come to foretell the future.'

The Emperor opened his door. He saw the corpse standing there, and beyond, in the darkness, thousands of hideous, leering faces. Among them stood Masferigon.

'Do you not know me?' the god asked him.

The Emperor screamed.

Later, Masferigon wandered alone through the empty city. He wept. He began to regret what he had done. He wished he might find some survivor to instruct, to start again on the way to contentment. He prayed to the other gods, to Shon Atasha, the most powerful of all.

His prayer was answered. He was moved to search every house until, at last, he found two boys locked in a foul shed. They were twin brothers, hidden away because their parents thought them idiots. Indeed, one had no mind left. He had never dreamed as other people do. Therefore the dark spirits had not recognized him, and had spared him.

He stood in the sunlight, his mouth slack, his eyes rolling. Masferigon changed him into a kind of animal and set him to guard the empty city forever.

The other brother was filled with visions. He saw so many things that when he tried to speak of them, his words came out in a confused babble. His dreams were so beautiful that even the dark spirits had drawn away from him.

He stood in the sunlight, blinking, his face filled with rapture. He recognized Masferigon. He had dreamed of the valley, even as the god had.

Masferigon straightened the boy's speech, and sent him out into the world as a storyteller, to describe the beauty of the valley and tell how it had been lost.

Then the god lay down in the empty city, sleeping a sleep close to death. He did not dream, but merely waited, as he waits now, for the last age of mankind, when his valley will be as it once was.

His tale done, the storyteller waited while a few copper coins were tossed on his cloak. The crowd began to drift away.

'Is this all my story is worth?' he asked in a quiet voice.

There was a moment of silence. Then a couple more coins clinked in front of him.

'We like stories of heroes and great battles,' one man said. 'Tell us one of those and maybe some silver will fall, if the tale is well-wrought.'

'No,' said the storyteller. 'I only know one tale. I have told it. I leave it with you as a warning.'

Then he was gone in the blinking of an eye, like a burst bubble. A woman cried out in alarm, but was hushed. The people stood still and silent for a long time.

The storyteller and his cloak had vanished. All that remained were the copper coins, dark against the pavement.

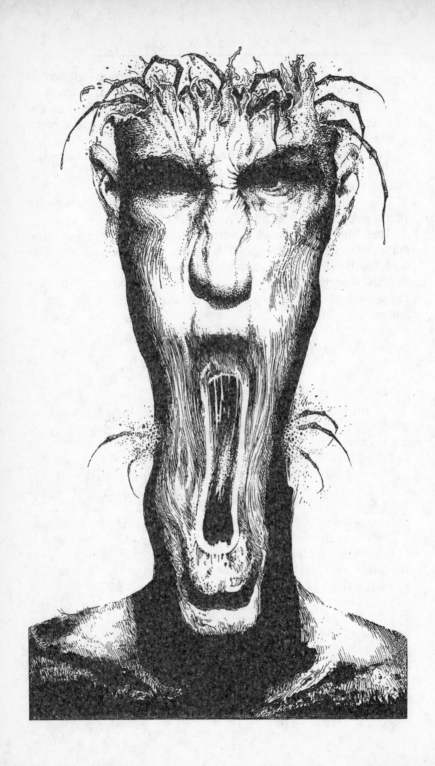

SILENT SCREAM

Samantha Lee

Samantha Lee's first published story was 'The Island of the Seals' in The 18th Pan Book of Horror Stories. *Since then she has published a fantasy trilogy, a novel-length version of* Dr Jekyll and Mr Hyde, *and a futuristic fantasy titled* Childe Rolande, *amongst other full-length works. Five of her short stories have been aired on London's Capital Radio and others have been published in four issues of* Fantasy Tales, Final Shadows, Space, Spectre, The Fontana Book of Monsters *and elsewhere. Her latest project is a television series called* Possession.

THE rats came up through the floorboards, big, fat hairy things with tails pink as unlinked sausages. They skittered across the floor in a tidal surge, feral eyes shiny as skinned grapes in the light-bulb's naked glare.

She wriggled in the restraining jacket, trying to press back into the wall, tearing feverishly at the inside of the sleeves with quick-bitten fingernails. Her feet made little kicking patterns, crumpling the hospital-smooth bedlinen, ripping it out of its carefully folded corners.

When the whiskers appeared, light as thistledown, over the edge of the cot, she began to whimper, veins cording her neck, legs suddenly damp with the spurt of unretainable urine. The warm, salt smell, more aromatic than blood, reached the nose of the pack leader. He halted a handspan from her naked ankle and sat up, sniffing the air.

Behind him, his minions clambered over the counterpane in a sea of undulating flesh, the souls of other, earlier victims staring out of the bright eyes as if to say . . . 'Your turn, your turn.'

'Go away, go away,' she cried out in her fiercest, loudest voice.

But the chief rat only smiled, curling pink lips back over pinker gums, dropping on all fours and ducking under the ward-issue gown to run up her leg and sink sharp white fangs into the soft, exposed flesh of her inside thigh.

Blood spurted, pumping from the vein in her groin.

No pain. Not yet. Just disbelief – and the sound of her voice screaming as the rest of the monsters swarmed up to cover her in a blanket of squirming bodies.

'Jesus H Christ . . . what's going on?'

The cell door opening, two men in white coats rushing in. Salvation. She wept with relief as, none too gently, one held her down while the other administered the injection.

The rats scattered at the men's approach, disappearing into the white walls, melting back through the floor while the hole through which they had so mysteriously emerged closed over. The Red Sea closing over the cream of Rameses' Charioteers.

She lay back, body soaked in sweat and piss, sinking down into the blessed blackness of the drug, the coarse faces of her deliverers swimming out of vision, voices grumbling about the mess that would have to be cleared up later on.

Castelli Worst case of DT's I ever seen. Look't the way she's squirming around in there. You'd think something was eatin' her alive.

Petrowski The demon drink, Charlie, the demon drink. She's been tippling for years. Be sure your sins will find you out. You ought to know that, Charlie, you being a good catholic and all.

Castelli How come a nice old lady like that gets to drinking in the first place? Nice home, nice family, nice life. I don't geddit.

Petrowski Maybe it ain't always been so nice. Old man Glassier says she was in one of them camps during the War. Maybe she drinks to forget?

Castelli Lotta crap talked about them camps y'ask me. Could'na been as bad as they said. Old lady like that, peeing her pants. It ain't seemly.

Petrowski She ain't so old. In her sixties. Says so in her notes.

Castelli Jesus, she looks eighty if she looks a day.

Petrowski Yeah, well, the booze ain't too good for the complexion, Charlie boy.

Castelli Ain't too good for the sheets neither. Nice old lady like that. You think she'd be ashamed.

For a moment she was at peace.

Then the dreams started. Dreams worse than the hallucinations. Closer to reality. Harder to bear.

It was the winter of '42. She was sixteen and back at the camp.

The rats were there too. They had eaten the foot off a three-day-old baby before the mother, a girl not much older than herself, had woken from the sleep of starvation and beaten them off in a frenzy of hate and fear.

The child had died soon after, from shock and loss of blood. And the mother, a stick figure with huge shadowed eyes, ugly in her grief, had gone insane, clutching the wizened scrap to her milkless breasts until the flesh turned putrid and began to dribble down the front of her prison issue tunic.

All this had taken time. But in the dream it happened instantaneously, the baby's body melting into green slime punctuated by pockets of putridness which exploded into small ulcerated craters and from which inch-long worms wriggled their way onto the mother's emaciated chest.

One morning the woman too had been dead, the child still clutched to her bosom. They had buried them later that afternoon – if you could call it burial – thrown into a common pit, covered in quicklime to keep the plague away.

It had been a beautiful morning in early May. They say there are no birds at Auschwitz. But birds had been singing that day as they'd tipped mother and child into the trench.

Mozart had fared no better.

But at least he hadn't had to put up with the rats.

Rats everywhere, thriving on dead flesh, sharpening their teeth on human bones, turning on each other when the corpses got too skinny, cycling and re-cycling themselves in an obscene orgy of cannibalistic gluttony.

It was her horror of the rats, her fear of what they might do to her after she was dead that made her decide to live . . . at all costs.

TRANSCRIPT OF INTERVIEW BETWEEN MRS IRMA LONGFORD AND JOHN PAUL GLASSIER, RESIDENT PSYCHIATRIST, MOUNTVILLE STATE PSYCHIATRIC UNIT, NEW STANTON, USA.

Dr G. You understand, don't you, Mrs Longford, that your drinking is only symptomatic of some other, deeper problem?
(SILENCE)

Dr G. (ctd) Mrs Longford. We can't help you unless you help yourself. We know you've been through a bad time. But it's over now. It's been over for fifty years. Maybe if you talked about it you could, you know, lay the ghost?.
(SILENCE)

Dr G. (ctd) Mrs Longford. I know this is hard for you. Often, when things happen . . . like happened to you . . . deprivation . . . a feeling of life being out of control, it leaves us scarred, ashamed even, because we didn't behave . . . perhaps . . . as well as we ought. There can even be guilt about being alive when others died. It's a common trauma. We often see it in the wake of a natural disaster. An earthquake for instance or a flood. After the relief wears off people are often left with a hollow feeling. 'Why me?', they say. 'Why did *she* die while I'm still here?'. Some individuals go mad under the strain, get strange notions, in extreme cases persuade themselves that they've somehow been the cause of the disaster, that it's their fault so many others died. I had one man in here, after an airline crash, who was convinced that he'd somehow made a pact with the Devil, that he'd sold his soul, that *that* was the only reason he was still alive. Guilt is understandable. It's a post-traumatic symptom. But therapy can help Mrs Longford. If you'd only just co-operate, talk about it. This is not the dark ages, we can help you. But you'll need to meet us half-way.
(SILENCE)

Dr G. (sighing) Very well, Mrs Longford. If you won't co-operate, I can't make you, though I can't understand why you won't try. If you won't think about yourself, think about your children . . . your grandchildren. Think

how hard it is for them to watch you go through this. Their sympathy could go a long way to helping you to a permanent cure. They love you Mrs Longford. Wouldn't it be better all round if they knew the truth?
(MUFFLED LAUGHTER, CHILLING IN ITS LACK OF HUMOUR)
Dr G. (stiffly) Right Mrs Longford. It seems there's no more to be said. Your son will be here in a few minutes to sign the release form. (Sound of papers being shuffled) And remember Mrs Longford, you're a hopeless alcoholic. If you ever drink again, you'll die, do you understand?.

She sat by the window, smocking a dress for Marsha's youngest. The needle flew, in and out, in and out, piercing the flesh-coloured silk into a series of knots and ridges. The puckered pattern brought to mind the scars of those inmates who'd undergone vivisection (no anaesthetic naturally. Jews weren't human, after all, and one needed the chloroform and drugs for 'our brave soldiers on the front'). She shook the thought away, concentrating instead on her hands. Wrinkled as they were and marked with blotches brought on by too many winters spent in Miami while Jack was still alive, they were as nimble as they had been when she was sixteen years old. She had been sewing the night the soldiers had come and dragged them from the house. Loud voices and louder boots, clamping on the cobbles in the lamplight. And the neighbours, peering through the windows, glad it wasn't them. 'Never did like those Varmann's anyway. Too uppity.' Sewing linen for her bottom drawer in anticipation of a normal sixteen-year-old's future. Marriage and children. Happy Ever After.
   She looked again at the silk, mind hooking onto items sewn long ago, in afternoons while Blucher snored and she, plagued with nightmares even then, would leave her lover asleep to search the bodies of the dead for anything the guards might have missed. A button perhaps or a piece of string. That body, stumbled over, still clinging to life. The eyes, staring from the half-eaten face (the rats again) begging for release. A sudden moment of forgotten tenderness and the hiss of the life-force escaping the punctured lung as she drove the sewing scissors home. The gratitude in the eyes

as the light died. So unlike those other eyes, the rat's eyes of her dreams, reflecting the thousand upon thousands of souls, driven to the long barrows, expecting the kiss of hot showers, blessed relief from the vermin that had flourished in the cattle-wagons, receiving instead the acrid embrace of gas filling the chambers.

'I am become death', she thought, fingers flying, wondering why she hadn't used the scissors to kill herself.

Those who *had* died, climbing over the bodies of their own children to claw at the doors, were the lucky ones.

For the rest, the slow torture of starvation, slave labour, or worse . . . collusion, enjoyment even . . . absolute power corrupts . . . What became of the human soul under such conditions? She looked out at her grandchildren, playing on the lawn, their bright laughter hanging like liquid gold on the clear Autumn air.

There were some who believed that the soul grew stronger under duress, that the greatest feats of heroism took place in the dirt and deprivation of the world's torture cells.

She knew better. In the stink of the camps humanity sank to rat-level, willing to betray any confidence, invent any blasphemy, commit any act in order to survive another day.

Some had even been known to sell a virgin daughter to a Camp Guard for a lump of sour bread.

Out of the corner of her eye she saw the head appear round the leg of the sofa. Impossible. She hadn't had a drink in days. But there was another one, under the table, and a third, slithering out of the wainscoting, flat as a blintz, inflating itself, balloon-like before scuttling in a sideways jig towards her.

She jumped up, flinging the sewing from her, clambering unsteadily onto the rocking chair, beating at the air with clawed hands as the rodents scurried up her nylons, tiny paws puncturing fabric and flesh, seeking purchase in their inexorable climb towards her throat.

'Hello. George. Is that you? Can you come home, dear? I'm afraid it's your mother. She's had another one of her turns. Yes. I *know* you're in the middle of a meeting . . . but it's more serious this time . . . No. No, I'm quite sure. There isn't a drop in the house . . . She's in bed now. She's paralysed

down one side and she can't speak. The Doctor says he
thinks she's had a stroke . . . You'd better come home,
George (crying) . . . I've had to send for Father Flynn.'

Bless me, Father for I have sinned. It's been forty years since
my last confession.

When I took the faith, Jack said it didn't matter what I'd
done. I could confess and it'd be alright. I never did, of
course. Saved it up for the end. And now I can't talk. Who
ever said life was fair? I've paid my dues. I've been a good
mother, a good wife. We're different people when we're
young. We can change. I've done my bit. And I've been
punished. Every day waiting for the knock on the door. The
dreams. The rats.

The ones who died deserved to, weak, gutless, pathetic.
Begging to be tortured, longing for it. Victor and victim,
master and slave, the good and the evil, opposite ends
of the spectrum. But are they, you with your beads and
your mumbo jumbo? Isn't it bad to be so weak, so stupid,
placing your fate in the hands of others, begging for death,
hungering for pain. And isn there something fine . . . Holy
almost . . . about inflicting it?

Torture is the oldest art. The most basic to our nature.
Orchestrating the note of the scream, thin and high for
exquisite pain, deep and vomit-gurgling for agony.

And the power . . . holding them there . . . like God,
between life and death, allowing them to die . . . eventually,
because by then they want to, because life is too hideous to
contemplate without eyes or breasts or genitalia.

Bless me, Father for I have sinned.

I have my mother to thank I suppose, weak, silly woman.
I might never have realized my penchant for pain if she
hadn't sold me to that pig, Blucher. He took me to the
cells to frighten me, to show me what would happen if I
didn't perform. But I wasn't frightened . . . just curious . . .
and aroused, I suppose. He got more than his bread's-worth
later on.

Afterwards he took me because it pleased me, excited
us both. And because I came up with such good sug-
gestions. Kindred spirits. But he was a pig all the same.
Ham-fisted. No finesse. And he died like a pig too, torn

limb from limb when the war was over and the allies were at the gates.

Those allied soldiers. So naive. Jack even crying for what I'd suffered at Blucher's hands. And all those who knew the truth too dead to tell.

Mrs Longford, respectable war-bride. Pillar of the community. Living example of the finer family values. Such a *nice* old lady.

The damn rats have been the only fly in the ointment. And now there's something even worse. Lately I've started to decipher a sort of twittering among their squeaks, like a radio turned down low. Voices without words, just below the level of comprehension. As though any minute now they're going to start to talk. To cry out. To accuse.

Amazing how humanity clings to life. Why? When what follows can be no worse than what they leave behind. I've seen life held in limbo inside a lump of flesh until it was no more than a that, a flayed, disfigured mound of guts and sinew with no throat left to voice its silent screams, no tongue left to thank me when I persuaded my lover to let it die.

In those days death was the most natural thing in the world. Living was hard. Still is. Death is my salvation. Away from the rats of cannibal conscience.

Absolve me Father, you in your black shroud, absolve me, now and at the hour. . . . Give me peace.

Oh, Holy Mother of God, what *is* this? The black cassock sprouting hair, whiskers slithering out of the pores, nose lengthening, twitching, sniffing, thirsty for blood. Keep your claws off me. Don't touch me. Stay away. Stay away . . .

Poor tortured woman, thought Father Flynn, what had she gone through, what memories would she carry with her to the grave? He leant forward and placed his hands on the narrow shoulders, pressing the frail old bones back into the crisp linen pillowcase.

Her eyes looked out at him in abject terror, toothless mouth gaping, spittle drooling. A wicked-looking old face, he thought, immediately ashamed that such a thing should have sprung to mind, so unlike that of the innocent eighteen-year-old whose portrait smiled from the mantelpiece, safe at last on the arm of the man who had found her in the the filth of the concentration camp and brought her to America to be his wife.

Irma Longford screamed once and fell back, and Father Flynn, feeling his own weight of years heavy on him, allowed his head to sink on his chest and wondered about the meaning of it all.

Later, at the graveside, he would speak of her many qualities, of the good she had done during her time on earth, of her humanity, her loving family who would miss her and the fact that, without her, the world would be an emptier place.

'She is at peace now', he would say, piously. 'Gone to her just reward.'

She woke in total darkness, the air damp and warm, tinged with a smell not unlike the foul fumes that had belched from the smoke-stacks daily above the gas-chambers.

Under her back she could feel the earth shuddering, as though somewhere, beneath her day-old corpse, a dormant volcano was preparing to erupt into life.

She had won. The struggle was over. The rats had gone. They couldn't touch her now. She felt as though a huge weight had been lifted from her soul.

So this was Heaven. Back to the womb. Nothingness. Emptiness. Peace.

In the darkness, a face swam before her. Her mother's face, the eyes dark and beautiful, her throaty voice lulling the six-year-old Irma to sleep with a song in yiddish.

The ground ceased its shuddering and began to heave. It bucked like a bronco in the darkness, tossing her from side to side, bouncing her off the satin shell of the casket as she'd once flung herself from wall to wall in the padded cell.

A sharp protrusion dug into her back. A jagged splinter of wood. An earthquake? No. Something was trying to get in, burrowing up through the bottom of the coffin.

Before she heard the scrabbling of the soft furry paws or heard the murmur of the far-away voices, she knew what it was and she screeched like a banshee, trying to sit up, banging her head, falling back again half-stunned. Desperately she rolled over onto her stomach and heaved, pushing at the unyielding wood with her narrow shoulders, trying to angle her way out through the lid and hold the floor together at the same time. Anything to stop them getting in, getting at her.

A hole opened in the casket beneath her. An abyss. She couldn't see it but she could feel the soft, wet nose, the tickle of whiskers under her palm. And the voices, louder now, calling up dark memories in the dark. Her mother, apologizing, begging for mercy; the twins, deliberately infected with rabies, screaming obscenities as they tore each others faces off; her best friend's shriek as the aborted foetus slithered from her butchered body; Blucher calling her name, turning accusing eyes on her as she joined his murderers helping to tear his body to shreds.

The rats burst through the coffin, bringing with them the red glow of Hell's cauldron. And in that glow she saw that they were no ordinary rats. Instead of animal heads, they had human faces, human voices, a human desire for revenge.

She had one brief glimpse of her mother the last time she'd seen her, face half-eaten before she'd plunged the scissors in. And then the surge of furry bodies swarmed over her, burrowing into her armpits, her groin, her mouth, silencing forever the scream that she knew would flow from her torn throat for all eternity.

STORE WARS

Garry Kilworth

Garry Kilworth's latest collection of short stories is Hogfoot Right and Bird-Hands. *He began his writing career by winning the 1974 Sunday Times/Victor Gollancz short story competition, and his collaborative novella, 'The Ragthorn' (with Robert Holdstock), won the 1992 World Fantasy Award. In between, he has published five short story collections, such as* The Songbirds of Pain *and* Dark Hills, Hollow Clocks, *with individual appearances in major anthologies and magazines such as* Fantasy Tales, Best New Horror 2 *and* The Year's Best Horror: Fourth Annual Collection. *Of his fifteen novels, recent titles have included* Hunter's Moon *and* Midnight's Sun, *as well as books for children and young adults.*

NO one really knows how the conflict started.

The store was closed for business, it being the morning before the Turn of the Century Sale. The doors were to be opened precisely at noon, 1st of January, 2000.

Some of the customers had been there since the previous evening, braving the night air, the street frosts, armed only with vacuum flasks full of coffee, nips of brandy and thick sleeping bags. Time takes on a different meaning in such circumstances. They made the remarkable discovery that the night is not all darkness, but that twilight lingers long and comes again early. The globe actually turns quite slowly. It is people who move fast. They had entered a world of idle hours. Around them the streets were almost silent, the night winds turning scraps of paper into small live creatures on strange urgent business elsewhere. Philosophies were formed, accepted, discarded. Old grudges shrank to insignificance and promises of reconciliation were born.

They found they had time to reflect on their lives, to make
decisions on a change of direction, on marriage, on divorce,
on leaving their job at the insurance office or bank and
hitting the road. In the early hours of the morning, lifelong
friendships were formed with people behind them in the
queue. There were even affairs begun, and some ended.
They found you could live more in a single night than in
many years of ordinary time.

Then, as the noonday opening came within sight at last,
they remembered why they were there.

There were always bargains to be had at Maccine's sales:
washing machines for a fraction of the retail price, just-out-
of-style dresses and suits, sports' gear that had last year's
colour on their motifs.

Within the building, all was not well however.

Animosity had been building up between floor and department managers at Maccine's, the world's largest store, for
as long as people could remember. The company fostered
rivalry between the managers, and consequently, the departments. Substantial prizes were given each year for the highest
takings at the till. Maccine's believed in the reward system.
They boasted jokingly that no employee had been flayed or
hanged for close on a century.

Competition was fierce and bloody. Staff had, in the past,
been known to sabotage rival departments. There was the
time when the sprinkler system had been tampered with
and was deliberately activated one morning by a person
or persons unknown. Men's Tailoring suffered a terrible
time when hydrochloric acid instead of water sprayed their
stock and staff. There was at that point some difference of
opinion between Men's Tailoring and Hardware regarding
the entitlement to sell workmen's coveralls. Then there
was the incident when tiny needles tipped with neurotoxic
poison were found fixed to the telephone earpieces of a
new little corner department known as Ribbons and Bows,
whom Haberdashery called the 'upstarts'. Three people
spent seven months in hospital, seriously ill with nervous
system disorders.

Managers had been known to have had fistfights in restaurants, when they came across deadly rivals unexpectedly
while out with their wives. Junior staff formed departmental

gangs outside the workplace and wore silk windcheaters with *Bedroom Furniture Dragons* or *Lions of Curtains and Draperies* in such clashing colours as, say, purple lettering on yellow fabric. These gangs fought pitched battles in the street, their members often getting arrested for carrying concealed weapons.

The inter-departmental messengers carried, in the main, sacks of hate mail between managers. Ex-Viet Cong immigrants were recruited and a booby trap called the 'bamboo bed' began to appear in dark corridors. This fiendish device was a spring-loaded trellis covered in spikes, which flew up from the floor when triggered by an unfamiliar foot. There-was one famous booby trap, where a young woman from Clocks and Watches put a dozen assorted poisonous sea snakes, each just over twelve inches long, into the cistern of the Garden Equipment manager's toilet. A banded yellow-black bit him on the left cheek as he was in the middle of his morning ablutions.

Although people were reprimanded, no one actually lost their job in any of these incidents, and truth to tell the company actually encouraged inter-departmental conflict. They felt it showed keenness. Inefficiency was not tolerated, nor were mistakes which cost the company money. For incompetence of any nature you could be out by your ear within the hour. However, nobody ever actually got the sack for unruly behaviour in the cause of patriotism for one's department.

There were vast spy networks. People who had transferred from one department to another, but who still retained old loyalties, were constantly passing secret messages back and forth. One member of Glassware 'fell' in front of a train while on her way home from work and the store detectives, the only impartial group in the building, were convinced she was pushed. Glassware had apparently discovered she was an agent for Porcelain and Pottery, having left the company and rejoined for the express purpose of feeding her old department with information.

There were religious differences it was true. Perfumeries, Electrical Goods and Hardware were one-hundred percent Catholic, and Protestants were in the high majority in Lingerie and Sporting Goods, but there were many other

departments where the mix was thorough and the two
Christian groups amicable. The Restaurant, Groceries, and
the Coffee Shop on the 101st Floor had a strong Islamic
element, while Pharmaceuticals and the Dispensary were
almost entirely Hindu. There were occasional problems
which might have been traced to extreme religious prejudice, but the only real fundamentalists were in the packing
department, way down in the basement, and in no strategic
position to assist an escalation of the fighting.

Much the same could be said about any racial disharmony:
there was little evidence to suggest that people of different
races at the store persecuted each other. Those who were persecuted were minority departments like Men's Socks and Ties
and Ladies' Fripperies. The staff in these small departments
were bullied and hounded by all, and only rarely was there
a token member of such sections invited on a quiz panel,
or to form part of any sports team. They were of course
continually campaigning for their 'rights' and occasionally,
when a strong leader arose amongst them, there would be
an assassination, usually carried out by some redneck from
Sporting Goods.

Naturally every member of each department considered
his or her floor to be superior to all others. The battles at
the till were fierce and customers searching for an item which
was not to be found in the department where they were
enquiring after it would be quietly directed to a rival store
further down the street, rather than to the floor in Maccine's
that stocked the object. The majority of the counter staff were
young and hotblooded, and they carried their grievances on
their shoulders. They might hate their department manager,
but at least he or she was one of them, and not a stupid
Nailbender (Hardware Department Assistant) or a dirty
Gluesniffer (Stationery Department Counter Clerk).

Feelings were running high on the day of the sale. There
were big prizes to be won and only the night before Sheet
Music had encountered Cassette Tapes at a seasonal dance.
There was supposed to be a truce on, over the sale period,
and both sides avoided contact for most of the evening.
However, Miss Rona of Sheet Music, and Mr Blake, of
Cassette Tapes, were caught canoodling behind a pillar.
Mr Smith of Sheet Music asked them quietly who the hell

they thought they were, Miss Montague and Mr Capulet?, thereby showing that though he had a passing familiarity with Shakespeare, his had not been a completely thorough education. There was nothing wrong with his boxing technique however, and he let Cassette Tapes' Mr Blake have it on the chin, at the same time bestowing a curse on his house.

The fight escalated, until broken bottles, can openers and furniture were employed, and the dance floor was littered with wounded warriors. Individuals from other departments were drawn into the rumpus, some never went home that night. One or two never went home ever again. The casualty departments of the hospitals worked overtime.

The following morning the first sign of really serious trouble came just after the ten o'clock coffee break, when a young man new to Men's Underwear accidentally got out of the elevator on the wrong floor. His own department first saw him again a few minutes later when the elevator doors opened and his lifeless body dropped at the feet of their Mr Williams, who screamed energetically until Mrs Denthrop-Jones slapped his face. The corpse was wearing nothing but a sequined G-string, wound tightly around its throat.

'Lingerie!' cried the department manager, and despite the fact that Mr Williams said it could be a frame, that just because an item of ladies' undies was used as a weapon did not necessarily mean that Lingerie was responsible, the manager despatched a commando team to raid the guilty department. 'Shut your face, Williams,' cried the department manager, 'or I'll you'll find yourself demoted from floor supervisor before you can say kiss my ass. I *know* your boyfriend works in Knickers and Bras, so don't give me that crap about how it might be somebody else! You're just trying to protect Simpson.'

This was all true enough.

The commando team was led by a man who was a sergeant in the National Guard, their Mr Ackroyde, a high-flyer and rising star in Men's Underwear. His sales figures were magnificent and his fervour in promoting his department during coffee breaks was unequalled. There were four ex-marines with him, older men who had seen service in Vietnam and Grenada. Their first stop was Sporting Goods, where they rushed from the elevator into the room, grabbed some weapons, and back into the elevator before the doors closed. Each of them had snatched a golf club, or a climbing ax, and Mr Ackroyde himself had managed to grasp a crossbow with two bolts in the side clips.

On route to the battle the elevator stopped to let on a white-haired bespectacled little man with the demeanour of a Swiss toymaker. A ripple of fear went through the five-man attack force as they quickly made space for Mr Vandyne, a counter clerk from an elite department. He looked at their weapons and then into each of their faces with an expression of contempt. They coughed quietly and shuffled around staring at their feet until Mr Vandyne got out. Only then did they break into loud animated discussion again.

They came out of the elevator into Lingerie in true heroic style; yelling their famous battle cry of, 'Briefs and buggery!' they laid about them with their deadly tools. Mr Ackroyde pinned a Miss Feversham to the wall with one of his bolts, but unfortunately missed his target with his second shot. His team mates felled at least eleven counter staff before they were overpowered.

Rage is not a good companion in war. Unfortunately their blind anger had not allowed them sufficient time to plan their escape. One needs a cool head when forming strategy on the battlefield. Though it had not been their original intention to forfeit their lives, it was in the end a suicide mission. The women of Lingerie wrested the weapons from the hands of these border raiders and then carried out some unspeakable tortures on the poor individuals. There was no such thing as rules of war in Maccine's: you took *no* prisoners. The girls simply screeched, 'No quarter!' and proceeded to do inventive things with pins and clips on male skin. Once the blood began splashing the designer foundations, they ceased their cruelty and put the raiders out of their misery. The bodies were piled into the goods elevator and sent hurtling down to Packing with labels that read, 'To be despatched to the Dead Centre of the City. (Joke!)'.

In the meantime, Sporting Goods, (or Jock's, as they liked to call themselves), were incensed at the audacious theft of their items. Being gentlemen, they sent someone to Men's Underwear (or Shreddies) to complain.

He came back wrapped in several, quite separate, thermal undershirts.

The Jocks armed themselves, but first they intended to pay back Shreddies on a one-for-one basis. Ronnie (the Jocks were on first names) rang down to Men's Underwear, using the outside phone, and pretended to be the Fire Officer. In thick accents Ronnie asked the callee to look out of his nearest window, to see if he could detect smoke from the lower floors. The poor shmuck did as he was asked and was almost decapitated by a medicine ball dropped from Sporting Goods. It certainly broke his neck and he flopped out of sight to a cheer from the Jocks.

One of the Four Horsemen was now in full gallop.

At fifteen minutes past ten, alliances were made. Sporting Goods phoned, in-house, Lingerie and proposed that they join forces to wipe out Men's Underwear. The two departments had always been on reasonable terms (considering they both worked for Maccine's) partly due to the fact that Lingerie employed fairly empty-headed females who went for unintelligent but muscled males, and Sporting Goods was full of such men, who in turn appreciated the sexy undergarments worn by the ladies of Lingerie.

Unknown to these two allies, Men's Underwear had contacted Kitchen Improvements and Bathroom Appliances. Now armed with bread knives and clubs fashioned from faucets, they waited to repel the onslaught expected from above.

Amazons from Lingerie used the fire escape and entered Men's Underwear from the windows screaming like banshees. The Jocks used the large service elevator, knowing their front rank would be cut down, but hoping the rear troops could use their bodies as a shield.

The ensuing battle was swift and vicious and blood flowed in rivulets down the glass showcases; splattered on the display figures (Men's Underwear called them 'mannikins') wearing Hawaiian shorts and the new undershirts with the Macho 'drop armholes'; sprayed the counter busts of a male midsections wearing men's knickerbriefs. Lingerie and Sporting Goods finally retreated, having failed to take

Men's Underwear by storm. They left many dead behind them, some being their own but the majority wearing black silk underwear with designer labels sewn to the *outside* of the fabric. (Hey, when you strip off, you want your lover to *see* the House of Cedric crossed keys!)

All the departments in this battle regrouped afterwards and counted their losses. All declared they were by no means beaten, that they had a lot of fight left in them yet, by golly. Banners were fashioned. Pennants were raised. Soon they were ready to do battle again, and set about contacting other departments throughout the huge complex, to gain support for their causes.

At precisely eleven o'clock, the General Manager arrived at the store to find that practically every department in the building was either under attack, or in the process of an aggressive act. Only one solitary department had not yet joined the conflict, and this particular section held itself aloof from what was now a company war. The worst area was the roof, where a terrible carnage was still taking place. Once in his office the General Manager became aware of bodies falling past his window. His secretary had been waiting for him to arrive for the last quarter of an hour. She said she was terrified and wanted to leave the battle zone, but had at the same time this inexplicable though undeniable urge to have sex with him.

War, he told her, did that to some people.

When they had finished, she said sadly as she buttoned her dress that they might never see one another again, but the General Manager made light of the situation, saying it would be over before next Christmas. Seriously, he told her, there will be peace before the twelve o'clock onslaught of customers. I hope so, she replied, throwing her laddered tights into the wastepaper basket, I sincerely hope so.

The General Manager then set about trying to restore order. He called in some of the Members of the Board of Directors to assist him in settling differences. The Unions too, were contacted, and sent representatives to form with the Directors a kind of peace-keeping force. This amalgamated group called themselves the Unprincipled Negotiators, or UN.

The UN risked their lives journeying through corridors,

up and down elevators, along passageways, into rest rooms,
looking for the leaders of the various factions. They carried a
huge banner which read GENERAL MANAGEMENT AND
UNION OFFICIALS to deter ambushers whose bloodlust
blinded them to the fact that there were non-combatants
still in the building.

At first the UN believed they were in search of department
and floor managers, but the war had gone beyond that stage.
New generals had arisen, popular leaders not chosen from
the official hierarchy, but whose charismatic personalities
made them prominent amongst their kind. The supreme
leaders, one would have to call them Field Marshals at this
point in the war, were – on one side – Hardware's strategist
warrior queen, the iron lady of Pots and Pans, Bo Driscoll –
and on the other – the cunning intellectual from Magazines
and Periodicals, Fletcher J., Jnr, whose left pinkie knew more
about tactics than Julius Caesar and Napoleon put together.

The UN finally got these two sitting at a table together,
the tall willowy figure of Bo Driscoll and the short but feisty
Fletcher J., who glared at each other with such hatred the
General Manager foresaw that the exercise would turn out to
be a useless one. Indeed, both parties swore that the conflict
had reached a stage where they could no longer control their
armies, that the fighting would go on until the last counter
assistant stood amongst the bodies of the enemy and planted
a victory banner.

'Genocide!' cried one.

'Genocide!' repeated the other.

The General Manager saw only one path left to him. He
telephoned the President of the company, who was on a
business trip to the capital.

'We need your voice,' said the General Manager. 'We've
done a hook-up to the speakers system throughout the
building. You have to make a speech, plead with the two
armies, get them stop before they destroy all our stock . . .'

'Plead with them?' boomed the President. 'Never!'

Instead he made a telephone call to the one department
that had so far remained neutral, the department of which
Mr Vandyne, the white-haired little man encountered by the
Men's Underwear commando unit in the elevator, was proud
to call himself a member.

The reason GUNS & RODS had not participated in the war so far was not because they were pacifists or anything wimpish like that. They had kept out of it because there was nothing in it for them. They were the ultimate department, in terms of force. Their firepower was unequalled, devastating. They were an utterly cold and ruthless breed, with contempt for all other mortals. The Department Manager would not recruit anyone whose medical report did not bear the words 'sociopathic tendencies' or 'history of psychopathic disturbances'. Their greatest pleasure, was in firing weapons on the indoor range. Their second greatest pleasure was in stripping down the guns afterwards, oiling them, and putting them back together again. Shooting things was their *raison d'être*, big game fishing their only hobby. When a customer came in and asked for anything smaller than a 12 gauge shotgun, a .45 handgun or said they wanted to fish for trout, the counter clerk would curl his top lip and openly sneer. Middle-aged grandmothers who had found themselves in the department by accident when looking for Babies' Clothes, had walked out with make-my-day magnums rather than continue to face the disdain of the staff.

The deadly beauty of the goods they sold, with their shiny blue gunmetal barrels and hardwood butts, was so superior to anything else the store had on offer that the counter clerks (who called themselves 'weapon salesmen' or 'gunsmiths' in the bars outside the store) looked with dreadful scorn on the rest of the company staff. The latter were as cockroaches to them.

The President's telephone call unleashed these hounds of hell, who came whooping and yelling from their cages, wearing baseball caps reading 'Born to Decimate', brandishing pump-action repeater overandunder 12-gauge shotguns, and waving vicious-looking hunting knives with bloodgrooves on the blades. Each member of GUNS & RODS had been promised a substantial raise in salary if the machine of war was stopped within quarter of an hour.

Until this point, although there had been some damage to the goods, much of the stock was still in a saleable condition. By the time GUNS & RODS had blasted their way through counters and doors, laying about them with wanton carelessness, peppering washing machines with shot, shattering televisions, puncturing pots and pans, there was little left in the way of whole items. GUNS & RODS had their *berserkers* who at the first sniff of a fired cartridge, leapt on clothes counters in a frenzy, and used their hunting knives to tear suits and dresses to shreds. They came in firing indiscriminately and went out blasting with abandon. Not the least terrible amongst them was the maniacal figure of Mr Thornton Vandyne, the pupils of his eyes like tiny mad mosquitoes, as he emptied two .45 automatics at anything that resembled a human shape.

When Bert Wilkins, the Chief Security Officer, crawled mortally wounded to the main doors at noon and opened them as the clock struck twelve precisely, the waiting hordes trampled him underfoot. New friendships disintegrated. Fresh loyalties were crushed without hesitation or remorse. It was every man, woman and child for themself. The waves of customers kept coming until the store was full of people. At first they ran around with wild eyes, their thoughts tuned to bargains. Then gradually their feet slowed to a stop, their thoughts became more regulated. Slowly, slowly the idea that all was not right with Maccine's settled like dust upon their feverish brains.

A kind of universal daze came over the crowd, as they stared about them at the smoking ruins of Maccine's interior, the soles of their shoes crunching fragments of crystal into the carpet. There was nothing left to buy. Nothing worth having, that is. All that remained, amongst the corpses, were the useless shards of a former shopper's paradise. The devastation had been total. A holocaust.

It was the end of all cheap things.

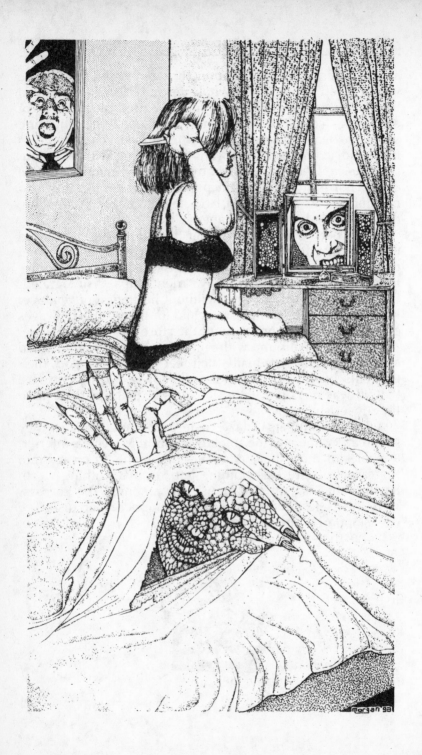

DADDY

Earl Godwin

Earl Godwin, Parke Godwin's brother, was an enthusiastic fan of horror fiction who unfortunately died before he could pursue a writing career. The story reprinted here (from Charles L. Grant's Shadows 7) *is the only one of the author's so far published, although several were completed, and it has been optioned for filming.*

I stay away from singles bars. I never was good at clever small talk, and I'm at my fumbling worst when the whole idea is to strike up a relationship with a woman. That's why I choose neighbourhood haunts where the serious drinkers gather to pass the evening in comfortable ambience. However, the thought is always tucked away in the back of my mind that I just might meet a special lady who could laugh aside my clumsy, inarticulate style and find charming the rather eccentric limitations of my bachelor life.

I met her in spades.

It had been raining and there was a chill in the air, so I sat in the back of the crowded bar in my raincoat nursing a straight bourbon. There were a lot of women in the place, some very attractive, but not that special one with whom I'd consider dancing through a night's fantasy. In life I've settled for some very ordinary women. In my dreams I always go first-class.

She came in with a man, and they threaded their way back through the crowd until a waitress seated them in a booth right next to my table. The man hung up their raincoats and she stood next to me, shaking the water from her dark, shoulder-length hair. A drop landed on my upper lip; I slowly licked it off, staring at her.

They weren't happy: this I could see right away. Worry

traced its path across her darkly beautiful features. This was a queen, not just worthy of my idle fantasy but one for whom I could work my whole life to wash the torment from that exquisite face and replace it with happiness. I don't say that easily, because I consider myself an accredited critic of beauty. I'm a photographer, and even if my sexual successes have been among the mediocre, I have a sharp eye for real beauty, and this creature with her eyes that leaped out and grabbed you would steal the heart out of a polar bear. The man? Who knows? I wouldn't remember him if he fell on me.

I tried not to stare. Her eyes flicked over me for a preoccupied instant and then away. I listened to the soft, tense tone of their conversation. He was saying things like, 'Tired of it . . . had enough . . . impossible.' I couldn't make out much. Most of it was in whispers and I don't hear well. They raised their voices slightly. The conversation was becoming more intense. The man leaned over the table, his face strained and angry, hers desperate and afraid. She hissed something that sounded like an ultimatum. He jumped up and shouldered his way through the crowd to the front door. I looked quickly at the woman. Her expression was one of weary defeat. It seemed to add years to her face.

Alone and nervous, she fumbled her way through several matches until she managed to light her cigarette. I caught her eye and raised my shot glass in a sympathetic toast. She started to raise hers, but the glass was empty. 'I seem to be abandoned and the gentleman had all the money.' She flashed a vulnerable smile.

I signalled the waitress. 'May I join you?'

'By all means.' Her confidence had returned, but there was still that air of vulnerability about her that excited me. I prayed I wouldn't overplay my hand.

I have a book at home called *How to Pick Up Women*. There are hundreds of opening lines for starting a conversation; I couldn't remember a single one of them. We looked at each other for an awkwardly long time until I blurted, 'Was that your husband?'

'No.'

'He sure ran off and left you like a lone duck.'

'No, just a friend. It's not important now. Do you have the time? I have to go soon.'

I felt my hopes plummet. 'It's nine o'clock. Please – don't go. I love talking to pretty ladies.'

She looked at me sharply, an appraising glance. 'Aren't you the charmer.' Then she fumbled with another match. I leaned over to steady her hand.

'*Eres muy caballero.*'

'You're Spanish?'

'I've been a lot of things. Do you live around here?'

I hadn't expected that. My pulse started to hammer faster. 'Yeah. I've got a studio apartment a couple of blocks from here. I'm a photographer,' I added for no good reason.

'Oh?' Her fingers drummed lightly on the table.

'Yeah. Uh . . . I'd like to take some pictures of you.' Oh Jesus! I winced inwardly to hear that tired old line come out of my mouth.

'I'll bet you would.' She ground out her cigarette in the ashtray, stood up, and reached for her raincoat. My heart sank; she was leaving. She put her coat on and fluffed that wonderful hair out around her shoulders. I sat staring up, hypnotized by her. She was older than I thought at first, pushing forty but still an incredibly beautiful woman. I would have said younger when she first came in, perhaps a trick of the light. But now she was leaving, the kind of woman ministers leave home for, and I'd never see her again. Jesus.

She smiled at me. 'Your place?'

I couldn't believe it.

I was all thumbs and stupid remarks as I tried to appear suave while attacking the suddenly impossible task of putting on my raincoat. She leaned against the booth with a tired patience and glanced up at the clock. She finally helped me with the coat before someone had to cut me out of the damned thing. We walked out of the bar with her in the lead, and I gave a few friends a debonair wave, as if leaving with the finest fox in the house was old stuff for me. Taking her hand, I couldn't help thinking how I'd almost let her get away from me.

My studio apartment was quite naturally a mess. I turned on a light and watched her as she picked her way through a maze of lightstands and reflectors. My furnishings were rather sparse, but I did have a studio couch and a couple of easy chairs. The kitchen area was in the rear corner of the big room, away from the window. The sink was full of vintage dishes and maybe some new life forms.

She moved around and studied the pictures on the walls as I fixed a couple of drinks and turned on the stereo. 'Very pretty women. How many have you slept with?'

'All' would have been a great answer, 'half' would have been half true. 'None of them,' I muttered.

'I love honesty,' she laughed. Then in a husky whisper as she came to me: 'It makes me feel so warm toward a man.'

We were standing in the middle of my front-room studio with the stereo low and the dim light struggling against the chilled gloom of the big room. She took my hand and guided me to the bedroom in the back of the apartment.

I kissed her full lips. They felt soft and full of promise, parting under mine, searching with her tongue, bringing me to quick readiness. I didn't rush. I'd been waiting a lifetime for this and I was going to enjoy the hell out of it. We undressed each other, pausing to caress favourite parts. Her large breasts were straining to be touched. She stroked and teased me and I pushed her gently back onto the bed – not in a hurry. Hell, I could have foreplayed with her until the cows came home. She was the one in a rush. She cried out then, a sound of relief and hope and something like fear, wrapping her legs around me as we rocked together in abandon. She held me like a vice with her arms and legs, squeezing me tight.

'No, honey, stay. I want it all.'

I came and felt a surge of relief flood through me. For her that was it: show's over. She rolled me off her and stood up. 'Thank you.'

Odd thing to say after an interlude like that. I rolled over and found myself staring up into the wickedest gun barrel I'd ever seen.

'I don't get it. We were having a good time. What gives?'

She stood naked before me, unsmiling, with the pistol levelled at my head. She looked stricken. 'Please. I haven't much time and I'm going to need your help. Don't ask questions, I don't have the answers. You have to deliver my baby.'

I must have looked classically stupid with my jaw down around my ankles. 'You're not pregnant.'

'I am now and you're the father.'

I managed a laugh like a choking gargle. 'Aren't we a little premature? I mean like this stuff usually takes nine months.' I laughed again, feeling ridiculous, sitting on the edge of the bed naked as a baseball. But there was nothing funny about her rage or the fear it came out of.

'Stop laughing, goddamnit! I – ' She gasped in pain. The pistol dropped from her hand and she fell face forward, curling into a fetal position, holding her stomach. I picked the gun up and dropped it into a drawer. Rolling her over onto her back, I couldn't help notice that she looked even older than I thought the last time. I couldn't explain any of it, the whole thing was beyond me, but I had the feeling that what was happening here was as unique as it was awful.

I showered and dressed. She was moaning and rubbing her stomach when I got back to her. I stood by the bed looking down at her. There was a grotesque aspect to the situation now. I watched in helpless horror as the woman's belly began to swell – a little at first, then faster, as if someone were blowing her up with an air pump. And all the while her hair was greying like flickers of light in the dark mass of it. Sagging, wrinkled skin and brittle bones, long past the ability to stretch against the obvious labour pains, punished themselves to do what they were made for. She looked – she *was* now – sixty years old, the sound of her breathing like a saw in wood.

'Help me, please! Oh God, it's almost too late!'

She gave a low animal growl and drew her knees up against her breasts, her hands clamped on the headboard. The gasps were coming every couple of seconds – and then I could see the first sign of a small head.

She'd asked me to help. Me? In a normal birth I would have been useless as pants on a bird. Here I was a blithering idiot. I could only stand frozen and helpless as the nightmare unfolded in front of me. The baby's head and shoulders protruded now; the woman writhed like a trapped fish. Unintelligible gibberish escaped from her withering lips. Then, somehow shaking out of the trance, I grasped the slippery little shoulders and began tugging, pulling life out of death. The woman was actually shrinking now, falling in on herself, seventy-five, eighty years old. She'd stopped moving by now, gone stiff, gone beyond that, *way* beyond it, and the smell emanating from the decaying mess of her was almost too much to bear. I had the baby almost all the way out. Only the feet were inside. By the time I cleared them, the thing on the bed had been dead a very long time. The smell was sickening. I fought the need to vomit, stumbling into the bathroom for a fresh razor blade to cut the umbilical cord binding the baby to something that didn't quite make it out of the body.

It was a girl. Remembering old movies, I held her up by the little feet and gave the tiny buttocks a sharp smack. Her gasp and yowl started her breathing.

My daughter.

I carried her into the bathroom and washed her down with lukewarm water. Then, messed with blood and other matter I'd rather not think about, I stared at my reflection in the mirror. He looked like I felt, every bit of it. And he was a father.

I wrapped the baby in a blanket and the now unrecognizable remains of my date in the sheets. What to do with the gruesome bundle was a problem. I couldn't take it to the police . . . Sure, they'd believe me. Sure they would . . .

The baby was crying. It was hungry. I collapsed by the picture window in the front-room studio with her in my arms as she nursed at the makeshift bottle I scrounged from my photo equipment, some milk from the icebox and – hell, why not? – an unused condom from a pack in the dresser.

What the hell was I going to do? The shock was wearing off, replaced by exhaustion. I wearily placed the bundle on the floor next to my chair, adjusted the bottle for her to work at it, and sat back with a very deep sigh. I'd had a hard night.

I watched the rain sifting past the streetlights as the drops splashed on the pavement. Cars plowed through puddles and sent sheets of dirty water up on the deserted sidewalks. The clock across the street said midnight. I yawned and looked down at the baby. She was happily pulling away on her bottle, watching me with clear blue eyes. A little while ago they were barely open and still milky, unfocused. God help me – she'd grown.

I fell asleep in the chair, lulled by the soft drumming of the rain against the window. I must have slept for over three hours when I snapped awake suddenly, more out of a sense of guard duty than from any particular noise. The rain had stopped but the streets were shining wet, and I caught the reflection of the stoplight on the corner in the damp sheen of the sidewalk. I remembered and sat up.

The blanket was empty and the bottle lay next to it. Behind me I heard faintly the soft tread of tiny feet. Turning, I could just make out the small form coming toward me out of the dark. My hair rose; I jumped up, knocking over the chair. She approached with careful child-precision. She was wrapped in a sheet that trailed behind her, and her dark hair was tousled down around her bare shoulders, and she pulled at my pants leg, urgent and trusting.

'I'm hungry, Daddy.'

I went into the bedroom, picked up the bundle of bedding, and carried it down to the dumpster in the back alley. And I disposed of the remains of that thing I had made love to. The mother of that thing in my apartment. I wasn't thinking; clear-cut thought was impossible. I walked back into the apartment. The little girl was standing by the window, peering out.

'Where'd you go, Daddy?'

'I just threw your mother in the garbage. From what I knew of her, she ought to feel right at home.'

Her eyes weren't that young anymore. She pulled her curls away from her shoulders and shook her head. A beautiful child. She didn't look anything like me. I made her a sandwich and a glass of milk, watching her as she ate – six or seven years old, only I knew better. She wasn't that many hours old. I retreated to my chair by the window and stared hopelessly out into the wet streets. Then she was at my side.

'What was my mother like?'

'I don't know. We didn't spend much time cultivating a relationship.'

She giggled, pressing my hand in her two small ones. 'I love you, Daddy. You talk funny.'

She leaned over and kissed me with a little hug. I felt myself go soft but I couldn't let her know it. We held onto each other as a fresh sheet of rain beat against the windows and made little wet rainbows out of the blurry neon signs across the street. We talked together about nothing much until finally, just before daylight, we both drifted off to sleep.

The roar of a bus outside the front window woke me with a start. I yawned and stretched; a glance at the clock across the street said it was a little after 8 am.

'You want something to eat, Dad?'

A pretty adolescent girl carried a plate of eggs into the dining area. 'C'mon, Dad. I know you're hungry. The one without the sausage is mine. I hate sausage.'

I wasn't in shock anymore but still not ready to accept this thing as it was. She sat down and scraped eggs off into her plate from the skillet.

'What are you staring at, Dad? You act like you've never seen me before. C'mon – eat up before it gets cold.'

While I ate, I studied her: seventeen or eighteen now, well formed, rapidly becoming the woman I had been with the night before. She devoured her food hungrily and downed a glass of milk in one pull, leaving a white mustache on her upper lip. I leaned over and wiped it off.

'Thanks, I'm always so messy. Okay if I do the dishes later? *All Quiet on the Western Front* is on TV, and I've never seen it. It's a classic.'

Whoever, whatever, from wherever, these things were born with some memories. I waved my hand helplessly. She could do whatever she wanted as far as I was concerned. The only thing she couldn't do was leave this apartment. I'd have to see to that. Until whatever was going to happen . . . happened . . . I'd just sit tight.

The morning passed in front of the television as we watched Lew Ayres in a dated but vivid story of a doomed German infantryman in World War I. She sat with her eyes glued to the screen. I couldn't help admire the beauty budding, blooming in front of me. She was full-bodied now, the woman I'd loved and watched give birth to her about sixteen hours before. The same woman.

The movie ended. She stood up and stretched, her breasts straining against the sheet that fit her a lot better now. She caught my glance. 'Like what you see?'

I felt the surge of heat. I must have blushed. 'Sorry. You're very beautiful. But I shouldn't have been staring.'

'Were you in the war?'

'I was in Korea,' I mumbled, glad for the change of subject.

She sat down again, drawing the sheet up around her. 'Men don't have much to look forward to, going off to war all the time. I'm glad I'm a woman.'

I thought, *Honey, they've got a lot more to look forward to than you do, any way you slice it.*

In a moment she went over to the stereo, sifting through the records, smiling over her shoulder at me. 'Got an idea.' She put on a record and came to me, holding out her hands in invitation. 'Let's dance, Daddy.'

I moved with her to the music, feeling the same power begin to sap at me as the night before. She pressed against me and hummed in my ear. I wrapped my fingers in that lush head of hair and pressed my face to hers, completely lost to the moment. She tilted her head back and looked up dreamily through seductive half slits of eyes. Her lovely mouth was so close to mine.

'I love you, Daddy,' she whispered.

Her mouth came up and I mashed mine down on it. That one second none of the sick, bizarre truth of this thing was going to rob me of the one moment a guy like me remembers all his life. Then, as she writhed her body against me, I felt something else, something cold. As if I were detached, across the room watching, I saw myself pressing back against her urgently thrusting body, sucking at her mouth, the mouth I remembered. A flash of her mother darted through my mind, the woman, the old woman, decaying before she was even dead. The same woman kissing me now. I saw the whole monstrous thing for what it was and pushed away from her so hard that she fell backward onto the floor, frightened.

'Get off of me!' I screamed. 'Don't touch me. What are you? I don't think there's a *word* for you.'

Tears of fear and rejection welled up in her eyes, a last piece of the fast-fading little girl in her. 'I'm sorry,' I said at last. 'I shouldn't have done that. But . . . do you know what in hell you are?'

She sighed resignedly and got up, adjusting the sheet

around her, slipped over to my liquor cabinet and fixed us
both a drink. She handed me the glass, holding me with
those eyes, the total woman now, cycle complete. 'Yes. I
know what I am. Does it matter? I know you want me.'

'You're my own daughter.'

She sipped at her drink. 'I've been a lot of men's daughter.
Does it bother you?'

'Damn right it bothers me. You can't possibly think I can
treat this like your everyday affair.'

I saw the lost look in her then, the same as the night
before, only now I knew what it was: the sense of too little
time already running out. 'You'll just let me die.'

'I don't know what I'm going to do.'

I collapsed in the easy chair by the window. She moved to
it and looked out at the rain. It was still blowing against the
glass. The watery reflection did sad things to her face. She
already looked much older. I felt I had to say something.

'How long has this been going on? How could it ever
start?'

'Does it matter?'

'You've got to admit it's an awful lot for a man to accept.'

'I don't remember how it started. A long time ago, hundreds of years. You wouldn't believe it.' I heard the despair,
saw it in her maturing face. She knew this was going to be her
last night. I wasn't going to let her out of the apartment.

With a set of handcuffs sometimes used as a prop, I cuffed
her to the radiator in the bedroom and made sure she was
comfortable. She didn't fight it; maybe she figured it was
time. I wasn't actually killing her, only allowing her to die.
I guessed about six more hours would do it.

I'll say one thing for her, she never begged. While I
cuffed her to the radiator, she just watched me with a
weary resignation. When I started to leave the apartment,
she was crying – softly, trying to hide it from me. Somehow
I couldn't just close a door on her.

'Look . . . I'm sorry.'

'I love you, Daddy.'

'Don't say that.'

'Why not? That's part of it. Can't there be that much beauty
to it, and can't you believe that much?'

I closed the door between us.

Mostly, I just walked in the drizzling rain, stopping now and then for a drink in one of the bars I knew. I wanted to get drunk and blot out the whole impossible thing. I ended up in the bar where I'd picked her up the night before. I realized now that it wasn't a different woman at all; she was always the same. I sat nursing my drink, glancing at my watch now and then. Two hours . . . a long time yet. I couldn't even feel the drinks.

Just going to let her die, aren't you?

A friend came over to my booth. We talked for a while, how's business, that sort of thing.

How does it feel to be God?

I played the juke. All the songs sounded the same, but who listened? The hallway to the men's room was crowded with drunks. I fumbled my way through. Clear the way for The Lord Who Giveth and Taketh Away.

The mirror in the john was the sort that really tells you what you look like. I never should have looked. *Hey, you've seen it all before, a guy doing all the impossible things to keep a beautiful woman.*

I love you, Daddy.

What kind of guy would deliver a baby and dispose of a corpse every night for the rest of his life?

I love you. That's part of it. Can't there be that much beauty?

I walked out of the bar and headed up the street toward my apartment. It was raining harder now, and I pulled the collar of my raincoat up around my neck as I turned down my street, knowing when I got up in the morning I'd have to raise a little girl to womanhood. I climbed the stairs and walked down the hall to my door.

And then at night, make love to your own daughter so she can live one day to do it all over again. The full cycle of life a man goes through once, three hundred and sixty-five times a year. But the guys I knew, those guys back in the bar, how many of them ever found a woman like this?

You tell yourself: nobody is God. They can call it what they want – incest, Dracula's daughter, whatever. Me? I was going for it. I opened the door to my apartment and shed my raincoat, dropping it on the floor, and walked over to the stereo to put on something soft and dreamy. I walked into the bedroom; there she was, still wrapped in the sheet, the most beautiful woman in the world at the late end of her prime, still . . . the impossible best. Her head came up when I entered the room. She looked at me uncertainly a moment, reading me surely, reading me right, then a slow smile curled that seductive mouth. Hell, I'd need a decent nursing bottle and baby food.

'Hurry, Daddy, or we'll be too late.'

THE DARK FANTASTIC

Adam Nichols

Adam Nichols hails from Canada. He made his publishing debut in the UK with 'Dead Bird Singing in the Black of Night' in the Spring 1982 issue of Fantasy Tales. *Since then, his stories have appeared in the USA, Australia, Canada and France. His debut fantasy novel is published by Millennium in 1994, with a second already under contract.*

YOUNG Peltrie goes helter-skelter through the tangled thickness of the greens. Their thorny suppleness catches and snaps at his little legs and he would cry out, tell them to stop it, if he dared. But he does not dare. Furious Black-Eye and Big are too close. He can hear the rush of those two behind him now. Much too close. The big leaves of the greens shower sudden stinging water down upon him, and, spluttering, he helter-skelters on through the ropey limbs and twisty trunks of them.

But Big was some wonder! thinks Peltrie, remembering as he runs. *Great showering wonder* . . . He skitters on, his mind full of the bright remembrance of that moment, that one, only, precious beyond precious moment of it when Big had shown . . .

In the small openness of Black-Eye's lonely glome in the deep Green it had begun, in the early evening with the Here of day dying and the Beyond of night about to be born, with Black-Eye spinning, spinning, his bones and feathers rattling and buzzing in the dying light, the blue coruscation that auraed him growing sparky-bright, his dark eyes wide afire with vision of the Beyond-Beyond. And little Peltrie scrunched up close and secret, but open as a flower to the wind when Big had come.

A sighing of long, lightbright limb and shimmer was Big, summoned by Black-Eye's power not just from the Beyond of the night – anybody could do that! – but brought from Beyond-Beyond, which lies past night and day, or before it, where flesh is not flesh, where the Now of life is different, different and flowing suddenly with wonders such as Big. And every hair on Peltrie's head had shivered erect. His bones shimmered in his flesh. His flesh jellied on his bones. Involuntarily, he had arched out of his concealment to hover there for one bright moment of clear, betraying sight in front of Black-Eye.

Aiee . . . What a great wonder was Big!

Fleeing Black-Eye's wrath, Peltrie skims down a sloping slope, trying to do it as he knows Black-Eye would, tacking along the looping shudders and twisty patterns of shattered rock and earth and limb and the flowing shimmer-force of the greens. His bowels shake with terror and joy and the body-knowing of quickness in flight. From behind, the rush of Black-Eye and Big is louder and nearer. Peltrie feels a sudden liquid flush of fear and rides it ecstatically, also as Black-Eye would, rides it out and down over the slope to the waiting water below.

The water is coolness, shadowed in the dying light by the big leaves of the greens. Drip, drip, drip, from the funnelling leaves into the pool the water goes, making a mazey and intricate pattern of expanding ripple circles on the surface. Greens above, skeltered greens reflected below in the pool. And in the midst of the reflections, the big calm eyes of a solitary eppie, long, furry limbs submerged, furry snout resting on the liquid surface of the water, watching with open-wide, round eppie eyes.

'Help me help me help me,' Peltrie implores, his breath coming in sharp, painful gasps.

The eppie snorts uncomfortably.

'Master Black-Eye and Big . . . Oh help me sweet eppie, help me please!'

Round eyes gaze unblinking. Tufted ears flicker.

Peltrie leans down and out over the water, his own bare body yearning upwards towards him in reflection. 'Please, eppie, lend me sanctuary in your pool. Oh *Please!*'

Round eyes still gaze unblinking. Tufted ears still flicker.

But the eppie does not flit way into the depths. The pool does not darken. Peltrie chances it. Black-Eye and Big are almost upon him now. From behind, he can sense Black-Eye's hot presence. Straining to do it right, Peltrie lowers himself into his own dancing reflection in the eppie's pool. The big open-wide eyes blink once, but it is all right; the eppie only sighs a long, snorting sigh and moves not at all.

Tanni sat, leaned back against the rough, hot face of an upthrust of shattered rock, fanning herself with her hand. She gazed about her at the thorny green tangle of vegetation that hemmed in their makeshift camp. It seemed . . . alive somehow, alive with a strange pulse and shimmer. Staring at that jumbled, green chaos, she felt a febrile shiver go through her and a little stab of something that might have been terror or exaltation. Or perhaps some eerie compound of both.

'Stinking heat . . .' said a voice, startling her.

'What?' she said, looking round.

It was Biss, walking over from the centre of camp and throwing himself tiredly down by Tanni's side, 'I said . . . the worst thing is this horrible, sticky, *stinking* heat.' Biss shifted himself to a more comfortable position against the hot, cracked surface of the rock against which they both now leaned, and wiped the sweat from his forehead on the sleeve of his Guard's tunic. 'I hate it!'

Tanni nodded in commiseration.

Biss ran a hand through his thinning, grey-speckled hair and sighed. 'A long hard plod for a first day. Travelling in this wretched, tangled-up place is like thrashing through a rubbish heap.' He lifted the big canteen which he had brought with him and took a long, gulping swallow. 'I hope Commander Tolke knows what she's doing. I don't fancy being lost down here. Whatever does she expect to *find* in all this chaos?'

Tanni reached for the canteen, took a sip. The water was flat tasting and blood-warm, but at least it helped wash away the aftertaste of the dry field-ration supper they had just eaten.

'The light never really penetrates down here properly,' Biss continued. 'Everything seems smothered in dank haze.

And everything's so tangled up I never know where to put
my feet.'

Tanni nodded.

'Feels almost like you're working your way through some
sort of giant, mouldered-up corpse, doesn't it?' Biss said.
And then, looking at her, 'Hoi, are you all right?'

Tanni sighed and shrugged and nodded and sighed again.
'Yes,' she said. 'Sure. Just tired is all.'

Biss looked at her doubtfully. 'You sure?'

Tanni took another warm sip from the canteen, looked
across at him, and smiled. 'Sure,' she said, trying to sound
convincing. 'Just tired.'

Biss did not look very convinced.

'What about that bloated thing we passed this afternoon?'
Tanni said quickly, before he could ask anything further. 'The
thing all covered with fungi. Looked like it could almost be
some crazy sort of . . . of house almost. Do you think Baily
really saw something move inside it like she said she did?'

Biss shrugged. 'Who knows? You'll have to ask Baily.
Makes my belly crawl just thinking what might have been
inside that thing.'

Tanni glanced around their encampment. It was a smallish
area of hastily cleared ground, littered with mouldering
slabs of pale rock and the white, twisted-up stubs of the
plants they had torn and hacked away to make camp. And
beyond, hemming them in on all sides, was a solid, green
tanglewood of vegetation. Most of the company just sat; the
heat made them all short-tempered and sluggish and too
tired to do much of anything. To her left, Tanni could see
a few die-hards tossing the bones, betting, and urging each
other on. On the far side, somebody played a slow melody
on a little flute. But there was no sign of Baily.

Tanni yawned and rubbed her eyes. Overhead, the bellies
of the clouds glowed a dull carmine, lit by the setting sun,
but down here the light was fading. The greenery hemming
the camp was fast becoming shadowy dim.

'Whyever did you volunteer for this wretched Downside
expedition?' Biss asked. 'This is your first expedition. You're
young. You could have done something easy, something like
the Windeater Peaks, maybe . . .' He reached the canteen
back from Tanni, drank, and sighed a long sigh. 'I wish

I'd stayed Topside. My head aches from the stinking hot air
down here and my belly feels like a sack of irritable red-birds
has been stuffed into it!'

Tanni stayed quiet. She did not know quite how to answer
Biss. In some ways, she hated it here as much as he did. The
moist, hot thickness of the air gave her a perpetual nagging
ache in the back of her head. And it stank. Each breath
seemed to rasp at her nostrils. Sitting there, she yearned
for the open air and the long, clear vistas of the Topside
clouds. She thought of the view from the veranda of her
mother's big rotunda, the clean, sloping lines of Mount
Shree going down to the undulating backs of the clouds
beneath, the chain of the Peaks upthrust like islands amidst
the cloud-swirl, the beauty of the evening, sky purpling
darkly, a scatter of crimson glowholes where the cloud layer
was thinnest set blazing from underneath by the submerged
and setting sun.

Topside, it was all light and coolness, all clear, airy distance
and straightness, and the eternal, rolling beauty of the clouds
below.

Here, it was all a thick green tangle of plants, shattered old
rock, foetid little pools, pervasively gloomy, hot and cramped
and miserable.

And yet . . .

And yet there was something about the orderliness and
the space and the light of Topside life that left her obscurely
dissatisfied. There was something missing, something she
could not put name to. And that had been the real reason
she had volunteered for Commander Tolke's Downside
expedition. To find a name for the nameless something
that was missing from her Topside life.

Silly. Too silly to confess to Biss at any rate.

She had not named that nameless something so far by coming down here. But something *was* happening. Somewhere in
all this heat and confusion, in the organic chaos that was so
unlike the ordered, airy openness, the cleanness of Topside,
there was something that called to her. But what voice was
it? What voice could it be in this wretched, clammy, dark,
disordered and dangerous place? She did not know.

A hand on Tanni's shoulder brought her out of her revery.
Biss turned her and pointed towards Baily, sauntering back

from relieving herself behind the thatch of scrub creepers and shattered rock on the camp's periphery that Tolke had ordained as the latrine area.

Biss waved, caught Baily's eye, beckoned. 'Let's find out if she really did see anything.'

Baily came forward a couple of steps, skidded precipitously, slapped at something on her upper arm, and screamed.

The camp erupted. Scatterguns sprang into sight. Baily, still screaming, jittered hysterically into the clearing. Something black and shiny, the size of a big hand, scuttled along her arm and burrowed into the flesh of her left breast, chewing through the tough fabric of her Guard's tunic as if it were paper. Blood flooded up in a dark, wet rush. Baily flapped frantically at the thing with both hands, spun about, and collapsed face down in a shivering heap on the ground.

Tanni leaped from where she had been sitting and scrambled to Baily's aid.

'Don't touch her!' Commander Tolke called out, her deep voice carrying clearly even through the confusion. 'Don't *touch* her!'

Tanni slid to a shaky halt.

Writhing face down on the uneven ground, Baily moaned. Her back arched spastically. Tanni heard something go *crunch* in Baily's breast, and a sudden wash of dark blood soaked the ground.

Baily lay still.

Tolke came up, scattergun in hand, and put a foot cautiously against Baily's still shoulder. In one quick movement, she kicked, tipping Baily over on her back, and leaped away. Baily's left breast was an oozing, open hole in which the black thing nested. Tolke aimed a long scatterburst at it and the thing exploded into sodden, sooty fragments. So did what remained of the left half of Baily's torso.

Tanni stared down at the bleeding, dead thing that had once been her comrade, a torn slab of wet red meat now, lying still. She felt her heart kick against her ribs. Her stomach clenched and heaved. Turning, she stumbled to her knees and retched.

Standing over Baily's body, Commander Tolke breathed

a long, ragged sigh. 'I warned you all how dangerous it is down here,' she snapped, turning, addressing the rest of the company who shuffled about, shocked and silent.

'It happened so *fast*,' somebody murmured.

Tolke glared at them. 'Baily was good, better than most, but she got careless. And you only need to get careless *once* down here.' She pointed to Baily's remains. 'That's what happens! This is *not* a nice place. I tried to tell you, but none of you really ever believed me, did you?'

Silence.

'*Did you?*'

More silence.

Tolke looked at what was left of Baily and shook her head. 'Get her cleaned up as best you can and bury her. Deep. I don't want her ending up being something's breakfast tomorrow.'

Nobody moved.

'Do it!' Tolke snapped, designating four of the nearest to the job and then stalking off.

Tanni shivered. Her hands shook. She felt a physical, nauseating repugnance for this wretched place overwhelm her. She saw again the black, scizzoring limbs of the thing, the liquid redness of poor Baily's dark blood, the hard white shards of splintered bone, and shuddered. How could she have ever thought there was anything down here but chaos and disaster? Still shaking, she stumbled quickly into the midst of the camp, looking for Biss, needing suddenly to feel the closeness of others about her, to feel protected from the darkened threat that hemmed them all in.

With a liquid twist in the thick water of the eppie's pool, Peltrie gazes up behind, to the place where he has just been.

Black-Eye himself stands there on the water's verge, his large hands clenching and unclenching, the blue, knotted veins of them shining. His bones and feathers chitter in a shiver of anger, and about him flares a blue glow, shimmering into surly red at the edges, easy to see now as the Beyond of night draws near. His eyes are hard, obsidian furies. Behind him, a little up the slope, Big hovers splendidly.

'Twisty little maggot-child,' Black-Eye hisses. 'Strip your skinny limbs of flesh, I will. Send you bare-boned and cold into the dark.'

Peltrie shivers.

'Give him up into my hands,' Black-Eye says coldly to the eppie, reaching. 'He has gone too far this time, spying on my most secret of secret things, and is mine now to do with as I wish!'

The tufted ears of the eppie arc backwards, close against the sleek furred skull, but the round eyes continue their unblinking, calm gaze.

Big draws close and Peltrie, wavering in the water, shivers harder. He feels himself jellying apart again under the pinwheel fire of Big's gaze. The water spangles eerily about him.

The glow about Black-Eye brightens and his hands shimmer with liquid bluefire now. He arches down toward the eppie. 'Relinquish the maggot-child to me now, eppie. Now!'

The eppie's eyes flatten out slightly, but it stays still and unmoving in the water. The pool itself begins to darken and grow chill.

Black-Eye flicks a talony hand against the surface of the pool and bluefire runnels across the top of the water. Peltrie feels the singe of it approaching him and scudders away as best he can.

And then a strange thing happens. A *strange* thing.

Big, sliding the air, sizzles the bluefire off into the night's Beyond.

Black-Eye stiffens, turns slowly to face Big. The bluefire pops and sputters into nothing in his hands. There is a long, slow moment of hard silence. Then, in a quick dance, Black-Eye's hands begin to form a binding pattern, looping and winding dizzyingly, drawing Big back, entwining him in the pattern.

Big shrugs it off.

For the first time ever, Peltrie sees something like fear in Black-Eye's face. Irascible Black-Eye, for whom young Peltrie forsook his own folk, so bright was the yearning in him, whom he has haunted and hounded for most of a season now, skulking in the Green and spying on secrets, refusing to be frightened away. Black-Eye, who has haunted and hounded him in turn, and for whom he, Peltrie, had never been enough of a thorn to warrant much heed. Until now. Solitary, distempered old man, from whom Peltrie has managed to learn much, but not yet enough. Black-Eye, showing the face of fear.

'No!' cries Black-Eye to Big, stiffening with a rattling tension. The blue glow about him shrivels momentarily. 'No. You cannot. You *will* not.'

Big moves in a slow, sinuous roll. Showers of tiny coruscating globules pelter down upon Black-Eye. They leave bright static trails in the air as they arc, and smouldering bursts of hot smoke where they land.

'It was *me* who summoned you,' Black-Eye cries in fright-fury, fending the brightness of the globules into nothing. 'Not the maggot-child. Not *him*. *Me!*'

Big shimmers menacingly.

Black-Eye takes an unwilling step backwards. Another. He glares one last, impotent glare, and the open black fury of that glare brings a sharp nausea stinging through Peltrie.

And then Black-Eye fades, dwindling into the darkening Beyond of the night.

Dwindled, but not gone. No, not really and trully gone. Shivering, Peltrie knows this, knows it with a blood deep certainty. Black-Eye accepts no defeat lightly. And Black-Eye never forgives.

The next morning, with Baily's death still uppermost in everybody's mind, the whole Squad moved forward with very great care, and with much glancing over shoulders and examining of ground. Wherever possible, they avoided the thicker and more knotted growths of plants and tried to make a way along the jumbled spines of the shattered, rocky outcroppings that marked this stretch of Downside territory. It was rough walking, but safer.

Biss had drawn point duty, with the rest of them in a loose wedge behind. They were working their way slowly upslope, panting through a confusion of shattered rock. It was a long, sweaty trek, and Commander Tolke called a rest halt once they reached the crest.

Tanni, on the left flank of the wedge, leaned gratefully

against the rough edge of a boulder and sighed wearily. This Downside country through which they travelled was utterly huge and wild and disordered. At moments, she had felt a creeping terror move through her.

And yet she still felt that strange, inexplicable, seductive Downside voice calling to her. And standing now, she could feel an odd tenseness, an excitement almost, as if something, she knew not what, was about to happen.

Tanni watched Tolke shrug off her pack, rummage through it for a second, then take out the leather map case in which she kept the meticulously penned glider surveys that were their only source of orientation down here. With the map case tucked under her arm, Tolke started to clamber up to the ridge crest where Biss crouched, hunkered down wearily in the shade of an outcrop of pale, splintered rock.

'Explorers!' Tanni overheard somebody near her mutter. 'Maybe I've gone skanky, but I don't see *nothing* down here worth looking for.'

'It's nothing but a stinking shambles down here!' some one else agreed.

'What *are* we lookin' for, Commander?' a third, bolder voice asked from across the other side of the wedge.

'I'll let you know when we find it,' Tolke called back quietly, not looking up from where she squatted now, map in hand, gazing out across the far side of the ridge. 'In the meantime, save your breath. You're going to need it.'

'Wonderful,' came a grunted response from somewhere down the line. 'Just what I like to hear, that.'

'Only thing Commander Tolke's looking for,' somebody whispered, 'is furthering her own career!'

Tolke shifted from her position on the crest and came striding back down to where she had left her pack. 'None of you lot seem to realize it,' she said, addressing them generally, 'but we're making history here. It's been three generations since the last Topsider walked this stretch of country. We'll be famous when we get back. All we need is . . .'

At that moment, Biss, still on the crest, interrupted. 'Commander,' he called softly. 'Commander, come and *see* this.'

From her position on the left flank of the wedge, Tanni could make out Biss clear enough, but she had no view of what it was that Biss had suddenly spotted.

Tolke moved up and hunkered down next to Biss.

For a long minute the two of them crouched there in silence. Then, slipping back a few paces, Tolke motioned to the two sides of the wedge. 'Fan out along the crest of the ridge,' she whispered. 'Silently. And keep down.'

Tanni edged upwards and worked her way between the boles of two trees, after first making carefully sure there were no unpleasant surprises lurking there for her. Downslope, on the other side of the ridge, the land opened up into an extensive valley. Though a damp haze of heat hovered over everything, Tanni could see that the valley itself was choked with vegetation. But it was not the view of the tangled greenery in the distance that caught her attention. It was something much nearer.

A lone man.

He was a skinny, wrinkled old man. Long, grey-white, ropey strands of hair hung damply across his shoulders, and sparse white whiskers prickled his face. He had bracelets of white bone around his wrists and ankles and a kind of intricate necklace of scarlet feathers and blackened bone dangling across his breast. But for the bone and feather adornments, he was stark naked. His skin, though wrinkled and folded like the rind of a dried fruit, gleamed with an oily sheen in the light.

A lone man . . .

As far as Tanni knew, nobody had ever met a Downsider before.

The man stood quietly less than fifty paces downslope from them, hands at his sides, feet apart, looking up towards their position. His face was half shrouded by the ropes of grey-white hair, but his eyes showed clear. They were big eyes, set wide apart over an arched nose, and black and sharp as a bird's.

Tanni felt instinctively that she did not like those eyes.

'Can he see us?' Tanni heard someone whisper near-by.

'What *is* he?' somebody else asked.

'A Downsider, air-brain,' came a whispered answer. 'Anybody can see that. I *told* you there had to be . . .'

'Shush!' Tolke hissed. She stared down at the man below. Her eyes widened, then narrowed thoughtfully.

'Downsiders,' she muttered, as if to herself. 'A naked savage. It's pitiful.'

Tolke shouldered her way across the crest of the ridge. 'Hoi!' she called to the lone man below. 'Hoi, you!'

'You sure this is safe?' Tanni heard Biss ask in a hard whisper.

'This is too good to pass up,' Tolke replied. 'Nobody's ever talked with a Downsider before. Think how it will look on my expedition Report! Besides, he's alone. What could he possibly do to us, well armed as we are?'

Peltrie drifts somnolently in darkness. Slowly, he feels recollection flood through him and he remembers, remembers Black-Eye dwindling into the darkening Beyond of the Green and he, Peltrie, easing out of the liquid safety of the eppie's pool. He remembers Big, lightbright and shimmering above him and so beautiful in the dimming dusk of evening that it made his belly ache with a painful, wondrous ache.

He remembers Big reaching, reaching gentle as the breeze, yet strong, strong, so huge and so strong. Wondrous being, spirit being, being from the Beyond-Beyond.

And Peltrie remembers the fear, the fear that jittered through him as Big took hold and tore him through the intricate convolutions leading to the Beyond-Beyond. This was not as he had imagined. This great, tearing blaze of agony and disintegration was not what he had imagined at all. Peltrie had twisted and scrabbled, desperate to be free of Big's hold, had fought with sudden, hysterical strength as he felt himself coming apart, felt his skin peeling like flaked bark from a tree, the long, wet, fibrous strands of his muscles flapping free, felt the network of his veins shred loose like rotted twine. One long scream he had been, one long agonized scream as his very bones were twisted and splintered apart.

Drifting, Peltrie remembers, but remembers smiling. For when it all had gone, with everything peeled, shredded, splintered away from him, then came the wonder of the Beyond-Beyond, aching wonder beyond words, beyond clear remembrance even, but still ringing clear in him somehow for all that.

And nothing will ever, ever be the same again, Peltrie thinks.

He sighs a long, gentle sigh and opens his eyes. He is himself again, intact. He feels the liquid pulse of his blood flush through him. He feels the air, warm and moist as a soft hand, lap about him. He is himself, yes. But, he knows, he is not the same self he once was.

Turning his head, he sees that he is lying on the verge of the eppie's pool. The eppie, furred head bobbing on the pool's liquid surface, blinks up at him slowly. But it is a new eppie Peltrie sees, a strangely different eppie. A blaze of delicate light pulses about the creature's head. The light is sunglow yellow, merging to sparks of violet at the edges. The eppie blinks again and the light pulses in tune with the blink.

Peltrie shivers. 'Sweet eppie,' he says softly.

About him, the Green glows and pulses with a similar blaze. It is a new Green, a radiant Green, all intricate leaf and branch and the leaping sparkle of sunglow.

And then, before him, Big comes, a brilliant, painfully beautiful Big. Peltrie's abdomen knots up in exquisite agony at the sight. In the full light of day, Big shines as would a firebrand in the dark.

Peltrie tries to move, to lever himself up from his prone position. But he is too weak. His muscles are lax and sore. His bones feel like thin green twigs, twisting and flexing in odd, useless ways.

For an instant, Peltrie feels a sharp prick of fear. What is wrong with him?

But Big hovers splendid and calm. With a sigh, Peltrie eases himself back down. It will come, in time. All he needs now is time to recover himself.

Gazing up at Big, Peltrie smiles tiredly. 'What a great wonder,' he hears himself murmur. 'What a great wonder . . .'

They moved quickly up and over the crest of the ridge and then downslope into the greenery on the far side. Commander Tolke kept them in the same wedge formation they had used for most of the day, but now the old man moved at the tip of the wedge, guiding them.

Tanni did not understand any of this.

The old man had talked with Tolke, squatting on his heels, his dark, bird-like eyes intent, and the next thing any of them knew Tolke had been all afire to plunge into the jungle below.

So plunge they did.

But Tanni did *not* understand, and the muttered grumblings she heard round about her confirmed that she was not the only one confused by this seemingly inexplicable impulse of Tolke's.

Tanni was amazed at how easily the old man flitted in and around and through the serried tangle about them. Gone were the cantered outcrops of shattered rock they had followed all morning. This was real jungle they were moving through now, thick and dim and close.

Watching his wrinkled, pale buttocks flash into view, disappear, flash into view again, Tanni cursed. She could not match, none of them could match, the old man's agile scamper. The ground was a tricky litterpit of dead branches and squishy fungus. Thorny tree limbs spiked at her like grasping hands, rasping against the tough fabric of her Guard's tunic. The trees themselves leaned at odd angles, drooped and throttled by an intricate dangle of lianas.

They moved forward as best they could, guided by the old man's silent hand signals, until he brought them to an abrupt halt, hands held out, the bone bracelets on his wrists and ankles rattling into stillness. 'Close now,' he hissed. 'Close.'

Close to *what*? Tanni thought. The tiny hairs along her arms and at the back of her neck prickled uncomfortably. For one brief and startling moment, Tanni thought she could discern a faint blue glow pulse the air about the old man. She shook her head, blinked. The glow was gone.

At Tolke's whispered instructions, they fanned out, several paces between each of them, and moved cautiously forward.

Tanni felt her pulse flicker and speed up.

Moving over a fallen and twisted up tree limb, Tanni missed her step and her right foot splashed ankle deep into scummy, black liquid. Something small and dark scuttled there. Her heart kicking wildly, she leaped sideways, smashed her elbow painfully against the rough trunk of a tree, and was brought up short, panting.

The others were ahead of her by now, but she did not rush

to catch up. Standing there, alone, she felt something strange begin to happen.

Though she was only now perhaps fifteen paces out of step with her companions, she somehow seemed irrevocably isolated from them. She felt totally alone in the pulsing gloom of the jungle, and, once again, the eerie Downside voice of this place was unexpectedly calling to her. The jungle shimmered about her in a dark chaos. She breathed it in, feeling something stir inside her responsively. There was nothing like this Topside.

She took a breath. Another. She felt the blood sing in her ears, heard the jungle sing in response. She felt frightened. She felt exhilarated. She did not know how she felt.

From somewhere up ahead, a scream split the air.

Tanni jerked, and then leaped forward, skidding to an abrupt stop when she found herself at the sudden edge of a small clearing.

Crouched there, concealed, the first thing she saw was Commander Tolke, splayed out on the ground. Tolke's face, those parts of her body that her Guard's tunic left uncovered, were purpled and splotchy and swollen like some overripe fruit. Blood trickled from her mouth. Her eyes, sightless and dead, bulged strangely. Even as Tanni watched, horrified, Tolke's left eye burst with a soft wet *thwopp*, oozing jelly and sodden red tissue down her dead cheek.

Standing next to Tolke's still form was the old man. His arms were held rigidly before him, the bone bracelets rattling. Once again, Tanni thought she could glimpse an elusive blue glow simmering around him. His dark eyes were locked on something in the clearing. 'Kill him,' he hissed. 'Kill him now. *Now!*'

Tanni turned and saw a round pond in the clearing before her. Lying prone nearby, propped weakly upon one thin arm, was what appeared to be a small, naked boy.

The old man gestured behind him, as if clawing something out of the jungle at his back. He made the motion once, twice, three times, all the while staring fixedly towards where the small boy lay.

For a long moment the jungle was strangely still. Then the abrupt, clattering whine of a scattergun lit the air. Tanni could see the bright swarm of deadly little flechettes shimmer towards the boy, and she felt a momentary, inexplicable pang of sorrow for him.

But the flechettes ghosted away into impossible vapour at the last moment and the boy continued to lie there, unharmed. From down by the old man's right, from where the burst of scattergun fire had come, somebody let out an agonized wail, and the undergrowth was thrashed into sudden, brief agitation.

Then all went silent.

The old man stood, shivering, his bones and feathers making a weird music. 'Kill him!' the old man shrieked. 'Kill him! All of you. *All of you!*' He clawed the air behind him as he had before, again and again, making great, furious, sweeping motions with his rigid arms. *'Kill him!'*

Tanni felt her hands move as if of their own accord. Her fingers tingled unpleasantly as they gripped hard against the stock of her scattergun, brought the barrel up to a sighting position. She found herself sighting down towards the figure of the boy before her, squinting through the vee sight of the gun at . . .

Squinting at . . .

In an instant the strange compulsion that had gripped her dropped away, ignored, unimportant, eclipsed. Unthinking, she burst from her concealment, the scattergun tumbling at her feet, forgotten. 'Do you see it?' she cried out, to everybody, to nobody. 'Oh! Oh . . . Do you *see* it?'

Peltrie feels them skulking towards him through the simmering, shimmering Green, Black-Eye in the lead drawing the rest along with him. Peltrie feels his pulse skitter frightenedly. Who are they? From where has Black-Eye summoned such strange aid?

He tries to rise, to shift himself, before they burst through into the little clearing about the eppie's pool. But he cannot. He is still too raggedly weak. The best he can manage is to raise himself up on one thin arm.

Black-Eye stands there. 'Maggot-child!' he hisses.

Peltrie can only stare weakly. The eppie is submerged into its pool. And Big? Where is Big? No lightbright shimmer hovers near. No Big.

Black-Eye grins hugely. His bones and feathers whirl and

clatter and sing. The blue glow of him stutters the air into angry life around him as he reaches behind, hand clawed into a grasping fist, and draws forth the first of his new allies.

She stands there, this new one, pointing a queer and shining stick at Peltrie. He can see the slight, pale glowing that is hers become enmeshed in Black-Eye's hard blue radiance. Black-Eye motions, his arm rocking. The shining stick is pointed. A clattering whine sizzles the air and a bright swarm of small, deadly things leaps out of the stick at him.

Peltrie shivers, and, hardly knowing how he does it, fends the dangerous little things off, skittering them away into nothing. *Big*! he shrieks soundlessly. *Big* . . . Peltrie's heart thumps painfully. *Big*!

Black-Eye glowers, his eyes dark points of fury, and gestures again peremptorily at this new ally of his. The stick is dutifully raised and pointed.

Peltrie whimpers, tries to scrunch himself down.

And then, with an angry *hoosh*, Big shows.

The shining stick splinters apart. Black-Eye's new ally screams once, then flops to the ground, bloating like an overripe fruit.

Peltrie gasps.

Black-Eye's fury is so great that it sends scalding blue tendrils of light coursing around him. He stands over the still form of his fallen helpmeet, arms locked rigid, bones rattling. 'Kill him,' he hisses, directing another of his new-found backers towards Peltrie. 'Kill him now. *Now*!'

From Black-Eye's right, there comes once more the strange clattering whine and small, deadly things leap out at Peltrie again.

Peltrie fends them off, panting.

And Big deals with this second of Black-Eye's allies.

Peltrie shifts his position, trying to prop himself up higher, trying to grasp what is happening. He can feel Black-Eye's backers out there in the Green, each one subsumed under Black-Eye's power, waiting, waiting to be used. But innocent, Peltrie begins to see, innocent of why they were brought here until too late. Innocent, yes, and in some strange, sad way, blind to the dark wonders that Peltrie lives for, blind to Black-Eye's glowing blue anger, blind to Big.

Blind to Big! How can anybody be blind to the great wonder that is Big?

But not all of them, Peltrie now realizes. There is one, hunkered down to Black-Eye's left, one who can almost see. Almost. Peltrie can sense her straining, can catch a glimpse of the glimpse she catches of Black-Eye's angry blue glow . . .

'Kill him!' Black-Eye shrieks, bluefire skuttering across his fingers. 'Kill him! All of you. *All of you!'* Again and again, he claws the air behind him, the bluefire lighting the Green behind him, making great, furious, sweeping motions with his rigid arms. *'Kill him!'*

Peltrie shivers fearfully, feels Black-Eye's allies, all of his new allies, squirm into life at this beckoning. Even the one Peltrie has just marked, the one who can almost see. He feels her shift, this one, feels her hands clutch the shining stick she carries, hands that move to Black-Eye's angry will.

'Big . . .' Peltrie calls soundlessly. *'Big!'* Peltrie does not know what he is doing. He does not think this. He feels it. His belly feels it. Reaching out, he senses her squinting through the vee sight at him. 'Big,' Peltrie implores. 'Make her *see.* Show yourself to *her!'*

Peltrie feels Big flower in sudden, wondrous brilliance above him. Black-Eye flinches away. But not her. Not *her.* She bursts from her concealment in the green. 'Do you see it?' she cries, her voice cracking through the clearing like invisible lightning. 'Oh! Oh . . . Do you *see* it?'

The pattern Black-Eye has been weaving unravels, fizzling through his fingers with the wavering bluefire of his anger. 'No!' he stutters. *'No!'* The bluefire surges up in him again. Peltrie sees it gather like a great, glittering cloud and cowers away from it instinctively.

Above him, Peltrie feels Big move and shift and reach out subtly to Black-Eye.

Black-Eye's fury gathers about him, coalescing. One talony hand comes up, sweeps down, flinging the bluefire of his terrible anger at Peltrie.

Nothing happens.

Black-Eye gags. He tries again. And again. The bluefire clings to him, turns on him, compacts on him.

And then, quite simply, Black-Eye erupts, riven by his

own bluefire fury, showering the eppie's clearing with dark, smoking, wet wreckage.

From above, Peltrie feels something emanate from Big, something which, if it were audible, and if Big were a person, might sound like . . . soft laughter.

Tanni blinked, shook her head, blinked again. Her ears rang strangely. There, above the boy, hovering . . . like nothing she had ever seen, ever imagined . . .

Lightbright shimmer of beauty.

She stood there, staring, unable to move.

'Tanni!' a voice called from behind her. 'Tanni.' The voice was Biss's, though shaken and wavery, not Biss's usual drawl. 'Come on, girl, move! We're getting *out* of here!'

But Tanni stood rooted as a tree.

'What's the matter with you, girl?' Tanni felt a hand reach to her shoulder from behind. 'We've got to get out of here.'

'Don't you see it?' Tanni asked, not taking her eyes from the wonder out there before her. 'Don't you *see* it?'

'See *what*? Are you crazy?' The hand wrenched Tanni about, shook her. Tanni found herself staring into Biss's face, white and shaken. 'Snap out of it,' he said. 'Snap *out* of it and come along.'

But Tanni only shrugged out of Biss's grip. 'It's too late for that,' she heard herself say, and, saying it, suddenly realized that it was true. It *was* too late.

If she had never come down here, if she had never left Topside . . . But she *had* come down here. She *had* heard the small, strange Downside voice singing to her, singing of darkness and mystery, of things she had never imagined in the airy heights and ordered structures of Topside. And she had seen that lightbright, hovering beauty out there, whatever it was. And now, somehow, nothing would ever, ever be the same again.

Big, a hovering flower of radiance, reaches out. Peltrie feels him touch the woman.

Peltrie does not understand.

Again, from Big, comes the something that might be laughter, or might be something much stranger. Big turns to him. There are no words, Big does not talk, but somehow

Peltrie understands. It is as if Big poses him a question: 'Why did I choose you over Black-Eye?'

Peltrie blinks. He has not had time yet to ask himself that question. He has been too immersed in the wonder of it all. Why indeed?

In answer, Big shows him a lightning rapid vision: of Black-Eye, Black-Eye weaving and twisting and fashioning, always fashioning the world to his own will. Drawing the mystery out of the darkness and binding it. And then Peltrie sees himself, open as a flower to the wind, eyes bright with wonder at that same mystery. Drawn to it, not drawing it to him. And finally, he sees the strange woman in the clearing, and sees the same wide eyed wonderment on her face too.

And feels, from Big, a great wash of cherishing fondness.

Peltrie shivers in mute wonderment.

Tanni took a step away from Biss. Another.

'Tanni!' he cried to her.

But it had all somehow slipped away now, the Guards, the Topside clouds.

A voice was calling to her. Calling sweetly. Calling mysteriously. Tanni gazed at the great hovering beauty there at the pool. The small boy underneath smiled at her. She smiled back.

A momentary pang of terror shivered through her. *What am I doing*? she thought.

'Tanni!' Biss cried again. '*Tanni!*'

Tanni glanced round once, for the briefest of instants, and then, to Biss's enduring astonishment and dismay, Tanni was gone, simply gone . . .

Tripping the dark fantastic with Peltrie, in the company of Big.

THE VIEW

Michael Marshall Smith

Michael Marshall Smith won the British Fantasy Award for Best Short Fiction in both 1991 and 1992. His stories have appeared in several volumes of Dark Voices, Best New Horror 2 *and* 3, The Mammoth Book of Zombies, Narrow Houses, Darklands *and* Darklands 2, *amongst others. His first novel,* Only Forward, *was published by HarperCollins in 1994.*

THE first glimpse Mark had of Northwood Hall was the most misleading, because it was funny.

With less than a week to go before the lease on his current flat ran out, Mark's flat-hunting was taking on an air of increasing desperation. There was nothing on the market, and the price Mark was hoping to pay had already provoked outright laughter. If pushed he could retreat back to his parents' house in deeper Essex, but it was bad enough looking from a base in North London. Trekking in from the suburbs would be a real drag, and after months of unremitting heat and light, summer had called it all off overnight and wintery autumn had dropped like a stone. Mark actually much preferred winter's darkness and shadows, but the accompanying rain made dogleg tube journeys and fifteen-minute hikes even less of a fun way to spend an evening.

LetsMove Letting was the third agency Mark had tried. He turned up at the Archway address to find that it was part of an estate agents. Within five minutes he had been bundled up and into a yellow convertible Mercedes, which was then aimed down a selection of the surrounding roads by the extraordinary letting agent.

Mark had seen yet another flat where the heating and

hot water didn't work 'but could be fixed, definitely' and
was on the way to the only other property LetsMove had
on offer before he'd really had time to draw breath. The
agent's name was Steve, and he managed to combine quiet
camp with being an Essex wideboy in a way Mark had not
only never previously encountered, but would have thought
utterly impossible.

They were somewhere in Upper Holloway when Steve
flourished the wheel over to the right and pulled the car
into a long circular driveway.

Even at first glance it was a bizarre place, a huge '30s
block that somehow looked as if it should be sat stolidly
not far from the front in a seaside resort that time had left
far behind. Hidden from the road behind a line of trees in the
middle of North London it looked massive and anachronistic.
Its six storeys with regular deco-style balconies were faded
and peeling pink and yellows, but the building somehow
gave the impression that in any photograph of the road it
would come out in black and white. Two huge wings at right
angles converged on what was presumably the lobby, and as
the car drew up the drive two very old people and a nurse
emerged.

Christ, thought Mark, biting his lip to fight off the giggles,
I'm being taken into residential care.

'Now you may like this, you may not,' said Steve. 'Who
knows.'

He parked the car, in the sense that he stopped somewhere
apparently at random and got out, and Mark followed him as
he marched off towards the main doors. The closer you got,
the bigger the place seemed to be, and quieter. Crouched
massively beneath the leaden sky, it was rather difficult to
come to terms with.

Steve led the way into the lobby, which was dark and
decorated largely in shades of brown. To the right was an
old wooden reception desk, which despite Steve's claims to
the contrary looked as if it had not been used in decades.
Mark looked down the two corridors which led off into the
distance. They were deserted.

'Now,' mused Steve, leafing through his keys, 'What
number are we? Oh yes: 614.'

Six hundred and fourteen? For God's sake, thought Mark,

close to giggling again. I can't live here: I'm about forty years
too young. How can I tell people my address is '614'?

Even the lift was extraordinary, a spacious cupboard with
floor indicator lights of original thirties-style numerals.

'Now, there are about two hundred flats in the block.'
observed Steve, swinging unpredictably into Estate Agent
mode. 'We are managing agents for about eight. Well I say
"we", but it's me really. I look after Northwood Hall. I'm
forever letting one or other of them.'

I can imagine, thought Mark. If the average age of the
occupants is anything like that the of pair outside, the turn-
over rate must be pretty high. There's probably an ambulance
round the back with its engine running 24 hours a day.

'Are there any, er, younger people in the building, at
all?'

'Oh yes,' Steve frowned. 'Well, there were. They caused
a bit of a stir though.'

Mark didn't really know how to pursue the topic, and
waited out the remaining moments as the lift crawled up
to the sixth floor in silence.

The lift opened out into a corridor which somehow
expanded the strangeness of the building into new realms.
It was a hotel corridor. Rather narrow and a murky green,
it stretched off to the left, bearing round and disappearing. Mark followed Steve along it, passing room numbers
in gold numerals on doors, half expecting to see a 'Do
Not Disturb' sign hanging off one of the knobs. He very
quickly lost track of where they might be on the floor,
becoming immersed in a feeling of placeless faded grandeur.
Abruptly Steve stopped, and thrust a key into the door of
room 614.

For the first few minutes Mark honestly didn't know what
to make of it, and then realized that thinking of the flat as a
hotel suite was genuinely the place to start.

The bedroom had floor to ceiling mirrored cupboards on
one wall, and french windows on the other which gave
out onto one of the balconies he had observed from below.
Delaying that for later inspection he moved into the en suite
(for God's sake) bathroom, which was done out entirely in
something which if it wasn't marble was as good as. He was
genuinely surprised not to see a small wicker basket with

a complimentary bar of soap and tube of toothpaste by the washbasin.

The next room along the corridor was another bathroom, which held a shower and toilet. It was after finding that the shower was one of the power variety and that it instantly gave hot water, that he first began to take the place more seriously.

The flat was arranged as rooms off a long lateral corridor that eventually gave into the lounge. Mark wandered into this after giving the much smaller second bedroom a glance. He didn't need a second bedroom, of course, but the flat was within his price range, and he'd doubtless be able to find some use for it. Perhaps he could finally have a piano again, if there was any way of getting it up this high.

Steve was lurking listlessly in the lounge. Like the rest of the flat it was painted white, with recessed and upward-pointing light fittings. The furniture was stolid rented accommodation standard issue, right down to the rather strange and predominantly orange forest scene reproduction on the wall, but acceptable. Emerging at a slight curve from the far end was the kitchen area, which had a washer-dryer, fridge, freezer. It was spotless.

Oh dear, thought Mark, turning round to go back for a second pass, this place has actually got all the right bits. Back in the lounge he wandered over to the window.

'Lovely view,' said Steve, 'that's because we're so high up, you see.'

It was certainly a view. In the not too distant distance was Alexandra Palace, with buildings and part of the hill visible in front, and the effect of the whole panorama was very striking in a way which wasn't easy to define.

Mark found himself frowning, and, unsure why, he turned his back on the window and discussed the letting details with Steve, becoming increasingly sure that it was going to be hard to reject this place.

Finally he walked back into the bedroom. It was rather full of the double bed, which he sadly had no more need for, at least at present. But now that he was living on his own it didn't really matter, because he could set his desk up in the lounge and work in there. He opened the French windows and stepped out onto the narrow balcony, leaning on the rust red handrail.

High above traffic noise, it was very quiet, almost eerily so. Below was a car park, sparsely occupied. Drawing his eyes slowly up the wing to the left he looked in windows. All of the rooms he could see into appeared to be lived in, in the sense that there was furniture in them, but they also looked dark and somehow almost as if they were in storage. Steve had said that the building was pretty well full: perhaps it was just the atmosphere and size of the building as a whole that dwarfed the chairs and tables whose corners poked into view in the unlit rooms.

And then, of course, there was the view. Mark was not a particularly view-orientated person, finding that after a couple of weeks one tended not to notice that kind of thing, but it was there all the same. From the balcony there was about 120 degrees of unrestricted View. There was so much of it, in fact, that it seemed slightly oppressive, and strangely close to. The impression was not so much of a vista as of a city crowding closer, seen from a turret of isolation.

Shaking his head and smiling at himself Mark stepped back into the bedroom and closed the windows. Out of Steve's sight he did some serious thinking.

In some ways it was far from ideal. Taking one flat out of two hundred in an enormous '30s, well, monstrosity, whose other occupants were clearly for the most part on the 'do not sell these people life insurance' list, was not exactly what he'd had in mind. On the other hand, it had all the amenities, it was recently decorated, the hot water worked, he could afford it, and he could have it immediately. Mark was a little puzzled at the way he had to keep thinking of advantages to point out to himself, and at his reluctance to accept that they overcame some unspecified misgiving he seemed to feel.

Riding back down in the lift, he asked Steve what he had meant by a 'bit of a stir'.

'Oh, well they were a bit – well I'll tell you. She was a prostitute, basically.'

'Basically?'

'Yes. But not really on a one-to-one basis.'

'Ah.'

'And that's what caused the trouble, really. Coming back with five men in tow, not ideal, is it?'

'No, I can see that might excite comment.'

'Well it did.'

The lift reached the lobby and Mark stepped out, looking at the reception, which was supremely deserted.

'And the other?'

'Other what, sorry?'

'You said the girl was . . . and so on: there was someone with her, was there?'

'Well apparently. Don't know much about him. They're long gone, anyway. So: what's the verdict?'

'I'll,' Mark paused for a moment. 'I'll take it, I think.'

'Jolly good. Oh look, here's Terence. Terry you old tart, what are you up to?'

A stocky sunburnt man with a pencil behind his ear, about four-foot-eight tall and dressed in pink singlet and fluorescent green shorts, sailed past the bemused Mark.

'Oh this and that, this and that,' he sang, disappearing out of the front door.

'That's Terence,' confided Steve, 'he's the plumber.'

'Is he.'

'Who's this yob, then?' enquired Terence, sailing back in again, pausing to take in Mark's long black coat and dark clothing. 'Find him on a National Front march, did you?'

'You old tart,' laughed Steve, heading off towards the car. 'Very good plumber, though.' he added, to Mark. Back to biting his lip, Mark suddenly decided that any place that could pack so much bizarreness into one visit had to be worth a try.

It was only much later in the day, amidst a general feeling of relief that the problem of where he was going to live had been sorted out, that Mark realized that in all the time they had spent in the block Terence the plumber was the only person they had seen.

The following Thursday Mark pulled into the sweeping entrance drive of Northwood Hall, with a car-full of stuff and the beginnings of a headache. The intervening time had been a dull flurry of bill paying and packing, and he was glad that the last hurdle was now in sight. Taking his leave of the old flat had been a thoughtful affair: while it held many bad memories of the last few months with Gemma, if one looked far enough back it held good ones too. She had helped him move in there, and though they'd mainly only seen each other at weekends, the flat spoke of her. Leaving it seemed to say a final farewell to the time when they'd been together, to a time when they'd shared a space, however infrequently. It was sad saying goodbye to Susan, his flatmate, too: a year of sharing the same kitchen with someone breeds a strange kind of closeness.

There was no one to help him move in today, sadly, and Mark got out of the car and stared morosely, hands on hips, at the mountain of stuff to be lofted piecemeal up to the sixth floor in the lift. Dave had said that he might look in about seven, but Mark really wanted to be into tidying by then. He screwed his eyes tight against the headache and then resignedly opened the boot.

It took twelve trips, and when Mark finally shut the flat door for the last time he was hot and had very cold metal nails hammered into his forehead behind each eye. Wiping his forehead with his arm he stepped into the kitchen to unpack the paracetamol he had bought specially and with what he regarded as alarmingly grown-up foresight.

Swilling them down with a glass of water he wandered back into the lounge, glad that the room was currently piled high with boxes of his stuff. On first walking into the flat he had been struck forcibly by its clinical and sterile anonymity, but knew it was bound to seem like that, and that it would feel much less so when his books were out and his word processor enthroned on the table near the window. He walked into the corridor, slowly looking round his new domain.

He'd tried to get a chance to look around the flat again in the intervening couple of days, to gauge what furniture he'd need to buy and generally think himself into living there. Two phonecalls to LetsMove had proved fruitless. Steve had been unavailable, and the person answering the phone had been unable or unwilling to help. When Mark had called at the office on Wednesday afternoon Steve had again been absent, and the person who had handed Mark the keys without a word had been less than forthcoming on when he might reappear. Mark had simply wanted to extend him the courtesy of thanks for his help: clearly that was no longer the done thing.

The flat was much as he remembered it. It was still a hotel suite, or holiday flat, and he still found it a little hard to believe that he was about to start living there. But on the other hand it was still large and clean.

As always he unpacked and rigged the stereo first: in the silence it seemed an even better idea than usual to have music to unpack to. He started with some U2 and Bangles, but both seemed to rebound flatly off the walls, sounding empty and thin. He tried the Brandenburg Concertos as he sorted stuff out in the bedroom, but even they for once sounded a trifle too jolly. By the time he was putting his books onto the bookcase in the lounge he was onto Bach solo violin sonatas, which though beautiful, are not the sort of stuff you crank up in the car on a hot summer afternoon. Anything else seemed to sound desperate and forced: claiming these rooms for his own was clearly going to take a little longer than usual.

At seven Mark was perched on the sofa with a cup of tea with a book. Everything was in place, the boxes were stowed, and yet Mark found himself vaguely wondering what time checkout would be in the morning. He seemed to have made very little impression on the flat, on its space. Even the large bookcase he'd bought secondhand seemed isolated against the wall: the surrounding white seemed to make too much of it, to make it stand out more sharply than its worth could support.

The doorbell rang ten minutes later, and Mark opened the door to find Dave standing outside. He smiled tightly, said hello quickly and then walked in. Mark followed him into the lounge, surprised.

'Is anything wrong?'

Dave sat on the edge of the sofa.

'No, no. Weird place you've got here, though.'

'Yeah.'

Mark fetched a beer from the kitchen and handed it to Dave, who accepted it with a slightly warmer smile. After fifteen minutes or so he became sufficiently relaxed to reveal that his initial manner was a result of having got off at the wrong floor. He'd been unable to find his way back to the lift and so had sought out the stairs. He'd been in the building tramping down corridors for about ten minutes, and had found the experience rather unnerving.

Conversation never really got off the ground, and Dave rose to leave a few minutes later. Shutting the door behind him, Mark walked him to the lift.

'I mean, look,' said Dave, turning round to face the way they'd come, 'Look down that corridor. It's like a film set.'

Mark looked. The narrow corridor, dark but with intermittent pools of light, stretched out in front of them, ending in a door at the end. The pool of light there was slightly stronger, making it look very much like the door to The Room at the Top of the Stairs.

'Yes. Thanks for pointing that out, Dave. I've got to live here.'

Dave laughed thinly.

'Oh, I'm sure it'll be fine.'

'Mm. I'm having a sort of flat-warming thing on Saturday: coming?'

There was a slight pause before Dave answered, but he did so genuinely enough.

'Of course. Though what you need is a building-warming.'

Mark smiled, and Dave got into the lift and started it on its journey downwards. Before he walked back to his flat Mark looked at the stairwell. Even this was a little strange, somehow looking like stairs on board a ship. Probably it was just the slight '30s styling, the rounded contours.

Back in the flat Mark stood at the window, waiting for Dave to emerge at the bottom. Several minutes elapsed, and he was beginning to worry that he had got lost again when Dave came out of the door at the bottom, shoulders hunched, walking quickly away. Mid-evening, on impulse, he phoned Dave and asked him something.

'No,' Dave said, his voice sounding warmer over the phone than it had in the flat, 'I didn't see anyone at all.'

It always took Mark a few nights to get used to a new bed, and so he wasn't very surprised to find that he was unable to get to sleep. After a while he got up and made himself a cup of tea: though the evening was rather warm and muggy he always found that tea helped him to get to sleep. Back in the bedroom he opened the French windows and stepped out onto the balcony for the first time since moving in.

Though it was after one the sky was still quite light from the glow of the city. Alexandra Palace sat blockily on the horizon: perhaps it was the fact that the hill brought the horizon in so close that made the view seem strangely closed in. It was quiet apart from the murmur of night traffic, and still, in a humid sort of way. Mark sipped his tea and looked out over the trees and houses and for a moment had a peculiar feeling. It wasn't London he was looking at. It wasn't London, and yet it was familiar.

It *was* London, of course: the landmark was there in front of him. But something seemed odd, as if he were looking at the town from a different angle, seeing something out of the corner of his eye. The lushness of the trees and blue black of the glowing sky seemed supernormally intense, like a badly-lit stained glass window.

Shivering slightly, Mark let his eyes drop down the wing to his left: no lights were on. He closed the windows and tried to get to sleep. Eventually he succeeded.

Next morning at work Mark found himself tired and irritable. The little sleep he'd got had been fitful, and threaded with dreams which he couldn't quite remember. He seemed to recall a scene in which he stood out on the balcony and looked down at the city below, but this time knowing what city it really was. He wasn't sure whether this was a bona fide dream segment or simply a confused memory of having stood there, seen through the prism of his other dreams.

His mood didn't last long, however. Ely Associates, his current workplace, was by far the nicest place he'd worked since he'd turned freelance. Originally hired in to design and typeset the annual report, he had now been there nearly three months, and wouldn't be entirely surprised if an offer of a permanent job were to be eventually forthcoming.

And if it did, it was quite likely he'd take it. The office was relaxed and good-humoured, the MD Howard Ely laid-back to the point of being horizontal. After some of the bastards he'd worked for, Mark found that the idea of a boss who wandered into the main office, announced that it was too hot to work, said that he was going home and suggested they follow suit, was very appealing. Especially when this was combined with somehow running a very, and increasingly, successful business. His PA Wendy was precise and efficient whilst still friendly, and the other four men in the office were all genuinely good to work with, with the sole exception of Egerton. The self-styled Finance and Administration Manager ('for which read "accountant",' Chris had said on Mark's first day), Egerton was a real pain, a self-important busybody who clearly thought of himself as senior management. As everyone including Howard seemed to view him with cordial dislike, Egerton shut himself in his office for much of the time, smoking heavily and only emerging when he felt the need to be irritating in the body of the office instead of over the internal telephone system.

But best of all was Julie. She was in charge of marketing, and hence the person Mark tended to work most closely with. They got on very well, and from time to time Mark had found himself glancing at her and thinking how wonderful it would be to have that easy laugh and unselfconscious elegance in his life outside the office as well. She was the first person he had really liked since meeting Gemma five years ago, and now that Gemma was gone . . .

But in the meantime she was a good friend and a nice person to work with, and Mark had no intention of pushing it. He'd seen Gemma pushed too many times, and seen her fall. Getting someone to fall was easy. It was only when people jumped of their own free will that you stood a chance of being happy. Unless it turned out Julie was interested in him, he was content with the way things were.

The morning passed off easily enough. Mark was currently revamping the company's promotional material, and the angle he and Julie had cooked up between them had been greeted with relaxed enthusiasm by Howard and serious praise from Brian, the most senior employee. Mark and Julie went round the corner to the local Italian for lunch to celebrate, and when they were at the coffee stage Mark looked up at one point to find Julie looking at him. She quickly dropped her eyes and continued her amusingly told tales of woe concerning her wayward flatmate, but not before Mark's chest had had time to tighten with a welcome excitement.

The afternoon went a little slower, mainly because Julie was out of the office at a client's. Mid-afternoon Mark phoned LetsMove largely on a whim, in the hope of hearing Steve's no doubt bizarre reaction to being thanked. The agent, however, was again – or still – unavailable.

'Is he likely to be back this afternoon?'

'No.'

'Tomorrow?' Mark persisted. Something in the manner of the un-named person he was speaking to made him lean forward on his desk.

'No. Mr Jones no longer works for us.'

'Oh.' Mark was very surprised. 'Has he left, or . . .'

'Is there a problem with the property, Mr Royle?'

'Er, no. No.'

'Then I'm afraid I must bid you good afternoon.'

The connection was severed abruptly, leaving Mark open-mouthed. Clearly strange things were afoot in the world of estate agents, and Steve was *persona non grata*. Maybe he'd filed something incorrectly, or run off with the plumber.

Before he left Mark reiterated his invitations to everyone to come to his flat-warming the next day. In the interests of harmony and buoyed up by memories of lunch with Julie, he even issued a first invitation to Egerton, and received a look of surprised gratefulness that rather took him aback. Walking the couple of hundred yards to the tube Mark found himself feeling genuinely happy for the first time in what seemed like months. The job was going well, he liked the people he worked with and they seemed to like him. And there was Julie.

There wouldn't, in truth, be that many other people at the flat-warming. Dave would come, with his girlfriend, and there were one or two others, but it would certainly be a fairly cosy affair. Though Mark knew that he wasn't socially inadequate he'd never really been able to open himself up to people, with the result that forming close friendships didn't happen often. He had a couple of people from school who he regarded as good friends, but one was a doctor and the other was bumming round Australia, so they were both as good as dead. With other people he found himself presenting a strange protective persona of aloof independence, and doing so with evident success. Most people seemed to think he was aloof and independent.

Maybe it was living in London, amongst so many people, so much rushing about, so many minds and disparate desires crowded amongst the streets and buildings. As he sat patiently, waiting for the Northern Line to remember that it was supposed to be a means of transportation, Mark made a promise to himself, an early New Year's resolution. He would make some proper friends.

By the time he got back to Northwood Hall, Mark was feeling rather autumnal and melancholy. It was not an entirely disagreeable feeling, but he wished all the same that there was someone he could ring up to talk to. His parents were out of the country, and the last time he'd tried talking to Gemma on the phone his head had filled with images of vast disused warehouses and arid Texan plains. He wished he had Julie's home phone number: confirming her invitation would have been a good excuse to contact her for the first time outside the office.

Another evening alone. He sat at the table in the sitting room and tried to do some work. Before long he was staring out of the window at the view, which was by now a blue-black panorama speckled with yellow points of light. Realizing that work was already at the point of dimishing returns Mark got up and walked to the window. So many windows, so many houses. On impulse he got his coat and left the flat to go for a walk.

Walking down the driveway towards Hornsey Lane, Mark turned and looked back up at Northwood Hall. The many windows were predominantly dark, only a few bursting yellow out of the edificial walls. By now Mark was beginning to wonder if all of his fellow inmates were bedridden: after two days he still hadn't seen a living soul, nor heard a sound. Not the ideal place for him to be living, the way he was currently feeling. Perhaps that had been the basis of his initial reluctance to take the place.

As he turned a corner Mark caught sight of someone else walking some distance away. Somehow he seemed to have a lot of space in front of him, and behind. He looked exposed and alone.

The night was cold and in the end Mark only walked to the nearest off-licence, bought some cigarettes and then came back. It was after ten by then, and the streets were dark and surprisingly deserted. As he looked in the windows he passed it was strange to see how few lights were on, almost as if the rows were just fronts with big hollow rooms two storeys high behind. A few windows were flecked with blue reflections of television, with occasional warm rectangles above, but for the most part it was like walking small among dark brick mausoleums. The space between them seemed somehow to be part of the dark sky towering above, and Mark felt exposed and alone. The wind picked up slightly, casting branches across the orange streetlights.

Walking back up the drive Mark noticed that none of the lights on in the building had gone off: the pattern of yellow was the same as when he'd left. It would be easy to believe that no one else lived in the building, that the lights were on some complex timer switch designed to ward off burglers. Waiting for the lift to complete its interminable journey back to ground level he checked the post again, fruitlessly. Though he'd been careful to let people know his new address as soon as possible, no one had taken advantage of the knowledge yet.

When the lift deposited him at the sixth floor Mark decided on a whim to walk the long way round to 614. He turned left and set off in an anti-clockwise direction. There was nothing to see, only an unrelenting hotel corridor of shut doors, but he found himself wanting to put off the moment of getting back into the flat.

After about fifty yards he heard something. Stepping quietly down the corridor he leaned towards the left wall, listening. Eventually he found the source: from within Room 620 came the faint sound of a television. Mark listened for a moment, trying to work out what the programme was, and hence what age the occupants might be, but was unable to make out enough of the words. Then suddenly there was a click and the corridor was completely silent again. Mark hesitated for a moment, overcome with an absurd desire to knock on the door and introduce himself. But the silence from within unnerved him and he moved on.

Mark was about to make the turn which would eventually

bring him into his own stretch of corridor when he heard
another sound, this time from the room that he was actually
passing. It came from nowhere, with no buildup, and Mark
felt his chest go cold for a moment, and then relax. The
sound was of a woman's laugh, rich and throaty, the sound
of a woman laughing with uncomplicated enjoyment. Mark
looked at the door. Room 627. Feeling a complete idiot, he
prepared himself, and then knocked on the door.

There was no reply. He waited for a moment then knocked
again, even more timidly, and heard only more silence. He
gave up and walked quickly down to his own flat, feeling
stupid.

The flat accepted his return with cold indifference, and he
wandered into the lounge like a stranger. The objects and
mementoes which he'd placed in the room looked out of
place, disconnected, like the possessions of someone who'd
died. Once facets of a life, now just a collection of unrelated
things, so many of the memories they stirred were at best
mixed blessings. A postcard Gemma had sent him a year
ago, saying how much she loved him. A mug he'd made in
a school art class, with its evocation of a set of friends and a
sense of community long since dead. A small stick of rock.

The rock was a reminder of his last full-time job, which
had involved, amongst other things, running a residential
convention. The rock was the worst memento of all, a
reminder of a very bad time. One evening Mark had gone
down to the bar, and tried to socialize with the people there.
The staff from the office stood in two groups, and he had
tried to join them. Conversations had been going, and he
moved to the edge of one of them, drink in one hand, his
other in his pocket, ready to be friendly.

And they wouldn't let him in. He felt people turn away
from him, sensed the way that they were standing in such a
way to exclude him from every group, seeing them encased
in a warm sheen of solidarity that deliberately excluded him.
In the end he gave up, sat out the evening, and retired to
his room just as the night was warming up for everyone
else. As he sat on his bed feeling dangerously unhappy,
feeling depression take flight within him like a flock of
mad orange birds, he thought he heard a whispering in
the corridor outside his room. He got up and opened the

door: but there was no one there, though in his head he heard laughter disappearing into the air.

He'd never told anyone about that, didn't know anyone he trusted that much. At most levels he knew that he'd just been tired and lonely and unhappy, and had projected that onto people he didn't like. He kept the rock to remind him to fight against letting his life slide down that sort of track again. But sometimes he wondered if it had been a glimpse of something that really was.

Sitting with a cup of coffee in his large bare sitting room Mark felt himself worryingly close to tears, and made a small silent vow to himself. Tomorrow, at his party, he would open himself up to someone. Finally there was someone he liked, someone he felt he could trust, felt he could love. He was tired of being lost, of being alone. Tomorrow he was going to let Julie know how he felt. She was beautiful, she was funny, she was interesting, but those were adult things. All he needed was to hold her hand. He felt nervous and vulnerable, conscious of stepping out on the kind of emotional limb he felt too young and small to survive anymore. But the worst that could happen was not bad enough. He was going to do it.

Mark woke up at midnight, to find himself still on the sofa. It took him several bleary moments to realize he'd fallen asleep there, and to summon up the energy to head towards the bedroom.

Suddenly the phone rang. He picked up the handset on autopilot and mumbled his number. There was silence for a moment, then, sounding far off and faint, the sound of female laughter. Then the phone went dead.

Mark sat up straighter and shook his head, heart beating hard. He picked up the phone again. Instead of the dialling tone there was only a very faint tidal sound. He replaced it, then picked it up again. This time the dialling tone buzzed loudly in his ear.

Mark screwed his eyes shut, then opened them again. He felt very spun out, half asleep, extremely disorientated and also slightly frightened. He was no longer particularly sure about what he'd heard on the phone: perhaps he'd just misheard someone's response to getting a wrong number.

'Please replace the handset and try again.'

Mark swore loudly, dropping the handset which he'd forgotten was still under his ear. The prim voice of the recorded announcement was all the worse for being the only voice he'd heard all evening.

'Please repla . . .'

Once in bed, he fell asleep again quickly. But a couple of hours later he found himself standing on the balcony, leaning on the railing and looking out over the view. He was wearing only boxer shorts but the air was warm, even humid. There were still a lot of lights on, plenty of people awake and doing things behind their glass and lace curtains. Mark found himself wondering how many muggings he was watching, how many rapes.

He let his gaze run down the next wing again. Behind those windows anything could be happening, or nothing. When his eyes reached the parking area below he was surprised to see a small knot of people standing, waiting for someone to get out of a large old car. A tall woman eventually emerged, and the others followed her to the entrance.

Interesting, but not very. Mark turned his attention back out to the town again. After a few moments he found himself yawning, and turned to go back inside. Suddenly he heard a sound from outside the flat door. It was the sound of the lift doors opening. He heard the sound of several sets of footsteps coming along the corridor. They seemed to get closer and closer, and then stopped. There was a long pause and then there was a knock on his door. Moving slowly and reluctantly, heart beating hard, Mark walked through the bedroom and into the hall. The knock came again. He reached out towards the handle and slowly turned it. He pulled the door open quickly. There was no one outside.

Bewildered, Mark stuck his head out into the corridor. It was empty, and absolutely still. Shaking his head, he retreated into the flat, and shut the door. He had just put the chain lock back on when he heard the sound of rich laughter from immediately behind him. He turned quickly and woke up, sweating.

He leapt out of bed and checked the door. The chain lock was on. Then he walked back into the bedroom and out onto the balcony. The car was not in the carpark, could never have been. The space was taken by a Nova which he had noticed on the way back from the off-licence. Mark turned away and went back to bed.

Sainsbury's on Saturday afternoon was a nightmare. Mark had known it would be, but it was the nearest place that he could get everything he needed in one fell swoop. He still hadn't fully recovered from the night before, and wandered round the aisles in a daze, buffeted by careering families.

Alcohol, soft drinks, cheese, dips. Bloody nibbles, sodding crisps.

As he loaded party raw materials into the trolley Mark began to feel more and more depressed. He shouldn't be doing this by himself. There should be someone with him, to turn it into exciting preparations instead of just a chore. It was like buying something for yourself as a treat. Whatever it was would be nice to have, but the very fact of having to do something like that made you feel exposed and lonely and vulnerable. Most of his CD collection was like that: to be taken home and listened to alone. The act of buying cheered you up, but the realization that your life needed such artificial cheer, that you were tending a life-support system, depressed you even more.

By the time he was negotiating his trolley towards the car Mark felt terrible. Part of it was due to nervousness: he meant to stick by his resolution of the night before, and found the prospect frightening as well as exciting. What if she wasn't interested? Mightn't it be better to have the dream than try for the reality and find it didn't exist, that he'd made something of nothing and would have to stay alone?

He really wished that he wasn't having the party. He wasn't in the mood, didn't feel up to it. It wasn't the kind of thing he normally did, and why should he be celebrating moving into that morgue anyway?

'Having a party, are we?'

Startled, Mark looked up from the boot of the car and saw Steve, leaning against the side of the building. Mark was very surprised to see him, and shocked to see him looking the way he did. Something had happened to the strangely dynamic man who had shown him round Northwood Hall: he looked tired and very pale. The difference in a week was incredible.

'Yes, I'm . . . well just a moving in thing, really.' He ground to a halt, then remembered. 'I tried to call you.'

'Hm,' said Steve, leaning up from the wall with some apparent effort, 'shouldn't think you got very far.'

'No. What happened?'

'Oh, nothing much.' Closer to, the difference in Steve was even more pronounced. He looked as if he was wasting away. 'Bit of a *contretemps*: they thought I wasn't looking after something properly. Blamed me for some problems they were having. But it will sort itself out.'

'Oh. Well, it wasn't anything much. I just wanted to thank you.'

'No trouble. How are you finding it?'

Mark paused.

'Not so good, actually. Sleeping problems, bit weird, that kind of thing.'

'You'll soon get used to it. Still, must dash.'

He turned and started to walk slowly away. On a sudden impulse Mark called after him, asking a question he hadn't even known he wanted the answer to.

'Steve . . .'

The man stopped, and half turned.

'The young people, when did they move out?'

'Oh, they didn't move out.'

'But you said they were gone.'

'Oh, they're gone, alright. They just didn't move out.' He turned to face Mark. 'He killed her. Cut her up in the living room. Then killed himself in a rather spectacular way.'

'Christ. When was this?'

'Oh, a long time ago. Ten years.'

When the drinks and eats were spread out in what he judged to be a suitably perfunctory fashion – he didn't want to seem too neurotic about such things – Mark had a shower and set about getting ready. As he dressed he cast his eye around his room.

The idea of a flat-warming was a farce. This place was never going to feel warm. Coming back to the building after his conversation with Steve he'd walked up the drive with something akin to dread. He'd gone up onto the building's roof and stood looking out over the grounds, the communal garden which was empty and looked like it had been so since the day it was fashioned. It was like looking at a sepia photograph of people you know are already dead: mildly interesting, but pointless.

He'd still seen no one in the corridors, never seen any mail in the slots in the lobby. The cars outside seemed to change places during the day when he was out, but that was all. The building was dying, in its last throes: he was mad to be living here. He knew he was getting down again, retracting from the world he shared with others into the one he'd bitterly built for himself.

As he carefully did up his tie he listened to the sound of the CD he had playing in the other room. It was an album he'd bought himself as a treat, and it sounded tinny and forced, like the happiness it had brought.

By seven fifteen he was ready. He'd shaved carefully, put on the clothes he felt smartest in, done all he could, and he had fifteen minutes still to wait. Not that people would come on time, anyway. It would be a miracle if anyone appeared before eight. Shoulders slumping he opened the French windows and stepped out onto the balcony.

It was already dark outside, but with a strange lack of cold reminiscent of the dream he'd had the night before. Mark leaned on the rail and looked out across the city.

Alexandra Palace was gone.

Mark had stared unseeingly at the mid-horizon for several moments before he realised what was different. When he did he reeled back as if struck, before turning to face the view again. It was definitely gone. Usually it dominated the view, sat square in the middle. Now it simply wasn't there. But there was no blank space: the rows of lights and houses covered the area. If anything they seemed more dense, and as if there were more lights on.

As he stared uncomprehendingly at the scene he focused on a window in a nearby block: in one of the squares of light he could see the silhouettes of a man and a woman. The man struck the woman across the face. In the next window along stood a woman loading a gun, sobbing. In the building behind Mark saw a child thrown against a wall and rebound brokenly. From his left came the sound of a siren, going the other way. He looked back at the centre of the horizon. What the fuck was going on?

Suddenly he heard a noise from below, and looked down. A car had pulled into the drive and was parking. After a moment another, larger and older, car pulled in and parked next to it. From the first car emerged all of the guys from the office, who stood around waiting for the occupant of the second car to get out. Mark felt his heart tighten with a dizzy excitement as the door opened and Julie got out. Even in the near darkness, lit only by light seeping from the Hall's few lit windows, he could see that she looked fantastic.

Moving quickly, Mark turned back to the bedroom and headed for the door, planning to meet them at the lift so there would be no chance of them getting lost in the way that Dave had. He had gone only a few paces when something struck him. It was pretty well pitch dark in the room, and he had to turn a light on to even navigate his way across the bedroom. Yet when he'd dressed he'd been looking at himself in the mirror, and the light had been perfectly acceptable. That seemed sudden even for the falling of a winter's night. Mark glanced across at his bedside clock. It said 9.50 in red.

Nine fifty? He'd only been out there two minutes: how the hell could it be nearly ten o'clock? And if it was, how come no one had come earlier? Mark stepped quickly back out onto the balcony. He looked down at the driveway. Julie was walking towards the lobby, confidently striding with her customary long-legged grace. The others followed, Howard, Brian, Chris, Nick and Egerton. Five of them.

Mark ran quickly to the front door. As he fumbled to open it he looked across into the living room, at the food and drinks laid out in silly rows, a mute testament to sadness. They might as well be wax replicas arrayed in a museum no one ever visited. He opened the door and ran out into the corridor.

The green carpet was new underfoot, and the gold numerals sparkled on the doors. One of them on the left was opened wide, and he stopped and looked inside. The featureless room spread out impossibly in both directions, with an unbroken window that ran for fifty feet. Mark slowed to walk past an old black and white television whispering quietly to itself and stepped up to the window. There in daylight lay the city, with every window open and every room empty.

Finally he understood about the view, knew what city he was looking at. It was a city that had been there all the time. He had been right after all.

He ran along the wall until he found another door and opened it. Back in the corridor he ran towards the lift for a few yards, then stopped as he heard its approach. He turned and ran back down the corridor. He ran and ran, past the hallway that led down to the room at the top of the stairs, down more corridors, and the faster he ran the newer the doors became, the brighter the paint. The sound of the approaching lift got louder and louder, terrifying him.

The time was past, it was too late: he had no use for whatever might be in that lift. The city outside was the one he'd seen in his dream. The city was London. He hadn't just been tired, and depressed: he had seen the ways things actually were. From the Hall you saw the truth, that every city is a foreign place, and that you are the stranger everyone points at behind your back. He'd fallen behind the city everyone conspired to maintain, a shared place where there were rules and kindness, and found the real world.

He'd been right about the convention, about the conspiracy to dislike him, about the sniggers he saw in girls' eyes. Those glimpses might be dismissed as paranoia in the shared world, but here they were the truth. Here he was right.

When you realize what's really behind all the windows, see how right you are, you can never change the view back again. Not when you've seen that everyone *does* hate you, that the world *does* face in at you and tower over you, that deep in every shadow is a new pain. Healing a paranoid is nothing to do with showing him the error of his ways: it's getting him to ignore the truth he's seen. Mark knew he could never forget.

Running out of breath, his chest heaving, he saw that he had come full circle, that he was looking down the corridor to the strangely lit door. And he saw the number on it, and saw that it was his own. He stumbled towards it and turned the handle. Inside was the featureless room, and a body. Howard Ely lay stretched out on the floor, hammered into it. The awkward placing of the limbs and the flatness of the head, mercifully face-down, could only have come from a fall of many storeys. As he looked up from the blood seeping from the underside of the body Mark noticed that it was night again, the view a riot of seething yellow squares. Timeless night, low afternoons and small hours alone: those were the only times left.

He ran out into the corridor again and all was quiet apart from the whispering of all the people who didn't like him, a tidal rustling that felt like a shiver in the mind. He turned the corner and was not surprised to see the corridor curving away like a wheel, for this was one circle he knew he could never break.

He heard a sound from behind a closed door and moved towards it. It was room 627, and when he opened the door he heard the sound of warm, rich laughter. The hall was sickly with the smell of copper, the air warm and red. His head hammering with someone else's headache, a headache that would never go away and had finally become too much to bear, Mark stumbled into the room at the end. The confined space was humid and claustrophobic, melting with the heat of six bodies. Julie laughed again as she looked at Mark, bending her body to the will of the men around her.

Mark thought that there would be no way out, that the corridor would have disappeared, or that it would run in a circle for ever. But he found his way to the balcony quite quickly.

The ambulancemen cleared away the mess long before the guests arrived to find that there would be no party.

THE SALESMAN AND THE TRAVELLING FARMER'S DAUGHTER

C. Bruce Hunter

C. Bruce Hunter works as a journalist and educator in North Carolina. He is the author of a number of short stories, which have appeared in five issues of Fantasy Tales, Alfred Hitchcock Mystery Magazine, Ellery Queen Mystery Magazine *and* Whispers. *The following story is the latest in a series which began in* Fantasy Tales *(with 'The Travelling Salesman and the Farmer's Daughter' and 'The Farmer and the Travelling Salesman's Daughter') and is set to continue in* Dark Voices.

BRIGITTE stared in fascination through the tiny window. She couldn't quite make out the faraway people, but she knew what they were doing and even what they were wearing. She had spent so much of her short life tending crops and animals on the same kind of tree-specked slopes, looking down at them now was almost like flying over her own home.

'They're very small, aren't they?' said the old man sitting beside her.

She nodded without taking her eyes away from the scene.

'They remind me of the merchandise I sell.'

'Are you a salesman?' the girl asked, turning to him with wide eyes. 'What do you sell?'

'Things,' he smiled. 'Things for collectors. There are people who will pay me a great deal of money for the right things.'

He leaned forward and pulled a tattered leather satchel from under his seat. Unbuckling the straps that protected its contents, he rummaged in it for several seconds then pulled out a small glass globe and held it up for her to see.

He quickly placed it in the hand she'd held out without thinking. She clutched it tightly and gazed into the little tableau that was imprisoned inside it.

'Oh, it's so pretty,' she said.

'It's not as pretty as you are,' the old man said, placing a hand on her knee. She pulled her leg away, and his hand retreated, but she never stopped looking into the little globe she held in her hand.

It showed her something she knew well . . . a farm house and a pasture with grazing sheep, and if she looked very close she could barely make out three farm girls like herself. They were sitting together as if talking while their sheep grazed the afternoon away.

'Shake it,' the old man said.

She did, eagerly, and the clear liquid sky burst into a blizzard of tiny white flakes that danced in the light from the plane's window then slowly settled to cover the farm with a sprinkling of plastic snow. Brigitte giggled as she watched the scene come to life.

'You may keep it,' he said with a casual wave of his hand. Beads of perspiration suddenly appeared on his forehead when he saw her smile change to a frown.

'I mustn't,' she said, holding the globe out to him.

'Nonsense.' His hand was on her knee again. 'I have a daughter at home just like you. She would love a toy like that.'

Brigitte smiled. Surely this old man was not one of those her father had warned her against when he put her on the plane. This was a nice man. If he had a little girl like her, he must be nice.

He patted her knee then turned his attention to closing his satchel and returning it to its place below his seat.

'Will someone be meeting you at the airport?' he asked.

When she shook her head, he looked surprised.

'You mean you'll be all alone?'

She nodded timidly.

'But that won't do,' he said. 'New York is a dangerous city. You'll need someone to look after you.'

'Tomorrow my aunt and uncle will come for me,' she tried to explain. 'They couldn't come today because . . .'

'That simply won't do, to be alone in a dangerous city all night. I know what. I'll look after you.'

'You mustn't,' she said. 'My father told me . . .'

'But your father isn't here, and I am. I'm a father, too, remember? Since my daughter isn't here, I'll look after you, and you can keep me company.'

Brigitte didn't say any more. She sat back in her seat, clutching the globe the old man had given her and trying to think what to do.

She was a little afraid of him. He seemed out of place, with his old fashioned black cape and a crop of shaggy grey hair that framed a pale, thin, angular face. He was like someone out of an old movie that had no colour. Still, he really did seem a nice man. He had done nothing to bother her during the eight hours they had sat together. And he had given her a nice toy. Perhaps it would be all right to trust him. He was kind and gentle, just like her own father.

She glanced at him from the corner of her eye. He had leaned back and closed his eyes and was smiling broadly. He really didn't seem a bad man.

She turned to the window and looked again at the farms below. If she looked real hard, she could make out the people tending their fields and animals. Then she looked at her new toy, with the three farm girls like herself, huddled together to keep warm from the plastic snow that had settled around them.

She shivered a little as she thought how big and strange the city would be. She didn't even know how to get from the airport to the hotel. Maybe it would be good to have someone take care of her until her aunt and uncle came to pick her up.

Brigitte stood hesitantly at the door of the hotel room. The old man had already gone in. He was unpacking some things from his satchel and stuffing them into one of the drawers of the dresser in the corner.

The room was old, like her own bedroom. But it was big and cold and shabby. It depressed her to think of spending the night in such a cold, lonely place.

'Come in, little girl,' the old man said. 'It's not a fancy room, but it's a good place to sleep, and that's all it needs to be.'

She crept into the room and lowered her suitcase to the floor beside the bed. It was a small bed, not nearly big enough for both of them, and it was the only place in the room to sleep.

'Don't worry,' he said as if he knew what she was thinking. 'I'll find another place to sleep. But you must be tired now. Why don't you lie down and rest.'

She really was tired and the bed looked inviting. She was still afraid, but she had already decided that she would trust the old man. So she took off her hat, laid it on the dresser beside his satchel and sat on the bed.

It was soft and creaked slightly under her weight. She looked up at the old man. He smiled and nodded. With a deep sigh, she slipped off her shoes and lay back against the small, hard pillow at the head of the bed.

'Do you want to take off your coat?' he asked softly.

She pulled it closer around her and looked fearfully up at him.

'No matter,' he said, and he moved quickly to the door and closed it. 'Go to sleep and I'll be sure no one bothers you.'

She felt a heavy lump in her pocket. It was her new toy. She pulled it out and held it up high so she could look at it. The plastic snow swirled a little, and the farm girls looked as if they were very cold. She turned the globe upside down then right side up again. The snow once more became a blizzard, and she smiled as she watched it swirl through the liquid sky above the little farm.

She tried to keep her eyes open to watch the snow, but they were tired and kept closing. The bed was so soft that it felt like it was moving gently under her. Through the window she could see real snowflakes fluttering through the air outside. That made her feel even colder. She pulled her coat more tightly around her and held her new toy close to her breast while she allowed her eyes to close and the motion of the bed to caress her.

She shifted her weight slightly to make herself more comfortable. The motion of the bed became a floating sensation that soon obscured everything else, making it difficult for her to tell what her body was doing. But she didn't care. She continued to relax, and as her muscles loosened, she became aware of a sound.

It was faint and low, like the sound of a chair being drawn across the floor. It came for a few seconds then stopped. Then it came again and stopped again.

Brigitte imagined the old man moving furniture around in the room, straining to get the heavy pieces where he wanted them. The legs of the chair and dresser dragged roughly against the hardwood floor then stopped as he gathered the strength to pull them a few inches more. At first she could barely hear the sound, but each time it came it was stronger and louder, closer and closer.

Finally the image faded under the onslaught of its own steady rhythm. Brigitte no longer needed the old man to explain the sound because she realized what it really was. As it became louder, the pieces of furniture broke into jagged fragments. The fragments faded from her imagination and were replaced by the knowledge that somewhere, someone was beginning to snore.

As slowly and gently as that knowledge had come, it, too, faded away. And the sound faded. And Brigitte drifted into a grey silence that lifted her like a breeze that was too gentle to feel.

The grey gradually turned to white, and the white took on almost imperceptible patches of blue. But the white held back the blue as a mountain of ice imprisons the watery colours that lie deep inside it.

It was a cold white. Brigitte could feel as well as see it. The cold started in her legs and moved slowly upward. She tried to look down to see what was happening, but she had no eyes with which to see. She drifted through the white as if she were a disembodied soul, unable to turn away, unable to shut out the cold and light.

The white-laced-with-blue surrounded her. It was a cold crystalline white that pressed against her and held her suspended in a world of frozen mist. Yet it softened at her touch, parting to receive her and closing behind as she passed.

Brigitte did not resist; there was nothing to resist. She gave herself to the mist and floated with it, or rose, or fell, there was no way of telling because the white was everywhere the same.

In time the patches of blue came together and formed an

icy blur that flickered, faded and flickered again. Each time it
became more solid. And each time it came closer as if it were
reaching out for her.

The blue slowly faded into shades of green that pulsed and
danced and retreated and teased. Then finally the green took
form in the distance and stayed there.

She couldn't quite see what the green was. The white still
obscured it. But as she drifted closer, the mist cleared and
she could see more clearly.

It was a pasture, much like the ones where she had
grown up. A scattering of sheep wandered and grazed in
the pasture. Farther away, a little farm house still hid itself
in the mist, but in the pasture, three little farm girls sat as if
talking to pass the time as they minded the sheep.

The three little girls turned to look at Brigitte, but they
showed no joy when they saw her. They just stared blankly
with sad faces and empty eyes.

The old man watched the little girl twist nervously in her seat.
An attendant had shown her into the waiting lounge and left
her there. For a quarter of an hour she had sat impatiently on
an impersonal blue chair, holding her ticket in her hand and
watching the suitcase that sat on the floor at her feet. He had
watched all of this without speaking.

'Are you afraid to fly?' he finally asked.

She looked at him but didn't answer.

'Did your father tell you not to talk to strangers?' he
asked.

She nodded.

'He was right,' the old man said. 'I know because I'm a
father, too. I have a little girl at home just like you.'

The little girl smiled.

'We live on a farm,' he said, and after a brief pause, 'Let
me show you a toy I'm taking home to my little girl.'

He pulled a glass globe from his pocket and shook it. At
that her eyes sparkled. She got up from her seat and came
and sat down beside him.

He held the globe out to her. She cupped it in her
hands and giggled as she watched the tiny flakes of snow
swirl and dance. They began to settle slowly onto a little
farm that had a house like the one she lived in, and a

tiny pasture with sheep, and four little farm girls just like her.

She was so enthralled by the scene that she barely felt the old man's hand on her knee.

AND THE SPIRIT THAT STANDS BY THE NAKED MAN

Peter Dennis Pautz

Peter Dennis Pautz has been writing and selling fiction for some fifteen years, just a little longer than he's been the executive secretary of the Science Fiction and Fantasy Writers of America. His full time occupation is as a family therapist, specializing in clinical hypnosis. Most of his writing has been horror, but a few of his novels, published under pseudonyms, are outside the field. With Frank Herbert he edited a Nebula Awards *anthology, and with Kathryn Cramer* The Architecture of Fear, *which won the World Fantasy Award in 1988.*

THIS time I was a lover of nature and lens, a despiser of mind and distortion. Whether in the midst of a tungsten-lit studio or fondling a remote cable, yards away from the leaf-reduced suns glittering across the spangles of a gneiss outcropping waiting for the contrast to enter from the far side of blur, I worked patiently, steadily. A velvet fist checking my heart, determined for the arrival of accomplishment: to come close enough to the borders of perfection to force the intervention of the muse. Any muse; hostile or benevolent. One that would gently stroke my work to completion, or a snarling beclawed thing to wrench me by my entrails from my art, curling and twisting in bloody frustration.

But only on the outside, by the flesh exposed to humanity. Not within, not reaching the heart's core, not that god-seeking bit of souled muscle. But *god* is not the word it once was for me.

A spirit or daemon or peri, blessing the earth with some holy visitation, or locked to a rotting and eternal penance,

causing terror and pain to the living, offering sanctity only
in death.

It does not matter.

Only the presence of that immaterial being matters, the
proof.

And the power to draw it out.

The Art.

This time my name is Sigmund Ringfeldt, photographer;
former artist, musician, poet, novelist, sculptor, *ad infinitum*,
ad interim. I always think of myself that way: a continuous
stream of creative styles, a lifetime searching for a medium
of perfection. The tools are mine, all mine. A clever eye,
masterful hands, an adjustable mind. But that is the problem.
They're mine; they belong to me. Not gifts, not inspiration.
Rather a matter of mechanics. A juxtaposing of sounds, a
delineated blending of hues. With no more genius than a
child rearranging the standard pieces of a tinkertoy set,
melding colour and shape into interesting new designs,
but never into anything beyond . . . comprehension. I am
always conscious of process, the means to the ends. There
is simply never any magical touch (or rent).

Yet even with these thoughts tumbling again through my
brain, snapping and falling like a never-ending set of stacked
dominoes, I work.

Water and fixer swirled in the trays beneath my hands and
new images bled into the world, slowly, carefully. But still by
a process as basic to me as zipping my trousers in the dark.
That, too, is mechanical, never touched by –

Finally an interruption! I smiled at the relief, and reached
across the black enamelled sink for the phone.

'Hello?' It was always a question. 'Ringfeldt here.'

'Jerry, it's Max.'

'The name's Sigmund now,' I said seriously. 'Why can't
you get that straight? Jerry was the pianist.'

'I can't get used to it because it's only changed four times
since then.' Max huffed into his receiver, just loud enough
to hear. 'And first names stick with the faces. How many
goddamned people do you know change their name every
time they change a job?'

'All right, all right.' I grinned. Max was a tiny little gent, barely taller than a broom handle and only twice as wide. I could picture him sitting behind his desk in his 42nd Street office, palm flat against the centre of the mahogany, pushing out his frustration and not getting very far.

Max didn't say a word, obviously waiting for me to ask why he was wasting his time calling all the way to the Pennsylvania woods. We played the game often, and I knew it was about to begin again: jack of tirades, master of all.

It was my turn to give in first. 'What've you got to make us rich this time?'

Max sighed. Apparently he'd stopped pushing. 'No contest this time,' he paused before adding, 'Si.'

'The West German and French delegations to the UN have asked the Guggenheim to stage a special exhibition of American photographers, *and* they both specifically asked for your complete folio.' I could tell Max was excited. His agent's paced voice barely sped at all. He was concentrating and enunciating the words individually, as if each was a valuable print in itself. It almost wasn't a spiel at all. But when I didn't answer, he said, 'Si, are you there?'

'Yeah.'

'Well?'

'Well, what?'

'Christ, Jer – ' He blew a larger breath into the mouthpiece. 'Damnit, Si. It's the goddamned Guggenheim! By diplomatic request, no less.'

'So?'

'*So?*' He hollered. 'Do you know who the hell called me to arrange for all this?'

I put the completed prints I was still working on into the final wash and let the phone dangle down my chest for a moment. A few seconds swishing them around and I tore the gloves from my hands and gradually raised the phone back to my ear. Max was still silent.

'I guess it was the Guggenheim,' I said. 'They'd have a lot of hassles rearranging their schedule, but I guess they'd do it for the UN. The chief curator won't be – '

'It was the christing State Department.' Max was up to his full-fledged bellow. It was all either of us said for quite a while. Only the sound of Max's heavy breathing could be heard on the line.

'The State Department?' I realized I was still holding the rubberized gloves I'd taken off and threw them into a corner of the black formica countertop. I didn't like it. Whenever political forces came into contact with art, it suffered, became propaganda, or a tool, or something equally manhandled. 'I'm sorry, Max,' I said at last. 'Tell them no.'

'It's too late.' I thought it might be. 'I already said they could count on you. The folio's on the way, minus whatever you have on hand that you want to send.' He was speaking quickly again. 'Or whatever you want to do up special for the showing.'

'I said no.' My throat cracked with irritation. 'Call them and tell them you want the stuff back. Immediately.'

'I can't,' he said.

'Why the hell not?'

'We need the money. When the staties called they doubled the standard Guggenheim showing royalty, and promised at least another ten thousand in sales. That's over and above whatever the Europeans want for themselves.'

'Wait a minute.' I was getting angrier by the minute, but had my voice back down to a civil tone at least. 'Who needs the money? There's still plenty in the accounts.'

'I know – '

'You said there would be enough for the next two years if I watched the travelling.'

'That's right.'

'Well?'

'There was another call.' He sounded embarrassed.

'Well, don't make me ask, will you?'

'Potterman called last week.' There was a long pause.

'And?'

'He found the spot.'

I hate New York. In fact, I hadn't been caught between those crushing concrete splinters since I was Ronald Waterjack, poet, living far beneath my means down on Water Street, eating rice and greens, forcing a life-style, waiting for a flash. I'd sold an average of four books for each of the three years there. Even tried to continue after my devastating failure in England. (Failure, of course, to write.) Oh there'd been the usual critical and financial success, but still

I failed. With lovely little rhymes of humans and airs and Stonehenge.

But lacking again the spirit I sought, a spirit that would open itself to me. Any spirit.

Those years in Soho had almost killed me. Almost driven me to be mollified as a technician, a chimp at a typewriter, a breeze in a bagpipe. But still it had only taken one sentence from Max to bring me running:

'This time you've got a guide.'

I'd been afraid to ask who, telling him only that I'd be there by three the next afternoon. Yet by the time I stepped from the cab in front of his uptown office I wanted to scream the question up at the penthouse window. *Who?* Who has seen them and may still utter a mortal sound?

As I entered the lobby and headed toward the immaculately caged elevator, I was torn by the thought that anyone could know of their existence, *actually know*, and remain a mere director to their infinities. Not a new Michelangelo, a Paganini. But rather a Clyde Beatty, 'Presenting for your education and mystification, the great, the magnificent muse, the purveyor of all light and life . . .'

When the elevator operator asked me what floor, I don't remember what I said, but it must have been, 'Penthouse, please,' since I soon found myself before Max's front door, rapping the brass knocker set squarely on the woodstained steel facade.

Immediately, without a hint of scraping bolts or jangling padlocks, it swung inward, bursting upon the atoll sunrise of Katherine Tully's gorgeous smile. As if knowing that she couldn't look better, she wore the simple blue dress with the tucked-in waist that I liked so much, crowned by nothing more than her shoulder length fall of tawny hair. Why it should seem (or matter) to me that she dressed the same for each of my visits was unfathomable. We'd never said more than a few dozen words to each other, but even now our eyes flicked away from the other's gaze, escaping like hastily written love notes on a blushing wind.

'Hello, Mr Ringfeldt,' she said, stepping aside to let me enter. 'Max will be right out. Please, come into the library and I'll bring some tea.'

Closing the door – and silently bolting two of its larger locks

– she led me down the short hall to a set of double doors, slid
them open, directed me inside, and promptly disappeared
amid a slight swish of blue that I couldn't help but notice.

There's something about that woman! I considered asking
her again to model for me. After all, how many hundreds of
times could she say no? I shrugged; it would be hopeless.
She had already turned me down too many times, for too
many mediums. 'It's not my place,' she would say. 'I'm not
a model.' Then she'd blink those luscious eyes and smile
my soul away. Yet somehow I had to agree with her. No,
she wasn't a model. It would be impossible to match her to
canvas or rhythm.

But wasn't that all the more reason to try?

(Still I knew I would ask her again, today, before I left.)

With fantasy and I resolved to the impossible and familiar,
I scanned the new acquisitions on the agent's walls: a new
oil by Parradini, a piece of ghastly metalwork by that Polish
gut mapper, two matching ceramic vases by someone as
yet unknown, even by me. Clients' items obviously, but
impressive nonetheless, for their variety and extravagance
if nothing else. Max Copek was a true patron of the arts,
a showcase of a promoter who did not shy away from
artistic in-breeding. Some of his best sales were between
clients. When you had the vision, the taste, or whatever it
really took to recognize the marketability – and sometimes
the aesthetic value – of work like this, you could pick and
choose who you handled and who you shipped off to Third
Avenue. (A sobering thought to any artist.)

Max whirled into the room. 'Now, what the hell's all this
about pulling out of the Guggenheim show?' His voice was
sharp, crisp. He was not going to broach any argument. He
hadn't even looked at me yet, and didn't until he rounded
his ornate seventeenth-century French desk, shuffled papers
needlessly from one draw to another, and twice tapped
the phone, like a lanky grandmother correcting a trucu-
lent child.

Meanwhile I moved to the large Tudor chair facing the
desk head-on across a large expanse of sea-blue carpeting.
I was certain the historical juxtaposition of the furnishings
was accidental, but could never quite convince myself that
someone – either Max or Katherine – hadn't an unconscious

battle plan in mind for the room. Sir Owen would have been proud of some of the victories made there, but this time there would be no battle, only a tallage.

'Forget it, Max.' His head came up, his mouth opening wide for a bellow, when I realized my mistake and quickly cut him off. 'No, Max. I mean go ahead with the show. Forget I ever said anything about pulling out.'

His expression did not change. He leaned back in his chair, smoothing the long sparse hairs across his head, and said, 'Okay, fine. But why the change of heart?'

'Come off it, Max. You know full well I intend to follow up on Potterman's report.'

'But you don't even know what he said yet!' The words were shot with irritation. 'You could wind up treading water under the Fulton harbour, or playing Daniel Boone with the bears in the Catskills, for Christ's sake.'

I bent back into the soft cushions and slowly shook my head. I'd eventually get what I wanted, even if I had to weather another one of Max's torrential storms. But surprisingly he quieted almost immediately.

Max had a distasteful twist to his mouth, but I could also make out something I had never seen before, something around the corners of the eyes. Not belief, but suspicion, which was disturbing enough on that pragmatic granite-face.

'It's good, isn't it?'

An exasperated sound pursed his lips.

'Are you going to tell me or not?' I was getting angry. I wanted to scream at him, to make him *tell me*. The feeling startled me. This was my deathsearch after all, but I'd never lacked such control before.

Then Katherine floated into the room bearing an engraved tea service and my temper thankfully faded. I relaxed back into my chair and watched her glide the tray onto the corner of Max's desk and begin pouring the rich liquid into Limoges cups. Max gazed at me, completely unruffled, and for once there was no gruffness in his expression. He seemed gentled, though with an ever so slight tensing just under the surface. He was definitely uncomfortable.

Neither of us said a word until Katherine was finished filling the cups and was about to leave. Max sighed, kept his eyes locked on me, and said softly, 'Katherine, I'd like you to stay for this, if you don't mind.'

I was past being embarrassed about my search in front of the people involved, but Katherine had never been told a thing. However, if it meant her continued presence, fine. When we had first met several years ago I'd stammered and generally acted like a fool, begging her to pose for me, for a day, an hour. Of course, she had declined, without a single flicker of reproach. So, I thought baring my heart to her – in this far more artistic sense – should be no worse. At the most she would think me deluded.

And why should Max and I be the only ones?

So quietly that I had to turn around to make sure she was still there, she sat against the wall next to the door, in a sparsely tufted chair that I could not place by epoch or culture. It was the effect she always carried with her: leeching the timeliness out of all around her as if to add to her own lack of immortality.

For a moment I was glad that she had never sat for me. She was too real, too much a focus. The art and the creator would be ignored in the light of her actuality.

Looking back at Max, the question must have flashed across my face as if I had never been distracted.

'Katherine will be going with us, Si,' the agent explained. 'She's agreed to pose. In fact, it was her idea.'

The remark couldn't have stunned me more if he had said that she was the muse herself offering to model, but I rejected the contradiction immediately. A god motivates from within, down the arm, through the eye. It doesn't sit on a rock and sell club soda.

This ghastly image made me aware that I had spun around and was staring at her. She blushed, but did not lower her eyes; it would have been too much a denial. Of what I wasn't quite sure. There was silence for a moment, then her voice broke softly. 'Just there,' she said, barely loud enough to be heard. 'Nowhere else, and only this once.'

I looked back at Max. What she'd said was unimportant, not critically, but as if it was so obvious that I need not have heard it.

Max said, 'I want her to know exactly what she's getting herself into.'

'If she doesn't know, why did she offer to pose?' We spoke as if she wasn't in the room, but I could not bring myself to care. She was somehow no longer unattainable. Rather, now she had spread herself, free and giving, and was slightly tinged by the position.

'Sanders talked her into it.' Max hesitated. 'Well, in a way.'

'Sanders is the guide, I take it.'

The agent nodded. 'He's waiting in the other room.'

'Well, bring him in! Why are you dragging this out.' I was getting irritated again. Too many things were changing too quickly. But Max's next words belied my anger, showing only his concern for everyone involved: 'I'll be going along, too, Si. I have to.'

I waited for what seemed like hours, weighing factors. It didn't take long to see that there was simply no choice in the matter. We'd be a party of four. A bridge club off to find a god.

Sanders was a short, stocky man with grey hair and a peppered moustache. We could have passed for the same age, but in his case that was nothing to be proud of. As he began to talk, it was obvious that he was almost ten years younger than he looked, just entering his late fifties.

When Max finally asked Katherine to bring him in, I prepared myself again for my little soul-baring. I'd only told even this vague outline of my search and its short, almost empty, history to a handful of people. To Max, of course, and a few others: Potterman, that infernal matchmaker between man and desire, and two other trackers that I'd found a long time ago, before hiring Potterman; men that, as it turned out, knew nothing and had nothing. I'd always felt it necessary to relax these pained and empty people, to show them I too believed in at least the potentiality of what they sought, but that was never there.

Sanders moved with a slight shuffle over to another period chair next to Max's desk, quickly doffed a worn and grease-smudged cap and nodded to me. It seemed a strange kind of acknowledgement, a fraternal greeting from one doomed soul to another. I only hoped he was right.

He glanced pitifully at Katherine for a moment while she

reseated herself, and then at Max when he said, 'Sanders, I
know Potterman explained exactly what's going on here, but
I want you to hear it from Mr Ringfeldt directly.'

His eyes came back to me and for a second I couldn't speak.
I almost gagged when I realized that Sanders was smiling at
me; the welcoming, reassuring smile of a mortician holding
open a crypt door. Swallowing the sensation I began quickly.
'I'm looking for god,' I said simply, waiting for a reaction
that did not come. 'It needn't be christian or benevolent or
even anthropomorphic. Just a spirit, a supernatural being of
any kind. But I do want absolute, definite proof . . . and
contact.'

'Why?' said Sanders; it was barely a whisper.

'That's my concern.' I said it a bit too sharply, and relented.
'The way you . . . the way some men have to breathe, to eat,
I have to find something outside mortal life.' I paused, looked
away then slowly returned to stare deeply into his placid
eyes. Somehow they made me go on more than I wanted to.
'I've been at it for a very long time; a longer time than even
I like to remember.' My voice broke, and suddenly, softly, I
felt Katherine's hand slide down over my shoulder. I don't
know what she felt then, but a hushed gasp escaped her. A
lengthy tremble rattled along her fingers and she withdrew
them. I shuddered, trying to remember that moment, that
comfort; failed, and forced myself to continue.

'Once, only once, I may have found it. I'll never really
know.' The words came slowly. 'The years and years of
searching before that time had been too much on me. I
was insane, locked in an asylum in England, where my
last friends brought me for seeking life. It was barbaric. Not
in a cruel way. Rather from the lack of understanding, the
intolerance. I was locked up like an animal, caged, sometimes
in a padded cell, sometimes in a filthy little cubicle with flies
buzzing around me incessantly. Filthy, blue and yellow flies.
And spiders.' For a moment my vision clouded over with the
memory of it.

'I was also restrained on occasion. Physically.' I felt a
smile crawl lightly across my lips at the thought of that
mild imprisonment, and the mood broke. 'He came only a
few times – my god. A very few times. At least that's what I
thought.' My eyes refocused. Sanders slumped form cleared

once again in my sight. 'But I was crazy at the time. I read a
report years later, written in part by the head doctor at the
asylum. I was sure he was referring to me. He called me his
"pet lunatic".

'And I may well have been. I'll never know. The only proof
I ever had of that entire time is a bruised and battered body.'
I saw Sanders glance at the flattened side of my skull – the
result of an early form of trephining – and the tiny dent left
in my neck; that same look I've seen many times before. 'I
remember the beating he gave me, but the doctors told me
I must have done it to myself. Beaten my head against the
floor, the wall, rammed my body into the corners of my
room, racing around like a lunatic until I finally fell from
my bed and twisted my spine.

'They came when they heard the noise, but it was over
by then. I was a crumpled, pierced sack of broken bones.
I collapsed at one point and they thought me dead for
hours. The coma I slipped into lasted months, during which
time they took the opportunity to learn much about bone
reconstruction and tendon alignment.

'They moved me out of the asylum once they thought I was
dead. Into a surgical hospital. I don't think my "pet" doctor
ever knew that I lived. I was simply out of his hands, and
he had more important things to do.'

The room was completely silent. Looking over my shoulder, I found that Katherine had moved back to her chair
against the wall, but I knew before I actually turned. Sanders was still slouched in his chair, staring at me with an
almost disinterested look on his creased face. Eventually Max
moved. He coughed, breaking the dead calm laying over us,
and said: 'Let's get out of here. I'm buying dinner.'

Half an hour later we sat down at a dark corner table in one
of the East Side's more subdued restaurants. It was as if we
were in stasis; no one spoke, except Max, and then only to
order our meals: New York cuts for himself, Katherine, and
Sanders, the chef's salad for me. Trust Max to be one of the
few people who would remember my vegetarian proclivities,
even under the present circumstances.

We remained that way – utterly silent – until the food
arrived, and strangely enough we all fell to with zest.

Little more than halfway through, Sanders popped another large slice of meat into his mouth, glanced once at me, sighed, and removed a stiff, glossy rectangle of paper from his jacket pocket. Katherine and Max lowered their utensils simultaneously and stared at the off-white back of the photograph as he handed it low across the table to me, obviously diverting his gaze even from its blank side. I could feel all their eyes on me as I took it and flipped it over.

Even before I touched it I could tell it was a print from one of the old Argus 240s, a camera produced at least a decade or two before the beginning of the last world war. The nine symmetrical steps on the tab, the truncated corners where the tiny clamps of a field printing box had been used; both were unmistakable. But all the details of texture and materials burst unheeded from my mind when I turned it over and fell into the image.

It was dark, and watery, and cold. A glory not of scene, but of impression. A river filled the vast centre, reflecting only scantly the tiny pinpoints of star- and city-light from far across the smooth ebony surface. Rough planking touched both edges, tentatively on the left, almost non-existently on the right. Small patches of icy snow crusted over the very ends of the beams, yet brought a freezing stillness to the air rather than the water. I shivered then, and heard weathered old boards crack beneath my feet. A light, insistent lapping swilled around the pilings from farther below. Frozen granules sprinkled into my eyes, yet they never blurred, they never teared, never looked away –

– until a roiling pain seared through my arm, and then my eyes. The picture was gone, stolen from my hand. Max held it flat against his chest. Katherine's nails tore through my coat sleeve like a fistful of tiger thorns.

My absolute agony must have shown blatantly on my face. My arm – with the hand that had just moments ago held that wonderful, blessed image – was outstretched before me, stiff and pleading toward Max. While he locked a steadying grip on it, lowering it back to the table and away from his heart, Katherine slowly eased the cutting pressure of her hand to rub gently and soothingly along my screaming muscles.

Max handed the photograph back to Sanders. 'It happened to all of us the first time,' he said. They both studiously

kept from looking at it; at some price I was just beginning
to understand. Pocketing it, Sanders turned his attention
back to his plate, took another bite of his steak. And in that
moment, I hated him: for his possession, his knowledge, and
most of all for his free acceptance of flesh. Flesh that had
walked, or swum, or . . . flown.

My mind drove one horrible thought through me: *Flies!*
And the memory of those days – and nights – compelled
me to gain control again. Max's hand withdrew, patting me
once like a good comrade. Katherine's slid down to my hand
and rested there. I stared at her and she nodded, almost
imperceptibly, then looked at Max.

'I think Sanders should explain.'

'Explain?' I cried. 'You can't explain that. Those images are
. . . magnificent. They're almost *godly*, in and of themselves.
If I didn't know better I'd swear it was a . . . a . . .'

'Stieglitz?' offered Sanders.

'Why, yes!' He was absolutely correct. Stieglitz was fascinated by water, especially in its winter forms. His first
masterworks were of snowstorms, frozen ponds, icy rivers.
'Or even Steichen. Though by the time of that,' I said,
gesturing reverently to his coat pocket, 'he was concentrating
almost as much on portraiture as on water scenes. More,
in fact.'

'While Stieglitz returned to the theme,' Max added.

I signalled agreement. 'By the end of the war, Steichen
was bouncing back and forth between water and faces. He
spent the rest of his life searching uncertainly for something
he never quite caught again. Something in those faces that
he could not find.'

'It wasn't there,' Sanders broke in quietly. 'It was in the
water.'

'My father was a ferry captain,' Sanders began, popping
the last morsel of bloody meat into his mouth and sitting
comfortably back in his chair. 'He was a senior runner by
the time they retired most of the ferries. That must have
been . . . oh . . . in the late thirties, just after they finished
the Lincoln Tunnel. He was just about hitting fifty when the
midtown docks were closed down and he was transferred
down to the Barclay Street Ferry, on the Jersey side. Even

those ferries only ran up through the mid-fifties.' His head sank a little toward his chest. 'But Dad was dead almost ten years by then.' This last was said seemingly without regret. Sanders paused then and stroked his bristly moustache with the calloused pads of his fingertips.

As he began again, I found myself listening to him as if he were an echo. The words bloomed full-blown in my mind, reverberating mightily between my own anticipation and Sanders' hidden fears.

'Dad was a gruff kind of a guy. He didn't get along well with folks.' The man chuckled, obviously trying to lighten his own mood and memory. 'He got into a couple of real bad ones before the transfer. Wound up in the hospital for months himself when he said a few choice words about a set of brothers' mother. Had his head beaten in against a bulwark. Nerve damage, the doctors said. Never heard another word after that. So the line put him by his lonesome on emergency night duty; stayed that way even down in Hoboken. By that time they were running from Jersey only over to 23rd, Christopher, and Barclay Street. But every once in a while they would need some emergency passage at night for a patient from Newark over to Bellevue or something. That was Dad's job: picking up wharf splinters and harbour crabs, waiting at dockside for something to do. It wasn't long before he'd be coming home soused every morning.

'I was in my teens then, almost out of high school. I used to get up at four, walk down to the corner, and catch him staggering down the street. He'd stink to hell. The brine and the booze combined into an odour that made me gag every time I got near him. It'd take a while, but I'd finally get him quieted down, and bring him into the kitchen, and get him cleaned up. My mother had been sickly for as long as I could remember and needed her rest, so I always managed to get him into his own bed without waking her.

'It was a real pain, getting him quiet sometimes. He could always talk, even if his words became a bit slurred and run-together after a couple of months, but he thought no one could hear him, I guess, shouting like he did. Couldn't hear himself, of course, but every once in a while he'd start in braying out some old song, probably thinking he was barely mouthing it, and he'd be screaming to beat the band.

A couple of times I had to clamp my hand over his mouth when he'd start while getting into bed, too drunk to see the hand signals I was waving at him.' He hesitated and took a deep breath, looking straight into my face. 'He'd glare at me then, with those rum-blinded eyes of his. Hated me for holding him down. But there were tears in his eyes the whole time. Once he held my fingers down over his lips as he cried. I could feel his teeth cutting into his lips, but he held it down tighter and tighter while he sobbed. The blame wasn't in his eyes then. They were closed, looking in at something he couldn't keep and was afraid to let out.'

As Sanders searched for something to fumble with, and finally settled on his napkin, the waiter returned. Max ordered two bottles of a stout burgundy – obviously for Sanders' sake – and asked Katherine if she was all right.

It was apparent that they had both heard at least some of all this before, but I couldn't guess what Katherine's connection could be. The weary man across the table from me was relating events that must have occurred at least a few years before her birth. Yet she was indeed a little pale, the lovely skin around her eyes a little tight.

'Would you rather we finished this somewhere else?' Max asked her.

She shook her head, and reaffirmed her grasp on my hand.

The wine came, was poured largely, all around, and Sanders again took up the burden of his narrative.

'That was all even before the troubles on the dock itself. When the war started the ferries were being used more, shipping supplies directly over to the temporary navy docks down by the Battery. It was more – what they'd call nowadays – cost effective, I guess. But for the first time in years the managers of the line were worried about keeping enough trained crew about to make sure the ferries all ran for as long as they were needed, or made money. They couldn't find the crewmen they had laid off five – ten years before. They was all in the service, piloting PT boats or somesuch. So a couple of apprentices were hired.

'The complete novices were assigned to learn from Dad, though only one at a time. Talking to him and making yourself understood was a major chore and not many took to it right off. And those that didn't, he just wouldn't take. One at a time was hard enough. He didn't want any wise-assing going on behind his back.

'They still didn't have any runs at night, though. Those Jersey Longshoremen managed to get off their entire load every day by five, so he still didn't have no work. Just getting the new boy used to the boat was all. Checking him out on steering around the dock, tearing down the engines, and like that. A few learned quick and were transferred to the other ferries over on the East River and places he never did know where. Some were slower, or just there at the wrong times, I guess.

''Cause they died. Six of them, all told.'

Sanders took a large swallow of his wine, then bent over his glass, staring into its dark ruby surface. Katherine's hand fidgeting on mine was the only other movement. When no one interrupted, he went on:

'I don't know Dad's side of it. He never tried to tell anyone any part of what happened, except for at the inquests for the two bodies that were found, but the Star Ledger was full of it. One had disappeared when his back was turned. He remembered seeing a light, foamy swishing in the water when he looked for the kid, but there was nothing until the Water Police dredged beneath the dock the next day. A rib cage was all they found. Freshly picked and the right size.

'The other one was even worse. The papers had a complete transcript of what my father wrote down for the court. Probably the longest thing he ever wrote in his life: "We was on the dock. I had Jerry cleaning the engine and he had the pieces spread right around the dock. I was showing the kid how to seal the point wires when he stands straight up and looks out to the river. I yelled at him, but he didn't hear me. I know I was yelling 'cause I could feel my throat vibrate. Then his eyes turned white. Didn't look like they rolled back. They just turned white all a sudden. Jerry took a step, tripped on the parts he was working on not a minute afore and landed on the edge of the dock. He felt the edge, grabbed the edge, and then jumped into the water. He had his back to me. He went right under. When I seen he wasn't bobbing back up, I grabbed a pike and poked around under the dock and the *Louisa Mae*. I snagged him and pulled up what was left. Never seen barnacles do that to a man. Good kid he was too.'

'I memorized it,' Sanders said, shifting uncomfortably in his seat. 'Half the meat on the body was gone. A whole leg, too. The final report mentioned animals and unknown shifting rock formations, because of the way the bone ends and muscles were grinded up. Dad never believed it though, I could tell. He knew there was something in the water.'

Still seeming to search his wine, like his father must have searched that black dock water, he remained silent for quite some time. Max and I sat silently, waiting for him, giving him the room he needed, but Katherine was becoming more unsettled by the moment. I was anxious to hear what he had to say specifically about the photograph, yet her nervousness was so intensely urgent it charged back my own impatience. Her fingers tightened, then loosened on mine, repeating the cycle every few seconds. Her thumb rubbed a rough sidestep on the back of my hand, while she virtually glared at Sanders.

Straining against the tension visible in her lips, she suddenly released the harshest words I've ever heard from her. 'Tell him about my father,' she commanded him.

'*Your* father,' I said, utterly surprised.

Again, she simply nodded, never taking her burning gaze from the ferry captain's son.

Without raising his head, Sanders drew a large, deep breath, and held it a moment. Throwing back the rest of his wine, he no longer had a place to stare, and to avoid Katherine fastened his eyes on mine. It made me distinctly uneasy, but I've known infinitely worse in my delirium of so long ago, and thus was capable of meeting it. He smiled lightly, but it quickly left his face.

'When your Mr Potterman called me last week he said he'd read about those men, boys, dying under the docks. He wanted to come see me at the house. I tried to put him off; it was all over years ago. But he said he would meet me there the next afternoon at three, and he hung up before I could say anything else.'

Katherine was fidgeting once more, sitting far back in her seat and huffing loudly, but Sanders ignored her.

'I don't know why – I work all day at Haverstrum's

Plumbing; I'm shop steward there – but I didn't go to the plant the next day. I'm alone now, except for Robbie, my oldest boy. The girls are both married. Robbie's a graduate student at Keane State, and when I told him I was staying home, that I didn't feel good, he offered to stick around. He's a good kid. But I told him I'd be okay. As soon as he'd left, I climbed up into the attic and started pulling all Dad's gear out of his old footlocker: tools I've never seen, his old seaman's mac, stuff like that. At the bottom was the sextant case he'd had since he was a kid. The sextant was long gone, but he kept all his most important papers there. Well, I carried the case and his logbooks down to the living room and just looked at them for a while.

'By the time Potterman came, I knew what it was he would want. He was reading through the logs for the forties when I couldn't take it anymore. I pulled the photo from underneath the cushion I was sitting on and threw it on the book he was looking at. I remember yelling at him to take it. I'd stared at it the whole afternoon once I'd found it, right up till he knocked on the door. Don't know why I hid it. But I couldn't keep it from him; it seemed so important. I wanted to be rid of it too.

'We sat there for over an hour while he just looked at it. Didn't stop until it was so dark he couldn't see. Then he stood up and tried to walk out the door with it.

'I almost killed him.' He glanced guiltily at Max for a moment, then brought his eyes back to me in an instant. 'I tried to hit him over the head with a marble ashtray. I don't remember picking it up. It's just that when I saw him walking away with it I couldn't let it go. I only hit him on the shoulder; lucky, I guess. The photo fell and I grabbed it up before he could move. He looked strange for a few minutes. I thought he might fight back or drop dead. Couldn't tell which. Finally he just said he knew someone who would pay five thousand dollars to hear about it. To be taken to where it was shot. He held out a card to me, and when I didn't move to take it, he dropped it on the floor. I called him a couple of days later. Neither of us have looked at it since that night. But you can't have it. It's – '

'Shut up,' Katherine hissed at him, as he halted looking

for a word. 'Just shut up about that damned photo. Tell him about my father!'

Sanders leaned back in his chair and slid down, shaking his head. A dull haze crept over his expression, as if his mind had vacated the ruins of his skull, leaving only memories.

Max reached across the table and stroked Katherine's hand where it was still clutching mine. She looked at him and relaxed, a pair of tears rolling gently out of the corner of her right eye.

'Katherine's father was the last apprentice,' Max explained in hushed tones. 'The night Sanders' father died in 1947, they were working together. According to Katherine's mother, who pieced the story together over six months of listening to mumbles and ranting dreams, Jake found himself walking toward the end of the dock, not knowing where he was going or why, when Sanders' father tackled him from behind. They wrestled horribly for a while, kicking, gouging, Jake trying to get away into the water and the captain trying to stop him. Finally, he broke away and jumped in, but Sanders went right in after him.

'The screaming brought a night guard running from the main terminal. When he got there, the captain was gone. And so was Jake's right hand. It was ripped off just above the wrist.'

In a tightly controlled voice Katherine picked up the story. Telling it somehow must have granted her the strength to hear it again.

'That was in November,' she said, speaking softly in the thankfully hushed corner of the restaurant. The waiter approached once, but Max warned him off with a curt wave of his hand. 'Six months later I was conceived.' A short, bitter laugh caught in her throat. 'Mom said she didn't know how it could have happened. He was so distracted, so . . . I don't know, lost somewhere else that he hardly ever slept. He walked around the docks all night. Oh, he'd never come out and say it, but she could always smell the dirty water on his clothes.

'Even when he was in the hospital for two months after the accident, he left once. Just walked out and took a bus down to Hoboken. The security guard found him collapsed just inside the locker hallway when he was making his morning rounds.

'It was worse after he came home. He'd snap out of it for a day or so every couple of weeks, but most of the time he would just sit around the house during the day. An old padded chair Mom had from her mother was moved into the corner at the back of the living room, and he sat there all day long, not saying a word. The doctors thought it was some kind of shock; a lot of the soldiers they were working with then had the same thing, but they still didn't know what to do about it.

'Mom tried locking the bedroom door at night so he wouldn't take off, but he almost killed himself dropping out of the window one night, so she finally gave in and let him go whenever he wanted. He always came back.' More tears started rolling down her cheeks then, and she managed to say again, 'He . . . always . . . came back,' before falling quiet. Her shoulders and arms rocked with the sound of her sobbings and I gripped her hand tightly. Not sure what else to do, I looked over at Max, who squinted his eyes and shook his head so slightly I was not completely sure I had seen it.

After a few minutes Katherine lifted her head and felt at her face. A faint tracing of mascara carved a black line down the side of her nose and came away on her fingers. Her eyes appeared a murky red. She tried smiling at us, but it came across like a weary grimace and she knew it. Excusing herself, she patted my hand as she rose and headed off toward the ladies' room. We all watched her go. I felt more drained by her story than by anything Sanders had said, but her absence was even worse. Fiercely tensing my thighs was all that stopped me from following her.

'One night he just didn't return,' Max said in ending. That seemed to place a shroud of silence on all of us. Sanders remained slouched down in his chair. Max, with his arm braced along the top of the table, just stared at the centerpiece. Every nerve in my body was afire, impelling me to run to those docks, to scream after Katherine that I'd find the answers to her frightful loss, to do some impossible thing with my hands and throat. I knew that she had been with Max for almost the last decade, gracing his office with her mild ease and consideration, but I'd never had the slightest inkling that they were as close as became apparent that night. He had the story from her mother's lips; he knew her reactions and her needs enough not to intrude upon her now. It was obvious that he loved her very much, and somehow the thought of sex did not enter into it. And that made it all simple enough to accept.

Just as I had to accept – by some unspoken agreement among the four of us – that we would not wait long before visiting those wharves.

The next few days were spent purchasing new equipment: boxes and hand-helds, meters, reflectors, floods (which somehow seemed the least appropriate of all), tripods, slaves, and all the other soulpaint of my medium. Finally though I left it all sitting in my hotel closet, and sent home for my finger-worn Hasselblad. Taking those state-of-the-art chrome and electronic icons in my hands for these purposes seemed absurd, raging like some noisome feedback in the middle of a Bach fugue. At least that's what I told myself over and over again. But the desperate need for a small familiarity to accompany me into that pit was the final pressing jolt that put my house and lab keys into the hands of a Park Avenue messenger service.

(I wondered if a man's god could be bonded.)

The shades were drawn shut and the curtains tightly occluded the daylight when a knock interrupted my memories. I was sitting in the farthest corner from the windows, lost in the shadows and the perilous and misty tenancy of a long life. Left well behind were the carriages and the stench of horses of that 'populous and smoky city' that proffered only remembrances of bound wrists and barred casements. And of one dear woman for whom, though she was not and could never be mine, I gave my life and my insanity.

I forced myself to hesitate before answering the rapping. It came only once, but was nonetheless insistent for that. Nothing was less than insistent these days.

Without checking the peephole, I opened the door and was surprised to find Katherine bearing my equipment case, slung over one shoulder with the grace of a pelerine capelet. She smiled warmly at me and stepped in, laying the case on the corner settee as a sidethought before sliding sensuously onto the loveseat just inside the archway.

'I made Max let me bring it over as soon as it arrived,' she said, aware of how foolish I felt still standing by the opened door. I hadn't known what my mood would be by the time the messenger returned – whether I would be locked in my room measuring patience with a heady port, or roaming the streets drinking the living rays of the sun while I could – thus I asked him to make his delivery to my agent's. Katherine's presence, however, paroled all questions from my consciousness, leaving only a vacant confusion. Softly I closed the door (against my upbringing) and moved silently beside her, granting her the topic.

She waited a moment, then lowered her gaze to her lap. On anyone else the pose would have seemed coquettish or affected, but I could tell she was genuinely embarrassed. 'I want to pose nude for you.' Her eyes came up. 'Tonight.'

Wanting to protest, I no sooner muttered some half-hearted argument when I saw what she already knew – that I had been composing the various angles and contrasts haunting my mind from Sanders' snapshot, and I had already decided sometime during the last two sleepless nights that all the possibilities came down to that.

Pale skin, brown timber, and black water.

I nodded, and asked her what Max had said.

'I haven't told him.' She leaned back limply into the cushions. 'I thought about it all night, and decided that it's best if he doesn't know.'

'But I promised him before he let me meet Sanders. You were there.' I was not actually concerned one way or the other. Max was a convenient focus, however. A point of diversion from the question I most wanted to ask. I understood my reasons in the *au naturel* configurations held in my mind's eye – and was mildly disappointed there was no prurient interest involved – but as to Katherine's motives I was reluctant to inquire. Was she seeking some sort of revenge for her father's death? Or was there a more simple need, an understanding, that she sought to lay to rest? In either case what could she do, naked and defenceless, against the gods?

'Max won't know,' she said. 'I told him Sanders had called and agreed to tomorrow night. I don't want him there. So it will have to be tonight.'

I did not argue. Sanders was necessary, to lead us to

the correct spot and for nothing more. Max, on the other hand, was an unstable element. His spectating could easily be a bastardization of my plans, my needs. I would not miss another opportunity. This time even Katherine was expendable, and I did not want Max about to complicate matters.

I could not wait any longer.

This time any sacrifice was acceptable. Just to get within arm's – or throat's – reach.

There must have been the usual swollen and ragged masses grinding their way through Pennsylvania Station that night, but their basic dissonance kept them from my notice. Across the river, a scant few minutes ride from that cauldron of mortal life, lay something without and beyond each. The contrast was simply too great, the mind could not withstand the transformation, so I saw only Katherine, linked to my side by a doubling chain of death and desperation, and Sanders, an immortal Moses, leading again.

I remember nothing of the PATH train or the quiet walk through the Hoboken station. My companions must have guided me like a blind man on his way to cathedral, once more to plead for eyes.

The first visual memory I have of that night is the inside of the railway terminal. It was a vast, arch-ceilinged waiting room, as smoked and dingy as some of the bombed-out churches of Europe. Outside a confusion of windows the abutted tracks of the Erie-Lackawanna and Conrail tracks fed into the darkness of northern New Jersey. Two sets of electric cars sat there, one a polished silver, the other a dull and dark moss green. The latter was the kind of carriage I remember from my first days in the United States: filthy levered wicker seats, sliding wooden doors with large iron handles.

Along the rear wall of the station, twin stone staircases climbed above a deep-set niche to meet at a set of heavy double doors that led to the street level. The tiny juice bar and newsstand were closed hours ago and less than two dozen people sat within the building. A few were already boarding the 11.30 outside.

As we stood poised in that black cavern, I followed Sanders' gaze up another, smaller stone stairway off to the left. Above

the portal at its summit, carved in the Gothic granite, were
the words 'Barclay St Ferry'. Katherine was still holding my
arm, but released it when Sanders removed my case from
his shoulder and thrust it out at me. We stood there locked
in individual memories, some real, others imagined. I could
hear as if from a long way off the scuffling of feet and the
banging of heavy doors. Several minutes later the trains
outside pulled off with a screech of complaining wheels and
tortured track.

Sanders lit a blunt cigar, took enough puffs to keep it going,
then looked at it disgustedly and stubbed it out on the iron
armrest of a nearby bench.

'Well, let's go,' he said. 'It's only a couple of hundred feet.
Up them stairs.' He set off without looking back to see if we
followed. Katherine and I moved in step until she noticed it
and broke the binding rhythm.

When he reached the platform before the doors, Sanders
motioned us to be quiet and waited for us to join him. 'There's
a security office around the first corner to the right once we
get in there,' he whispered. 'Watch the doors and how you
walk. He's an old gaffer and spooks easy.'

'Doesn't he know we're coming?'

'No. He's already thrown me out of here a couple of times.
The docks are kind of rotten in places and he's worried about
losing his job if there's an accident.'

'Is there any chance he might come upon us down there?'

'Not if we're quiet,' Sanders explained. 'He only does two
rounds a night. The rest of the time he sits in that office. We'll
be all right until two or so.'

Katherine made no response to any of this. She did not
even look at us. Signing agreement to the stocky guide, I
eased open the heavy glass-panelled door and we entered
a series of long crisscrossed corridors. The walls were a
two-tone institutionalized green, light above and dark below.
Closing the door softly, we moved behind Sanders without
making a sound. As he approached the first intersection, he
waved us to a halt and edged around the corner. A moment
later he reappeared and we hurried past. For another five
minutes we worked our way through a repetitious maze of
halls and doorways, until finally we came upon a dead-end.
Flanked along one wall stood a few dozen lockers. Opposite

the unused khaki metal boxes, spaced out a hundred feet or more apart were two sweating doors, large translucent panels in their upper halves.

Sanders led us to the first one and nudged it open. Quickly we stepped through and lost even the light from the dull and widely spaced bulbs suspended along the building's hallways. Only the glass at our backs contained any illumination, and it projected not at all into that blackness.

Commanding us with a single word, 'Wait!', I could hear Sanders breath stop. Katherine's had been too shallow to hear since we stood in the waiting room.

Slowly, as if it were cautiously approaching on wary pads, a weak lapping came from far beneath our feet and to the fore. The gentle sound of unmoving water meeting stolid pilings. A susurrus without movement.

Our eyes adjusted gradually to a wide sprinkling of light far away, directly on the horizon. And it was only at that moment when I realized we were again outside, perched twenty feet or more above the river, staring across at the lower realms of Manhattan. Below and beyond the rough and weathered plankings rustled the black waves and all they contained. A pit no light would ever penetrate. For a second, a deep depression flooded my heart as my fingers closed on empty air. Then a shaft of gold shot across the upper catwalks of the dock and pointed out the upper rungs of a ladder. Sanders' footsteps crept away toward the ladder, and I could hear his breathing again. From its new position at the end of the walkway, the flashlight beam guided the way for Katherine and I.

'Walk easy,' Sanders said, in a normal voice now that we were beyond the confines of the terminal. 'These upper planks are rickety as hell.'

Soon we were climbing down the ladder to the wider dock, surrounding the actual landing for the ferries. Some new two-by-fours had been lashed to the weaker rungs and I guessed that Sanders had been out here making preparations for some few days now. As we descended, the greasy smell of exhaust fumes left deep in the beams above our heads by more than a half-century of idling stacks abruptly gave way to the flat, briny odour of the wharves' lower reaches.

Boards creaked sharply under our feet. At this level a

gibbous moon could be seen hanging over the far city. No reflection touched the water, and before more stumbling about began, I hefted my equipment case and removed the battery-powered tungsten lamp I always kept there for extreme low-light conditions. I thumbed on the toggle and its low 50-watt bulb fed back about twenty feet of the harshly creased docking with its ebony border. Swinging the light to Sanders' instructions revealed the three storied open-ended box we stood in. Flat, smudgy brown and green slats lined the walls on both sides, walkways set on thick pilings at their feet. We stood on the northernmost of these, a wide expanse of unmoving river and a slight incline of muddy bank separating us from its twin. The walls ended a bare dozen yards or so out past the bank; the docks twice that distance beyond the enclosure. All that could be heard was the constant lapping, but always at a small distance and never underfoot. And with never a ripple in the water.

It was perfect! The thirsty night, the sound without movement. I wished painfully for that phantasmal sense that had led me to my incarceration in that filthy British asylum. Desperately I desired to feel that approach of the preternatural, to call it to me; but a mental blockade had been driven into place along with my returning sanity. This time I would have to depend upon my hackles alone. Or so I told myself until I glanced at Katherine.

Already she had stepped to the very end of the dock, out into the dark of the water and the night. Her light jacket had slid from her back before she had stopped. As I held the light on her, her skirt dropped also; her eyes gazing out far into the river. A small breeze stole across my cheeks – chilling my dry skin – carrying a repetitive mumble from where she stood. The words were indistinguishable from one another, but the tone carried the gently weaving texture of a chant, childlike and imploring.

Sanders, forgotten until now, had come to stand next to me and whispered, 'I won't stay.' He knew he didn't have to say this is it. 'I'll be back for you at one-thirty.' With that he left. For a long time afterward, I seemed to hear the creaking of the boards above my head – barely noticeable as I watched Katherine continue undressing – intermittent footsteps coming closer, then retreating from the scene before me.

Katherine's clothes ultimately rested behind her, completely discarded. Without taking my eyes from her, I snapped a diffusing panel over the lamp and set it on the edge of the dock, far enough away to barely light her pale form. Slowly I slipped up behind her, and bending, retrieved her clothes. As I did I saw a pinkish patch, the size of a guinea and shaped like an urn, lay nestled in the inward curve of her spine. I reached out a finger to touch it.

Her back quivered. Her hips shot forward, pulling the rosy mark away. Accepting the unconscious scold, I straightened and moved her clothes back to the foot of the dock.

My camera was cold as I lifted it from the case. In the meantime, Katherine had turned and was now reclining on the very brink of the planking, her back all but projecting out over the black water. She seemed an offering, a willing virginal self-sacrifice. Bent on one elbow, her long legs stretched and canted slightly behind her, I found myself incapable of movement. Her skin had the shimmery, glistening quality of a Japanese goldfish pool; her breasts and thighs a translucence blended of blue water and rose sunlight where veins and arteries carried the elements of earth and sky, not mere blood, nor mere life. The moon, far above and riding the mountainous crenellations of the forgotten city paled into a tarnished reflecting patina next to the purity of her hair, both nestled and free.

I hesitated. Suddenly I wanted very much to take her away from these wharves, but the beauty and power surrounding them were given eternity by her movements, and I knew I could not stop. If her body could enwrap such desire, her pose such soulful palpitations, what could the soul of a god evoke? I had to know.

Memories of her gruesome story – and Sanders' – fought the absolute rapture before my eyes as I began, unconsciously, to photograph her. The environs were almost forgotten, focusing more strongly in her very being. An ancient quatrain ran through my mind:

> From the hag and hungry goblin
> That into rags would rend ye,
> And the spirit that stands by the naked man
> In the book of Moons defend ye!

And at that moment something moved behind her. A furtive music filled my mind and the camera dropped from my hands. Before my eyes became too glazed to see further, I thought I saw a wall of hands, streaming and running with black river water, snake over Katherine's body. Caressing and tugging lightly at her flesh those groping pairs of arms began rolling her over the edge of the dock. Arms with insistent fingers; all but one. That last severed at the wrist.

My sight left me then, but I could feel my legs treading down those rough planks. I tried counting the steps, savouring each, while the blessed darkness gradually smothered the rest of my senses. Their calling cadences blocked all sound, until a shattering explosion ruptured that godly envelope that only a moment before was smothering me in holy death.

Gunfire screamed down from the walkway far above in the darkness. Mundane consciousness returned and I saw Katherine in the water, descending limply. I broke into a short run and lunged in next to her body just before it was pulled beneath the surface. She must have been released immediately though, for her now buoyant form crested heavily into me, as if she had been used as a barricade. Sputtering, I pushed her out of my way and dove, again and again. But however long I remained under the water I found nothing, except once the foremost piling of the dock.

Finally I lay floating, numbed with despair. Vaguely I sensed hands pulling me from that miasma of life and eventually managing to labour my body back onto the coarse wooden boards of the dock. I stumbled away, ignoring the bare outlines of Max's and Katherine's faces as they hauled me away down the wharf and up the ladder to the suspended walkway. Slowly I came round and moved more daintily. My senses cleared slightly as we gained the building once more, but as we left the landing below I thought I could hear laughter from the black waves behind us, but decided not. A thousand years ago, or even a hundred, I might have cried. But not this time. For now I would wait a while, mercilessly, and then I would keep on searching.

Next time perhaps I would be . . .

What?

It doesn't matter really. As long as I keep searching, and as long as I stay sane enough not to let another Carfax escape me.

STEPHEN JONES was born in 1953 and is the winner of two World Fantasy Awards and two Horror Writers of America Bram Stoker Awards, as well as being a nine-time recipient of the British Fantasy Award and a Hugo Award nominee. A full-time columnist, television producer/director and genre film publicist (all three *Hellraiser* films, *Night Life*, *Nightbreed*, *Split Second* etc.) he is the co-editor of *Horror: 100 Best Books*, *The Best Horror from Fantasy Tales*, *Gaslight & Ghosts*, *Now We Are Sick*, *The Giant Book of Best New Horror*, *H.P. Lovecraft's Book of Horror* and the *Best New Horror*, *Dark Voices* and *Fantasy Tales* series. He has also compiled *The Mammoth Books of Terror*, *Vampires*, *Zombies* and *Werewolves*, *Clive Barker's Shadows in Eden*, *James Herbert: By Horror Haunted*, *Clive Barker's The Nightbreed Chronicles* and *The Hellraiser Chronicles*, and is the author of *The Illustrated Vampire*, *Dinosaur* and *Frankenstein Movie Guides*.

DAVID SUTTON was born in 1947 and has been writing and editing in the fantasy and horror genre for more than twenty years. He has edited, produced, and contributed to a wide range of small-press publications, most notably for The British Fantasy Society, and is the winner of the World Fantasy Award and eight British Fantasy Awards. His short fiction has been published in such books and magazines as *Best New Horror 2*, *The Mammoth Book of Zombies*, *Final Shadows*, *Cold Fear*, *Taste of Fear*, and *Skeleton Crew* amongst many others. He is the editor of the anthologies *New Writings in Horror and the Supernatural* volumes 1 and 2 and *The Satyr's Head and Other Tales of Terror*, and co-compiler of *The Best Horror from Fantasy Tales*, four volumes of *Dark Voices: The Pan Book of Horror*, and the *Fantasy Tales* series. He has completed three horror novels, *Earthchild*, *Feng Shui* and *funfair*.